MW01154902

Pro Football
Expansion

Published by Jim Gardner

This book is fiction.

Copyright © 2022 by Jim Gardner

All rights reserved.
Fair comment rules apply, but generally no part of this book may be copied, reproduced, scanned or distributed in any electronic or paper form without permission of the author.
Please do not violate this author's rights.

ISBN: 979883602401

Pro Football Expansion

Jim Gardner

AUTHOR'S NOTE:

Written with apologies to the 1976 New England Patriots; the only team that season to beat the Oakland Raiders. For the sake of this work of fiction I had to make a few slight alterations to history.

CHAPTER ONE
Humble Beginnings

October 15, 2000

It was almost as if we had been brought out of a time capsule. Most of the 1976 Hawaiians returned to the place where we had played the team's first ever NFL game a quarter of a century earlier. We ranged in age at this date between 46 and 60.

We were the same people, of course. Most of us still didn't look like we had ever been pro football players. It wasn't that we were necessarily in bad shape. We had simply gotten older.

The scene was Aloha Stadium on the outskirts of Honolulu although officially it was in Aiea across Kamehameha Highway from Pearl Harbor. Our first NFL regular season game took place one day shy of the first anniversary of the stadium's grand opening. The stadium looked essentially the same as it did when it was brand new although some changes had been made. The stadium had actually undergone a major renovation as a result of a severe rust problem some years earlier. The floor of the stadium was still lined with artificial turf although not the same turf we had played on. The only real conspicuous change from the grand opening was the scoreboard was different and included a Jumbotron screen.

Technically speaking, it had only been 24 years since our first NFL game on September 12, 1976. More specifically, it had been 24 years, one month and three days since we kicked off to begin our NFL tenure, but this was regarded as the silver anniversary since it was the team's 25th season in the NFL. All members of that 1976 team, including those cut or signed during the season, were invited to be reintroduced to the crowd prior to the October 15, 2000, matchup between the Hawaiians and the Memphis Grizzlies; a fellow 1976 expansion franchise.

October 22, 1975

I still recall getting the news. The WFL Hawaiians were working out at Honolulu Stadium in preparation for a two-game road trip to Charlotte and San Antonio. We carried on as normal even though we knew that the World Football League was on very shaky financial ground. Many of us figured that the problems would be resolved if we stuck it out. We, at least, were part of a franchise that was actually drawing good crowds and generating revenue.

During the practice the ax fell. We received word that the WFL had just officially folded. We no longer had reason to practice. Although I didn't say anything, a part of me wanted to continue the workout. It was as if by doing so we could will the league into continuing to exist.

With nothing else to do, we showered and dressed. The locker room was devoid of frivolous conversations and horseplay this time. There were sounds of equipment being shed, showers running and muffled conversation. Nobody was talking about what movies they wanted to see, what nightclub acts were worth checking out or what restaurants had the best food. Even the seventh game of the World Series, which featured the Boston Red Sox and Cincinnati Reds and would get underway shortly, was not mentioned.

Afterward some of us gathered outside the locker room to discuss the latest developments. It was a numbing experience. I can't recall too many times in my life when I felt so insecure and lonely. Most of my teammates would never play pro football again.

As I engaged in conversation my eyes panned the wooden confines of Honolulu Stadium. The facility on the corner of King and Isenberg streets had played a major role in my life. I had played three years of college football, one full year of pro football and part of my second pro season at this facility. The brand-new Aloha Stadium welcomed us about six weeks earlier.

I broke away from my now ex-teammates and took a moment of solitude in the middle of the field. I looked around the antiquated stadium and relished all the cherished memories.

The baseball infield was still present. Normally by this time grass would have been planted on the section of the infield that was overlapped by the football field. There was no need for it this time since the final baseball game signified the end of all competition at Honolulu Stadium. Since the Islanders' final victory in September, giving them their first ever Pacific Coast League Championship, the facility was used only as a practice facility for the Hawaiians.

I walked along the makai sideline in front of the right field screen. Although I had spent my years with the University of Hawaii and Hawaiians stationed on the mauka sideline when I wasn't on the field, my first game at Honolulu Stadium in July 1970, had me on the makai sideline. I came over as a member of a California high school all-star team to take on a group of Hawaii high school all-stars. At the time my immediate future was at USC where I had visions of playing home games in the iconic Los Angeles Coliseum, Rose Bowl matchups and national championships.

The stadium and general Hawaii environment left a lasting impression that superseded any glories I could have realized at USC; something very few would understand. I transferred to the University of Hawaii after one year at USC with nary a regret alhough with occasional trepidation regarding whether this really was the right move.Everything fell into place. I played three wonderful years for the University of Hawaii and graduated just in time to be a charter member of the Hawaiians of the World Football League. For both teams I played in front of enthusiastic, appreciative fans decked out in tropical attire. I could hear the vendors hawking "cold beer," "hot dogs," "peanuts" and an assortment of other delicacies. I could also

4

smell the corn on the cob and occasionally got a whiff of somebody's hand-rolled cigarette, which contained something other than tobacco.

As I patrolled the mauka sideline I reflected back almost exclusively on my tenure at the University of Hawaii. The majority of our home games were on Saturday nights although we did play the occasional day game. As opposed to the likes of UCLA, Notre Dame and Ohio State whom I would have opposed at USC, I faced the likes of Montana, Pacific, the University of California at Santa Barbara and Grambling in Hawaii. For good measure we did square off against the occasional Division I school such as Nebraska, Stanford and Washington.

In my mind's eye I could see the girlfriend I had my senior year who was part of the cheerleading contingent. Although as a player I kept my focus on the field, I did catch occasional glimpses of Carol as she jumped, twisted and yelled in sync with her colleagues as her long blonde hair danced with her every move. Her routines included a kick that would have put the Radio City Rockettes to shame.

I had also watched several Hawaii Islander baseball games and even played a few baseball games at this facility on the university's team even though we had our own field on campus. It was a great place to be a player and a fan.

Suddenly my final appearance at this old friend marked the end of an era in Hawaii. Our final workout that was cut short was the stadium's final official function after half-a-century of use. As it turned out, I would never again set foot on this hallowed ground until after the facility was razed and turned into a public park.

Honolulu Stadium had served Honolulu well although it had outlived its usefulness. I still loved the single-tiered facility with its billboards running around the perimeter plugging sponsors such as Jolly Roger, Datsun, Bea's Drive-In, the Chart House, Coppertone and Finance Factors.

At least the stadium went out in a blaze of glory in early September when the Islanders won their championship. A fly ball to Jim Fairey in right for the final out gave the Islanders the championship after game six of a best-of-seven series against the Salt Lake City Gulls. The entire crowd then stood and sang *Aloha Oe* and then the lights were turned off forever. Its only function after that was workouts for the Hawaiians. I never dreamed that the condemned stadium would last longer than the team working out on its turf. I kept my hopes alive until there was finally no hope for the World Football League.

Of course the primary issue was not the stadium. There was a group of football players suddenly out of work.

The NFL had announced in 1974 that Tampa and Seattle would be expanding into the league in 1976. This obviously gave those cities plenty of time to prepare. It wasn't until December, 1975, that Memphis and Hawaii were also named as new franchises.

From what I understand, Commissioner Pete Rozelle began considering expanding the expansion even before the WFL folded. Rozelle had apparently spent long hours discussing the feasibility with other league officials in the days leading up to the WFL's official demise. He also met secretly with NFL team owners after the WFL folded to get their approval which was mandatory for expansion.

Some of the criteria were already met since the teams being considered already had uniforms and equipment. It was also presumed that they could continue playing in the stadia they had used during the WFL days.

The NFL acted quickly to prevent fire sales of uniforms and equipment. Based on fan support prior to the dissolution of the WFL, NFL officials considered the Memphis Grizzlies, Birmingham Vulcans, Southern California Sun (whose home field was in Anaheim) and the Hawaiians for possible expansion into the NFL. Less than a week after the news that the WFL no longer existed, officials from these four franchises were asked under terms of absolute secrecy if they were interested in expanding into the NFL in 1976.

They all responded in the affirmative. That meant that two cities, and possibly all four, would be denied entry. The NFL wanted to ensure that all necessary criteria were met, especially financial backing and solid fan bases. The expressed willingness to field a team was simply a critical first step.

Somehow the plan remained esoteric. Through the entire month of November there wasn't a single leak. Negotiations went on among the NFL and officials in Memphis, Birmingham, Anaheim and Honolulu. The media somehow were never apprised.

On Monday, December 1, the NFL decided to award a franchise to Memphis. The decision was kept under wraps until it decided which other WFL city would fill the remaining vacancy.

Birmingham was all but completely eliminated. The NFL decided that the first franchise would be either Memphis or Birmingham with Memphis getting the nod since it was further than Birmingham from existing franchises in Atlanta and New Orleans. It wasn't that Birmingham would have stolen fans from either city. The league simply wanted franchises as far apart from existing franchises as possible. The league eliminated Birmingham after naming Memphis since Birmingham and Memphis were from the same region.

Geography was the primary reason Hawaii got the other franchise. Southern California was eliminated because the team played its games in the same general area as the Los Angeles Rams.

Had the league had to make this decision two decades later Hawaii almost definitely would not have been awarded a franchise. Southern California probably would have easily been given the nod since there were no longer any franchises in the Los Angeles area. Fortunately for Honolulu, the possibility of Los Angeles ever not having an NFL franchise was considered to be insane in 1975.

The two additional franchises were officially announced on Wednesday, December 3. Residents of Birmingham were reportedly outraged while Anaheim residents barely flinched since they still had the Rams just up the road and the Chargers a little further down the road.

Memphis residents were thrilled and Hawaii residents were overwhelmingly exuberant. After losing Hawaii's only pro football franchise in more than 25 years exactly six weeks earlier, local residents were shocked by the dramatic step up in stature. The WFL had been a worthwhile venture and might have survived had it not come to be during such a woeful economic time, but the NFL truly was the better of the two leagues. As much as I had believed in the WFL, I probably would not have signed with a WFL team had I been drafted by a WFL franchise other than Hawaii.

With Hawaii being expanded into the NFL, that was the answer to my prayers, right? It guaranteed that I could stay home, right?

Wrong!

Dallas technically held the NFL rights to me since the Cowboys drafted me in 1974 simultaneously with Hawaii taking me in the WFL draft. Since this was an expansion and not a merger situation like when the AFL merged with the NFL, the league ruled that I belonged to Dallas.

Hawaii threatened to challenge the ruling in court. The league quickly and quietly mediated since the Cowboys said they were willing to fight. An agreement was reached that the Hawaiians would retain the rights to me in exchange for surrendering their top college draft choice to Dallas. It was a minor coup for the Cowboys since they hadn't actually taken me until the third round in 1974.

I was elated. I honestly would not have minded playing for Dallas but I was in a better frame of mind playing in Hawaii. I was in on the ground floor of something very exciting. Most importantly, I was staying home.

With a minimum of haggling I signed a contract for 1976 for $63,000. That was not a bad sum of money in those days, especially when taking into consideration the fact that I was back with a team given up for dead two months earlier. For trivia buffs, I was the first player ever to sign with the NFL Hawaiians.

During what turned out to be only an ephemeral period of unemployment and uncertainty when the World Football League folded, I was hired by a local independent TV station to host a weekly sports highlight show. It was the prototype sports highlight show with a lot of emphasis on local sports. I wrote the show myself and narrated videotaped highlights, asked questions to guests when I had them and even did the occasional editorial on subjects such as the intensifying controversy surrounding the University of Hawaii basketball team which would ultimately lead to the program being put on two years' probation. The show was a lot more difficult to do than it appeared. I still enjoyed the challenge.

With my feet firmly planted in Hawaii I bought a condominium on Ala Wai Boulevard in Waikiki. It was a comfortable two-bedroom dwelling. I invited a former college teammate, Bill Trimble, to rent the second bedroom.

Bill graduated from UH one year after me. He was a wide receiver who had been invited by a few teams, including the Hawaiians, to try out as a free agent. He decided to simply hang up his cleats. With a degree in business administration, Bill took a job as an assistant manager in a Waikiki restaurant.

Being under contract to the Hawaiians did not mean that I could take things for granted. My contract was null and void if I did not make the team. That meant extra hard work to ensure my being in good shape when training camp began in July.

To sum up football simply in terms of running, passing, blocking and tackling is making it much too simplistic. Being a good football player requires being in excellent physical shape. Anybody can play a pickup game on the playground. There are ions of differences between a simple pickup game and the game one watches on television.

An individual's inability to cut it as a football player is often attributed to his failure to keep himself in proper physical shape. An individual with good speed and hands is useless if he doesn't have the stamina to play a full game. Not only does he slow down but his lack of conditioning makes him dangerously vulnerable to injuries.

Throughout my career I took every precaution to make sure I didn't fall into that category. I joined a local gym and worked out several times a week to keep myself in as good a shape as possible. I vigorously pedaled the exercise bike, lifted weights, did wind sprints at a nearby field and ran several miles. Although the facility provided treadmills, I did my running outside through the streets of Honolulu or else Aiea, Pearl City and Waipahu, depending on which facility I went to.

This is not to suggest that I was the epitome of discipline. I was a smoker back then. I was also known to drink beer although I was not a drunk.

The aforementioned are not admissions I am proud or happy to make. They are simply the truth which I cannot rightfully deny. When I thought about it later in life, I could not understand how I managed to find pleasure in smoking and drinking.

Looking back, I am amazed that I had the discipline to work so hard. I was a part of a clique that took advantage of the local nightlife. It wasn't that I was spending a lot of time in bars or at parties but I did have my indulgences. Somehow, without necessarily realizing it, I had the discipline to utilize moderation. I was not normally one to wake up with a hangover.

8

It was fortunate that I had lived frugally. I wasn't extremely parsimonious although I didn't throw my money around. During my first WFL season I made $35,000. That was a healthy sum for somebody in Hawaii who turned 23 during the season. I still spent my money wisely, eating out only at places I was accustomed to while I was a college athlete on a scholarship and not at the more epicurean facilities where one paid substantially more for ambience or orchids in the Mai Tais. Although I was more financially secure than I had been as a college student, I still wanted to be the same person my friends had known. Eating a double cheeseburger at Chunky's, a waffle or an omelet at Jolly Roger, a pastrami on Jewish rye at the Waikiki Deli, a bowl of saimin at Zippy's, a hot dog at Izzy's or a pizza at Red Lion or Chico's was still good enough for me. If I wanted a steak I usually went to Sizzler instead of something more upscale.

There were occasions when I splurged although I didn't go overboard. I didn't date during my rookie season since I was smarting from the enigmatic exile elsewhere of the girlfriend I'd had through my senior year in college and needed time to recuperate while also not eliminating the possibility of her return. Primarily I played football, spent time with friends, kept to myself and stayed out of trouble. I spent some money but saved a lot.

Largely to adjust to the departure of my girlfriend, I spent Christmas, 1974, with my family in Montebello, California. It initially was my intention to stay only for the holidays but I wound up staying for about five months after I was offered a job as a host at a restaurant. It was fairly easy money since I was primarily being exploited as a pro football player. There was even an autographed picture of me in front in case anybody didn't know who the guy in the tuxedo at the front entrance was. It really started to get embarrassing and, quite frankly, probably very few people in southern California were impressed about being greeted by a pro football player from a team in Hawaii in an upstart league.

While in California I worked out to stay in shape I also went to Dodger and Angel games when baseball season started, allegedly "worked" at the restaurant and then returned to Hawaii to prepare for the start of my second WFL training camp.

The money I'd put away during my rookie season and my stay in California paid off during my second season. League financial problems meant that the payroll was occasionally delinquent. The league was functioning primarily under a single financial umbrella to protect the weaker franchises but was floundering.

Where my frugality helped was it prevented me from having to take a fulltime job when the WFL folded. Knowing that I was going to get a shot at the NFL, along with my weekly sports highlight show, enabled me to dedicate several hours each day to staying in shape.

One afternoon shortly after I signed my contract I was the keynote speaker at the Honolulu Quarterback Club meeting at the Flamingo Chuckwagon on Kapiolani Boulevard. I made the obligatory remarks about how thrilled I was to be playing for the NFL version of the Hawaiians, which was very true, and talked a little about my background. After that I fielded several questions.

"How do you think the team will do?" was one such question.

That was an interesting inquiry. I was still the only player at this juncture officially bound to the team.

"It's hard to say," I replied. "All I know is Coach Walker has a reputation for getting the most out of his players. I think we'll have a fairly competitive team."

Chuck Walker had coached on the college and pro levels for several years although this was his first opportunity to be head coach for a pro team. Previous tenures even included time under Vince Lombardi. He admitted to emulating Lombardi without always consciously doing so. Like Lombardi, Walker was one who got his players to reach back and find what might not have been known about his potential had the player not made the extra effort to find it on his own.

"What are the chances of you guys going to the Super Bowl?" was another question.

It should be noted that most questions from the Honolulu Quarterback Club were meritorious. There were, however, obvious exceptions. It took a lot to keep from responding condescendingly to a question regarding the odds of an expansion team with only one player currently on the roster getting to the Super Bowl.

"We'll get there eventually, I hope," I responded diplomatically. "As far as the first season goes, even that is always possible. Any team should play as if it has just as good a shot as anybody of going all the way. If we work hard and play up to our potential, who knows?"

The latter response appeared in one of the local newspapers. Coach Walker saw it. He actually called me to verify it. When I admitted that I had been quoted accurately he said he hoped all of his players had that attitude.

"Of course you still have to make the team," he added lightly.

CHAPTER TWO
Building a Team

The preseason roster gradually filled. The team acquired players during the expansion draft and rookie free agent draft. Counting myself, the roster would grow to 64 players if everybody drafted agreed to report to the team which they ultimately did.

First was the expansion draft. Tampa Bay, Seattle, Memphis and the Hawaiians took turns drafting unprotected players from the 26 existing teams. Each expansion team could select 39 players. That meant that 156 players would wind up going to expansion teams. Each existing team stood to lose an average of roughly half-a-dozen players.

The rookie free agent draft came in April. The 26 existing teams drafted in 17 rounds back then. The four expansion teams were awarded 25 rounds.

Hawaii was the last of the expansion teams to draft in the expansion draft. Everything was inverted for the rookie draft as far as the expansion teams went so Hawaii had the first pick there.

Which meant that Dallas actually had the first pick, thanks to me. We didn't draft until the final selection of the second round.

Our first pick in the expansion draft was Marv Nelson. He was a nine-year veteran guard from Grambling. His entire pro career had been spent in New Orleans. He was one of the original Saints so this would be his second stint as a charter member of an expansion team.

The second pick was Steve Bender out of UC Santa Barbara. He was a quarterback whom we took from San Francisco. He played from 1962 through 1970 for Washington and then was traded to San Francisco.

We went to defense for our third choice. Jim McDaniel was a defensive end taken from Oakland. He would be beginning his eighth year out of Maryland, starting his career in Pittsburgh in 1969 before being dealt to Oakland after two seasons.

Our final expansion choice was wide receiver Tom Prisbrey. He had played in a couple of games for Atlanta in 1975 and spent the rest of the season on the taxi squad. He played college football at Cal Poly-Pomona after serving two years in the Marines, including a year in Vietnam.

Prisbrey was an arbitrary choice. By the time our 39th pick came around Coach Chuck Walker looked at the list of remaining unprotected players and there was nobody left who impressed him. He asked his assistants if there was anybody they liked. When they expressed no preferences Walker decided to take the first player his eyes fell on. That is how Prisbrey won a trip to Hawaii that seemed likely to be very short.

In April we drafted our rookies. Theoretically I was the first player Hawaii selected in this draft. When we finally got around to our actual first choice the team selected quarterback Joe Billingsley from Brigham Young University.

For the record, our final pick was Mitch Marchetti; a kicker out of Colorado. He would be competing with at least one other kicker, since the team had also taken Raul Ortega from New England in the 32nd round of the expansion draft.

Two players from the University of Hawaii were selected. Cornerback Randy Sterling was selected in the 19th round. Defensive end Edmund Kupau was claimed in the 21st round.

The Hawaiians drafted one other player with local ties. Tight end Craig Kamanu was taken in the 24th round. He played high school football for Kamehameha, then opted to play college football for Washington State.

Another 50 or 60 names would be added to the roster before training camp opened in July. The team was very determined to sign a large group of rookie and veteran free agents. Two were signed shortly after I was since they were not tied to any existing NFL team. Cornerback Eric Hamer from Oregon State had played for the WFL Hawaiians in 1975. Safety Rich Hasegawa had played for the WFL Hawaiians in 1974 and 1975 and had also been my teammate at the University of Hawaii.

Our top choice in the expansion draft moved to Honolulu almost immediately. Marv Nelson was anxious to begin his tenure with an expansion team for the second time in his career.

I was taken by Marv's congeniality when I met him shortly after his arrival. He was very smart and self-confident. My first conversation with the large Black man made me feel as if I had known Marv my entire life. The only people who ever had trouble with Marv were those who played on opposing defenses.

Marv had no children. That made moving easy for Marv and his wife Karla since they didn't have to uproot any kids. Marv figured he had a couple of good years left, never dreaming that as a player and coach he would still be with the team a quarter century later.

Nine years in New Orleans seemed to test Marv's patience. He accepted the team not doing well during its first few years but losing seemed to be the pattern for this team. The Saints almost seemed like the pre-1969 New York Mets since their whole purpose when taking the field seemed to be to lose. By the time the Mets had been in the league nine years, however, they had already won a World Championship. The Saints never even broke even during their first nine years.

"I remember how excited I was when we scored a touchdown on the opening kickoff of our first game," Marv recollected bemusedly. "I thought that was a sign of things to come for us. After nine years in New Orleans I never got excited again. We won only two games last year. That's one less than we won my rookie year. I hope this team will know how to win."

12

I loved Marv's attitude. He was excited about the new opportunity and he was hungry. He was dedicated to winning.

Linebacker Ed Jennings also moved to Hawaii shortly after being taken from Philadelphia in the eighth round of the expansion draft. Ed had played five years in Philadelphia after playing college ball at California.

Why Philadelphia left Ed unprotected in the expansion draft is an enigma. He was one of the best linebackers in the game and still very much in his prime. The Eagles' mistake was expected to be our gain.

I suppose Ed could be described as the stereotypical alumnus from California. He had long wavy medium brown hair and a fairly liberal perspective.

Ed wasn't married but his girlfriend, Jennifer Rhoden, lived with him. She had silky brown hair that ran to the middle of her back. She and Ed began dating during their junior year at Cal and began cohabitating the following year. She went with him to Philadelphia where she managed a boutique and then accompanied him to Honolulu.

Although Ed had moved to Hawaii, he didn't get close to any of his new teammates right away. He was friendly but distant. He preferred getting to know people gradually on his own terms.

While waiting for training camp to begin I spent many evenings watching the Hawaii Islanders in their first season at Aloha Stadium. At the time they were still the top farm club of the San Diego Padres; a partnership dating back to 1971. While I enjoyed watching the baseball games in front of me, even sitting with a few friends I had gotten to know while watching the Islanders at the old stadium, I also looked at the field and visualized the stadium in its football configuration. I was very excited about representing Hawaii in the NFL.

Assuming I would make the team, I would actually be paid to play a game I initially played as a means for fitting in in a new environment. During the summer of 1966 I moved with my family from Azusa, California, to Montebello which was several miles away.

In all likelihood I would have gone out for football had I stayed in Azusa. It simply seemed more imperative in Montebello. I have no doubt that there were excellent coaches in Azusa but I don't know that they would have done what my varsity coach in Montebello did. He was the one who helped me to transform from a jaded kid to a fairly dedicated football player.

The first friend I made in Montebello was a tall, lanky kid named Steve Phillips. He lived a few doors down from me and would be playing football as a junior at the brand-new South Valley High School. Steve was never a starter although he did get his share of playing time and played well when he was in there. He was a split end; now referred to as "wide receiver."

Steve and I spent time throwing the football prior to the start of football drills. Although we did remain friends, we drifted apart when football drills began. He was reunited with friends from his class who had also transferred to the new school and I was meeting new people in my class. He was part of South Valley's charter varsity team while I initially expected to be a part of the "C" contingent but was told to report to the "B" squad since I had too many exponents (points based on height, weight and date of birth) to play on the "C" level.

First we did a week of two-a-day conditioning drills in gym shorts, T-shirts or topless, and football cleats. We kicked off the second week with our first practice in full pads.

Early in the practice we had a tackling drill. We had two lines of players. A player from one line would lie down as the ball carrier while a player from the other line would lie down as the tackler a few feet away. The two combatants would remain head-to-head until the coach gave a signal.

"Set! Hut!"

On cue the two gladiators would rise and charge. One would try to run through and the other would try to make the tackle. Since they were charging in a very narrow area it was almost impossible for the ball carrier to get through.

It didn't matter how good the tackle was. Assistant coach Tom Caesar was never satisfied. Each encounter was succeeded by myriad disparaging remarks often laced with expletives and slang references to the female anatomy. Sometimes Caesar would focus his displeasure on the ball carrier and other times he would focus on the tackler. Often he had unpleasantries for both.

I began this drill near the end of the ball carrier line. That gave me plenty of time to observe before my first turn. Although I had never played football except for flag football during physical education classes in Azusa and had rarely even watched football on TV, I quickly picked up what I observed others doing. My focus was on going hard, keeping low and driving hard even after contact. I expected to be tackled but I was determined not to be easy.

"Okay, Dockman and Lybacher," Caesar called out, reading the tape on the fronts of our maroon helmets when my turn came.

Mike Lybacher and I took our places. Lybacher was a sophomore tackle who was slightly larger than me and somewhat flabby, I observed. He would ultimately be a second-string player who would give up football after one season.

"Set!" Caesar called out. "Hut!"

I charged Lybacher with every ounce of strength I had. I went in low and we banged hard before Lybacher got his arms around me. He held on while I tried to break loose. My legs kept churning and I lunged forward before finally going down.

"I guess that wasn't too bad, Dockman," Caesar growled grudgingly. "It wouldn't have been so easy if Lybacher wasn't such a pansy."

I was miffed and I am sure that Lybacher was not especially pleased with the lack of approbation. He actually did a pretty good job of tackling me. Caesar simply wasn't going to admit it.

Dutifully I took my place in the tackling line. As I waited for my turn I grew increasingly irritated with the way Caesar constantly questioned his players' masculinity, courage, sexual preference and/or personal pride. My new teammates were actually having some pretty impressive collisions. Just once I wanted to hear something positive.

When my turn came I was determined to make a tackle that Caesar could not help but . . . not condemn. As I took my place I noticed I would be squaring off against a guy named Purcell. He was an end who was about two inches taller than me and about my weight. He was a sure-handed sophomore who would start every game until he broke his arm late in the season.

"Set! Hut!"

Larry Purcell charged with the same intensity as me. He came in low but I was even lower. My momentum actually enabled me to lift him slightly off the ground and throw him down hard. It wasn't so much that I hit him hard although I definitely did. It was simply leverage and momentum.

I was very impressed with myself. I was certain that Caesar would be impressed.

Caesar was suddenly in my face. I thought I had given him what he was after and he was dressing me down, telling me about how I was going to be putting opponents in the hospital if I tackled like that. Suddenly he was portraying himself as a humanitarian who cared about the physical well-beings of other players although he never even bothered to check to see if Purcell was all right. Purcell was slow to rise but not injured.

Being somewhat of a red ass after spending most of my life in a rough section of Azusa, I was fuming.

"I quit!" I suddenly exclaimed and stormed off the practice field.

My disposition only got worse as I approached the locker room. By the time I reached the "B" locker room I felt as if I could run my fist through the metal lockers.

Fortunately I wasn't quite angry enough to try. Instead I vented my anger by heaving each piece of clothing and equipment. Everything I had been wearing wound up in various parts of the locker room floor after being heaved against the lockers across the room.

What I hadn't paid much attention to on the practice field was the presence of the varsity's head coach. Marcus Farnwell tore himself away from his own squad to check out his future prospects. I had noticed the tall athletic looking man with the maroon baseball cap with the gold "SV" locked together on the front but didn't give him much thought. I had no idea who he was.

Farnwell opened the door of the "B" locker room at about the time I had completely stripped down. He had a bemused expression at the sight of my football clothing and equipment strewn about. He looked at me with a semblance of a grin that somehow calmed me. He enigmatically came across as being nonjudgmental.

"After you've showered and dressed I'd like for you to stop by my office for a minute," Farnwell said evenly.

I nodded and headed to the shower. By this time I had deduced that the sandy-haired man was a coach of some sort.

Farnwell greeted me congenially in his office. He introduced himself as he shook my hand and invited me to sit in the chair on the opposite side of his desk. It turned out that he was not only the varsity head coach, he was also the school's athletic director.

At no time did Farnwell try to talk me out of quitting. Doing so probably would have turned me away from football forever. He simply asked me questions about my background and how I felt about my new environment.

"Would you like to stick with football?" he finally asked.

I thought for a moment. I had been somewhat enthusiastic about playing. I simply didn't care for Caesar's tactics. To this day I know he was wrong. Making it a point to condemn everything might have been a good motivating tactic for some but it discouraged others. Farnwell and other coaches I had through college and the pros understood there were times when a player needed to be pushed and times when he needed to be praised.

"I would like to play," I conceded, "but I don't like the way that coach out there treats everybody."

Farnwell agreed that Caesar's tactics were extreme. He said he didn't really know Caesar since this was a new school and he didn't know most of the staff that well except by their reputations, having been recruited to move to the new school from Arcadia. He also pointed out that the "B" head coach, Paul Ratherber, was a more rational coach who had been away because of a family emergency. He would be back by the end of the week.

"What position do you want to play?" Farnwell asked.

If I still had any anger inside me, it was superseded by my feeling totally stupid. I hadn't given much thought to what position I might play. I believe I may have thought that positions were assigned to us. I knew very little about football aside from the fact that the center hiked the ball to the quarterback who either passed to an end, ran or handed the ball to somebody else. I knew that guards blocked and there was a position called "tackle" which didn't make any sense since I knew that everybody on the defensive unit could make a tackle. I honestly had never heard of a defensive end, middle guard, linebacker or safety.

"Have you ever played any kind of football?" Farnwell asked.

"Just for PE. I was usually an end."

16

"I see. How fast can you run?"

"I don't know," I said, not recalling any specific times although I had run against the stopwatch. "I stole some bases in baseball. That's all I really know."

Farnwell pondered for a moment, tapping his fingers on his desk.

"Well," he said, "if you were stealing bases then you're probably pretty fast and you seem to be pretty tough. You'd probably do a good job in the backfield. Do you think you might work out at quarterback?"

I didn't respond right away. Coach later told me he wished he had a picture of the incredulous expression on my face. The suggestion of my being a quarterback was beyond my expectations.

"Can you pass?" Farnwell asked.

"Sure," I replied, recalling the rare instances in PE when I played quarterback and passed with fairly consistent accuracy from the pocket and even under pressure.

"Okay. We'll try you at quarterback. If that doesn't work out we can probably turn you into a pretty good running back. I'll tell Coach Caesar that you're to work at quarterback. You go put your stuff back in your locker and be ready to go this afternoon."

And so I did. Not only did I have renewed enthusiasm for football but with a sense of purpose as well.

I worked hard at my position and started throughout my freshman year on the "B" squad. Often I also started as a defensive back and was the team's punter.

By my sophomore year I was the varsity's starting quarterback and became a starting defensive back near the end of the season.

For my junior year I became our punter in addition to being a two-way player and even added being a placekicker by the time my senior year rolled around. There were games when I was on the field for every single play.

My last two high school games linked me to my future and my past. My second-to-last high school game was the previously mentioned all-star game at Honolulu Stadium. At the time I didn't know I was in the stadium I would play in as a collegiate and for the first segment of my pro career. I actually thought the trip to Hawaii was a one-time thing. As much as I enjoyed being in Hawaii, my immediate future was at USC. I did not fathom that I would even consider transferring to Hawaii after my freshman year.

An all-star game at Citrus College in Glendora, California, was my last high school game. Glendora was actually my birthplace and was right next to Azusa. It was one of my rare visits to my old neighborhood after my family's move to Montebello.

Whatever accolades I might have received as a high school, college and pro football player can be traced to one day in September 1966. That was the day a very compassionate football coach took a moment of his time to provide an angry and somewhat confused young man with a compass. That compass made me a better athlete, a better student and, eventually, a better person in general.

When June rolled around I grew eager in anticipation of training camp. I still had a month to go. I intensified my workouts and continued enjoying my free time.

There were always different women for me to date along the way. For the most part there was nothing atypical. The only thing out of the ordinary was about a week before training camp opened up when I met a young visitor to Hawaii who turned out to be the daughter of a high-ranking league executive.

Two things made this encounter less than typical. The first was that it didn't take me long to discover that she was totally full of herself, obviously believing that Daddy's stature gave her some type of opulent entitlement. The second was that assistant coach Greg Wilson saw me out with her and tried to convince me later that I was "skating on thin ice" if I continued to see her.

That was vintage Wilson. He was generally a nice guy who looked a lot like Steve Allen. I simply did not respect him as a coach. Whatever half-baked ideas he had when he saw me in a pizza parlor with the league executive's daughter were ideas that only he could have contrived. Despite his vehement attempt to discourage me from seeing this young woman further, the only reason I didn't ask her for a second date was because I was sick of her before the end of our first date.

I suppose that seems callous. I was still nice to her throughout the date and when I ran into her afterward. It's just that even before we sat down in a nightclub after leaving the pizza parlor I had already ascertained, because of her uppity attitude, that this was our last date. When she immediately ordered a Chi Chi, drank it like water and unilaterally gestured to the waitress for another, I also ascertained that our only date would not be an especially lengthy affair. As soon as it was socially acceptable I escorted her to her hotel room, kissed her goodnight, walked away and met up with some friends who were actually *fun* to have around. Counting the pizza parlor, I think our date lasted about 90 minutes.

But this was just before it was time to report for training camp. Despite the ladies I had dated over the previous six months and the ladies who were still out there, I was ready to turn my attention to football.

18

CHAPTER THREE
Training Camp

Training camp officially began the minute July 5 arrived. Our mandated arrival time was midnight the night before the official opening of training camp.

I spent the hours prior to my arrival at Aloha Stadium. Although nervously anticipating the opening of my first NFL training camp, my roommate and I went to the Hawaii Islanders' game against the Sacramento Solons. The Islanders lost, 11-5, but the fireworks show after the game was great. Afterward I drove Bill home and raced to camp with a little time to spare.

Part of the preseason preparation included securing a location for camp. The year before as a WFL franchise we used a resort in Makaha. The year prior to that we trained in Riverside, California. Neither locale seemed suitable for the NFL Hawaiians.

Several sites were considered. Initially there was consideration given to constructing temporary quarters at or near Kahuku High School and using the school's athletic complex. This was on the north side of the island about as far as one could get from the distractions in Waikiki. Walker wanted something as far away from the evil temptations of Waikiki and, especially, Hotel Street in Downtown Honolulu as possible.

Kahuku was shot down for several reasons. The most compelling was that public schools in Hawaii resumed in August. There would be an overlap between the start of school and training camp. The presence of pro football players after school started would pose a distraction for students and faculty.

Brigham Young University a few miles down the road in Laie was even briefly considered. The school's administration momentarily expressed a willingness to consider leasing part of the campus to the Hawaiians until a few realities came in to play. In 1976 it wasn't uncommon for pro football players to smoke. Then, as now, it wasn't uncommon for them to drink and it definitely wasn't uncommon for them to have colorful vocabularies. Since the Hawaiians could not realistically guarantee that the players would not smoke, drink or swear on Mormon property the BYU idea was dismissed for eternity.

Other islands had facilities but they were an absolute last resort. Walker wanted camp on Oahu so that those with families on the island could spend time with them. Although those affected would not get much time with their families, Walker believed that even a little quality time with family could enhance a player's morale and performance.

An agreement was finally reached with the Federal Government!

More specifically, the team was able to lease a large field at the Kaneohe Marine Corps Air Station as it was known in 1976. It was considered to be a major coup. It didn't hurt that Walker's cousin was a colonel assigned to the base although the nepotism angle allegedly played a very small role in the agreement. It simply didn't hurt the team's chances.

Officials from the team worked quickly to arrange to have a sufficient camp built on a field on the base. Buildings were constructed around the perimeter for housing and meetings. There were also locker rooms, a dining hall and weight rooms among the amenities.

A watchdog group tried crying "foul" over this. The group questioned the wisdom of a football training camp being constructed at taxpayers' expense but it was all done at the team's expense. Everything from the structures to the plumbing to the electrical outlets was on the Hawaiians' dime. There was some government expense since we were using government land but the cost to the government was at the bare minimum. The team's majority owner, a local businessman named Cec Heftel, made extra sure that this could be done without this becoming a white elephant for the taxpayers. On top of that, the Marine Corps was welcome to use the facility whenever the Hawaiians weren't using it.

A single-story dorm was constructed for veterans. This included communal bathrooms and showers and a laundry. Each room had two twin beds, a desk and chair, and two large lockers. The rooms were small, leaving very little room to move around.

There was a barracks for the rookies. It was built in the tradition of military barracks with bunk beds on both sides and lockers. A long table with benches on both sides ran down the center.

Obviously the rookies didn't get much privacy. As camp wore on and chunks of rookies were eliminated the barracks gradually became eerily palatial.

Technically I was a rookie in the NFL. However, since I had two years' experience in the WFL Walker granted me, as well as other WFL veterans, veteran status.

Meals were prepared by off-duty Marine cooks hired and paid by the team. Those hired had to give written assurances to the base commanders that they would live up to their full responsibilities in this endeavor since this was considered to be a goodwill agreement between the Hawaiians and the Marine Corps. There is probably nothing in the world more disciplined than a United States Marine.

Primarily we remained within the confines of our training facility when on base. We were allowed access to a bowling alley and movie theater but had little time to bowl and almost no time to sit through a movie. A member of the coaching staff was allowed to go to the PX each day to purchase beer, soda, snacks and other supplies for the team to enjoy.

We were also advised in very strong language that any player who violated any of the agreements with the base would be subject to severe

20

disciplinary action. It goes back to the arrangement being a goodwill agreement between the Hawaiians and the Marines Corps.

There were 116 of us in camp that first day. There were 51 rookies, 46 who had played professionally exclusively in the NFL, five who had played in both the AFL and NFL, seven who had played professionally only in the WFL and seven who had played in both the NFL and WFL. Among the veterans, we had a combined total of 319 years of professional experience, averaging 6.25 years. The veterans combined for 21 Pro Bowl appearances and 13 Super Bowl appearances.

Quarterback Steve Bender had the most seniority with 14 years under his belt. With rookie Joe Billingsley in camp, the team was hoping Bender had at least one or two good years left while Billingsley served as backup and got the feel of being in the pros.

The first morning reminded me of my first WFL camp two years earlier. As an expansion team the camp was comprised of players who hadn't bonded yet. There were those who had been teammates in college and the pros and others were acquainted from having opposed each other. There was still no phalanx of those returning from the previous year's team the way there would be in subsequent years. We were a group of virtual strangers.

There were seven of us from the previous year's Hawaiians team but it wasn't the same. We were all simply given an opportunity to try to stick with an NFL version of the old team. Past glories with the Hawaiians bore little significance. Whatever we might have achieved before was done in a league that was considered inferior to the NFL.

We spent the first morning getting physicals. They were conducted by the team physician and two off duty Marine Corps doctors the team hired. I suppose that is why some players compared this to the induction physicals they were subjected to during the days of the draft.

Only one player didn't pass the physical. Defensive tackle Chuck Morgani, after seven years with Washington, Denver and St. Louis, had problems with his knees that were irreversible. One more hit could have crippled him for life. He was regretfully given an airline ticket and flown to San Francisco that day. It was time for him to move on to another chapter in his life in his hometown of Novato, California.

During the afternoon we got our equipment. Various piles of pads were scattered around a locker room. Each player was issued knee pads and thigh pads which fit inside special compartments in the uniform pants.

Also issued were girdle pads to pad the hips and shoulder pads. Those who had experienced rib injuries were issued rib pads. This was a few years before the flak jacket was introduced.

We were issued solid white helmets. Brand new gold helmets with the team logo on each side and colored piping in the middle would not be issued until our public scrimmage July 24.

The team's equipment manager and his assistants dutifully recorded the numbers printed with indelible ink on each piece of equipment in our possession. As our equipment was recorded, we were issued two pairs of practice pants and two practice jerseys. The pants were solid white and were identified by indelible numbers inside the waist band. The jerseys were solid white with brown numbers and solid brown with white numbers. Everybody received one of each except for the quarterbacks who received two solid red jerseys with white numbers.

There was a lot of duplication of numbers. Officials took steps to ensure that no more than one of any number was issued for offense and one for defense. The number and color of the jersey enabled the coaches to keep track of who was doing what. The offensive players were identifiable during the morning drills by wearing white jerseys. The defensive players wore white jerseys in the afternoon.

We were assigned numbers when we were signed. Each player was asked which number he preferred with priority going to who was signed the earliest. Since I was the first player signed, I had no problem securing my traditional number 22 which I began wearing on my high school baseball teams and had also been wearing for football since my freshman year at USC. Had another offensive player requested 22, he would have had to settle for another number by virtue of having signed with the team later than I did.

A rookie defensive back named Jim Morrissey also had number 22. If we both made the team, Morrissey would be the one to choose an alternate number since I was signed first.

It is amazing how attached an athlete can be to a certain number. Although most players probably aren't especially particular about their numbers, for others it is a simple superstition. Steve Bender told me he never cared what number he was in baseball and basketball but his football number always had to be 10. That was also my number as a high school quarterback.

And if they had assigned me a different number than 22?

I suppose I would have survived. A different number would not have zapped my strength or slowed me down. I was simply most comfortable with 22. I believed that it looked right on me.

Our first meeting took place that first night. The entire team initially crammed into the room where the offense would conduct its nightly meetings. Since the room was filled to roughly double its normal capacity there were several players and coaches standing around the perimeter.

Coach Walker stood at the podium up front. He was an outstanding coach but looked more like a chemistry professor or a banker or something in that line. His salt and pepper hair was combed straight back and was slightly thin on top. He was a thin man who wore wire-rimmed glasses and looked slightly older than his 48 years.

Walker had been an outstanding halfback at Oklahoma State. A severely dislocated shoulder his senior year ended whatever thoughts he may have had of playing professionally.

After taking one final drag off his Winston and crushing it out, Walker flashed a smile. It was sincere the same way he was sincere when he breathed fire at us.

"For those of you who haven't met me yet," Walker began, "I am head coach Chuck Walker and I would like to officially welcome you to the Hawaiians."

Walker introduced the rest of the coaching staff. There were nine assistants. All were personally selected by Walker except for his top assistant, Greg Wilson. Walker gave Wilson grudging approval at the behest of somebody in the front office. Wilson, as I said, was a nice guy but with few football leadership skills. Although he was technically second in command in the hierarchy, his duties required little else but to be there as Walker's yes man during camp. During games he spotted from the press box and, to his credit, did very well. Aside from that he was about as useful as a surfing instructor in Kansas.

"You are all here because you deserve the opportunity to try to make this team," Walker continued after he finished introducing the coaches. "I don't care if you were the first man drafted or the last free agent signed. Those who perform the best are the ones who will still be with us in September."

We had all been given handouts. The handouts comprised a detailed list of team rules including off-limits establishments; most of which were reputed to be hangouts for gamblers.

"Gambling is not legal in Hawaii," Walker stressed. "I assure you, there is gambling in Hawaii. There is a crime syndicate here. One of the ways it funds itself is gambling. People all over Hawaii spend their money on parlay sheets and other forms of betting on football games. Don't jeopardize your career by getting involved with gambling."

Once we had covered the handout we got into working on our playbooks. The offense stayed in the room and the defense moved into another meeting room.

Despite having an offensive coordinator, Walker conducted the offensive session the first night. He stood at the blackboard and diagrammed plays while we drew them in our playbooks.

Most of our plays had Hawaiian names. It was a way to help us identify with the community. They were common football plays but with names indigenous to Hawaii.

Much of the first session dealt with the kama'aina series. These are plays similar to the legendary Green Bay sweep and can be run from a variety of formations. The ball carrier runs around an end behind two pulling guards and one or two backs, depending on the formation.

Walker was a firm believer in doing what he believed would work regardless of what was trendy. We never used the wishbone, which was primarily a college formation, but he would not have hesitated to use it had he felt it would work. We used a plethora of formations, even what we called "the dotted I" which had the halfback directly behind the tailback who was behind the fullback. If there was something he saw on an elementary school playground that he thought would work, he would not hesitate to implement it.

One thing Walker stressed a lot was teamwork. All coaches do that, of course, but Walker stressed it much heavier than most.

"All the talent in the world means nothing if you don't play together," he stressed at least a few times that first night and would countless times for the rest of his career. "There are a lot of more talented teams in the NFL but you can beat any one of them if you play together."

That segued to our status as an expansion team. Very little would be expected of us.

With a few colorful words thrown in, Walker said such an attitude was unacceptable.

"We are not here simply to make a good showing. We are here to win. We won't win every game we play but we will not be satisfied with defeat. We will win, not by throwing in a lot of trick plays but by playing hard-nosed football. Our plays will be simple but effective if we pay attention, do our jobs and play as a team."

Walker paused, then laughed softly to himself.

"Why didn't I think to make that speech while the whole team was in the room?" Walker asked rhetorically, causing some muffled laughter in the room. "Okay, let's get down to business."

Our first day of camp was mild compared to what was to follow. Like most football training camps, we were governed by a rigorous schedule.

We were awakened at six o'clock by the sound of pounding on the door. There is nothing like being jolted from a sound sleep by a violent pounding on the door by a member of the coaching staff, usually Wilson.

After the first few days I reached the point where I could hear it coming. The pounding started down the hall and got louder and louder as it drew near. By the time it reached my door I was already sitting up or completely out of bed.

24

Breakfast began at 6:30 and lasted an hour. One of the cooks making a few extra bucks by cooking for us told me one day that he had recently transferred to Kaneohe. His previous two years were spent cooking for recruits in San Diego.

"I guess this must be like cooking for recruits," I remarked.

The Marine looked thoughtful for a moment as he looked around. He shook his head and smiled.

"The technique is the same, of course" he replied, "except there are a lot more recruits. Plus, you guys aren't wearing fatigues."

I looked around the room and took note of the eclectic mix. In this informal environment sat a group of football players wearing gym shorts, Bermuda shorts, blue jeans or whatever else suited them. Unlike the diners at the Marine Corps Recruit Depot, nobody was wearing fatigues. The only semblance of uniformity was simply a coincidence when two men happened to show up wearing blue jeans and similar light blue T-shirts.

"The big difference is the sound of the mess hall," the Marine said. "You guys are in here talking and laughing like you would in a civilian establishment. Recruits are absolutely forbidden to talk in the mess hall."

"Really? Not even 'pass the salt,'?" I asked.

"You talk, you walk."

After breakfast those who needed to have their ankles taped had that taken care of. That was also when half of the team lifted weights. Offense and defense rotated each day on using the weight room in the morning.

At nine o'clock we began our first workout of the day. These were fairly meticulously timed so that they would run exactly two hours. Occasionally they ran longer but never by more than about ten minutes. Deviating substantially would throw the entire day's schedule off track.

Lunch ran from 11:30 to one o'clock. At 1:30 we returned to our preparations for a workout. More taping was available for those who needed it. The weight room was used by whichever unit didn't use it that morning.

We were back on the field at three. Marine Corps personnel were usually present to watch a large group of men fighting for the right to play pro football so that we could be among the ranks of overpaid civilians.

Walker welcomed the base personnel. As paranoid as he could sometimes be whenever our sessions were watched, it was very unlikely that anybody ever joined the Marines simply to spy on the Hawaiians for the benefit of a favorite football team back home. Football coaches have been known to employ some innovative tactics to spy on opponents. Persuading somebody to join the Marines for this purpose was beyond comprehension so Walker didn't mind the audience.

Various members of the media were also frequently present. They simply needed to prearrange access to the base.

Dinner was at 5:30. This was also the time for modest hazing of the rookies. It was little more than getting the rookies to stand and sing. The singing was usually followed by jeers but it was all in fun. Most of the rookies even seemed to enjoy it. It was a way for them to bond better with the veterans.

At seven o'clock we had our meetings. Walker occasionally switched but he stuck primarily with the offense. Regardless of where Walker was, it was usually offensive coordinator Mike Tipton who drew up the new plays.

"Tonight we will start by diagramming our Wahiawa series," Tipton announced at the start of one such meeting.

While many plays had Hawaiian names, there was also a practical reason for why each play was so named. Wahiawa is a community in the center of the island of Oahu. A "Wahiawa" was simply a handoff up the middle.

An example of the play would be a "3 Wahiawa left." This meant the tailback would rush with the ball on the left side of the center.

A "4 Wahiawa" left or right meant that I or whoever was playing halfback carried the ball since the halfback was the four-back.

Before one reaches Wahiawa when driving from Honolulu, one will pass through Mililani. The close proximity to Wahiawa led to a series of draw plays up the middle bearing the Mililani name.

Then we had the Waikiki series. Since Waikiki is considered to be a tourist trap, the Waikiki series involved trap plays.

It seemed simple to me after five years in Hawaii. Some of the guys not familiar with Hawaii needed a little extra time.

Of course the left or right on such plays indicated the way the play was supposed to go. All a ball carrier looks for once he has the ball is daylight. It isn't unusual for a play up the middle to wind up going elsewhere if the intended hole gets plugged. Proper execution prevents that from happening but if a blocker misses his block or a defender reads the play and plugs the hole it will happen.

Our nightly meetings ended at about nine. That gave us three hours to unwind before curfew. Some guys relaxed in their rooms or the TV lounge. A few laundered street clothes. Some ventured off the base into neighboring Kailua or Kaneohe. Many sat outside and chatted while drinking the beer or soda which was picked up from the PX.

Usually I did the latter unless I was especially tired. I would sit in a large group near an aluminum tub full of beer and soda that was iced down. There would often also be supplies of chips, pretzels, peanuts and other snacks, courtesy of the team.

Monday nights were a different matter. Immediately after the meeting I drove to Honolulu to the TV studio on Kapiolani Boulevard. By ten o'clock I had pancake on my face and would tape my show for the following evening. Normally I was live but obligations to football, especially during training camp, mandated that some of my shows be prerecorded.

It wasn't as hard as it appeared since I made sure I was organized in advance. After taking time to read the newspaper each day and remaining in communication with the station, I had everything pretty well scripted. I also knew which video clips were available.

I began by going into a production room to narrate over the Major League Baseball highlights I had. I also talked about the week the Hawaii Islanders just had over a videotape of random highlights. I also did a narrative over clips of the Hawaiians training camp.

From the production room I went to the main studio and prerecorded the segments when I would actually be looking at the camera. The engineers would then edit everything in the proper order.

I was always finished by about eleven. That gave me enough time to drive over the Koolaus to the base with a little time to spare.

My teammates never saw my show during camp. A lot of them didn't even know I was doing a TV show. The show ran at 7:30 on Tuesday nights. That was when we were all in our evening meetings.

The first few days of workouts consisted primarily of conditioning. Agility drills, crab walks, grass drills, sprints and other grueling exercises were on the agenda. We also had various blocking drills, including various drills on the seven-man and two-man sleds, and tackling drills.

Football training camp produces a remarkable sight and sound. More than 100 men run around banging into each other, catching passes, slamming into sleds and doing an assortment of other drills in hope of being among slightly more than one-third who would still be with the team when we opened the season two months later. Amid the sounds one normally found on a Marine Corps air station were the sounds of blocking sleds, quarterbacks calling signals, pads colliding and players encouraging each other. Coaches were also very vocal, alternating between encouraging and berating players.

"Dig! Dig! Dig!"

"Hit that hole!"

"Okay, looking good! Looking good!"

"Hit the man! Don't kiss him!"

"Come on! You run like you've got a piano on your back! Let's move it!"

"That's the way to block!"

"You call that a pass? What do you have against a spiral?"

And so it went with nobody exempt from criticism or praise. The offensive players had to take part in open field tackling drills and the defensive players had to participate in downfield blocking drills since those skills would come into play on turnovers. Punters and kickers were also required to occasionally take part.

A total of 84 colleges were represented. There were the expected powerhouses, such as USC, Alabama and Notre Dame. There were also lesser-known schools such as Cal Poly, William and Mary, Vanderbilt, Azusa Pacific and Southeast Missouri which produce quality football players but are not considered to be breeding grounds for the NFL. There are occasions, however, when somebody from a lesser-known school rises to stardom while even Heisman Trophy winners from more well-known schools sometimes do very little in the NFL.

Not surprisingly, the University of Hawaii was the most represented school in camp with nine prospects. All eight of the others had been my teammates for at least part of my tenure as a Rainbow. Of the nine, five were rookies.

Only one Hawaii alumnus had prior NFL experience. Defensive tackle K.T. Smith played for Denver during part of 1973 and then resurfaced with Birmingham of the WFL over the next two seasons. My two other fellow veterans, safety Rich Hasegawa and defensive tackle Jimmy Souza, had played for the WFL Hawaiians.

Of the other schools represented, Kentucky, San Diego State, Syracuse and Washington had three alumni in camp. Fourteen other schools had two and everybody else had only one.

Walker had to fight to maintain his poise during the early days of camp. A sportswriter from a national publication asked if the reason there were nine Hawaii players in camp, as opposed to no more than three from any other school, was a ploy to put local people in the seats.

At the time we were doing agility drills and a few of the Hawaii contingent heard the ridiculous question. Hasegawa and I simultaneously turned our heads toward the reporter with looks that would never be mistaken for affection.

Walker held up his hand to let us know that we should go through our drills as if nothing had happened. The question was not only insulting to the Hawaii players but to Walker as well.

"The reason we have nine players from the University of Hawaii," Walker replied after taking a moment to lose the desire to respond with expletives, "is because there are nine players from the University of Hawaii who deserve to be here. Some of them won't make the team. They all earned the opportunity to try."

Walker paused. The media personnel were uneasily silent. They knew that Walker had more to say.

"The bottom line is that only the best players will make the team," Walker continued. "I don't care if they are all rookies or veterans or where anybody went to school. Those who can do the best for the team are the ones you'll see with us when the season starts."

I am sure it was no coincidence when Walker mentioned sportswriters at a joint meeting that night.

"There are a lot of good sportswriters," he said. "Occasionally you will encounter those who ask really stupid questions. Sometimes it is because

28

they're human and make mistakes. Sometimes it's because they're inexperienced. A few of them are just plain stupid. All I can suggest is you deal with them the best you can. Don't let them get to you. Just move on."

Ten years earlier I went to preseason workouts for the first time ever at South Valley High School. I have to reluctantly admit to having had no idea of what to expect. I thought we would be given equipment and proceed to run plays. I knew nothing about a solid week of conditioning drills.

We were on the field at eight o'clock. We ran sprints, did crab walks, hit the sled, did grass drills, did agility drills, did. . . . Our conditioning workouts at South Valley lasted only about 45 very long minutes. The time seemed interminable. The only time that passed quickly was the interim prior to three o'clock when we were back for more.

What I also remembered from that first high school preseason experience was walking stiff legged by midweek. Those who had played football before were more prepared and some even worked out during the summer months to try to get a head start. Even they were walking as if they had iron rods in their legs. Those of us without football experience especially were extremely pathetic sights.

When the weekend rolled around we were more limber. The coaches encouraged us to run on our own during the weekend. I did and so did some of the others. I was still somewhat in shock from spending a week doing what I never expected to do. I had kept my mouth shut since I didn't want anybody to know just how ignorant I had been. I think I was in college before I admitted to having been surprised by the week of conditioning prior to my freshman year of high school.

Secretly I wondered if I would play football beyond my high school freshman season. A decade later only two of us who were present that inaugural day at South Valley High were still donning the pads. We were both in the NFL.

Each full-padded workout for the Hawaiians was broken up into sections. The first 15 minutes were dedicated to calisthenics. After that we broke into units with the offensive backs and receivers in one group, the offensive line in another, the defensive line and linebackers in another and defensive backs in another. Occasionally the linebackers worked out with the defensive backs.

After about 20 minutes of this the offensive backs and receivers worked out with the defensive backs while the two lines and linebackers joined forces. This would last for about another 20 minutes.

For almost an hour afterward the entire squad worked together. I was at halfback which made me feel almost like an endangered species. The position was almost completely obsolete in the NFL but, as I pointed out, Walker was in favor of anything he thought would work.

The term halfback was once very common in football and can still be used. One simply hears it used very little as a result of offensive structures changing. Pro teams primarily have fullbacks and tailbacks although some teams refer to their backs simply as running backs. Occasionally a fullback will be referred to as a blocking back. There are also tailbacks referred to as halfbacks but their functions are different from mine.

My first experience as a halfback was in high school but on defense. As a two-way player I was a quarterback and defensive left halfback. The latter is more commonly referred to now as the left cornerback. The name has changed the way a split end is now a wide receiver.

An offensive halfback for the Hawaiians is the third back who sets up in the backfield directly behind the linemen. Since most pro teams now usually employ only two backs directly behind the linemen and occasionally only one, one rarely hears a player referred to as a halfback.

Again, Walker went with whatever he felt would be effective. During my tenure with the Hawaiians that meant utilizing the services of a fullback, tailback and halfback.

I was a halfback essentially because I functioned as a running back and wide receiver. As a running back I lined up in various spots behind the line. As a wide receiver I lined up wide to either side but always in a slot behind the line of scrimmage. I could still catch passes in my running back formation and there were plays when I lined up wide and went in motion before taking a handoff.

Had I been with another team I probably would have been strictly a wide receiver. I preferred my halfback position because of the diversity. I was a rusher, receiver and occasionally even a passer.

I also wasn't averse to blocking. I enjoyed blocking downfield and also in the trenches to help the other blockers open a hole. It is an awesome feeling when you lay a solid block on somebody and knock him out of the play. I guess when I chose pro football over baseball I subconsciously decided to be as complete a player as possible.

During our workouts some players were briefly called away for special teams drills. This included me since I was among those considered for returning punts and kickoffs. The special teams units were to be comprised primarily of younger players. Since I was only 24, I was a very viable candidate.

At the end of each workout we had what we dreaded most. That was when we did wind sprints or grass drills or both. At the end of a two-hour workout these drills seemed to run for an eternity.

Walker wasn't totally sadistic. There were teams that reportedly operated on the same schedule seven days a week but Walker believed that was excessive. Walker believed it was best for all concerned if he gave us a little time off over the weekend.

This was well thought out by Walker who was a bit of a psychologist. He believed a break in the routine would be better for morale and attitudes. The break would also give players time to heal minor aches and pains.

On Saturday we were excused after the second workout. Walker initially was going to allow only those with families in the area to sleep at home on Saturday nights. He modified that to include anybody who had a permanent residence on the island. That obviously meant that I could sleep in my own bed one night a week. Those without permanent residences still had the midnight curfew but could leave again after breakfast on Sunday. We were all required to be back in camp by midnight Sunday night.

What did I do with my time off?

Primarily I relaxed. I didn't have wild nights. I didn't even date during this period. I simply wanted to kick back without any obligations.

If the Islanders were home I went directly from the base to Aloha Stadium. I would nurse a beer while sitting down the first base line and cheering on the Islanders while chatting with friends I had known from previous seasons at Honolulu Stadium.

Islander games really did relax me physically and mentally. It was a diversion from football and an opportunity to mingle with people who were not involved with football.

When the Islanders were playing on the road I simply went home. My free time when not watching baseball was spent by doing quiet things that I enjoyed. A good book, a walk on the beach, or time in front of the TV kept me pacified. I also enjoyed stretching out in my king size bed and not having to get up at the crack of dawn.

The scenery was certainly better at home. There was rarely an opportunity to venture away from camp for any substantial period of time during the rest of the week. At camp I didn't see much other than football players and Marines.

Being home was a breath of fresh air. From my 14th floor lanai I could look across the Ala Wai Canal to Ala Wai Field and see groups of young men playing baseball. Outrigger canoes were being paddled in the canal and on the sidewalks below I could see walkers, joggers and bicyclists who had nothing to do with football or the Marines.

Off in the distance I could see Kaimuki and Tantalus. At the foot of Manoa valley I could see the University of Hawaii. These landmarks, which seemed so common, seemed incredibly foreign while I was toiling in camp.

One Sunday night Marv Nelson and I were late for curfew after attending an Islander game. Marv's wife usually dropped him off at camp but had another commitment this time. Since Marv also liked baseball, I picked him up at his Aina Haina home and we went to Aloha Stadium with every intention of making it back in plenty of time.

We stopped to eat after the game at the Bob's Big Boy in Mapunapuna since we still had plenty of time. What we didn't count on was the flat tire on Likelike Highway.

We reached the gate at 12:05. In order to get back on base we also had to show the sentries our credentials. The sentries were instructed to log the time each late player returned and turn the log over to the team. That was how we got caught.

The first infraction was a 125-dollar fine. Walker was sympathetic when he questioned us but he couldn't back down from policy. Each subsequent infraction was double the previous amount. Neither Marv nor I was late for curfew again.

Breaking curfew without getting caught wasn't impossible. It was still probably more difficult at our camp than at other camps. Being on a Marine base, there was virtually nowhere to go within the confines of the base. If one left the base, he had the guards at the gate waiting to take down his name and time of return.

Cornerback Mark Black came up with an innovative way of circumventing the curfew rule. He began by getting his blonde hair cut Marine Corps style. He then befriended a couple of young Marines. After bed check he slipped away and met his friends who took him to the EM Club.

The Marines were insurance in case somebody was checking for IDs in the club. They could bring Black in as a guest. The haircut enabled Mark to not look conspicuously like a football player breaking curfew.

Of course Mark's accomplices drank for free. The promise of free beer was all they needed to agree to assist Mark in his scheme.

Black never got caught as far as I know. Bucking the system was a way of life for him. He played football for four years at Oklahoma but claims he rarely saw the inside of a classroom. He even seemed proud of himself for it.

Of course Mark wasn't in a class by himself. Countless athletes turned the term student-athlete into an oxymoron. As one who actually took academics seriously, I was never happy to hear about athletes who attended school for four years without actually getting an education.

Sometime during our morning workout on July 16 I noticed a former teammate was missing.

"Where's Manfra?" I discreetly asked Kevin Salles, sadly sure that my inquiry was rhetorical.

"I was just wondering the same thing," the fullback from Middle Tennessee State who had been with Manfra and me in the WFL replied. "I heard that a few people got cut this morning. I guess he was one of them."

There were actually four casualties although Bill Manfra was the only nonrookie who was cut. Manfra was a very gregarious tackle who came to

32

the Hawaiians the previous season after a year in Cleveland. He may have been slightly out of shape when he reported to camp but not so much that I thought he would be among the initial cuts.

Different teams had different methods for cutting players. I'd heard of instances of players finding out they had been cut by discovering that their lockers had been cleaned out. That is about as ruthless as it can get.

Some teams have personnel directors or assistant coaches who make the cuts. Walker insisted on handling this unpleasant task himself. He didn't feel it was right to relegate something so unpleasant to somebody else. He felt that since he was the one who made the final decision on who got cut, it was his responsibility to give the bad news.

Whenever a cut was made there were actually three coaches involved in delivering the sad tidings. One would send the unfortunate player to Walker's office. Another would be with Walker in case the player threatened violence.

"I've literally had to cut hundreds of players," Walker was quoted as saying in a local newspaper a few years later. "It's about the most unpleasant task a coach has. Most players accept it although the disappointment shows. A few times I was called every dirty name you can imagine. A few have broken down and cried or even begged for a little more time."

The cuts that Walker had to make during the 1976 training camp were obviously difficult on Walker although he never really got to know these players. It got tougher in later years when he had to cut players who had been with the team for a few years. Walker was one tough, relentless cookie. He still gave his heart to virtually every player who spent so much as a single day with the team.

Like any pro football team, cuts are a necessary evil. Walker normally started making cuts toward the end of the second week. He figured by that time he could pick out the few who had absolutely no hope.

Until we got into our exhibition schedule there were no prespecified dates for cuts. They happened whenever Walker was convinced that somebody was not going to work out. It could have been for a lack of talent, lack of proper conditioning or a lack of heart.

Excepting disciplinary cases when cuts were more impetuous, all cuts were made after breakfast. Walker tried to make it as easy on the unfortunates as possible. He figured it was best to allow each casualty to get a good night's sleep and good breakfast before getting the bad news. Excepting those living in Hawaii, all casualties had flights of a minimum of five hours after being cut. That made for extremely long flights.

During that first training camp it didn't take us long before we figured out when cuts were being made. We knew at least one victim would depart whenever we saw Coach Wilson lurking outside the dining hall during breakfast. His job was to wait for each designated victim and inform the unluckies that Walker wanted to see them in his office and to take their playbooks. Those who got past Wilson knew they had at least a 24-hour stay of execution.

The further into training camp we got, the harder it was to decide whom to cut. There comes a point when those being cut are good enough to make the team but there simply isn't room for them. Some will turn up with other teams. Some will be recalled by the Hawaiians later if a spot opens up. Some will be kept on the taxi squad.

Walker tried to be as encouraging as possible when he made cuts. Even those cut early were asked if they would like to try to hook on elsewhere. Through an agreement between the team and the airline that handled our flights, each player was booked on a flight to either his home or the city of a team willing to give the player a look.

How secure did I feel?

I always worked hard. I never took it for granted that I had the team made. I knew it could all abruptly end if I didn't work hard.

My roommate during that first NFL training camp wanted me cut in the worst way. Robert Shibata and I were paired off because we were both halfbacks with pro experience. He was half Japanese and the other half was a potpourri of White nationalities. He grew up near San Francisco in Foster City and played college football at Pacific.

It took me about five minutes to ascertain conclusively that Shibata hated my guts. The only reason I can think of, in all humility, was because he was jealous of me for being a better football player. He knew that I had been a starter during my two years in the WFL. He knew about the Hawaiians giving up a top draft choice to keep me and he probably knew that I was number one on the depth chart even though I didn't even know about that until years later.

Shibata was with his fifth team in five seasons. He was with San Francisco his rookie season, playing in only three games and spending the rest of the season on the taxi squad. The following season he played in one game with Denver and spent the rest of that season on the taxi squad.

Finding no takers in the NFL after his release from Denver, the WFL prolonged his career. He spent one year with the Portland Storm and one year with the Chicago Wind. He was signed as a free agent by the Hawaiians shortly before minicamp in May in Palo Alto, California.

I suppose I should have been more compassionate toward Shibata. It is simply too hard to feel compassion for somebody who wants to make the team so bad that he is willing to spend a lot of time spreading rumors about you. According to what I was told, he tried to convince my teammates that I was some combination of drug addict, rapist, homosexual, child molester and a few other pleasantries. Had it occurred to him that I was living in Los Angeles County at the time of the Tate-LaBianca murders he probably would have tied me in with the Mansons.

34

From the very beginning I gave Shibata very little chance of making the team. He was fast and had fairly good hands as a receiver but those were the only attributes I could see. He couldn't block anything much more agile than a turtle, was a so-so tackler and did not hit the holes very well when rushing. He would have had a better opportunity to make the team had he gone out strictly as a wide receiver although even there he would have had very little chance. As soon as he was hit he was not one to fight for the extra yard.

Yet he hung on. I wasn't sure if Walker and his staff saw something in him that I couldn't see or if they hadn't gotten around to noticing Shibata's ineptitude. Perhaps Walker thought the man who was cut by four teams in as many years would improve.

The halfback I was fairly certain would make the team was Gary Giametti. He was the team's eighth round draft pick out of Long Beach State and looked good. He wasn't as fast as me but he was a good receiver and hit the holes well when rushing. He also wasn't afraid to block and tackle, meaning he left Shibata in the dust.

Gary was somewhat flippant initially although that was to be expected. Not only did he want to make the team, he wanted to start. Who could blame him for that?

I am one of those people who always loved to throw a football. Even before I began playing high school football it was something I loved to do. There was something about the way I could make it spiral and fly majestically toward its target.

What I never gave much thought to was my accuracy. It never mattered whether I was playing a simple game of catch or throwing to somebody running a pattern. I usually got the ball where I wanted it to go. It was like the hand of God guiding it.

How ironic it was that I couldn't do the same thing with a basketball. I played during my first two years of high school but didn't have the touch required to be anything more than a low percentage shooter. I was good on defense and could rebound but I definitely wasn't the one to go to if a hoop at the buzzer was needed.

But I could thread a needle with a football. Go figure!

My love for throwing a football carried into training camp. I usually threw the ball around some before our workouts to loosen up. Occasionally I would throw passes for a few minutes after our workouts to a few Marines who had been watching the workouts. It enabled them and me to have some fun.

What I didn't know was that some of the coaching staff was taking note of my passing ability, especially since I was dropping back and rolling out before unleashing my passes. I was simply doing as I had done in high school without giving it a second thought.

Toward the end of the second week offensive coordinator Mike Tipton approached me after an evening meeting.

"Coach Walker wants to see you in his office," Tipton said.

That's the kind of statement that makes a prospect's heart stop beating. At that moment I started sorting through my head about which football teams might have an opening for me after Walker sent me packing. Cuts had only just begun. Walker's policy of making cuts only in the morning wasn't known yet.

"Right now?" I asked.

"Right now," Tipton replied, finding mild amusement in my discomfort.

Tipton escorted me into Walker's office. Walker was casually leaning back in his swivel chair behind his desk. Also seated in the room were Greg Wilson and backs and receivers coach Craig Bennici.

"Have a seat, Jay," Walker instructed congenially.

I sat and looked at Tipton. He must have read the relief in my head once I realized I wasn't being cut. He smirked, getting Walker's and Bennici's attention since they seemed to have read the situation and also smirked. Wilson looked perplexed.

"Did you really think you were brought here to be cut?" Walker asked, beaming.

"Well, I wasn't sure," I admitted, smiling finally. "It certainly crossed my mind."

This was when Walker explained to me his policy of making cuts only in the morning except for disciplinary cases. The obvious compassion he had for those being sent home made me realize that Walker was much more complex than a simple martinet. He cared about those he cut and, as I would observe, he cared about those he didn't cut.

"Were you ever a quarterback?" Walker asked.

"In high school I was," I replied somewhat tentatively.

"We thought so," he said. "We've been watching you throw passes out there. You're got a good strong accurate arm."

"Well, thanks."

At this juncture we still had six quarterbacks in camp. They all seemed fairly healthy and were skilled enough from my point of view. I could not fathom why Walker was so interested in my quarterbacking skills.

"We have two things in mind," Walker said. "First of all, we want to create a few plays where you will pass to a receiver from the halfback position. Do you think you can handle something like that in the NFL?"

"Well, we had a few plays where I passed in college and in the WFL. I don't see why I can't do it in the NFL."

"Good," Walker replied brightly. "Of course it isn't a top priority right now. It's just something we may add during the regular season. First we want to get you used to working some at quarterback."

"What?" I asked abruptly, causing the coaches in the room to chuckle.

36

"A lot of professional teams have a backup or two for the regular quarterbacks," Walker explained. "We were looking for somebody to fill that role. With the way you pass the ball you seem like a good candidate. Are you with us on this?"

"So far, I guess. What you're saying, I think, is that I would be put in at quarterback if the regular quarterbacks get hurt."

"Exactly," said Tipton.

"You'd be a safety valve," Wilson added.

"Right," said Walker. "We're not sure if we're going to keep two or three quarterbacks this season. Regardless of that, the possibility of you having to fill in seems very, very remote. Just the same, we'll start having you run some plays occasionally in practice so you'll be ready in case we need you."

"Okay," I responded brightly.

"Just remember," Walker cautioned, "you're here as a halfback, not a quarterback. Whether you make the team or not is contingent on how you perform at halfback."

The following day part of the workouts were run with me at quarterback. Although it had been seven years since I quarterbacked my high school team, I felt very natural at the position that turned me into a football player a decade earlier.

As it was, Walker had several people prepared to play something other than their normal positions in case of emergency. He didn't do it to the point of it being a distraction but just enough so that those concerned were familiar enough with alternate assignments. Virtually every position had somebody capable of being a safety valve. Walker simply refused to leave any stone unturned.

During lunch one day I shared a table with Steve Bender, Ted Dietrich and Clint Abraham. The topic of discussion was baseball. We had all played for our high school teams. All but Clint had been pursued by professional teams.

"I had a lot of power," the black offensive tackle who had been a catcher for his high school team in Compton, California, said. "The trouble was, I struck out too much. If I got the bat on the ball it would sail but usually I was a sure whiff."

I had actually been drafted six times in baseball. I was drafted by Cincinnati out of high school. During my junior year in college I was drafted by Kansas City, being eligible for the draft while still in college since I had turned 21. The following winter I was drafted by Boston. Since that coincided with the football drafts I wound up having to choose among Boston, Dallas of the NFL, and Hawaii of the WFL.

It didn't end there. Possibly because of the WFL's shaky future, I was drafted by the Mets, Cardinals and Giants in subsequent drafts. I was nearly the final choice by the Mets and was literally the final choice by the

Cardinals and Giants. They were ostensibly merely interested in holding the rights to me in case I decided to turn to baseball.

My primary position in baseball had been center field. Since I was left-handed, I also played a lot of first base. In high school I also pitched on a semi-regular basis and continued to pitch on occasion in college. I had a fastball that had been clocked in the upper 90s. I also had a curve that "usually" broke, a changeup and could even throw the occasional knuckleball.

Ted was drafted out of his Bellingham, Washington, high school by the Washington Senators. He had been his team's center fielder. Had it not been for the football scholarship offers he said he definitely would have signed with the Senators.

Steve was never drafted in baseball simply because baseball didn't have a draft in his baseball days. The San Francisco Giants made a substantial effort to sign him after his glory days as a third baseman for his high school in San Jose, California, but not substantial enough. What he wanted most of all was the opportunity to get his college degree. Since the Giants were not willing to help him with that, he accepted a football scholarship to the University of California at Santa Barbara.

Sitting at a table close enough to hear the conversation was Gary Giametti. The rookie approached me on the way to that afternoon's drills.

"What high school did you go to?" he asked.

"South Valley. Why?"

"And you pitched and played center field?"

"Yeah," I said.

"Now I know where I'd seen you before. It's been bugging me since the day I met you. Do you remember playing a game in Lakewood when you were brought in from center field to pitch?"

"Yeah, kind of," I responded tentatively. "The way I remember it, we had a two-run lead, there were two outs and the bases were loaded when I came in. Is that the game you mean?"

"That's the one," Gary replied cheerily.

"You were there, huh?"

"Of course I was. Who do you think hit the home run off of you?"

"Oh geez," I moaned, stopping in my tracks and looking incredulously at Gary.

"That was you?"

"That was me."

I vividly recalled working the count to a ball and two strikes. I tried to sneak a curve on the outside corner by him. Unfortunately the curve refused to curve, preferring to simply hang for an eternity as if the ball was a masochist begging to be clobbered. Gary blasted it over the left field fence to win the game for his team.

38

What made the incident memorable for me was it was the only grand slam home run I ever surrendered. I had given up other home runs but none with the bases loaded.

"That was the first varsity home run I ever hit," said Gary who was a sophomore at the time while I was a senior.

"Glad I could help," I deadpanned.

This encounter enigmatically marked the beginning of a friendship between Gary and me. We were competing for the same position and that had kept a barrier between us. We were still competing but had both grown secure enough to be friendly.

The third week of training camp was brutal for cuts. Between Tuesday and Friday there were 17 prospects given tickets home.

Five of those cut had previous pro experience ranging between two and seven years. Among the dozen rookie hopefuls were two from the University of Hawaii. Free agent guard Kalani Kanoe was among Thursday's casualties. Cornerback Randy Sterling was waived on Friday.

Walker believed it was wrong to keep players in camp who had no chance of making the team. If he knew somebody had absolutely no chance, either because he wasn't good enough or if the remaining players at his position were simply that much better, he figured it was best to let the player go. That gave the player an opportunity to find another team that might be able use him.

Kanoe fell into the latter category. The guard position was simply too top heavy. Barring injuries, Marv Nelson and Bill Stanek were expected to start when we opened the season. Jim Kohl also looked like a sure bet and there was stiff competition among Greg Henry, rookie Randy Hubert, Brian Purl and WFL Hawaiian veteran Abraham Foster. Of the eight guards remaining in camp, at least three were likely to be dismissed before the start of the season.

Two halfbacks were cut on Friday. One of them was Keith Parker, a seven-year veteran out of Portland State. He definitely had experience in packing his bags after stops in Philadelphia, San Francisco, Pittsburgh, Miami and Kansas City.

The other halfback was Fred Landers, a rookie out of New Mexico. He was a decent running back but wasn't much of a receiver.

Obviously this reduced my competition to three. Giametti was one. There was also Kent Oglethorpe, a tall 15th round draft choice from Ohio State, and Shibata.

"Hey Dockman," a center named Keith Fradella called as he approached after an afternoon workout. "Somebody's looking for you."

"Who?"

"Some Marine. Oh, there he is," the nine-year veteran taken from Minnesota in the expansion draft reported, pointing to a Hispanic Marine in street clothes about 20 feet away.

I wasn't sure if this was somebody I should have recognized. He didn't look at all familiar to me.

"Were you looking for me?" I asked congenially.

"Jay Dockman?"

"Yeah."

"From Azusa?"

It was getting eerie. A decade had passed since my family moved from Azusa to Montebello. How strange it seemed to run into somebody who connected me with Azusa.

But I didn't readily recognize this individual. I couldn't ascertain if this was somebody I had fought with or with whom I had been friendly. Azusa wasn't a bad place, but in the section where I had lived either was possible.

"I did live in Azusa," I admitted. "I moved away from there ten years ago."

"I know," the Marine said. "Do you remember me?"

"I'm not sure."

"Jim Martinez?"

"Jim Martinez?" I repeated enthusiastically, shaking his hand.

Like a lightning bolt it came back to me. He was the little brother of my old friend David Martinez. David was my age while Jim was a few years younger. Jim graduated from high school in 1973 and entered the Marine Corps for a three-year hitch in January, 1974. For 18 months he was stationed at Subic Bay in the Philippines which included an opportunity to play two seasons on the base football team. He was then transferred to Kaneohe where he would remain until his separation from the Marines, which was scheduled for January, 1977.

I told Jim that I had a schedule to keep but that I wanted to spend a little time with him. He agreed to return at nine o'clock so that we could rendezvous after the evening meeting.

We spent a couple of hours at the EM Club on base. I was there as Jim's guest and we enjoyed a few beers. The last time I had seen him he was still playing Little League baseball.

My most memorable, and nearly fatal, experience with Jim took place in 1963. Jim's brother David and I were walking to school together when we stumbled across two boys who appeared to be about our age trying to relieve Jim, who was eight, of his lunch money.

David and I squared off against the two boys. I knocked one boy down and made the mistake of turning my back on him to stare down the other boy whom David had been fighting. The boy I had knocked down snuck up from behind and stabbed me in the side with a switchblade.

40

My answer to where I was when President Kennedy was assassinated is that I was in surgery. I was stabbed just a few hours before Kennedy was shot.

Obviously I recovered from the stabbing. although it took some time. I didn't return to school until February.

At the EM Club Jim told me he had watched the Hawaiians work out on occasion.

"Why didn't you approach me before today?" I asked.

"Because I didn't know who you were. I never knew your last name in Azusa. I knew there was a Jay Dockman playing for the Hawaiians. I just didn't know it was somebody I used to know."

An arbitrary phone call to his family the night before enlightened Jim. David happened to be there and told Jim who I was.

David graduated from high school in 1969. He was drafted in 1971 and was sent to Vietnam but returned unscathed. He went to college for a year, then got married and took a job as a welder. He was living in Duarte.

Like any facet of society, a pro football team is not immune from adversity. Our first test of such had nothing to do with sex, drugs, illness or even anything where culpability rested on a player. It dealt strictly with the demented views of a member of the coaching staff.

Defensive coordinator Joe Bancroft was hired by Walker primarily based on his reputation. The stocky, balding coach who had been a successful coach at schools in Texas, Louisiana and Arizona was not somebody Walker knew except by his record. Walker was still impressed enough after interviewing Bancroft that he hired him. Although Bancroft had no prior coaching experience on the professional level, Walker made him defensive coordinator because he was considered to be the most qualified among the defensive coaches.

Walker could have found out exactly what he needed to know had he asked Bancroft his feelings about Martin Luther King, Malcolm X, Stevie Wonder or even George Jefferson. Since those figures have little to do with football, Walker didn't ask. Nor was he aware that Bancroft had never worked on a coaching staff that included Blacks.

Until he was hired by the Hawaiians.

Offensive line coach Jerry Meacham, linebacker coach Max Crawford and defensive back coach William Pickett were all Black. Within the first few weeks it became painfully obvious that Bancroft was unhappy that the coaching staff was 30 percent Black. It became especially evident to Crawford and Pickett since he was superseding their defensive proposals.

Bancroft had coached black players before. That was a different matter. Bancroft was among those who believed that Blacks were genetically strong physically which made them ideal for athletic competition and manual labor.

Bancroft was not an especially warm person anyway so his contempt for Blacks might not have been obvious right away.

Walker realized what he had on his hands when Bancroft literally asked why there were Blacks on the staff. It should be noted, though, that Bancroft used language that was far less polite. When Bancroft expressed his perceived notion that Blacks did not have the intelligence or sense of responsibility to be coaches, Walker immediately fired him.

This all went down about three days before the team's public scrimmage at Kailua High School. Walker was absolutely livid and everybody could see it.

At our meeting that night we had everybody in the same room. Walker walked in and moved directly to the podium at the front of the room.

"If anybody here has any problem about having to play with people of other races," Walker began in a tone that did not betray his anger, "I want you to get the hell out of here right now and save me the trouble of having to kick you off the team later."

Walker looked around with a scowl that was not contrived. The silence was deadly. At this point very few people were apprised of what had gone down. Bancroft was last seen at our morning workout. Later there were rumors circulating that he was gone from the team but no confirmation and no known reason.

"We have one fewer member of the coaching staff now because of one's racist attitude," Walker continued. "As far as I'm concerned, Joe Bancroft doesn't even exist. Bigotry has no place on any team in my charge."

That said, Walker softened his tone.

"I blame myself for this. I probably should have seen something when I interviewed him but I obviously didn't. I apologize to anybody he may have treated more harshly because of race."

Walker paused and looked around the room again. He was generally a reasonable man even though occasionally it was easy to forget that aspect of him. His goal simply had been to build as good a football team as was humanly possible by giving everybody a fair opportunity to make the team. He wasn't going to keep or cut a player based on his race.

"There are a lot of factors taken into consideration for who makes this team and who doesn't," Walker stressed. "How well you fit in with the team depends largely on how well you play but it doesn't stop there. Each person has character flaws and we can accept those to a point. Racism will absolutely not be tolerated and neither will anything else that disrupts the team. If you disrupt the team, you're gone."

Walker stepped back and grimaced. It was obvious that he was deeply affected and weighed his words carefully. In subsequent camps he included his views on racism during the opening night meeting. In this camp he apparently entered camp believing racism would not be a problem.

"Those of you who make the team will be representing Hawaii," Walker finally continued. "Hawaii is one of the most racially diverse places in the entire world. If there is any player, coach or anybody else affiliated with the team who feels he can't function with people of other races, now is the time to walk out. There is no spot on this team or in this community for a racist. Any questions?"

Perhaps adding insult to Bancroft's injury, although not for that purpose, his former position was filled by a Black man. Max Crawford assumed the role of defensive coordinator. Since there wasn't an opportunity to hire a new linebacker coach, Crawford continued in that capacity as well.

As for Bancroft, his coaching days probably ended that day. At least I never heard anything about him again. He was probably too busy burning crosses to send the team a postcard.

The night before our public scrimmage Russ Allen began a tradition. He arbitrarily grabbed a group of rookies, recruited a few veterans with wheels, and led a caravan to the Shakey's on Kamehameha Highway in Kaneohe. I drove Russ's lifelong friend Norm Richards since I only had room for one passenger in my Porsche. Marv Nelson, Rich Hasegawa and Ed Jennings put a few rookies in their cars. As I recall, there were 16 of us livening up the pizza parlor.

This became an annual tradition although it didn't always take place the night before the scrimmage. It was always on a Friday night, though. A handful of us would grab as many rookies as we could fit into our cars and take them out for pizza. Initially we went to Shakey's until a Pizza Hut opened that was closer. We made a lot of noise, I guess, but we also spent a lot of money, tipped well and never tore the place apart so we were always welcome.

This gathering was one of many ways that Russ led the team. He motivated a lot of people to do well.

One of the best things to happen to the NFL Hawaiians took place on January 4, 1975. That was while the Hawaiians were of the WFL vintage but it was also the day that Russ, while driving his Pontiac on South Boulevard near Detroit, wound up in a head-on collision. There were no fatalities or serious injuries but Russ suffered a broken left foot and a broken right leg.

Good for us!

I suppose I should qualify that. Russ had just completed his fifth season at the time of the accident. He had gone to the Pro Bowl twice and one Detroit sportswriter referred to him as Detroit's greatest defensive player since Alex Karras in his prime.

Naturally Russ was incapacitated for a little while. He played the 1975 season although not at full strength. It appeared to team officials that Russ had lost his edge.

The Lions should have been more patient. Instead they left Russ unprotected in the expansion draft. The Hawaiians snapped him up.

What the Lions surrendered was not only an outstanding football player but a leader as well. By the time he reported to camp he had regained everything he had previously lost. Virtually everybody could see early on that Russ was going to anchor the defense.

Russ encouraged everybody. He was the epitome of a team player. He was so secure with his own ability that he would even go out of his way to assist those who were competing for his position. He would ride those who didn't seem to be going all out.

"That's not the way to make the team!" I would see him holler in his quest to encourage a young hopeful to put more of himself into it. "Come on now! Keep that head up! Drive! Drive! You can do it! Show me what you've got! That's the way!"

Russ also had his lighter side. He was usually the catalyst for getting the rookies to sing during the evening meals. He also snuck into the rookie barracks one morning while they were still sleeping and found creative ways to make shaving cream sculptures on their bodies. A few rookies woke up and watched and giggled as Russ performed his artwork.

And then there was the chocolate syrup in the soap dispensers. Nobody knows who was responsible. There was a lot of speculation that Russ had something to do with it.

Russ moved to Hawaii with his wife, Ellen, about a month before the opening of training camp. They sold their house in Michigan and bought a condominium at the corner of Beretania and Punahou streets in Honolulu. This was on the same parcel of land as one of the gyms where I worked out. Occasionally I saw him pumping iron but I didn't meet him or know that he was one of my teammates until I saw him when training camp opened.

July 24, 1976 was when the NFL Hawaiians made their first public appearance. The venue was Kailua High School.

This was our intrasquad scrimmage. This would wind up being an annual event at a local high school, usually on the windward side of Oahu because of its close proximity to the base. We did venture elsewhere occasionally including to neighbor islands.

Admission in 1976 was a mere two dollars. That was a reasonable price, even then, especially when considering that this was a charity event. The team's only profit was whatever exposure it got. After paying for the use of the field the proceeds went to local charities.

By the time the scrimmage rolled around there were 94 left on the active roster. Aside from one who didn't pass the physical on opening day, the remainder of those no longer with us had been cut. Nobody had left the team voluntarily and, perhaps miraculously, nobody was to be held out because of injury.

Our routine the morning of the scrimmage was similar to that of any other morning. Our workout, though, was done at half-speed without pads and only lasted about an hour. We were also divided up according to which unit we would represent.

After lunch we lounged around. There were no restrictions on us as long as we were dressed and ready to board the buses by 5:30. Our briefing for the scrimmage took place the night before.

I left the base for a few hours. I even considered going home but thought better of it. I drove through parts of Kailua and Kaneohe simply to revel in the ephemeral freedom. I also took a walk on a beach in the Aikahi section of Kailua and then had a Big Mac for a pre-scrimmage snack.

For this scrimmage we wore our game uniforms for the first time. They were actually uniforms from the WFL Hawaiians but they were identical to what we would be wearing as the NFL Hawaiians. That meant that the uniforms of both units were identical except that one unit wore white jerseys while the other wore brown.

The only difference between what we were wearing that night and what we would wear during games was the players' names were not sewn on the backs of the jerseys. The exceptions were those of us who had been with the Hawaiians in the WFL. The following week we would play our first exhibition game in brand new uniforms complete with names on the backs.

We left the base shortly after 5:30 and headed toward Kailua High School. It was not at all like the bus rides we would take on the road. On road trips we were on air-conditioned tour buses instead of the gray Marine Corps buses with drivers in fatigues.

It was a quiet trip as players and coaches focused on their assignments. The scrimmage was taken as seriously as a game since careers were on the line. Everybody knew that this scrimmage would represent the last time a handful of hopefuls would work out with the team. Most, if not all, of those cut Monday morning would never play football again.

We went through the main business district in Kailua. Most who spotted us recognized us as their representatives in the NFL. A few car horns honked as the occupants waved. A few people on the sidewalks waved including one Polynesian male of high school age who raised his index finger to lend his support. There were also a few cries of "Go Hawaiians" and one diehard fan, apparently transplanted from San Diego or possibly an alumnus of Pearl City High School or even my own beloved South Valley High School, who yelled "Go Chargers."

On the high school field in the Pohakupu section of Kailua we limbered up and warmed up. A lot of people were already in their seats when we arrived. Officials speculated that "as many as a thousand" might show up but the actual attendance turned out to be almost ten times that many. A lot of people wound up watching in a standing room only situation.

Coach Walker supervised the scrimmage. Greg Wilson headed the team in white jerseys and Mike Tipton ran the team in brown. The teams were appointed by position and according to the depth chart.

45

As players we never knew how the teams were divided up. Positions on the depth chart were known only to the coaches. Throughout training camp, they mixed everybody up during the workouts so that nobody could be completely sure of who fit in where. It would become a little more apparent once the exhibition games started since the top members usually got the starting nods. Even then it wasn't indelibly carved in stone.

The ambience was similar to an actual game. The yard lines were marked and three local high school officials were hired to keep order on the field. The scoreboard wasn't turned on but there was a public address announcer to help keep track of who did what. Music was provided by the Royal Hawaiian Band during breaks in the action. The local Shriners sent clowns to help entertain the kids in the bleachers.

It was still a scrimmage and not a game. That is obviously why the scoreboard was not turned on. Tipton's offense started on the 20-yard line and ran ten plays from scrimmage and then Wilson's offensive squad did the same thing. After this cycle was repeated a few times there was a break while kickoff, punting and field goal units got some work. Then we went back to the offensive and defensive units getting in some work before calling it a night.

This was the only intrasquad affair where it was permissible to sack the quarterback. The coaches considered not allowing it before deciding that the scrimmage should be as close as possible to actual game conditions. The officials were still instructed to blow the whistles if the quarterback was in somebody's grasp before he was brought down whenever possible. This was well before the NFL implemented an "in the grasp" rule. There was also no blitzing.

I was on Wilson's team so I was in a white jersey. I rushed twice for nine yards and caught four passes for 66 yards. I also had a good kickoff return of 29 yards and returned a punt for eight yards.

Kent Oglethorpe was the other halfback on the white team. He rotated with me so that we each got three series. Gary Giametti and Robert Shibata did the same on Tipton's brown squad.

Marv Nelson was on my team. Other white teammates included Rich Grummon — taken in the expansion draft from the Giants; Craig Kamanu, Jeff Kerner, rookie quarterback Sid Crosley — a 22nd-round draft choice out of Wisconsin; Ed Jennings, Edmund Kupau and Kupau's main obstacle toward making the team, Gavin Pratt. Pratt was a third-round draft choice out of Arkansas and somebody who appeared ready to instantly transfer from All-American to All-Pro.

If this scrimmage was any indication, Steve Bender was a lock for starting quarterback. For the quarterbacks this was the most intense competition they had faced thus far, if for no other reason than they no longer had their protective red jerseys. Bender completed five consecutive passes on the brown team's first ten-play series for 68 yards. This included a five-yard touchdown on the ninth play to tight end Danny Klaas, a five-year veteran taken from Buffalo in the expansion draft.

Bender's performance may have been bad news for Frank Joseph. The seven-year veteran quarterback out of Colorado State had spent virtually his entire career as a backup with the Jets. Bender was believed to have already been earmarked as our starter and his near perfection during the scrimmage not only increased Joseph's chances for a season on the bench but even his chances for not making the team. With Joe Billingsley drafted so high it appeared that Joseph was going to have to hope the team would keep three quarterbacks if Joseph didn't ultimately beat out Bender.

Joseph actually played well. He completed five of seven passes for about 84 yards (final yard totals were estimates and not official since it was only a scrimmage).

My 26-yard reception during my first series turned out to be the longest play from scrimmage. From our 31-yard line I caught a pass from Joseph near midfield. I got to their 43 before I was brought down by cornerback Hyrum Van Every, a three-year veteran from Adams State who was taken in the expansion draft from Cincinnati.

There were some pretty impressive gains on both sides. All six quarterbacks seemed to do well and the running backs often picked up huge chunks of yardage. Of course that also meant that Walker was going to blame the defenses instead of crediting the offenses.

If it was any comfort to the defenses, Walker was likely to find reasons to lambaste the offenses. Of special merit seemed to be tailback Ozzie Roberts of the white team. The fourth-round draft choice out of Austin Peay carried seven times for 64 yards but he also fumbled twice, losing one.

The crowd seemed to enjoy the scrimmage although I am sure there was some disappointment among those who expected an actual game. Good plays were always rewarded with enthusiastic cheers. It didn't seem as if too many people left before it was over.

Near the end I relaxed on the sidelines since I knew I was through for the night. It wasn't like the end of a tight game where one focuses hopes on the defense holding the opposition. I talked and joked with my teammates. I also signed autographs for a few kids.

"I noticed that you throw left-handed," a Japanese kid of about ten named Darren observed as I wrote my name inside the bill of his baseball cap.

"You're pretty observant," I responded cheerily.

"Well I was just wondering," he said, "how come you throw with your left hand and write with your right hand?"

That was an interesting question for which there was no logical answer.

"I really don't know," I replied. "All I know is Babe Ruth was the same way. I've also got a sister who throws right-handed but writes left-handed. "

While the scrimmage didn't have the significance of the signing of the Declaration of Independence exactly 200 years and 20 days earlier, it was a fairly historical event. Just the same, I didn't think of it in terms of being historical until a few years later.

On the bus ride back to camp I felt good about my performance. That meant that my day at home was going to be that much more enjoyable. I looked forward to a night of sleeping in my own bed and roughly 24 hours in an atmosphere devoid of dining halls and communal showers and bathrooms.

Sitting next to me was Sam Grubb. He was a rookie free agent safety out of Florida State.

"How'd you do?" I asked.

"Pretty good, I think. I was in on some tackles and made one unassisted tackle. I also broke up a pass."

I couldn't judge how well he had played. I was primarily focused on myself since a scrimmage is in many ways an individual test. Having endured camp this long suggested that he was a fairly good football player. He might very well have performed well but was it enough?

Apparently not. Grubb was among the six players cut after breakfast on Monday.

I happened to run into Grubb as he was preparing to leave the compound. It was the first time I had ever encountered somebody who had just been cut. It is something that is simply too awkward under normal circumstances and I admit to feeling ill at ease when our paths crossed. He shrugged his shoulders and flashed an uncomfortable smile.

"I guess I didn't play as well as I thought I did," he said.

That wasn't necessarily true. As unfair as it might have seemed, the coaches were committed to getting the squad down to 90 or fewer before the first exhibition game. Those cut were not necessarily incapable of playing in the NFL. I have no doubt that throughout the history of pro football there were players cut who never returned who might have made the Hall of Fame had they not been affected by a game of attrition.

"What are you going to do now?" I asked.

Grubb took a breath. He was trying to take it in stride but I could see that he was hurting inside. Playing pro football could have been a lifelong dream for him. A lot of players who get cut are losing the thing that means the most to them.

"Go home and figure it out, I guess," Grubb finally replied after pondering my inquiry. "Walker was cool about it. He told me if I keep myself in shape, he'll see about giving me another shot next year or maybe some other team will be interested. I'll take a little time to think about it. In the meantime, I need only six more credits to get my geology degree. I think I'll take care of that."

At least he had something in mind for what he could do. A lot of guys who get cut are totally unprepared for life among the mainstream.

"What was your name again?" Grubb asked before we parted company.

"Jay. Jay Dockman."

"Jay Dockman," he repeated. "I'll remember that. I'll be looking for you when I watch the Hawaiians on TV."

"I still have to make the team."

"You will," he said brightly as we shook hands and he headed to the van that would deliver him and a few other casualties to the airport.

Grubb was more sure of my fate than I was. In 1976 I was virtually untried in the NFL and couldn't know if I would make the opening day roster until the roster was finally set. Even so, that only guaranteed that I would draw my first paycheck. I still needed to work hard to ensure that I would stay for the duration of the season. It always paid to be at least a little bit paranoid.

By the time we finished our morning workout, Grubb was probably somewhere over the Pacific en route to his hometown. I didn't know what city he was from or even what state he was from. I only knew that he played college football at Florida State.

Grubb's professional career might not have gone beyond the few weeks he spent in Hawaii. Although it would be little consolation to him and others who came up short in their quests for pro football careers, their presence in camp meant that they were very good football players. With but a few exceptions, anybody who spent so much as a single day in camp was there because he deserved the opportunity.

Of course I didn't give it much thought while I was still playing. I saw players cut whom I thought were still pretty good football players but I never really looked at the overall picture until after my career was over. For most of those who accepted invitations to try out for a pro football team it meant that they must have been pretty good football players in college. In some cases they were probably even better than some of the players who got to stick around. No coach was absolutely perfect in selecting the right players.

As it turned out, Grubb was the only player cut loose that day with no previous pro experience. Fullback Kevin Salles, who had been with the WFL Hawaiians in 1975, was let go. Also released were quarterback Robert Flannery, linebacker Robert Glass, tailback Paul Franco and cornerback Hyrum Van Every. All except Van Every had been signed as free agents.

On the plus side, we got through the scrimmage with no serious injuries. If the season were about to start we would have nobody on injured reserve or with any other disabled status. Instead we still had half-a-dozen exhibition games coming up to increase our chances of having debilitated players before our season opener.

CHAPTER FOUR
The Exhibition Season

The exhibition season finally approached. Among the survivors were those whose NFL careers would not get beyond the preseason. The end result of each game was that the roster would be gradually reduced.

Our schedule in camp eased up. We held full workouts only in the mornings. They often ran longer than previously since our schedule wasn't quite as regimented. The workouts still never went longer than two and-a-half hours.

We were still in training camp status. For the three home games, which were played on Saturday nights since our schedule was not regulated by national TV, we rode a chartered bus from the base to Aloha Stadium and then returned to base as a unit. Those of us with local housing were then excused until midnight Sunday night.

Our first two exhibition games were at home against San Francisco and San Diego, respectively. I was eager with anticipation, especially before the San Francisco game. After four weeks of training camp, I was anxious to have some competition. It was also very exciting to see the uniforms of an established NFL franchise on the same field as us.

This was theoretically the Hawaiians' NFL debut although our official debut was still six weeks away. The game seemed like a miracle a little more than nine months after pro football in Hawaii seemed to be lost forever. On that day I thought if I was going to wear a pro football uniform again it would be as a Dallas Cowboy.

Aloha Stadium was sold out. Each time we ran on the field the fans gave us a rousing cheer. It was intoxicating.

Unfortunately for the fans the early exhibition games place little emphasis on winning. They are competitive but primarily about seeing who does best under game conditions. The coaching staff is concerned with giving everybody a fair chance to show what he can do.

With few exceptions, nobody played more than a quarter in our first game. We still had 88 NFL wannabes including five quarterbacks. Walker didn't want to cut somebody who didn't get a fair opportunity.

There was some rotation on plays from scrimmage. Generally speaking, those who saw considerable action in the first half saw little or no action in the second half. Several of us, myself included, were allowed to shower and change into street clothes at halftime. We could then return to the sidelines or watch the rest of the game from the dugout seats behind the south end zone. We could also sit in the baseball dugouts which flanked the dugout seats.

I played almost exclusively in the first quarter. The exception was that I was still on the punt return and kick return teams throughout the first half.

Because of the number of hopefuls still with us, there were two units for each special team; one for each half.

But all of this was for the opening exhibition matchup. With the roster shrinking each week and the regular season approaching, the coaches adjusted accordingly. The two special teams system lasted through the fourth game although more guys each week played in both halves. As the exhibition season wore on the projected starters gradually increased their playing time.

That includes yours truly. I played through most of the first half during our second exhibition game against San Diego as well as our third contest in Washington.

At least in Washington it was a day game. That meant not having to wait all day.

As a pro I was always psyched up almost from the moment I got out of bed on game day. That meant time dragged on for night games.

In high school all of my games were at night but I was preoccupied with school if our game was on a Friday or working my job if a game was on a Saturday. I was always more relaxed on game days in high school, never feeling overly anxious throughout the majority of the day. It wasn't until about three hours before game time that I would drift into a pregame zone.

When I was in college we were sequestered on game days. That is when I started feeling anxious as soon as I woke up. In high school I had my normal responsibilities to carry me through but in college I was in a football-all-day mode.

As a pro the let's-play-now mode became more prevalent. This included the regular season when we had Monday night games. As much as I tried to distract myself, my mind was almost always on that night's game.

We beat San Francisco, 21-17, although it was hardly noteworthy in the first of six exhibition contests. My focus was on playing well and I believed my job was secure for another week once it was all over. I rushed once for six yards and caught one pass for 17 yards. I also returned two punts for a total of 16 yards.

San Diego got the better of us, 20-16, although the loss bore no more significance than the victory the week before. It was more significant that we won in Washington because it marked the halfway point of the exhibition season. Although everybody was still fighting for roster spots, more emphasis was placed on winning as the exhibition season progressed.

And then came the Rams. This was our final exhibition home game.

What made this matchup memorable was the presence of a tight end named Lance Redmon. He was beginning his fourth year with the Rams after playing college football at UCLA. He had also been my teammate at South Valley High School.

Lance was a year ahead of me at South Valley and was a member of the school's charter varsity team. When I moved up to the varsity the following year he was one of my primary receivers. He was strong and hard as a bull to bring down. He was also blessed with extra-large hands, making it easier for him to grasp the football.

Like me, Lance had been a two-way player. He was actually strictly a defensive end his sophomore year and then started on offense as a junior.

Lance and I also teamed up in baseball. He was primarily a third baseman but caught on occasion, meaning he was occasionally behind the plate when I pitched. He was also the team's most powerful hitter. Once he hit three home runs in a game and each one was a tape measure shot that would have made Mickey Mantle envious. It amazed me that he was overlooked in the baseball draft.

I saw Lance the day after my high school graduation when we both happened to show up at the same party. After that our paths never crossed again. I saw him play football on television a few times with UCLA and the Rams but that was it.

During our warmup I spotted my former teammate on the other side of the field. We obviously couldn't sit down and have a chat but I watched him warm up when I could and I suspected that he did the same with me. At one point we did get close enough to make eye contact and subtly nod at each other.

I also got his attention near the end of the game.

"Jay Dockman in at quarterback," the public address announcer reported as I took my place behind the center after Walker decided to give me a brief look at quarterback under game conditions late in the game.

As I checked to make sure my teammates were properly positioned, I caught a brief glimpse of Lance on the makai sideline. Although he had obviously seen me play quarterback in the past, his expression told me he wasn't expecting it here.

But who was?

Nobody except my teammates. Prior to the game everybody was advised that I would take a few snaps at quarterback. It was the only time I did so during the exhibition season.

After the game, which we lost, I searched for my old teammate. It only took a few seconds before we were face to face for the first time in six years.

"What's this? You're back at quarterback?" he asked good-naturedly.

"Only as a safety valve," I replied. "But it sure was fun quarterbacking in a game again. The last time I did that was in a high school all-star game at Citrus College."

I talked to Lance for only a couple of minutes on the way to our locker rooms. We were able to talk for a few more minutes before we were to board our respective buses. Lance introduced me to a few of his teammates. I introduced him to a few of mine.

52

There wasn't much time. What I did learn was that Lance married Darlene Reed from my class at South Valley after his rookie season with the Rams. A year later Lance and Darlene Redmon were blessed with a baby boy. They had recently discovered that they would be adding a second child in April. It was the type of thing I hoped to experience in the future once I was with the right woman.

"Have a good season," Lance said as we shook hands before boarding our respective buses.

"You do the same. We'll make Coach Farnwell proud."

At two-and-two we flew to Memphis. This was the so-called World Bowl game. There were no prizes involved. It was simply a matchup between the two teams brought into the NFL after the WFL folded.

Or perhaps I should say it was a matchup between two sets of uniforms from the WFL. Most of the players were not with their respective teams when the teams operated out of the WFL. By this time the Hawaiians had only five players from the WFL team and Memphis had only three.

But somebody wanted to make something out of virtually nothing. I suppose it was appropriate to show that something was salvaged from the WFL. The preseason World Bowl continued beyond my eventual retirement in a home-and-home format.

We won that first contest. That made us three-and-two in the preseason. However, the most interesting aspect of our sojourn to Memphis was what took place the night before the game.

We flew to Memphis with four halfbacks still on our roster. Before our bed check we had only three. Robert Shibata decided to simply pack up and leave.

Eric Hamer happened to spot Shibata walking through the hotel lobby with his suitcase. Eric asked him where he was going.

"I'm going to where I don't have to be a yes man," was Shibata's curt reply. He went outside, caught a cab and was never seen or heard from again.

Shibata was probably lucky that he lasted as long as he did. He may have sensed that and quit to spare himself the indignity of being cut for the fifth time in five seasons. What he actually did was save the team some money since his leaving the team on his own meant that he had to furnish his own transportation home.

Because of Shibata's unilateral decision to leave the team we entered our final exhibition game with 55 active players, not counting three with injuries, fighting for 43 roster spots. Those 43 roster spots represented the right to make history in our first-ever NFL regular season game eight days later.

The flight home from Memphis was pleasant. The periods between the game itself and the time prior to practice were always somewhat relaxing.

We couldn't turn back the clock and undo our screwups that could cost us jobs and the cuts were not made until a couple of days later. There was nothing to be gained by worrying about what might happen next. Just enjoy the flight and the camaraderie of our peers while we still had the opportunity.

Marv Nelson, Ed Jennings, Gary Giametti, Danny Klaas and I stood in the aisle about halfway through the flight. The conversation turned to people with unusual last names. Ed recalled having a teacher in elementary school named Mrs. Ruhle.

"It wasn't so much the name," Ed admitted. "It's just that she was so mean. Behind her back we used to call her Mrs. Ghoul."

"That's pretty ironic," I remarked. "We had a Mr. Ruhle at my school when I was in fifth grade. He was the meanest teacher in the school. Everybody used to call him Mr. Ghoul."

I only had one encounter with Mr. Ruhle since I didn't actually have him as a teacher but was already well-apprised of his cantankerous demeanor. He was often seen grabbing boys who misbehaved by the shirt and even occasionally by the hair in the days long before the ban on corporal punishment. We used to dread when he had playground duty.

My clash with the volatile Mr. Ghoul took place in the cafeteria during lunch. As he stood at the front of the cafeteria seemingly distracted in conversation with the janitor, I committed the heinous crime of popping the bag from my ice cream bar.

Mr. Ruhle didn't even flinch. He seemed oblivious to my act of decadence.

By the time I had eaten most of the chocolate coating off of my vanilla bar the dreaded teacher came over. As I worked on the vanilla ice cream portion of my dessert he towered above me and asked if I was the one who had popped a bag.

"Yeah," I replied with a somewhat flippant smile, surprised that he quickly seemed to pinpoint the culprit from about 50 feet away when he hadn't even been looking in my direction.

Without warning Ruhle lifted me out of my seat. He was holding me by the armpits and speaking loud and fast while he held me aloft, swung me around and shook me. It took every ounce of strength I had to hold on to my ice cream. Had I lost my grip it might have flown into somebody's face.

What I found out later was that Ruhle had shaken me so violently that my arm swung around. My ice cream bar actually struck his back. He had vanilla ice cream on the back of his dark blue sport coat. I was elated when a classmate told me what I had done to the tyrant.

Along the course of our conversation Marv mentioned that he had never known anybody named Dockman. It sounded like a common enough name but none of us had ever known anybody named Dockman. The only Dockmans I had known were related to me.

54

"What kind of name is that? British?" Ed asked.

"It's contrived American," I replied.

"What do you mean 'contrived American?'" Gary asked.

"It's a name that was actually created in America," I explained. "There might be other Dockmans who aren't related to me but the Dockmans in my family have a name that was created in America about, oh, 35 years ago."

I explained that I am actually the grandson of a German immigrant. His birth name was Wolfgang Heinrich Bismarck.

My grandfather was born in Hamburg, Germany, in 1893. When he was 18 he and a friend, on a lark, made their way to Liverpool, England, and got jobs with the White Star Line. My grandfather's formal education was probably no more than the equivalent of fourth grade but he had learned shipyard skills. His father had been a shipyard worker and my grandfather was taught at a fairly young age by his father and others at the shipyard.

Despite my grandfather's lack of formal education, he had a reasonably good grasp of the English language. His ability to communicate, albeit not always without difficulty, and his shipyard skills paved the way for his employment with White Star.

My grandfather's companion stayed in Liverpool a few months and decided to return to Germany. My grandfather set his sights on America. He got White Star to allow him to work his way across the Atlantic on one of its ships.

He thanked his lucky stars for his good fortune until the day he died in 1982. He was initially assigned to sail to America on the Titanic. He was switched to a later voyage on the Olympic two days before the ill-fated Titanic was to depart.

Cognizant of what had happened to the vessel he was originally to sail on by the time he set sail much later since White Star decided to refurbish the Olympic in the wake of the Titanic disaster, it was a very solemn voyage for him. His downtrodden feelings were partially because he knew he probably would have gone down with the Titanic.

Primarily, though, he thought of those who did go down. He was working on the dock as Titanic was loading passengers and cargo. He was a good-natured individual who joked with some of the passengers in either English or German. He figured that all but a handful of those he encountered verbally and visually wound up on the floor of the Atlantic.

When my grandfather caught sight of the Statue of Liberty he decided it was time to move on. Fate had spared him. He was in America. His goal was prosperity.

My grandfather worked an assortment of jobs in his new country, splitting his time between New York and Pennsylvania. His goal, although he was never sure why, was to settle in California.

While in Pennsylvania he met my grandmother, Liesl Brigitta Dettweiller. She had migrated with her parents in 1905 when she was ten. She met my grandfather in 1915 and they were very devoted to each other although they didn't marry until 1919.

My grandfather served on a troop ship in the Navy during World War I. There was some reluctance to take him since the enemy happened to be from the very country in which my grandfather was born and raised. He convinced the powers that be that his allegiance was to his new country.

It wasn't until 1923 that my grandparents finally moved to California. They settled in Long Beach where my grandfather worked in the shipyard. Their first child, Robert, had been born in 1921 in Pennsylvania. He was followed by Ruth in 1923 and Harold in 1925. My dad, Jerry, was born in 1928. After that came Arlene in 1929 and Warren in 1932.

As the United States moved precariously close to World War II, anti-German and Japanese sentiment was flourishing. My grandparents finally decided early in 1941 that it would be prudent to change the family name. Something German might not have been a concern except that the name Bismarck was dubious. Otto von Bismarck had been the chancellor of Germany's First Reich.

When my grandfather returned home from his job at the shipyard my grandmother would often greet him by saying, "The dock man is here." As my grandparents pondered a new moniker, that salutation stood out. By the summer of 1941 Wolfgang and Liesl Bismarck legally became Walter and Lisa Dockman although they often addressed each other by their original first names for the rest of their lives.

Our final preseason showdown was in Green Bay.

Of all of the preseason games, this was the one where winning was most important although there were still players who were on the precipice of making the team or not making the team. I put myself in that category even though I had started every preseason game and generally played well. Our projected starters would play the majority of this game since a victory was expected to give us momentum going into the regular season. It was still a final opportunity to showcase ourselves.

There were still seven of us with ties to Hawaii. There were some mutterings about locals getting preferential treatment. I am honestly certain that local ties meant nothing.

The fact is, local players still with the team were, like everybody else, playing their hearts out. Safety Rich Hasegawa was very impressive. He didn't have any interceptions but he had broken up several passes and made several tackles.

Cornerback Eric Hamer was also doing well and wasn't truly a local product. His tie to Hawaii was limited to the 1975 season with the WFL Hawaiians after playing college football at Oregon State. He had one interception to his credit and also had broken up several passes and made his share of tackles.

Defensive tackles K.T. Smith and Jimmy Souza were holding their own. Smith was even leading the team with two and-a-half sacks.

Edmund Kupau was still fighting for a defensive end spot. Unfortunately he twisted his knee on the opening kickoff of the Memphis game and was doubtful for Green Bay. It wasn't certain if his injury would hurt his chances for making the team.

Tight end Craig Kamanu was doing well, having four receptions for 55 yards and a touchdown. He was aggressive and an effective blocker.

Seven other players with local ties had already been cut. Three had played for the Hawaiians in the WFL including guard Abraham Foster who got the ax after the Memphis game. The other four had played for the University of Hawaii.

Everybody was expected to go full speed when given the opportunity against Green Bay. This would be the toughest of all cuts. Those cut would be players Walker would prefer to keep. It was simply that notorious game of attrition.

Who would or would not get cut was a topic of discussion over dinner the night before the game. Gary Giametti, Rich Hasegawa, Craig Kamanu and I used our per diem to dine at a moderately priced restaurant near our hotel where I ordered corned beef and cabbage.

"You have the least cause to worry among us," Rich insisted.

"How can you be so sure?" I responded. "It could work that you three will make the team and I'll be watching from the bleachers."

"But you've started every preseason game and you're starting tomorrow," Gary pointed out.

"It doesn't guarantee a thing," I insisted simply because it didn't. "Walker might decide to keep you and Oglethorpe. We don't know what Walker's thinking. We could all make the team or we could all be cut."

"True," said Rich. "But they went to a lot of trouble to get you. They gave Dallas a first-round draft choice to keep you in Hawaii and you haven't exactly been dogging it on the field."

I was grateful for Hasegawa's sense of logic. I hoped that Walker would employ the same logic if he couldn't think of any other reason to keep me on the roster.

Why we were having this discussion is probably because we were nervous. We had lasted this long and still had one very formidable hurdle before the roster was finally set. There was no guarantee that any of us would be on the field for the season opener.

Craig didn't say much. Of the four of us, he seemed to be the most vulnerable. With Rich Grummon virtually guaranteed the starting tight end spot and Danny Klaas likely to be his backup, Craig's best hope seemed to be if we carried more than two tight ends. We didn't know how many at any position Walker was planning to carry. Walker himself probably wasn't completely sure.

This was my first trip to Green Bay. Of the three cities we visited during the preseason, I had only previously been to Memphis since it had been a WFL city.

In Washington there is much one can see. The White House, the Capitol, the Smithsonian, the Washington Monument and the Lincoln Memorial are available among other attractions.

Of course we weren't there as tourists. Our business was football. We had enough time to have a light workout, eat, sleep, play the game and head to the airport. We might as well have been in Siberia for all of the sightseeing we got to do.

Green Bay can be an interesting place to visit. It has restaurants, residential neighborhoods, gas stations, bowling alleys, movie theaters, golf courses. . . .

Oh sure, there is more to Green Bay than that.

Or is there?

The fact is, the most historical place in Green Bay is probably the very site where we would take on the Packers. Forget George Halas, Bronko Nagurski, Jim Thorpe and legends of that caliber. I believe it was Vince Lombardi's Packers who raised the bar for pro football's current standard of prominence.

As I ran my personal tradition of pregame laps around the perimeter of Lambeau Field I felt that sense of history. This was the field where Lombardi transformed a group of losers into a force virtually unbeatable. This was the former stomping grounds of Paul Hornung, Max McGee, Jimmy Taylor, Forrest Gregg, Henry Jordan, Jerry Kramer, Jim Ringo, Ray Nitschke, Bart Starr, Dave Robinson and Fuzzy Thurston. This was the field where most opponents once arrived believing they could beat Lombardi's Packers, then left wondering how they could have harbored such a fantasy.

The field may have been best known for the legendary 1967 Ice Bowl game. Fortunately my first taste of Green Bay football was while it was still technically summer. I would not be shivering on the sidelines while the defense was on the field. Nobody, at least if they were sane, would be wearing ski masks, gloves or thermals this time. As the fans headed to their seats there wasn't a down jacket in sight.

As I finished my last pregame lap around the field Walker and Steve Bender were talking casually near the tunnel connecting the field and the locker room. Both seemed to have faraway looks.

"If you're looking for the ghost of Vince Lombardi, he's over there," I said, pointing to the Green Bay sideline.

"Did you talk to him?" Walker asked lightly.

"Yeah," I replied. "He told me to get the hell off of his side of the field."

58

Walker smiled and shook his head reflectively. He looked over at the Green Bay sideline. I could tell that he was reminiscing about his days with the legendary coach years before.

"The man left us six years ago, almost to the day," Walker said. "I wonder if anybody will ever know how he truly was. All you ever hear about him sometimes is how hard he pushed his players. They should spend some time talking about how his players were like sons to him. He was definitely tough to live with much of the time. He also had one of the biggest hearts of anybody I've ever known."

I sat stoically in front of my locker in the minutes before we took the field. Physically I felt perfect. Mentally and psychologically I was ready. I still was all too aware of what this game meant. Some of those currently wearing the white Hawaiians jerseys with the assortment of colored trimmings would never wear those jerseys again. Of those destined to be waived in about 48 hours, a few of them, if not all of them, would never play pro football again.

In all humility, I was aware of the odds being in my favor to make the team. The team did give up a lot to get me and I did start every preseason game. Those factors suggested, but did not guarantee, that I would remain with the team.

The most compelling factor was statistically. I had rushed eight times for 41 yards and one touchdown through the first five games. I had also caught 14 passes for 229 yards, leading the team in both categories. I had returned five kickoffs for 161 yards and 12 punts for 176 yards: the latter including a 63-yard return in Washington. I had also completed three passes in three attempts against the Rams for 34 yards.

But I didn't want to get overconfident. Overconfidence would lead to complacency. If my career was going to end prematurely, I didn't want it to be because I got stupid and lazy.

Feeling fairly secure about my chances while still taking nothing for granted, I felt for the guys who wouldn't be sticking around. Those who would be cut were good enough to play in the NFL. It would be attrition, not lack of effort or ability, that would destroy their careers.

I looked to my right. Gary Giametti sat a couple of lockers down, a cigarette burning in his left hand while he rubbed his forehead with his right. His reddish-brown hair had a very oily texture. He was a good-looking guy with a moustache similar to mine since it drooped just a little below the corners of his mouth.

Gary took a drag off of his cigarette and looked at me. He raised his eyebrows in a manner that said nothing and also said everything.

"Ready?" I asked softly, breaking an almost total silence in the locker room.

Further down the row sat Kent Oglethorpe. He was a nice guy although very quiet. I liked him and regretted the fact that he seemed most likely to be cut among him, Gary and me, although I didn't like the thought of Gary being cut and I absolutely hated the idea of myself getting cut. Kent was simply too tall and skinny for a position that required one to be a running back as well as a receiver. He was a good receiver. His undoing was that Gary and I were more powerful as runners. Gary and I also had lower centers of gravity.

"All right, let's play some good football today," Walker called as he moved to his spot in the center of the locker room. "Who's going to lead us this time?"

A handful of hands shot up. Walker chose Oglethorpe to lead us in *The Lord's Prayer.*

"Our Father who art in Heaven," Kent began reverently before the rest of the team joined in, "Hallowed be Thy name. . . ."

Some were kneeling. Others stood and the rest sat. I believe that even our most irreverent players took part to grab whatever help they could get.

"Okay!" Walker called enthusiastically at the conclusion of the prayer. "This is our final tune up before we start playing for keeps. We are asking you to do one thing; play clean, hard, smart football. That's all we will ever ask of you on the field. Your dedication to playing clean, hard and smart will determine your success. Now let's go."

We were very consistent in one area in particular. There is no way to check but we were probably the only team in NFL history to lose the coin toss in all six of its exhibition games. Our captains might just as well have gone to midfield and said, "Put the coin away. We'll kick and defend that goal."

Actually it is supposedly better to lose the toss anyway. There is allegedly an advantage to putting a fired-up defense on the field first.

I suppose there is some truth to that. Our defense got off to a flying start with the opening kickoff. Eric Hamer hustled down the field and forced a fumble. Green Bay recovered but had to start on its own nine-yard line.

"That's the way to charge, Hamer!" Walker exclaimed as Eric returned to the sideline, fighting the urge to crack an "I am absolutely full of myself" smile.

Eric was radiant even if he did succeed in trying to look nonchalant. Although there were no guarantees, his chances for making the team had just increased. It was an awesome hit and more was in store from both sides of the field. Both teams had players taking advantage of this final showcase to avoid unemployment.

The Packers went nowhere and we methodically drove toward the end zone when we took possession. Larry Scott eventually picked up four yards

60

to Green Bay's 18 and fumbled. Fortunately he managed to scoop the ball back to himself.

Giametti, briefly subbing for me, made a leaping grab of a pass at the two on the very next play. He was hit immediately and fell forward to the one.

"Way to go, rookie!" Ted Dietrich called enthusiastically as he helped Gary to his feet as I returned to the field. "Great catch!"

"Good job, Gary!" I told him as he headed to the sideline.

Fullback Jeff Kerner climaxed the drive on the next play. He exploded up the middle for the first score of the game.

Green Bay marched quickly down the field. The Packers tied the game on a 14-yard pass in the end zone.

I guess I took the touchdown personally. I took the ensuing kickoff on the four and refused to be brought down.

Of course I had a lot of help. Greg Henry knocked a would-be tackler on his derriere. Nearby Stuart Arroyo, a center drafted in the seventh round out of Marshall University, cut a defender down. I also recall streaking past Giametti as he kept an enemy player distracted.

I thought I had it made. As I crossed midfield I saw nothing but end zone ahead of me. It took me totally by surprise when I was hit from behind at the Green Bay 30.

It was a 66-yard return. I wasn't satisfied with it.

"How in the hell did he catch me?" I asked in utter disgust as Dietrich and Danny Klaas helped me to my feet.

"Don't sweat it, Jay," Dietrich responded as he whacked my derriere. "That was a helluva return."

"I thought sure I was going all the way," I muttered as I headed toward our huddle. A football player's ego can obviously be very fragile.

Our drive lasted one play. Tailback Larry Scott took the handoff on a 3 Wahiawa right. He was hit just behind the line, broke loose and scampered 30 yards for a score. We led 14-7 with 2:48 left in the first quarter.

Green Bay tied the game in the second quarter. The Packer punt returner fielded a punt at his own nine. Hasegawa had him in his grasp a couple of yards later but lost his hold. The return man was finally brought down by Ray Jablonski, the punter, at the Green Bay 45. It was a 36-yard runback. The Packers ultimately scored.

Near the end of the half, we saw an example of why Bender had such longevity in the NFL. We got the ball on our own 24 and went into a two-minute drill.

Except we only had about half that much time.

Specifically, we had 1:03 to go 76 yards or at least get into field goal range. We had two time-outs available.

"We can do it," Bender said encouragingly as we huddled. "Do your jobs and we'll be leading at the half."

Bender hit wide receiver Joe Slater who went out of bounds at our own 49. He followed that up with a pass to Dietrich at the Green Bay 25. We were two-thirds of the way after only two plays.

Unfortunately Steve was sacked for a seven-yard loss. We called time out with eleven seconds left. Steve and Walker both decided to take one quick shot at the end zone.

We had been running in our double-double formation. Dietrich and Slater were wide to the right and left, respectively. I was in the slot on the right while Giametti was in the left slot. Bender was protected by Kerner if anybody penetrated the line.

"Okay, we've got to run this play quickly so that we've got time to kick a field goal if we don't make it," Bender said when he returned to the huddle. "Double-double tsunami on two. On two. Ready?"

"Break!"

The tsunami was a play where all receivers went long. It was a Hail Mary with a localized name. If Bender couldn't find an open receiver quickly he was going to throw the ball away to leave us time for the field goal attempt.

I streaked toward the end zone. The blitz was on but Steve eluded it long enough to get the pass off. As I approached the end zone I looked back and Steve spotted me. I leaped up about five yards into the end zone and was hit but I hung on to the ball.

It was my first receiving touchdown of the preseason. There were two seconds left so we did a very good job of getting the play done quickly. We would have had time to try a field goal had the play failed. Instead we had a kickoff and went into the locker room with a 21-14 lead.

Neither side scored in the third quarter. With 51 seconds left in the period we began a drive on our own three. By the time the final period was almost one-third over we had gone the full 97 yards.

There were a few key plays. On third-and-three at our own 24 Bender read a blitz and called an audible; the 3 Mililani left. This was a tailback draw. Scott picked up four yards for a first down.

Bender avoided a heavy rush on the next play. He hit me on a swing pass on about the 30. I got all the way to our 45 for another first down.

On third-and-five at the 50 Bender hit Slater who went out of bounds at the 31. They were livid on the Green Bay sideline. They insisted that Slater brought only one foot down inbounds.

Had this happened a couple of decades later the Packers could have thrown a red flag to demand a replay. This was unheard of in 1976 and it was just as well for the Packers. The films eventually showed that Slater managed to get both feet down. It wasn't by much but the officials had called it correctly.

The drive climaxed at the three with a 4 kama'aina right, meaning I was the ball carrier on our customized version of the legendary Green Bay sweep. With a convoy of blockers ahead I ran around right end and dove into the end zone, scoring my second touchdown of the game and third of the preseason.

For the rest of the game I played only on punt returns. The two-touchdown cushion made Walker decide to give the nonstarters a little more playing time. The score wound up being 34-14 since Joe Billingsley scored on a one-yard quarterback sneak as time expired. We didn't bother with the PAT since there was no point to it.

That final drive did not go over well with some of the fans. As we left the field we could hear a few of them, most likely encouraged by ingestion of large quantities of Wisconsin consumables, accusing us of running up the score.

The fact is, we weren't not running up the score. Had this been a regular season game we would simply have run out the clock. In this case we had two series with guys trying to make the team. You don't make the team by downing the ball when you are given an opportunity to show what you can do. The Packers could also have had a few defensive players trying to prove their worth and wouldn't have had that final opportunity had we simply downed the ball.

Walker always made sure there was no misunderstanding. He always met with the opposing team's head coach before the game. During the preseason it didn't matter if we were winning or losing by 50 points. He felt that players on both teams should have every opportunity to play to the full extent of their capabilities.

It was a happy flight to Honolulu. We savored the victory and the four-and-two preseason.

But this was the end of the line for some.

On Sunday, September 5, I woke up confident that I had made the team. I couldn't say that for an absolute certainty but I was reasonably confident.

Whether I made the team or not, I wouldn't find out officially until the following day. It almost seemed like a cruel irony that the following day was Labor Day. Those who worked jobs befitting the average American were getting that day off. On that same day there would be good football players finding themselves out of jobs.

Going into Green Bay, Walker must have had an idea of who would stick with the team. I am sure that is the way it is with most pro coaches. There are still cases when two players are competing and the one who remains is the one who performs better in the final exhibition. The other will be placed on waivers. There is also the possibility of being waived, claimed and having the Hawaiians revoke waivers to keep the player on the taxi squad if not the regular roster.

Another possibility is that a person a coach is certain will be cut will perform so brilliantly that the coach is forced to reconsider. An injury to another player can also grant a fringe player new life.

Whatever my fate was, I was not going to worry about it 24 hours in advance. On this morning I reveled in the joy of waking up in my own bed. It had actually been a very short sleep. Our chartered jet landed at the Kaneohe Marine Corps Air Station at about midnight. By the time I got everything situated and arrived at home it was about two o'clock. I went to bed at about three and was up at 8:30.

What was different was that for the first time in two months I would sleep in my own bed two nights in a row. For the rest of the season I would sleep in my own bed except for when I was on the road. Regardless of whether I was in my own bed or a hotel room bed, it sure beat the puny training camp bed.

Some players remained at the training camp facilities. After the final cuts the remaining players had until Saturday to find other digs. Those who opted not to rent houses or apartments would stay in a hotel as part of an advertising exchange with the team. The players would still have to pay for the rooms but at rates below what the tourists were paying.

As a sign of my liberation, I was going to spend the day at a beach party. Don Simmons, an attorney friend who had passed the bar a few months earlier, was our host. He had an oceanfront home in Kailua that he rented with an option to buy.

Don and I struck up an instant friendship when we met during my junior year at the University of Hawaii in December, 1972. He had graduated from Castle High School in Kaneohe the same year I graduated from South Valley but was so academically gifted he had even earned a handful of college credits before his high school graduation. He took a heavy caseload in college which enabled him to graduate within three years from Chaminade College which was a small Catholic college a short jog from the University of Hawaii. He would ultimately earn his law degree from the University of Hawaii.

When I met Don he was still a student at Chaminade. On top of his academic prowess, he also knew how to party. I was a good student but could only be so if I kept my festive life in moderation. Don was the rare type who could stay out all night and still ace his exams.

It was a Friday night at a bar on University Avenue called the Blue Goose when I met Don. Dozens of students were having a good time at the establishment in Puck's Alley just across the freeway from the university. We had just completed the football season the previous Saturday by losing to Stanford. I had planned on going to the University of Hawaii's basketball game against Pacific Lutheran at the Honolulu International Center but decided instead to get a jump on my finals.

I was sitting at a table by myself. In front of me were open books, notes and a Budweiser while I actually studied in this notoriously rowdy establishment. For whatever reason, the ambience seemed perfect, probably because finals were far enough away that I didn't feel any pressure. Had we been closer to finals I would have done my studying in a quieter atmosphere. Under the current conditions I was undaunted.

At the table next to me was a group of five males apparently celebrating the fact that it was Friday. I was fairly oblivious to the festivities until the ringleader came over to me.

"Have you ever tried a flaming hooker?" asked the tall, slender stranger with shoulder-length dark brown hair.

"A what?"

"A flaming hooker. It's a shot of 151 with a little vodka to make it burn. It's on me if you want to try one."

Having no urge to resist since it was during a wilder period of my life, I allowed this individual to buy me the strange beverage. On Don's instruction I lit the drink, threw it down and set the glass down with some of the blue flame still visible inside the glass. It was a horrible tasting concoction which I chased with a gulp of beer. I suppose I was just initiated into some convoluted fraternity.

Although my first flaming hooker also wound up being my last, I was also through studying for the night. I moved over to Don's table and joined the party. One putrid beverage marked the beginning of a lifelong friendship.

Almost four full years later I spent the day after our final exhibition at Don's. It was a party comprised of as many as 30 mutual friends. I unwound from the drudgery of two months of training camp by playing volleyball on the beach, swimming in the ocean, socializing and barbecuing hamburgers.

I simply enjoyed the opportunity to return to a relatively normal existence. I loved being a football player. I also enjoyed life away from football. I relished the opportunities to spend an entire day without seeing or hearing from any of my teammates or coaches. I was with other friends; some of whom I had known since college. I was the only pro football player in the bunch and that was a refreshing change. I was even the only one who had played college football.

Among the females in attendance was a cute, sleepy-eyed lady with long blonde hair. I knew I had seen her although I couldn't place her. I sat next to her in the sand.

"Where do I know you from?" I asked.

"Don's office," she replied without hesitation.

That explained it. I had been up to Don's office on a few occasions when we were to meet for lunch or a beer prior to training camp. She worked as a secretary at the law firm. Although I had never spoken to her, I had noticed her since I always had to walk past her on my way back to Don's office.

This encounter put me back in circulation for the first time since just before training camp. Laurie Pyne was attractive enough and seemed fairly nice. Before the party ended I had her phone number. A date appeared imminent.

But that would be later in the week. I had to hope I was still a pro football player when that happened.

CHAPTER FIVE
Officially Underway

It was Labor Day. As I drove to the day's workout, listening to a tape of the Moody Blues without really hearing it, I prayed that I would not be a casualty.

I was fairly certain I had made the team. My stats during the exhibition season should have secured my spot. I had even climaxed it with an excellent game in Green Bay. I still did not want to be too cocky. My heart was beating a little faster than normal, I'm sure.

Although training camp was officially over, our next few workouts would be at the base. This was primarily because most of my teammates were still living on base. With the conclusion of the Hawaii Islanders' regular season the workers at Aloha Stadium could work unmolested to switch the stadium to the football configuration. The Islanders were in the Pacific Coast League playoffs but all of their postseason games, thanks to some financial improprieties by the general manager which made it impossible for the Islanders to return to Hawaii, would be in Salt Lake City.

The grim reaper was striking at about the time I arrived at the base. The unfortunates who had toiled all summer to survive this day were sent to Walker. As it worked out, eleven players were placed on waivers. That was actually one fewer than previously expected. Safety Jack Densemore was placed on injured reserve after breaking his ankle in Green Bay.

Of those placed on waivers, a few would remain with the team on the taxi squad. Those injured or on the taxi squad did not count against the active roster.

Only one rookie was cut. That was Oglethorpe. With a smile which seemed to be in gratitude for having been allowed to try, Kent sought some of us out to wish us luck during the season before he headed to the airport.

"I'm glad I gave it a shot," the ever-congenial free agent said as he shook my hand. "It's time for me to move on to other things."

Cornerback Jerry Morehouse was among those waived. The fifth-year pro out of Notre Dame was taken from St. Louis in the expansion draft. He was claimed almost as soon as his name hit the waiver wire and Walker granted Morehouse's request to not revoke the waivers. St. Louis grabbed him back, meaning he would play in our home opener after all but on the other side.

Another former Cardinal, fullback Gene Kappes, was claimed by Memphis. With Kerner virtually assured the starting fullback spot, Kappes and rookie Danny Edwards were battling for the backup role. Initially Kappes seemed favored. In the end Edwards had simply outplayed Kappes who also was granted his wish to not have his waivers revoked.

As we prepared for our NFL regular season debut we had an active roster comprised of 14 rookies and 29 veterans. This included a few of us who had pro experience strictly in the WFL. One rookie and five veterans made the roster as free agents. Of the rest, 23 of our 39 choices from the expansion draft and 13 of our 24 picks from the rookie free agent draft made the team.

And then there was me. Although my two prior years were spent with the Hawaiians without ever having played so much as a down elsewhere, I was still listed as technically acquired in a trade.

None of the final cuts involved players with Hawaii ties. That status could change later. Officially we were charter members of the NFL Hawaiians. That distinction was eternally irrevocable even if we never played a single down. Being on the first-ever opening day roster guaranteed our spot in history.

Kamanu, no doubt, heaved the biggest sigh of relief. Hamer also seemed surprised to have been selected over Morehouse and Hasegawa's chances for making the team improved with Densemore's broken ankle although it was always possible that Densemore would have been cut. Kamanu was believed to be the underdog in battling Klaas for the backup tight end spot. Craig came on strong in the end, though, and got the nod. Klaas ultimately agreed to remain with the taxi squad. If Kamanu faltered, Klaas was ready to roll.

There were a lot of smiles at camp. We were careful, though, since we were sensitive to those who didn't make the team. Those leaving us were shuttled quickly to the airport. Those who accepted offers to be on the taxi squad if they were not claimed stuck around. As it worked out, only Morehouse and Kappes were claimed and flew to the mainland that night after telling Walker they preferred to be on active rosters instead of having waivers revoked and accepting posts on the taxi squad. Nobody blamed them for that.

"You are the ones we want," Walker announced during a meeting after the final casualties were advised of their unemployed status. "You are the ones we believe are most qualified to open the season as Hawaiians. Congratulations."

For the moment there was an ambience of relief in the room as we waited to begin our film sessions which would precede the day's light workout. There were 43 players who would suit up against St. Louis plus ten who comprised either the taxi squad or were injured. The latter tally would drop to eight by the end of the day with the departures of Morehouse and Kappes.

A few of you came up to thank me for allowing you to be on the team," Walker continued. "I appreciate the gratitude but it is inappropriate to thank me. You are with the team because you earned the right to be. Nobody was chosen over a better player."

From there we watched the films of the Packer game. Walker, as always, ran the offensive film. The assistants stood nearby to make their comments although Walker was easily the most vocal among the offensive coaches. That's the way it would always be.

This wasn't a fire and brimstone session. Walker was very constructive as he pointed out mistakes. I think he wanted to focus on building us up for our NFL debut.

"What you just saw here included some good plays by a handful of players who are no longer with us," Walker said as he turned off the projector. "Those final cuts were tough. You men beat out some outstanding talent. You can justify your spots by sticking it to the Cardinals on Sunday. Now let's get to work."

We only had a light workout, sans pads, on Monday. Tuesday through Friday were scheduled to be for contact workouts. Thursday would also be our first workout at Aloha Stadium.

On Tuesday evening I called Laurie Pyne. She seemed nice enough. I didn't even mind that she turned out to be about three years older than me. She actually looked like she was about three years younger. I invited her to have dinner with me on Friday night and she accepted.

I picked Laurie up right on time at her apartment on Prospect Street in Honolulu's Makiki section. She looked nice in a blue dress with aloha print and her long blonde hair worn loosely. Don told me she had been extremely excited about our date.

That made me wonder something I often wondered about women who were with me. Did she like me for me or was it because I was a football player?

It didn't matter. Laurie was cute and seemed nice but I didn't view her as a permanent fixture in my life. For all of her positive attributes, there was something eerily strange about her that I couldn't pinpoint right away.

We dined at the Pottery Steak House on Waialae Avenue in Kaimuki. It was so named because the plates and other dishes were made of pottery. The establishment served a very delicious steak.

Laurie was friendly yet somehow withdrawn. She also didn't like Hawaii and was planning to return to her home in Ohio in November. She had arrived in Hawaii in November, 1975 and decided that one year was all she needed.

"Have you ever been to Ohio?" she asked.

"No, never. I could have gone my senior year in high school. Woody Hayes tried to recruit me and invited me to visit Ohio State but I already knew that I didn't want to go to school there."

"Why not?" she asked, seemingly surprised.

"Nothing personal," I replied. "A lot of it had to do with the fact that I was a quarterback and Woody doesn't like to pass. I couldn't see myself just taking snaps and handing off. Besides, I was pretty set on USC at the time."

"USC? I thought you said you went to the University of Hawaii."

"I did but not until my sophomore year. I went to USC my freshman year when I decided that I wanted to get out of California. I arranged a transfer to Hawaii."

Laurie and I didn't have much in common. She was a staunch Republican while I was an Independent who wasn't averse to voting Democrat. She was the daughter of a retired Army officer and had brothers who were Army officers and believed we should have continued fighting in Vietnam while I believed that we should not have been in Vietnam in the first place. She also didn't believe she could get away from Hawaii soon enough while I loved Hawaii and couldn't imagine living elsewhere.

Despite the fact that about the only thing we had in common was that we were not vegetarians, we had a pretty nice time together.

On Saturday morning I rose early. We were scheduled to have a light workout at Aloha Stadium late that morning. Since I had a few hours to kill I walked down to the Jolly Roger Restaurant on Kalakaua Avenue for breakfast.

The only significant football first that rivaled the 1976 experience was my first game as a high school freshman. That was ten years earlier, almost to the day, and I was the starting "B" quarterback at South Valley High.

For the record, the date was September 23, 1966. It was a Friday so I spent the day in school. Normally on the day of a game I had very little trouble focusing on classwork but things were very different on the day of my first game. I could have gotten just as much benefit from what was being taught in the classroom had I stayed home. I was grateful that no tests were scheduled that day.

Our game was in South San Gabriel and we lost the toss. Since I wasn't a starting defensive back that day that meant I wouldn't be taking the field until our opponent's drive finally stalled near midfield and they were forced to punt, enabling me to finally take the field as a punt returner. Even then I wound up with a less than memorable debut since the punt was away from me and downed on the South Valley two.

With our backs against the wall Coach Ratherber allowed me to get my feet wet by calling for a quarterback sneak. My first play as a quarterback showed me rushing for a two-yard gain. Those two yards eradicated some of my apprehension.

We picked up a first down at the 13 before I finally threw my first pass. That was a simple swing pass to the tailback, Frank Zercher, at the 14. Zercher picked up three more yards to the 17.

The completion, albeit for a mere four yards, seemed to take away what was left of my apprehension. I was suddenly sure I could handle being a quarterback. It was pretty brash confidence stemming from a drive that had thus far picked up all of 15 yards.

I actually completed my first four passes for a total of 55 yards. I also scored my first touchdown that night, keeping on an option play in the third quarter and scampering four yards to the end zone. I also returned one punt for 16 yards but neither of our opponent's two kickoffs came my way. On offense I wound up with eleven carries for 94 yards, thanks largely to a 61-yard gain on an option play which took us from our own 38 to the one.

Of course I had to accept the bitter with the sweet. What appeared to be a guaranteed touchdown after my sizable gain was nullified when I threw an interception in the end zone two plays later. It was one of two interceptions I threw that night.

We won that game, 13-6. I completed 15 passes in 24 attempts for 204 yards and a touchdown.

What I also recall was the overall ambience of the typical "B" game in California. It was the prelude to the varsity game. Virtually none of the student body was in attendance until much later.

At kickoff it was still daylight. The sparse attendance was comprised primarily of parents and siblings of the players, the "B" cheerleaders and very few others.

A decade later Aloha Stadium would be different. It would have very few empty seats when the Hawaiians made their NFL debut, I knew. The question was how attendance would be for our six subsequent home games.

It would all boil down to how well we played. Hawaii fans seemed very fickle. With Hawaii's high cost of living, sports fans found better things to do than support teams that didn't play well. Winning mattered but it wasn't just that. Fans might still support us if we played well even in defeat. If we began a pattern of losing by four or five touchdowns with sloppy play the bulk of our fans were going to stay home and watch the NFL on TV.

As I consumed my sausage, eggs and hash browns I thought about the significance of the game I would play a day later. The prospect of playing my first ever regular season NFL game was very, very exciting.

The NFL took an enormous chance on awarding Hawaii a franchise. If we didn't draw fans we could wind up as the NFL's version of the Milwaukee Brewers who moved to Milwaukee in 1970 after one season as the Seattle Pilots. I never considered the possibility of relocating in 1976 but realized much later that my teammates and I might have wound up mollifying the disappointed fans in Birmingham in 1977 if we didn't draw good crowds in Hawaii.

Or we could have found ourselves playing in Phoenix, San Antonio, Wichita, Indianapolis, Brooklyn, Irwindale. . . .

In 1974 I played my first professional game in Orlando, Florida, for the WFL Hawaiians. That was also exciting but not like this. The thrill of my first game as a pro was partially diminished by the uncertainty of what was going on with my girlfriend. All seemed very well between us when I left

Hawaii for training camp in California but I only heard from her once after that. As exciting as the initial pro experience may have been, I wondered if I would still have a girlfriend when I returned to Honolulu. That issue will be described later.

We held our light workout as scheduled. An air of excitement permeated the air. Ten and-a-half months after pro football seemed to be lost to Hawaii forever Hawaii not only still had a team but had risen to the ultimate level. In about 24 hours the NFL standings would include an unprecedented entry from Hawaii.

It was at this workout that it was officially announced who would be starting and who would be on what special teams units. There were no real surprises among the starters since almost everybody had been working out in starting and backup roles.

"Okay, Jay. You got the start."

Those words came from Giametti, my backup. It was good of him to take the congratulatory attitude. I would like to believe that I also would have had the situation been reversed.

I would also be on two of the special teams. I would be returning kickoffs and punts.

"I don't think we could be more prepared," Walker announced at the end of the workout while we gathered around him at midfield. "You all worked really hard. It isn't just a football game tomorrow. It's a very historical event. Hawaii has never hosted a regular season NFL game. The game sold out yesterday morning. About 50,000 people will be coming to stand and cheer and go crazy. If you give them what they want . . . they will be back. We want to play well enough to continue putting people in these seats. Let's show the world that we're for real."

On that note Walker dismissed us. It was easy to see that the team was up. I think it showed that we believed in ourselves. It was a question of whether we would outplay the Cardinals.

I was dying to get started but the game was still a day away.

At home I tried to relax. I watched some of the Hawaii Islanders game against the Salt Lake City Gulls as they battled for the Pacific Coast League Championship. Since we were deprived of watching the Islanders in person, we at least had them on TV.

Later I switched to football. The University of Hawaii was playing at San Jose State on TV. The game wasn't interesting enough to ease my excitement about our NFL debut. The Rainbows ultimately lost 48-7.

I hoped it wasn't an omen.

The 1976 Hawaiians were officially introduced to the public that night at a banquet held in the Hibiscus Ballroom of the Ala Moana Hotel. Players, coaches, staff members, wives, girlfriends and dates of the players and

72

coaches were assigned seats in the front of the room. Members of the general public forked out 15 dollars a plate to fill out the rest of the room. It was a benefit for a few local charities so the cost was tax deductible.

There were no-host cocktails. Walker considered declaring prohibition for the players and coaches, then decided there wouldn't be a problem as long as everybody used common sense. He sternly warned of dire consequences if anybody embarrassed the team.

Dinner was superb. We dined on tossed salad, mahi mahi almondine, steamed rice, peas and carrots, and chocolate cake with white icing for dessert.

Presiding over the banquet was Ed Podolak, the team's general manager. He and his wife sat directly to the right of the dais at the elevated head table. On the opposite side of the dais were Walker and his wife.

Also among those at the head table was Les Keiter, the team's play-by-play announcer who acted as master of ceremonies, and Earl McDaniel who was the general manager of KGMB Radio and would be the color commentator for our home games. During road games Keiter would work solo.

Elsewhere at the head table were Governor George Ariyoshi and Honolulu Mayor Frank Fasi and their wives. It was considered to be an upset that they both showed up while knowing that the other would be present. It was beneficial that they sat at opposite ends of the table. It was no secret that Hizzoner and the Guv didn't always work and play well together. At no time that night did I observe them getting to within ten feet of each other but there was also no discernable friction.

As everybody was finishing dessert, Keiter introduced Podolak. Podolak made a concise address of gratitude for the public's support. He then turned the dais back to Keiter who introduced McDaniel who expressed a few concise thoughts and then McDaniel introduced Walker.

Walker was a very confident public speaker. He didn't waste words, preferring that his audience not be put to sleep. He gave his own brief welcome and expression of gratitude before introducing his coaching staff.

"Now I would like to introduce you to the team," Walker continued, drawing a nice round of applause. "I should point out that 116 players came to training camp when we opened July 5. Those you meet tonight are the ones who proved that they have what it takes to represent the team and all of Hawaii when we take the field tomorrow."

We were briefed at our workout that day on how Walker was going to handle the introduction of players. He was going to go down the list in numerical order. He started by saying the player's number and name, at which point the player would stand and receive polite applause. Walker then gave the player's position and made a brief statement about the player.

"Number 22, Jay Dockman," said Walker when my turn came. This was my cue to stand while Carl Rodgers sat. "He's one we are glad to carry over from the World Football League team. He will be our starting halfback tomorrow and is expected to have a very bright future with the team. He's also a local product since he played his college football at the University of Hawaii."

Walker was a very tactful individual. He didn't make any specific promises. He summed it up by placing the burden on himself, saying, "Unless I am a very poor judge of talent, I honestly believe that we have some outstanding football to look forward to this season."

"Right on," Marv Nelson, sitting to my immediate left, said just loud enough for anybody within a few feet of him to hear. I smiled at the remark while Clint Abraham, sitting directly across from Marv at the round table, nodded and smiled at Marv.

After the introductions came a highlight film. Most of the highlights were from the exhibition season although individual highlights of players with their previous teams were also mixed in. In subsequent years the highlight film would consist almost entirely of highlights from the previous season.

This was one of the rare instances where Walker presided over a film session without berating any of the players. There wasn't a single negative remark although, out of reflex, the sight of Walker presiding over a film session probably made most of my teammates and me cringe.

Actually he hadn't been too hard on us during the exhibition season when we watched game films. There would be times over the years when he would berate us so mercilessly that it was probably very fortunate that nobody had heard of Dr. Jack Kevorkian yet. At this juncture we still were not apprised of just how ruthless a film critic Walker would ultimately prove to be.

Kickoff for our official NFL debut was at ten o'clock, Honolulu Standard Time. That was the way it was for our home games that early in the season. When the rest of the country went to standard time our kickoffs were moved to eleven o'clock. The TV networks, which spent millions for the rights to televise NFL games, mandated our early starting times.

I went to bed at about midnight. Not wanting to take the slightest chance of oversleeping, I had bought an extra alarm clock. I set it and the original for slightly before six, strategically placing the two clocks on opposite sides of the room and far enough away from where I slept that I couldn't simply reach over and turn them off in my sleep.

In my excitement I didn't need either alarm clock. I woke up at 1:50 and went back to sleep. The routine continued at 2:38, 3:57 and 4:14.

When I woke up at 4:32 I decided it was time to forget about sleep. I was too wound up to stay in bed.

I got dressed and sat in the living room. This was long before Nick At Nite and other cable entities since cable TV was a fairly recent innovation. There was nothing on TV except HBO, which I didn't feel like watching. Since this was roughly a decade prior to my conversion to the Church of Jesus Christ of Latter-day Saints I passed the time primarily by drinking coffee, smoking cigarettes and trying to stay focused on the paperback book I was reading. Since I was so focused on the game, I think I averaged about 20 minutes per page. I could have written the book faster than that.

Years later it amazes me that I once found pleasure in smoking. I simply can't recall what the attraction may have been. I know better now but in 1976 it seemed completely natural to find pleasure in smoking, drinking beer and engaging in other vices. I suppose it all seemed all right because I was unenlightened and it was also pretty commonplace back then. In 1976 it was no big deal to smoke while waiting in line at a bank, grocery shopping or engaging in other indoor activities. We weren't allowed to smoke at the Neal Blaisdell Arena but that ordinance only went into effect earlier that same year.

At seven I left for the stadium with my roommate riding shotgun. Conspicuously absent was Bill's girlfriend but that had nothing to do with the fight they had the night before. I only managed to scrape up three tickets which I gave to Bill, Don Simmons and his girlfriend, meaning I managed to get one more than I would normally be allotted. Bill's girlfriend, Cherie Monbouquette, would attend a couple of games later in the season although, being a fairly recent immigrant from France, she knew practically nothing about football and had virtually no interest in the game. Football at the time was known almost exclusively in North America.

We entered the parking lot through Gate 4 and parked in the players' parking area adjacent to the tunnel leading to the north end zone. Bill joined some friends at a tailgate party in another part of the lot. I headed down the ramp to the tunnel.

There was always a very special feeling whenever I made this walk. As I moved deeper through the tunnel toward the north end zone the green artificial surface grew closer, as did the goal posts at the two ends of the field. Initially I caught sight of the orange seats and baseball dugouts on the opposite end of the stadium, then the blue seats, baseball press box on the loge level and finally the yellow seats in the uppermost section.

The word "HAWAII" was painted in block letters in the north end zone. It was flanked by a painting of the Hawaiians helmet in the mauka corner and a white University of Hawaii Rainbow Warrior helmet with a muscular menehune running with a football inside a rainbow in the makai corner.

In the south end zone the word "ALOHA" was flanked by a St. Louis Cardinal helmet in the mauka corner and a Texas A&I helmet, which was an upcoming home opponent for the University of Hawaii, was in the makai corner. After each visiting team had played its game, its helmet would be washed out and the next opponent's helmet would be painted in. It was something that the Hawaiians executives wanted and paid for. The University of Hawaii and its opponents were included as a courtesy that was also paid for by the Hawaiians.

I discovered that only four of my teammates were in the locker room when I arrived. Frank Joseph and Mark Black had arrived together only a few minutes ahead of me and were starting to undress by their respective lockers. Rich Grummon was a peculiar site in the trainer's room, smoking a pipe while sitting on a table in his underwear as an attendant taped his ankles. Marv Nelson was sitting by his locker in gym shorts and his game jersey while casually smoking a cigarette.

Marv nodded and smiled as I approached him.

"How's it going?" I asked softly to respect the reverence of a pregame locker room.

"It's a new life for me," he replied just as softly. "I spent nine years in New Orleans and we never got anywhere. I've got a really good feeling about this team."

I got out of my street clothes. I got into my blue gym shorts and a Los Angeles Dodger T-shirt and hat and began my traditional pregame run around the field.

The stadium was ready for Hawaii's NFL debut. There were orange pylons marking each corner of the end zones, hash marks in spots designated for both college and pro football on the field, long aluminum benches on both sidelines and tables for Gatorade at the 50-yard line. I could see a few bodies up in the football press box above the mauka sideline even though kickoff was still almost two hours away. The large scoreboard in the north end zone was flanked by the word "ALOHA" on one side and an electronic likeness of a pack of Salem with the team names and scores on the other. There was a message already welcoming early birds even though the gates would not actually open until almost a half-hour later.

As I began my final lap the St. Louis team in street clothes emerged from the north tunnel to head for the locker room on the makai side of the south end zone. A few nodded slightly as I ran past including Jerry Morehouse who had been my teammate a week earlier and who exchanged a quick handshake with me as I jogged past.

Most of the Cardinals were in reverie, focusing on avoiding the prospect of losing to an expansion team in its NFL debut. They had flown roughly 4,000 miles to face us. The last thing they wanted afterward was a flight home that seemed like 40,000 miles.

"Have a good game today," I unconsciously said to a large Black player who smiled lightly as I ran past him near the south end zone.

"Same to you, man," he replied.

I suppose I meant it. As long as Hawaii finished on the upper end of the scoreboard I wouldn't mind if he personally had a good game. The better they played, the better we would look if we beat them.

Most of my teammates had arrived by the time I returned to the locker room. Some had actually been in the hospitality room prior to this; a facility I didn't know at the time was available to us since word leaked out slowly. About half of the team had actually arrived at the stadium before I did but were in the hospitality room with wives or girlfriends and children.

The closer we got to game time, the more I focused on a pregame tradition that I began in high school. Several of my teammates shared in the tradition by relieving themselves every five minutes or so. It wasn't so much a matter of being overly hydrated. We were simply dealing with nervous energy.

Others had their own ways of dealing with pregame jitters. A few listened to radios or tapes. Walker permitted this as long as they used earphones so that those who preferred a more quiet ambience would not be disturbed.

There were those who meditated. Some studied playbooks even though everybody should have had his assignments down. Phil Hoddesson read from *The Book of Mormon*. Jimmy Souza read from *The Bible*. Kerner read a *Sports Illustrated*. A few others checked out their game programs.

"Hey, that's me," I overheard Hamer say to Morrissey, pointing at the program they were looking at together. I still wonder if Eric was genuinely surprised that his spot on the team allowed him to have his picture in the program.

As we did for the home opener every year, we entered the field earlier than normal prior to the opening kickoff. This was so the entire team could be introduced to the crowd. During the rest of the season only the starting offense or defense would be introduced on an alternating basis but the entire team was always introduced in the home opener.

Individual teammates were introduced in numerical order except for the starters. The starting defensive unit was introduced after the nonstarters and then the starting offensive unit. The team formed up in the south end zone and each player ran to midfield as his name was called.

"At halfback, number 22, from the University of Hawaii, Jay Dockman."

Like the rest of my teammates, I received roaring approbation from the crowd of 49,718. It was a wonderfully warm feeling.

Along the way the Cardinals gradually trickled down to the bench on the makai sideline. After our introductions were completed the PA announcer introduced the St. Louis starting offense. Overall the Cardinal players were greeted with quiet. There were some boos, a smattering of applause and about half-a-dozen fans on our side of the field loudly asking, "Who cares?" after each player was introduced.

The Waianae High School band quickly marched on the field. Waianae was selected in a random drawing to perform the National Anthem and halftime show. All local schools interested in performing, including those from neighbor islands, had their names randomly drawn. Seven local high schools were selected for seven regular season games. Two more were chosen in the event that we hosted two playoff games. If one or both of the latter schools didn't get to perform as a result of us not qualifying for the playoffs, they would have the first options for 1977.

Time was of the essence for the pregame festivities. The kickoff had to take place right at the top of the hour to accommodate CBS. We were running slightly ahead of schedule as we prepared for the coin toss.

Bender, Marv, Allen and Rodgers moved to midfield for the coin toss. St. Louis won and elected to receive. We chose to defend the north end zone.

For the only time since turning pro I wished I was on the kickoff team. That is how anxious I was to get started. With the exception of my appearance in the Hula Bowl, I hadn't played on a kickoff team since high school but felt like I needed to be on the field now.

"Get 'em off the field quick," I said somewhat lightly to defensive end Jim McDaniel. "I can't wait to get started."

As our kickoff unit and their kick return unit stood in place, an official wearing a headset, white referee pants and a red shirt stood on the 25-yard line on the Cardinal side of the field with his arms folded. This told the officials that CBS had yet to come to us. I stood in front of our bench and jumped up and down a few times to try to work off some of the excitement. I held my helmet in my right hand and was dying to put it on and run on the field.

The official with the red shirt cranked his arm in a circular motion to signal that CBS was with us. Fans in the St. Louis and a few selected other markets were going to get the nation's first televised look at Hawaii's regular season NFL presence. The game was also shown in Hawaii since it sold out barely well enough in advance to be shown locally. It was the only home game that season that would fall into that category.

It was very exciting. Eric Guinn prepared to kick the Hawaiians into history. I jumped up and down a few more times.

History?

Yes it was. It didn't rival the signing of the Declaration of Independence, the Emancipation Proclamation, Germany's and Japan's surrenders to end World War II or even Hank Aaron's 715th home run but it was still history. Honolulu had always been a minor league sports town but now it had a major sports franchise.

Guinn approached the ball and boomed it toward the south end zone. A Cardinal kick return specialist caught the ball cleanly at about the five. He headed upfield as the crowd encouraged our kickoff unit to bring him down quickly.

Kyle McWherter, a defensive end taken from Kansas City in the expansion draft, hit him on about the 20 but the return man spun away. As he was trying to regain his balance he was hit almost simultaneously by Ken Gilbert, a rookie out of San Diego State, and the rookie Jim Morrissey who was also our starting right cornerback. The play ended at the St. Louis 26.

"All right! Good enough!" Walker barked. "Let's get out there, defense!"

The latter part of Walker's direction was redundant. It is simply what most coaches do automatically after a kickoff. He called on the defensive unit even though the starting defense was already heading to the field. Everybody affected seemed to know that he was not going to send the field goal unit out although he would not have hesitated to do exactly that if he believed it would cross up the Cardinals. He would have sent out a team of Girl Scouts if he felt that that would be effective.

"Let's go, defense!" I called. "Three and out! Whaddya say? Three and out!"

I simply could not wait to get my licks in. During the series I stretched, jumped up and down, and did a few short sprints behind the bench.

There was a balminess in the air. I wasn't sure if it wasn't simply my nervous tension. Nervous tension probably did play a role but it did turn out to be more humid than normal. I noticed the night before that planes were approaching the runways from the east. That meant Kona conditions which meant virtually no wind, making it hot, humid and miserable.

We didn't get a three and out. St. Louis was primed to draw first blood. The Cardinals picked up two first downs and had first and ten at our 31.

"Tighten it up out there! Tighten it up!" Walker hollered, cupping his hands around his mouth to amplify his voice. "Let's plug up those holes!"

The Cardinals ran a sweep around left end that picked up seven yards before Morrissey brought the ball carrier down. They next play went up the middle with K.T. Smith making the stop . . . and knocking the ball loose!

"Fumble!"

"Loose ball!"

"Get it! Get it!"

"We got it!"

"Ours! Ours!"

One fumble brought our sideline to life. The crowd also got into it with every vocal Hawaiian and Hawaiian fan trying to let the officials know that the Cardinals turned the ball over to us.

It all proved fruitless. One of the Cardinals' linemen fell on the ball. I felt incredibly let down; perhaps as much because I was dying to take the field as my desire to win. Third and one.

"Come on, you guys! Get the ball!" I cried out.

The Cardinals tried a fullback draw. Allen plugged the hole quickly. The play lost two yards.

"That's the way to do it, Big Russ!" Greg Henry cried jubilantly while standing next to me on the sideline.

It was fourth and three at the 24. The Cardinal field goal unit took the field. It would be a 41-yard attempt.

A yellow flag abruptly shot in the air.

"What happened? What happened?" Walker wanted to know, pacing an erratic pattern on the sideline.

"All right! It's against them!" Abraham exclaimed, thrusting his fist in the air.

The Cardinals were charged with unsportsmanlike conduct, creating a huge roar from the crowd and our sideline. One of their linemen was alleged to have tried to mix it up with Norm Richards although I wondered if the lineman simply caught the official's attention while reacting to something Richards provoked. If that was the case, nobody on our side was about to set the record straight.

Since the penalty came after the play was blown dead it was still fourth down. The difference was the Cardinals needed 18 yards from the 41 for a first down. They were also no longer in reasonable field goal range although a 56-yarder was not impossible.

"Punt return unit, let's go!"

With 11:17 left in the first quarter I took the field for the first time ever in a regular season NFL game and positioned myself at the five. Normally I went back no further than the ten but I wanted to get a good jump if the ball were to come down in front of me. Anything inside the ten I would let drop and, I hoped, let it bounce into the end zone.

Unfortunately the St. Louis punter did his job well. He was going for the coffin corner. The ball flew out of bounds at the six. That was about five yards short of the punter's goal but good enough.

Despite the Cardinals' philanthropic gesture of jumping offsides before Bender's incomplete pass on the opening play, we played the opening series in expansion team fashion. On second down Scott gained all of one yard. Bender was then sacked at the eight. It was fourth and eight. We had no choice but to punt.

Ray Jablonski got off a halfway decent punt. A fair catch was made at the Hawaiians 49. The Cardinals had excellent field position.

Fortunately the defense tightened up. The Cardinals went nowhere and were forced to punt again.

Unfortunately their punter was akin to a golfer who shoots a hole-in-one. He put the ball to where I couldn't get to it with a reasonable effort and the ball headed toward the end zone.

I tried to block one of the Cardinal wideouts streaking downfield after I knew I wasn't going to be able to field the punt. I managed to slightly impede his progress but it wasn't enough. I had to keep one eye on him while also being careful to stay away from the ball. All I could do was bump him toward the sideline but he still managed to continue. He downed the ball at the two.

Perhaps our first series had been a fluke. Perhaps its futility could be attributed to debut nerves.

All I really know is we looked a lot better on this series. We moved the ball this time.

Scott got us some breathing room with a nine-yard run. Kerner fought for two more yards for a first down at the 13.

Two plays later from the 18 I got my first official NFL carry. I shot through the hole off right tackle, was hit at the 22 but stayed on my feet to the 25. We had another first down.

Oh what a rush of adrenaline!

A couple of plays later I picked up our next first down. Running a quick slant from the left slot, I caught Bender's pass just before I was hit. I picked up all of five yards to the Hawaii 37.

Not only was this my first NFL reception, it was the Hawaiians' first official reception. Bender hadn't been getting much protection although that is not as negative as it sounds. We had only attempted a few passes.

As we continued our drive the crowd became more vocal. The Cardinal defense also became more aggressive. It was coming at Bender hard and forcing him to hurry his throws or scramble. He still maintained the poise of an All-Pro and kept the drive alive.

For the record, the first touchdown for the NFL Hawaiians was scored by Rich Grummon. The tight end out of Syracuse made a leaping grab of a pass in the right rear corner of the end zone as time expired in the first quarter.

The fans went nuts! They had been in a perpetual crescendo as the 98-yard drive continued from north to south. When Grummon made his leaping grab while a defensive back tried in vain to deflect the ball the stadium exploded.

"Way to go, man! Way to go!" I exclaimed as I ran over to Grummon from the center of the end zone. Grummon spiked the ball and accepted the congratulations of the offensive unit as we ran off the field in triumph and the extra point team jubilantly ran on. The Hawaiians, NFL vintage, were showing the world that we were capable of playing serious football.

"All right! Good job, men!" Walker lauded, slapping some of us on our backs. "It's a good start but we still have three quarters to go."

I grabbed a cup of Gatorade while kicker Eric Guinn was successfully splitting the uprights. As I gulped it down I looked at the large scoreboard that was halfway up the bleachers on the north side.

Scott seemed to be thinking like me as he sipped his Gatorade.

"Look at that, guys," he said to Abraham, Carl Hayer, Marv and me at the Gatorade table. "We drew first blood."

"That's good for now but we can't let down," Marv cautioned. "It doesn't mean a thing if we're not on top after four quarters."

No doubt Marv recalled the way his former team's NFL career began. A touchdown on the opening kickoff got the Saints off to a promising start. Unfortunately there were few highlights after that. Through nine seasons in the NFL Marv never experienced a winning season. That experience probably encouraged Marv to try extra hard to keep everybody on this expansion team motivated. The last thing he wanted was to play on another expansion team whose growing pains were comprised of very little growth and a lot of pain.

We began the second quarter kicking toward the north end zone. The return led us to believe we were about to pad our 7-0 lead.

The St. Louis kick returner fielded the ball about three yards deep in the end zone. He hesitated, then brought it out.

"Get him!" I barked viciously as my teammates on the kicking team zeroed in on him. "Inside the 20!"

Hasegawa was downfield like a shot. He hit the ball carrier hard at the 18. Rich and the ball carrier went down in a hurry while the ball shot up in the air.

"Fumble! Fumble!" I cried out while several teammates, coaches and fans made similar calls.

The ball hit a few yards toward the north end zone and took a strange bounce, heading back toward Rich who was raising to his knees. He popped up and narrowly beat a Cardinal player to the ball. He dove on top of the ball about a yard behind where he made the initial hit.

A few players on both sides jumped in while I unconsciously held my breath. It appeared to me that Rich had made the recovery although I was also a very partisan source and several yards away. It was up to the officials to sort things out.

Suddenly the referee pointed toward the north end zone. The stadium erupted. First down, Hawaii, at the St. Louis 17.

"Offense! Offense! Let's take it in!" Walker called as the offensive unit jubilantly ran past to the field.

Hasegawa was running off in triumph. He slapped fives with a few of us along the way. A week earlier he appeared to be on the cusp of making the team or not. Now he had answered the call by making a big play. It was a very proud moment for my fellow former Rainbow.

"Let's put up more points, Jaybird!" I heard Scott call enthusiastically as he ran about two yards behind me toward our huddle.

"I'm not arguing," I replied, looking back at Scott with a grin of anticipation. At that moment I didn't believe that even the Pittsburgh Steelers could beat us. In retrospect, this was incredible optimism regarding

82

a team whose official NFL history had comprised exactly 15 minutes, eight seconds.

When I reached our huddle at just inside the 30 I happened to look toward our sideline. Walker was slapping Hasegawa's shoulder pads with the palms of his hands. Walker's smile was so big that nobody in the stadium could have missed it.

The turnover led to some points although in a very unconventional manner. We ran a few plays and had a first and goal at the four.

"Split right, slot right," Bender directed in the huddle. Three Wahiawa right on two, on two. Ready?"

"Break!"

I lined up in the slot on the right. Bender took the snap on cue. I shot toward the middle to lay a block on a linebacker as Bender handed off to Scott who shot through the hole between Hoddesson and Marv and got down to the one. . . .

Scott dropped the ball!

"Loose ball! Loose ball!"

About half-a-dozen of us in the vicinity dove for the ball. Unfortunately the enemy recovered.

This is the kind of thing that can have a very demoralizing impact on a team. When you start a drive with a sure touchdown in sight the last thing you want to do is come away empty-handed, especially by turning the ball over. The momentum suddenly switched to the Cardinals.

The Cardinals were obviously cognizant of the sudden shift of fortune. All eleven defenders seemed to jump in unison. As I rose to my feet I noted the jubilation on their sideline. There were a lot of smiles over there; something I didn't anticipate seeing on our sideline.

I ran off the field while our defense ran on. I grabbed a cup of Gatorade and observed Scott sitting on the aluminum bench.

"Oh man, oh man, oh man, oh man, oh man," he muttered softly to himself as he stared at the ground and shook his head. "Man, oh man. What did I do that for? I can't believe it."

"It's all right. Shake it off," Bender calmly instructed him as he bent over and placed his hand on Larry's back. "It'll all work out."

Bender was right. On the second play from scrimmage Richards shot through the line and tackled their running back in the end zone. We scored as an indirect result of the initial turnover after all. We had a 9-0 lead.

What's more, we were getting the ball back. The safety meant the Cardinals had a free kick. Our kick return unit huddled and agreed to return the kick to the left.

The kick was up. It was heading toward me.

"I got it!" I called loudly, signaling Dietrich to run ahead to block.

I fielded the ball at the 25. Dietrich and Giametti both did nice blocks a few yards ahead of me to give me running room. Other teammates did the same further up field.

After vaulting over a couple of Cardinals who had been laid out I took off. Suddenly I was flying like a rocket up the makai sideline with nothing but end zone in sight.

Suddenly I was at the 50, 40, 30. . . .

And the crowd was going crazy again! I didn't notice it at the time but recalled it later. Few things are more thrilling in football than something that gets the crowd on its feet and screaming its approbation.

As I approached the 25 I spotted a white jersey. It was their punter running over to either try to tackle me or else push me out of bounds.

I made a slight cut to the inside as I slowed up a little and saw him get nothing but air and fall on his face. My elusive maneuver was enough, however, to enable another Cardinal to catch me from behind. I went down on the 15.

We were up by a mere nine points but the crowd was loving it. After a sluggish start we were making some big plays that were keeping our fans awake.

Unfortunately our drive moved all of one yard. That seemed pretty pathetic. Guinn came on the field to attempt a 31-yard field goal.

Even that was exciting. The ball hit the left upright and then went over the crossbar.

"That's good enough," I heard Walker sigh. I could almost feel his heard skipping a beat as the ball hit the upright.

We had three scores but were only leading 12-0. The Cardinals were very much alive.

The Cardinals went to work. They put together a drive until it finally stalled at the Hawaii 18. They settled for a 35-yard field goal with 3:23 left in the half.

And that's when we went to work. It was almost as if the Cardinals insulted us by having the nerve to kick a field goal on our turf during our NFL debut.

After a kickoff out of the end zone to put us on our own 20 we proceeded to move the length of the field. Bender showed us what a 14-year veteran quarterback could do. The drive included a 26-yard pass to Dietrich and a 25-yard pass to me that gave us a first down at the St. Louis 27. After another couple of plays, as well as an illegal procedure penalty against us, Bender hit Slater for a 24-yard pass to the five.

Kerner took care of the rest. He slammed into the end zone on the very next play. With the extra point we were up 19-3 with 18 seconds left in the half.

84

That's the way the half ended. After a short kick return the Cardinal offense downed the ball and ran to their locker room. The newly expanded Hawaiians held a 16-point lead and got a nice ovation as we left the field.

In the locker room I relieved myself, drank some Gatorade and sat in front of my locker. It felt good to have a 16-point lead although that is far from insurmountable. It was still a lot better than trailing by 16 points.

I thought about what the situation meant. I was happy with the overall outcome of the first half, but the second half was still an enigma. What happened then could set the tone for the rest of the season. If we won it could give us momentum that we could keep as long as we continued to play well. If we blew it we might wind up in a funk that could be hard to overcome.

Of course it was still one game. Just the same, a positive start was better than losing a few before finally getting into the win column. So much of this game is psychological. Winning this game wouldn't get us into the Super Bowl but our collective psyche would be at a healthier level.

And if we blew our 16-point lead . . . .

I didn't want to think about it.

"Your opponents are in their locker room making adjustments," Walker reminded us. "They're analyzing your strengths and working on how to overpower you there and they plan to exploit your weaknesses."

Walker paused to take a drag off of his cigarette. It gave him a moment to think about what to say next.

"You've held your own for 30 minutes. We need you to do that and more for another 30 minutes. They're getting beat by a team that wasn't even in the league last year and that is making them hungry. They're being humiliated and some teams would surrender at halftime but not these guys. They're going to come at you like a nest of angry hornets so you have to be ready. We need a peak performance out of you for 30 more minutes with good, clean, smart football."

As if on cue, an official stuck his head in the locker room.

"Two minutes, Coach," he said.

Walker nodded and subtly waved to acknowledge.

"All right, men," Walker said to begin his conclusion. "We'll be receiving. That means that we can strike first blood of the half. Let's go."

We let out a collective roar and filed out of the locker room to head to the sideline. I felt the same level of excitement I felt at the beginning of the game. At least this time I wouldn't have to wait to take the field.

Things didn't go according to Walker's directive. Our opening drive of the second half produced virtually nothing. Just as we did on our opening drive of the first half, we ran three virtually futile plays and had to punt.

As expected, the Cardinals showed signs of life. Their offense appeared to have made the adjustments Walker mentioned and began moving the ball.

That wasn't a cue for us to panic.

And we didn't.

Their quarterback dropped back. Jennings broke through the line and charged into the backfield.

"Get him, Ed!" I hollered while standing behind our bench.

The quarterback managed to get the pass off concurrent with being hammered by Ed. It actually wasn't a poorly thrown pass despite the degree of difficulty but safety Ben Blakely played it perfectly. He cut in front of the receiver and picked the pass off at the Hawaii 31.

I am sure the crowd roared its approval. I can't verify it because from where I stood the crowd was drowned out by those of us on the sideline who roared our approval. We were beginning to smell victory. We wanted it really bad!

Blakely stumbled a little as he was catching the ball. He only managed to get six yards to the 37 but that was perfectly all right. We had the ball. We were 63 yards away from another score with 10:04 left in the third quarter.

The crowd was thinking victory. We wanted to give it to them. It would be a wonderful opening chapter in the epic of the NFL Hawaiians.

And so we drove. Grummon probably had the most impressive play of the drive. On second and three from our 44 he caught a pass on a quick slant just beyond the line of scrimmage. It looked like he was going to get a yard, at most, but he was a tough customer. He broke away from a pair of would-be tacklers and picked up a total of 14 yards.

It was Grummon again on second and nine from the St. Louis 19. He caught a pass five yards deep in the end zone for his second touchdown of the game.

"Yeah!" I cried out with my fists in the air near the goal line where my teammate from a week earlier, Morehouse, had me covered like flypaper. I was a little embarrassed when I realized who my defender was since I honestly wasn't trying to rub his nose in anything.

Morehouse looked at me with a subtle grin of resignation.

"It's okay, Jay. You guys are earning it."

We gave each other friendly whacks on the back before I ran to our sideline. Jerry stayed on the field to defend against the PAT.

The extra point was good. We led, 26-3, with 6:22 left in the third quarter.

But the game was far from over. The Cardinals knew that as well as anybody. On the subsequent drive they seemed to find the holes in our defense. After a series of rushes and short passes they had a second and seven at our 17.

Their quarterback dropped back on the next snap. He spotted one of his running backs open on the left sideline just inside the ten. He fired to the back who made the catch and sidestepped Morrissey.

Rodgers was nearby. He caught up with the receiver and brought him down just short of the goal line but he wasn't able to prevent the receiver from reaching out, enabling the ball to break the plane before any part of his body touched the ground. The Cardinals had their first touchdown of the season with 1:48 to go in the third quarter. With the extra point we still held a 26-10 lead.

Although the momentum had shifted in the Cardinals' direction for the moment, I was still feeling pretty good. The entire experience of playing on an NFL team in Hawaii was overwhelming, especially since we were doing so well. A year earlier I was wearing the same uniform but in a league that was admittedly inferior to the NFL and I was trying to help my team win while hoping the league would stay afloat. The contrast was so overwhelming that I was almost tempted to ask somebody to pinch me. This was not the Jacksonville Express of the World Football League we were facing like we did 364 days earlier in our first-ever game at Aloha Stadium. This was the St. Louis Cardinals, an established and respected franchise of the National Football League.

During the closing minutes of the third quarter and the opening minutes of the fourth both sides had quick series that achieved very little aside from making the two defenses look good. The Cardinals capped their series with a 62-yard punt to our three yard line.

We huddled in the back of the north end zone. Bender, who was generally all business, presided in our huddle in a cocksure manner.

"It looks like we've got 97 yards to go," he began. "That's perfect. We'll cover the 97 yards and kill most of the clock in the process."

That's virtually what we did. Whether Bender's demeanor loosened us up or not, I don't know, but anybody who didn't know our history would find it hard to believe that we were not a veteran NFL franchise with the way we moved the ball. We marched down the field a chunk at a time with the ecstatic crowd cheering us on.

The drive included only two passes which was just enough to prevent the Cardinals from keying on the run. I had a 25-yard reception near midfield and stayed inbounds to keep the clock running. Dietrich caught a 16-yard pass.

Two plays after Dietrich's reception Larry Scott ran it in from the nine. The extra point extended our lead to 33-10 with 5:31 left to play.

Need I mention the crowd?

There are few things more gratifying to an athlete than the sight of the home crowd on its feet and cheering raucously. Arms were being raised, hands were being clapped, those who could whistle did so and everybody seemed to be smiling. It was awesome.

We loved it although there was an unwritten football protocol that mandated that the players pretend not to notice; at least while there is still more than a minute or two on the clock and the outcome with at least a semblance of a doubt. Baseball players could wave to the fans after making an outstanding play or hitting a home run. Football players really weren't supposed to do that. Waving to the fans with more than five minutes remaining wouldn't have got anybody fined or suspended by the NFL but you can be sure that Walker would have had something to say about it.

We could still loosen up a bit on the sideline. As the offensive unit sat on the bench and sipped Gatorade, we could let our guards down a little. The Cardinals were still technically alive but needed a total collapse on our part. They needed a minimum of three touchdowns and a field goal.

"This is great; just great," Carl Hayer said enthusiastically as the huge tackle from Washington wiped the perspiration from his face with a white towel.

"I'm happy," Marv added. "I think we've already shown that we're better than any of the Saints teams I played on. We won a few games during the nine years I was in New Orleans but I don't think I felt this happy and optimistic after a victory since I was still at Grambling."

"I just want to keep this momentum going," Scott said. "I wonder if Cosell's going to say anything about us tomorrow night."

"Who cares what Cosell thinks?" I chimed in.

"Right. He'll probably blame the whole thing on the Cardinals," Hayer replied jocularly.

"Or maybe he'll be so impressed with us that it will render him speechless," I suggested lightly.

"That'll be the day," Marv chuckled.

The Cardinals, to their credit, continued to play hard. Just before the two-minute warning they scored a touchdown to pull to within 33-17 but the game was as good as over. We recovered their onside kick and, after a quick first down with the backups inserted, Frank Joseph took a couple of snaps and knelt down while the crowd gave us a standing ovation that actually began immediately after we recovered the onside kick.

Our opponents were gracious in defeat. We were the same in victory. We shook hands on the field as we headed toward our respective locker rooms, wishing each other luck the rest of the way.

"It wouldn't be that much of a surprise to see you guys in the Super Bowl," one of the Cardinals told me.

"Well thanks but that's a pretty lofty goal," I replied humbly although I was all in favor of playing in the Super Bowl.

"I'm not kidding," my now-former opponent remarked. "Jerry Morehouse . . . . You know. . . . The guy who got cut from your team the other day and came back to us. He told us that we had better be ready to play because you guys aren't like the typical expansion team. He said there is some All-Pro talent on this team."

88

He seemed sincere and it warmed me. I was glad that we had earned that much respect. It also ostensibly meant that we had won legitimately. It wasn't a matter of the Cardinals getting burned because they took us lightly.

As I approached the tunnel leading to our locker room in the south end zone I finally acknowledged the fans. Many were still standing and cheering and I casually waved to them. A few reached over the barrier between the bleachers and the tunnel and I quickly shook their hands as I moved past.

We were all smiles in the locker room. All may not have been right in some parts of the world but our locker room was a temporary refuge from that. We were the only team in the NFL to have won every game in its entire existence. We were very glad that we didn't join our fellow expansionists in Seattle, Tampa and Memphis in starting our history with the expected defeat.

At the time I thought that we were the only expansion team in NFL history to win its debut game. I found out later that the Minnesota Vikings had done that in 1961, scoring a 37-13 victory over the Chicago Bears. It was one of only three victories for the Vikings that season. I was hoping that we would fare better than that.

Backup center Stuart Arroyo volunteered to do the postgame prayer which was an actual prayer and not a team recitation of *The Lord's Prayer* the way our pregame prayer was done. Afterward we began our tradition of giving out a game ball. This was something we would do after every victory. The recipient would be somebody who had done something noteworthy although it didn't necessarily have to be the player who rushed for the most yards or made the most receptions. It could have been somebody who made a key sack or interception or even a rookie or somebody else making his first start who played a good game. Sometimes more than one player was awarded a game ball.

The recipient was usually awarded the game ball by Walker although he rarely unilaterally made the decision; often consulting his coaches or occasionally even some of the players. On this occasion the four team captains were given permission by Walker to make the presentation. Marv, Allen, Bender and Rodgers stood in the middle of the locker room. Bender was holding the ball.

"Like a lot of teams," Allen announced loud enough for everybody to hear, "we're beginning a tradition. Each victory means that somebody will get a game ball. I hope we give away dozens of game balls before I'm through playing."

That brought enthusiastic applause from the players and coaches. The overall well-being we all felt was impossible to describe.

"This one is extra special," Marv added once we were quiet again. "This one is historical."

"Right," Allen agreed. "The four of us put our heads together and decided that there was only one candidate for today's game ball."

Bender held the ball up. I could see that "Hawaiians versus Cardinals" was written in magic marker along with the date.

The four captains moved over to Walker who was standing off to the side smoking a cigarette near where I was standing in front of my locker. His eyes widened in genuine surprise.

"This was our first victory," said Bender. "It was because of your coaching that we got it. Let this symbolize the first of at least a few hundred victories in Hawaii."

Steve handed Walker the ball amid a spontaneous roar of approval. Walker opened his mouth but initially couldn't speak. The honor blindsided him. He understood the special significance of this award and the high hopes that it represented.

"I honestly don't know what to say," Walker said once he had finally composed himself, holding the ball with both hands while staring at it the way a child admires a new puppy for Christmas. "You men made this all possible. We play one game at a time and . . . we're off to a helluva good start."

There were more raucous cheers. Walker handed the ball back to Bender. "I want everybody to sign the ball before you leave," Walker said. "I've got a very special place at home where I'm going to keep it."

With that he smiled and waved before heading to his office.

As I gradually shed my perspiration-soaked uniform I looked to my right. Carl Rodgers was stripping down and gave me a smile as our eyes met. On the other side I exchanged a similar wordless encounter with Jeff Kerner.

Both were smoking victory cigars. There were several such cigars being smoked, courtesy of Rich Grummon who brought a whole box of them in anticipation of our victory. Even guys like Stanek, Jurgens and McDaniel were smoking cigars even though they were normally nonsmokers. Although I was a smoker then, I declined the cigar that Grummon offered me. There would be times when I would smoke them after a victory but I didn't really care for cigars.

The media people came in. Reporters were allowed in the locker room in 1976. In later years when female sportswriters demanded equal access our locker rooms became off limits to all media. Media personnel were still given access to players and coaches but only in the area behind the south end zone; on the turf near the tunnel leading to the locker room or else in the dugout seats or baseball dugouts.

What the reporters encountered on this historical day was a very effervescent locker room. We didn't boast but we were still very full of ourselves. Although most of the journalists seemed to focus their attention on Walker, Bender and Grummon, some went around getting random quotes from the rest of us.

"It's a great way to start a franchise," I said to Ferd Borsch, a local newspaper reporter.

What I really wanted to say was that we were invincible; that nobody could beat us. That was the way I felt at that moment. Fortunately I knew better than to make such a stupid statement. The last thing we needed was a statement that would fire up the Chiefs whom we would be facing in Kansas City the following week. A quote like that could also fire up the Cowboys, Raiders and Bengals whom we would face later in the season.

A reporter named Mark Samples from United Press International asked me if the dissolution of the World Football League was a blessing in disguise since it enabled Hawaii to have a National Football League franchise.

"I can't say something like that," I replied cautiously. "When the WFL folded a lot of good football players found themselves out of work and most of them will never play football again. It's wonderful that Hawaii got a franchise but I can never say that the World Football League folding was a good thing. I would be very happy playing in the WFL if it still existed."

CHAPTER SIX
To the Road

It was a Monday. That was our normal day off after a Sunday game. Why was I at Aloha Stadium in my uniform?

Actually it was Marv and me. We were dressed in our uniforms to tape a commercial for a local dairy.

It took us longer to get dressed than it took us to actually shoot the spot. Technicians had already installed the proper lighting and camera in the locker room. Marv and I put on our uniforms, which the team provided specifically at the request of the ad agency, and headed to another locker room. Our hair was then tousled and slightly dampened to give the impression that we had just completed an intense game.

This done, we sat on stools in front of the camera. We were both given glasses of milk. When the director said "action" we were to look at each other and smile while clinking our glasses together.

The spot obviously taxed our acting abilities to the max. The director had us repeat the sequence three times to ensure that everything wound up on tape correctly. After that we were through. Less than ten minutes after we'd finished putting our uniforms on we were taking them off.

It was actually a 30 second spot but there was no spoken dialogue. The first 25 seconds of the finished product had individual tight shots of Marv and me playing the game the day before. A camera operator and sound technician had been allowed to roam the sidelines during the game.

Marv and I didn't know about the camera operator and sound technician. Only part of the coaching staff knew. The rest of us simply assumed they were part of CBS or a local TV station. Keeping their identities away from us prevented the possibility of distraction.

The finished fast-paced product had shots of me running and catching passes and Marv throwing blocks. The final action clip, which was simply a lucky break since the camera happened to be in perfect position to catch this, had Marv throwing a downfield block that enabled me to run past. All of these clips included embellished sounds of grunts, groans and collisions.

For the final five seconds the spot cut to the locker room. Two gridiron gladiators toasted victory with glasses of milk as a graphic of the dairy's logo appeared on the screen in front of us. Marv and I were both milk drinkers although we honestly didn't drink milk right after a game. Gatorade or water was more likely and a beer usually came into play somewhere along the way.

Throughout my career our routine between Sunday games was fairly constant. We were off on Mondays but had to report at nine o'clock on Tuesday morning. If the next game was on grass we reported to our Marine base training ground. If we were going to play a home game or an away game on artificial turf we practiced at Aloha Stadium.

Tuesday always began with films of Sunday's game. This did not entail simply sitting in a room and watching until the reel emptied. Walker manned the projector for the offensive unit and beaucoup instant replays were on tap, as was the case with whoever ran the defensive unit's films. If somebody screwed up an assignment Walker ran it back and forth at least a few times. He also did the same thing if somebody did something especially well although he was a lot less generous with the compliments than he was with the criticism.

Walker wanted to review the films first thing because he was a firm believer in moving forward. He took care of whatever he needed to do from Sunday's game and that was generally that. As soon as the projector was turned off Walker made his closing remarks. After that we started preparing for the following game.

For most of the next hour we sat in a meeting. This included diagramming new plays and whatever other business Walker felt was imperative. Then we got dressed, sans pads, and would be ready to start the day's workout by about eleven.

The Tuesday workout was primarily for getting loose. It generally lasted about 90 minutes. I was usually home by about three o'clock after a weightlifting session. That gave me time to put the finishing touches on the TV show that I would be doing live that night.

On Wednesday we also reported at nine o'clock. We began this session by watching films of our upcoming opponent's previous game. Each team was required to issue its forthcoming opponent films of its previous game. That was a very strict league rule.

Our workout on Wednesday was in full pads with the focus on offense. The workout usually lasted about two hours but sometimes stretched as long as two and-a-half hours. I often wrapped up the day by lifting weights at the gym I belonged to in Pearl City.

On Thursdays and Fridays we also reported at nine o'clock. Sometimes we would watch films of a previous game we had with our upcoming opponent although that was obviously not possible this early in our history. There would also be meetings to discuss that day's agenda, any new plays that were being added or changes in existing plays, travel itineraries and anything else that needed to be discussed.

The Thursday workout focused on the defense. On Friday we focused on both the offense and defense before wrapping up the workout with special teams drills.

If our next game was going to be on the road we usually left on Friday. Often we could still go home after the workout, depending on what time our flight was. If we were heading to the airport after practice we had to have somebody drive us and our luggage to practice since we had no place to leave our cars. A truck would be waiting to transport our luggage and we would take a bus to the airport after practice.

Prior to trips when we had time to go home first, we obviously had to have somebody drive us to the airport. We still took our luggage to our workout where the truck would be waiting to transport it to the plane. Our aircraft was always on the opposite side of the airport from the main terminal. We got to our aircraft by utilizing a facility just off of Lagoon Drive.

If our Sunday game was at home we were to be on the field at Aloha Stadium at ten o'clock on Saturday morning, sans pads. If we were away we did the same thing at an arranged time in the stadium where our game was to be played. In both cases it was simply a final walk-through of our game plan.

Our second game of the season was in Kansas City. This would be on artificial turf so our sessions would be at Aloha Stadium. In 1976 more than half of the teams in the NFL played on artificial turf. Only our games in San Diego, Oakland, Denver and Cleveland would be on grass.

In all of my years of playing for Walker I can safely conclude that he was a master psychologist. This included the way he conducted film sessions.

The worst time to watch films was after we had routed an opponent. With a few dozen swelled heads Walker made sure we were humbled. Every nitpicky thing he could find he harped on obsessively. If a ball carrier didn't make enough of an effort to break a tackle or if a lineman didn't open a hole wide enough Walker often breathed fire.

If we won by a narrow margin Walker pointed out mistakes although he wasn't too hard on us. He was especially civil if we lost a hard-fought tight game. He would point out mistakes with an understanding of the human element. Just as he focused on bringing us down to earth after a rout, he wanted to build us up after a tough loss. The important thing was to have us ready to play the next game. That was simply good coaching.

Of course there are mistakes and there are stupid mistakes. Win or lose, stupid mistakes were never overlooked. The more stupid the mistake, the more likely Walker would lose his cool.

There were often light moments. Walker didn't mind us having a few laughs as long as it didn't get out of hand. One such opportunity came when Bender dropped back. Left guard Bill Stanek rose to block, then lost his footing and fell forward on his face. The defensive tackle ran past and hit Bender just as he released the ball. The sight of Stanek falling on his face for no apparent reason brought some laughs.

"That wasn't funny," Bender called out jocularly. "That hurt."

"What happened, Stanek?" Walker asked lightly. "Did a gust of wind hit you?"

94

I unwittingly did my part to keep my teammates sufficiently entertained. On a pass play when I was designated to run a cross pattern I slipped and fell as I was making my cut.

Walker had previously reviewed the film. He always knew what was coming up.

"Dockman," he called prior to the play turning up. "This is one heck of a pass pattern you are about to run."

That got everybody's attention. Instead of the play itself, everybody would be watching the dark jersey with the 22 on it. Game films are not like what one sees on TV. They come from a single camera which provides a panoramic view of all 22 players on the field from high in the stadium.

I was lined up wide on the left, slightly behind the line. Dietrich was wide to the right on the line. He would be running a post.

The fact that Bender completed a pass to Dietrich was barely noticed. Walker, in the spirit of levity, ran the film to the point where I fell down, then reversed it to where I was standing, then to where I was down so that I was up, down, up, down, up, down. . . .

Of course it wasn't especially funny except for the way Walker presented it.

"Now Jay," Walker began lightly after he'd gone through the cycle about half-a-dozen times. "No matter how many times I run it back I still can't find the banana peel you slipped on."

If we had played a good game Walker often used opportunities to keep everybody loose. Pro football was a serious business. It was also fun when we played hard and well.

For whatever the reason, I called Laurie on Thursday night. I will probably go to my grave not understanding why. I didn't dislike her but I also wasn't especially crazy about her. She and I had practically nothing in common. Why was I pursuing a second date?

I suppose I was being nice. Although I had no real interest in her, I asked her if she wanted to go to a movie the following week.

"You're not available tomorrow or Saturday night?" she asked.

"I'll be in Kansas City. I'll be back late Sunday night. How's Monday work for you?"

"That sounds fine," she agreed.

So I had a date for Monday for which I was neither excited nor repulsed. Laurie was attractive and seemed fairly normal. There was still something different about her that I couldn't put my finger on. Perhaps that was what compelled me to call her.

I enjoyed being a football player. However, if my parents made a list of things they hoped I would do professionally athletics would never have made the cut. They didn't even want me going to college for academics, let alone athletics. They were so bitter about my decision to play college football and baseball that they flatly refused to attend any of my games until they finally relented and flew to Hawaii to see me in the Hula Bowl.

What my parents had in mind was a military career. It was what my dad's brothers did and what my dad would have done had he not been wounded in Korea and medically retired shortly after I was born.

Why did my parents insist that I was doing America a great disservice by not going into the military?

It dates back to my paternal grandfather's experience. In the days preceding corporate greed, Vietnam and Watergate it was not unusual for an immigrant to begin with very little and live a happy, prosperous life in this country. My grandfather came over with a few learned skills and was able to provide a decent lifestyle for his family.

This instilled a deep sense of patriotism in my dad and his siblings. My uncles Robert and Harold joined the Army right after high school. Both were part of the Normandy invasion although with different units. Harold was killed while approaching the beach. Robert got through unscathed and served in the Army until his retirement in 1969.

My dad joined the Army after graduating from high school in 1946. Along the way he was stationed in Ft. Benning, Georgia, and was sent down to Florida for maneuvers in 1949. That was where he met and married my mom.

Despite the fact that my parents had known each other for less than a month when they got married, they had a good marriage. It was very puritan since my dad was the sole provider and my mom stuck by him even during lean times. The idea of my mom ever getting a job was totally out of the question.

It was in January 1952 that my dad's military career ended. A mine explosion near where my dad was patrolling in Korea killed three of my dad's buddies and wounded my dad and two others. Since my dad was furthest from the explosion among the casualties he was the least seriously wounded. It was still enough to cause permanent damage to his legs and back and force an end to his dreams of being a 30-year man.

After his discharge and recovery he took a job as a butcher in a meat locker in Azusa and occasionally took side jobs to help make ends meet. A few years before we moved to Montebello he took his butchering skills to the Alpha Beta grocery chain, working initially in Covina before transferring to Pico Rivera in 1966.

My dad's younger brother Warren slightly altered tradition and joined the Navy after his high school graduation in 1950. He saw combat from destroyers during the Korean and Vietnam conflicts. He was a master chief who was still active in 1976, stationed in San Diego.

That explains the zealous patriotism on my dad's side. My mom's sense of patriotism stems primarily from my dad. It wasn't as if my dad didn't allow her to exercise free speech or form her own opinions. She simply agreed with him, or at least took his side, in this case.

My mom was born Norma Louise Smith in Fort Myers, Florida, in 1931. Both of her grandfathers were native Britons. Her paternal grandmother was from Mexico and her maternal grandmother was full-blooded Seminole. This obviously makes me 50 percent German, 25 percent English and one-eighth each of Hispanic and Seminole.

Put another way, I am 100 percent American and my parents never hesitated to insist that my obligation was to defend the country that my paternal grandparents and three of my maternal great-grandparents migrated to during the early part of the 20th Century. Apparently the freedom of choice was limited to what branch of the service I would join. By opting to go to college instead of the military I caused my parents to actually consider me a dissident who gave America a black eye.

Of course there was a lot of dissension going on at the time. Hordes of people in my age group, including several in uniform, vehemently opposed the Vietnam War. We were actually supposed to believe that the mere fact that the United States decided to go to war justified everything.

What is ironic is my paternal grandparents supported my decision to go to college. We kept the conflict between my parents and me away from them but I would like to believe they would have taken my side had they known. They came to America looking for a better opportunity and that is what I was doing when I opted for college.

While my parents didn't disown me, they were obviously not supportive of my being in college. When I was at USC I was allowed to go home whenever I wanted to but they never asked questions about any facet of school. They were also unwilling to provide any financial aid although I didn't need any since I was on an athletic scholarship that took care of my school expenses. I had also spent a few years working to put money away for other expenses.

Inwardly I believe my parents knew I was not wrong. They were simply so extremely ingrained in their military ideals that they would never admit it. The distance between my parents and me played a minor role in my decision to transfer to Hawaii after one year at USC. Primarily my decision stemmed from a general desire to go away to school. I had fond memories of my brief experience in Hawaii the previous summer for a high school all-star game. Coach Farnwell put me through the proper channels to help me arrange my transfer.

Getting back to my dad's side of the family, I had relatives fighting on both sides in Europe during World War II. This includes Normandy where a cousin of my dad's was part of the German contingent.

I met this first cousin once removed during a family gathering in the summer of 1973. It was a somewhat awkward association since he spoke no English and my grandparents saw no benefit in raising their children to speak anything but English. Only my grandparents could communicate with this cousin in German. He was, however, fluent in French. This enabled me to converse with him since I was also fluent in French. I asked Hans Bismarck about living in Germany during the Third Reich. He told me that a lot of Germans revered Hitler but he observed more people acting out of fear than reverence.

What was sad was the cool reception Hans received from my parents, aunts and uncles. It was primarily a language barrier, I knew. There was still some trepidation about how to deal with somebody on the other side of the war, especially since he had been a part of the same battle that killed one of my uncles.

Hans didn't like being in that battle any more than anybody else did. He fought for Germany because he had no choice. He didn't hate Americans. Unlike the diabolical animal running Germany, he also didn't hate Jews. He had many Jewish friends although most of them had enigmatically disappeared by the time he found himself in the German Army.

Having relatives in America put added pressure on Hans. There had been no contact for several years although Hans always knew where part of his extended family was. He had been afraid to mention having relatives on the other side of the Atlantic for fear of being labeled a traitor. Paranoia ran deep under Hitler.

It wasn't until a few years after the war that Hans learned that he had had two cousins fighting against him. One of his brothers and two other cousins were fighting on the German side but only Hans was at Normandy when two American cousins invaded.

During our only meeting Hans and I conversed throughout the day. He had a good sense of humor and took an interest in my life as a college student and as a baseball and football player. He was vaguely familiar with baseball since it was played in parts of Europe. The American version of football was virtually unheard of in Europe at that time. He had seen pictures but that was about all.

The team was in pretty good spirits as we prepared for our odyssey to Kansas City. We were confident after knocking off the Cardinals. We followed that up with a solid week of practice.

"You made history by winning Hawaii's first ever NFL game," Walker stressed at the end of Friday's workout. "Knock off the Chiefs and the momentum will continue. The entire state of Missouri will hate every last one of us. That's perfectly okay with me."

We absorbed Walker's words as he stood in the middle of us near the south end zone at Aloha Stadium. Most of us were on one knee although some, along with the entire coaching staff, opted to stand. Everybody's eyes were riveted on Walker.

98

"We leave at five," Walker said to begin wrapping up his pep talk. "We should be in Kansas City by about six or six-thirty tomorrow morning, Kansas City time. Be at Air Service by four-thirty this afternoon."

Walker asked if anybody still needed transportation to Air Service. A few guys raised their hands. Arrangements would be made for them.

"We're going to have to figure out a solution to the transportation situation," I heard Walker remark to Greg Wilson as we headed to the locker room. "If there's no place for them to park their cars some of our single guys and married guys whose wives work are going to have to scramble for rides every time we travel. We don't need that kind of distraction two days before a game."

"Couldn't we just go to the airport by bus immediately after practice?" Wilson asked.

"It wouldn't help. The same guys would have to scramble for rides to the stadium. Same problem, different location."

Karla Nelson would be my driver. I wasn't sure whom to ask for a ride. I was going to ask McDaniel since he lived reasonably close to me until I remembered that his wife worked. Jim, it turned out, would be catching a ride with Stanek.

It surprised me when Marv asked me if I wanted to ride with him and Karla. Since Karla worked I figured that he would be scrambling for a ride. Karla had arranged to get off early so that she could drive Marv, Eric Hamer and me to the airport.

Marv and I met for lunch at the Zippy's on King Street in Makiki after practice. As we were placing our orders, Eric happened to show up.

Eric and Marv ordered plate lunches. I opted for a bowl of saimin and an order of fries. Eric and I were at this same Zippy's as WFL teammates about a year earlier when I ordered a bowl of saimin and put pepper and Tabasco in it just to see how Eric would react. He thought it was pretty gross but I discovered that I preferred my saimin that way.

"What's this? Cajun style saimin?" Marv asked as he observed me spicing up my lunch.

"You got it," I said good-naturedly. "This is the way it's done in the deepest part of southern Japan. They also speak Japanese with a drawl."

Eric didn't say anything. He simply shook his head with a smile of disbelief.

While we ate Marv mentioned that he felt like a rookie. Sometimes a veteran says that because he made rookie mistakes. Marv was referring to his level of enthusiasm.

"This team is going to win," he said. "We've only played one game and already I can tell that this team is better than any of the Saints teams I played on."

"How long were you with the Saints?" Eric asked.

"Nine years. Nine . . . very . . . long . . . years. I was there at the very beginning and it was nine years of losing. It really wears you down, man. I accepted it at first because we were a new team, but we didn't get much better. Sometimes I thought we were getting worse. Last year we had our worst season ever."

I also felt good about our team. I wondered, though, how realistic our chances were to be in the playoff hunt.

"Do you believe we can make the playoffs?" Marv asked as if he could read my thoughts.

"Of course I do. If I didn't I wouldn't have any business being on the field."

"How about you?" Marv asked, looking at Eric who was placing a forkful of rice in his mouth. "Do you believe we can make the playoffs?"

Eric swallowed. His face initially looked as if he didn't quite understand the question.

"Sure," Eric replied although he sounded tentative.

"At this point everybody should believe they can make the playoffs," I added. "The other expansion teams, Memphis, Seattle and Tampa Bay, all lost on Sunday. They should still believe they can make the playoffs."

"Right," Marv agreed.

"Do you think they will?" Eric asked, looking primarily at me.

"I have no way of knowing," I replied. "All I know is there are 30 teams in the NFL and all of them have shots at making the playoffs. The sportswriters always make their preseason predictions about who is going to do what and most of them have all four expansion teams finishing last in their divisions simply because that is where expansion teams traditionally finish."

"We can blow that theory all to hell," Marv added. "We don't have to finish last. We don't have to finish second-to-last. If we can play well enough we can get into the playoffs. If we don't win the division we've got a shot at the wild card. Those sportswriters are picking the Rams and Steelers and Raiders and Cowboys to win their divisions but they don't win just because the sportswriters say so."

I added that in most cases the sportswriters are right but not always.

"Last year they said the Cowboys were a year away," I recollected. "Whom were we watching in the Super Bowl last January?"

"The Cowboys," Eric replied, "but they didn't win."

"No but they sure played a helluva game," Marv said. "I've watched all ten Super Bowls and the last one was the best of the bunch."

"And it was between one team that most sportswriters said would be there and a team they believed was a year away," I added. "There will always be teams they believe will get in who don't and teams they believe have no chance who wind up making it. How many people thought the '69 Mets would not finish near the bottom, let alone win the World Series?"

100

"Probably none," Eric answered.

"Except the Mets themselves," I said.

"Right," Marv added brightly. "They had to know they could do it. If they didn't know it they wouldn't have done it. Teams that don't believe they can win always lose."

"Exactly," I said. "It doesn't matter what the sportswriters say. Some of them wrote some pretty flattering stuff about us after we beat the Cardinals. It was a good victory but it doesn't mean we're a good team and it doesn't mean we're a bad team. I also don't think it will mean a whole lot if we blow the Chiefs out of Kansas City or stink up the place. We've got Denver next week and later in the season we've got Oakland and Dallas and Cincinnati and a few other teams that should be pretty tough. How we fare against those teams will be the best indicator of what we can do."

As I did the week before, I snuck peaks at our opponents as we went through the pregame warmup. Once again it was a milestone since we were playing a previously established NFL team in a regular season game. The difference this time was that this team had been to two Super Bowls including the first one. Another difference was we were also playing in a previously established NFL stadium.

I also looked at the fans as they gradually arrived. It was a reasonably warm day so the fans weren't bundled up the way they would be later in the season in Kansas City. The fans were dressed similar to what the fans in Honolulu wore with many in shorts and t-shirts. The only difference was that I didn't notice any females in bikini tops like those often seen at Aloha Stadium.

We made a statement a week earlier. We could make an even stronger statement by beating the Chiefs. The anchors of the sports highlight shows could even feel compelled to use the word "contender" when talking about us that night if we pulled this one out.

Back in the locker room prior to when we would run out before the opening kickoff I marveled at how good I felt. I felt ready to roll.

The night before Marv, Steve Bender, Ted Dietrich and I went the baseball game between the Kansas City Royals and Chicago White Sox at Royals Stadium which was on the same parcel of land where Arrowhead Stadium sat. It was a computer snafu or something that enabled the Chiefs to play a home game during the same weekend when they Royals were home. The Royals and White Sox agreed to play a Sunday night game which was rare in 1976. Otherwise there might have been a chaotic mess had there been a baseball and football game simultaneously on the same parcel of land. I'm guessing that a handful of fans made a day of it, watching the Chiefs and then traveling across the parking lot to see the Royals.

Going to the baseball game was very relaxing for me. I enjoyed the game which the Royals won, 6-5 by scoring the winning run in the ninth but now I was feeling the pregame jitters again.

I stood up and did a couple of squats. I couldn't simply sit. Neither could Bender who did stretching exercises in front of his locker.

Eric Hamer seemed to be in reverie. He was bent over with his forehead resting between the thumb and index finger of his left hand. He was a free-spirited individual who often didn't seem to take things seriously. This close to kickoff he ceased to be the free spirit.

Richards had a portable cassette player with headphones plugged into it. An open cassette case next to him told me he was listening to a Hawaii group known as Country Comfort. He was sitting on the floor with his eyes closed. His mouth was silently moving to suggest that he was either praying, talking to psych himself up or singing along with the music.

Walker stood in the middle of the room. We gave him our full attention. For the eighth week in a row, we started with a tradition that continued through the years.

"All right," said Walker. "If you're an atheist, bear with us. I need a volunteer to lead us in *The Lord's Prayer*."

Bender led us. During the regular season the volunteers before each game and the postgame prayer afterward casually raised a hand. During the exhibition season there were considerably more eager volunteers among those fighting for the elusive roster spots. They were ostensibly trying to impress Walker or God or both.

I admit to rarely volunteering. I wasn't much of a Christian in those days although I didn't realize it.

"I think we're ready," Walker remarked at the prayer's conclusion. "Whaddya say?"

Walker's inquiry produced a plethora of responses that raised the decibel level. All responses, I believe, were in the affirmative.

"All right then!" Walker called. "Last week we broke the hearts of eastern Missouri! Let's do the same for western Missouri!"

We began filing out. Some made pitstops on the way. I dashed out and took a quick look around at the reported 60,984 whose dreams for the day I fervently hoped to crush.

"Look at these idiots," I said lightly, but seriously, to Phil Hoddesson. "They paid good money to see their team lose."

That was simply a statement which helped me to keep my psych level up. Nobody in the crowd heard my remark. Some still had a few words for me.

"You stink, 22!" I heard from somewhere in the lower level. "You're a bum, Dockman!"

It was great. The crowd was a mixture of apathy, boos and disparaging remarks singling out my teammates and me. Favorite targets were punter

Ray Jablonski and defensive end Kyle McWherter who had played in Kansas City the previous season.

"You're a reject, Jablonski!"

"Hey, McWherter's on the other team! The game's in the bag!"

Even linebacker Bob McWilliams wasn't immune. He played in Kansas City five years earlier and wasn't entirely forgotten.

"Hey, McWilliams! Couldn't you hook on with a good team?"

We loved it. After all, it wasn't our home crowd. They could try to link us to the Mansons or Hitler for all we cared. We just wanted the fans in Hawaii to like us.

And to send those taunting fans home disappointed.

I stood on the sideline as the starting defense stood in the end zone waiting to be introduced. I basked in the warmth of the sun. Of course it is noteworthy that it was still officially summer although fall was only two days away. I reminded myself to enjoy it while I could since most of our remaining road games were expected to be under less favorable weather conditions.

"Feeling up for the challenge?" Scott asked as he stood next to me. The Black running back from LSU had his trademark crooked smile that made him look somewhat goofy but also suggested confidence.

"I'm ready to go," I replied. "After we beat the Cardinals I couldn't get to Kansas City soon enough."

Larry and I slapped fives and stood silently while the defense was introduced. The crowd wasn't too hard on our guys although McDaniel was jeered pretty hard. We could only surmise that his status as a former Raider was grounds for animosity in Kansas City.

"And at left cornerback, number 38," the public address announcer called to close out our defensive introductions, "a rookie out of Villanova, Jim Morrissey."

Morrissey ran to join his ten colleagues at midfield.

"He just had to mention that Morrissey's a rookie," I heard Abraham mutter. Nobody doubted that the Chiefs were aware of Morrissey's rookie status. We simply hated to hear it announced since it suggested vulnerability. If Morrissey played up to his capability it would be no problem. The Chiefs were expected to test him.

Morrissey was actually one of two rookies on our starting defense. The other was Gavin Pratt, the right end out of Arkansas. Pratt was expected to begin his career as a backup but wound up in the starting lineup when Jon Jurgens went down. With the way Pratt played we knew he wasn't going to surrender the starting spot easily when Jurgens was healthy again.

We broke what appeared to be a longstanding tradition. After six exhibition games and one regular season game we finally won the toss. For the first time in our brief NFL history we were going to receive the opening kickoff.

I took my post at the goal line. Dietrich was to my right. Giametti was about 15 yards in front of me. Slater was to his right in front of Dietrich.

The kick was made. It was closer to me than Dietrich as it moved end over end in a high arc.

"I got it!" I called.

"To the right, Jay, the right!" Dietrich instructed, reminding me that we were going to have blocking to the right.

I took the ball about two yards deep in the end zone. I slanted to the right, noticing the hole the blocking created. Slater hit a man so hard that he went down and his momentum caused him to turn a back roll and raise back up again.

It wasn't Slater's fault that this is the man who tackled me at the 27. When he rose up he was in perfect position to make a textbook tackle. There was no time for me to react except to try to run over him. He put his shoulder right into my midsection, wrapped his arms around me and brought me down.

As I stood up I noticed Giametti about five yards behind me. He was on one knee and slow getting up. I ran over to him and arrived simultaneously with the trainer.

"What's wrong, Gary?" I asked.

Gary shook his head and made a grunting sound. He'd had the wind knocked out of him. As soon as he recovered he left the field under his own power to a smattering of applause.

The offensive unit left the field shortly thereafter. We got the opening kickoff with high hopes of drawing first blood. Instead we did a three and out. Perhaps it wasn't such a blessing to receive the opening kickoff.

"Geez, you guys. You didn't even break a sweat," was Walker's salutation as we ran off the field.

I grabbed a cup of Gatorade and downed it in a couple of gulps. I sat on the bench, then got back up. I hadn't really exerted myself and didn't need to sit.

"Let's go, defense!" I hollered, amplifying my voice by holding my right hand at the side of my mouth. "Get it back for us!"

Kansas City began its drive on its own 34-yard line. The Chiefs seemed to have prepared well. They cut through our defense like a knife cuts through butter.

It looked like the drive was going to finally stall. The Chiefs had third and five at our 34. It was obviously a pass situation. That meant we were looking for the pass while knowing that they might try to cross us up with a rush.

They did neither. K.T. Smith ended the mystery when he got called for encroachment.

I sat on the bench and noticed Walker. I could literally feel every expletive known to man on the tip of his tongue. He stood with his jaw clenched tight and arms folded. His only outward release was when he spit on the turf.

At least we got a break. The measurement showed that they were still short of a first down. When they tried to bust through McDaniel threw the ball carrier for a one-yard loss.

The Chiefs wisely opted for a field goal. Everybody seemed to agree that a 37-yard field goal was the right call.

Except for many of the fans, of course. There was a lot of booing among those who were certain that one yard against our defense would be a piece of cake.

The kick split the uprights. The Chiefs held a 3-0 lead with 8:14 left in the first quarter. The fans seemed to be okay with that.

"Let's see if the offense can move the ball this time," Walker muttered as I ran on the field with the kick return unit.

We actually did. I returned the kick to the 27 for the second time in as many returns, making me wonder if the 27 had some type of magnetic effect on either me or any of the three guys who brought me down.

Whatever the case, we opened by going to the air. Bender hit Grummon at about the 45. Grummon fought for an additional four yards to the 49. Two plays later Bender fired a strike to Dietrich inside the 30. Ted broke a couple of tackles and headed toward the end zone.

I did my part. One of the defensive backs was in pursuit. I plowed into his midsection at about the 15, knocking him down as Ted ran past. He was finally knocked out of bounds at the four.

"Way to go, man! Way to go!" Marv jubilantly greeted as Ted reentered the field. I stuck out my hand to slap five with Ted as we headed toward the huddle.

Scott went up the middle on the next play. He wound up inches from the goal line.

Kerner finished the job through the left. The burly fullback from Stanford was hit at the line, then bulldozed through to the end zone. We had the lead with 4:52 left in the quarter.

Kerner got up. He handed the ball to Hayer.

"Spike it!" Jeff instructed.

"Uh," Carl replied, puzzled. "Oh, what the heck."

Carl spiked the ball. He played as hard as anybody but wasn't one to call attention to himself. Stanek, who also made a key block on the play, might have bit a chunk out of the ball and swallowed it had Kerner given it to him. Carl was a little more modest.

"All right! Now we're rolling! Now we're rolling!" I exclaimed as I ran off the field.

Walker had a smile on his face. That sure beat the scowl after the previous series. The first series was so ephemeral that it was easy to forget we had even had that series.

"Great drive, men!" Walker said as he slapped some of our backs and shoulders. "Just remember there is still a long way to go."

I sat on the bench next to Abraham as I sipped more Gatorade. The extra point increased our lead to 7-3. For the moment I felt pretty good.

"Now if the defense can hold them," Clint remarked. "We score again and have a 14-3 lead in the second quarter."

Clint made it seem so simple. Just hold them and score. Unfortunately the Chiefs probably had something else in mind.

My guess is that the Chiefs worked overtime watching films of our defensive unit. They found holes that the Cardinals couldn't find a week earlier. They very methodically moved downfield for the second drive in a row. Walker had stopped smiling.

They had a first and ten at our 22. They called a pass which Richards seemed to read. He bolted through the line, forcing the quarterback to scramble.

"Get him! Get him! Get him!" I encouraged, jumping to my feet.

The quarterback saw that he was about to be nailed. He wisely tucked the ball into his midsection as Norm mauled him like a grizzly.

"Yeah!" I exclaimed, pumping my fist in the air.

It amounted to a nine-yard unassisted sack. Had the quarterback eluded Norm; Norm's Pop Warner, high school and college teammate, Russ Allen; had penetrated and would have done the job.

The Chiefs were undaunted. They completed a 14-yard pass to the 17 to give them a third and five.

Another pass was called. McWilliams blitzed. The quarterback was forced to scramble again. This time he got the pass off, finding his receiver in the right rear corner of the end zone as the crowd erupted. With the extra point the Chiefs held a 10-7 lead with two seconds left in the quarter.

"(Expletive deleted)!" I said.

"All right, all right," Walker called in a calm tone. "We'll have to figure out why they're moving the ball so easily on us."

For the moment the offense had to focus on retaking the lead. We began the second quarter with the ball on our own 20 after Dietrich killed the final two seconds of the first quarter by fielding the kick in the end zone and returning it to the 20.

It wound up being a less than auspicious drive. I began it with my first carry of the game, losing two yards. It was very discouraging to see a hole and charge, then suddenly find a red jersey in my face.

Dietrich made an interesting play on third and four. Bender threw a quick pass to him at the 32. That was more than enough to get us a first down but Ted decided to move laterally to try to maneuver around a defense back. He wound up backtracking and going down at the 30.

They measured. We had the first down anyway. Ted knew he'd almost blown it for us. The look of relief on his face was priceless.

Bender hit me on the next play. I caught the ball near midfield, took a few steps and was brought down at the Kansas City 48.

I bounced right up and underhanded the ball to an official. I was clapping my hands as I reached where our huddle was forming.

"Okay, okay. Let's keep moving," I said enthusiastically. I was pumped.

Grummon was the next target. Unfortunately a defensive back cut in front of him at the 36 and intercepted the pass. The defensive back stumbled a little, preventing him from getting any momentum. He was brought down by Kerner and Grummon after only a three-yard return.

Fortunately nothing came of the Chiefs' drive except for a couple of first downs. The highlight was that they punted to the seven, pinning us back. We then didn't do much on our series and also had to punt.

The Chiefs were finding the holes again. They weren't making any substantial gains. They were going three or four yards at a time. That was enough to keep the drive going.

They plowed in from the three with 1:48 to go in the half. Hamer, who had just been sent in, twisted his knee on the play. He was trying to cut the ball carrier off before he reached the end zone and injured himself trying to cut when the ball carrier cut.

This was also bad for the team since Eric was out for the remainder of the game. He was not a starter but all players are crucial. Eric was a good special teams player. He also filled in very well if Morrissey or Black needed a break. He was also the sixth defensive back in our dime defense.

We couldn't worry about that. We simply had to adjust. With us trailing 17-7 Dietrich took the kick five yards deep in the end zone.

"You've got room to run!" I hollered, not sure he even heard me as I ran forward to help with the blocking.

I laid a block but couldn't hit the defender solidly. I tried to force him to my left to give Dietrich room on the right. He fought off the block and brought Ted down on the 22.

We wanted to score before halftime. We would settle for 17-10 with a field goal but 17-14 would be even better. Although we were clearly being outplayed by the Chiefs, we figured we could beat them if we managed to shift the momentum.

Our drive lasted exactly one play. Bender tried to hit me over the middle. Unfortunately the ball was tipped at the line and the ball's course shifted. A safety picked off the diverted pass at the 38 and returned the interception to the 25.

The people in attendance were thoroughly enjoying their Sunday afternoon. Their roar of approval was annoying proof.

It was Bender who made the tackle. He never shied away from contact. As I ran off the field I thought about how sick I was of hearing the crowd roar. This wasn't Aloha Stadium, so cheering wasn't allowed, at least in my mind. The things I was muttering under my breath are things I would rather not repeat. I wanted us to silence the crowd.

Unfortunately I wasn't going to get the silence I wanted right away. On the third play of the short drive, which included Morrissey getting flagged for roughing the passer when he hammered the quarterback a little too late on a blitz, the Chiefs ran it in from the five. The gap had widened to 24-7 with eight seconds left in the half.

"We've got to break this one," I told Dietrich as we ran to our places in front of the end zone. I was angry about the game turning into a rout. I desperately wanted to change that with a score.

"You're right," Ted agreed. "We've got to take it all the way in. If all we do is get to field goal range we'll eat up the clock."

"Right. And if we down it in the end zone Bender'll just take the snap and drop to a knee."

Football is an emotional game. It is a game that brought out the best and worst in me. I hated to lose. I hated that we were looking bad in the process of losing.

They didn't squib it like I was afraid they would. Instead, the kicker sent the standard high end over end kick. It was heading my way.

"I've got it!"

I caught the ball about two yards deep in the end zone. Up ahead I could see Dietrich running to cut down anybody in a red jersey entertaining thoughts of tackling me. Ahead of him were various clashes of white jerseys and red jerseys.

Within seconds I was past the 20. Somebody in a red jersey had broken through and approached me from the right. I straight-armed him and seemed to stave him off. Unfortunately there was the Chief on my left. I was so preoccupied with the defender on my right that I never saw him. He hammered me at the 30.

I got up slowly. I wasn't hurt but I was angry. I very badly hoped to shift the momentum. Of all of the kicks I'd returned in high school, college and the pros I had only one touchdown to my credit and that dated back to my sophomore year in high school. For some reason I believed it was mandatory that I score a touchdown on this particular runback nine years after my only other kick return touchdown.

"Are you all right, 22?" an official asked as he took the ball from me while I sat on the 30-yard line and pondered. "Are you all right?"

"Yeah," I muttered as I rose to my feet. "I sure wanted to put seven points on the board before halftime, though."

The worst thing about it was we would be kicking off to start the second half. I didn't know what the Chiefs captains' individual grade point averages in college had been. I was certain, though, that they were smart enough to know that receiving would be the better option.

108

There were several defensive players huddled around Allen in the locker room. I grabbed a cup of Gatorade as I sat in front of my locker. Although Allen was speaking in a low tone, I could hear him.

"We're giving too much ground. We've got to tighten up and plug those holes. When we make a big play to push them back we've got to keep the pressure up. We can't allow them to make up for it on the next play. We've got to shoot them down, guys."

Of course the offense wasn't having a division championship day. Our passing game wasn't too bad despite the two interceptions. Our rushing attack was going nowhere. I found out later that we had eight carries for ten yards in the first half. That doesn't win games.

Walker came in and stood in the middle of the room. He seemed unsure of what to say. He took a drag off of his cigarette and looked down as he exhaled the smoke, then looked up again.

"We've been together for two-and-a-half months now. In practice and in games I've seen you play some superior football. Today is not one of those days."

Walker's tone was actually not demeaning. He sounded weary. The words stung because they were brutally honest.

"I know you can play better than this. Offense, let's have a rushing game to balance our passing game. With what we did in the first half nobody's going to believe we have running backs on the roster."

"Defense," Walker continued, "you're giving them too much ground. You lock the door on one play and hold it open for them the next. If you push them back once, push them back again. I believe you're better than these guys but you're chasing 17 points. If the defense shuts them down and the offense moves the ball we can put together one great comeback."

Walker continued his spiel. Along the way an official poked his head in, caught Walker's eye and held up two fingers to indicate two minutes to kickoff.

"What do you think, Jay?" Jennings asked me on the sideline as our kicking unit got into position.

"I think if we don't play better in the second half we're going to be playing before 50,000 empty seats next week."

"Yeah? Well I guess we'd better pull it out then."

"Capital idea," I said, cracking a semblance of a smile even though I was not in an especially good mood.

The Chiefs picked up a couple of first downs on the opening series. When their drive stalled they punted to try to pin us back. With footballs shaped the way they are they sometimes take strange bounces.

This was one of those times. I watched as the ball hit inside the five. I expected the ball to go into the end zone for a touchback. Instead it bounced toward me and nearly hit me. The Chiefs downed the ball at the 12.

"(Expletive deleted)," I muttered under my breath.

Actually the Chiefs thought they had the ball. A couple of them tried to argue that the ball had touched me. The ball missed me but only by inches. I was so certain that the ball was going to bounce into the end zone that I calmly stood with my hands on my hips. I suddenly had to dart out of the way as the ball came right at me while I stood on about the ten.

"Man, that was close," I said to Hasegawa while a couple of Chiefs argued in vain. "That was one weird bounce."

"Did it touch you?" Rich asked discreetly.

"Not quite but it was very close. If I was in their shoes I'd be arguing, too."

We showed our resolve from the very start. Scott picked up five yards up the middle and I went off right tackle for four. On only two plays we were only a yard short of our entire rushing output from the first half. We had third and one on our own 21.

"Dietrich!" we heard. It was Kamanu coming in to signal Dietrich to go out. We were going to a two tight end formation.

Bender met Kamanu to see what play Walker had sent in.

"Walker says for you to call it," Kamanu said.

And so he did.

"Dotted I, one Mililani right. On one, on one. Ready?"

"Break!"

Bender had called his own number. He was going to run a quarterback draw.

And he executed it perfectly. He moved back as if he was going to hand off, then turned and shot through the line. He picked up two yards in one of the rare times that he called his own number.

Marv and Kerner pulled Bender up.

"Just remember who was blocking for you, my man," Marv remarked jocularly. "It was Phil and me. If it wasn't for us you'd be in hot water with Walker for trying to run the ball yourself."

I happened to look over at our sideline. Walker was standing with his hands on his hips and shaking his head with a puzzled grin on his face. He was among those who couldn't believe that Bender would actually call his own number. Bender was still effective but past his prime and had problems with his knees. Nobody including the Kansas City defense expected Steve to carry.

We got back down to business. After two more plays we had a third and three at the 30.

A screen was called. Bender did a play-action fake to Kerner who barreled into the line. Scott glided toward the right sideline, as did Clint and Marv.

110

I also figured in the play. I lined up on the left flank, then went into motion. My post was near the sideline alongside Clint and Marv.

"Go!" we heard Scott call. That meant that he had caught the pass just behind the line. That gave the green light to Marv and Clint to charge upfield with me.

I got a decent block on a defensive back a few yards downfield. It wasn't a game breaker but good enough. I kept the defender outside while Larry shot past.

A pair of Chiefs brought Larry down but not until our 48. First and ten again.

"Good block, Jay," Larry commented as we moved toward our huddle. "That was perfect."

The drive continued. I managed to break a couple of tackles when I carried later in the drive and picked up eleven yards to the Kansas City 26. A couple of plays later Slater caught a 19-yard pass that gave us a first and goal at the four.

My spirits were up but guardedly so. It felt good to be only 12 feet from a score but there was still a long way to go. I wondered if the touchdown that I hoped was inevitable would shift the momentum our way or if it would compel the Chiefs to make the necessary adjustment that would shut us down the rest of the way.

Bender fired a quick strike to Grummon. Rich caught the ball at the two and fought his way through the final two yards, finally brought down just barely across the goal line. It was his third touchdown in two games.

"All right, men. That's a start," Walker chided as we ran off the field. "We still need a couple more scores. Let's do it."

With the extra point we had narrowed the gap to 24-14 with 5:03 left in the third quarter.

Both offenses seemed to be through for the third quarter. In fact, very little happened until the fourth quarter was about half over. It was great that our defense was holding the Chiefs at bay but our offense wasn't holding up its end of the deal.

Kansas City punted from our 40 and the ball went into the end zone for a touchback. That gave us the ball at our 20 with 8:12 left to play.

We needed at least two scores. We didn't have to hurry at this juncture but we had to be mindful of the clock. On any play that didn't stop the clock we needed to huddle quickly and get to the line.

On second and seven at the 23 Scott picked up ten yards before running out of bounds at the 33. Bender followed that up with a pass that was tipped. I made a diving lunge for the ball about 15 yards downfield but a Kansas City defensive back got closer. Fortunately he couldn't hang on.

I rose up and heaved a huge sigh of relief. An interception could have broken our backs. I had no doubt that Bender was at least as relieved as I was.

Scott rushed for seven yards to give us a third and three at the 40. He followed that with five yards to the 45. First down and the Kansas City fans were getting nervous.

Bender rolled to his left and fired a pass that Grummon caught at the 36. Rich was hit and brought down immediately. We were 44 yards closer to the end zone than when we started the drive.

Scott's number was called again. He was hit behind the line but broke the tackle. He picked up five yards to the 31.

I was next. Bender hit me with a pass just inside the 15. I tried to run around the defender. He dragged me down at the ten. We had another first down with 4:40 to play.

"All right, this is the way to play," Bender remarked in the huddle. "We've got plenty of time to put this away. We just have to keep going."

The Chiefs seemed to read the next play. They stuffed Kerner for a two-yard loss.

Scott followed by picking up four yards around left end. We had third and goal at the eight.

Next the Chiefs put on a charge as Bender dropped back to pass. He was hit but not before getting the pass off. Slater caught the pass at the two near the left sideline. He dove into the end zone with 3:06 left.

We were pumped. Dietrich and I were the first to converge on Slater as he lay looking content in the end zone. We hurriedly lifted the rookie from Baylor to his feet.

"Good job, Slater," Dietrich said. "That's the way to get it in there."

I looked back. Bender was on his feet, undaunted. He was running over to congratulate Slater.

"Good catch, Joe. Way to go," Bender said in a restrained but sincere tone as he shook Slater's hand and slapped him on the back.

With the extra point we were down by only a field goal. If our defense could get the ball back quickly we would have plenty of time to get in position for a field goal if not a touchdown. I believed the offense could now move at will.

Things seemed to go our way with the ensuing kickoff. The kick bounced out of the end zone. Since nobody had touched the ball, no time ran off the clock. Even one second could prove to be critical in our quest to overtake the Chiefs.

"Now let's stop 'em, defense!" Walker called as the defense ran on the field.

Nobody was sitting on our sideline. Every Hawaiian player and coach, including Hamer who was in street clothes and behind the bench on crutches, was standing. We all held high hopes that, at the very least, the Chiefs would run three plays and then punt. Ideally, they would turn the ball over.

"Hold 'em, defense! Hold 'em!" I barked.

112

"Let's go, defense! Do your job!" Grummon called.

"Russ! Carl! Jim! K.T.! Get the ball for us! Whaddya say?" was Bender's plea.

It all went for naught. The Chiefs picked up three first downs while we exhausted our three timeouts and the two-minute warning. When we could no longer stop the clock their quarterback took a couple of snaps and knelt down.

There wasn't anything we could do. We shook hands with the victors as we headed to our respective locker rooms.

You guys were tough," one of the Chiefs told me.

"But you guys were three points tougher," I replied with a forced smile on my face. "See you in November."

Contrasting the previous week, the locker room was not the least bit festive. Nobody was smiling and there was practically no talking. Some of us lit cigarettes but there were no victory cigars.

Our quest to conquer the western portion of Missouri obviously fell short. A week earlier we were basking in the glory of being the first expansion team in 15 years, and second in NFL history, to win its debut game. In the locker room everybody had been laughing, slapping backs and shaking hands. This time around we spoke in hushed tones with a mediocre 1-1 record.

Walker took his customary spot in the center of the locker room. He asked for a volunteer for the postgame prayer. Hoddesson did the honors.

When the prayer ended Walker thanked Phil and looked around the room. The ambience is almost impossible to describe. We had played hard; played to win. By losing we had shown a more vulnerable side to ourselves.

"Men, I don't want to comment on the game until I've had a chance to look at the films," Walker said. "The truth about how well we played or how poorly we played will come out then. Obviously there are areas in which we need to improve and we'll work on that. The thing I want you to remember is that nobody expected you to go undefeated. We might lose a few games but we can win several more before the season's over. It depends on how hard we work and how much we improve."

Walker paused. One could see traces of torment on his face. Defeats always took their toll on him, I would discover over the years. In games when we played well but still came up short much of his anxiety was out of empathy for us.

"We've got Denver next week," Walker continued. "My impression is that the Broncos are better than the Chiefs. What they're going to see, though, is a much-improved Hawaiians team on our home turf. You can make it happen. All you have to do is put in a good week of practice and keep your head in the game. We can learn from what happened today."

There was a trace of a smile on Walker's face. He gave his head a nod as if to add an exclamation point to his words. He was already trying to build us up for Denver.

"For now," he said, "get whatever first aid you need, get showered and dressed. Relax and unwind on the way home. Take care of your personal business tomorrow and have a good day with your families. Be ready to go to work on Tuesday."

As I gradually shed my uniform I replayed part of the game in my head. I wondered how we could have allowed ourselves to fall behind the way we did in the first half.

Granted, we staged an impressive comeback effort in the second half. It obviously wasn't enough although it may have been enough to bring back whatever fans who were having second thoughts about attending the Denver game the following week. Whether we lost by three points or 50 points, we had tallied one for the loss column.

I assumed that members of the media would write glowing accounts of our comeback effort. I suppose it said something for us when we refused to simply go through the motions in the second half. We went down with a fight. The bottom line was that we shouldn't have allowed ourselves to fall so far behind in the first place.

There were media personnel in the locker room again. They spoke primarily to Walker although some circulated to get quotes from players. I managed to avoid contact.

I suppose the only winners in our corner were the gamblers who bet on us. The Chiefs had been 13 and-a-half point favorites. We beat the spread but that meant nothing to my teammates and me.

Flights after losses always seemed longer than normal. We weren't like the Rams who could lose a game in San Diego and be back in Los Angeles within an hour of taking off. If the Rams were kicking off a game in San Diego, or even San Francisco, at the time we were departing from Kansas City they would play the entire game and be back in Los Angeles before we would arrive in Honolulu.

It still wasn't a bad flight. Walker's words probably helped since he didn't lambaste us. Since we hadn't lost a regular season game up until this point, with Walker we weren't certain of how he would react in the immediate aftermath. Some teammates I had over the years told stories of coaches on the high school, college and even pro levels who went ballistic after a loss. Walker, while proving very capable of going ballistic, responded in a very rational manner. He knew that the reason we lost wasn't because we didn't take the field determined to win.

We were a new team. We were just getting used to playing together. It would take some time. With the exception of Bender and Dietrich who had been teammates since 1969, none of our offensive unit had had enough time to understand his compadres' strengths, weaknesses and tendencies and the same could be said for the majority of our defensive unit. There were guys on both sides of the ball who had been teammates at one time or another but we hadn't had time to gel as an overall unit.

There was a lot of mingling on the plane. It was easier to do on these flights. In college and in the WFL we flew regularly scheduled commercial flights. The NFL Hawaiians struck a deal with an airline that agreed to renovate one of its DC-8s for the Hawaiians to use. It was all first-class seating and the Hawaiians name was printed on the fuselage and the logo was on the tail.

The aircraft was used almost exclusively by players, coaches and a few other team personnel. Also included were some of Honolulu's media personnel including play-by-play announcer Les Keiter. The airline provided the cockpit crew and four flight attendants.

I talked to Hoddesson during the flight. It is somewhat interesting to note that I had a cigarette in one hand and a beer in the other since he was one of two members of the Church of Jesus Christ of Latter-day Saints on the team. Somehow the conversation turned to his religion which I would join nine years later although it was the last thing I believed I would ever do in 1976. I asked him if the average member looked down on those who smoked and drank.

"We're not the ones who make the judgements," Phil replied. "Everybody makes his peace with God in his own time."

"So you don't think those of us who smoke and drink are bad?"

"I can think of a lot worse things you can do," he said somewhat lightly. "There might be members of the Church who will condemn you for it but they're not supposed to."

This was the first time I ever really talked to Phil. He was such a startling contrast to the team's other church member, Joe Billingsley. Phil was a congenial, soft-spoken individual whom I never heard swear or saw get angry. Billingsley was brash and wasn't averse to unleashing streams of expletives although when I met up with him several years later he had become more devout.

Phil was married with two boys and two girls. His wife was from his high school class in Orem, Utah, who waited faithfully for him when he served a mission in, of all places, Hawaii. They were married about six months after Phil returned, not fathoming that the site of his mission call would also be one of his stops in the NFL.

Darcy Hoddesson was a very beautiful statuesque woman with dark hair and dark eyes. She was one who smiled easily and left a very positive impression. She was a friendly unpretentious woman who had been a head cheerleader and homecoming queen in high school. By profession she was a registered nurse although her career was on hold at the time to dedicate herself to being a stay-at-home mom while her devoted husband closed out his NFL career.

CHAPTER SEVEN
Buck The Broncos

As promised, I picked Laurie up on Monday evening. She asked what movie we were going to see.

"I thought we'd check the newspaper together and make a joint decision," I replied pleasantly.

And so we did.

After a painstaking process, that is. That was when Laurie started showing her true colors. She panned virtually every movie that was playing for reasons that made absolutely no sense.

Somehow, we finally agreed to go to Waikiki and see *The Return of a Man Called Horse* starring Richard Harris. I had seen the original and figured that the sequel would also be entertaining.

It was a good movie.

Only Laurie didn't like it.

In fact, she didn't like anything. She was showing a total contrast to the person I had had a pleasant dinner with ten days earlier. She complained about everything she could think of all the way to the theater and while we were in the theater. The only time that she wasn't bitching about everything was while the movie was playing. I guess I should have been grateful for that.

When I mentioned on the way out of the theater that the movie turned out to be much better than she believed, which it was, she did not concur. She gave a seething editorial all the way to my car.

I got Laurie back to her Prospect Street apartment as fast as I could. Ever the alleged gentleman, I walked her up and waited for her to get her door open before I bid her good night and left. I don't know if she expected a good night kiss but she wasn't getting one.

Afterward I went to the Nest for a beer. Don was sitting at the bar so I joined him.

"Were you out with Laurie tonight?" Don asked.

"Yes," I replied wearily, by now slightly amused by the entire experience, "and I will never take her out again."

I gave Don a brief summary of that evening's experience. He listened and shook his head. He wasn't the least bit surprised that I was writing her off.

"I think she's a lesbian," Don said. "She doesn't like any of the guys who take her out. Every time she has a date she spends the next workday complaining about him."

"At least you know what you can look forward to tomorrow," I said dryly.

Walker exercised substantial restraint during the films on Tuesday. He knew we felt bad about losing a game we would have won had we played just a little better. Rather than yell, he spoke in even tones about our mistakes which were numerous. There were times, however, when he couldn't restrain himself when something happened that he didn't like.

On one play during the second half Hoddesson missed his block which was rare. The films suggested that it wasn't so much Hoddesson as it was the man he was trying to block doing a great fake. Hoddesson went after him, the defender shifted abruptly and Hoddesson wound up on his face.

Fortunately the defender misread the play. We didn't go up the middle, so the defender didn't figure in the outcome.

That didn't matter to Walker.

"What were you doing, Hoddesson?" Walker called in a tone that was far from congenial. "Is that the way they taught you to block at Utah State?"

That produced a few stifled giggles. Hoddesson had learned nothing at Utah State because he went to BYU. Walker had the right state but wrong school.

"You are reputed to be a nice guy off the field and I'm glad," Walker continued, himself not being especially nice at the moment. "You don't have to be so damn nice on the field. If that play had gone up the middle the ball carrier would have been creamed."

Walker seemed obsessed with Phil who sat uncomfortably a few feet away from where I sat. Walker kept showing Phil's fall, running the play back and forth, as the defender scooted around him.

"Hoddesson, you've got more time in the NFL than almost everybody on the team," Walker continued. "You're supposed to be above this kind of thing. What do you have to say for yourself?"

The congenial former LDS missionary hesitated.

"Well?" Walker prodded.

"Hey, I got faked out. I'm sorry. It won't happen again."

"Geez," Walker muttered. "The guy's only in his 30s and already he plays like he's senile."

The fact that Hoddesson played almost flawlessly the entire game meant nothing. Walker saw the mistake and that was all that mattered to him. With all of the restraint Walker had exercised, Phil's mistake probably came at a time when Walker could no longer hold it in. Walker's wrath probably covered about a dozen mistakes committed by various members of the team up to that point.

What was good was that Hoddesson was secure enough not to allow something like this to bother him. He may have been a little shaken but didn't show it. He knew he was a good player and that he played a good game.

And he truly was a nice guy off the field. He could also be a nightmare on the field for those playing against him.

118

Phil wasn't the only guy to be lambasted during the films. Walker got on Scott for not seeing a hole open and Giametti for being too slow to block during a kick return. He also got on a few others for various infractions. Phil simply got raked over the coals worse than everybody else.

"Don't sweat it, man," Kerner said to Phil in the locker room.

Phil shook his head and smiled. He seemed undaunted. He admitted, though, that he was surprised to have been singled out so brutally for one simple miscue. Everybody seemed to agree that Phil's overall performance was worthy of an All-Pro.

One new play was being added. This was the Kalaupapa left or right. This was the play Walker had told me during training camp would eventually come. The play was to be run similar to a reverse. I was to line up in the slot, most likely on the right to accommodate my being left-handed, and go in motion. Bender would take the snap and roll to his right, handing the ball to me on a reverse.

Once the ball was handed off it would appear as if I was going to rush around left end. That was designed to draw in the defensive backs, allowing the receivers to get open. I was then to pass to the first open receiver I spotted.

With the defensive backs abandoning the receivers, assuming they would do what we hoped they would do, was the reason the play was called Kalaupapa. Kalaupapa is the location of a somewhat legendary leper colony on the island of Molokai. The coaching staff hoped the defensive back would think the play was an end sweep and abandon the receivers as if the receivers were lepers.

Of course once we'd burned somebody with the play the other teams were going to know we had it. We could still do it successfully on multiple occasions but its best chance for success was the first time we tried it.

Walker worked us extremely hard in preparing us for the Denver game. We were probably too sporadic in our execution in Kansas City. Walker wanted to sharpen us up, especially since he believed the Broncos were better than the Chiefs. We also did more than the usual amount of conditioning during the week. It was suspected that the defense was too tired at the end of the Kansas City game. Had they had more energy Walker believed they would have prevented at least one or two of the Chiefs' final first downs and gotten us another shot on offense.

Hamer watched from the sidelines. He was day-to-day but each day made him more doubtful for Denver. By the time our Friday workout rolled around we knew that the cornerback with black Prince Valiant hair would not see action at least until we took on San Diego.

In one of the Friday newspapers one of the beat writers wrote a reasonably nice article about us. He said in his opinion we were actually fairly good "for an expansion team."

Walker referred to the article during his post-practice pep talk on Saturday.

"I want you to ignore this crap," he insisted. "These sportswriters are generally nice guys but too often they try to pass themselves off as experts. The publicity might help to put people in the stands, and we can use that kind of support, but don't let the article cause you to overrate yourselves. This guy just wants to win a Pulitzer Prize by referring to us as 'pretty good for an expansion team.'"

"Ignore what is written regardless of how good or bad they say we are," Walker continued. "Most of all, ignore this 'expansion franchise' garbage. We've got two games under our belts and have shown at least a little ability to play well. If you spend a lot of time thinking about being an expansion franchise you'll start playing like an expansion franchise. You are a bona fide NFL franchise. The expansion franchise label is nothing more than an excuse for losing. We play to win here."

True to form, I woke up early on Sunday and decided not to go back to sleep. It was 4:30. That meant five and-a-half hours until kickoff. I wanted to play *now*.

I took a quick shower and dressed. Faded blue jeans and a red aloha shirt were the uniform of the day in my civilian attire. I put on white socks but, adhering to a Japanese custom that was prevalent in Hawaii, I wouldn't put my blue boat shoes on until I was ready to leave.

My roommate was up. I could hear the shower in his bathroom. He was scheduled to work at six so he obviously had to miss the game. I gave passes to Don Simmons and his girlfriend and also scraped one up for my Marine Corps friend from Azusa, Jim Martinez.

As the coffee brewed I checked outside to see if the newspaper had arrived. The paper boy was about to drop the paper just as I opened the door. He almost jumped out of his skin.

"Sorry, I didn't mean to startle you," I said as eleven-year-old Jeremy Ching regained his composure.

"Nah, it's okay," he replied, displaying a flustered smile. "You gonna win today?"

"We'd better. Are you going?"

"Nah. No tickets."

"Oh," I said. "I wish I'd known but it's too late to get you tickets. See me before we play Dallas if you want to go. I'll get you and whoever in your family wants to go tickets if I can."

"When do you play Dallas?"

"In two weeks. We go to San Diego next week and then we'll be home against Dallas."

"You gonna beat the Cowboys?" he asked with a somewhat sly grin.

"It would sure be nice."

That exchange killed another minute or two. It was still too long before kickoff.

My breakfast consisted of two apples and however many cups of coffee. I was too wound up to eat anything substantial and my cooking skills left everything to be desired anyway. I passed the time by eating my apples, drinking my coffee, smoking too many cigarettes and forcing myself to focus on the newspaper.

"You're up early," Bill remarked when he emerged to go to work. "I don't remember you getting up this early for our games in college."

"Most of our college games were at night," I reminded him even though I knew he was simply being jocular. "Besides, we always stayed in a hotel the night before a game, even at home."

"We sure did. The good old days."

They were good days. Outside my living room window I looked at a point between the Ala Wai Canal and the Koolau Mountains and could see the light standards at Honolulu Stadium still standing majestically. This was more than a year after the Islanders' final victory that shut the lights out forever and about eleven months after the WFL Hawaiians held their last practice on its turf. The facility where Bill and I were teammates for all three of my seasons for the University of Hawaii was scheduled for demolition the following week.

The college experience, on and off the field, was a crossroads of youthful frivolity and adult responsibility. As a pro I was pretty much on my own as an adult. Some of the things I did with my peers suggested that I still hadn't quite outgrown my childhood.

"Have a good game," Bill said as he left.

"Thanks."

I returned to the newspaper but avoided the sports section. I didn't care to read anybody's analysis of what we were up against and that was what would be on the front page of the sports section. Instead I read about the most recent presidential debate. Incumbent President Gerald Ford was declared the winner of the debate but polls showed that Georgia Governor Jimmy Carter was still favored to win the election.

Ford was under investigation. The Watergate special prosecutor was investigating whether Ford had accepted secret funds from two maritime unions between 1964 and 1971.

Elsewhere in the world, a Soviet mail pilot flew his aircraft to Iran and requested asylum in the United States. A few years later anybody going to Iran to request asylum in the United States would probably have been shot.

I did check the sports section although I disregarded anything having to do with the NFL. The University of Hawaii Rainbow Warriors met Pacific the day before in Stockton, California, and did little to boost the hopes of the team's faithful fans. Hawaii jumped to a 12-0 lead before suffering a 21-12 defeat.

It hadn't been a good day for my Los Angeles Dodgers. They lost to Cincinnati, 4-3. Pinch-hitter Mike Lum, an alumnus of Honolulu's Roosevelt High School, doubled in the eighth inning and scored what proved to be the winning run on Ken Griffey's single.

Not that it mattered. The Reds had already clinched the National League West, holding a ten-game lead over the Dodgers. The New York Yankees had just clinched the American League East. The Kansas City Royals and Philadelphia Phillies were on the verge of clinching the American League West and National League East, respectively.

At 6:30 I decided to roll. Traffic was still light so I was pulling into the stadium parking lot at a little before seven. I parked my car at about the same time that Hayer arrived with his wife and two boys.

"Going to breakfast?" the big tackle from Washington asked.

"Breakfast? What breakfast?"

"The buffet in the hospitality room. Didn't you know about it?"

I admitted that I didn't. I wondered if I may have missed a mandatory team ritual had Carl not filled me in.

As it turned out, it was simply an optional affair for players, coaches, wives, and other guests. A buffet was set up in the same room where we watched game films. The spread consisted of scrambled eggs, bacon, ham, sausage, hash browns, rice, rolls, fruit, juices and coffee.

The buffet was ready three hours before kickoff. Since most of the players would not be eating that close to game time, only the married players with spouses in town were told about it prior to our opening game two weeks earlier. The rest of us found out gradually by accident.

I was impressed when I saw the buffet. I was also modestly miffed that I wasn't told sooner. Knowing about this facility's accommodations meant that I could leave home a little early. That beat watching the clock at home.

"Good morning, Jay. Ready to play?"

Walker was the first to address me as soon as I arrived. This gentleman who a few hours later would be running up and down the sidelines berating players and officials appeared extremely personable at this juncture.

"Ready to go, Coach," I replied congenially.

"Good. Good. Get yourself a bite to eat. Just be careful not to eat too much."

"Right."

I grabbed a small plate and helped myself to a roll and a little bit of pineapple and a cup of coffee. The eggs and other items on the buffet were tempting but I knew better. One hard shot to the gut or simple overexertion would cause me to toss the entire thing. I didn't believe that what looked appetizing on the buffet line would look quite so appetizing when deposited in regurgitated form on the artificial turf. That could also put a serious dent in the stadium's concession revenues after I killed the spectators' appetites.

I sat with the Hayers and looked around the room. Bender was sitting in a corner having a seemingly serious conversation with Dietrich and Tipton. All business was Bender's way. He did have a sense of humor. He just didn't show it often. He rarely showed it on the field although he was also very even tempered.

Dietrich was looser. He was a lot like Bender in the sense that both would give the shirts off their backs to those in need. While Dietrich generally took football seriously, one could also include him on the list of possible suspects if somebody pulled an anonymous practical joke.

Bender's wife was sitting with her two daughters at the table next to where I was sitting. She was a very good-natured woman, more willing to display a sense of humor than her husband was. She was also starting to worry about a slight weight problem although she was far from unattractive. At 35 she was a year younger than her husband and had been with him since her sophomore year in high school. They got married prior to her junior and his senior year at the University of California at Santa Barbara.

Jennings came in with his live-in girlfriend. Jennifer didn't say much and there was some speculation that she was anti-social. She actually turned out to be very gregarious but preferred to get to know people on a gradual basis. She was a lot like Ed in that regard.

By eight o'clock I was doing my customary laps around the perimeter of the field. Once again our opponents arrived while I was running. Quarterback Norris Weese, who had played for the Hawaiians in the WFL two years earlier, smiled and waved as I approached.

"Still doing those laps, I see," he called.

"It's become a superstition. I'm afraid I'll break a leg if I don't."

Norris smiled again and casually waved before disappearing into the tunnel that led to the visitors' locker room. Another player addressed me before I went into the Hawaiians' locker room. This turned out to be a defensive back whom I would see a lot during the game.

"I don't know if I like coming here or not," he said. "The weather's great but these ten o'clock kickoffs really suck."

"Yeah, I know. I wouldn't mind so much except that I go to bed afraid I'm going to oversleep."

It wasn't often at this stage of my career that I engaged in conversation with an opponent before a game. Later as I got to know the opponents better or when I encountered a former teammate I would say hello and address them by name but I avoided anything lengthy. They had their pregame agendas and I had mine.

K.T. Smith led us in *The Lord's Prayer*. The tar-black defensive tackle from the University of Hawaii may have been looking for extra spiritual incentive against his former mates. As was previously mentioned, his only prior NFL experience was in 1973 with the Broncos.

A couple of other teammates had done time with Denver. Bob McWilliams was dealt from Kansas City to Denver after the 1971 season and stayed for three seasons. Hoddesson, who was dealt to Denver from Dallas in 1970, had three of his five Pro Bowl seasons with Denver. If Phil had been a little younger the Broncos would never have allowed us to get him in the expansion draft.

"We're on our own turf, men," Walker reminded us after the prayer. "The game is pretty close to a sellout so you've got a good crowd on your side. The Broncos are ready but we're more ready. I believe we can take them. Let's go."

One thing I missed about high school and college football was the team charging on the field together. In the pros it almost seems as if that kind of thing is beneath us. Most of my teammates took the field at the same time but at a jogger's pace, not a charge. A few hung back for a moment to visit the urinal one last time or to make a last-minute adjustment.

Black actually lit a cigarette as we began filing out. He hotboxed it down, stomping it out in the tunnel that led to the field. He exhaled a few times to ensure that there would be no stream of smoke in view of the fans before trotting out to the field.

The starting offensive unit was introduced after Denver's defense. As I stood with my fellow offensive starters I looked at the Denver players as they stood on the makai side of the south end zone for their introductions. In that corner of the end zone a replica of the Grambling helmet was painted since Grambling was the University of Hawaii's next foe. On the mauka side of the south end zone on the other side of the word "ALOHA" the blue Denver helmet was painted.

A strange thought came to me while I looked at the replica of the Denver helmet as the last few Bronco defenders were being introduced. The fans might have loved it had I suddenly started jumping up and down on the Denver helmet.

Walker, on the other hand, would have demanded my head on a platter. He wasn't one for excessive flamboyance, especially if it was something that was certain to fire up an opponent.

It wasn't necessary for me to jump on the Denver helmet image to fire up the fans. After acting cadaverlike during the Bronco introductions they roared to life. All eleven of us were greeted by raucous cheers.

124

"Okay, men. It's our game to win!" Allen called enthusiastically as the offense ran to the sideline after the introductions. He shook my hand and whacked me on the back as I went by, giving the same treatment to a few of the other offensive starters.

We were hyped, naturally. Football is not a game for the lackadaisical. There was an assortment of encouraging words, helmet slapping and other displays of enthusiasm. Some of us had eager smiles on our faces; smiles of eager anticipation that we hoped would climax with smiles of victory.

"A lot of points today!" I called as I arbitrarily slapped a few of my teammates on the shoulder pads.

"Let's do it, man!" I heard Marv say to Stanek.

"Hit! Hit! Hit!"

"Let's score 40!"

"Hammer these suckers!"

Of course this type of scenario was probably going on across the field. No doubt the Broncos had been reminded at least a dozen times that two weeks earlier we treated the Cardinals to a very long flight back to St. Louis. Our season opening victory made a statement that the Broncos were expected to heed. They would not take us lightly. We were already proven to be a team capable of winning.

After the Aiea High School band played the *National Anthem*, the captains went to midfield. We reverted back to our old habit of losing the toss.

"Well, what the hell," I sighed. Two weeks earlier we lost the toss but won the game. In Kansas City we won the toss but lost the game. If losing the toss means. . . .

Of course there was still that trivial matter of actually outplaying the opponent. That is often known to be a factor in the outcome.

We were short-handed on defense. Besides Hamer being out with a twisted knee, defensive end Gavin Pratt was out with a twisted foot. The rookie from Arkansas actually twisted it the day before when he misnegotiated the steps leading into one of the baseball dugouts when he wanted a drink of water. His foot had swollen up to practically twice its normal size. Kyle McWherter was starting in Pratt's place.

Walker was livid when he learned about Pratt. He hated it when his players got hurt, especially when the injury had nothing to do with football. He was so cautious that he insisted that my contract have a provision prohibiting me from surfing from the beginning of training camp until after our final game since he knew that I loved to surf in my spare time. It almost made me wonder if he was going to put a provision in Pratt's next contract prohibiting him from going up and down stairs over the same period.

We kicked off. The ball was fielded about four yards deep in the end zone and downed. The Bronco offense took the field and immediately picked up enough yardage on each play to sustain a fairly impressive drive.

"Come on, defense! Don't give in to them!" Walker barked. "Let's be heads up out there!"

A fact of life in the NFL is that each offense will score periodically. It isn't like I recall from high school where there would be powerhouses which rarely allowed opponents to score. In the NFL points are going to be scored regardless of how good the defense is.

And our defense was good. With Allen, Jennings, McDaniel, Rodgers, Richards and the others I knew our defense was solid. They would still surrender points. It was up to the offense to score more points than the defense gave up.

"Turn it over, defense!" I called, sitting on the aluminum bench when it was obvious that I would have to be patient before getting my first licks in. There were no extremely large gains being surrendered. Just enough to keep the drive alive.

A three-yard run around left end climaxed the drive. The ball carrier went into the end zone virtually untouched. The Broncos led 7-0 with 9:17 left in the first quarter.

"All right, all right. Let's not panic," Walker implored as the extra point sailed through the uprights. "There's plenty of time for us to outscore them."

If our kick return was any indication, we were going to need all the time we could get. Denver's kicker nearly put the ball into Andromeda. The ball was heading a few yards to the right of Dietrich.

"Take it, Ted!" I called which was utterly redundant. I was on Ted's left and the ball was to his right. It didn't seem likely that he was going to ask, "Shall I take this one, Jay, or do you want to run all the way over here and take it?"

Redundant instruction happens in most sports. Teammates, coaches and fans call on somebody to do the most obvious thing he needs to do just in case his brain cells suddenly died. People call on a ball carrier to "run" even though it is very unlikely that when a running back took a handoff he was going to simply stand there unless he was given more specific instructions. The redundant instruction is simply spontaneity.

Dietrich caught the ball at the goal line of the north end zone. Perhaps I should have given him more specific instructions. He might have thought that I meant for him to pick up only eight yards. An eight-yard gain on a play from scrimmage is good. When it's on a kick return. . . .

Actually it wasn't Ted's fault. It was a combination of one of Denver's men doing an outstanding job of shooting downfield and a few of our guys doing a not very outstanding job of blocking. That was also coupled with the ball being kicked so high, giving the defender a little more time to move.

126

The defender shot around Sterling Burgess, the offensive tackle from San Diego State whom we took from Green Bay in the expansion draft. He did the same with Kupau and Slater. He headed toward Dietrich from Ted's right and dove at him since that was the only way he was going to be able to get a hand on him. He tripped Ted up at the eight.

I had no idea of what was going on until I saw the game films a couple of days later. All I recall was trying to block a defender and hearing the whistles.

"What happened?" I asked nobody in particular as I stood and looked around near the 15, uncertain of how much time had lapsed on the play. "How far'd we get?" I asked before seeing the ball being spotted at the eight. "That's it? Oh geez!"

Perhaps instead of telling Dietrich to take the ball I should have reminded Burgess, Kupau and Slater that blocking was acceptable and even encouraged.

We huddled in the north end zone. We were all a little shocked by the short return. Nobody ever expects to take a kickoff and get pinned back like that.

"All right, all right. We'll get through this," Bender insisted, reading everybody's mind.

Walker wanted him to start with a Kaneohe left. This was an off-tackle play that called on Kerner to carry the ball. If the tailback was to be the ball carrier it would have been a Kailua left and a Waimanalo left would have designated me.

Kerner took the handoff and picked up six yards. Walker had probably been thinking that the Broncos would key on Scott and he probably would have been right. Our opponents had to learn to be prepared to take on more than one running back.

Of course Scott was our premiere running back and he got the call on the next play. He ran around right end, was hit just beyond the line of scrimmage and broke the tackle. By the time they got him down he had picked up seven yards to give us a first down at the 21.

I was nearby when Larry went down. I reached down to help him to his feet.

"Nice job!' I said enthusiastically, whacking him on the derriere before we ran to the huddle together.

"Okay, okay. We're looking good so far," Bender observed before calling the next play. It was a 3 Wahiawa left which picked up only one yard. Scott got a better chunk of real estate on the next play, going seven yards to give us a third and two at our own 29.

Third and two often suggests a running play. Bender saw Denver's defense geared up for the run and called an audible. He hit Grummon near the left sideline at the 41. Grummon fought off defenders until he was brought down at the Hawaii 48. It would be Grummon's only catch of the day, but it was pivotal in this drive.

Seeing Grummon and Scott fighting for the extra yardage on their respective plays must have inspired me. I got the call on the next play, running through the right. I must have been hit three or four times but kept charging. By the time I went down I had picked up six yards, getting us into Denver territory.

I don't know if it was vanity but I was starting to notice the crowd. The 46,283 in attendance seemed terribly disappointed at the time of our anemic kick return. Having picked up 46 yards since then, meaning we were halfway to the end zone from where we started, the crowd was getting more vocal. After six plays we were averaging almost eight yards per play.

Dietrich did his part to electrify the crowd. He made a leaping grab of a pass at about the 22 near the makai sideline. He broke a tackle and was brought down at the 16. The crowd expressed its approval.

Unfortunately our drive stalled. On consecutive plays Bender tried to hit Slater and then Dietrich in the end zone. The defensive backs seemed to be sandbagging, holding back to give the impression that Slater and Dietrich were open before moving into position. In both cases the passes were nearly picked off.

"They're trying to get cute," I heard Bender say to Hoddesson as the huddle was forming. "Maybe a pump fake will knock them off balance."

Giametti ran in, sending Scott out. We were going to our double double. Dietrich and Slater would be split to the right and left respectively. Giametti would be in the slot on the left and I would be in the slot on the right. It was a formation for obvious pass situations.

Bender took the snap and dropped back. He did a pump fake to nobody in particular since he had four of us in the end zone. He tried to hit Giametti.

The pass was batted forward. It fell fast but I made a diving attempt from the side. I was still about 15 feet short. It was fourth and ten.

"What happened, Steve?" Walker asked as Bender approached the sideline.

Bender shook his head. He was obviously disgusted.

"They were just ready for us, I guess, " he said mournfully. "Maybe I should have called an audible on one of the first two plays. I don't know."

At least we got something for our effort. Guinn split the uprights from 33 yards out. We were down 7-3 with 2:41 left in the first quarter.

"All right! We've got points on the board now!" Walker called out optimistically, clapping his hands. "Those three points'll help us! Let's stick it to them, defense!"

The defense did its job fairly well. The Broncos still picked up a couple of first downs. They were going for a third when Jennings stuffed the ball carrier for a yard loss on third and one at our 39. The Broncos opted to punt.

I stood at our ten. I didn't expect to get a return unless the punt was extremely short. I wanted to focus on preventing the Broncos from downing the ball before it went into the end zone.

The punt was to my left and behind me. I tried to watch both the Bronco coverage and the ball. I tried to block one of the Broncos but was so worried about what the ball was doing that I wasn't able to get a solid shot at him. I obviously couldn't allow the ball to hit me since then it would be a live ball.

Fortunately the ball didn't hit me. Unfortunately the Broncos downed the ball at the two. The same Bronco I couldn't lay a solid block on was the one who prevented the ball from going into the end zone for a touchback. That play marked the end of the first quarter. We ran to the south end zone since we were obviously changing direction.

Bender stayed on the sideline to have a few words with Walker. I happened to notice Marv nearby.

"I think we can pick up the 98 yards, don't you?" I said in a somewhat serious tone although discreetly to prevent any nearby Broncos from getting fired up over my display of confidence.

"Yeah, sure," Marv replied. "The ground game's going good and Bender's going to find his passing game. We'll get down there, man."

Scott got the second quarter off to a good start for us. He picked up eleven yards.

After an incompletion I got my first reception of the day. I caught the pass on the 30 or 31 even though I had a defensive back on my tail. He wrapped his arms around my midsection and dragged me down at the 33 near our sideline.

"Great catch, Jay! That's the way to play it!" I heard Walker call as I got up.

Denver helped our cause prior to the next snap. One of their linebackers charged in prematurely. He wasn't able to stop before he ran into Abraham, knocking Clint to the sitting position.

"What the.. . ," Clint muttered angrily before looking at the big picture from where he sat. "Well, okay. We'll take the five yards."

I was actually afraid that Clint or one of the other linemen had moved. They hadn't so Denver got called. We had first and five at our 38.

Scott picked up about five and appeared to have the first down. The officials brought the chain out. We were a few inches short.

The honor of picking up those few inches fell on my shoulders. A Waimanalo right was called.

Bender handed off smoothly. I charged through the line amid the grunts and cracking sounds from those in the trenches. I knew I had the first down and kept moving forward, feeling myself being hit and hearing more cracks as my equipment met their equipment. I threw my shoulder into a defender and broke his tackle. I crossed over midfield and was tackled at the Denver 48.

"All right, Jaybird!" I heard amid the whistles and the cheering crowd. It was Marv as he approached me before he and Clint pulled me up. "That was some runnin', baby!"

"Way to go, Jay!" Clint cried.

"Hell, you guys were the ones who opened the hole," I pointed out. They had done their job superbly. That was honestly why I was able to get as far as I did.

Hoddesson patted me on the back as I headed for the huddle. Scott and I exchanged slap fives.

"Good job," Bender said, maintaining his stoic presence.

The drive continued, much to the delight of our frenzied fans. They were cheering wildly for every gain. On the scoreboard an animated cheerleader appeared, waiving her pom pons over her head and calling on the crowd to follow her lead.

"Go! Go! Go! Go! Go! Go! Go!"

On second and nine at the 30 Bender did a play action fake. He fired a bullet to Slater who clutched the ball at about the 15. He maneuvered around one defender before being brought down at the nine.

I helped Slater up and whacked him on the rear. I could hear a baritone-voiced fan sitting near the front row on the mauka sideline.

"Way to go, Hawaiians!" he cheered amid the cheers from the rest of the crowd.

"Geev 'um, guys! Geev 'um!"

The following two plays netted us only one yard. We were well into the red zone. We had moved 90 yards and my heart was set on not settling for another field goal.

I didn't have to worry about what Walker would decide on fourth down. On third down Bender made the scenario moot when he drilled a pass into Dietrich's numbers in the back of the north end zone. Ted was hit immediately but held the ball.

Touchdown!

The extra point made it a 10-7 game with 9:07 left in the half. For the first time that day we were leading. All we had to do was still be leading 35 minutes and 53 seconds later.

I took my helmet off on the sidelines as I usually did. I grabbed a towel to wipe my face and then chugged a cup of Gatorade. We'd had two sustained drives and I was in every play. I had worked up a fairly good sweat on this typically warm and humid day in Hawaii. Playing on the artificial turf raised the temperature even more.

"How're you feeling, Dockman?" Tipton asked as I chugged a second cup of Gatorade.

"As long as we're winning, I'm happy," was my cheery reply.

"Good, good. Just remember to take a little time to sit while you're on the sideline. We've got a long way to go. We need you to conserve your energy."

I sat on the bench and watched the defense try to hold our opponents. Most of the offense was on the bench. The others were either walking around or talking to other players and coaches about their assignments.

Dietrich was sitting a few feet away from me. He was happy, of course. He had just scored his first touchdown of the year.

We could all smile a little. We couldn't laugh and joke but since we had the lead it was okay to flash a respectable smile.

Unfortunately the defense was having a rough go. The Broncos were driving, threatening to regain the lead and their right to smile. Rodgers even got nailed for pulling the facemask, giving the Broncos 15 free yards as if they weren't racking up enough yardage on their own.

The Broncos got all the way to the 16. The officials took time out for a measurement. It would either be first and ten or fourth and inches.

"Short! Short!" Kamanu barked; primarily wishful thinking since he was on the sideline about 25 yards away and couldn't possibly see the outcome.

Craig was right but not by much. They only missed by a few inches.

"All right, defense! Let's hold 'em!" Marv implored while standing near me with a cup of Gatorade in one hand and his helmet in the other.

They were going for it. No surprise there. That is exactly what I would have wanted to do had it been us. I just hoped that the Broncos' effort would be in vain.

By this time our entire team was standing. Perhaps to show the defense that it had my confidence, I put my helmet on in anticipation of taking the field after the play.

The Broncos went to a long count. I thought they were simply trying to draw our guys offside and would take the delay of game penalty if our guys didn't jump, still keeping them in easy field goal range. They might also have been waiting for the play clock to wind down and then snap the ball after lulling our defense to sleep.

They snapped the ball. They were running a draw play. They might have made it but McDaniel seemed to have seen something that tipped him off. He was off like a shot and dropped the ball carrier for a two-yard loss, producing a thunderous roar from the crowd and his teammates on the sideline. The scoreboard flashed the word "BEAUTIFUL" in letters large enough to cover the entire scoreboard before making way for Jim's name and likeness.

"Yeah, Jim! Way to go, baby!" I hollered as I started for the field. It was on the field where I could usually allow my exuberance to flow freely.

131

"You da man! You da man!" I heard Marv call as he ran nearby.

Jim trotted off the field with a somewhat boyish grin and look of serenity on his face. I slapped fives with him as our paths crossed. Jim was somebody who had earned an appointment to the Naval Academy out of high school. Due to his opposition to the Vietnam War, he dropped out after one year and opted for the University of Maryland. The flawed Tonkin Gulf Resolution had just cost the Broncos a first down.

What both offenses had shown thus far was an ability to move the ball almost at will. There hadn't been a single three and out. Both teams had one drive which produced touchdowns and one drive that eventually stalled with our stalled drive producing a field goal. The Broncos also had one drive that eventually led to a punt.

We were hoping to put together another sustained drive that would climax with another three, if not seven, points while running down the clock. With the ball at our own 18 we were at our best starting point of the day.

After two plays we had third and eight from the 20. I guess we had a flare for the dramatic since we had to convert with long yardage to avoid a punt.

Bender, who was the epitome of ice water veins, hit Slater at about the 37 along the left sideline in front of Denver's bench. The cocksure rookie from Baylor picked up another ten yards before being brought down by two defensive backs.

On the following play I made a reception that will never appear in the record books. It was a 17-yard play to Denver's 36. I was hit and dropped in the middle of the field. I got up feeling pretty good. Dietrich was there to shake my hand and slap me on the back.

"Penalty marker on the play," I heard over the PA system. Normally I try not to arrive at any conclusions. This time I had a negative feeling in my gut.

"Don't tell me it's against us," I moaned as I gradually made my way back to the original line of scrimmage. Denver's reaction told me the play was going to be nullified. I watched as the referee prepared to. . . .

Yup. Five yards. Instead of first and ten at the Denver 36 we had first and 15 at our own 42.

"Illegal motion," the referee announced. "Number 33, offense. Repeat first down."

Scott had gone in motion. Unfortunately he turned forward before the snap.

"Don't sweat it," I said to Larry, knowing he felt bad about his iniquity.

"Yeah, we'll get it back," Kerner added somewhat lightly. "Just remember, this isn't Canada. The rules here are that you can't go forward until the snap."

I don't know if that made Larry feel any better. He did rush for six yards on the next play, giving us second and nine at our own 48.

As it turned out, I got my 17-yard reception back. I made a leaping grab over the middle at the Denver 35. I was hit while still in the air and pinwheeled over but hung on to the ball for a first down.

Bender hit me again on the following play. I had the defender beat as I made a routine catch near the right sideline just inside the ten. The only downside to the play was my momentum with the angle I was running caused me to run out of bounds at the seven. Still, we were only 21 feet from a touchdown.

Make that 36 feet. Just as the ball was to be snapped we got flagged for delay of game. Despite how far downfield we were, as we headed back to the huddle I was sure I could see the veins popping out of Walker's neck. He stood with his arms folded and jaw clenched tight. That pose meant he was in his most livid state.

Kerner got us halfway to the goal with a six-yard rush.

"Jay! Jay!" I heard.

I looked back and saw Giametti running in with a play. I ran off, slapping Gary's hand as I headed off the field. I didn't mind coming out for a play or two since that was not an uncommon practice. What I didn't relish was standing on the sideline with Walker in a bad mood. I hoped that Kerner's six-yard gain had eased Walker's disposition.

Walker gestured for me to stand nearby. He was going to send me back in with a play if we didn't score right away.

Giametti ran a quick slant. Bender hit him on the chest while a linebacker also hit him. Giametti's effort netted us three yards, giving us third and goal at the three. It was Giametti's first reception as a pro.

"Let's run from the dotted I," Walker said to me, obviously hoping that three running backs directly behind the quarterback would loosen the defensive line. "Three Mililani left."

"Got it!" I replied brightly and ran toward our huddle. "Gary! Giametti!"

Had we started the next play on the one or two we would have had six points.

Unfortunately we were on the three. Scott's two-yard gain on the draw play gave us fourth and goal at the one.

A field goal would have been easy. From this distance Guinn could have put the ball through with his eyes closed. The fans didn't seem to want a field goal.

"Go! Go! Go! Go! Go! Go! Go!"

I looked back and noticed that the field goal unit was not taking the field. I agreed with the crowd. I wanted a touchdown.

We ran a Kailua right, meaning Scott was carrying. He leaped up and came down amid a mad stack of Hawaii and Denver players.

Unfortunately he narrowly missed breaking the plane. Our 82-yard drive came up less than six inches short of a touchdown with four seconds to go in the half.

If you ever wonder what a football player looks like when he feels absolutely sick, check him out as he runs off the field after a long drive that winds up inches short. The fans were sitting in a stunned silence, possibly wondering if the current scenario was the result of the Denver defense doing its job or the Hawaii offense not doing its job. I wanted to pick up the Gatorade bucket and slam it to the ground. I wanted to throw my helmet down. I wanted to kick the bench over. I wanted. . . .

All I could do was trot off the field and hope that the futility of the drive would not be a factor in the final outcome. Most of my teammates felt the way I did.

Nobody said a word. We looked at each other on the sideline. Our expressions said it all. They were blank to match the drive.

On the field Denver prepared to run out the clock. Normally in a situation such as this the quarterback will simply take the snap and drop to his knee. Since that would have put the Broncos dangerously close to a safety the call was for a quarterback sneak.

For a second or two I thought the quarterback was going to wind up doing the longest touchdown run in NFL history. His intention might have been to simply move forward a few yards and fall down. Instead he decided to try to break away. He picked up 13 yards before Blakely nailed him.

"What the hell was he thinking?" Arroyo wondered out loud.

"Seven points," Hayer replied laconically.

Fortunately he didn't get his seven points. Instead, we held a 10-7 halftime lead. We were given moderately enthusiastic applause as we exited the field. Although I wasn't thinking this at the time, we were giving the fans a very exciting football game.

"Let's not get down," Bender encouraged us in the locker room. "We've still got the lead. Let's be heads up in the second half. We can beat these guys."

As I sat in front of my locker I weighed Steve's words. I was feeling downtrodden because of a drive that didn't produce the desired result but I preferred to put it behind me and focus on trying to extend our lead. We couldn't allow the drive to set the tone for the second half. It was still our game to win.

"Hang in there, men," Walker called as we prepared to return to the field. "You've got the lead. You can keep it if you keep your focus. Let's be smart out there. Let's go."

I admit that I felt better. The 12-minute break enabled me to clear my head. Instead of dwelling on the 82-yard drive that produced no points, I was ready to play some serious football.

We had the first crack although we didn't do much with it. Dietrich fielded the kickoff three yards deep in the end zone and brought it out to the 24. The drive, which produced one first down on a pass to Dietrich at midfield, got only as far as the Denver 46.

Something like that does have its upside. Getting to the Denver 46 meant that we could pin the Broncos back. Jablonski did exactly that with his first punt of the day. The ball bounced out of bounds at the Denver two.

I sat on the bench. I was joined by Kerner, Bender, Scott and Dietrich. We discussed what was working, what wasn't and what we could do to improve overall.

Coach Bennici was using a small chalkboard to diagram possibilities. The discussion seemed to take several minutes. It seemed like the defense had had enough time to get the ball back. When we finished our discussion Denver's offense was breaking out of a huddle. The Broncos had first down at our 40.

What the hell?" was Dietrich's response to the situation. His concise remark befit us all although it wasn't as big a surprise as it might have seemed. We had kept our eyes on the field as we discussed possibilities with Bennici, so we had some idea that the Broncos were driving.

The Broncos didn't possess the ball much longer. One play to be exact. The quarterback dropped back, threw a perfect strike down the right sideline and watched as his receiver raced for the end zone. Black tackled him but not until he was crossing the line.

It was a 98-yard drive. We had done one earlier and I had been impressed. This one didn't have the same impact on me.

The extra point was no problem. We trailed 14-10 with 7:59 left in the third quarter.

Black was livid with himself. Every expletive ever created, that was what he was calling himself under his breath. As I ran out for the kickoff I could hear him as our paths crossed. I could tell by his crude vernacular that he was inconsolable.

It appeared from where I stood that Black actually had his man pretty well covered. It was simply a perfect pass. Anything less than that and the ball would have dropped incomplete or been intercepted.

That was no consolation to Black. It also didn't detract from the fact that we were chasing four points.

We knew our job. We were to score a touchdown and stay on top. What could have been simpler?

Once again the kick went to Dietrich. He caught it about three yards deep in the end zone again. He hesitated, then charged out and was brought down at the 21.

"Okay, let's bounce up there," I heard one of the officials say. There were actually five of us fairly close together. There was me, the guy I blocked, Ted and the two guys who tackled him. "Everybody okay? Good."

We ate up some real estate to begin the drive. Kerner went up the middle for ten yards. The officials took time out to measure.

The marker came down about halfway on the football. The referee stood erect and sharply signaled toward the north end zone to indicate a first down. The crowd roared its approval.

I carried next and managed only two yards. Scott more than made up for it by picking up 17. We had a first and ten at the 50.

Unfortunately we started to unravel. I ran a cross pattern and looked for Bender. He was trying to scramble away from the white jerseys that infiltrated our backfield. He wound up sacked at the 40.

Bender next hit me at the Denver 46. I straight-armed one defender and spun around another. For my trouble we picked up an additional four yards after the catch. It was third and two.

And then third and seven!

Marv got a little too anxious. The snap was on three. Marv jumped on two.

"Ah, man. I can't believe it," Marv said angrily to nobody in particular with a painful expression on his face.

"It's all right," Hoddesson said, patting Marv on the back on the way to the huddle. "We'll make it up. Just forget it, okay?"

Bender tried to hit Dietrich at about the 25. The pass was batted down. We were forced to punt.

"All right, men. Let's not panic. Let's not panic," Walker instructed as we dejectedly ran off the field while the punting unit ran on. "There's still plenty of time for that winning score. Defense, we need you to shut 'em down this time."

Kerner, Dietrich and I grabbed cups of Gatorade and sat on the bench together. We were all perspiring profusely. Some of the perspiration came from the agony of being behind. We knew we could beat Denver. We simply had to find the way.

How odd it seemed. I happened to notice the scoreboard as the results of other games were being flashed. Tampa Bay and Memphis had lost while Seattle, who enigmatically would switch conferences with us in 1977, was losing. The other three expansion teams were still looking for their first victories and were hoping to have at least a couple by the end of the season. We were hoping to get our second victory in three weeks of NFL existence. We, a lowly expansion team, wanted to be in the playoff hunt.

"We've just got to find a way to pull this out," Kerner muttered while Dietrich and I nodded in agreement. "There's an awful lot of talent on this team. I know we can beat these guys. We just have to do it."

I agreed. I didn't know if we would beat Denver. I did know that we could. I wanted it very badly.

If we came up short it wouldn't be our punter's fault. For the second consecutive time Jablonski was credited with a 44-yard punt that wasn't returned. This time the ball didn't bounce out of bounds but Hasegawa did an outstanding job of getting downfield. He downed the ball on the Denver three.

"All right, Ray!" I hollered, getting up to join my teammates in greeting Jablonski as he left the field. "Great punt, man! Great punt!"

Hasegawa, who was my teammate for the sixth consecutive year, returned to the sideline.

"Way to hustle down there, man!" I greeted with the same enthusiasm I had shown for Jablonski. Had Rich not hustled downfield, Jablonski's punt, while still impressive, would have bounced into the end zone. It was obviously far better to have a 44-yard punt and no return than a 47-yard punt that went into the end zone.

After two rushes and a pass the Broncos were on the 20 anyway. It was first and ten.

"Come on, you guys," I muttered to myself on the bench. "Get us some field position."

It looked like the drive would stall. On a play off right tackle Jennings held the ball carrier to two yards. On the next play Allen threw the ball carrier for a one-yard loss. It was third and nine at the 21.

"Let's go, Norm! Jim! K.T.!" I called as I rose from my seat, arbitrarily calling the names of the defensive players including Hasegawa who assumed his role as a nickel back in an obvious pass situation. "Ben! Mark! Ed! Let's hold 'em!"

This would be a great opportunity. A punt with a halfway decent return would mean starting our drive near midfield.

McWilliams blitzed as the quarterback rolled slightly to his right. McWilliams actually had him in his grasp. The momentum would have brought the quarterback down but Bob had to fight off a block and reroute himself, preventing him from getting a clear shot.

Just as the quarterback was going down, he got the pass off. The receiver caught the ball at the 38 and was hit immediately by Hasegawa and Blakely. We'd played it well but they played it just a little better.

Had this scenario repeated itself years later McWilliams would have been credited with a sack. In 1976 there was no "in the grasp" rule.

When time ran out in the third quarter they were still driving. It would be second and four at our 31 as they attempted to move toward the north end zone. Allen came over to the sideline as we changed direction. He looked frustrated and embarrassed.

"What the hell's going on?" Walker asked impatiently.

Russ shrugged. He obviously didn't know the answer.

"You've got to tighten things up, Russ," Walker continued. "They're already in field goal range. We don't even want to give them that."

Russ nodded. There wasn't much he could do but nod. He ran down to preside over the huddle prior to the beginning of the final period.

Soon the Broncos had a first and ten at the 18.

"Geez, what's with our defense?" Walker wondered out loud. "If these guys were playing for free they'd still be overpaid."

The Broncos rushed for two yards. They followed with a pass in the end zone which Rodgers broke up. It was third and eight at the 16.

That raised our hopes. Either we were taking the momentum back or clsc Rodgers had merely delayed the inevitable. I was hoping the defense would take a stubborn stand similar to what the Denver defense took at the end of the first half.

"Hasegawa, 33 nickel!" Walker barked, indicating we were going into our nickel defense with three down linemen and three linebackers. Smith would come out.

"Come on, defense. Turn it over," I said to nobody in particular while flanked by Bender and Hoddesson.

To the surprise of nobody, Denver called a pass. The quarterback rolled to his right and saw McDaniel penetrating, then reversed direction.

"Get him!" Bender commanded.

"Don't let him get away!" Marv barked from nearby.

"Sack, sack, sack!" I called.

The quarterback wound up in the arms of Richards. He tried to break away but McWherter also got a grip on him. He went down at the 23 for a seven-yard loss.

"Yeah! Way to go, defense!" I called amid the other cheers among my teammates and the crowd.

The Broncos did manage a 40-yard field goal to increase their lead to 17-10. They were probably grateful for the three points. We were grateful that they didn't get more.

To win the game we needed two scores with at least one of them being a touchdown. We also needed for our defense to shut the Broncos down. I figured it would also be beneficial if we started things with a good kick return. If they kicked it to me. . . .

I would settle for decent field position.

The kick was high. For the first time that day it was even in my territory. I caught the ball and prepared to head upfield, then noticed what appeared to be about 50 white jerseys charging in my direction. Since I also discovered I was also about eight yards deep in the end zone I decided it would be prudent to take the touchback. No way would I get even as far as the ten if I tried to run.

Giametti was on the ground at about the 15 after throwing a fairly decent block just before the whistle blew. I ran up to him and helped him up.

"How come you didn't run it out?" he asked.

"Did you see where I was when I caught the ball?"

"No. I was throwing a block. Where were you?"

"About eight yards deep and nowhere to go."

"Oh," he said and ran off the field.

Scott got us off to a good start. He charged up the middle to the 35. I was sure he was going to have a 100-yard game. He was having some sizable gains.

Hayer set us back a little. The sumo-sized tackle jumped before the snap. We had first and 15 at the 30.

It could have gotten much worse. Bender dropped back to pass and Denver had a blitz on. Bender somehow managed to elude his chargers but others were penetrating. Steve scrambled and ran out of bounds on the makai sideline near the Denver bench. He actually managed to gain a yard.

After Scott's six-yard gain Bender hit Dietrich over the middle for close to the eight yards we needed. I was sure we had a first down.

Walker was also sure. Unfortunately he and the officials had differing opinions on where the ball should have been spotted.

"What in the hell are you doing? Why are you spotting it way back there?" I heard Walker ask almost frantically. "He had at least another two or three feet."

The chain came out. We were short by about two inches.

Bender held up his thumb and index finger to show Walker how close we were. I think secretly he wanted the crowd to see it. He wanted the crowd to influence Walker's decision.

"Go! Go! Go! Go! Go! Go! Go!"

Obviously the crowd took the bait. So did Walker. He wanted to get out of the stadium alive.

Scott got the call. He charged to the Hawaii 49. First down!

In all of the excitement I forgot about a special play in our repertoire. Walker sent it in.

"You're on, Jay," Bender said in the huddle before calling the Kalaupapa left. I don't think there was ever a time in my brief professional career when I was more nervous. Not counting our preseason game against the Rams, this was my NFL debut as a passer. If I muffed the pass Walker might not ever call on me again. If I completed the pass we had another weapon in our arsenal.

Bender handed the ball to me as I ran parallel to the line of scrimmage. I spotted Dietrich and fired the ball to him. It was a perfect spiral that he hauled in at the 30.

If I did anything wrong on the play, it was that I didn't wait long enough. The defense fell for the decoy and the defensive backs started playing for the run when I took the handoff. Had I waited another step or two they might not have recovered in time to catch Ted. In this case they did, bringing him down at the 24. It was still a 27-yard gain.

My overzealousness paved the way for my first NFL touchdown. On the very next play Bender hit me inside the ten near the left sideline. It wasn't until I saw the film clip that I realized what a difficult catch I had made. The ball was actually slightly behind me. I had to jump and twist back a little before coming down with the ball. I jockeyed around a defender and ran into the end zone unmolested.

The roar of the crowd washed over me as I spiked the ball. I was a team player, but I have to admit that my first NFL touchdown affected my ego. Like anybody else who ever played football on any level, this was something I dreamed about.

But then we had to attend to the business at hand. Guinn tied the game at 17 with his PAT. There was 8:21 left.

Defensive coordinator Max Crawford was giving the defense a pep talk while the kicking unit prepared to take the field. I grabbed a cup of Gatorade as I always did after returning from the field. Although I couldn't hear what Crawford was saying, he was obviously imploring the defense to shut the Broncos down.

The Broncos were still able to move the ball. Not only did they gradually move closer to scoring position, we were reaching the point where the clock was a factor. We had to shut them down as quickly as possible.

They wound up with a third and two at the Hawaii 27. I guess they got a little cocky because they tried to get the two yards by going up the middle. With Allen at middle linebacker that is often tantamount to a Volkswagen playing chicken with a train. Russ plugged the middle and the Broncos had fourth and two. The play ended with 3:13 left in the game. The clock continued to run.

The Broncos kicked a 44-yard field goal to give them a 20-17 lead. There was 2:37 left.

"We've got plenty of time," Walker pointed out. "Use the time and your time outs wisely. Know where the sidelines are."

I took my place on the goal line of the north end zone. Dietrich, as always, was back with me.

"We can pull this out," he said as he and I did our traditional slap five exchange.

"I'm game," I agreed. "Let's do it."

The kick was clearly going Ted's way. I did the redundant by calling for him to take it and ran ahead to cut down a white jersey. I was just getting in a solid lick when I heard hollering that stopped my heart.

"Fumble!"

"Loose ball!"

Ted was hammered at the 13. The ball popped straight up in the air. Ted desperately tried to retrieve it. A Denver player fell on it first.

A sick feeling washed over me. Not only were we not going to start a drive, Denver was 39 feet from a touchdown. With three time-outs left and the two-minute warning we still had hope if we could either prevent them from scoring or limit them to a field goal. A touchdown meant it was as good as over.

We stopped them, or so it appeared. With fourth down and less than a yard to go for a first down McWilliams jumped offside. That gave them the first down and enabled them to run out the clock. At least they didn't rub our noses in it by going for the touchdown.

On whom do we hang the blame? I wondered as I shook hands with our opponents and left the field.

The fact is, the Broncos won and the Hawaiians lost. We were 1-2 with two losses by three points apiece. In one game we simply failed to come back enough. In the other we did come back, only to let it get away.

After the prayer which was offered by special teams coach Ken Holcomb, Walker addressed the team. There was a long silence.

"Men, we'll find a way," he finally said. "We know you've got talent. We know you can play. We just have to find whatever link is missing."

Walker spoke for a couple more minutes and then let the media in. A couple of reporters went straight to Dietrich.

What vultures, I thought.

For the second consecutive week it was a shellshocked locker room. Blowouts are embarrassing but losses in tight games are often harder to accept.

Unlike the week before when we made the mistake of falling too far behind and being forced to fight our way back, this game was more competitive from start to finish. In the end the outcome was exactly the same with us coming up three points short.

The media would say we were making a good showing for an expansion team. I suppose that was a pretty accurate assessment. We still couldn't afford to be satisfied with that. We had one victory in three tries and that didn't seem good enough to my teammates and me.

Yes, we were an expansion team but I had grown to resent the label. I wanted to believe that we were somewhere above the prototype expansion team. The playoffs were a longshot and I'd probably be committed if I publicly suggested that we might make the Super Bowl. I still wasn't ready to throw in the towel three weeks into the season and I hoped my teammates shared my determination.

A local sportswriter came over just as I was ready to head to the shower. This was somebody I had known since my days at the university. He told me he was impressed with the way the team looked.

"Thanks but it still isn't good enough," I replied, shaking my head mournfully. "It's great to play well but we expect to win."

At least it was another victory for some of our local gamblers. The Broncos were favored by six and-a-half points. If beating the spread was what mattered we would be undefeated.

Personally, I wished everybody who bet on our games would lose their shirts.

For whatever it was worth, Ted Dietrich and I had the first two 100-yard receiving games in the team's NFL history. Ted caught six passes for 108 yards. I caught five for 105. It was hardly consolation although they were examples of the Hawaiians' capability of playing good football.

We were still looking for the first ever 100-yard rushing game. It surprised me that Scott didn't quite make it. The newspaper the next day reported that he had 18 carries for 94 yards. Had Dietrich not fumbled. . . .

No, I didn't want to go there. Ted didn't lose the game for us. He played a good game. The reason we lost was because as a team we didn't do well enough. We win as a team and lose as a team. The 100-yard games were meaningless for Ted and me because we didn't win.

I found out several months later that Carol Lafayette was at this game. She was sitting in the orange seats along the mauka sideline on about the ten-yard line near the south end zone. It was the first time she saw me play in person as a pro.

The orange seats are the seats closest to the field but they extend for several rows. Carol was up near the top row of orange so I probably couldn't have spotted her even if I had tried. I also didn't normally look into the stands during a game.

Who was Carol Lafayette?

During my senior year in college she was my girlfriend. I had last seen her when I left for my first pro training camp in mid-1974.

I met Carol during the final week of the second summer session of 1973. I had been working out in preparation for the start of football drills the following Monday. I climaxed the workout with a run of about seven miles through Manoa valley. This ended with four laps around Cooke Field on the University of Hawaii campus.

After my run I sat in the bottom row of bleachers and watched the cheerleading squad go through its preseason drills on the sideline.

Perhaps I should qualify that by saying I *pretended* to be watching the cheerleading squad. My eyes were riveted to a pretty sophomore with long golden blonde hair. The rest of the squad was totally devoid of presence.

Eventually I struck up a conversation with a congenial man who sat near me. This turned out to be the pretty blonde's father.

Obviously the blonde was Carol Lafayette. We wound up being introduced by her father. A few nights later we went on our first date together. It was the beginning of a very wonderful relationship.

There was nothing atypical about us as a couple. We did things on campus, went to movies, went out for pizza, went to concerts and did other things couples our age did. We had our ups and downs and were generally very content to be in the company of each other. It is also noteworthy that

142

Carol was a very virtuous young woman and I respected that aspect of her the way I respected her in general.

Things happened while I was at my first pro training camp which took place in Riverside, California; things which still had me in the dark in 1976. When I returned to Hawaii after making the team and playing the team's first two games on the mainland, I found the Lafayette's Hawaii Kai home vacant and up for sale.

I knew something was wrong since I hadn't heard from Carol since the early phase of training camp. All I could do when I found the vacant dwelling was sit stunned in my car, not even pulling into the driveway. I found out later that her father, who worked for an airline, was abruptly transferred to the mainland and that triggered a chain reaction which led to Carol leaving the island.

Carol's best friend and neighbor, Stacy Miyamoto, offered to fill me in but I told her not to bother. As much as I felt lonely and betrayed at first, I decided that if Carol wanted me to know where she had run to she could be the one to tell me. I was baffled although surprisingly not especially angry, somehow convincing myself that Carol needed to be away more than I needed her with me, and it was better for her if I left her alone. I didn't believe that I needed to know where Carol was although, in reality, I most definitely did.

Carol's disappearance triggered my tradition of running pregame laps around the field beginning with our first home game in 1974 at the old Honolulu Stadium. The run was simply a pretext which enabled me to watch the bleachers in case Carol happened to turn up. Since I didn't know where she was, I also did this run before road games but to no avail.

By the time my second pro season started I had given up on Carol but the run had become a tradition if not a superstition. At home and on the road, I did this run before every exhibition game, regular season game, playoff game, Super Bowl game and Pro Bowl game I ever played in. Rain, snow, dome or sun, not performing this ritual would have been unthinkable.

Although I wouldn't admit it during the 1976 season and wasn't consciously aware of it, Carol was the veritable love of my life. There was no way that I could find a woman better suited for me. I was living up to my reputation as a ladies man and seeming to enjoy it, even convincing myself sometimes, although I was actually very miserable without Carol. Primarily I was letting go of somebody I believed would never be back.

CHAPTER EIGHT
Charging Into San Diego

What to do in the offseason?

That seemed like a remarkably premature question three weeks into the season. What I would probably do, I reasoned, was take a little time off, begin a grueling workout schedule to prepare for the 1977 season, have some fun, make occasional public appearances, and continue my TV show.

Yet I was driven to do more. I knew when I retired my name would go down in the archive in regard to yards gained, passes caught, touchdowns scored and whatever else was pertinent to my career. I knew that that was the way football fans would remember me. I saw more potential in myself than simply that.

In retrospect, I can't fathom why I was looking so far down the road. It seemed like a mature thing to do and I don't view myself as having been especially mature at 24. I may have been sophisticated in certain areas but not when it came to looking further than a few days down the road. I was at the stage when I thought I would always be a pro football player; that setting money and other securities aside for the future was simply a formality. Although my next birthday was less than a month away, I still didn't even fathom turning 25.

Regardless, I took the time to visit the University of Hawaii. How strange it seemed to stroll across the campus again. Almost a year had passed since my last appearance on campus.

More than two years had passed since I took my last final before graduation. That meant that there were still several undergraduates who were on campus during my undergraduate days. Nonetheless, the faces I saw were unfamiliar to me.

The campus was pretty much the same as before. The only conspicuous difference I noticed was the new Campus Center structure near the Sinclair Library. Hawaii Hall, Dean Hall, Spalding Hall and everything else were very familiar.

I took a moment to sit and ponder after two pretty coeds vacated Dockman Bench.

Dockman Bench, Gracie?

Okay, there was no formal acknowledgement by the university and I did not have the authority to unilaterally name an inanimate object in my own humble honor. I assure you that there is such a structure as Dockman Bench. Knowledge is esoteric but it definitely exists.

Dockman Bench is located across from where the Hamilton Library was eventually built. It is outside a small kiosk between Keller and Bilger halls where one can patronize a series of vending machines. It is actually on the Keller Hall side of the kiosk and is the bench closest to the walkway that runs in front of Keller Hall.

If you should encounter Dockman Bench, please be seated. It is open to the public.

How did it become Dockman Bench?

That dates back to the spring of 1972. It had somehow become a favorite spot of mine to sit and study between classes. A group of friends would also congregate in the vicinity and somewhere along the way I started claiming the bench as my own.

"You act like you own that bench," a teammate named Carl Evans remarked.

"I do," I replied lightly.

"Well then maybe we should call it Dockman Bench."

That's how it started. I didn't create the name although I did what I could to keep the alleged legacy alive. My friends even began referring to it as Dockman Bench, as did Carol Lafayette when she became my girlfriend more than a year later. It was also my understanding that word had spread during this period and students I didn't even know were referring to it as Dockman Bench.

It was a spot I used often through graduation. A small minority of students even used Dockman Bench as a reference point.

The bench brought back some fun memories during this 1976 visit, as did the overall campus.

I was also reminded of one of the reasons I hadn't spent much time on campus since graduation. There were simply too many memories of my old girlfriend. Carol and I were only together for my senior year but virtually every inch of that campus bore some type of memory of her. Being there reminded me of something missing from my life.

And so I focused on putting her out of my mind. As I mentioned, her disappearance ultimately led me to hustling other ladies. I didn't realize at the time, though, that I was simply using the young women I was out with as band aids to cover my wounds.

My most recent date was no help at all. I smirked in disbelief at my memory of the previous Monday evening. Laurie was a pretty woman but a negative personality. Carol was prettier, at least according to my taste, and was infinitely better in the personality department.

Don Simmons and I had a beer at the Nest the night before as I licked my psychological wounds from the Denver game. He told me that Laurie no longer worked at the law firm where he was employed.

"Friday afternoon she simply packed up her things and announced that she wouldn't be back," Don said, chuckling in a tone that seemed to say, "Typical Laurie."

"No notice or anything?" I asked rhetorically.

"Nothing at all. That didn't stop her from going to the company picnic on Saturday. The boss was so ticked off at her for, first of all, quitting without notice and then showing up at the picnic that he tried to humiliate her. When everybody was together, he made this big announcement. He said, 'I guess you know that Laurie Pyne no longer works with us but she is here to grace us with whatever attribute she thinks she has. For the life of me I can't think of any attributes she might have but it's obvious that she is pretty impressed with herself. All I know is she'll be going to Ohio soon and, as far as I'm concerned, Ohio can have her.'"

All of this was done as Laurie stood by. It obviously hadn't been a very kind speech and the boss probably should not have given it, especially when he ultimately ended it with a lewd remark that made everybody laugh while Laurie blushed. Just the same, Laurie can't say that she didn't bring it on herself.

But Laurie was out of my life even though she was still in Hawaii. She would be in Ohio by the time our season would end in Cincinnati and Cleveland. I definitely had no plans to look her up.

For the moment my focus was at the University of Hawaii. The reason I was on campus was to go to the admissions office. I filled out an enrollment form for the spring semester as a graduate student. On top of everything else I had planned to do in the offseason, I would be a student again for the first time in two and-a-half years.

Walker did not give rave reviews of our performance when we watched the game films on Tuesday. It started quietly enough since it began with the opening kickoff where Denver downed the ball in the end zone. The next thing the offense saw was Denver's kickoff after the Broncos' touchdown.

That's the way our film sessions worked. The offensive and defensive units had their own films but all special teams segments were included in both units' films since each special team often included players from both units.

The segment of our kick return clearly showed why Dietrich only managed eight yards. The man who tackled him seemed to have been ignored by Burgess, Kupau and Slater. Walker laid into Burgess and Slater pretty well. Kupau was watching with the defensive unit and would hear about it from Max Crawford. Something told me he would eventually hear about it from Walker as well.

"I don't know what you guys were thinking," Walker chided to Burgess and Slater.

"Slater, your being a rookie is no excuse. And Burgess, you've been to the Pro Bowl. How you got there is beyond me."

During the kickoff I had thrown a fairly good block so I should have been relaxed.

I wasn't although it wasn't a fear of Walker venting his wrath on me. I was feeling bad for Burgess and Slater even though I knew that there was no excuse for either of them or Kupau not picking the man up. Among the three of them one of them should have at least slowed him down.

146

"It's almost like you gave him the key to the city or something," Walker continued. "Statistically it makes Dietrich look like he didn't do his job because he got a return of only eight yards. He winds up looking bad because you guys didn't seem to want to block for him."

Walker was hot and cold the rest of the way. He got on guys who didn't do what they were supposed to do. He also pointed out instances when somebody did something well.

When both units had finished watching their films Walker decided to conduct a joint meeting. This wasn't necessarily unusual. What he wanted to do was try to discuss with us a few things which could have been reasons we were 1-2 instead of 2-1 or even 3-0.

"Some things we're just not doing right and we need to work on rectifying those things," he said. "I want to win and I know you guys want to win. You're a better team than the standings show."

Walker looked down at his clipboard. He had written a series of stats.

"We have a much better rushing game than our opponents. We are averaging almost a yard per carry better than our opponents although they have 36 more carries than us. Through three games that is an average of a dozen per game. They have also thrown a dozen more passes so our opponents obviously have the ball more."

Walker stressed that the number of plays or time of possession were often misleading. Our opponents had combined for only 35 more rushing yards than us and we had outpassed them in terms of completion percentage and total yards.

"The key is, in the previous two games the Chiefs and Broncos did just enough to be one field goal better at the final gun. It's not a problem with the defense and it's not a problem with the offense, nor is it a problem with the special teams or the coaching staff. It's a team problem and we all have to get better."

Walker segued to our turnover ratio. We'd had two interceptions over our first three games. We had only fumbled twice but lost both of them.

"That's not bad," Walker said. "We're averaging one and-a-third turnovers per game. That's not bad at all. We know that occasionally they're going to pick off a pass or we'll lose a fumble. The trick is for the defense to suck it up to keep our opponents from capitalizing on those turnovers and the offense to shake it off, put it behind them and go from there."

Walker pointed out that turnovers often result from good defense. It isn't always a matter of poor offensive execution.

"But our ratio still favors our opponents," Walker continued. "We have intercepted one pass. We have caused four fumbles but recovered only one. Our opponents have committed only two turnovers and both of those were St. Louis. There has been nothing since then."

Walker covered a variety of areas. Among other things, in each game that we played we had more penalties than our opponents. This included the Kansas City game when we had only three penalties. The Chiefs were only penalized twice. It appeared to have been one of those games where the officials were content to simply allow us to play the game.

"The bottom line is, you're a much better team than your record shows . . . or at least you should be," Walker insisted. "Of the two games you lost you should have been able to pull out at least one of them. There had to have been a way to put more points on the board."

During a weightlifting session following Tuesday's light workout I thought about what Walker had said. I agreed with him that we were a better team than our 1-2 record suggested. There was something about this team that made it seem not at all like an expansion team.

Not that I was an expert on expansion teams. The closest I had ever come to playing on an expansion team was when I played for a brand-new high school. Just the same, I honestly believed that we were not in the same mold as other expansion teams. I can't validate what I believed went on in other expansion team programs but I believed that the players believed they weren't expected to win too many games. Although we weren't talking about the Super Bowl, everybody on the Hawaiians seemed to believe that winning was a very real possibility with us.

Walker gets a lot of the credit. There was something about the way he handled us. Without shoving winning down our throats, he somehow instilled that winning attitude into us. That means the winning didn't surprise us and losing was not something we merely accepted as an expansion team.

There would be some personnel changes in San Diego. Offensive tackle Vince Daniels and guard Jim Kohl were activated from the taxi squad. Daniels was from Cal Poly-San Luis Obispo and was taken in the expansion draft after two years in Cleveland. Kohl was from St. Louis although he played his college football at Georgia. He was also taken in the expansion draft after two years in Baltimore.

Tackle Horace McMichael and guard Greg Henry were placed on waivers. Both would ultimately clear waivers but stay with us on the taxi squad. McMichael was a rookie drafted in the 13th round out of Florida. Henry was from Tarzana, California, and had played college football at Cal State-Northridge.

What was especially sad about this was that Henry had been talking about the trip to San Diego since the opening day roster was set. He had played in San Diego in 1973 and 1975 and had looked forward to playing against his former team. Members of his family were planning to drive down from the Los Angeles area.

Hamer and Pratt would be back in action. Unfortunately we would be without the services of Dietrich. It turned out that on the play where Ted fumbled the kick return he was hit so hard that one of his ribs cracked. He

148

would miss the San Diego game and possibly the game the following week at home against Dallas.

This was a semblance of a break for Giametti. Slater would start at wide receiver. Giametti would be Slater's backup as well as mine.

Injuries are always an unfortunate part of the game. We went through our normal routine with the personnel we would be using in San Diego. All of our practices during this week would be at our training camp site since we would be playing our first regular season game on grass.

On Wednesday night I called my parents. I invited them to the game in San Diego. They actually surprised me by accepting. I suppose they were starting to come around.

This, of course, would be the first time they would ever see me play in the NFL. They had seen me play in the WFL when we played the Southern California Sun at Anaheim Stadium but that wasn't an especially long trip from Montebello. The commute to San Diego was more than 100 miles.

Unfortunately I would not have an opportunity to spend much time with my parents. They would drive down to San Diego the morning of the game and go directly to the stadium. We would only manage to visit for a few minutes after the game before I would board the bus that would transport my teammates and me to the airport.

My parents might not have been willing to make the trip were it not for my 14-year-old brother Craig. He was the one who really wanted to see me play. This was to be the only opportunity of the season since we didn't have any games scheduled in Los Angeles.

Craig was theoretically following in my footsteps. He was a freshman at South Valley High School. He was a quarterback and defensive back, just as I had been ten years earlier, although he was on the "C" team while I began my high school career on the "B" squad. Craig was expected to play the same positions on the "B" squad the following year.

For whatever the reason, I had always been Craig's hero. Obviously there was much about me that he didn't know.

Or maybe he was simply willing to accept me for what I was.

It must have been 10:30 pm, Pacific Daylight Time, when we touched down in San Diego Friday night. About an hour later I entered my hotel room. That gave me a whopping half-hour until curfew.

I didn't give that much thought. I went to the lobby and purchased a couple of Coors beers; a luxury for people who lived in Hawaii since Coors still wasn't available in Hawaii. I sipped the beers while watching TV and reading *Shogun*.

We had our light workout at San Diego Stadium, as it was known in 1976. Not only was this the home of the Chargers, it was home to the San Diego State football team and the San Diego Padres.

I had been to this facility once before. In September, 1969, I drove down with a high school football teammate and our dates to see the Dodgers play the Padres. The Dodgers began the four-game series very much alive in the first year of divisional formats while the Padres were in their first year of existence.

Not only did the Padres win the day I was there, they won the other three games of the series. The Padres were not quite in the same category of futility as the 1962 New York Met but they still weren't very good in 1969. It almost seemed as if they had held back all season in anticipation of this four-game series.

Although the Dodgers were still technically alive, this series was pivotal. It was the series Dodger fans pointed to when the Atlanta Braves eventually won the National League West while the Dodgers wound up settling for fourth place. Years later my mouth still gaped open when I thought of how a group of alleged doormats virtually knocked the Dodgers out of contention.

I looked at a section of seats behind the end zone and recalled my visit seven years earlier. We had purchased general admission tickets . . . and sat in the field boxes adjacent to third base.

"Do you need help finding your seat?" a pretty usherette asked on the concourse leading to the field level.

"Oh, no thanks," I replied confidently. "We know where they are."

Obviously at 17 I wasn't the epitome of integrity. I suppose the Padres were just happy to have four fewer empty seats. Back in those days the Padre attendance figures suggested that the people of San Diego didn't even know they had a baseball team. Since all of the Dodger games in San Diego were televised in Los Angeles that year I knew ahead of time that we could sit almost anywhere in the stadium without somebody claiming the seats we were sitting in as their own since a lot of emphasis was placed on the number of empty seats during the telecasts.

Getting back to football, our workout was excellent. Although it was a light workout there is often something about the way a team goes through its paces that tells whether it is ready or not. Having lost two in a row since our debut victory, the general attitude seemed to be that we would not be denied a third consecutive time. We were going to take our anxieties out on the Chargers.

San Diego Stadium was ideal for football. In 1976 it was a five-tiered, horseshoe shaped facility. Only the area near the scoreboard was devoid of seats.

150

On the other hand, a sellout crowd for baseball meant that some fans were going to be stuck in some pretty crummy seats. The top deck above center field was hardly choice.

But we were obviously there for football. Those same seats weren't so bad for football even if they were probably nobody's first choice.

"A lot of people are going to be screaming for the Chargers here tomorrow," Walker reminded us after we had gathered around him at the end of the workout. "I say we concentrate on not giving them what they want. Let's get back on track."

After Walker dismissed us we straggled toward the locker room. I was with Kerner and Grummon. Walker was just ahead of us.

"Hey, Coach," Grummon called, causing Walker to stop and turn. "Do you notice how quiet this place is right now?"

"Yeah? So?"

"That's how quiet it's going to be tomorrow during the game," Rich said brashly. "Everybody'll be thinking about the money they wasted coming here expecting the Chargers to beat us."

Walker grinned. He pointed his index finger at Rich.

"I'm going to hold you to that," Walker cracked.

Late that afternoon I was on board a destroyer at the shipyard. My uncle was stationed on that ship. Officially he was a master chief radioman. He was actually his ship's chief master-at-arms.

Warren and my Aunt Marilyn picked me up at the hotel so that I could have dinner at their place. Warren asked me if I wanted to visit his ship first.

"Sure," I replied, masking my ambivalence to avoid hurting any feelings.

Destroyers aren't especially large ships although they have crews of a couple hundred. My uncle showed me the mess deck, pilot house, signal bridge and gun turrets, among other amenities.

Being a Saturday, most of those on board were in a duty status. Some of the looks I got told me it was well-known that Chief Dockman's nephew was a pro football player. Overall I wasn't especially well-known outside of Hawaii at the time but I sure wasn't anonymous on this San Diego-based destroyer.

Actually my first inkling of how conspicuous I was came when I first boarded the ship. My uncle immediately introduced me to the officer of the deck.

"Lieutenant Cashman. I'd like for you to meet my nephew, Jay Dockman."

"Of course. The football player," the lieutenant responded brightly as he shook my hand.

Had the exchange taken place four or five years earlier the lieutenant might have referred to me as "the draft dodger." My dad called me that a few times in a not very endearing manner.

I was introduced to a handful of my uncle's shipmates. I was, I believe, being exploited to a small degree although I tolerated it. I greeted everybody congenially and answered a few questions about Hawaii, the NFL and the next day's game.

The watch on the quarterdeck had just changed as we prepared to depart. The messenger of the watch did a double-take as we approached. His eyes widened in recognition.

"Hey, you're Jay Dockman," he observed.

It was hard for me to respond. I was in full agreement.

"That's what they tell me," I replied jocularly. "Do I know you?" I asked as I extended my hand to the youthful looking sailor.

Art Camacho was from Hawaii. He graduated in May from Honolulu's McKinley High and spent most of the summer in basic training in San Diego. He finished basic training a few days too late to catch our season opener. His leave did enable him to be in attendance for the Denver game.

"Sorry we weren't able to put together a victory for you," I told him.

"It's okay. It was a good game. I also used to go to your games a lot when you guys were in the WFL. I even remember you playing for the Rainbows."

The sailor's leave ended and he reported for duty on the destroyer only two days earlier. He hadn't been on board long enough for it to register that the chief master-at-arms had the same last name as me.

"Are you going to the game tomorrow?" I asked.

"I don't have any tickets. Besides, I don't even know how to get to the stadium here."

There was a bus service to the stadium. The big problem was the ticket situation. The game was sold out.

"When I get back to the hotel tonight I'll see if there's a spare ticket lying around," I promised. "I can't promise anything but I'll see what I can do. I'll call and let you know if I find one, okay?"

Normally I wouldn't have worried about somebody I didn't even know getting a ticket. In this case it was somebody from Hawaii several hundred miles from home who remembered seeing me play as far back as my college days. I felt an ephemeral kinship with him.

This was my uncle's third tenure in San Diego. This was where his career began in 1950 and where he planned to remain until his retirement in 1980. He had served at various commands in the area including time as a recruit company commander and an instructor at the Naval Training Center. He was stationed in Norfolk, Virginia, between 1954 and 1958, during which time he met and married my aunt.

My uncle did spend time in Hawaii. It was a common port of call for the ships he was on. He was also assigned to a ship homeported at Pearl Harbor from 1966 to 1969 and followed that up with a year of shore duty at the Barber's Point Naval Air Station.

152

I have to admit that it was a little awkward spending the evening with my aunt and uncle at their home in the Mission Beach section of San Diego. They were obviously family but I barely knew them. I had last seen them at a family gathering more than three years earlier. With my uncle stationed at various points around the world, that was one of only about half-a-dozen times I had seen them.

Their two daughters were there. Karen was a senior in high school and very popular. She was so much younger than me that I had barely noticed her during our few previous encounters. During our most recent meeting she was getting ready to start high school while I was about to begin my senior year at the University of Hawaii. She had long blonde hair and tantalizing blue eyes. Her boyfriend had been a defensive back in high school but was now a freshman at San Diego State and no longer engaged in sports.

"So what are you doing here on a Saturday night?" I asked Karen as I enjoyed the roast chicken my aunt had prepared.

Karen shrugged with a tight grin. She later confided that she had grudgingly acquiesced to her parents' request that she stay home and spend some time with her visiting cousin.

Laura was a freshman in high school. She was also a blonde although her long hair was a darker shade than Karen's. Like her sister, she was friendly but unsure of what to make of her enigmatic cousin. Often during dinner she seemed to be trying to size me up.

Karen drove me to the hotel so we had a chance to get to know each other. She confided in me about how hard it had been for her to be a military dependent. Her first ever day at school was at Subic Bay in the Philippines. Her family then moved to Hawaii where she went to school for almost four full years.

"I was almost eleven when my dad got transferred to San Francisco," she said. "By that time I was old enough to be happy where I was and hated having to move. It was even worse last year when he got transferred down here."

"You don't like San Diego?" I asked.

"Sure, it's okay. It's just that I get adjusted and like where I am and we move. I have to make friends all over again. If he gets transferred again, he can go without me."

An explosion in Korea prevented me from having such a nomadic lifestyle. Of course I was never glad that my dad had been wounded so severely that he was forced into a medical retirement from the Army. Had he got to be the 30-year man he intended to be I would have been forced to live all over the map like my cousins.

Instead we wound up in Azusa when my dad was retired from the Army. The reason we wound up there is that was where my mother and I were when my dad got wounded.

My mother was pregnant when my dad shipped out to Korea. Rather than stay in the vicinity of Fort Ord while my dad was overseas or go all the way to Florida to be with her own family, my mom moved down to Azusa where one of my dad's sisters was living. That way there was a relative available for when it was time to take my mom to the hospital. I arrived at about four o'clock the morning of October 23 in nearby Glendora.

With my dad medically retired he had no choice but to settle down as a civilian. Azusa seemed ideal since my mom had already settled there even though it was originally intended to be a temporary change of venue. It was also reasonably close to Long Beach where my paternal grandparents lived.

I was up at a little before six on Sunday morning. I stayed in bed as long as I did because I forced myself to. I recalled waking up during the three o'clock hour and being tempted to go out. I was ready for kickoff.

After I showered and dressed I went outside. It was a cool morning in San Diego but not uncomfortable. Something in the air even reminded me of October mornings in Montebello more than 100 miles to the north. Although six years had passed since my last experience of an October morning in southern California, I still recalled the ambience.

How my life had changed in those six years. It was at about this time six years earlier that I began thinking about the possibility of transferring from USC to the University of Hawaii. Since that time I made the move, played three solid years of football for the University of Hawaii, graduated and was in my third year of pro football in Hawaii. Somewhere along the way I proclaimed Hawaii to be my home.

I went back inside and into the hotel coffee shop. Two teammates who had also been college teammates were present. I joined Rich Hasegawa and Jimmy Souza.

Although he wasn't saying anything at the time, Souza didn't feel his position on the team was secure. The Waipahu native who had been a year behind me in college, might only have made the team in the first place because Hank Prendergast broke his ankle at the end of the exhibition season. Prendergast was expected to be activated in another week or two. Unless there was another injury that put somebody else on the shelf, somebody was going to be waived. Souza and Ken Gilbert seemed to be the most likely candidates.

When I am running my pregame laps I am thinking about the game I am about to play. Often, though, I allow my mind to take a few minutes to focus on the stadium in which I am playing.

This was the last day of baseball's regular season. At San Diego Stadium the baseball infield was still in place even though the Padres had played their last home game and were closing out their season that day in Los Angeles. Since the Hawaii Islanders in 1976 were still the Padres' top farm

154

club, there were guys I had watched play in Honolulu who had played on this turf. Some had very brief tenures in the majors while others stuck around longer. At the time names of former Islanders like Bill Almon, Dave Freisleben, Dan Spillner, Mike Champion and Dave Tomlin came to mind.

None of the aforementioned would go to the Hall of Fame. Almon, Spillner and Tomlin would wind up with respectable journeyman careers that would carry into the 1980s. Champion's career wouldn't be quite as illustrious but he would have his moments.

A heavy weight was placed on Freisleben's shoulders a couple of years earlier. The stocky right-hander was considered to be a primary key in the Padres' transition to a higher level.

I recalled 1973 and the numerous Islander games I attended at Honolulu Stadium. I was always most enthused if I was able to attend games where Freisleben pitched. It was almost as if victory was assured whenever he was on the mound.

Prior to the 1974 season I was reading a baseball publication that gave summaries of each team's prospects for the year. The analysis for 1974 began with "Dave Freisleben had better be good." Although the Padres had other talented players such as John Grubb and Dave Winfield and had just acquired Willie McCovey in a trade with the Giants, everything seemed to rest on Freisleben's shoulders.

Much to the surprise of many of us in Hawaii, Freisleben started 1974 in Hawaii. By the end of April he was called up to the Padres. He had a reasonably respectable season and on this particular day he would wind up 10-13 with an ERA of 3.51.

Unfortunately he would never live up to the earlier hype and would pitch his final game in 1979, winding up with a 34-60 record and a 4.30 earned run average. There could have been myriad reasons for why he didn't wind up with a better career. I would speculate that the pressure from the hype early in his career played a role.

Kyle McWherter led the team in *The Lord's Prayer*. Walker stood in the middle of the room and addressed the team afterward.

"Men, you've had as good a week of practice as you've had since July. You've worked hard and it shows. The other coaches and I noticed how substantially improved you are. Now let's take that to the field. Practice is one thing but today we play for keeps. Let's pick up that second victory, okay? Let's go."

We filed out with the stating offense hanging near the end zone to be introduced. Slater would be the first player introduced since he was filling in for Dietrich. With Stanek also sidelined Kohl would be starting at left guard. That was quite a coup for Kohl. The cocksure black man spent the previous three games on the sideline in street clothes and game jersey as a member of the taxi squad. Suddenly he was not only on the active roster but in the starting lineup.

As I waited for the introductions I caught a glimpse of my parents sitting in the bleachers behind the Hawaiians bench along with my aunt, uncle and cousins. With them was my brother Craig. Even from where I stood in the end zone I could tell that Craig was radiant.

My parents, I suppose, were guardedly enthusiastic about my career at this point. I suppose it helped that I didn't drop out of school the day the draft ended so they realized I wasn't going to school to sabotage the country. It would not have made sense to go to college just to avoid the draft anyway since my lottery number was 339. I would not have been drafted whether I went to school or not.

Bender, Marv, Rodgers and Allen went to midfield. As had been the case in Kansas City, we won the toss. A pattern seemed to have formed since in all four of our regular season games the visiting team won the toss.

Special teams coach Ken Holcomb gave us a briefing. Everybody on the kick return team gathered around him.

"Okay, nothing fancy," he instructed, looking each of us in the eye. "Let's just head straight up the middle but don't blow your assignments. Remember you're being filmed. If you let somebody get through like what happened last week, Walker will have a seizure. Okay, let's do it."

As bizarre as it might seem, that was actually inspirational. The mere mention of an adverse reaction from Walker was motivation enough. He didn't always lambaste us for our mistakes when we viewed the films but he usually made some kind of an issue out of them. The best thing to do was to simply not screw up since there wasn't a single mistake that wouldn't be caught on camera.

We took our places on the field. I stood on the third base side of the baseball infield which was where the goal line was. With Dietrich out, Ozzie Roberts was my running mate.

"Ready to go?" I asked Ozzie as we continued the ritual Dietrich and I began by slapping fives.

"Ready to go," Ozzie replied confidently.

San Diego's kicker got off a good kick. I moved a step to my right and about a yard in the end zone.

"I got it!" I called, then caught the ball and headed up the field.

Giametti got me off to a good start. He popped a guy so well that I could hear the crack of equipment colliding. Gary stumbled and fell but not until knocking the Charger down.

Kamanu and Slater also put together outstanding blocks. They were practically side by side when they knocked enemy players out of the picture. It was as if they were Moses parting the Red Sea. They had redeemed themselves for their shabby job on our first kick return against Denver.

156

Finally I was tackled around the ankles. I tried to shoot past a Charger who had been knocked to his knees but to no avail. He lunged out and tripped me up, causing me to go down on our 38. It was still decent field position.

"All right, Jay! Way to go!" I heard somebody call although I don't know who delivered the approbation or even if it came from somebody on the field or on the sideline. All the while I received pats from teammates running on and off the field.

In the Denver game Scott missed out on a 100-yard game. He began this game as if he was determined to not be denied again. He shot through a hole opened by Abraham and Marv and picked up ten yards.

"Yeah, first down!" I called as soon as the whistles blew the play dead, looking at where the ball was spotted and the yard marker.

"Gotta be!" Kerner agreed enthusiastically.

The officials were a little less biased. They insisted on measuring. The chain was stretched out and the marker came down at about half the length of the football. The referee pointed in the direction of what had been right-center field but was now the end zone we were heading toward, meaning a first down.

"All right!"

"Yeah!"

"First down!"

These were some of the enthusiastic cries from the Hawaiians on the field. We were truly pumped up in a game that was less than a minute old.

"Okay, kids, let's settle down," Bender implored as we formed up in the huddle. "We've still got a long game to play."

Bender called Scott's number again. This time he was going up the gut.

It was almost as if Larry was insulted when the officials insisted on measuring for the first down after the previous play. He shot up the middle as if he had been catapulted. He was so quick that the only guys in the trenches who got their hands on him managed nothing more than the feel of his jersey. Larry picked up 21 yards before a pair of defenders finally brought him down at the San Diego 31. With all of about a minute expired Larry had two carries for 31 yards.

"Right on, man!" I cheered enthusiastically as Grummon and I helped Larry to his feet. At the same time the referee stood erect and signaled a first down.

"What, they're not going to measure this one?" Larry cracked in mock sarcasm as we headed to the huddle.

We picked up our third first down in as many plays when Bender hit Grummon near the left sideline at the 15. Rich was hit immediately but twisted his way forward for another yard.

Unfortunately the drive stalled. A pass to Scott inside the ten was batted away. Scott rushed for four yards to the ten and then Bender threw a pass out of the end zone when he couldn't find an open receiver. It was fourth and six.

Nobody was shocked when Guinn ran on the field with the rest of the field goal unit. We needed to put points on the board even if it was less than what we wanted.

We were kicking ourselves on the sideline for not getting a touchdown.

"Don't get down, men," Tipton implored when he couldn't help but notice us muttering to ourselves. "There's still plenty of time to rack up the points. It was a good drive."

On the bright side, Guinn converted on his 27-yard field goal attempt. With us having drawn first blood I grabbed a cup of Gatorade and sat on the bench.

The Chargers got a fairly decent kick return. The ball was fielded about four yards deep in the end zone and the return man never hesitated. We had a chance to get him inside the 20 but a combination of timely blocking and elusive running dashed that hope. Kevin Zanakis brought him down at the 22.

Initially it appeared that the Chargers were going to have their way with our defense. They picked up a couple of first downs. They had a first and ten at their own 47.

"That's far enough!" Walker called. "Let's tighten it up out there!"

The Chargers only managed one yard on the next play. They got called for illegal procedure before they could get the following play off, giving them second and 14 at the San Diego 43.

A pass was called. Their quarterback saw that his receivers were covered and threw the ball to where it dropped about ten yards from the nearest receiver.

This was Allen's time to shine. The odds were that the Chargers would attempt to pass.

I stood up to try to encourage our defense with body language.

"Okay, let's go hukilau!" I heard Allen call, getting a chain reaction.

"Yeah, hukilau!"

"Hukilau! Hukilau!"

"Hukilau coming right up!"

Hukilau was the word we used for blitz. If our guys used the word it didn't necessarily mean that a blitz was coming. The vocalization was meant to give our opposition something to think about.

Allen blitzed. The quarterback tried to scramble but Russ was relentless. He got his arms around the quarterback and dropped him at the 31. It was a 12-yard loss, giving them fourth and 26.

"All right! Punt return team!" Walker called with a huge smile on his face.

With a huge smile also on my face I anxiously ran on the field with the rest of the punt return team. Pushing them so far back after they nearly

158

reached midfield had to have had a demoralizing effect on the Chargers, I believed. I figured a touchdown on this drive would dash their confidence further.

We broke out of our huddle. I started heading back toward my designated spot about 40 yards downfield from the line of scrimmage. Hasegawa ran alongside me since he would be playing at a deep safety spot about ten yards in front of me.

"Hey, Jay. Do you think they might try a fake punt?" Rich asked lightly.

I actually tilted my head back and laughed out loud. A fake punt on fourth and 26 was so ridiculous it was funny. We were very loose.

But hopefully not too loose.

Things were still not going San Diego's way. The Chargers only got a so-so punt. It wasn't a line drive but it also didn't have much hang time. I was officially credited with fielding the punt at our 34-yard line, making this a 35-yard punt.

"Go for it, Jay!" I heard Hasegawa call.

I took off. It looked like I had a lot of real estate.

After a few yards I began to encounter blue jerseys and helmets. Somehow I managed to pick up another five yards before going down. It was first and ten at our 44. That's a great place to start a drive.

That's also close to where the drive ended. On the second play Bender had blue jerseys in his face. He spotted me downfield and got the pass off. Unfortunately he was off the mark and threw the ball slightly behind me. I was running away from the ball and leaned back to try to deflect it. I fell down as a defensive back picked the pass off at the San Diego 34.

I watched helplessly from the ground as my opponent took off with what was meant to be my first reception of the day. Fortunately he didn't get very far. Grummon pulverized him at the San Diego 41.

So much for that drive. Things were now going San Diego's way. I ran off the field. As I approached our sideline I caught up with Bender.

"It's all right, man. We'll get it back," I said as I patted him on the back. I felt like I had to say that. That is exactly what he would have said to me had I turned the ball over.

I was actually a little angry with myself, not Steve. I just hated when we turned the ball over. Had I been able to lunge back a little more I might have prevented the interception.

"Let's go, defense! Get it back!" I hollered as the Chargers broke out of their huddle and approached the line.

I watched as the Chargers ran off left tackle. The ball carrier picked up five yards before McWilliams, Allen and Morrissey combined forces to bring him down. It was second down at the San Diego 46.

"Geez," I said to Hoddesson as I grabbed a cup of Gatorade and prepared to sit on the bench. "That interception seemed to fire them up."

Of course a turnover will have that effect. The offense will always be fired up to capitalize on the break.

Two completions on consecutive plays gave them a first down at the Hawaii 29. They tried going up the middle and managed three yards.

Jennings shot through the line on the next play. The quarterback scrambled to his left and managed to get the ball off just before Ed hammered him. The ball fell untouched.

"All right, Ed! That's good enough!" I called out.

The Charger offense lined up on third down. We figured another pass was on the agenda. Hasegawa was on the field as the nickel back.

"Hukilau! Hukilau!" I heard.

It was no bluff. Hasegawa blitzed and got to the quarterback. The quarterback was on his way down when he got the pass off. Whether there was a receiver reasonably close to where the ball was thrown was a matter of debate.

"Grounding!" Walker yelled. "That was intentional grounding!"

Several of us were yelling. Walker simply superseded us.

"Where's the penalty flag?" Walker demanded to know. "He threw that ball away! What game are you guys watching?"

Of course we all wanted the yellow flag. The penalty would have taken them out of field goal range. Unfortunately there was no penalty and San Diego's placekicker split the uprights perfectly from 43 yards. The game was tied.

"Okay, forget it," Walker said. "Let's focus on getting the lead back."

I took my place on the end zone line as I prepared to receive the kickoff. Roberts, who was a very aloof individual but not unfriendly, was to my right.

The kick was coming to me again. It was as if the kicker had dead aim. I was able to catch the ball on the exact spot where I was standing prior to the kick.

"I got it!" I called to prevent a misunderstanding.

I caught the ball and shot forward. Roberts did a good job of laying out a defender at about the 15. I could also see Giametti holding off a tackler wannabe.

As I approached the 30 I tried to elude a defender by cutting to my left. He may have anticipated my cut.

Suddenly I was down on the grass at the 30. I didn't even recall being hit. It was simply a matter of one second being up and running and the next second I was down with my tackler lying on top of my thighs. Whistles were blowing and then I felt the force of another body on top of me.

"Late hit! Late hit!" I heard Daniels call.

I wasn't hurt but I could tell that the hit was way late. I didn't see the official throw up his flag but I did see it land.

160

"Come on, let's bounce up there, men," one of the officials directed as I felt bodies shifting and getting up. "Okay, 22. Are you all right?"

"Yeah, I'm okay," I replied as I rose to my feet.

The Chargers were charged with a late hit. That was worth 15 yards. We had first and ten at our 45.

We didn't waste any time in giving most of the yardage bonus back. Abraham was cited for holding, giving us first and 20 at our own 35. Scott then lost two yards on a sweep.

"This way, guys!" Walker called sarcastically, pointing toward the end zone we were supposed to be heading to. "Do you want to try moving this way?"

If I hadn't taken the game seriously I might have laughed. Walker's sarcasm was fairly amusing.

On the next play Bender hit me on a cross pattern on about the 43. There was a defender right there and I tried to elude him by bellying back toward the line of scrimmage. He and another defender brought me down at the 40. It was third and 15.

Giametti came in and Grummon went out. This was obviously a pass situation. That didn't automatically mean we were going to pass but the odds heavily favored it. We were going to line up in a double single with Giametti and Slater wide and me in the slot.

"Walker says for you to call it," Giametti told Bender.

Steve momentarily studied our line of scrimmage and sized it up with how far we had to travel. He then dropped to one knee and looked up at us in the huddle.

"Okay, I want this. I don't want to punt," he began, then called the Pali Lookout. This was a play where the receivers run to just past the first down marker where they would turn and wait.

The play worked perfectly. Bender hit Slater right on the numbers at about the San Diego 45. Slater wanted to be doubly sure so he managed to squirm for a couple more yards even though he was in a defender's grasp as soon as he made the catch. We had the first down.

That conversion worked wonders. We all lit up. I was the first to get to Slater, since my pattern had been on the same side of the field as his reception.

"Great effort, Joe," I cheered vibrantly as he bounced up and accepted my handshake.

Giametti then showed up to offer his accolades.

"Awesome, man, awesome!"

It was indicative of how strong the rookie from Baylor actually was. He was roughly my height but not quite as heavy. Had he gone down at the point of his reception he probably would have had the first down although he would have been close to not making it since he ran about a yard short of where he was supposed to run prior to his reception. His strength showed in his ability to get the extra yardage after he was hit.

Scott picked up three yards to the 40. I then got my first carry of the day, picking up five yards to the 35. On that play Kohl blocked a linebacker out of the way as routinely as a dust mop moves a gum wrapper around a sales floor.

"Helluva block, Jim!" I said, whacking him on the rear as we approached the huddle.

On third and two Bender figured they were looking for the run. He called a play-action fake to Scott and then hit Kerner at the 20 for another first down, stopping the clock with 23 seconds left in the quarter when he was knocked out of bounds. Scott then closed out the quarter by picking up four yards.

We moved toward the opposite end zone, meaning we would be playing on the baseball infield which would no longer be visible during the Chargers' next home game.

I trotted down alongside Marv, Slater, Kerner and Abraham.

"We should be able to at least pick up another field goal," Slater remarked.

"I want a meal, not a snack," I retorted in only a partially light tone.

"What?"

"We don't want a field goal. We've already settled for one of those," Marv said to clarify my remark. "We want a TD."

"Oh," Slater replied.

When play resumed we continued to flow toward our primary goal. Bender called a Kaneohe left which had Kerner carrying through the hole on the left. Kerner picked up five yards, giving us third and one at the eleven.

"Waimanalo right," Bender called in the huddle.

This was essentially the same play to the opposite side. The difference was that I would be carrying instead of Kerner.

I picked up three yards although those three yards are not included in my game, season or career totals. It was a free play since one of the Chargers jumped offside just before the snap. The five yards gave us a first and goal at the six instead of at the eight.

Much to our chagrin but not a surprise, the Charger defense turned up the heat. Scott went up the middle and managed only a yard. On the subsequent two plays Bender was under pressure while being unable to find an open receiver and had to pass out of the end zone.

The field goal unit ran on the field.

"Damn!" Marv exclaimed, speaking for virtually the entire offense as we ran off the field. We weren't angry about going for the field goal. Once again, we were upset with ourselves for not scoring a touchdown.

162

Those of us on the sideline stood and watched. Guinn predictably converted the 22-yard field goal.

"Okay, men, shake it off," Bennici directed, taking note of the frustrated expressions of the offensive players. "There'll be plenty of opportunities for touchdowns."

"We've already had two opportunities and had to settle for field goals," Abraham replied sharply.

"Just take it easy," Bennici instructed calmly, patting Clint on the back. "You've got the right attitude and the momentum. Take that fire to the field. You'll blow these guys away."

I sighed, sipped my Gatorade, and looked at the scoreboard. The 6-3 didn't look especially impressive. At least the right team had six.

Guinn's kickoff was fielded about five yards deep in the end zone. The Chargers made no effort to run it out. They would start at the 20.

"Next time kick it a little shorter," I heard Hamer kid Guinn on the sideline. "When they down it like that I don't get to hit anybody."

I smirked at that remark. I also found it somewhat refreshing. It seemed to epitomize the team's overall frame of mind. We were ready to play.

San Diego picked up a couple of first downs and got to midfield before having to punt. I was determined to have a runback. I was charged up.

I took the punt at the ten and ran forward. I didn't see the San Diego defender move in from my left side. He hit me at the 18. He hit me so hard that I was literally airborne before I crashed to the ground with him on top of me. It was one of the rare times I was hit that hard in the open field. It was also the second time that day that I was hit when I didn't expect it.

"Wow, where did you come from?" I asked lightly.

"I jumped out of the stands, actually."

"Oh. Helluva hit."

Meanwhile I could sense that up in the bleachers my mother's heart had skipped a few beats. It amazed me that she worried about me on the football field but had preferred that I join the military where I was sure to be shot at.

We wasted no time in letting the Chargers and their fans know we were dead serious about winning this game. We opened with a 3 kama'aina left. Scott didn't go down until he had picked up 22 yards to the 40. He was really outdoing himself.

I got the call next. Grummon and Hayer opened up a nice hole for me on the left side. I shot all the way to the San Diego 46. We had picked up 36 total yards on only two rushing plays.

"We're hot to trot now, baby," Scott remarked as he and Kerner patted my back as we got ready to huddle.

The Chargers dug in. They held Scott to two yards up the middle; a phenomenal feat when considering the kind of day Larry was having. On

163

the next play they were in Bender's face and his pass to Slater dropped untouched.

"Okay, let's get it done," Bender remarked in the huddle. The expression on his face told me there was no doubt that we would.

And we did. Bender hit Giametti near the left sideline at the 21. Gary raced for ten more yards before being knocked out of bounds. We had a first down with 5:17 left in the half.

"Giametti!" Grummon called as he ran on the field, sending Gary out. The two slapped fives as their paths crossed.

After two plays we had third and ten at the eleven. Kerner had rushed to the nine but Bender was pressured in the pocket, tried to scramble and was sacked at the eleven.

"I sure hope we're not going to have to kick another field goal," Kerner remarked as we headed back to the huddle.

I nodded. Every three-point drive was helpful but no team wants the placekicker racking up all of the points. We needed touchdowns.

San Diego helped us a little. The Chargers' encroachment penalty gave us third and five at the six.

Bender had to scramble again on the next play. This time he got the pass off. I was near the back corner of the end zone and shifting toward the center. The ball was about to pass a few yards in front of me so I dove. . . .

Touchdown!!!!

I had reached out while parallel to the ground and managed to get a firm grip on the ball. I pulled it in to my chest just before I hit the ground. I kept the ball high enough against my body so that it wouldn't appear as if I had trapped the ball.

Of course when one scores a touchdown one ephemerally becomes the most popular player on the team. Giametti was first to run over to me.

"Great catch, Jay!"

Next came Grummon, Marv, Hoddesson and a few others. We triumphantly ran off the field as the PAT unit replaced us. As our paths crossed, I slapped fives with Daniels, Billingsley, Edwards, Guinn and a few others. Walker, bearing a smile as large as an aircraft carrier, slapped me on the shoulder and shook my hand.

"I love that kind of effort, Jay. Way to go."

The PAT was successful. We had a 13-3 lead with 3:48 left in the half.

I grabbed a cup of Gatorade. Nearby I noticed Allen trying to fire up the defensive unit. All of the starters were present except for those on the field with the kickoff team.

"Let's really tighten up," Allen directed. "Don't let them score. Let's do three and out. If we get the ball back quick enough we'll have time for at least a field goal."

San Diego began on the 20 after downing the kickoff in the end zone. The lack of a runback kept the clock as is. I was grateful since I wanted another score before halftime.

But the Chargers insisted on moving the ball. They picked up a couple of first downs and had first and ten at their own 46.

"Let's go, defense! Get it back for us!" Bender called.

Allen took matters into his own hands when the Chargers got a play off just before the two-minute mark. On the Hawaii 45 he made a leaping interception. He was actually fairly fast for a man his size and headed toward the end zone.

"Go, baby, go!"

"Move it!"

"All the way, Russ!"

Russ broke a few tackles. He was finally caught from behind and dragged down. By that time he had a 37-yard return, giving us a first down at the 18 with 1:46 left in the half.

The offense ran on the field. We wanted to get a play off *right now*. It blew a little of the wind out of our sails when we realized we were at the two-minute warning. There may have been a TV time out anyway with the change of possession but the two-minute warning guaranteed it.

Of course the Chargers were also anxious. When we lined up after the break one of their linebackers tried to anticipate our count. He started to charge in, then saw we hadn't snapped the ball and tried to hold up. His momentum carried him into Hoddesson.

That put us at the 13. Bender then hit Slater with a quick pass at the ten. Joe maneuvered his way to the six for a first down.

Walker decided to go to the air again. I was in the end zone near the goal post when I heard the crowd roar. I turned and saw Bender trying to scramble before being sacked at the 14, leading to a crescendo from the crowd.

I won't tell you what I said. Suffice it to say it was a good thing I wasn't wired for sound by NBC.

Undaunted, Bender hit Giametti on the following play. Gary had to jump to get the ball at the three. He was hit from behind immediately but hung on to the ball.

That made it third and goal. We called our second time out with 17 seconds left in the half.

"Man, we've got to get six," I said to nobody in particular. I knelt down in the huddle and turned to watch Bender and Walker conversing several yards behind me near the sideline.

Bender came back and called a 3 kama'aina right. Scott took the handoff and followed his blockers, including yours truly, around right end. It looked like he was going to score but an alert defensive back shot through and met Larry at the one.

We called our final time out. There were ten seconds left.

"Don't even think about it, Walker," I heard Marv mutter. We all wanted a touchdown. We were only three feet away.

It was reminiscent of the Denver game. At the end of the first half we went for a touchdown and failed, then ultimately lost by the three points we would have had had we kicked a field goal instead. I am sure I wasn't the only one in the huddle hoping the memory would not make Walker reluctant to take the gamble this time.

The field goal unit never budged aside from Guinn warming up by kicking a football into a portable net on the sideline. Bender finished conversing with Walker and headed our way.

If we don't make it this time Walker's never going to gamble again, I thought as I watched Bender approaching the huddle.

"Let's take it in," Bender directed evenly, calling the 3 Wahiawa right.

Bender took the snap and handed off to Scott. Scott leaped up and over and. . . .

Touchdown!!!!

Of course we did our part to make sure the officials didn't blow the call. Grummon, Kamanu, Marv, Bender and I all raised our arms. The officials concurred our perfect diagnosis.

The extra point gave us a 20-3 lead with five seconds left. This touchdown was doubly important since we would be kicking off in the second half.

Actually the interception was the most veritable key. The Chargers might otherwise have driven for a touchdown of their own while running the clock down. That would have narrowed our lead to 13-10 with the Chargers possessing the momentum and receiving the second half kickoff.

"Your lead doesn't guarantee a thing," Walker warned in the locker room. "Right now it's better to be in our shoes than their shoes but you can't let down. We need 30 more minutes of solid football from you and then we can breathe easy."

Scott, it turned out, had an exceptional first half. He had eleven carries for 64 yards. It looked like he was going to have his first 100-yard day for the Hawaiians.

Giametti was our leading receiver to that point although that isn't saying much. He only had two receptions for 44 yards.

It was good that Gary was seeing some action. He had several relatives who had driven down from Lakewood and other parts of the Los Angeles area. As I recall, he had ten tickets for parents, one sister, one set of grandparents, an aunt and an uncle, his girlfriend who was a junior at Long Beach State and her parents.

166

The Chargers took the kick return from the two to the 17. McWherter shot through and made a tackle that caused one's teeth to hurt.

"Yeah, baby! Right on! Right on!" a jubilant Allen cried when McWherter made the hit, pumping his fist in the air. "Let's go, defense! Let's get out there and put it to 'em!"

Russ was a fun guy to know. He was among the hardest hitters on the field, yet gentle as a lamb off the field. He was a good conversationalist with a great sense of humor. He was also the most vocal supporter of whoever was on the field.

The entire defense seemed to be fired up. Of course we didn't want to blow our 17-point lead. McWherter's hit definitely got us off on the right foot for the second half and sent the Chargers a message.

On third and seven our defense played for the pass. The quarterback dropped back and had to scramble. Rodgers was in hot pursuit on a safety blitz.

"Get him, Carl!" I called among the other encouraging calls from teammates.

"Don't let him get away!"

"Move it! Move it!"

"Go Rodgers go!"

Carl got him. Richards also got in there. They brought the quarterback down at the eleven. It was fourth and 16.

"Good job, defense! Outstanding!" I heard Walker call as the defense ran off the field and I ran on with the punt return unit amid slap fives.

I was pumped. I knew that the rest of the team was pumped. We had shoved it down the Chargers' throats to blow away any hopes they may have had to get the second half off to a good start. We were certain to begin our first possession of the half with excellent field position.

We had savored the taste of victory three weeks earlier and wanted it again. Among the reasons we wanted this game, aside from the obvious, was that a victory would give us momentum with Dallas coming to Honolulu the following week.

My mind was made up. Our offensive unit would not even take the field right away. I was going to return the punt for six.

I guess the San Diego punter was afraid I would do just that. He shanked it. The ball went out of bounds at the San Diego 37. It was a 26-yard punt.

The San Diego crowd was not pleased. The booing was very prevalent. I almost felt sorry for the punter.

Almost!

"All right, let's do it," Bender directed in the huddle as he prepared to call a play.

Whatever Steve had in mind, it didn't work. His pass was picked off in the flat. The San Diego crowd that had been booing a couple of minutes earlier was roaring its approval.

I have to give Bender credit. He made a textbook tackle at the San Diego 45. Had it not been for that the Chargers would have had six points.

That fired up the Chargers. They were starting this drive with excellent field position. Before I knew it they had a first down at our 29.

The crowd was into it. They knew that a touchdown would put the Chargers back in the game. Even a field goal would help since they would be only two touchdowns behind although they naturally preferred the touchdown.

So we started dashing their hopes. Jennings and McWilliams converged on the quarterback, sacking him at the 41.

"Yeah! Yeah! Yeah!" I hollered, leaping to my feet and moving toward the sideline.

That's the way to do it!"

For an encore Ken Gilbert, a rookie out of San Diego State, dropped a San Diego running back for a three-yard loss.

"All right!" Marv exclaimed as he stood next to me. "Local boy comes back with a vengeance."

"Yeah, it's good to have a guy who knows his way around the field," I remarked. "It's probably very nostalgic for him."

Of course we could get a little too pumped up. Richards suddenly found himself in San Diego's backfield before the ball was snapped. He wanted another sack in an obvious passing situation. Since he made contact he was cited for encroachment.

"Use your head, Richards! Use your head!" Walker barked in exasperation.

Norm stood with his hands on his hips in the defensive huddle. I could see him roll his eyes and shake his head as soon as he was penalized. He was angry at himself.

We were in our dime defense. With a third and 20 on the 39 the Chargers may have been in field goal range. I think Walker was willing to concede a field goal and give them a little yardage. He simply didn't want them getting a first down and a shot at a touchdown.

As expected, the Chargers passed. With six defensive backs it was hard to get a man open. The quarterback set up in the pocket and got the pass off just as he was hit by Richards.

It was a good pass. The ball hit the receiver in the hands just inside the 20. Unfortunately for him, Blakely arrived simultaneously with the ball and hit the receiver at the perfect moment. The receiver was not able to hang on.

"Right on! Right on!" I exclaimed, putting my helmet on running onto the field. I crossed paths with Blakely and slapped five with him.

168

"Take it all the way, Dockman," he said.

Of course I was more than willing to comply.

Actually it hadn't been guaranteed that they wouldn't attempt a field goal at the 39. Since they dispatched their punting unit to the field, we countered with our punt return unit. Had they gone for a field goal the defensive unit would have stayed.

The punter went for the coffin corner. He kicked it to his right and actually came fairly close to achieving his objective. The ball hit inside the five but didn't go out of bounds until just after it had crossed the goal line. It was close but not close enough. We would start at our 20.

We began our drive with two incomplete passes. Bender then hit me at the 40 for a first down. I couldn't accept the mere 20 yards, though, and tried to elude the defensive back by bellying back as I cut across the field. I was brought down at the 37. It was the second time that day that bellying back cost me yardage. It was still a first down.

Scott rushed for six yards to our 43. Bender then hit Slater at the San Diego 43 to give us another first down. Two plays later Bender hit me at the 24 amid heavy traffic.

I caught the ball and immediately heard and felt the contact. There was so much noise from the collisions between our equipment that it seemed as if the Chargers had emptied their bench to bring me down. The films would show that I was tackled by only two players.

"Dockman!"

I heard my name as I approached the huddle. Giametti was coming in to relieve me. I trotted toward the sideline.

"Good catch," Gary said as we slapped fives as our paths crossed. I took my place close behind Walker, knowing he was going to send me back in after one or two plays.

Giametti caught his first pass of the second half. It was a quick slant which he caught at about the 21. He managed to get to the 17 for a seven-yard gain.

Scott ran around right end. He managed only two yards to give us a third and one.

"They'll probably be looking for Larry again," I heard Walker say to Greg Wilson through the headset he was wearing. "We can probably count on Kerner for the first down."

Walker turned and looked at me. He reached his right arm in my direction. Instinctively I moved toward him as he put his arm around my shoulder.

"Run a two Mililani right," Walker instructed.

"Got it," I replied sharply and ran toward where our huddle was forming. "Giametti!"

Walker had called the right play. Kerner bulldozed up the middle for two yards. We had a first down at the 13.

Scott kept our momentum going, picking up seven yards between his next two carries. We had third and three.

A good defensive effort prevented us from going any further. It also prevented me from scoring my second touchdown of the game. Bender tried to hit me in the end zone. The ball was batted away by a defensive back and nearly intercepted by a linebacker. The linebacker wasn't expecting the ball to be batted in his direction and he accidentally batted the ball up in the air as if his hands were made of bricks. He lunged helplessly as the ball dropped incomplete.

I was knocked down in the scramble. As I rose to my knees I saw our field goal unit running on the field. I wanted to go for it but, however grudgingly, I understood.

At least the San Diego players and fans were frustrated. They weren't pleased about being outplayed by a franchise that wasn't even remotely considered for the NFL a year earlier.

Guinn's kick split the uprights. Of course it was only slightly longer than a PAT. I figured I probably could even have made it even though I hadn't done any placekicking since high school.

Still, it wasn't Guinn's fault that we didn't make a longer kick for him. The members of the offense were taking the blame although you can also credit the Chargers for tightening up on defense. Although nobody was saying so, we all believed the most Guinn should have been allowed to kick was a PAT.

Just the same, those three points would make it that much harder for the Chargers to catch us.

The Chargers picked up a couple of first downs after starting on their own 24. Once they got past midfield the defense bore down. They found themselves with fourth and 12 at the 50.

We put on a moderate rush on the punt. It was just enough to hurry the punter. He got the punt high but not as far as he wanted. I called a fair catch at the 15. There were 57 seconds left in the third quarter.

Bender wanted a touchdown bad. We opened the drive with a couple of incomplete passes. The first one he threw away after nearly being sacked. The second one the defensive back literally batted out of Slater's hands. It was third and ten. Nobody expected us to run.

We didn't. Bender dropped back. He found Grummon near the left sideline and hit him at the 26. He was hit immediately but had the first down. We were content to let the clock run down. Only 15 minutes to our second victory in NFL franchise history.

As we changed directions one saw a growingly optimistic group of Hawaiians and a somewhat shellshocked group of Chargers. Bender ran to our sideline to converse with Walker. One of the Charger defensive captains went over to their sideline.

170

I watched as Bender conversed with Walker with Joseph and Billingsley standing by. Walker looked incredibly relaxed. A 20-point lead with only 15 minutes left seemed to work wonders for Walker's blood pressure.

"Look," I said jocularly as the rest of us formed a semblance of a huddle. "Walker's even smiling."

"Nah, it's just gas," Kerner deadpanned, cracking everybody up. With our 20-point lead at this stage we could afford to loosen up a little. We still had to be cognizant of the fact that our lead was not insurmountable.

Bender ran in from the sideline. The linemen bent over with their backs to the line of scrimmage. The backs and receivers bent over facing the linemen. Bender crouched down and looked up at his teammates. We could stall a little since NBC was still in commercial.

"Okay, we'll mix it up a little but primarily we want to run off as much time as we can," he said before calling the play.

We worked the clock well. After two carries by Scott gave us a third and four, Kerner picked up five yards up the middle for a first down. Scott then went up the middle for three to get us up to the Hawaii 40.

"Okay, I think they expect nothing but rushing plays from now on," Bender observed with his usual self-confidence. "Let's burn them in the air."

I lined up on the right flank obliquely behind Abraham, then shifted to the slot. On the snap I ran a flag pattern.

There is something enigmatically magical about the moment a quarterback locks his eyes on a receiver. You know he is about to cock his arm and come to you. I welcomed the opportunity.

The ball hit me right on the numbers at the San Diego 42. There was a defender right there, but I simply outran him while swiveling my hips a little to elude another defender. I kept running until the first defender I eluded caught me from behind. By that time, I was at the 12. It was a 48-yard gain.

I bounced up. We were 36 feet from expanding our lead. A field goal would have looked impressive on the scoreboard but that wasn't what we were after.

"Helluva play, Jaybird!" Marv cried out as I headed toward our huddle. Bender shook my hand and there were a few slaps on my back.

"Come on, Chargers! You're making it too easy for these guys!" I heard a fan holler from one of the sideline seats. Normally one cannot decipher individual remarks like that while on the field. In this case we could because most of the rest of the crowd was eerily quiet. Some of the fans were even already in their cars and heading home.

We continued toward our goal. A short pass to Slater, a rush by Scott and an encroachment penalty against the Chargers gave us a first and goal at the one. We figured we could pick up a yard in four plays.

As it worked out, we only needed one play. Scott took the ball and leaped into the end zone. He penetrated so far that it wasn't necessary for us to raise our hands to help the officials. Some of us did anyway.

We ran toward the sideline as a unit. I was clapping my hands, as were Kerner and Abraham. Marv displayed a jaunty run with both fists thrust in the air. Bender's emotional display consisted of a smile.

"Good job, men," Walker remarked, whacking a few of us on our derrieres as we went by.

Guinn's PAT was true. We had a 30-3 lead with 10:21 left.

"I guess we'd better not blow it," Allen said lightly as he put his helmet on to prepare to take the field after the kickoff.

"Damn right you'd better not blow it," Marv replied, flashing a laughing smile. "I want to go home two and two."

"Yeah," McDaniel added. "When was the last time you played on a team that didn't have a losing record this far into the season."

Marv reflected back on his nine years in New Orleans. He shook his head with his smile still planted on his face.

"I think I was still at Grambling," he remarked, drawing a round of laughter.

We were loose. That didn't mean the Chargers couldn't still win. Four unanswered touchdowns with extra points would give them a 31-30 lead. It wasn't likely but possible if the bounces went their way and our defense collapsed. The clock still did not favor a team with a 27-point deficit.

"If we blow this one we'll have to commit a joint seppuku in the locker room," I remarked dryly as the kicking unit prepared to go to work.

"A joint what?" Jennings asked.

"Seppuku," I repeated. "It's referred to a lot in *Shogun*. We'll have to disembowel ourselves. Otherwise we go back to Honolulu where our fans will beat us to death. We'll all be lying dead somewhere between the tarmac and Lagoon Drive."

"You're probably right," Ed agreed lightly, running on the field after Guinn's kick went out of the end zone.

The Chargers picked up a first down at the 39 on their second play from scrimmage. It was a 19-yard pass after an incompletion but they couldn't pass on every play. They rushed for three yards to the 42, then Pratt got called for encroachment to give them a second and two at the San Diego 47.

Pratt made up for his faux pas on the snap. He ran right through the block and tackled the running back for a two-yard loss.

The Chargers went back to the air on third and four. Hasegawa played it perfectly at about the 30. He cut in front of the receiver, knocked the ball away and nearly wound up with it himself. He did a brief juggling act before the ball dropped to the ground.

In a tight game this would have been a heartbreaking moment for those of us on the sideline. In a game as lopsided as this we actually giggled at the

172

sight of the ball bouncing in Rich's hands like a hot potato. Each unsuccessful Charger effort moved us closer to victory.

"Punt return unit!" Walker barked.

I was enjoying myself so much that I forgot it was fourth down. I jumped off the bench and put my helmet on as my colleagues and I ran on the field.

When the Chargers sent out their punting unit the boos could be heard in Tijuana. I was actually surprised that they opted to punt. I was watching for a fake. Since they were down by four touchdowns with a little more than eight minutes left they wouldn't have had much to lose by going for it.

They did punt, much to my surprise. The punt hit inside the 20, then bounced backward and was downed at the 25. Even a simple punt was working against the Chargers. The punt netted only 30 yards even though this wasn't really the punter's fault. There was 7:58 left.

The fans were starting to make a beeline for the exits. Some had already left but now they were lining up en masse to get out.

We headed toward the end zone. After about half-a-dozen plays Walker put in some of the reserves. Joseph took over as quarterback, Edwards at fullback and Roberts at tailback. There were also changes on the line.

I stayed in for the time being since my backup, Giametti, had also been the wide receiver backup and got considerable playing time. It wasn't until we had second and five at the five that Giametti came in for me.

As I ran off the field I took note of the empty seats. More than half of the crowd had left. It made me proud.

"Good game, Jay," Walker greeted, shaking my hand and patting me on the back.

"Thanks, Coach."

I stood on the sideline and continued to marvel at the empty seats.

"Man, we sure cleared this place out," I remarked to Mark Black.

"Good," Black cracked. "I never liked San Diego anyway."

Edwards eventually plunged in from the two with 1:43 left. The extra point gave us our 37-3 margin of victory.

The Chargers weren't able to move the ball and we took over for the final seconds. Billingsley took a turn at quarterback and ran a few short yardage plays, then dropped to his knee on the final snap. When the clock ran out we were officially 2-2.

"All right, man!" Abraham cheered.

It felt good to leave the field a victor again. I shook hands with some of the Chargers, guardedly sympathetic toward them. They were gracious but I sensed that they were shellshocked.

"We knew you were good," one of the Chargers commented to me. "We knew you could beat us but you just killed us. Who's next for you guys?"

"Dallas," I replied. "We've got Dallas at home next week."

"I believe you guys might just beat them."

"I hope you're right."

I was feeling pretty darn good. We even had a better record than the Steelers who were now 1-3 after falling to the Minnesota Vikings.

We had our postgame benediction. Slater did the honors.

"Okay, thanks, Joe," Walker said afterward. "Now, game ball. I don't know what the official total was but I know that we had a 100-yard rushing effort today."

Walker tossed the ball to Scott. That produced enthusiastic cheers from everybody. It had been a true team effort but Larry's effort was one that stood out. Larry officially carried 24 times for 114 yards. That gave him 81 carries for 369 yards through four games. He was on a pace to carry for more than 1,000 yards on the season.

I only carried twice for 19 yards. That gave me 12 carries for 65 yards on the season.

Obviously I had a better yards-per-carry average than Larry did although that is misleading. The defense was usually not keying on me on the rush, so they were often caught off guard.

I caught five passes for 95 yards. That gave me 17 receptions for 333 yards on the season. I moved into the team lead by default since Dietrich had to sit the game out. He had 15 receptions for 255 yards.

It was a nice visit outside the stadium with my nuclear family and other relatives. There wasn't much time before the bus left for the airport but it was pleasant.

My brother Craig was the most enthusiastic member of the entourage. As a young teenager it meant a lot to him to watch his older brother play in the NFL. Whenever I spotted him in the stands during the game his smile seemed to be perpetual.

It was a happy flight home. It wasn't as if our 2-2 record sent the champagne corks flying but it sure beat our flight from Kansas City two weeks earlier.

I read more of *Shogun*, although it wasn't easy. It was a fairly good book but one that requires full concentration if one wishes to follow the plot. On a plane full of laughing, joking football players is hardly the proper ambience for that.

"Ho, look at the size of that book," Black remarked as he walked down the aisle toward where I was sitting. "Does it have a lot of pictures? I've never seen a book that size before."

I looked at Black and grinned. I think it was for his own interest that he inquired about pictures.

"No pictures," I replied. "Just a lot of pages full of words."

That probably killed whatever interest Mark might have had in the book. I got along with him okay but he wasn't one who could discuss academics with you. If it didn't concern football he liked to discuss which bars he liked and where to go pick up girls. I don't think I ever saw him read anything that didn't have pictures. In fact, I don't think I ever saw him read anything that didn't have centerfolds.

I suppose *Shogun* would have been better suited for offseason reading. I bought the book the previous Thursday with the idea that I would have a large chunk of it read by the time we touched down in Honolulu Sunday night. Amid the distractions on two flights between Honolulu and San Diego (the latter of which was very lively), meeting relatives and my mind wandering from the book to Sunday's game, I guess I did well to get as far as page 114. Since the book had 1152 pages and I had a plethora of responsibilities and recreation planned I figured I might be about halfway through by the time we played in Oakland. That was three weeks away.

"Can I borrow that after you're done?" Jennings asked during the flight.

"Sure," I replied brightly. "Of course we both might be retired by the time I get through."

CHAPTER NINE
Lasso Them Cowpokes

"This is a nice car," Ed Jennings commented as I drove toward our workout at Aloha Stadium. Normally he drove himself but his girlfriend needed the car they shared so I agreed to give him a lift.

"Thanks," I said. "It's one of the few lingering reminders of the World Football League."

As I watched the traffic on the H-1 Freeway I could see out the corner of my eye that Ed was looking at me quizzically.

"You mean you bought this while you were in the WFL?"

"Nope. It was part of my signing bonus."

Being hotly pursued by three professional sports franchises gave me some leverage in 1974. When I decided to sign with the Hawaiians I impulsively included a 1974 Porsche and a $5,000 bonus on top of my salary demand. I asked for the $5,000 to cover the income tax on the Porsche.

The Hawaiians were reluctant to include the car but offered little resistance. Two days after we reached our verbal agreement I went to the Waikiki hotel where the team had its temporary headquarters to sign my contract. My brand-new Porsche and the bonus check were waiting for me.

Being only 22 at the time, I was probably much more impressed with myself than I should have been. The economy was a shambles, tensions in the Middle East had us in an energy crisis, the White House was disgraced by Watergate and Patricia Hearst had recently been taken hostage by a terrorist group calling itself the Symbionese Liberation Army. At the same time I was on top of the world as I neared my college graduation prior to the beginning of my pro football career.

Getting back to 1976, we were back at Aloha Stadium where our next contest would be. As usual, we began the week in the hospitality room.

We were effervescent. We had just humiliated the Chargers on their home turf, sending their fans home in a discontented daze. The giddiness from Sunday was still apparent with guys joking, laughing and playfully pushing each other.

"All right. Let's get to work," Walker directed as he led his staff into the room.

Nothing can kill a party faster than the sudden appearance of a scowling head football coach. The room was suddenly quiet except for the sound of a few dozen men moving to their respective sections to watch the films and Joe Slater popping his bubble gum.

The lights went down. Walker prepared to turn on the projector for the offensive unit. Slater popped his gum.

"Slater!" Walker barked. "If I hear that bubble gum pop one more time you're going to wear it on your nose for the rest of the day!"

The room was dead silent. Walker broke the silence a few seconds later. "Do you hear me? Huh?"

"I hear you, Coach," Slater replied obediently.

That was the introduction to how the film session was going to go for us. Walker nitpicked all the way through. There wasn't a single play where he didn't find some reason to belittle somebody. I don't think there was anybody in the offensive meeting who wasn't singled out at least once.

My alleged faux pas came on a pass to Slater. Walker felt that I could have blocked the man who eventually tackled him inside the ten-yard line.

"Slater could have had a TD, Dockman," Walker said in a way that was not fire and brimstone but still got under my skin. I knew at the time that I could have blocked the man but at the angle I would have had to take I would have had a hard time keeping from clipping him. "Why didn't you block him?"

"Because I was afraid I'd get called for a clip," I replied honestly. "I didn't have a good angle on him."

Walker hesitated. The fact that we did score a touchdown to end the first half on this drive did not seem to impress him. I think I put him in an uncomfortable position where he wanted to lambaste me for missing the block but had to concede to my reasoning.

"We can't be making these mistakes against the Cowboys," Walker finally said as he resumed critiquing our performance.

That was the phrase of the day. Walker must have uttered that very phrase at least 50 times during the session.

"That'll teach us to beat the crap out of somebody," Rich Grummon facetiously remarked in the locker room after the film session mercifully ended.

I suppose we were all a little dazed by the critique. Walker did hand out compliments during the session including high praise for my diving catch in the end zone.

"That's what I like to see!" Walker called vibrantly. "A lot of guys would not have bothered but you opted to dive for the ball and came up with it. That's great football, Jay. Plays like that mean we score touchdowns more and settle for field goals less."

It still seemed that for every compliment Walker dished out there were at least a dozen complaints. Sometimes he issued a dozen complaints on the same plays where he issued praise.

"Maybe we should start sandbagging," Clint Abraham suggested. "From now on we don't pull ahead until the final minute."

It was that kind of a day. Walker continued his martinet demeanor during the workout. It was only a light workout without pads but Walker acted as if he was going to suddenly expect us to start tackling.

There were some roster changes. As expected, defensive tackle Hank Prendergast was activated. He was a veteran out of Southeast Missouri who played the first four years of his career in Philadelphia before spending one season each in Baltimore and New Orleans.

To make way for Prendergast, Souza was placed on waivers. Jimmy was a Waipahu native who was with the 1975 WFL Hawaiians. He always believed he would be the one let go as soon as Prendergast was activated.

It was always sad when a teammate was cut during the season but it was especially sad in a case like this. Jimmy had been a teammate during my final two seasons at the University of Hawaii, giving us a very special bond. I hated losing him as a teammate and seeing his career come to an end. There was always the possibility of him hooking on with somebody else, but he ultimately never did. His entire NFL career spanned four games.

After the session was over I lifted weights and then gave Jennings a ride home. As I normally did, I got off the freeway at Punahou Street but turned right toward Beretania Street like I would normally do if I was going straight home. I forgot to turn left toward Manoa to take Ed home.

"We can't be making those mistakes against the Cowboys," Ed remarked lightly about my failure to miss the turn.

Ed wasn't even there when Walker made the remarks during the offensive film session. Walker used the phrase enough during our light workout that our defensive players would also be uttering the phrase in their sleep. I guess Walker was a believer in equal opportunity hackneyed phrases.

I enjoyed showing the highlights of our game on my TV show that night. I had to use a lot of restraint to keep from dedicating my entire show to the Hawaiians but there were other NFL games as well as the University of Hawaii's loss to Grambling. That's not to mention the preview of the baseball playoffs which would be getting underway later that week.

"It's the Yankees and Royals in the American League and Phillies and Reds in the National League. I think the Reds are strong enough to make it to the World Series again although the Phillies won't be easy."

"In the American League you have the Yankees in the postseason for the first time since the 1964 World Series and the Royals in the postseason for the first time ever. I think the Yankees will prevail although that is not etched in stone. The Royals are very capable of pulling it out."

Walker was pretty brutal on Wednesday and Thursday. We began Wednesday's session by watching films of Dallas's game in Seattle. While we were embarrassing the Chargers, the Cowboys were in Seattle and falling to an early 13-0 deficit that gave Seahawk fans a false sense of security. By the time the game ended the Cowboys had scored 28 unanswered points. It was almost as if the Cowboys had conspired to give the Seahawks and their fans false hopes.

"If you find yourselves leading the Cowboys by two touchdowns, don't let up," Walker directed. "Don't let up if you are leading by three touchdowns or four or five. This is a team that can rebound from virtually any deficit as long as there is time left on the clock."

Just in case we missed anything, we saw the same films again prior to our Thursday workout. This was hardly normal behavior although in our fifth week of our first NFL season we could not truly ascertain the norm yet. History would prove that this would be the only time that we ever watched the same films on two consecutive days.

Of course Walker presided over the offensive session. He had scrutinized the films pretty well before we saw them. He knew every defensive player's tendencies. There was a lot of, "Watch the way this man shoots to the inside," or, "He really likes to blitz," or, "He knows how to use his hands," and other observations before the films would prove that Walker knew exactly what he was talking about. It got to where it seemed as if the players we were watching on film were acting on Walker's instruction.

There was also a lot of rhetoric, such as, "Stanek, this man will glide right past you with that move of his if you're not careful," or "Don't let him do that to you, Abraham," or "Be heads up back there, Kerner," or "Don't let him stick to you like that, Dockman and Dietrich." It was as if we had already made the mistakes before the Cowboys had even arrived in Honolulu.

Walker was actually fairly civil during these two film sessions. At least he didn't raise his voice much although he couldn't very well lambaste us for the Seahawks' mistakes. He made up for the lack of decibels during the actual workouts.

Naturally the Wednesday workout focused primarily on the offense. The Thursday workout focused primarily on the defense. With the way Walker was breathing fire one would have thought that we had the worst offense in the NFL on Wednesday and the worst defense in the NFL on Thursday. It almost seemed as if Walker screamed and hollered in perpetuity on those two days. Had we been working out at the Marine base the base commanders might have asked Walker to tone it down so that they could hear the fighter jets taking off and landing.

"You can get away with that third-rate performance in San Diego," was a common remark over those two days, "but you can't get away with it on Sunday. The Cowboys are coming! Do you hear me? The Cowboys are coming!"

I have little doubt that a few miles up the road at Tripler Hospital somebody suddenly came out of a coma with the immediate knowledge that the Cowboys were coming. Had Walker yelled a little louder a few cadavers might have left the lab to head to the box office to buy tickets.

"How bad do you think Walker wants this one?" Jennings asked me as we enjoyed a late lunch after Thursday's workout. We were at Hawaii's first Taco Bell which had opened earlier that year on Kapahulu Avenue.

"Pretty bad, I guess," I said as I poured sauce on my taco. "I think we had better win just to keep him from committing suicide."

"Yeah, really," Ed remarked in agreement. "I've never had a coach get that worked up over a single game."

"Neither have I."

Ed took a bite out of his burrito. He bore a ponderous expression as he chewed.

"What do you think?" he asked. "Do you think he has some vendetta against the Cowboys?"

I thought for a moment, shrugged, and shook my head.

"Probably not," I replied. "I think it's just that they're going to be our toughest opponent to this point."

"Yeah, you're probably right. He just wants us to know that the Cowboys will be a lot tougher than the Chargers were."

"I think we were all aware of that anyway. He doesn't need to scream and yell like that to make us believe that."

Walker began to mellow on Friday. He shifted his strategy from the previous in awe of the Cowboys to something more encouraging to get us to believe in ourselves. In order to beat the Cowboys, we had to believe we could. Walker knew that and so did the rest of the coaches and players.

On Saturday Walker was hyper almost to the point of giddiness. He was there to greet everybody with kind words and a big smile as we arrived for our light workout.

"Watcha say, Jay?" was his salutation to me. "Are you ready to corral them Cowboys?"

"Better believe it," I replied, glad that Walker seemed to have some faith in us again.

Walker had no ill feelings toward the Cowboys. He was actually very friendly with Cowboy Coach Tom Landry. He simply saw this game as a magnificent opportunity for us. If we could beat the Cowboys we would be above .500. The victory would also give us great momentum for our encounters with Houston and Oakland.

I suppose I was prematurely worked up. On Saturday night I found it almost impossible to sit still. I tried reading the afternoon newspaper but kept daydreaming. I couldn't concentrate on the TV and didn't feel like listening to music.

The baseball playoffs would have helped keep my mind at bay. Unfortunately the opening games were not televised in Hawaii. None of the three network affiliates opted to televise the games for reasons known only

180

to them although one station made a last-minute decision to televise the next day's American League matchup.

Unfortunately that didn't affect Saturday. With no destination in mind, I got in my car. After driving an indirect route that would make one wonder if I was trying to shake somebody on my tail, I found myself at Kelly's Coffee Shop on Kamehameha Highway. It was a decent enough place to eat and my being there reminded me that I hadn't had any dinner. Somehow my being there even helped to calm me a little.

"The Cowboys are coming."

Yes they were, I thought to myself as I enjoyed my roast beef dinner. They had actually been in town for about 24 hours and would be squaring off against us the following morning.

I was hoping to make the Cowboys sorry they came.

I arrived at Aloha Stadium at just about seven o'clock on Sunday morning. Within minutes I was in the hospitality room to enjoy a breakfast of fruit, juice and coffee.

"Ready to go?" Walker asked as he approached me from behind and placed his hand on my shoulder. I hadn't even noticed that he was in the room.

"Of course" I said in my best cocksure tone, partially because it was true and partially because anything negative would have been the wrong answer.

"Good. I know we're going to get a good game out of you," he remarked before going over to Hoddesson who was sitting with his wife at a nearby table.

Of course I wanted to win as badly as Walker did. I also personally wanted to play well and not just because I had given out eight passes. I kept my promise and gave my paper boy passes for him and his dad. There were also passes for Bill and Cherie, Don Simmons and his girlfriend Eileen, and two passes for Jim Martinez.

Right on schedule at eight o'clock I was running my pregame laps. The empty stadium essentially represented the calm before the storm. We knew we could beat the Cowboys. Something told me that the Cowboys would not be taking us lightly. Our rout of the Chargers seven days earlier definitely got their attention.

What a strange contrast it was between us and our three fellow expansion franchises. We were hoping to finish the weekend at 3-2 to give us the momentum to be 5-2 by the time we finished playing Oakland. Tampa Bay, Memphis and Seattle were still looking for their first victories.

Our injury report indicated that Pratt would probably play but not start. Kupau would start in his place. McWilliams was listed as doubtful because of a shoulder injury.

The Cowboys had arrived just a few minutes before I began my run. The players were already in their locker room. As I was finishing up my final lap their head coach came out of the tunnel from the locker room to look at the field. Since our paths crossed I stopped briefly to say hello.

Tom Landry was wearing a white shirt and tie. I thought he might dress more casually in Hawaii, choosing an aloha shirt over his more traditional attire. His only concession to Hawaii was that he opted not to wear his sport coat.

"You guys are going to be tough," he said with traces of sincerity.

"Something tells me your team won't be easy," I replied.

It was the old game of never badmouthing an opponent but there was truth in what we both said. We were going to take the Cowboys seriously. The Cowboys were going to take us seriously.

Marv led us in *The Lord's Prayer*. Walker stood at his usual post in the middle of the room. He appeared slightly ill at ease while trying to force a confident smile.

"Men, we've had a good week. You worked hard for this game. There isn't a single doubt in my mind that you can rise to the occasion."

Walker paused. He arbitrarily looked at half-a-dozen or so of his players.

"This is our biggest game yet," Walker continued. "I know you're ready. Let's send them back to Dallas in shock."

That was the pregame speech. I joined my teammates and coaches by immediately leaving the locker room and heading to the sideline. About ten of my teammates stayed behind to take care of last-minute preparations. The starting defensive unit hung out in the south end zone to be introduced.

I grabbed a cup of Gatorade and looked at the crowd to briefly divert my mind. Two convincing victories and two narrow defeats by a combined six points suggested that we were playing well. That, I reasoned, was why we had such overwhelming support. I would be surprised to find out later that the game did not quite sell out. There were about 150 unsold tickets.

As our defense was being introduced I looked across the field at our opponent. This was not a common opponent by any stretch of the imagination. They were men no different from the men on my own team, yet they were Dallas Cowboys. The name alone, led by their stoic head coach, inspired awe.

Of course we wanted to beat them and we probably had extra incentive. This was, after all, the team we had watched duke it out with the Pittsburgh Steelers in the most recent Super Bowl. Although the Cowboys had won only one of the first ten Super Bowls, they had been to three and the two they didn't win went down to the wire. They were also consistently in the hunt during the seasons when they didn't get into the Super Bowl. A lot could be said for the Hawaiians if we could beat a team of this stature.

182

This was also the NFL team that drafted me in 1974, only to lose out to the WFL Hawaiians. I was still very grateful to the Cowboys for their willingness to allow me to stay in Hawaii a year earlier when they owned the NFL rights to me. I was aware, though, that they didn't make the deal simply to accommodate me. Primarily they made the deal because they had the manpower which indicated that they didn't need me. The number one draft choice they got in exchange for me also had its appeal.

The Cowboys looked like royalty. Perhaps it was the royal blue trim that went with their silver pants, white jerseys and silver helmets. There was something about them that commanded respect.

And I wanted to beat them sooooooo bad. It wasn't anything personal. Beating the Cowboys would tell the world that the Hawaiians had arrived.

"I'm very impressed with what I've seen of this team," Landry was quoted as saying about the Hawaiians. As much as I liked him and respected him, I wanted to beat his team so badly that he would assume the fetal position and suck his thumb simply by watching *Hawaii 5-0*. I wanted him to be haunted by anything having to do with Hawaii.

Dallas won the toss and naturally elected to receive. With the trade winds blowing from the northeast, as usual, we would defend the north end zone.

Guinn teed up the ball at the 35 as 47,912 anticipated a very exciting game. Some of those in attendance were Cowboy fans; primarily military personnel from Texas and vicinity who were stationed in Hawaii. We would have our largest TV audience to date since CBS would be showing this game throughout much of the South as well as in other select areas. The Cowboys always drew viewers.

Unfortunately none of the viewers would be in Hawaii. The game was blacked out in Hawaii because it didn't sell out.

Guinn's kick was fielded at the one. The return man headed upfield in a seemingly flawless effort. I watched in horror as the Cowboys executed to perfection the art of upfield blocking.

"Come on! Somebody get him!" I called from an area behind the sideline.

It was Pratt, back in action with a vengeance, who brought the return man down. The tackle wasn't made until the return man had reached the Dallas 42.

Just in case the 41-yard return wasn't enough to damage our psyches, we had a man down. Kevin Zanakis was very slow in getting up at about the Dallas 35. He was blocked just as he was about to make the tackle and was kicked in the head by the ball carrier as he ran past.

Fortunately Zanakis would be okay although he would have to sit out a few plays. He was starting in place of McWilliams who wound up not even suiting up.

The Cowboys wasted no time in moving the ball. They actually got a little help from us right away when their four-yard rush was nullified by McDaniel jumping offside just before the snap. It was a free play and they naturally accepted a first and five at the 47 instead of second and six at the 46.

"Great start! Great start!" I heard Walker call sarcastically. "Let's try to keep our heads in the game, McDaniel."

Jim was probably a little too anxious. I know I was. I must have been up and down about five times during the drive.

"I want to get in there right now," I said to Hoddesson as I sat next to him.

"Take it easy," he said with an amused smile as he patted me on the back. "We'll all see plenty of action."

The Cowboys picked up a couple of first downs before their drive stalled. They had second and eight at the Hawaii 30 before throwing two incomplete passes; the latter of which was beautifully broken up in the end zone by Rodgers.

"That's the way to play it, Rodgers!" Walker called. "Way to stick with him!"

The Cowboys sent their field goal unit out. Their kicker was not unfamiliar to me. Although I had never faced him in high school, he was playing not too far from where I lived at the same time that I was playing for South Valley High. Even in high school he was capable of splitting the uprights from 50 yards out.

But not this time. The 47-yard field goal attempt was wide to the right. That produced a roar of approval from our crowd.

"All right, offense! Let's get on that scoreboard!" Walker directed as members of the offensive unit ran onto the field.

We started the drive by moving backward. We wanted to make a statement by going to the air immediately. The Cowboys made a statement by sacking Bender at the 22.

So we went right back at them. Bender hit me in front of the Cowboy sideline. I caught the ball at the Hawaii 38 and was hammered immediately and knocked out of bounds. It was third and two.

One of the Cowboy defensive backs apparently believed that I had caught the ball out of bounds. He seemed very livid as he pleaded his case. A couple of his teammates and Landry tried to restrain him but they didn't get the job done soon enough.

A yellow flag suddenly shot up. The crowd roared its approval. The Cowboys were hit for unsportsmanlike conduct. We had a first down at the Dallas 47.

"Man, this is going to be one very intense game," Marv remarked with a wide grin on his face as we moved forward to our new huddle position.

We decided to air it out again.

184

Unfortunately the Cowboys came at Bender hard. He was forced to scramble and did make it back to the line of scrimmage before running out of bounds at the Cowboy sideline.

It was a costly play. Slater tried to throw a block when he saw that Bender wasn't going to be able to get the pass off. He wound up with a neck sprain and would be out for the rest of the game.

This meant that Giametti would do double duty for the second week in a row. He would be Dietrich's backup as well as mine.

Scott went through the right and fought for four yards to give us a third and six at the 43. Carl Hayer then put us in a third and eleven situation when he jumped too soon.

"I can't believe I did that," the big tackle out of Washington muttered with a pained expression on his face.

"It's all right. We'll get it back," I said.

We did get the yardage back although not enough for a first down. Bender eluded a Cowboy blitz and threw a quick pass to Giametti at the 44. Gary got to the 38 before he was brought down. We were still a yard short of a first down.

"Come on, Walker. Let's go for it," Larry Scott pleaded quietly as the officials were spotting the ball where it was obvious without measuring that we were a yard short.

"Field goal unit!" I heard Walker bark. Grudgingly I joined my offensive colleagues in running off the field while the field goal unit ran on.

I stood and watched as Billingsley crouched down to field the snap. The ball would be spotted at the 45, making this a 55-yard attempt.

The snap was true. So was the hold and Guinn got the kick off. I watched the ball sail and heard the crowd roar as the official raised his hands over his head. We had a 3-0 lead with 7:49 left in the first quarter.

"All right! All right! Not a bad start!" Walker called. "Kicking unit, don't give them a return like last time. You be ready to stick it to them, defense."

The kicking unit didn't have to do much. Guinn's kick bounced into the end zone. The Cowboy return man downed the ball, giving them first and ten at the 20.

Guinn was still smiling as he ran to the sideline. The field goal he had just kicked was the longest of his career. His previous best was 54 yards from when he was with New England.

I sat on the bench and drank a cup of Gatorade. I was a little more relaxed now that I had been in the game. I still couldn't wait to get back out for more licks, but I could contain myself better now that I had seen some action.

The Cowboys weren't in any hurry to let me back in. They picked up a first down at the Dallas 43 before our defense bore down. The Cowboys picked up three yards to the 46 then Rodgers batted down another pass.

"Yea, Carl!" Abraham bellowed, waving his fist in the air. "You da man, baby!"

On the next play the Cowboys attempted to pass. Allen blitzed but was headed off in the backfield. Prendergast got through and sacked the quarterback at the Dallas 37.

The crowd loved it. So did the Hawaiians on the sideline. We were all yelling as Prendergast casually got up after his triumph. He was happy to have made such a key play, we knew, but he wasn't one to beat on his chest on the field.

I took my place inside the Hawaii 25 in preparation to receive the Dallas punt. I temporarily got a case of butterflies. Things were going well for us so far but this was not an ordinary team we were playing. A 3-0 lead is never insurmountable against anybody and definitely not the Dallas Cowboys.

The punt was short. I was tempted to call for a fair catch but was too psyched up for a huge runback. I fielded the ball at the 31 and managed a mere five yards. I was actually hit right after I caught the ball but somehow broke away before being hit a second time and dropped at the 36.

We started moving again. I caught a pass on the opening play from scrimmage in front of the Dallas bench for five yards. I tried to twist for more yardage but had to settle for what I got.

On second and five Scott carried on a sweep around left end. He picked up 12 yards to give us a first down at the Dallas 47. Our crowd loved it.

Kerner was next. He caught a pass over the middle at the 43. He managed to pick up seven more yards, breaking three tackles in the process. After only three plays from scrimmage we had picked up two first downs.

Unfortunately that was where our drive stalled. An incomplete pass that was nearly intercepted, a five-yard rush and then a sack back at the 36 gave us fourth and ten.

"(Expletive deleted)," I muttered under my breath as I watched from downfield as Bender went down. I had no choice but to run off the field.

Guinn's field goal attempt this time would be 53 yards; two yards shy of his previous attempt but he came up short. He wasn't smiling as he ran off the field this time. He was looking down and shaking his head.

"It's all right, man. Nobody makes them all," I said.

"Shake it off, Eric," Bender offered.

"It's okay. You'll get the next one," Hayer assured him.

The Cowboys were moving the ball again. This drive would produce our second casualty of the game. On first and ten at the Dallas 46 the Cowboys completed a pass at about the Hawaii 35. Morrissey brought the receiver down at the 33 but came down hard on his elbow. X-rays showed no broken bones but he was finished for the day. Hamer would finish the game at right cornerback.

186

We still held our 3-0 lead when the quarter ended but it wouldn't take the Cowboys long to get on the board. A 46-yard field goal tied the game with 14:36 to go in the half.

For the first time this day we would be receiving a kickoff. Ozzie Roberts continued the role of deep man with me even though Dietrich was back in action. Walker reasoned that Roberts was younger and more durable. He also believed that by allowing Roberts to return kickoffs he would feel more like a part of the team.

Ozzie and I stood a few yards apart on the goal line. The kick seemed to be slicing toward Ozzie.

"Take it, Ozzie!" I called as I ran forward to head off a defender. I wound up throwing one of my better blocks at an unsuspecting Cowboy although it was partially his fault. As I headed him off near the 15 he decided he was going to vault over me. I had gotten down low and raised up as he leaped. I actually managed to flip him over since his leap enabled me to get the kind of leverage that would make a judo instructor proud. I was told later that CBS showed my block three times on instant replay.

By the time my judo-style block was complete Ozzie had shot past. He was finally brought down at the 31. Since he fielded the ball on the goal line he was credited with a 31-yard return.

We got the crowd excited again. After an incompletion Bender hit Kerner at the Hawaii 48. Jeff crossed midfield and was brought down at the Dallas 48 for a first down.

The following play could have sent Walker into cardiac arrest. Bender spotted Giametti open over the middle and cocked his arm. He was hit as he was releasing the ball, however, and the ball missed its intended target. It went into and out of the arms of a defensive back.

Of course the defensive back was not amused. He probably started trying to make his return before he had possession and the ball squirted out. He jumped up a couple of times to climax a play that he was going to see in his head during the entire flight back to Dallas.

Bender called another pass. This time he hit Dietrich at the 24 near the mauka sideline. Ted raced to the ten before he was knocked down and out of bounds. That had our fans out of their seats.

The Cowboys dug in. Scott went up the middle and was stuffed at the line. Kerner went off tackle for three but Bender's pass to me on third down was nearly intercepted in the end zone. It was time for Guinn to redeem himself.

This was not much more than a chip shot although sometimes the shortest field goal attempts can be the most difficult if the kicker is not in the right frame of mind. I am not sure if Guinn was still brooding about his previous attempt but he did convert. We led 6-3 with 9:02 left in the half.

I remained standing on the sideline for the kickoff. Guinn put his foot into it and kicked it all the way to the goal line of the north end zone. The return man then proceeded to show signs of another long kick return.

Actually it looked like Hasegawa was going to bring him down inside the 20. Unfortunately a Cowboy got in Rich's way and knocked him out of the play. Gilbert finally brought him down at the 34.

This game was very, very intense. That was probably because it was so close and the fact that we were playing a game which would enable us to make a very strong statement if we found a way to win this one. I don't believe I sensed this much tension among my teammates and me during our first four games.

I sat on the bench and drank a cup of Gatorade. I am not sure if it was superstition or fear of dehydration. All I know is I always drank at least one cup of Gatorade after each offensive series I was in. If we turned the ball over on the first play I still drank my Gatorade. If our opponent turned the ball over on the first play I chugged what was left of my Gatorade.

The Cowboys seemed to have had their Wheaties. They were picking up huge chunks of yardage. It was almost as if our defensive line wasn't even on the field.

But this was one of the keys to our hopes for victory. We knew the Cowboys were going to move the ball. We knew that they were going to put points on the board. Our hope was that the defense would contain them occasionally and that our offense would find ways to score and pull way ahead.

The Cowboys had a first down at the Hawaii 15 when they got called for delay of game. I was resigned to the idea that the Cowboys would score. I only hoped that our defense would hold them to a field goal.

Our defense did even better than that. The Cowboys did a short pass to about the 14. The receiver got to the nine and was hit by Hamer. The receiver fumbled and Rodgers was right there to fall on the ball. We had a first down at the nine with 6:11 to play in the half. It happened so fast and so far from where I was standing that I didn't even know that there had been a fumble until I saw the referee point toward the north end zone to indicate that the ball had been turned over.

Unfortunately we didn't do much to capitalize on the first turnover of the game. Scott picked up six yards up the middle but that was followed by two incompletions. One was coming to me but was batted down and the other fell incomplete after Bender was hit as he threw.

Jablonski made his first appearance of the game. He got off a good punt that took a bounce and was fielded at the Dallas 43. The return man got to the Hawaii 49. They had excellent field position.

Four consecutive rushing plays picked up a combined total of 24 yards. The Cowboys had a first down at the Hawaii 25. They then went to the air and wound up on the nine. It was as if the fumble recovery and our three-and-out never happened.

A four-yard rush up the middle gave them second and goal. They decided to pass on the next play but our defensive backs had the receivers covered. The quarterback wisely threw the pass out of the end zone.

Jennings blitzed on the next play. Prendergast and McDaniel also penetrated, forcing the quarterback to scramble.

And scramble he did. . . .

Right into the end zone! The Cowboys had just scored the first touchdown of the game on a play that we expected would knock them back about ten yards. I was feeling sick.

The extra point gave them the lead for the first time that day. It was 10-6.

After the extra point Offensive coordinator Mike Tipton immediately called the starting offense to gather around him. He wanted to encourage us to score prior to the end of the half.

"We've got to get downfield but we've also got to work the clock properly," Tipton stressed as Walker stood off to the side and observed. "We don't want to risk throwing three incompletions and giving them the ball back with plenty of time to score. We've got to mix in some running plays initially to keep them from focusing on the passing game. Use your timeouts wisely but otherwise don't be taking your time in getting to the huddle. Get the plays off quickly. Now everybody on the kick return unit, get out there."

Tipton spoke very fast and I am not sure he made himself understood as eloquently as he wanted. I know I wasn't quite sure of what he was talking about aside from the fact that he wanted to avoid going exclusively to the passing attack.

So did I.

I got to my post at the goal line in plenty of time for the kickoff. This time the kick came my way. I fielded the ball at the two and shot upfield. My teammates were doing a good job of blocking and I even broke a tackle at the 19. I was finally brought down at the 28 with 1:56 left in the half. It was time for the two-minute warning.

"Nice return," Dietrich said to me as he got to where we were huddling.

"Thanks," I replied although I was a little annoyed with myself. "I just wish I could have gotten us better field position."

"You did good enough. Don't worry about it," Scott added.

Bender conversed on the sideline with Walker and then reported to the huddle. We were going to start our drive with a rush.

"Three Wahiawa left on one, on one. Ready?"

"Break!"

Scott took the handoff and shot up the middle. It was a very determined effort. He picked up eight yards.

We called our first time out with 1:47 left. The eight-yard gain put us in a bit of a dilemma. Since we were so close to a first down we almost felt obligated to rush.

That's what we did. I got the call and went through the left. I picked up one crummy yard. We had third and one and huddled in a hurry, not bothering with a time out.

Kerner went up the middle and appeared to get the necessary yard. A timeout was called by the officials to measure. There was 1:05 left in the half.

Unfortunately we were still short. Rather than risk not making it and giving the Cowboys excellent field position that virtually guaranteed at least a field goal, Walker called on the punting unit. Most of the crowd probably understood but I detected some scattered booing.

Jablonski did his part. After allowing the clock to run down as far as possible he punted the ball all the way down to the Dallas 19. There was no return attempt. Dallas took one snap and the two sides went into their respective locker rooms for halftime.

I was angry. I might not have shown it but I was angry. I didn't feel as if we were playing as well as we should have.

Of course again, this wasn't just any opponent we were facing. I knew that whatever shortcomings we may have displayed were often being forced.

I wasn't angry at my teammates. I wasn't even angry at myself although I wasn't satisfied with the way I was playing. I was simply angry because I thought things should have gone better than they had been going.

All I could do was hope things would change in the second half. I made my trip to the urinal and grabbed some Gatorade, then met with the other offensive players to go over the adjustments we would make for the second half.

"All right, men," Walker called near the end of halftime. "I don't think there's anything I can tell you that you don't already know. Defense, we need you to hold them. Offense, you need to move the ball and score. You're a darn good football team. I know you can rally to beat these guys. Are you ready to do it?"

We were suddenly pumped up. We roared our responses in the affirmative just as one of the officials was poking his head in the locker room to advise us of two minutes before kickoff.

"Let's do it then!" Walker called and waved us to the field.

Naturally the crowd was still behind us. They cheered us as we left the field at the end of the first half and again when we returned. They understood that we had a tough task ahead. They also knew, as we did, that we were capable of pulling the game out and giving our best effort to make it happen.

"All right, Jay!" Marv called while slapping my shoulder pads on the sideline. "We gonna do it?'

"We are going to do it!" I heartily replied. "Let's geev 'um!"

There was an abundance of hyperactivity on our sideline. Players were slapping each other on the backs or shoulders and talking excitedly. We were trailing but we were psyched.

Working in our favor was the fact that we would receive the kickoff. Ozzie and I took our places in front of the end zone. Ozzie even smiled as we did our traditional slap five. He hardly ever seemed to smile about anything.

The kick was high and hooked toward Ozzie. He settled under it about a yard deep in the end zone.

"Run it!" I directed before running ahead to block. I spotted a white jersey angling toward Ozzie from my right and I turned to cut him off.

The defender tried to elude me by moving slightly to his left. I still got a decent chunk of him, knocking him further away than he preferred. That enabled Ozzie to move forward without the defender laying a hand on him.

Ozzie was ahead of me. I started going forward to try to catch up to him and run interference. I could see him breaking a tackle at about the 25 and continuing upfield. By the time I caught up to him he was in the grasp of two Cowboys who dragged him down at the 37. It was a good return.

I could feel the excitement in the huddle. I could even feel the crowd's excitement. They were thrilled that we trailed a team that was in the most recent Super Bowl by only four points. They smelled upset.

Bender called my number. I was to run around right end. I was determined to go all the way.

Unfortunately I came up about 60 yards short. A Cowboy defensive back and linebacker disagreed with my belief that I was entitled to a touchdown. The three of us went down together at the Hawaii 40.

It was still a halfway decent three-yard gain. Unfortunately we lost yardage when Stanek jumped prior to the next snap. Three Cowboys responded by charging across the line, hitting Stanek, Marv and Grummon. Tempers started to flare a little but the officials stepped in and quickly restored order.

And we had second and 12 at our 35.

"Come on, men! We can't afford to be making those stupid mistakes!" Walker reprimanded from the sideline.

After Scott carried to the original line of scrimmage, Bender hit Giametti at the Dallas 42. Gary was hit immediately and fumbled but Scott was right there to fall on the ball. There were a few other white jerseys and brown jerseys, including my own, in the ensuing pile but Scott held firm. We had a first down at the 42.

Scott went up the middle to the 36. It was a gutsy run since he was hit at the line. During every one of those six yards he had at least one Cowboy holding on to him. The crowd seemed to crescendo as Larry continued moving forward.

Since the Cowboys were ostensibly looking for another rush Bender called a pass. He hit me near the right sideline at about the ten.

I had to hit the brakes to keep from stepping out. That enabled a Cowboy defensive back to catch up to me and push me out of bounds at the eight. He hit me hard enough to knock me down but that was part of the game. The important thing was that I had a 28-yard reception.

And the crowd was in a frenzy! The fans were standing and cheering. We were only 24 feet from taking the lead.

The final eight yards were a little more difficult to obtain. After two plays we had a third and goal about a foot from the goal line. That was when Scott took the handoff and leaped forward.

"Yeah!" I hollered as I observed Larry coming down several inches in the end zone. My response was drowned out by the explosion of the crowd as the officials raised their arms in the air.

We ran off the field in triumph and watched Guinn split the uprights. We led 13-10 with 11:01 left in the third quarter.

On the sideline I took off my helmet, grabbed my Gatorade and sat down. There was a lot of smiling in the vicinity. We were doing a fair job of putting it to the Cowboys. Everybody seemed satisfied and that scared me a little.

"All right, guys," Allen called as he mingled majestically in front of the bench. "We're doing pretty well but there is still a long way to go. Don't lose your focus. Stay in the game."

That was the key. I sipped my Gatorade and looked at the scoreboard. It made me feel good to see that we had a three-point lead against a team like the Cowboys in only the fifth game of our NFL existence. The score would be flashed on the scoreboards of games in progress across the country and mentioned on NFL telecasts, raising the eyebrows of millions of football fans who were certain to be impressed. With 26 minutes and one second left to go I was reserved in how secure I allowed myself to feel. We led by only three points but it was far better than trailing by three points.

Of course leading the Cowboys by three points means less than leading most other teams by three points. Just ask the Seahawks who led the Cowboys by 13 points the previous week. The Cowboys were undaunted by their 13-point halftime deficit in Seattle. I should probably wait until we led by at least 33 points before I started to consider even remotely feeling secure.

Guinn kicked off. The ball sailed all the way to the goal line. The return man fielded it and headed upfield.

He didn't get far. Black made a very determined effort. He didn't even seem to break his stride as he encountered a blocker. He simply seemed to run through him before tackling the return man at the eleven.

192

"All right! All right!" I exclaimed, briefly thrusting my fist in the air. We had momentum. It appeared to me that Black's hustle would intensify our momentum.

Unfortunately again, this wasn't just any team. The Cowboys were a team who could regard such a short return as "just one of those things" to overcome. They proceeded to head toward the south end zone.

We gave them a push. Before their first snap Kupau jumped and bumped a tight end. That moved the ball up to the 16.

The rest the Cowboys did pretty well on their own. A few passes along with some impressive rushing attempts got them into Hawaii territory. Ultimately they had a third and three at the Hawaii 22.

A pass was attempted. Kupau and Jennings charged in. It would have been a sack had the Cowboys not had such an agile quarterback. He was hit hard but managed to get the pass off. Fortunately the ball dropped untouched.

"Hey, how about a penalty?" Walker called. "There was no receiver anywhere! That's intentional grounding!"

Unfortunately none of the officials seemed to agree.

"What's the matter with you guys?" Walker hollered, then turned around to compose himself before drawing a flag himself for unsportsmanlike conduct.

The Cowboy field goal unit was set. The snap was on target and the hold was perfect. The ball sailed through the uprights with plenty of yardage to spare. The game was tied again.

"Okay, the only solution is to score again," Walker directed, showing a flare for the obvious. "We're going to have to score every time we have the ball."

Although it was a tight game and I dreaded the thought of losing, I was actually having the time of my life. We had a good team and we were playing hard against one of the NFL's best. That made it fun.

The ensuing kickoff went to me this time. I fielded it at the three and shot upfield. There was space up the middle, I saw. I also couldn't help but notice an angry mob in white jerseys fixed on pulverizing me. I got as far as the 32 before I suddenly found myself on the turf.

"Okay, everybody up," the referee instructed in an even tone. "Is everybody okay? Let's bounce up and make way for the next play."

My tackler got up first since he was on top of me. The tall black man extended his hand and helped me to my feet, then whacked my derriere and joined his defensive unit.

"Are you okay, 22?" the referee asked as he took the ball from me.

"Huh? Oh, yeah, I'm okay. This is fun."

The referee seemed amused by my response. He cracked a smile as he spotted the ball on the left hash mark at the 32.

Unfortunately it was a three and out for us. We got as far as the 40, leaving us two yards shy of a first down. I felt slightly bewildered as I ran off the field.

At least Jablonski pinned the Cowboys back. He punted toward the sideline to prevent a return. The ball bounced inside the 15 and went out at the nine.

"How're you doing, Jay?" I heard at my right side as I stood drinking my Gatorade.

I turned and saw I was being addressed by Tipton.

"I'm doing okay," I replied. "I just want to pull this one out."

"Yeah, we all do," he concurred in an obvious understatement. "Are you able to get open out there?"

"Usually. They've got some pretty tight coverage so it's hard to get open by much but I do have some space."

As Tipton and I discussed some possibilities the Cowboys conducted another march toward the south end zone. When McWherter sacked the quarterback to give them a third and 14 at their own 28 we should have been able to stop them. The Cowboys were undaunted and completed a pass to the 44 to give them a first down.

By this time there was less than three minutes left in the third quarter. The Cowboys continued their drive for a few more plays, finding themselves at the line on a second and five at the Hawaii 40 with the clock ticking down the final ten seconds of the quarter.

A Cowboy running back shot around right end. He broke McDaniel's tackle, then did the same with Black. The next thing I knew he was heading down the sideline with nobody to stop him as the third quarter came to an end.

I wanted to utter every expletive known to man. I understood that these things happen in football but I couldn't stand the thought of it happening to us. After all, we were. . . .

Or were we actually the prototype expansion team? Could it be that we were destined to win only two or three games and that we just happened to get our victories early?

No, I thought. We couldn't be like Tampa Bay, Memphis and Seattle. We had something they didn't. I wasn't sure of exactly what that was but it made me believe in the team I was on.

The silver lining was that the Cowboys failed to convert on the extra point. A bad snap from center kept the score at 19-13 going into the fourth quarter.

"Okay, that's good," I overheard defensive coordinator Max Crawford uttering to nobody in particular. "The defense holds them the rest of the way, the offense scores a touchdown, we make the extra point and win the game."

194

Of course I thought to myself as I trotted out to my post on the goal line of the north end zone since we were changing directions. What am I worried about? All we have to do is hold them, score a touchdown, and make the extra point.

It always sounded so simple.

The kickoff headed my way for the second consecutive time. I fielded it about two yards deep in the end zone.

"Go for it, Jay!" I heard Ozzie direct as he headed upfield to run interference.

It was déjà vu. There was an opening up the middle with the familiar white jerseys heading toward me. Seeing a collective weight of more than a ton moving toward you at a full clip can unnerve a man. The thought of breaking through can be very exhilarating.

There were some pretty good blocks in front of me. It wasn't enough, though, since I was brought down at the 30. It was still a pretty good return.

There was a delay in the action. Giametti was down. He threw a block and the defender fell on Gary's ankle. Fortunately it was a minor problem that went away on its own and Gary left the field under his own power, getting the expected round of applause.

It didn't take long before I joined Gary on the sideline. Three plays and we were finished again. After Scott's run lost three yards to give us a third and 13 and Bender getting hammered as he released a pass that dropped untouched, we wound up having to punt again.

Jablonski punted to the 30. There was no return.

Dallas acted as if the return wasn't necessary. They drove downfield again. The drive was climaxed by a two-yard run for a touchdown with 7:20 left in the game. The extra point gave them a 26-13 lead.

"We can pull this out," I heard Bender saying to Bennici as I headed out to receive the kickoff. I was in full agreement. It was a matter of shifting the momentum back our way.

The momentum shift wasn't going to happen on the kickoff. I fielded the ball four yards deep in the end zone. I opted not to risk a runback. Not only did I not want to risk getting caught inside the 20 but we also had to preserve time on the clock. We needed two touchdowns and those were not likely to come quickly.

I began our drive by taking a pitch from Bender and moving around right end. I got to the 26 before being hit and dropped, giving us a second and four.

Scott was next. He ran through the left. He hit the hole so quickly that he had our first down without a single hand being laid on him. He wound up picking up eleven yards to the 37.

At this point we were giving those in attendance what they wanted. We were down by two touchdowns but we were not giving up. The crowd was responding with enthusiastic cheers.

We went to the air on the next play. Bender hit Grummon at the Hawaii 49. Rich easily crossed midfield before being knocked out of bounds at the Dallas 45.

Our drive showed signs of stalling. A couple of rushing plays gave us a third and seven at the 42. Obviously we were in a passing situation.

I was covered by one defensive back with another defensive back nearby. Bender passed the ball perfectly. I hauled the pass in at the 27 and was hit by the defender covering me and then the other defender. I still managed to fight my way for another two yards. This game seemed far from over.

Bender electrified the crowd even more on the next play. He hit Dietrich near the makai sideline at about the seven. Ted was pushed out of bounds at the four. It was first and goal and the decibel level continued to rise at Aloha Stadium.

A heavy rush greeted Bender on the next play. He wisely threw the ball out of the end zone.

We went back to the ground game. Kerner went up the middle but only managed a yard. It was third and goal from the three.

The tension was mounting. It seemed imperative that we score on this drive. It was partially because we were only nine feet from a score but also because we had chewed up a healthy portion of the remaining time. It was still technically possible to catch up if we didn't score on this drive but very unlikely.

And it had to be touchdowns. A 13-point deficit at this stage of the game meant that a field goal was almost equated with not scoring at all.

Bender met another heavy rush on the next play. He saw Grummon in the end zone and got the pass off. Unfortunately the pass was batted down by a defensive lineman a few feet from Bender.

I was also in the end zone but well-covered at the time. As the futile play ended, I noticed a yellow flag on the field.

The crowd roared when it was revealed that Dallas had been offside. The ball was moved half the distance to the goal line. It was still third down with a yard and-a-half to go.

Bender spotted Giametti in the mauka corner of the end zone on the next play. He fired the ball but a defensive back moved in and barely got his fingers on the ball, knocking it down at Gary's feet.

All of us were heavily soaked in perspiration as we stood in the huddle. Dallas had been heavily favored but we wanted this game badly. We figured it was now or never. The clock was stopped with 2:59 left and Dallas was certain to play a very cautious game and run as much time off the clock as possible if we had to turn the ball over to them on downs.

The call was a draw play but we lined up with Dietrich split wide to the right and myself in the slot on the right to suggest a pass. Bender took the snap and handed off to Kerner who headed up the middle. He fought his

196

way forward but came up half-a-yard short. The clock stopped with 2:53 left.

I remember my eyes being glazed as I ran off the field. It was hard to accept our hard-fought, 79-and-a-half-yard drive when we needed 80 yards. Had we scored we might have recovered an onside kick and scored again. We also might have kicked deep and hoped that the defense would force a three and out. We had two timeouts left plus the two-minute warning, but it was doubtful that we would have enough time for two scores even if the Cowboys failed to get a first down.

It was a moot point anyway. The Cowboys worked the clock and the field. They picked up a couple of first downs. By this time the clock was running out and our timeouts had been exhausted. The quarterback took the snap and dropped to his knee and the final seconds ticked away. There was nothing left to do but congratulate the victors on the way to the locker room.

Maybe it was a better game than I thought. At the time it didn't feel as if it had been such a good game. In retrospect, we were in the game up until the final few minutes.

We were simply outplayed.

At least we had two victories. Seattle and Tampa Bay both lost again. We were hoping to upset the Cowboys and rise above .500 while those two fellow expansion franchises were still looking for their first victories after five losses. Memphis didn't lose. The Grizzlies finally got in the win column by knocking off the Giants.

Some would say that victory was tainted. The Grizzlies and Giants had both been looking for their first victories of the season. Giant fans were probably certain that their team could finally get into the win column against a lowly expansion team. There was no joy in East Rutherford, New Jersey, on this day.

Except in the Grizzlies' locker room.

CHAPTER TEN
Here Come the Oilers

"The films don't lie."

That was Walker's observation as we watched films of the Dallas game.

Walker kept his composure. There were still numerous mistakes which he did not hesitate to point out.

"Linemen, you didn't protect the quarterback as well as you should have," Walker chided on one of the plays when Bender met a heavy rush. "We know that they're going to break through on occasion, especially a team like Dallas. What we can't accept is them getting into the backfield so much that they were having their mail forwarded there. It was too much to simply pass off as just one of those things."

There was no immunity from criticism for our quarterback. A second quarter pass that Bender threw that was nearly intercepted in the end zone had Walker's full attention. I was in the end zone, as was Giametti, but the ball was nowhere near either of us. The ball scored almost a direct hit on a defensive back who may have been out of position since he didn't appear to be defending against anybody. It actually appeared as if he was the intended receiver.

"Steve, I just don't understand this," Walker said mournfully as he froze the film with the ball about to hit the defensive back's hands. "You've been in this league since '62. You know better than this. The last thing you want to do is have a pass intercepted in the end zone. We just got lucky on this one."

Walker hesitated. I turned slightly in my seat and gazed at Walker out of the corner of my eye. He was glaring at the film that was still frozen.

"What I can't understand is why you were throwing in that area anyway," Walker continued after another few seconds. "Look at this. You've got Dockman in the right corner and Giametti over on the left. They have defenders with them but they both still appear to be in position to make a reception. Scott's over on the side there in perfect position for a safety valve. With three receivers to choose from why in the hell did you throw it toward the defender?"

"I didn't mean to," Bender replied. "It looked to me like Jay and Giametti were both covered, and I didn't see Scott. I tried to throw it out of the end zone but I lost my balance just as my arm was cocked. I took something off the throw."

It wasn't all negative. Walker knew that we had played hard. There were instances of second effort, breaking tackles and other noteworthy efforts that Walker praised.

"People are saying we played a good game," Walker reported at a meeting of the entire team after the films. "They're saying we played a good

198

game because they expected us to lose by about 50 points against the team that represented the NFC in the Super Bowl last January. Since you only lost by 13 points, they think you played a good game. Personally I'm not satisfied with that."

Walker took a breath. He pondered, looking into the eyes of about half-a-dozen of my teammates.

"I suppose in the grand scheme of things you did play a good game," he conceded. "Through five games you seem to have proven to just about everybody that you're better than what was projected. In our three home games you've drawn good crowds and will continue to do so as long as you play reasonably well, even in defeat. I just wonder, is that enough? Gary Giametti, is it enough for you to just play a good game?"

"No, sir," Gary replied, looking surprised that he was called on so abruptly.

"How about you, Ben Blakely? Do you come to the stadium thinking that all you want to do is play a good game?"

"No, sir."

"And you, Russ Allen. You play as hard as anybody in the league. You've been compared with Nitchzke and Butkus. I watch you pulverize ball carriers and thank God that I didn't have to face you when I was playing. Are you satisfied with simply playing a good game?"

"No I'm not, Coach."

"And why not?"

"Because I play to win," Russ replied without hesitation.

Walker nodded his head thoughtfully. He took a moment to ponder, then continued.

"That's right. We all play to win. We can finish two and 12 and point out that we are just an expansion franchise but that would be just a convenient excuse. I see this team rising above that. We can do anything we allow ourselves to do starting with Houston this Sunday. Then we go to Oakland and Denver, then come home for a rematch against Kansas City.

"After that. . . . Uh. . . ."

Walker looked toward his assistants who were standing off to the side.

"We go to Philadelphia after that," Wilson reported, showing that he at least knew our schedule if not much else. "Then we come home to play San Diego and Oakland."

"Right," Walker concurred brightly. "Then we close out the regular season in Cincinnati and Cleveland. Now which of those games are we not capable of winning?"

If there had been bookies in the room, they would not have given us much hope for victories over Houston, Oakland, Denver, Cincinnati and Cleveland. They probably also didn't expect us to do much against Kansas City since the Chiefs had already beaten us. If any of our guys agreed with what the bookies would have maintained, they weren't saying. No matter what kind of a team you play on, you can't take the field believing you can't win.

"Okay, good," Walker continued. "The key is execution. We play hard, we play clean, and we play well. The northern portion of Texas got the better of us on Sunday. We'll take it out on the southern portion of Texas this coming Sunday. Now let's get to work."

And work we did. Physically we didn't work any harder than we did the week before. Mentally we were more focused. Although nobody was willing to admit it, I believe that the week before the team was somewhat intimidated about its first ever meeting with the Cowboys as if we were a garage band competing against the Beatles. Although we obviously didn't win that game, the fact that we had the lead as late as the third quarter was a sign that we were capable of squaring off against just about anybody.

Nobody wanted to beat Houston as badly as Richards did. He wanted to pay them back for not protecting him in the expansion draft. The anger was feigned and Norm was actually happy to be in Hawaii, especially since it reunited him with his lifelong friend Russ Allen, but there were twinges of regret and resentment.

Norm played six years in Houston. During his first four years the Oilers won a grand total of nine games which included back-to-back seasons with one victory apiece.

Then the fortunes began to change. The Oilers broke even in 1974. In 1975 they didn't make the playoffs but banged on the door with a 10-4 record.

"I figured we were only a year or two away from the Super Bowl," he said in a light manner in the locker room as we dressed for Thursday's workout.

"And then Hawaii took you in the expansion draft," Abraham chuckled while dressing in front of his locker which was next to Norm's.

"Yeah, well, that's the way it works," Norm remarked thoughtfully, shrugging his shoulders and smiling. "Hawaii's a nice place to play even if it doesn't have a Burger King. At least I'm with a team that has a chance to win a few games. I think I'd be banging my head against the wall if I got taken by Memphis, Tampa Bay or Seattle. It'll probably be a few years before they start contending . . . at least judging by the way they look now."

The local media naturally wanted Norm's view on what it would be like playing against his former team.

"It's just another game," he said diplomatically. "I want to win but that's because I always want to win. There's no grudge involved."

I think he honestly wanted to believe what he told the media. Regardless, he had extra incentive for wanting to be at the top of his game against the Oilers.

Early in the week some roster changes were made. Jon Jurgens, the ninth-year defensive end taken from Baltimore in the expansion draft, was activated after being injured during the exhibition season. Kyle McWherter was waived to make room for Jurgens.

It was probably a tossup between McWherter and Kupau for who would be waived when Jurgens was activated. They were considered to be fairly even. The tiebreaker may have been that Kupau had beaten McWherter out for the starting nod against Dallas and played a solid game.

When a player is waived he will often disappear without a trace. Sometimes they are too embarrassed or hurt to face their suddenly former teammates.

McWherter was the direct opposite of that. With a smile firmly planted on his face he sought out as many players and coaches as he could to bid aloha.

I suppose it shouldn't have surprised me that the congenial Black defensive end did not depart anonymously. He was a very positive individual who got along extremely well with virtually everybody. Regardless of his misfortune, we were people he considered to be friends and he wasn't going to depart without a final word.

"Good luck the rest of the way, Jay," he said as he shook my hand. "You've got a great future here."

I admit to feeling awkward. It had to have hurt to have been waived, especially since he had played very well when called upon. I almost felt guilty for still having my job.

"Do you think you'll be able to hook on with somebody?" I asked.

"I don't know," he replied uncertainly. "When I get back to Kansas City I'll make some calls to see if there's a spot for me somewhere. If not, Walker told me the door was open to try again next year. You just might see me in training camp."

I honestly hoped I would if he didn't hook on with another team first. Besides being congenial, he had a good sense of humor. He was also worthy of playing in the NFL but lost out in this case simply because of the same old game of attrition.

We would still be short one defensive end against Houston. Gavin Pratt's bad ankle flared up against Dallas and he was out of action again. It almost made me wonder if Walker was going to lobby to have escalators installed in the baseball dugouts. Pratt would have squared off fearlessly against Godzilla on the football field but a few steps leading into a baseball dugout were much too dangerous for him.

Another linebacker was joining our ranks. James Malick was signed after being cut by San Diego. The last game the sixth-year pro had played in was the Chargers' game against us.

He had actually been waived the previous Wednesday. After he cleared waivers, the Chargers cut him completely loose. The Hawaiians flew him to Honolulu and signed him.

Malick was a good-natured Black man who played college football at UCLA. As he was getting to know his new teammates, he joked about the Chargers using him as the scapegoat for the rout by us.

"It was all my fault that you beat the crap out of us," he joked.

To make room for Malick, Vince Daniels was placed on waivers. It was simply another matter of attrition. Walker and his assistants decided the team needed to strengthen the linebacking corps. They decided the team could sacrifice one tackle. Daniels had the dubious distinction of being the sacrificial lamb.

Thursday afternoon I decided I needed a break from reality. I loved living in Honolulu and being a football player. Sometimes I still needed to break away.

I left Aloha Stadium at about 2:30 with every intention of going straight home. Instead, I impulsively exited the freeway at Likelike Highway and headed to the windward side. Rather than go into Kaneohe or Kailua, I turned left on Kahekili Highway and steered my Porsche toward rural Oahu. This area was occasionally referred to as "the country" by localites.

Ultimately I stopped at Swanzy Beach Park in Kaaawa. There was no reason for why this particular locale was chosen. It simply looked like as good a place as any to stop.

Although I had driven through Kaaawa a handful of times in the more than five years since my arrival in Hawaii, this was the first time I had ever stopped in any part of the small rural community. I sat at a picnic table on the grass near the beige wall which bordered the park and the shoreline.

Kaaawa is about 25 miles from Downtown Honolulu. It is light years from Honolulu in ambience. There was no sign of a freeway. The tallest structures I could see were two-story houses. The community was actually a fairly narrow area with the beach park and ocean on the east side of the two-lane Kamehameha Highway. On the opposite side of the highway was a sparsely populated residential area which ran to the base of the Koolau Mountains. The mountains seemed almost close enough to reach out and touch from the park.

The park was a nice retreat. Besides public restrooms and about half-a-dozen picnic tables scattered about, there was an asphalt basketball court and a softball field. There was also an assortment of coconut trees.

I walked across the highway to a mom-and-pop store to buy a pack of cigarettes and a beer, then returned to my previous post. I drank my Budweiser with the can still in a small paper bag while I drank in the sights and sounds of the vicinity.

202

Kaaawa, like most of Oahu's rural communities, had the laid-back ambience of most neighbor island communities. Honolulu, although geographically close, was another world. I took my shirt off and basked in the warm sun in virtual anonymity.

There were about a dozen people at the small park. If any of them recognized me, they didn't let on. A couple of young men were fishing, two others were tossing a football and two more were pitching horseshoes. A Polynesian woman in a one-piece black bathing suit sat on the wall and stared thoughtfully at the ocean. A Polynesian man sat at a picnic table about 25 yards away from me and openly drank from a quart bottle of beer while reading the afternoon paper. The only sounds were those of conversation, the clink of horseshoes hitting their mark or the thump of horseshoes missing their mark, and the occasional car passing by enroute toward Kaneohe or Punaluu.

I felt no more or less conspicuous than any of the other people at the park. My being in Kaaawa was an opportunity to temporarily break away from Jay Dockman, football player. That particular identity and all that went with it I could live with most of the time. I was even living up to my reputation as a ladies man with a date scheduled the following evening with a Western Airlines flight attendant. The previous evening I spent with a blonde tourist from Caldwell, Idaho, whom I met on the beach in Waikiki.

Although I might have met the two ladies anyway, my being a football player may have been something they found intriguing. For one afternoon in Kaaawa I reveled in the joy of trying to blend in without "football player" seemingly tattooed to my forehead.

Of course I loved being a football player. It was a wonderful privilege for which I worked hard.

Just the same, there was more to life than being a football player. I needed opportunities to let go and be something other than a football player. Had I been obsessed with being a football player 24 hours a day I don't think I would have loved being a football player quite so much.

The University of Hawaii wasted little time in getting back to me. When I got home Thursday evening I found that I had been accepted as a graduate student for the spring semester.

Yes, there was more to life than being a football player.

The official notification was actually a formality. I had earned my bachelor's degree not quite two and-a-half years earlier with a grade point average well above the 3.0 the university required for acceptance for graduate studies. There was no reason for them not to accept me. I knew when I applied that I would be accepted.

Still, it felt good to receive the official notification.

Saturday night was spent at Aloha Stadium. My roommate and I went to see the University of Hawaii take on Portland State. We were joined at the stadium by Jim Martinez, the Marine from my old neighborhood in Azusa.

Jim was scheduled to be separated from the Marines in January although he believed there was a good chance that he would be sprung in early December as a Christmas cut. He was planning to return to Azusa to work when he got home and then start school during the fall semester. He was even hoping to attend the University of Hawaii.

"Do you think I would get an opportunity to play football?" he asked. I shrugged and pondered for a moment as I stood on the concourse at halftime and sipped a beer. I figured that anybody who had the drive could play football.

"You've got nothing to lose by trying," I said honestly.

Jim had been a wide receiver and defensive back in high school even though he wasn't as tall as most players at those positions. He was in good shape and had technically missed out on only one season since he had played football the previous year at Subic Bay.

"You should call the university's athletic department and arrange to meet with the coach," I suggested. "He's a nice guy. He'll let you know if there'll be an opportunity for you."

"Can I mention your name to him?"

"Oh, sure," I replied somewhat lightly. "Larry usually doesn't mind admitting that he knows me."

Jim did meet with the coach. It was recommended that he begin at a junior college and then transfer after one or two years.

That is exactly what Jim ultimately did. He played two years at Citrus Junior College in Glendora and then transferred to the University of Hawaii. Although there was a different head coach when Jim transferred, he played his junior and senior years and even ultimately spent a few years with the Hawaiians after being signed as a free agent. When he was cut loose by the Hawaiians he played two years in Canada.

Obviously he had nothing to lose and a lot to gain by trying.

But that was in the future. Jim, Bill and I sat and watched the University of Hawaii Rainbow Warriors struggle to finally get into the win column for 1976. It was an interesting game with my alma mater trailing 10-7 at halftime before pulling out a 20-17 victory.

The officials' arms must have been tired when it was all over. They spent a large amount of time throwing yellow flags in the air. Portland State was penalized nine times for 100 yards. Hawaii was penalized 16 times for 186 yards.

Despite almost double the penalties levied against the Rainbow Warriors, it was Portland State's head coach who was disgruntled with the officiating. He even pulled his team off the field with five seconds left in the game. He said that Hawaii should award the game ball to the officials.

204

Gametime approached. I was ready to play. I wanted to end the day with Hawaii at the .500 mark.

For that matter, I wanted to end the day with Houston at the .500 mark. We began the day with two victories and three defeats. Houston began the day with three victories and two defeats.

I had gone through my pregame routine wistfully and loyally. Now I was standing behind the south end zone as the Houston offense was introduced. The 45,218 in attendance showed the Oilers being introduced about as much warmth as an out-of-town team can expect in most cities. Apathetic silence mixed with a few boos and a smattering of applause from the few Oiler fans in attendance.

There were actually 13 of us standing behind the end zone. Before our starting offense was introduced Jurgens and Malick would be introduced. Jurgens would be introduced because he was making his first appearance as an active player after being out with an injury for the first five games. Malick would obviously be introduced as a new member of the team. Both would be given leis at midfield.

And then it was our turn. Dietrich, Abraham, Nelson, Hoddesson, Stanek, Hayer, Grummon, Kerner, Scott and Dockman would be introduced in that order as the crowd roared its approval. We all ran toward midfield, were given our leis and waited for the final introduction.

"And at quarterback, number ten, from the University of California at Santa Barbara, Steve Bender."

As Steve jogged toward midfield the other ten of us stood and clapped while the crowd let out another roar of approval. Steve got his lei and slapped fives with some of us. We all got into formation with our leis hanging around our necks and ran our quarterback sneak to the sideline, sans ball, where we disposed of our leis.

"Okay, let's go!" I barked, slapping some of my teammates on the shoulder pads or helmets.

We were all psyched. Richards was so psyched that he spent part of the pregame hunched over the toilet. Regardless of what he told the media, facing his former team was not "simply another game" to him.

Captains Nelson, Allen, Rodgers and Bender went to midfield. With the Oilers calling while the coin was in the air. . . .

We won the toss!

"Right on!" I exclaimed, dying, as usual, to get my first licks in right away.

I stood at my normal post on the goal line. Houston would be defending the north end zone so I stood facing the primary scoreboard. Ozzie Roberts stood a few yards to my right.

The kick came. It headed Ozzie's way.

"Take it, Ozzie!" I called before running forward.

At about the time I was throwing a block into the first white jersey I saw, I heard the whistle. Ozzie had taken the kick about four yards deep in the end zone, sized up the situation and decided to down the ball. We would start at the 20.

The first play was a good indicator that we were playing to win. Bender hit Dietrich at the Hawaii 46. Ted fought for three more very determined yards before going down.

"Gain of 29 yards on the play," I heard the public address announcer report after crediting Dietrich with the reception and naming his tacklers. "First and ten Hawaii at the Hawaii 49."

The next couple of plays were good indicators that the Oilers were also playing to win. Scott was dropped a yard behind the line on the first play and then lost three yards on the following play. It was third and 14 from our own 45, compelling Walker to give an encore performance in sarcasm we had seen in San Diego.

"This way, guys!" he called, pointing toward the north end zone as we headed toward our huddle. "Try heading north for a change! You guys on the line should know that blocking is permitted in the NFL!"

Bender put his trust in me on the next play. He hit me over the middle at the Houston 35. There was a defender nearby who brought me down but not until I managed to get to the 32.

Two plays later we had another first down at the 21. Scott followed that up with a run through the right to the 12.

"Okay, Walker," I heard Scott mutter as we moved to our huddle. "We're heading north just like you said."

Scott had not been happy with Walker's sarcasm after he lost four yards on two carries. Although the criticism was levied at the entire offense, Larry seemed to feel the weight resting entirely on his shoulders.

Bender changed direction on the next play. He dropped back to pass to Grummon when he was sacked at the 18. Suddenly our second and one had changed to third and seven. We simply couldn't let this pitfall break us.

"Okay, 4 kama'aina left on one, on one. Ready?"

"Break!"

The Oilers were looking for a pass. We decided to keep it on the ground. I would be carrying the ball around left end.

I got good blocking in front of me but one Oiler did penetrate. He managed to get ahold of me behind the line but failed to grasp me securely. I turned the corner and reached the eleven-yard line before being brought down.

"First down! First down!" I heard Hayer jubilantly declare as I started to rise up.

The officials were not ready to concede Carl's declaration. They brought out the chain. The referee lowered the rod and. . . .

206

Those in the crowd were not blind. We had the first down by almost the entire length of the football. The crowd roared even before the referee stood erect and made his first down gesture.

One play was all we needed to get the crowd roaring again while putting points on the scoreboard. Bender came to me on a pass play. I caught the ball at the goal line and was immediately hit but didn't go down until I was a yard deep in the end zone.

"All right, Jaybird!" Slater exclaimed while he and Kerner helped me to my feet.

I ran to the sideline. Walker was all smiles as he held his hand out to shake mine.

"Good job, Jay!" he said. "Excellent drive, offense!" he continued, seeming to have forgotten his anguish from the early part of the drive.

"Yeah, we pulled out our compass and found where north was," Stanek jocularly remarked, getting a chuckle from Walker.

The extra point was good. We had a 7-0 lead with 10:29 left in the first quarter.

Scoring a touchdown in football is akin to hitting a home run in baseball. It is a team effort that comes about with the line blocking, Bender throwing a good pass and the other receivers spreading out the defense. Just the same, it was my touchdown. I was the one who scored it. As much as I acted humble, inwardly I was very full of myself.

It was back to business as soon as NBC stopped showing commercials. Guinn kicked off and the ball was taken at the four.

"Get down there! Get down there!" Walker hollered just in case anybody on our kicking team had contrasting thoughts.

Hamer fought off a block and headed for the ball carrier. He had him in his grasp at about the 15. Unfortunately Eric lost his grip and the ball carrier wasn't brought down until he reached the 29.

The Oilers wasted no time in playing tit-for-tat with us. They immediately ran through the line for about ten yards. The officials called time out to measure. It would either be first and ten or second and inches.

It was just short. They made up for it by picking up three yards up the middle to the Houston 42. They then moved into Hawaii territory and picked up a couple more first downs. Before I knew it, it was first and ten at the Hawaii 32.

The Oilers only picked up four yards between the next two plays. We were all hoping that the defense would hold them, if not turn the ball over, on the next play. If our defense could hold them we could limit the Oilers to a field goal attempt and still have the lead.

Unfortunately Houston was undaunted. The Oilers converted on a pass play which gave them a first and goal at the nine.

"Damn!" Walker bellowed, bending over as if he had a stomach cramp before raising back up again. "Let's go, defense! You're making it too easy for them!"

The defense seemed to have listened. The Oilers went up the middle and Allen greeted the ball carrier with open arms, dropping him for a one-yard loss. That was followed by an incompletion.

Unfortunately the next play was a completion. The Oilers executed a swing pass near the makai sideline. The receiver headed into the end zone for an apparent touchdown.

"Not so," said the officials. Black had bumped the ball carrier and got enough of him to force him to step on the sideline at the one. The receiver had already spiked the ball in jubilation, only to discover that he hadn't stayed inbounds. He tilted his head back and lifted his hands over his face in anguish.

It was fourth and goal. The Oilers were going for it. It was early enough in the game where just getting on the scoreboard didn't seem extremely critical; at least not with the ball on the one. A few yards back and they might have settled for the field goal.

I was standing at this juncture. One way or another I knew I would be taking the field after this play. I only hoped that we would take over on downs. As much as I enjoyed the challenge of returning kickoffs, the only way I would be returning a kickoff this time was if Houston scored.

The Oilers broke out of their huddle. Allen, McDaniel, and Rodgers all waved their arms to encourage the crowd to make some noise to make it hard for the Oilers to hear the quarterback's signals. The crowd was very obedient.

They got the snap off. It was a handoff through the right.
Touchdown!

I put my hands on my hips and looked at the ground in resignation. We didn't expect a shutout. It would have been nice, though, if we could have built up a better lead before allowing Houston to score.

Not surprisingly, the extra point was good. The score was tied with 5:03 left in the first quarter. All I could do was swallow hard and take my place for the kickoff. I couldn't undo what had been done.

The kick came my way. I took it at the six and headed upfield.

Sometimes a kick return can spark excitement among the crowd. Sometimes it is over almost as soon as it starts.

In this case it was the latter. I leaped over an Oiler that Giametti had knocked to the ground at about the 17. The next thing I knew I was being hammered from my right side. I went down quickly with my tackler on top of me. Jennings later told me that the play was so quick that the fans were just starting to cheer me on and then let out a collective groan almost immediately. We had a first down at our own 21.

208

I was slightly dazed; not physically but from the surprise of being hit when I didn't expect it. At least I got past the 20. I rose up as quickly as I could and huddled with the offense.

Kerner began our drive by going through the right for four yards. We wound up with second and one after Houston was called for encroachment.

Jeff got the call again and got to the 31, causing the officials to call for another measurement.

We were about three inches short. Fortunately it was only third down.

I got the call. I went through the right and managed to get to the 35. Marv and Clint did an outstanding job of opening the hole.

The Oilers stopped Scott for a gain of only one yard on the next play. As we were lined up on second down they shot themselves in the foot. An overzealous linebacker charged through and got a piece of Stanek.

We huddled up, having a second and four instead of second and nine. As I stood in the huddle I happened to look at the scoreboard. A happy looking cartoon figure appeared and then its body transformed into the word "Mahalo." This was the Hawaiian word for "thank you" in obvious gratitude for Houston's faux pas.

Bender's pass to Scott near the Hawaii sideline was batted away. That brought up third and four.

They'll probably be looking for a pass," Bender reported in the huddle. "Let's stick it up the gut. Double-single, slot right, 3 Mililani left on three, on three. Ready?"

"Break!"

The call was a draw play but in a pass formation. Dietrich was wide to the right and Slater was wide to the left. I was in the slot on the right. Kerner and Scott were in "I" formation.

Bender took the snap and headed back before handing the ball to Scott who went up the middle. Scott was hit at the line but broke away. He got all the way to midfield before being brought down. First and ten.

We continued to move toward the north end zone. Bender hit Dietrich with a pass at the Houston 34. Ted broke a couple of tackles before going down at the 28.

Scott was brilliant on the next play. He ran around left end for a nine-yard gain. Kerner then rushed to the 15 to give us another first down as the first quarter expired.

Bender ran to the sideline to converse with Walker while the rest of us changed sides of the field. I was impressed with the way we were playing.

"No way are we going to settle for a field goal," Marv remarked as we crossed midfield. "I smell a touchdown."

Whether Marv smelled a touchdown or not was not important. All I know is it only took us two plays to get the necessary 15 yards for the TD. Bender hit Grummon over the middle with a pass that Grummon took all the way to the one. Scott then went up the middle for the final yard. With the extra point we led 14-7 with 14:21 left in the half.

A hackneyed saying in sports is that "half of this game is mental." Believing in yourself is the key. At this moment I believed that the Oilers couldn't beat us.

Of course I am sure that there were players on the other side who believed that the Hawaiians couldn't beat them. I figured that they were simply being too cocky.

We kicked off and kicked again. The first kickoff was downed in the end zone but was nullified by a penalty. The newly acquired James Malick was overzealous and wound up offside. On the ensuing kick the ball was fielded two yards deep in the end zone and returned to the Houston 25.

"All right, defense. Pin them back," I directed in a low voice as I took my seat on the bench and watched as Allen, Rodgers, Jennings and company prepared to meet the Oilers in what I expected to be Houston's futile attempt to get anywhere. At the very least, I wanted three plays and a punt. A turnover would have been even better.

The Oilers decided to pass on the first play. Zanakis shot through the line and headed straight for the quarterback. The rookie from Washington State got the quarterback in his grasp. He was soon joined by Jennings who helped Zanakis finish the job at the 17.

That naturally brought a roar from the crowd. It also brought a roar from the bench. At that moment I figured the final score would wind up in the neighborhood of 60-7.

The Oilers rushed for five yards on the next play. They still had 13 yards to go for a first down.

My spirits were crushed when they completed a 19-yard pass. Their quarterback had good protection. Rodgers was the nearest defender to the receiver but the receiver still managed to haul in the pass at about the 35 and pick up a few more yards to the 39.

That gave the Oilers momentum. They continued to move downfield. Even a holding penalty didn't stop them. It was merely a temporary setback.

At third and five at the Hawaii 42 it looked like we had them contained. Allen blitzed and McDaniel got through from the left side. As the quarterback reacted by trying to escape to his left toward the Houston sideline Zanakis also penetrated.

"Get him!" I heard Walker holler above the roar of the crowd. "Get the (expletive deleted)!"

Unfortunately Houston's quarterback was of the mobile variety. He managed to get to the 35 before finally running out of bounds. That was two yards more than the Oilers needed for a first down.

The drive finally stalled. A three-yard rush and two incompletions gave them a fourth and seven at the 32. They kicked a 49-yard field goal to narrow our lead to 14-10 with 9:03 left in the half.

210

"All right, Hawaiians!" Walker turned and directed as I prepared to take the field for the kickoff. "They got the momentum on that drive but we still have the lead! Let's take the momentum right back and pad that lead!"

That was exactly what I had in mind. We scored a semblance of a moral victory by holding the Oilers to a field goal. If we could score a touchdown the Oilers would have to score twice before they could catch us.

I was so hyped that I focused on trying to will the kick to myself. I suppose I wasn't being much of a team player. I felt it was my responsibility to get us into good field position. I wanted Ozzie to simply block for me.

Ozzie may have had his own ideas. Regardless, my telepathy seemed to work. The ball was coming right to me. I fielded the ball two yards deep in the north end zone and charged out.

There was a lot of open space for me. I was regarded as one of the best kick returners in the game but, to be perfectly honest, all I really did was follow my blockers. That was actually more complex than it sounded. I had been returning kickoffs since my freshman year of high school a decade earlier so I had had a lot of practice.

I got to the 30 before I was brought down. I tried to sidestep a defender but he moved in the same direction and knocked me to the turf with him right on top of me. A 32-yard return was still pretty good.

We went to the air right away. Bender hit Dietrich just past midfield. Dietrich sidestepped a defender and got to the Houston 41 before being dropped.

My turn was next. Bender hit me on the left sideline at the 17. I was on a dead run and leaped up and caught the ball even though there was a cornerback matching me stride for stride. As soon as I had the ball he pushed me out of bounds.

Of course the crowd was not sitting on its hands. The roar of approbation was overwhelming. We were rewarding them with exciting football. We had gained 53 yards on two plays.

The final 17 yards were much more difficult than the previous 53. On three plays we only managed to pick up two of those yards. We settled for a 32-yard field goal. That gave us a 17-10 lead with 4:51 left in the half.

Houston tried to snatch the momentum away from us and succeeded to a certain degree. The Oilers returned the kick to the 20 and began a steady drive. They got all the way to the Hawaii 34 before the drive stalled. A 51-yard field goal attempt was wide to the left. Their momentum had come to a demoralizing end.

"You know what to do, offense!" Walker implored as I joined my offensive colleagues in running on the field. "We can work that clock and have a two-touchdown lead at halftime!"

It seemed so simple. It always does. It is always more complicated when the opposition has other ideas.

A pass to Grummon was batted down by a defensive back. Scott ran a sweep around right end that got us all of two yards for a third and eight. The Oiler defense was obviously very determined.

Everybody knew that a pass was in the works. I was lined up in the slot on the right. My job was to run to about the 45 which was just past the first down marker. I would be in the center of the field while Dietrich was to run to about the 45 near the right sideline. Slater and Giametti were to run similar patterns on the left side. Our only goal was to get a quick first down.

The blitz was on. Bender was forced to scramble and decided to run.

"Go! Go! Go!" he yelled to inform the linemen to abandon the pass blocking and move downfield. I immediately turned to face my defender and blocked him at his midsection.

Bender managed to get to the 43. That was still a yard short of the first down although that became irrelevant. Steve was hit hard and coughed up the ball. In the ensuing scramble the Oilers recovered at the Hawaii 40.

I felt sick as I ran to the sideline. I felt sick for myself because I wanted this drive to give us that coveted two-touchdown lead that might have been insurmountable if we could maintain the momentum in the second half. I was sick for my teammates because I knew that they felt similar to the way I did. I felt sick for our fans because they really loved to get excited when we did well. I felt sick for Bender because he wanted to win as badly as anybody and I knew that he felt as if he had let everybody down.

It was a brutal hit that Steve took. I didn't see it at the time because I was busy trying to block but I did see it during the film session on Tuesday. Steve was not the type of quarterback who would go into a slide as soon as he saw he was about to be hit. His goal was to pick up the first down and he was determined to not be denied. He was hammered and the ball was knocked loose in the process.

The Oilers obviously had excellent field position. If our defense could hold them to no yards the best they could hope for was a field goal. If they couldn't even achieve that the momentum would stay with us even though we still led by only a touchdown.

Houston did not squander the opportunity. Two first downs gave them a first and goal at the nine. The clock was stopped with 12 seconds left. They had, at best, two shots at the end zone before they would have to settle for a field goal. I had resigned myself to being satisfied with a 17-13 lead at halftime.

One play was all the Oilers needed. A pass rifled into the end zone and the ensuing extra point tied the game. There were seven seconds left in the half.

The ensuing kickoff was fielded by Ozzie eight yards deep in the end zone. Ozzie downed the ball on my direction although, in hindsight, that may have been bad advice. Had Ozzie run the ball out the worst thing that would have happened was that he would have been tackled somewhere.

212

Even if he had fumbled the odds were that there would be a mad scramble and time would have expired before either team could get off another play. The best scenario, however unlikely, was that Ozzie would have run 108 yards for a touchdown.

As it was, Bender took the snap and downed the ball. Both teams ran to their respective locker rooms. Our fans gave us an encouraging round of cheers as we left the field.

I drank some Gatorade as soon as I got to the locker room. I followed that up by eating a Snickers and washed it down with a Pepsi as I sat in front of my locker and tried not to reflect on what might have been. It was too discouraging. At the very least, I felt we should have had to settle for a one-touchdown lead. At the very most, I felt we could have had a two-touchdown lead. With the Oilers able to tie it up the way they did it also gave them momentum.

The focus had to be on what was and what could be. We were in a tie game with 30 minutes to go. We needed to be at least one point better than the Oilers when those 30 minutes expired. Whatever negatives there might have been in the first half, we had to disregard them. We were simply starting a brand-new game we had a chance to win.

"Don't lose your cool, men," Walker directed near the end of halftime after we had made some adjustments in our offensive and defensive game plans. "You can take these guys. They're a good team but I think you're even better. You can take them. Now let's do it."

We got up and headed to the field. The cheers washed over me as I ran from the tunnel to our sideline.

"Are you ready to play, Jay?" Bender asked as I stood in front of our bench and looked at the field which was currently populated only by the officials who waited for the teams' captains at midfield.

"I'm ready," I replied, glad that Bender was too mature to allow himself to be down even though it was his fumble that was the key in allowing Houston to tie the game.

Guinn kicked off toward the south end zone. There would be no excitement on this runback. The kick was downed in the end zone to give Houston the ball at the 20.

In the early stage of the second half the advantage went to the Oilers. They picked up five yards on the opening play; a rush off left tackle. That was followed by a swing pass which got them a first down at their own 31.

It appeared that we had them contained after the next two plays. A sweep around right end picked up six yards but the pass on second down fell incomplete. I felt confident that our defense would hold them on third and four.

The Oilers were going to pass. Richards broke through and pressured the quarterback. Since there were no receivers open the quarterback had no choice but to run.

Houston's quarterback was just fast enough to get around Richards. He also eluded Jurgens before turning upfield on the left side. He managed to get to the 43 before Morrissey appeared and compelled him to slide. It was enough for another first down.

"What's the matter with you guys?" Walker called angrily. "You should have had him behind the line of scrimmage! Instead, you gave him a first down!"

Walker shook his head and stood with his arms folded as the Oilers broke out of their huddle. The lambasting Walker gave the defense didn't seem to do much good. On the very next play the Oilers completed a pass across midfield to inside the 45. The receiver got down to the 36 before Blakely brought him down.

"Damn!" Walker muttered just loud enough for me to hear. His arms were still folded and a scowl was sculpted to his face.

Fortunately the drive stalled. Two rushes for a total of five yards and an incomplete pass gave them a fourth down at the Hawaii 31. The ensuing field goal attempt was perfect to give the Oilers a 20-17 lead.

"Okay, okay," Walker relented, trying not to clamp down on the defense too hard since he needed the defense fired up the next time the Oilers had the ball. "We'll get it back."

I headed out to my spot for the kick return. The fact that the Oilers were putting points on the board was not a shock to me. The Oilers were a rapidly improving team from the woebegone losers of a couple of years earlier. The key was for us to regain the lead and hold it.

As I waited for NBC to come out of commercial I took a deep breath. For the casual football fan we were giving them a very entertaining game. The game was making me queasy.

The kick was made when the network returned to live action. It was a low bouncing kick. I ran up like a baseball infielder charging a ground ball. I fielded the ball at the ten and charged forward.

At about the 20 I leaped over Giametti who had thrown a good block before losing his balance. He didn't know where I was since he was facing away from me. He started to raise up and just missed being kicked in the gut since I hadn't expected him to raise up and my foot missed him by no more than two or three inches. I got to about the 30 and was hit and hit again. The two defenders brought me down at the 33.

I went down in such a way that I was face down on the artificial turf. Had I not had a facemask I would have literally kissed the turf and possibly broken my nose. Nearby I could hear whistles blowing and footsteps coming to a stop. One of my tacklers was on top of me.

214

As soon as my opponent rolled off of me I rolled over and looked up. There were about eight players around me in either white or brown jerseys. One of my tacklers reached down to enable me to grab his hand. He pulled me up and whacked me on the rear before trotting off the field.

"Good runback, Jay," Hoddesson said as we formed a huddle at about the 23.

Our drive got off to a difficult start. Scott went through the right and was literally met by a wall of white jerseys. He wound up with no gain.

We fared better on the next play. Scott went up the middle. He picked up seven to give us a third down at the 40.

Kerner got the call. It was another rush up the middle. Jeff was hit at the line but kept plowing forward. At least three defenders had hands on him before he finally went down at the 43.

"That's a first down," I said enthusiastically as if the officials didn't agree with me.

They didn't . . . at least not right away. The officials brought the chain out to determine whether it was first down or fourth down.

The chain was stretched and the rod was set down. It came down on the rear portion of the football.

"Yes!" Marv exclaimed in a very loud whisper. At the same time the referee stood erect and pointed in the direction of the south end zone. That produced a roar from the crowd.

Our first down also seemed to fire up the Oiler defense. Scott went around right end for a mere yard. Bender then fought off pressure from the defensive line before firing a pass that Dietrich caught out of bounds. On third down Bender got another pass off but it was batted away behind the line of scrimmage. A defensive tackle then ran into Bender, knocking him back.

"Roughing the passer! Roughing the passer!" Walker called frantically from the sideline. I was about 20 yards downfield and I could hear him as clearly as I could have had I been standing right next to him. Walker had his right hand cupped at the side of his mouth while he pointed at the defensive tackle. "That's roughing the passer! Don't tell me none of you guys saw that!"

Perhaps we would have got the yellow flag had Steve fallen down. He stumbled back but kept his feet.

I ran off the field, as did the offensive players who were not on the punting team. I took my helmet off and ran my fingers through my hair. The hair was almost completely covered by perspiration.

Jablonski got off one of his legendary All-Pro type punts. He managed to punt it away from the return man. The ball hit inside the Houston 20 and took a few bounces before being downed at the ten. It was a 46-yard punt with no return.

I grabbed a cup of Gatorade and sat on the aluminum bench. I was flanked by Abraham and Scott. Almost all of the offensive starters were sitting on the bench sipping Gatorade.

"Is everybody okay?" Tipton asked rhetorically, bent over with his hands on his knees as his eyes circulated among us. "We're only down by three. We can take these guys. It won't be easy but you can do it. Just keep focused. Don't get overanxious. The points will come."

Our defense was doing its job. After a one-yard run Richards shot through and dropped the ball carrier for a two-yard loss. That was followed by a blitz that pressured the quarterback. He got the pass off but it was more than ten yards longer than the nearest receiver. Suddenly it was fourth and eleven.

I ran on the field with newfound enthusiasm and slapped fives with a few defensive players as our paths crossed while they ran off. It was an exemplary effort on their part. We stood to begin the next drive in excellent field position. We could even start in field goal range if I made a good enough return.

The punt was very high. I was tempted to call for a fair catch but my desire to put together a long return was too great. I caught the ball and looked upfield.

What I saw first was an Oiler charging from a few steps away. I reacted by running to my left, trying to gradually turn upfield in the process.

I was caught and wrestled down at the Houston 49. That meant a two-yard return since I took the punt on the Hawaii 49.

When I discovered that I had run about 20 yards for a mere two-yard gain I had a few things to say. I didn't hesitate to mutter a steady stream of expletives. My obscene monologue didn't do any good.

The Oiler defense continued to rise to the occasion. A first down pass to Dietrich was broken up. On the next play I ran through the right and got all of one yard, giving us third and nine at the 48.

We picked up a more sizable chunk on the next play. It was a pass and the Oilers knew it was coming. They rushed Bender who still got the pass off. I was a yard beyond the line as a safety valve and the pass hit me on the numbers. From the 47 I fought my way down to the 35 for a first down.

The Oilers were undaunted. They charged in on first down. Bender tried to get away and tucked the ball under his arm as if he was going to run. He was still brought down at the 37 for a two-yard sack.

Scott went up the middle next. He picked up five yards. It was third and seven at the 32.

It was a passing situation although there were no guarantees. Just the same, we did what was considered to be the norm.

Except that it looked like it was going to be a run since it was the Kalaupapa left. Bender pitched the ball to me and I headed toward left end.

216

I was nearly brought down behind the line but managed to elude the defender before firing a pass to Slater.

A defensive back cut in front of him and nearly intercepted it. He juggled the ball a few times before the ball dropped to the turf.

I stood with my hands on my hips. I kept my gaze fixed downfield. It might have appeared to the observer that I was glaring at Slater for not getting in a better position to catch the pass. I was actually staring at the spot where the ball was deflected as if I could will a different outcome to the play.

There was no point to that. I ran off the field as our field goal unit ran on. I stood and watched as Billingsley prepared to take the snap and set it down so that Guinn could tie it up for us.

It was a good snap and Billingsley got the ball down on the 39. Guinn got his foot into the ball and caused it to soar toward the south end zone. It looked like it would split the uprights. Unfortunately the ball hit the crossbar and bounced back to the field.

If I had a bad heart I would have collapsed already. My nerves were on edge because I wanted to win this game badly and we couldn't seem to get the breaks. The defensive players were giving their all. So were the offensive players but we still trailed by a field goal.

As I stood sipping my Gatorade I unwittingly found a momentary diversion. Normally I avoid looking directly into the crowd while the outcome is still in doubt but this time I couldn't help myself. My eyes happened to land on a cute Japanese girl who could not have been more than three or four years old. She did not seem to be especially immersed in the game but she did seem to be enjoying the frozen chocolate malt she was eating. As she put a wooden spoonful of her treat into her mouth I noticed that the area around her mouth was covered with chocolate. The sight of the display of childhood innocence even made me smile.

Suddenly I caught myself and realized that my focus had to be on the field. I turned around just in time to see Allen hammer a ball carrier. The ball squirted loose and players in brown jerseys and white jerseys dove into the same general area.

It took only a few seconds to sort everything out. Despite Black's enthusiastic pointing toward the south end zone, the referee raised his hand up with two fingers extended. Second down Houston at their own 36.

The Oilers followed up with a pass to their 41 to give them a first down. Two plays later they picked up another first down at the Hawaii 47.

But one play after that the Oilers didn't even have the ball. They passed and Morrissey picked it off at the Hawaii 28. He returned the interception nine yards to the 37.

"All right, rookie!" Grummon exclaimed as soon as Morrissey had possession of the pass. "Go! Go! Go!"

Suddenly Morrissey was the most popular member of the team. If we wound up winning this game his interception made a strong statement toward having him awarded the game ball. With 1:27 left in the third quarter I returned to the field with high hopes of Morrissey's interception becoming the final straw for the Oilers.

We wasted no time. Bender hit Dietrich at the Houston 42. He struggled for another six yards before being brought down. It was exactly the kind of play that the crowd wanted to see.

Kerner was next although he wasn't as successful. He went up the middle for a mere yard.

An incomplete pass stopped the clock with 21 seconds left in the quarter. We were technically in field goal range but it would be a long one. Besides, we didn't want to settle for a field goal. Our greed knew no bounds.

Bender connected with me on the ensuing play. I caught the pass at the 26 which was about a yard more than we needed for the first down. I managed to break away from the defensive back who was covering me and got down to the 14.

The crowd was jumping up and down and roaring its approval. I was feeling pretty darned happy as well.

That was the final play of the third quarter. I felt content as I trotted to the opposite end of the field. I looked at the scoreboard that hovered above the orange and blue seats in the north end zone. The scoreboard showed that we were still behind but I was confident that change was inevitable.

The heat was on. On the first play Bender was pressured. He couldn't find an open receiver so he threw the ball over the end zone.

We got a better result on the following play. Bender dropped back and spotted Grummon with a slight lead over a defender. Bender fired the ball and hit Rich on the numbers. He was hit and dropped immediately but had just crossed the goal line.

"All right!" I called, throwing both fists into the air as I headed toward Grummon from where I stood in the right corner of the end zone. I reached Grummon who had just been helped to his feet by Kerner. I whacked him on the back and ran off the field.

Walker was smiling for the first time in what seemed like an eternity. He had been scowling since about the first quarter. Now he was smiling with an outstretched hand and kind word for everybody.

"That's the way to play it," he said as we ran off the field. "Great job. I knew you could do it. That's the way to go. You're looking good."

The extra point was true. We led 24-20 with 14:40 left in the game.

I continued my ritual of grabbing a cup of Gatorade after returning from the field. I held my helmet in my left hand and my Gatorade in my right as I sat on the bench. I hunched over and thought about the game I was playing. It was a very hot game regardless of the weather. I was

218

perspiring profusely. As I stared at the ground I may have been trying to will us a victory.

If I was truly trying to will us a victory, I may have been doing an excellent job. The Oilers took too long taking the field for the kick return and wound up penalized for delay of game.

Houston's bad luck continued from there. Their kick returner fielded the kick about five yards deep in the end zone. Hamer charged downfield and eluded one or two blockers. He greeted the ball carrier at the ten and leveled him.

"Yeah!" Kerner exclaimed as he raised his fist in the air.

The second-year pro from Oregon State was not one who could expect All-Pro status. Hamer still was able to rise to the occasion and make big plays. The roar from the crowd was probably a wonderful reward for his effort.

I sat but not for long. I was simply too hyped to win this game. With the crowd perpetually roaring its approval the Hawaii defense did its part with flying colors.

Rush through the left. . . .

No gain!

Pass over the middle. . . .

Incomplete!

Pass near the right sideline. . . .

Forced to fire out of bounds after a heavy rush by Zanakis!

Houston was in trouble. The Oilers were forced to punt from deep in their own territory. We were expected to begin a drive at close to midfield.

I practically floated to midfield as I prepared to field the punt. I wanted a good return before the offense followed up with a touchdown to give us an eleven-point lead. That wasn't a guarantee of victory but it would sure make it difficult for the Oilers to catch up.

It was a good punt. It still wasn't so good that it would get behind me. I watched the ball arch up and then come down toward me.

"You've got room to run, Jay! Go for it!" I heard Hasegawa direct.

I fielded the punt at the Houston 47 and began to run. I didn't encounter anybody until I reached near the 40. I straight-armed a defender and scooted around him. I was finally hit from the side and dropped at the 36. It was a good return.

As I got to my feet I took note of the fact that we were 36 yards from a touchdown. I calculated that I wanted us to average about four yards per play. That might seem like a frivolous thought and I honestly would have been thrilled to score on the first play. I was simply thinking about how much time such a drive would eat up. There was still 13:22 left but if we could whittle off a large chunk on this relatively short drive the clock would soon become a factor.

Scott exceeded my hoped-for average. He ran a sweep around left end and picked up six yards to the 30.

An accurate pass from Bender ate up an even larger chunk of real estate. He hit Grummon over the middle. Rich was hit and dropped almost immediately at the nine.

Now the crowd was roaring as loud as it had throughout the entire game. Our fans smelled victory and so did my teammates and me.

It was Scott again. This time he went through the right. He got all the way down to the four.

I enjoyed the play especially because I threw my best block of the game. I had lined up on the right wing and ran obliquely toward Scott's projected course and hit the linebacker. I had to approach him from an angle so I had to be careful to keep my head on his front side to avoid a clipping penalty. The linebacker was so focused on nailing Scott that he didn't see me coming. I was able to maneuver him about three or four yards which kept him completely out of the play.

The linebacker seemed to resent the block. He shoved me as the whistle blew the play dead. He knocked me back a few steps and I started moving toward him to retaliate. Before I could Stanek and one of the officials got between the linebacker and me.

"Let's keep it cool, men," the official directed evenly as he held one arm straight out in my direction and his other arm toward the linebacker. "You men are playing a good game. Let's not mess it up by losing our cool."

Stanek had me in a semblance of an embrace. He gave me a couple of friendly taps on the back of the helmet and nudged me toward the huddle.

"What happened?" Bender asked.

"I guess he didn't like the way I blocked him."

"How you blocked him? What did you do?"

"I knocked him out of the play," I said in a somewhat arrogant tone. I felt as good about the block as I would have felt had I picked up the five yards myself.

A 2 Wahiawa left was called. Kerner was going up the middle. Kerner and Scott were lined up in the "I" formation. I was in the slot on the right.

Bender took the snap, and I ran a pattern that placed me in the middle of the end zone. I turned and watched as Kerner bulldozed his way up the middle. He got to the three . . . two . . . one. . . .

My eyes must have expanded tenfold as I spotted the ball hitting the ground while Kerner was in the grasp of three Oilers.

"Fumble!" one of the Oilers called from the side.

"Loose ball!"

"Get it! Get it!"

The ball was inadvertently kicked and took an erratic course into the end zone. I ran forward to try to recover it. I literally dove but it was a big club. About four or five men in either white or brown jerseys were diving for the

220

same parcel of land which featured a loose pigskin disguised as a pot of gold.

As I laid in a pile I heard a series of whistles blowing the play dead. I couldn't tell who had recovered but I knew it wasn't me. My head rested on the back of somebody in a white jersey. I could see part of a Hawaiians helmet directly below him. There were traces of movement below me with whoever it was who had recovered the fumble squirming to protect the ball and somebody else in the vicinity trying to take it away before the officials could sort things out.

It took several seconds to clear out the mess. The final analysis was the Oilers had recovered for a touchback. I can't begin to tell you how much that hurt.

One could easily credit the Oilers with causing the fumble. We could also be blamed for fumbling. From our own perspective it was a fine example of how not to play football. Turnovers committed during golden opportunities to break games open are not marks of good teams. Knowing that such things happen to even the best of teams was of no consolation. One could argue that the turnovers worked out to 21 points in the Oilers' favor since our turnover before the end of the first half led to an Oiler touchdown while possibly depriving us of a touchdown and this turnover also prevented us from scoring. For at least the second time that day we had managed to shoot ourselves in the foot at the least opportune time.

The scowl on Walker's face as we dejectedly ran to our sideline told us that he wasn't impressed with the fact that even teams like the Cowboys, Steelers and Raiders have things like this happen. Everybody prudently opted to avoid getting too close to Walker.

The ensuing drive lasted only five plays. That was what the Oilers needed to cover the entire 80 yards. They opened with a ten-yard rush up the middle. The clock was stopped for a measurement. They had the first down.

On the next play the Oilers managed only four yards. Unfortunately Blakely was cited for pulling the facemask. That gave the Oilers a first down at the Houston 49.

Two consecutive pass plays gave them two more first downs for a total of four on four plays. The first pass got them down to the 27. The second gave them a first down on the four.

The Oilers ran around right end on the next play. As the play was unfolding a yellow flag flew in the air. The play climaxed with a touchdown. I was hoping the Oilers would be called for holding.

Our luck just wasn't that good. We were offsides. The Oilers obviously declined the penalty. The extra point gave them a 27-24 lead with 7:56 left in the game.

"There's still plenty of time, men," Walker announced. "We're a resilient team. Let's get past this and pull the game out."

That was more than all right with me. It almost seemed redundant that Walker uttered those words. All of us, I'm sure, were thinking exactly along that line. It was still Walker's job to say and do whatever it took to pump us up.

The Oilers didn't kick toward the end zone. The kick was actually fielded by Slater at the ten near the right sideline. He ran forward before being knocked out of bounds at the 26.

It was time to go to work. It was the perfect opportunity if we could sustain the drive. A touchdown on one play was fine but I still preferred a drive of short spurts. We could milk most of the clock along the way.

Dietrich slanted in on the opening play. Bender hit him at the 30. Dietrich got to the 34 and. . . .

"Fumble!"

The ensuing scramble for the ball was far less dramatic than the recent one in the end zone. A defensive back fell on the ball virtually uncontested at the 39. I tapped him on the hip to prevent him from being able to get up and run. I could have leaped up and fallen on him and my frustration made such an act very tempting. Somehow I maintained a semblance of common sense and limited myself to simply tapping him. During high school, college, and pro football I never ever took what was considered to be a cheap shot at another player.

I felt sick as I jogged to the sideline. I looked up at the scoreboard and saw that there was 7:32 left. I also noticed a modest assortment of boos coming from the crowd.

Something like this will test a football player's character. The most natural impulse would have been to be angry at Dietrich. His fumble a few weeks earlier played a key role in our loss to Denver. His fumble this time could also prove to be pivotal.

But I knew better than to be angry at Ted. I was angry about the fumble but I fought the urge to be angry at him. I knew that nobody in the entire stadium felt as bad as he did. Although he had never been to a Pro Bowl, his stats generally indicated that he was worthy of selection.

How many times had I fumbled since I started playing football ten years earlier?

There was no way for me to answer that. There were too many for me to count.

Sometimes my own team recovered my fumbles and sometimes not. I was living proof that anybody who carries footballs for a living will occasionally cough the ball up.

Ted sat on the bench. Bender sat to his right, no doubt trying to provide Ted with some comfort. Ted was hanging his head with his helmet still on. Normally he took his helmet off on the sideline. I suspected that he subconsciously tried to hide from view by keeping his helmet on.

222

I walked over to Ted. I gave him a couple of pats on the back of his shoulder pads.

"It's all right. We'll get it back," I said, then walked away without waiting for a response. Only a victory would eradicate the sour taste Ted had in his mouth.

It took the Oilers three plays to pick up a first down at the 28. Two plays later they had a third and six at the 24. Their quarterback dropped back to pass.

There was no pass. Allen and Jennings saw to that. The two linebackers hit the quarterback and dropped him at the 32. My guess is as he set to pass and looked downfield he saw nothing but two brown jerseys coming right at him.

The Oilers were going to settle for a 49-yard field goal. If they converted we could still beat them with a touchdown and extra point but they would at least prevent us from tying the game with a field goal.

It didn't matter. The kick was very wide to the right. As soon as the ball was kicked it was obvious that the attempt would wind up way off its mark.

That gave us a first down with 3:49 to play. The clock was becoming an overwhelming factor at this juncture but we still didn't have to rush things. At the very least we could get into field goal range and send the game into overtime. Of course we preferred a touchdown with practically no time left but a field goal would keep us alive.

Scott opened the drive by going up the middle for three yards. We then decided to go to the air.

Bender threw the pass in my direction. I had my defender beat by a step or so as I headed toward the sideline near midfield. The pass was slightly off the mark so I slowed my pace slightly to await the ball.

My having to slow down also gave my defender an opportunity to catch up. He jumped in front of me and picked the ball off. In doing so he collided with me, knocking me down but in the process of going for the ball so there was no penalty. I sat and watched helplessly as he ran down the sideline virtually unmolested to the south end zone.

Just like that we needed two scores. The extra point was good so the Oilers led 34-24 with 2:58 left. Another shot in the foot. We were still alive but the lid on our coffin was closing rapidly.

"We can still do it," Tipton told us as the offense huddled around him while NBC showed commercials. He had to make his pep talk quick since some of us had to take the field for the kick return. "It won't be easy but you can do it. This is a great opportunity to show the NFL what you're made of. Let's score as quick as we can, get the onside kick and score again."

It was another of those talks that appeared redundant yet was actually effective. Tipton was thinking like most of us. It was reassuring to hear it from somebody with Tipton's authority.

Ozzie took the kick at the six. I ran ahead and laid a decent block at about the 15. Ozzie ran past as I kept the Oiler occupied.

Unfortunately there were ten other Oilers on the field. Hawaiians threw blocks with varying degrees of success. One Oiler succeeded in bringing Ozzie down at the 23.

Instinctively I looked at the scoreboard clock. There was 2:49 left. The scoreboard also showed that we had only one time out left.

Our first play was no help at all for two reasons. Bender was forced to scramble which used up precious seconds. He was ultimately sacked, moving forward to the 20 for only a three-yard loss but he wasn't able to get out of bounds to stop the clock.

We acted as quickly as possible in getting set for the next play. Bender hit me near the right sideline at the 34. I stepped out of bounds to stop the clock. We had a first down with 2:22 left.

Bender was forced to scramble again on the next snap. He probably should have conceded the sack and gone down quickly but that is next to impossible to ask of a dedicated quarterback. He wanted to make something happen and believed he could if he could get away. He managed to get back up to the 30 before being dragged down.

The play used up a lot of time and our receivers were downfield. There was no way for us to get another play off before the two-minute warning.

Once again I felt sick to my stomach. I wasn't conceding defeat but there was that gut feeling that we might not rise to the occasion. The turnovers appeared to be a vital difference between victory and defeat. If we didn't pull the game out it could be accurately argued that we had beaten ourselves.

Dietrich caught a pass at about midfield on the first play after the two-minute warning. He was near the sideline and saw that he had room in front of him. He decided to pick up a few yards before stepping out.

Ted was hit at the 43. He wound up out of bounds but not until after he was ruled down. The clock continued to run.

Bender tried to hit Giametti on the next play. The pass was intercepted at the 26. The defensive back ran the ball back about 20 yards before Marv and Hayer simultaneously brought him down. There was still 1:22 left but the game was as good as over.

There are few things in football that make one feel more helpless than watching the opposition's quarterback take a snap and drop to one knee as the final seconds tick off. Dejectedly I stood on the sideline and threw down a cup of Gatorade as I watched this anticlimactic drama unfold. We had our opportunities but obviously did not rise to the occasion.

It was a tough game to lose. I suppose one could say that we had improved over the previous week but that would have been faint praise. In the end we lost by ten points compared to the 13-point loss against Dallas.

224

We actually had the lead in the fourth quarter. That was an improvement from the previous week but what good was it? It is not a matter of who is winning during the final period. It is who is winning at the end of the final period.

The fact is, we beat ourselves. That is the worst type of defeat of all.

In the locker room Richards had a woebegone look on his face. He took off his jersey and looked thoughtful, then looked angry and appeared ready to heave his jersey. Before he resorted to that his expression softened.

It seemed as if all eyes were on Norm. Everybody knew how badly he wanted to win this game. Whether it was for vengeance or simply pride connected with facing a former team mattered not. Norm was going to have to take a little catharsis time so that he would be ready to go in Oakland. That game was eight days away.

And the Raiders were still undefeated!

I inadvertently caught glimpses at the scoreboard during the game. Along the way I saw that the Raiders had defeated Denver to remain undefeated. It was up to us to knock them off of their pedestal. Since our record was now 2-4 I don't think too many people expected us to do it, especially with the way we essentially gave the Oiler game away.

Walker came in with a strange expression on his face. It was almost a cross between angry and sympathetic. Tough losses like this always left him perplexed.

"Can we have a volunteer?" Walker asked.

There was a brief hesitation before Jurgens raised his hand. Walker nodded to him to give the postgame prayer.

"All right," Walker said at the close of the prayer. "I really don't have much to say at the moment. We obviously have some work to do. I honestly believe we have the makings for a fine football team here. We just need to gel and cut down on the turnovers. Take tomorrow to clear your heads and be ready to work on Tuesday. Remember that we're practicing this week at Kaneohe."

Walker took a look around at the woeful team that he had. He then left to allow the media access.

I tried to hurry out of my uniform. I didn't feel like talking to anybody. At the very least, I figured I would feel slightly refreshed if I could shower before facing the media. I was halfway undressed when Harry Lyons, a local newspaper reporter, came over to me.

"Did you know that you and Dietrich had more than 100 yards receiving again?" he asked.

I shook my head slowly while continuing to undress. This reporter was somebody I knew and liked. I was trying to accommodate him although I still didn't feel like talking.

"It doesn't matter," I replied in a subdued manner. "You can gain more than a thousand yards or a million yards. It doesn't mean a thing if your team loses."

Lyons nodded respectfully and moved on. He understood my reluctance to talk. His brevity was something for which I was grateful. My willingness to answer his question was something for which he was grateful. He and I had a mutual respect for each other.

During and after a game I rarely thought about statistics aside from what was on the scoreboard. As it turned out, I had six receptions for 107 yards. Ted had five for 133 yards.

Something told me that Ted cared about those impressive statistics even less than I did. Something told me his fumble was his most prevalent thought. The fumble did not lead to a Houston score but who knew what it prevented? I had no doubt that Ted was thinking that we might have ultimately scored the winning touchdown had he not coughed up the ball.

We were six weeks into the season with two victories and four defeats. That didn't seem very good to me.

Of course we were an expansion team, as we were continually reminded. We weren't expected to win too many games. I still didn't want to use that as an alibi. That almost seemed akin to being told we were too little to play with the big boys. I believed we were better than the prototype expansion team.

I thought about Tampa Bay as I sat quietly in my living room later that day. The Bucs, led by my old friend John McKay, were still looking for their first victory. We were two up on them. That still didn't make me feel better.

Memphis had only won one game. The other of the four expansion teams, Seattle, got its first victory that day. The Seahawks beat Tampa Bay in the battle of the winless.

At the risk of sounding disrespectful, I began to believe that other teams viewed games against the Grizzlies, Seahawks, and Buccaneers almost like weeks off. They couldn't take those teams too lightly but those three teams were not regarded as especially difficult to beat. Perhaps I was simply being arrogant but I believed that Hawaii was better developed than our three fellow expansionists. If nothing else, we proved from the very beginning that anybody who expected to beat us had better be ready to play. We had four losses but nobody was blowing us out.

Perhaps that was what was bothering me. It wasn't our woeful record but the fact that we lost games that could have gone either way. I believed we could have beat the Cowboys a week earlier had we simply dug in a little harder. I definitely believed we should have beat the Oilers. It wasn't that I disrespected the Oilers. I simply believed the Hawaiians were a team that could stand up to anybody when we weren't busy giving the game away the way we seemed to on this day.

226

I told as much to my roommate. Bill agreed that we looked good judging from what he had seen of us. Local sportswriters were generally giving us favorable reviews and the local fans seemed to like us. Still, we were winning only one-third of the time and turnovers essentially turned victory into defeat against the Oilers.

"Next Monday's the big test," I said as I slouched in a living room chair with my feet propped on the ottoman. "If we can beat the Raiders that will prove that we can play with anybody."

"The Raiders still haven't lost," Bill reminded me.

"They also haven't played us yet," I replied in mock cocksurety.

Bill shook his head and smiled although he understood my attitude. He had played football through his senior year in college. He knew that a football player had to believe in himself and his team to be of any value.

One of Bill's earliest memories of me was from late in his freshman and my sophomore season at the University of Hawaii. I was one of the most passionate believers in our chances to beat Nebraska in our season finale. Very few people were giving us any hope to even score in that game. I even heard somebody joke about simply mailing the Cornhuskers a 50-0 victory and saving them a trip.

I believed we could win. They beat us, 45-3 but I believed in my team. The Cornhuskers were better than us by a wide margin. I still believe we could have won that night in my beloved Honolulu Stadium.

It was time to unwind. After watching some television I went to the Nest to relax over a couple of beers and some socializing. Don Simmons was there, as was a small group of other friends. About ten of us went to a coffee shop a few blocks down Kalakaua Avenue after the Nest closed.

By about three o'clock in the morning there were five of us left. Don and I were accompanied by Melinda Clemons, Becky McLean and Karen Montague. The girls were waitresses in a Waikiki restaurant who shared an apartment on Kuhio Avenue. The five of us laughed and played near the shoreline of Waikiki Beach.

The remnants of a wave washed over Karen's feet. In mock anger she kicked at the water and splashed the rest of us. That started a chain reaction which had us all splashing each other. Before we knew it we had chased each other to where the water was about two feet deep. We actually started knocking each other down in the water.

I swear that nobody in our group was drunk. We were simply young and full of fun.

What made it a little more interesting was that Melinda and Karen were wearing dresses. Don and I were in blue jeans and Becky was in shorts. We all laughed as we frolicked in our street clothes in Waikiki's gentle surf in the middle of the night.

I suppose this was another reason to be grateful that I was playing for Hawaii. Had I wound up playing in Dallas it would have taken a day's drive to even get to the ocean. I was reasonably certain that nobody on the Rams, Chargers or 49ers were frolicking in the ocean in their locales in the middle of October. I was absolutely certain that nobody on the Chicago Bears was enjoying this form of recreation in Lake Michigan.

But the water was perfect in Hawaii's tropical setting. Normally I didn't swim in street clothes but a little insanity on occasion was acceptable. I suppose I would have been committed had I done the same thing in Lake Michigan.

We must have been an incredible sight for those still on the streets of Waikiki. It was about the time that the discos were closing when we left the ocean and walked the streets. We were so busy laughing and joking among ourselves while soaking wet that we didn't notice, or care about, the way people were reacting.

Perhaps we didn't appear especially peculiar. Perhaps we blended in. This was a section of Honolulu where the tourist population in ostentatious aloha attire was augmented by prostitutes, drunks, Hare Krishnas, and an assortment of other characters. What was so special about five young adults who decided to take a dip in the ocean fully clothed?

"Next time we should do this in tuxedos," Don remarked jocularly.

"Right," Karen agreed. "And we'll wear evening gowns. That'll get everybody's attention."

We wound up in the apartment the girls shared. We actually got in the shower together and rinsed the salt water off while fully clothed. The girls provided Don and me with towels to wrap around ourselves. They dried our clothes in their clothes dryer and changed their clothes. After Don's and my clothes dried we all went out for breakfast. It was about 6:30 in the morning before we called it a night.

I loved those girls. I still do even though more than two decades have passed since their extended Hawaii holidays came to an end. One by one they returned to their homes in California, Arizona, and Montana. It seemed ironic that three strangers could arrive in Hawaii at about the same time, get hired to work in the same restaurant and have so much in common that they decided to room together. There were differences among the three but they seemed more like sisters than friends.

There was never anything romantic between any of those girls and me. At the time I may have considered them too young since Becky and Karen were still only 18 and Melinda was 19. Just the same, I truly loved them. I always had a good time in their presence. Our impromptu swim in the ocean would ultimately prove to be my best of all experiences with them. For a few hours on a Monday morning they helped me to shed the facade of pro football player and simply join them for a good time. I would have had a wonderful time even if I hadn't been licking my wounds from a tough loss but I think that the fact that we had just lost a tough game made the experience that much more special. I needed to unwind.

228

CHAPTER ELEVEN
Raiding Oakland

It was about noon when I woke up on Monday. I actually smiled to myself. The fully clothed romp in the surf with Don and three cute females worked wonders. I had something positive to recall from Sunday instead of just the game.

When the newspaper arrived I checked the sports section. I saw where I was quoted in perfect context. Sometimes an exact quote will appear in a way that will give it a totally different meaning. John Lennon learned that a decade earlier when he suggested that more young people would attend a Beatle concert than go to church. It was something he should not have said. He was still taken out of context.

I looked at the stats. That was when I saw how Dietrich and I did in our 100-yard efforts. The eleven receptions for 240 yards between us did not detract from the defeat.

What wasn't especially impressive was our rushing effort. As a team we had only 95 rushing yards on 27 carries. That comes out to 3.5 yards per carry which wasn't too bad. It still didn't seem like much since the entire team didn't get beyond the 100-yard mark.

The Steelers finally got back into the win column after three consecutive defeats. They scored a 23-6 victory over the Bengals in Pittsburgh. That raised their record to 2-4; identical with ours.

Walker lowered the boom a few times during the films. Poor blocks, inept running, turnovers and a few other things aroused his ire.

"I just don't know what to do about you men sometimes," he said in exasperation. "Sometimes you look like a team heading to the Super Bowl. Other times you look like. . . ."

Walker didn't complete his thought. He didn't have to.

But we wanted to believe we were heading to the Super Bowl.

"You have two victories and four defeats," Walker reported when the films ended and the entire team was together. "Had you played just a little better on Sunday you would be three and three. Had you played just a little better in the other games you lost you would be four and two if not five and one. That would have given them something to talk about."

Walker took a breath. He shook his head just enough for it to be seen.

"You've won two games," he continued. "That's about how many an expansion team is expected to win. Is that it for you? Did you hit your peak in San Diego? Are you satisfied with an effort in games where people will say you *almost* won? Is it enough for you to put together three good quarters before falling apart in the fourth? Are you going to be satisfied with our two lousy victories even though we have eight games left?"

The room was silent. I am sure there were guys wondering if perhaps we had become complacent.

"I think you're a better team than that," Walker stressed. "If we can fix a few things we'll catch fire. I believe we can contend for a playoff spot. Is there anybody here who disagrees?"

Of course nobody admitted it if they did.

"Okay, men. It's up to you. We've got Oakland Monday night. Let's practice, practice, practice and show the Raiders what we've got. It's a wonderful opportunity to show every football fan in the country what we've got. For the first time in our history we are playing in prime time because somebody somewhere screwed up and scheduled us for a Monday night game. First-year teams aren't supposed to play on Monday nights but we were awarded a game and it's too late to change the schedule. This will be a wonderful opportunity to rise to the occasion and justify the mistake. Let's blow the doubters away."

There was an interesting column in one of our newspapers during the week. The writer expressed an opinion that the Hawaiians were much better than expected. I suppose we should have been grateful, especially since this was not a biased local sportswriter but somebody from New York. I also wasn't inclined to disagree

In retrospect, the columnist was right on. We actually were better than people expected. We had lost four of our six games, but nobody was blowing us away. The Kansas City game had all the makings of a rout by halftime, but we charged back and lost by a mere field goal.

As the columnist indicated, we were a gritty, determined team. He indicated that we came out hard and played to the final tick as if we could stand up to anybody.

"The uniforms are brand new to the NFL but the intensity and quality makes it hard to believe that this is a new addition to the NFL," he wrote.

Like a lot of people, the columnist seemed to be sizing us up almost exclusively with the other expansion teams instead of the rest of the NFL. While it's true that we were making a much better showing than our counterparts in Seattle, Memphis and Tampa Bay, I didn't want to be compared exclusively with them, especially since none of those teams were on our schedule.

More and more my resentment grew toward the constant references to us as an expansion team. I realize that that was what we were but I still felt as if we were at some level above that.

We were, I suppose, although our record was still an unimpressive 2-4. No glowing approbation by a sportswriter or anybody else can change the fact that that is a losing record.

Perhaps if we hadn't gotten off to such a promising start I might have been more receptive to the idea of being on an expansion team that wasn't expected to win more than a few games. After our illustrious debut against the Cardinals I believed that we were actually contenders. We fell into a deep hole but nearly fought our way out of it in Kansas City the following week, then came within an eyelash of beating Denver. After a convincing victory in San Diego we held our own against Dallas before our philanthropic effort against Houston.

I was willing to concede the Cowboy loss. I believed, though, that we should have beaten the Chiefs, Broncos and most definitely the Oilers. Not doing so was very painful.

Playing on a team that wound up with a losing record would not be unprecedented for me. I had played on a few baseball teams since I was eight that wound up with losing records and one of the two basketball teams I played on in high school had a losing record. All through high school and college football I never experienced a losing record.

What I never actually focused on for some reason was in pro football I had never experienced a winning record. The WFL team I played on in 1974 finished the regular season 9-11 but it didn't seem like a losing record, partially because we seemed to get better as the season progressed and we still made the playoffs. Counting our two playoff games we wound up 10-12 but had we beaten Birmingham in the semi-final and then knocked off Florida in the World Bowl we would have wound up 12-11. It was a semblance of a fluke, I guess, that we got into the playoffs but doing so and noting the overall improvement of the team prevented me from reflecting on the fact that we had a losing record.

In 1975 we were 4-7-1 when the plug was pulled on the entire league. I never really thought about the overall record since that was superseded by the dissolution of the entire league. Before the league folded I was still confident that we could wind up with a winning season. Since it was scheduled to be an 18-game season in 1975 we would have had to win five of our final six games.

Getting back to the article, it was good. It was also accurate. It also got everybody's attention.

"It was a nice article," Walker conceded during a team meeting. "Don't let it go to your heads. It's up to you to play like you are worthy of such praise. You can start Monday night in Oakland. Just because nobody else has beat the Raiders doesn't mean you can't."

With an extra day to prepare we had an extra day in pads. Our routine was normal through Friday. On Saturday we also worked out in pads with a workout similar to Friday's which emphasized both the offense and defense as well as special teams.

By working hard it wasn't a matter of working longer or more grass drills or Walker yelling louder. It was simply a matter of everybody focusing on doing their assignments as well as possible and paying attention.

Walker drove us. He was still careful not to go too far. He didn't want us getting down on ourselves but he also had to prevent us from getting complacent . . . as if anybody could be satisfied with our two-game losing streak.

"Great cut, Scott! That's the way to do it."

"A little harder, Nelson. Push it to the limit."

"Stick to that receiver, Morrissey! There you go!"

"Don't lose your poise there, Billingsley. We may need you to fill in."

Walker was that way with just about every play we ran that week. He criticized but constructively.

"I smell an upset," Rodgers remarked as half-a-dozen of us walked to our cars after Thursday's workout.

"That'd be sweet," Jennings replied. "This would be the perfect time to do it. Knock off an undefeated team on national television. That might even shut Cosell up."

"Well I don't know about that," Joseph cracked facetiously. "I got to know Howard pretty well in New York. It would take a lot more than that to shut him up. He won't stop talking until about three or four years after he's dead."

"Right," I offered. "He can deliver the eulogy at his own funeral."

"He'd better," Ed added. "Otherwise they'll have a hard time finding somebody willing to say something nice about him."

It was all in fun. Howard Cosell was the man that even a lot of football players loved to hate. Howard overall wasn't as bad as he was portrayed although he had his impossible moments. There were times when he ran off at the mouth so much that I wanted to. . . .

I gave James Malick a ride home on Thursday afternoon. He was still waiting for his car to arrive from the mainland and had to bum rides each day. We took turns picking him up at his apartment just off of Kunia Road in Waipahu and taking him home. It was several miles out of my way but I didn't mind the drive. I enjoyed the opportunity to get to know my teammate a little better.

James was a very congenial individual. He was married with a six-year-old boy and a four-year-old girl. The uncertainty of pro football, especially for somebody who was signed after being cut by another team, made his wife and him decide it was better to leave the family in San Diego until he felt secure about his future in Hawaii.

"That's the only thing I don't like about playing here," James lamented. "I don't like being away from my wife and kids but my boy's in first grade now. We didn't want to uproot him if it turns out that I'm only going to be with the Hawaiians for two or three weeks. We figure if I'm still with the team next year we'll consider moving over here. We'll see."

It wasn't an uncommon problem in football and other pro sports. It is hard for entire families to move to new locales where there are no guarantees. This is especially true with fringe players.

232

"What do you think of the team so far?" I asked.

"This team . . . is hot."

"You think so?"

"Oh, yeah. You've only seen it from the inside but I saw it from the outside. You beat the crap out of us in San Diego. Afterward we all just sat around in the locker room not saying anything. It was like we couldn't understand how we went out to play football and wound up getting run over by a train or something."

James and I had a common bond since we were both from the Los Angeles area. He was from Pomona which was several miles east of where I went to high school but was a reasonably short drive from my old neighborhood of Azusa. Pomona was best known as the home of the Los Angeles County Fair.

After I dropped James off I turned on the radio. Not a minute went by before a disc jockey got ready to give the score of game four of the World Series. The Cincinnati Reds had swept the first three games from the New York Yankees who were in their first World Series since 1964.

Quickly I shut off the radio. The game was over but it hadn't been shown in Hawaii. My plan for the evening was to simply kick back and watch the delayed telecast. Although the situation looked bleak for the Yankees, I was pulling for them to come all the way back. The Reds were the Dodgers' primary rival at the time and I felt an obligation to root against them, just as I did the year before when the Reds took on the Red Sox.

Just before I reached the Punahou Street exit of the freeway I turned the radio back on. As I maneuvered my way to the offramp I was distracted. I didn't hear the disc jockey preparing to give the score until he actually gave the score.

"The Cincinnati Reds seven, New York Yankees two."

So much for my plans for the evening. I watched part of the game anyway but couldn't get into it. Radio people simply didn't respect satellite delay.

On Saturday I turned 25. I celebrated in a way in which I would like to forget. Normally I didn't make my birthday an issue. This time I did with much regret.

For whatever the reason, I decided to let myself go. It was a Saturday night and there was no game the next day. All the Hawaiians had scheduled was a light workout at Aloha Stadium at one o'clock on and then we would fly to Oakland, arriving at about midnight, Oakland time.

Saturday was a different scenario. I didn't get into any legal trouble. My body still wound up very angry at me.

It was probably close to four o'clock in the afternoon when I got home from Saturday's meeting and workout at the Marine base. The first thing I did was put on *The Eagles' Greatest Hits* which I had just bought at the Kailua

Holiday Mart. While I enjoyed the music I packed for the forthcoming trip, drinking two beers in the process.

At six o'clock I went to the restaurant where my roommate worked as assistant manager. Don Simmons was there, as were Ed Jennings and his girlfriend Jennifer. We were also joined by Karen, Melinda and Becky; the three girls who frolicked in the ocean with Don and me during the wee hours of Monday morning. My roommate also joined us, making a table for eight.

On this evening the place seemed to be a magnet for my teammates. As I was ordering a plate of spaghetti and a beer McDaniel and his wife walked in. We invited them to join us just before Black, Joseph and Blakely showed up with Mark's and Frank's dates and Ben's wife. Suddenly the original party of eight had expanded by 100 percent.

I had two beers with dinner, giving me a grand total of four since I got home from practice. It seemed innocuous, especially since I had prudently chosen to walk to the restaurant which was only a few blocks from my condo.

After dinner most of us decided to hit the Waikiki nightclub circuit. My roommate had to stay behind since he was working. Also begging off were Blakely and his wife since they had other plans. That left a party of 13.

We hit three clubs. At each one I had two beers. That meant a total of ten beers between four o'clock and ten o'clock. Almost everybody else was drinking at the same pace and seemed pretty well in control. We drank ourselves into a festive mood but weren't especially rowdy.

The entertainers at each club insisted on singing *Happy Birthday*. That called further attention to the fact that a local football player and a few of his teammates and other friends were painting the town red. Since Waikiki is a place where the clubs are inhabited by tourists it gave some visitors a convoluted idea of what pro football players in Hawaii did in their spare time. It's not that it was unusual for football players in any city to tie one on but we defied the image that many fans had of us.

I didn't spend a single dime. My roommate bought my dinner as a birthday present. The other members of my party took turns buying my drinks.

My knockout blow was at the Nest. McDaniel decided to buy me a shot of Jack Daniels to go with my ninth beer. I didn't really want the shot but was loose enough to not turn it down. I threw down the shot and chased it with the beer.

As bad as that was, Don felt compelled to order another shot for me. I don't even remember throwing that shot and beer down. I was evolving into a catatonic state by that time. My last recollection of the night was throwing down the original shot of Jack Daniels. The next thing I knew, my roommate was waking me up at 11:30 on Sunday morning.

234

Jennings had rung up from the lobby to pick me up for the workout prior to our departure. Since the team was taking a bus to the airport immediately after the workout we were expected to find alternate transportation to the stadium. Ed's girlfriend would be dropping off Ed, Giametti and me.

I might have forgotten that I would be traveling had I not nearly tripped over my suitcase and garment bag I had left in the middle of my bedroom floor. Had I not done so I probably would have forgotten my luggage. In my severely hungover state it was all I could do to focus on getting dressed as quickly as possible and heading downstairs.

My condition was at least partially out of character. There were times when I drank more than I should have dating back to high school. Just the same, I was not one who liked losing control. I was now a living example of how easily alcohol could be abused.

If simply wanting to maintain my senses wasn't enough, the way I felt that Sunday was a strong deterrent to ever overindulging again. There had been rare occasions earlier when I woke up feeling slightly queasy from the night before. With the way I felt on the morning of October 24, 1976, making a comparison between the earlier hangovers and this one was tantamount to comparing a slight headache with a brain tumor. I was a total wreck.

"Are you okay?" Ed asked with amused compassion as he opened the trunk of the car.

"I don't know," I muttered, placing my luggage in the trunk. "I can't believe I drank that much."

Ed closed the trunk and we joined Jennifer and Gary in the car. Ed drove while I sat in the back with Gary. A cadaver would have felt better.

"Are you okay, Jay?" Jennifer asked.

I shrugged my shoulders.

"You really tied one on last night," Gary observed, having already been filled in. "I wish I'd been there."

"I wish I hadn't been," I replied dryly.

My tone was somewhat angry but I was angry only at myself. It was a lesson to be learned, at the very least. Nobody forced me to drink as much as I did. I made my decision on my own.

"I blame the University of Hawaii football team," I muttered, taking a faint stab at humor.

"Why would you blame them?" Gary asked.

"Because they had a bye last night," I replied. "If they'd played I probably would have just gone to the game."

We pulled into the Aloha Stadium parking lot and stopped near the bus that was parked adjacent to the main box office. We handed our luggage to the attendants who would put our luggage on the bus that would eventually transport the team to its waiting aircraft a few miles away.

235

When I got to the locker room I realized that virtually the entire team knew about my inebriate experience. Something in everybody's face told me that was true. I found out later that Black and Joseph wondered out loud with most of the rest of the team present whether I would even show up.

McDaniel came up to me as I put on my workout clothes. For a light workout my attire was comprised of blue gym shorts, a Los Angeles Dodger T-shirt and cap, and my shoes and socks.

"How are you feeling?" he asked softly.

"Like I've been poisoned," I replied facetiously.

"I can understand. I'm not feeling too good myself. I've never had that much to drink in my life."

I hadn't thought about it until that moment. Jim's indulgence must have taxed his system in unprecedented fashion. The defensive end was considered to be a veritable teetotaler compared to many of the rest of his teammates. Jim was the type of have a beer or two on occasion. Three beers in the same day was considered a media event. His consumption the night before was considered completely out of the realm of possibility.

"Everybody seems to know about last night," I said as Jim and I emerged from the tunnel to the field.

"That's because it was you," he said. "Everybody has seen you have a few beers but nobody ever saw you get smashed. If it had been some of these other guys nobody would have even thought twice about it."

Jim's remark alleviated some of the embarrassment but not the hangover. That was going to be around for a little while.

"I'm really sorry about buying you that Jack Daniels."

"Well you may have bought it but you didn't force me to drink it. I did that all by myself."

Jim shrugged with an embarrassed smile. He said he was almost glad that we were going away for a week. That would give his wife an opportunity to get over the night before.

"Valerie's really ticked off at me for drinking as much as I did," he said. "It'll take her the entire week to forget about it."

"But she drank as much as you did, didn't she?"

Jim shook his head.

"She switched to Pepsi after we left the restaurant."

Jim said his wife had had such a good time that she hadn't been aware of how much he had been drinking. It wasn't until after they had gotten home to their condo on Keoniana Street in Waikiki that she noticed. The first thing he did when they got home was go to the bathroom to toss his cookies.

It was a light workout. For that I was eternally grateful. We ran through some plays, sans pads, at half-speed. Based on what I was capable of doing that day that was probably full speed for me.

236

On one of our pass plays Bender slightly missed the mark. In a game or even a full contact workout I would have dove for the ball. In a half-speed drill I wasn't about to do that, especially on artificial turf. I got my fingertips on the ball but that was all.

Hasegawa was defending against me on the play.

"Pretend it's a bottle of Jack Daniels," he remarked jocularly as we jogged back to the line. "That way you'll never miss it."

I assumed the coaches also knew. They didn't say anything but I was sure that they knew. They had been around and knew that football players, as well as coaches, knew how to drink. They were probably grateful that nobody got arrested or into an accident.

How I envied the team's two LDS members; Hoddesson and Billingsley. I don't know what they did the night before but it was definitely more wholesome than what I did. I began to realize that there were many other ways I could have had fun without doing something that would make me forget how I got home and wake up feeling like I had slept in the sewer. It just wasn't worth it.

The shower after the workout was refreshing. The bus ride to the airport was not. I was very uncomfortable.

During the flight to Oakland I ate for the first time that day. I did a lot of reading to keep my mind off of the way I felt.

Jennings was sitting next to me. I declined his suggestion that I have a beer.

"Nothing cures a hangover better than beer," he said.

At the time I also believed that myth although I still refused to drink a beer. At that juncture I didn't care if I never touched another drop of alcohol. The strongest thing I drank during the flight was coffee.

I got up at about 8:30 on Monday morning. It was one of those times when I was initially taken aback by the strange surroundings before I realized that I was in Oakland. That had nothing to do with my alcohol consumption. It was simply one of the hazards of frequent travel.

After I showered I went downstairs for a modest breakfast. I was still queasy but not to the extreme of the previous day.

I spent the rest of the morning in my room. To pass the time I read more of *Shogun* and watched television. I went down for the pregame meal at 1:30.

As evening approached I was ready to play. So was the rest of the team. We were hyped to take on the undefeated Oakland Raiders.

We were not quite at full strength. Pratt was out again. McWilliams was at full strength and would be starting at right outside linebacker. That relegated Zanakis to backup duty even though he had played well against Houston.

It was going to be a cool night. That was to be expected in northern California in late October. It would be cool and even cold but not frigid.

I stood on the sideline and watched and listened as our starting defense was introduced. Each name produced the expected result.

"At left end," came the voice over the public address system, "number 82, from Maryland, Jim McDaniel."

Jim ran to the gathering post at midfield near our sideline. The expected boo birds were out to give my teammates Oakland's version of the aloha spirit. Had any of our players received something more congenial we would have wondered if the entire world had gone mad.

It may have been my imagination but it seemed to me that McDaniel got the loudest boos of everybody. It may have been because he was the first one introduced and some of the fans lost interest in the booing after the initial salutation. More likely it was McDaniel's status as a former Raider. It was as if the fans were playfully accusing him of treason by being taken in the 12th round of the expansion draft as if it was his idea to be left unprotected.

As our captains took midfield to lose the toss my body continued to remind me that less than 48 hours earlier I embarked on the worst drunk of my life. At the moment I was about to make my debut on Monday Night Football.

"How're you feeling, Jay?" Bennici asked as he stood beside me.

That was a typical question a coach would ask a player when a game was about to begin. Still feeling queasy and ashamed of myself, I naturally wondered if he was asking me if I was still hung over.

"Ready to go," I replied smartly. "Let's beat these guys."

Bennici grinned and smacked me on the back. He went over to Grummon a few feet away to inquire about his state of mind and body.

The Howard Cosell Show was officially on the air. Guinn approached the ball that was teed up on the 35 and put his foot into it. The ball hit about three yards deep in the end zone and rolled out for a touchback. The Raiders would have a first and ten at the 20.

I figured the Raiders would move the ball. Our defense was primed to play but a first down or two was inevitable. I sat on the bench to await my turn. If I didn't take advantage of an opportunity like this I would wear myself out. I would get my rush of adrenalin when I took the field.

The Raiders did pretty much what I expected them to do. They actually picked up four first downs by picking away. After a four-yard run that gave them a second and six at the Hawaii 34 our defense dug in.

A sweep around right end failed. McDaniel fought off a block and rudely greeted his former teammate with a one-yard loss.

This was obviously a pass situation although there are times when an offense will do the unexpected. With Oakland's Hall of Fame caliber quarterback Ken Stabler still in his prime the Raiders went by the book.

What the Raiders didn't count on were Jurgens and Jennings. They both converged on Stabler. They simultaneously hammered him as he released the ball. The ball dropped untouched to create a fourth and five at the 35.

"All right! All right!" I cheered, jumping to my feet. "That's the way to go, guys!"

It was field goal time. I was willing to concede the three points if we had to. I was hoping that our ability to shut down their drive would shift the momentum to our corner. I figured it could have a demoralizing effect on the Raiders although I knew better. If the Raiders were the type of team to surrender after a single drive fell short they would not be undefeated.

The Raider placekicker got the kick off. It was a line drive that appeared to be low.

"Short! Short! Short!" I heard Kerner holler.

The kick appeared to be short. Then it hit the crossbar and bounced over. It wasn't quite short enough. The Raiders had an early 3-0 lead.

"Okay, men! That's good enough!" Walker called. "Let's take the lead now!"

Walker's optimism would have produced snickers from the majority of the millions watching ABC at that moment. At this juncture of our existence we had proven only that we only won one-third of the time. Although we had lost to Kansas City and Denver by three points apiece and had played tough against the Cowboys and Oilers, the standings still showed that we had only two victories to go with our four defeats and were tied with the Chiefs for last place in the AFC West. Oakland was at the top of that same division with an undefeated record. The naysayers would wonder who Walker thought he was to believe we could actually lead against the Raiders, let alone beat them.

I wasn't a naysayer. I stood on the goal line in anticipation of my first taste of action against a team I admired. During my WFL days I actually became a Raider fan. I watched them on TV on several occasions and admired their apparent invincibility. The Raiders presented a challenge to my teammates and me that I felt determined to meet.

Unfortunately the kickoff produced very little excitement. I caught the kick about seven yards deep in the end zone. I wasn't going to rise to any occasion if I played stupidly. I downed the ball immediately, taking note of a very determined group in silver and black heading my way.

One play does not a game make.

Thank God for that. The first play from scrimmage went nowhere. Kerner went through the left and was rudely greeted at the line for no gain.

I didn't fare much better on the next play. I went around right end and picked up a whopping two yards. I resisted the urge to utter a stream of expletives as I rose up from the grass.

"Penalty marker on the play," I heard the public address announcer report.

Oakland was offsides. It was one of their defensive linemen on their right side; somebody who didn't figure in the outcome of the play. The first mistake of the day gave us a second and five instead of a third and eight.

Whether the faux pas fired us up is unknown. We were fired up anyway so the outcome of the next play might have been the same. Bender found Grummon near the left sideline. Rich caught the ball cleanly before the angle he was running caused him to run out of bounds at the Hawaii 45.

"All right! Now we're moving," Bender exclaimed under his breath as we huddled on the 35.

Steve called a 3 Wahiawa left. "On two, on two. Ready?"

"Break!"

Bender took the snap and handed off to Scott. Larry was hit at the line but broke free. He wasn't brought down until he had crossed midfield and reached the Oakland 48.

"Good effort, Larry! That's the way to go!" Walker hollered from the sideline to our left.

Larry managed only one yard on the next play to give us a third and two. My number was called next.

The play was a 4 Waikiki left. It was a trap. Stanek was going to pull to the left and I was to run right through the now-unprotected area. I would either find a hole because the linebacker was suckered into following the guard or I would be met by that same ravenous linebacker who would be drooling at such a golden opportunity.

Fortunately the linebacker keyed on Stanek. I don't mind admitting to a certain amount of apprehension as I awaited the snap. I was very, very careful not to give anything away as I lined up on the right wing and went into motion on cue before taking the handoff.

I did get hit but not until I picked up four yards to the 43. It was another first down for us.

As happy as I was to pick up the first down, I hoped that Bender and Walker knew better than to call the same play twice. At the very least, I hoped a couple of quarters would pass before the play was called again to give the linebacker time to forget that he'd been burned.

Better still, don't call it again for at least six days. That way we would be in Denver where a different linebacker would be primed to get burned . . . unless he was taking notes while ABC showed half-a-dozen replays of the Oakland linebacker getting burned.

It may have been a stroke of genius that a 3 kama'aina left was called. This was a power sweep around left end. Stanek would pull to the left again but the linebacker was expected to be slower to react after being burned on the previous play.

The play worked pretty well. Scott picked up six yards to the 37. The linebacker, as projected, held back and did not figure in the outcome of the play except by his absence.

240

We continued to move toward our objective. Our linemen were doing an outstanding job of blocking. That enabled Kerner to rush for six yards to get us another first down at the 31.

A quick short pass was next on the agenda. Bender hit Slater two yards beyond the line at the 29. Slater scrambled for an additional nine yards to give us our second first down on as many plays at the 20.

After an incompletion Scott went up the middle. He picked up roughly ten yards, covering half the distance to the goal.

It was too close to call. The officials brought out the chain. Had Scott's gain been about two inches shorter it would have been second down. Instead we had another first down just inside the ten.

We knew that the closer we got to the goal line, the tougher they were going to make it for us. The key was to overcome their determination with our determination. Thus far we were making a pretty good impression during our maiden appearance on Monday Night Football.

Scott went up the middle and managed only a yard. I decided to be optimistic and think of it as being a yard closer to our objective. Thinking that we had made "only one yard" seemed too pessimistic.

My positive thinking didn't do much good. Bender tried to hit Grummon with a pass. The ball was batted in the air by a defensive lineman and a linebacker picked it off at the seven.

A roar went up from the crowd although I wasn't focused on that. I was only about a yard or two behind the linebacker when he began moving upfield. I caught him and brought him down at the 12.

I did my job but there was no satisfaction in that. We had put together an impressive drive of 71 yards.

Unfortunately we had needed to travel 80 yards. When the drive was over we still trailed by three with 3:37 left in the first quarter. I was feeling pretty darn bad and it had nothing to do with my hangover.

I contained my frustration as I ran to the sideline. Dating back to high school, I was in my eleventh season. A three-point deficit late in the first quarter was hardly insurmountable. Given the end result of our drive, I wondered if what the entire country thought was true. Could it be that we were simply a lowly expansion franchise with no right to expect more than modest success on occasion? Was it impossible for such a team to beat a team like the Raiders?

"Let's go!" I called as I reached the sideline, not willing to concede. "Let's not get down!" I continued, slapping my teammates on the shoulder pads regardless of whether they were my offensive colleagues, defensive substitutes, the kicker or punter. "We can beat these guys! Let's believe in ourselves!"

I was hyped again. I hoped that I had everybody else thinking positive.

The Raiders began a drive. They picked up a first down at the Oakland 25.

On the ensuing play the Raiders completed a pass at the 37. Morrissey hit the receiver who immediately dropped the ball. Allen was just arriving and wasted no time in falling on it.

"Yeah!" I exclaimed, leaping to my feet and running on the field as I put my helmet on. I didn't even wait for the signal for our first down which came after I had left our sideline.

"Offense, let's go!" I heard Walker call redundantly. Half of the offense was already on the field.

Coach John Madden was livid. He insisted that the receiver did not have possession and the play should have been an incomplete pass. Their argument was in vain in the days before instant replay. I heard later that replays shown by ABC proved that the officials made the right call. It simply wasn't the call the Raiders wanted.

We had to put together a drive of 37 yards. The Raiders let us know from the very first snap that we were going to have to earn every inch of that yardage. Scott was met by a silver and black brick wall up the middle on the first play.

I was the next Hawaiian masochist. I went through the right and managed to pick up three yards before being hammered.

"We can get the first down. We can go all the way on this drive and we can win this game," Bender told us in the huddle before calling the play.

I played a major role in Bender's prophecy coming true. I ran a slant and caught the ball at the 28. I was hit immediately but not so decisively that I went down right away. I managed to fight for two more yards to pick up a first down at the 26.

The whistles were blowing and I was satisfied with myself. I knew that there were ten other players on the field who played a major role in my eight-yard gain but I felt as if I had done an exemplary job. Picking up the final six feet of that play came as a direct result of a gritty effort. That effort was the difference between a first down and having the field goal unit running on.

From the time we took the field after the fumble recovery I was very intent on getting the ball in the end zone. Since it was only the first quarter we didn't have to be watching the clock. I was taken by surprise when I learned that the quarter had ended.

It was first and ten at the 26. As far as I was concerned it was first and goal at the 26. My mind was made up that it wouldn't be enough to tie the game. Every point is always critical, especially when playing a team like the 1976 Raiders. This expansion franchise was not playing to simply avoid embarrassing itself. We were playing to win.

Of course the Raiders were also playing to win. On the opening play of the second quarter Giametti caught a pass a yard beyond the line of scrimmage. He was hit and dropped immediately.

242

I suppose the Raider defensive effort was impressive but not impressive enough. Bender hit Grummon with a pass at the five near the left sideline. Grummon took a couple of steps and then dove into the end zone just before a defensive back could take a shot at him.

Grummon bounced up and held his hands over his head. He was either signaling a touchdown or simply raising his arms in triumph with the ball in his right hand. He then spiked the ball.

Almost the entire offense converged on Grummon and then headed to the sideline. It was a moment of jubilation. We knew that if we continued to execute we could win.

To hell with the oddsmakers! We were feeling almost completely invincible at the moment.

The extra point made it 7-3. There was 14:18 left in the half.

"There's a long way to go," Tipton reminded us after he got the offensive unit sitting together. He walked up and down the bench, looking each of us in the eye as he passed. "I want to remind you of how good a team we are. Two weeks ago against Dallas we had the lead in the third quarter. Last week against Houston we had the lead in the fourth quarter. Let's take it over the top this time. If the defense does its job and you guys do your job there is no reason why we can't do it."

Mike paused. He looked up and down the bench with a very determined look on his face.

"This is what I want and what I hope you guys want," he continued before raising his voice a few notches. "When the fourth quarter is over I want for us to be holding that lead! You can do it! This is our game to win!"

Mike was so wrapped up in his talk that I felt as if he was even heard across the bay in San Francisco. He was, it turned out, as well as all across the country. ABC came back from commercial and the kickoff had taken place before the sideline camera and microphone featured Mike. His last couple of sentences were seen and heard in every home that had Monday Night Football on.

The lower rows of seats behind our bench even caught Mike's passionate address. There were a few catcalls and expletives sent our way.

Nobody responded to them. It was fairly amusing.

Our kickoff had been fielded at the eight. The Raiders return man initially had difficulty handling the ball. He still managed to get to the 29 before Hamer brought him down. Eric was proving himself to be a very valuable man to have on special teams.

The first play from scrimmage picked up five yards. Rodgers made the tackle but it was a costly stop. When he got up he was limping. He twisted his foot as he went down.

Rodgers limped off the field. He was taken to the locker room for X-rays and treatment. Hasegawa was sent in.

The Raiders went to the air on the next play. Hasegawa got his hands dirty when he tackled the receiver at the Hawaii 49.

I can't say that they were deliberately keying on Hasegawa. If they were it was a mistake on their part although it is natural to test a defensive back entering the game as a substitute. They tested him again and the end result of the next play was that Hasegawa had broken up a pass.

Of course the Raiders were not a team to raise the white flag. After a four-yard gain on the ground they got a ten-yard completion to the Hawaii 35 for another first down.

I was getting nervous. I looked at the scoreboard to catch a glimpse at our 7-3 lead. I wanted to hold that lead.

Our defense wanted to hold the lead as well. The Raiders tried running around right end and were rudely greeted by McDaniel, their former teammate. They should have considered themselves lucky to have gotten one yard.

They went to the air next. Blakely was in perfect position inside the 20 to break the pass up. He looked like a volleyball player spiking the ball over the net.

The next play ended their hopes for even a long field goal. Richards broke through quickly. Stabler saw him coming as he was getting set to pass but didn't have the mobility to elude Norm. Norm sacked him at the Oakland 42. It was fourth and 17.

"Punt return team!" Walker called.

I returned to the field. I wanted to have my first ever punt return for a touchdown. Although I had had some pretty impressive punt returns, I had never returned one for a touchdown even in high school. I decided that this was the perfect time for that.

But I also knew it was very unlikely against this team. The Raiders had one of the best punters in the NFL. He was going to punt it away from me.

And that is exactly what he did. The ball came down near the left sideline. I watched helplessly as it went out of bounds at the six.

I stood in the end zone and waited for the rest of the offense to huddle up. I figured if we could go the full 94 yards it still would not have a severe deflating effect on a team like the Raiders. It might have a deflating effect on their fans.

That included one acquaintance of mine in Honolulu. He liked the Hawaiians but had been a Raider fan since the beginning of their tenure in the American Football League. He lived and died with the Raiders the way I lived and died with the Dodgers. I wanted this guy to have a very miserable night.

"We're going for six," Bender instructed us in the huddle. "We're going the entire 94 yards. We'll eat up a lot of the clock in the process."

On the first two runs by Kerner and Scott, respectively, we managed six tough yards. The Raiders dug in on third and four.

244

The Raiders might have been looking for a pass. We didn't bother accommodating them. Scott swept around left end for seven yards and a first down at the 19.

We mixed up our plays and picked up a couple more first downs. We were proving to the world that we could move the ball against the Raiders but that wasn't proving much. We still had only a four-point lead and needed to add to it before we could think about having proven anything.

On first and ten from our 36 Bender dropped back and was met by heavy pressure. He was hit as he got the pass off and the ball went off course. A Raider defensive back was the first to the ball and seemed to have an interception. He juggled it a couple of times and then lunged forward as the ball was batted in front of him. The ball hit the ground just before he did. He laid face down for a second and then pounded his fists a few times.

We crossed midfield on the next play. Bender hit me near the right sideline at the 47. I was hit as I caught the ball but managed to hang on as I went down.

Scott went through the right for a paltry two yards on the next play. I followed with a sweep around left end. With an escort of Stanek, Marv and Kerner I picked up seven yards to give us a third and one at the 38.

We were where Guinn was capable of kicking a field goal but that was not what we were after. We were a new team that wasn't expected to do much but we were thinking like champions. Our goal was a touchdown. We had gone 56 yards and would not be satisfied if we settled for less than the remaining 38. We could also run out the majority of the clock before halftime.

Scott foiled our hopes to run out the clock on the next play although nobody on our side was unhappy about that. He went up the middle, broke a couple of tackles and continued toward the end zone. He was finally brought down at the 14. It was a 24-yard gain.

I had thrown a good block on the play. I didn't knock my man down but I held him back long enough to prevent him from making a tackle. He was actually so angry that he called me a few things that I won't list. It was actually an honor to have made him that angry. It clearly showed which side was winning and possessed the momentum.

One more play was all we needed. Danny Edwards came in at fullback and caught a pass at the six. The rookie lunged over for our second touchdown of the night. With the extra point we had a 14-3 lead with 2:36 left in the half.

"I love it! I love it!" Marv remarked on the sideline, slapping fives with every player he could find. "This team can stand up to anybody! Let's keep it up!"

Walker turned around. He looked like he wanted to remind us that there was still an entire half to go against what was one of the best teams in the NFL, then seemed to think better of it. I suppose he probably understood that we were simply hyped to play and not declaring a premature victory. We believed in ourselves but we weren't being cocky.

Guinn's kick was deep in the end zone. It was downed to give Oakland a first down at the 20.

We were in our nickel formation. We were still without Rodgers. Otherwise we would have been in our dime formation.

Oakland completed two passes before we got to the two-minute warning. They had a first and ten at their own 41. They, naturally, were going to try to score a touchdown while eating up the clock.

Blakely was the star of the next play from scrimmage. A pass over the middle near midfield was swatted away by him.

Oakland was undaunted. The Raiders completed a pass at the Hawaii 40 for a first down. They completed another pass at the 27 for another first down.

Blakely was the star again on the next play although this time for the other team. He broke up a pass at the 16. Unfortunately he was called for pass interference. Oakland had another first down.

Our defensive line dug in. By pressuring Stabler, they forced two incompletions. Augmenting the defensive line's effort was the effort of our defensive backs who didn't allow the receivers to get open. We had them covered even though we reverted back to our standard defense once they reached the 16.

On third down our defense rose to the occasion again. There was nobody open and Stabler was under heavy pressure. Prendergast got his arms around him and prevented him from being able to throw the ball away. A split-second later McDaniel arrived to finish the job, sacking Stabler for a ten-yard loss.

Oakland was going to have to settle for a field goal. The Raiders were going to run as much time off the clock as they could first to keep us from being able to put together a drive.

"Call time out! Call time out!" Walker frantically yelled, holding his hands over his head in shape of a T to get somebody's attention.

Suddenly Allen gestured with his hands for a time out. The referee waved his hands over his head to stop the clock. There were 47 seconds left in the half. Not only would that give us time to put together a fast drive but it would also give the Oakland placekicker an opportunity to think about what was expected of him. We hoped it would give him time to start thinking negatively.

We didn't quite achieve our objective. The kicker converted on the 33-yard attempt, stopping the clock at 43 seconds. McWilliams took quite a shot when he charged in to attempt to block the kick. He was very slow to get up and had to be helped off the field but wound up all right.

"Don't try to run it back if it winds up in the end zone," special teams coach Ken Holcomb instructed Ozzie Roberts and me before we headed to

246

the field for the kickoff. He's probably going to squib it but if he kicks it hard enough it should go all the way to the end zone. Just down it or let it go out of bounds. That way we pick up 20 yards without any time running off the clock."

My ego meant that I was disappointed. I wanted to have a big return but Holcomb was right. We needed the yardage but we needed to use the clock wisely in order to get those yards.

As Holcomb predicted, it was a squib kick. He kicked it hard and it bounced at such an angle that it headed toward the sideline to my right. It passed the pylon into the end zone before it went out of bounds. We still had those 43 seconds and two timeouts.

Our receivers couldn't get open on the first play. Bender was under moderate pressure. He threw the ball downfield to prevent an interception and stopped the clock with 36 seconds left.

Bender hit me on the next play on the 31. It was over the middle but I had a little room to run. I was finally wrestled down at the 40 and immediately called time out. There were 26 seconds left.

Bender hit me again on the next play. This time it was at the right sideline at the Oakland 37. I stepped out of bounds and stopped the clock with 18 seconds left.

Giametti was next. Bender hit him near the left hashmark at the 21. Gary was brought down in bounds at the 14.

"Time out! Time out!" everybody in a white jersey seemed to call once we realized the clock was still running.

The officials waved their hands over their heads. The clock finally stopped with three seconds left.

I ran off the field as the field goal unit ran on. It was a cool night in Oakland but we were sweating profusely. I believe we were playing as hard as we had played all season. After two consecutive tough losses we really wanted this game.

Guinn's kick went through the uprights. The half ended with us holding a 17-6 lead thanks to our ability to move 66 yards in 40 seconds, leaving enough time for a lead-extending field goal. We ran off the field amid a chorus of boos that may have been levied against the Raiders. Either way, we loved it.

There were still 30 minutes to play. I was very aware of that. We led Dallas at halftime and lost. We were tied with Houston at halftime and lost. The only advantage we had over Oakland that we didn't have over the Cowboys and Oilers was that the Raiders would need to score twice to overtake us. We also knew that the Raiders were more than capable of doing exactly that.

I still felt pretty good about what we were doing. I felt so good that I almost forgot that I began the game with a hangover from two nights earlier. I think I had finally sweated out the physical effects of my overindulgence. I was still pretty ashamed of myself but tried to put it behind me.

Rodgers was running in place in the locker room. That was a good sign. The X-ray was negative and there was no other discernable damage. A shot for the pain had him ready for the second half.

Scott had had a good performance and appeared primed for a 100-yard game. He had carried eleven times for 63 yards.

My stats were not bad. I had rushed three times for 14 yards. I had also caught four passes for 68 yards.

"One half is over," Walker told us just before we were to return to the field. "One half is not the full game. You have impressed a lot of people with what you did in the first half. The real test comes in the second half. You have stirred up a hornets' nest. Those hornets are angry. They want to sting you to death. You just keep playing your game for the next 30 minutes and those hornets won't hurt you."

We were to receive the second half kickoff. A score could have a deflating effect on the Raiders. We figured that they would score in the second half but if we could score as well, they were going to have to try to climb a very steep hill to catch up.

The half's opening kick went to Ozzie. He fielded it two yards deep in the end zone. He ran it out, getting just past the 20 to the 22.

That kick return, which was adequate but not spectacular, was the high point of our opening drive. It was a three and out comprised of two rushes for three total yards and an incomplete pass.

"All right, men. We'll get them next time," Walker assured us as we dejectedly went to the sideline. He knew that we wanted to put together a scoring drive as badly as he did. He wasn't going to lambaste us and have us mentally on a downward spiral.

Jablonski got off a fairly decent punt. It had a good hang time and was fielded at the 37. The Raider punt returner set out for a good run but managed only five yards. Hasegawa fought off a block and got through to prevent a longer return.

"All right!" I exclaimed, addressing Kerner somewhat lightly. "That's a U-H boy! He was my teammate in college! That's where the real talent is!"

I guess I had gotten over the fact that we had settled for a three and out on the opening drive.

Despite Hasegawa's good play, the Raiders had good field position. Our inability to pick up any first downs allowed them to start with only 58 yards to go to the end zone.

The Raiders rushed for four yards on the opening play, then McDaniel tackled the running back for a two-yard loss on the next play. He seemed to feel right at home in the stadium he had played in for five years. It was third and eight.

248

With the Raiders it wasn't any problem for them to go eight yards in a single play. They managed to get twice that on a pass to the Hawaii 40. It was first and ten.

A pass on the next play produced 12 yards and another first down at the 28. They followed up with a run up the middle for five yards and a four-yard run to the 19.

"Dig in, men!" Walker called. "Make them settle for a field goal!"

The Raiders ran through the right. Richards had a firm grip on the ball carrier and Jennings quickly joined in. It was in an area that would have made it close to the first down. The ball carrier fell forward for another yard to remove all doubt.

I had stood up for the previous play. I sat back down after they made the first down. I was hyped and wanted to get back on the field but needed to conserve my energy.

The Raiders passed for ten yards. It was close to another first down.

The officials called time out to measure. The measurement indicated that the Raiders had a first and goal at the seven.

It only took one play from there. The Raiders swept around left end and headed toward the end zone. McWilliams and Morrissey teamed up to tackle the ball carrier but not until he was crossing the goal line.

I looked down at the ground and shook my head.

"At least we still have the lead," I muttered, not convinced that I would still be able to make that statement later on. It depended on whether we could take the momentum back.

The Raiders converted on the extra point. We led 17-13 with 8:51 left in the third quarter.

"Don't sweat it," Walker directed, trying to make sure that we didn't lose our poise. "Let's expand the lead again. That'll frustrate 'em."

I stood on the goal line waiting for the kickoff. I was feeling angry. I had reached the point where I expected to win. I also expected the Raiders not to close in on our lead. I considered them to be out of line for scoring.

The kick went to Ozzie again. He caught the ball three yards deep in the end zone. Ozzie downed it.

We put together a drive that, timewise, was only slightly longer than our opening drive of the half. This one had a totally different result.

Kerner went up the gut and picked up five yards. Bender then hit Grummon on a slant at the 28. The tight end from Syracuse got to the 32 before being dragged down. We had our first first-down of the half.

Scott through the right on the next play. He fought his way to the 37.

A screen pass was called. I lined up in the slot on the right, went into motion to the left, then reversed direction. When the ball was snapped Bender dropped back and passed to me near my original spot. By that time Grummon, Clint and Marv had moved down the line to the right to run interference for me.

249

"Go!" I barked, telling my blockers that I had the ball and they could move upfield.

By the time I took a couple of steps Kerner had joined the trio.

My blockers did an outstanding job. Marv knocked a Raider on his derriere while barely breaking stride, then hit another Raider as I ran past. I also got some outstanding blocks from Kerner, Grummon and Clint. By the time I got to the Raider 30 I was by myself along the right sideline with nothing ahead of me but end zone.

I focused on the end zone except I occasionally turned my head to look to my left to make sure nobody was in pursuit. It appeared that I had everybody beat.

And I did. I reached the end zone unmolested. It was the longest touchdown of the season for the Hawaiians.

I wanted to throw the ball in the stands, then decided against baiting the crowd. Clint was the first teammate to reach me after doing an outstanding job of blocking. I gave him the ball and told him to spike it.

It was a major moment of my career. I was hoping that a touchdown on the fourth play of an 80-yard drive would send a message to the Raiders. I was pretty certain that the Raiders would be frustrated but not ready to surrender. At least it should have fired my teammates up.

"Great job, guys," Walker greeted with a wide smile as we approached the sideline. "Good pass, Steve. Clint, that's the way to block. Helluva run, Jay. That was good blocking, Jeff. Way to hustle."

I grabbed a cup of Gatorade while feeling aglow. I was aware of the team contribution of the play but I couldn't help but feel good about myself.

The extra point attempt made its predicted successful sojourn through the uprights. That raised our lead to 24-13. There was 7:17 left in the third quarter.

"We needed that," Marv said as he sat beside me on the bench. "We are playing some serious football. All we have to do is hang on for another 22 minutes."

I felt like all we needed to do was hold our breath for 22 minutes and 17 seconds. That amount of time remained unchanged after the kickoff was downed four yards deep in the end zone.

Oakland picked up a first down but then had to punt. We then picked up two first downs and had to punt. By that time we were into the fourth quarter. Our punt forced Oakland to start their drive on their own 13.

They didn't get far. One first down was all they got. On third and four at their own 38 they went to the air. Black nearly intercepted the pass about 15 yards downfield. What prevented it was when the receiver assumed the role of defensive back and swatted the ball away just as Mark was making the catch. Mark never had possession but a few black jerseys and white jerseys scrambled for the ball in case it was ruled a fumble. The officials in the area were blowing whistles and waving their arms in front of them to indicate it was an incomplete pass.

It was time for another punt. I stood at about the 20. I was very excited about the prospect of beating the Raiders. We still led them by two scores and time was gradually running out. There was still more than enough time for them. A long possession by us, if not an actual score, was essential to our quest.

At this juncture Oakland's punter had never had a punt blocked in his entire career. This would not be the exception. He got the punt off which I fielded at the 23.

It didn't seem as if I had taken more than two or three steps before I found myself rolling on the grass with somebody in a black jersey wrapping his arms around me. It turned out that I had returned the punt for eight yards but it sure didn't seem that long. We had a first down at our own 31.

Our first play suggested that our quest to score would not be any easier than before. Kerner ran off right tackle and managed only two yards.

We more than made up for it on the next play. Bender hit Slater at our 47 for a first down. The pass was perfectly placed with Slater well-covered near the right sideline. Bender threw it so that Slater had to extend his arms almost completely straight out to make the reception. Had he aimed for Slater's numbers the ball could have been knocked away or even intercepted. Slater and the defensive back were running as a single unit.

Scott swept around left end on the next play to the Oakland 46. He got us another first down on the next play when he picked up six yards through the right.

Going through the right worked so well on the previous play that Bender decided to try to burn that section of the Oakland defense again. This time I got the call. Marv and Clint created a huge cavity with their superior blocking and Kerner ran interference ahead of me. By the time I was brought down I had picked up nine yards to the 31.

The defense bore down after that. Scott went up the middle and got nowhere. On the next play he actually reached the 30 to get us a first down, then fumbled.

I dove for the ball. By that time the ball was being knocked around by players on both teams doing the same thing. When I went down I never even touched the ball. It seemed to magically shoot away from me.

It was Bender who ultimately recovered the fumble. That was good news for us. The bad news was he was on the 32. That would put us in a fourth and two.

The field goal unit took the field. I took my helmet off and stood on the sideline as I watched and practically prayed for Guinn to convert. A field goal would still mean a two-score lead but the best Oakland would be able to do with two touchdowns was tie the game.

Billingsley took the snap and set the ball down. Guinn approached and got the kick off.

I swung a clenched fist through the air as soon as the officials under the goal post raised their arms. It was a 49-yard field goal that extended our lead to 27-13. We needed to hold that lead for seven minutes and 46 seconds.

Oakland decided to move down the field quickly. Trailing by two touchdowns, we had reached the point where the clock was a factor although it still wasn't time for them to panic. After downing the kick in the end zone, they opened the drive with a 17-yard pass to the 37.

The Raiders moved into Hawaii territory on the very next play. I sat on the bench with half-a-cup of Gatorade in my hand as Oakland completed a pass at our 48. The receiver had room to run and headed toward the end zone as the crowd roared its approval.

The receiver only picked up an additional nine yards before being hit hard by Morrissey. I was relieved that the play didn't go further and looked down to heave a sigh of relief. That prevented me from seeing the final development of the play.

"Fumble!"

I jumped to my feet and watched the scramble. I saw a huge pile of humanity on the side of the Oakland bench but couldn't see the ball.

The referee stood above the pile. He seemed to be picking his way through the rubble of bodies.

Suddenly the referee raised up. He abruptly pointed to indicate that we now possessed the ball.

"Yeah!" I exclaimed, jumping up in the air and then running on the field as I put my helmet on and fastened the chin strap. I was also aware of a lot of booing among the crowd.

It was Black who recovered the fumble. I slapped five with him as our paths crossed.

"Way to go, Mark!" I called brightly.

Mark had recovered the fumble on the Hawaii 38. At this juncture it wasn't so important that we score. A score would have put the game completely out of reach but our focus was on using up the final 6:57.

The best thing about getting the ball back turned out to be that we were able to run off more of the clock. Even Oakland's encroachment penalty didn't help us to get a first down. We had a third and four at our own 44 and decided not to pass since an incompletion would stop the clock. Kerner went through the right and picked up three of the four yards needed.

I felt somewhat dejected as I joined the rest of the offensive unit in running off the field. The odds were more heavily in our favor with each passing second. We still could have slammed the door shut had we had a more sustained drive.

252

At least Jablonski did his part. He punted the ball and kept it away from the return man. The ball bounced a few times before Hamer touched it down at the eleven.

I grabbed a cup of Gatorade but didn't sit down. I was too hyped. There was actually nobody sitting on our sideline. We were all too jubilant over the prospect of a major upset, especially on national television, and too apprehensive about the possibility of blowing it at this juncture.

We went into our dime defense. This was a concession to the run or short passes. The Raiders might ultimately get to the end zone but if they only got a few yards at a time it might be too late by the time they finally got there.

Oakland took small chunks of real estate. After two plays they had a first down at their own 27. There was 3:41 left at the end of the second play and the clock continued to run.

An incompletion stopped the clock. The Raiders followed that up with a completion to the Oakland 41. The receiver stepped out of bounds to stop the clock with 3:12 left.

Heavy pressure from the defense forced Stabler to scramble and use up extra seconds in the process. After two plays of such pressure he had thrown two incompletions. It was third and ten with the clock stopped at 2:51.

There was more pressure on the ensuing play. Stabler still managed to get the pass off just before being hammered by Ed. The receiver was only eight yards from the line of scrimmage when he caught the pass and was immediately hit by Hasegawa. Rich got him down before he was able to maneuver his way out of bounds so the clock continued to run.

What else worked to our advantage was that the Raiders had already used two of their timeouts. They only had one left.

The eight-yard gain on third down compelled the Raiders to utilize their ground game to get a first down. They probably figured that our defensive setup was a concession for the necessary two yards. The running back picked up four yards to the Hawaii 47. They had the first down but weren't able to get off another play before the two-minute warning.

"Man oh man," I sighed, turning away from the field. "I don't know how much more of this I can handle. This is going to be the longest two minutes of my life."

"Ya gotta love it, Jaybird," Marv told me with a huge smile on his face. "This is what is beautiful about it. Ah ain't in New Orleans anymore."

I don't think anybody was happier about being with the Hawaiians than Marv was. Nine years of losing in New Orleans had that effect on him. We still had a losing record but we still seemed to be a pretty good team.

Action resumed. So did the pressure on the quarterback. We were able to put a heavy rush on him even though we were using only three down linemen and two linebackers. At least one and usually more of our front men got through. On each play one of the linebackers and occasionally one of the defensive backs blitzed.

The Raiders started with an incompletion before a 22-yard pass to the 25. The clock continued to run until an incompletion on the following play stopped the clock at 1:29.

A 16-yard completion gave the Raiders a first and goal at the nine. They finally used their final time out. The clock showed 1:20.

Two incompletions resulted in a third and goal with 1:07 left. Walker stood on the sideline posed almost like Jack Benny. One arm was across his chest with his hand on the bicep of his other arm. That arm was pointed up with his hand partially covering his mouth. After each play he looked up at the clock as if he could will more time away.

I was doing the same thing. After each play I looked at the clock.

Oakland finally achieved one of its objectives. Stabler sidestepped Hasegawa's safety blitz and got the pass off. He hit a receiver in the end zone.

The crowd was going crazy, believing now that the Raiders were going to find a way to put it away. No doubt they were preparing to stay for overtime.

No doubt there was pressure on the kicker since a botched PAT would have kept it at a two-score game with 58 seconds left. He didn't choke in the clutch the way I was hoping he would. The PAT narrowed the gap to 27-20.

"Hands team!" Walker barked.

Walker was calling for our kick receiving team which was comprised entirely of players who could handle the ball. This was used whenever an onside kick was an absolute certainty.

Roberts and I would still be deep. That might seem foolish in an obvious onside kick situation. Had we not placed anybody deep there was the possibility of the Raiders kicking the ball deep and running downfield to pounce on it. If all of our people were up close a kick like that would take us by surprise. The time it would take to recover from the surprise might be sufficient for them to beat us to the ball.

The predicted onside kick was made. Blakely fell on the ball and the game was as good as over. Bender took two snaps and the clock ran out.

Who would have believed it? A lowly expansion team with a 2-4 record and a national television audience scored a 27-20 victory over a previously undefeated team. Perhaps we really were better than we realized.

But let's not get cocky. The victory was impressive but it only improved our record to 3-4. The psychological effect still had the potential to carry us into the playoffs. It depended on how the other wild card contenders did since I didn't believe the Raiders would go into a tailspin that would prevent them from winning the division.

Ultimately it also depended on how we responded. We were a team that was making believers out of football fans across the country. We wouldn't look so impressive if we got overconfident.

For the moment we could savor the experience. It was a very jubilant locker room. We had just shocked the nation. From Maine to California to Alaska to Florida there were people whose mouths were frozen open after witnessing the antithesis of the rout they were expecting. For our own fans in Hawaii the delayed telecast was not yet started. Those who were fortunate enough to have avoided the loudmouths who belted out the score were in for an overwhelming treat.

As we went around patting each other on our backs and shaking hands in the locker room Walker stood in the center of the room. He had a smile as big as I had ever seen on him.

"All right. Settle down. Settle down," he called, bringing down the noise level as we turned our attention to him. "First thing's first. Who would like to volunteer?"

McDaniel, perhaps feeling inspired after we beat the team that let him go in the expansion draft, gave the prayer.

"Thank you, Jim," Walker said at the conclusion of the prayer. He held up the game ball. "One fumble set up a touchdown for us. Another halted one of their late threats. This goes to the man who caused those two fumbles."

Walker tossed the ball to Morrissey. The locker room erupted into more cheers.

I admit that I thought that I had earned the game ball. I also had to admit that the blonde rookie defensive back from Villanova had also earned the game ball. There was probably at least a dozen of our guys who did something to warrant a game ball. The important thing was the victory.

The bus ride back to the hotel was very entertaining. They usually are after victories, especially those that were previously considered improbable. Taking advantage of the fact that we had played on Monday Night Football, we had guys doing Howard Cosell impersonations.

"Perhaps the most unforeseen victory of the century," Kerner remarked in a fairly impressive effort. He didn't sound like Cosell but his inflections were perfect. "The Hawaiians have silenced their detractors by stunning the previously invincible Oakland Raiders. It was a truly remarkable effort as football fans across the nation sat in stunned silence and then admiration. Who would have thought that a fledgling NFL team from the very center of the Pacific could . . . ?"

"That's not what Howard was saying," Allen interrupted before doing his own Cosell impersonation that was equally as impressive. "The improbable victory by this defector from the obviously substandard World Football League defies all logic known to man. The evidence clearly confirms that the Oakland Raiders were on the take tonight. Obviously there is corruption in the NFL that will spread like a deadly cancer if left untreated. This reporter is calling on the NFL to investigate the obviously tainted game that was allowed to adulterate the benevolent name of *Monday Night Football*. If one man named Peter Edward Rozelle does not concur with this reporter's obvious finding and take appropriate action, it will be an outrage. We will have no choice but to call on the Federal Bureau of Investigation to weed out this deadly corruption starting with none other than Peter Edward Rozelle."

There were a lot of laughs. Nobody, including Cosell, dreamed before the game that we would be laughing after the game.

It is probably also worthy of note that I no longer felt hung over. I still resisted the temptation to indulge in even one beer. I went back to the hotel, got a bite to eat in the coffee shop and went to sleep with the TV on in my room.

All was well in my world again.

Several months later I discovered that I had a four-member fan club at this game. Carol Lafayette's parents and two younger sisters made the commute from San Mateo to see me play in person for the first time since the 1974 Hula Bowl.

Although the Lafayettes had to settle for end zone seats, they did get a good view of me since they arrived very early. I was still doing my customary pregame laps when they arrived, committing a minor NFL violation because we were not supposed to be on the field when the paying customers were present unless we had our uniform jerseys and pants on. Their seats were about a dozen rows up from the field.

Carol's youngest sister, 12-year-old Denise, wanted to run down to the front row to say hello. While I was courting Denise's oldest sister, Denise had loved me as a surrogate older brother. When I had to decide about with whom to sign among the Dallas Cowboys, Boston Red Sox and the Hawaiians she literally jumped up in my arms when I announced that I had decided to stay home. She wanted to be where she could watch me play football. Her father's transfer to San Francisco before my first professional game dashed that hope.

I had actually been very close to Carol's entire family. I had never felt so welcome in any girlfriend's home as I felt in the Lafayette household. I was treated like an actual member of the family.

Denise's idea to run to the bottom of the bleachers to say hello came a little too late. I was on my last lap and disappeared into the locker room. The next time Carol's family saw me I was in full uniform and not able to exchange salutations with anybody.

I don't know if I could have handled seeing them anyway. I still missed Carol even though I tried to convince everybody including myself that I didn't. I also missed Carol's family although I still had no idea of where they were at the time.

This was actually the only time since I began the tradition of pregame laps that I almost didn't do my pregame running. I was still slightly hung over from Saturday night and considered not doing the run.

I did the run because the last thing I wanted was for anybody to even remotely suspect that I was still feeling the effects of my overindulgent birthday celebration by not running my pregame laps. I also reasoned that if I couldn't run a few times around the field I wouldn't be much good during the game. It wasn't until after the same that I admitted to Ed and Marv that I had still been hung over when we got to the Oakland Coliseum. I had played a good enough game to where it didn't hurt to admit that I began the game at less than 100 percent.

"You played a helluva game," Ed remarked lightly. "You should always go out and get bombed two nights before a game."

"I think not."

CHAPTER TWELVE
To Denver

RAIDERS MEET THEIR MATCH!

That was the headline on the sports page of the Oakland newspaper on Tuesday morning. I was reading the account of the game on the bus to the airport.

"They're a good team," Raider Head Coach was quoted as saying. "They simply outplayed us."

Walker said it was a matter of the team believing in itself.

"We were only down by three in the first quarter but that long drive that ended with the interception could have discouraged our guys," Walker said. "Instead, they rolled up their sleeves and shifted into a higher gear."

My 63-yard touchdown was reported to be pivotal.

"All I did was carry the ball," I was quoted as saying. "Marv (Nelson), Clint (Abraham), Jeff (Kerner) and Rich (Grummon) opened the door for me. They threw some great blocks."

I felt it was very important to give credit where I knew it was due. Nobody goes 63 yards on a screen pass without some outstanding blocking.

The screen pass was my only reception of the second half. It gave me five receptions for 131 yards.

What surprised me was that Scott did not break the 100-yard mark in rushing. He had 25 carries for 96 yards.

The killer was his final carry. He lost two yards on the play. Had he gained two yards instead of losing two yards he would have finished with exactly 100 yards.

We didn't go home because we had just played a Monday night game with another road game to follow. There is a substantial difference in flying home after a Sunday afternoon game and flying to Honolulu after a Monday night game, especially if the following week's game is on the road.

A secondary factor was that we would be playing in Denver. That obviously is a much higher altitude than Honolulu and the weather would be much cooler.

It was a prudent move by Walker to have us stay on the mainland. He didn't want us going home to practice near sea level in a tropical climate before a game in possibly bitter cold at a facility appropriately named "Mile High Stadium."

What is also worthy of note is we didn't fly right to Denver. We boarded our plane in Oakland on Tuesday morning and flew to Salt Lake City.

Of course this didn't take the team by surprise. We knew exactly what we were going to do. We were advised several times dating back to the earliest days of training camp that we would be spending a few days practicing in Utah. To have not prepared us for this would have created a major distraction.

The reason we went to Salt Lake City, first, is because coaches are justifiably paranoid about spies. The closer one is to an opponent's home field, the more paranoid the coaches become. New plays, new formations, injuries and whatnot are things coaches prefer to be kept quiet. Injury reports are ultimately made public but they rarely tell the entire story.

We spent Tuesday, Wednesday and Thursday nights in Salt Lake City. On Wednesday, Thursday and Friday mornings we boarded a bus to the University of Utah for films, meetings and practices. Late Wednesday and Thursday afternoons we returned to our hotel near Temple Square.

On Tuesday I did my TV show for the first time ever away from Honolulu. Some of the show had already been taped since I was able to do the segment on the final two games of the World Series on Friday in Honolulu. Things would have been more complicated had the Reds not made a clean sweep over the Yankees and spilled the series into the weekend.

The rest of the show was slightly more complicated since it included a smattering of Sunday's NFL action and our game the night before. Our game was so impressive that it would be the highlight of the show. The hard part was editing the clips in plenty of time to get them and the voice tracks down prior to the deadline.

KSL-TV was contracted to assist in the process. Its studio wasn't too far from the hotel where we were staying. A technician edited the clips that I wanted and I put my notes together. With six minutes worth of World Series highlights in the can, I had 18 more minutes to kill since my show only included six minutes' worth of advertising.

The Hawaiians game got eight minutes and Sunday's NFL highlights got six. All dialogue was done over videotape from a production studio at the TV station. The remaining four minutes would cover introductions to each segment, introductions to commercial breaks, sports news briefs and the opening and closing segments of the show.

Rather than do the latter from a studio, we went a few blocks up the road to Temple Square. Each segment was done at different points in the vicinity with the Salt Lake Temple in the background. The closing segment was done literally from inside Temple Square with permission from LDS Church officials with the domed tabernacle in the background.

Once this was completed we returned to the TV station. Everything we had done was sent by satellite to Honolulu. It was then up to the technicians in Honolulu to put everything in the proper order for the show. From what I was told later, everything went smoothly.

The weather in Utah was about what I expected. It was cold by Hawaii's standards but cool by Utah standards for late October. It wasn't so cold that anybody was uncomfortable. With temperatures in the 50s, I wore a jacket when I went out but I actually saw a few localites walking around in shorts.

Hoddesson told me that the current conditions were not unusual but the weather in northern Utah was often unpredictable. Being a native of Utah, he said he came with an attitude that nothing would surprise him. He said that had we encountered frigid temperatures and/or heavy snowfall it would have been far from unprecedented for that time of the year. The nice thing was that, barring a sudden winter blast, we would be playing in similar conditions in Denver on Sunday.

This was our third road trip of the season or sixth when including our preseason games. How ironic it seemed that the only city we really got to spend enough time in to feel rooted was a non-NFL city.

During the preseason we went to Washington D.C., Memphis and Green Bay. What did we see in those cities?

Primarily only what we saw on the bus during drives to and from the airports, hotels and stadiums. There wasn't enough time to go sightseeing. The only semblance of a window of opportunity was a few hours the day before each game. Almost everybody was too focused on the game to care about the sights and sounds of the cities. A few may have gone sightseeing while others saw only the inside of bars. The rest simply took it easy.

Since the season began we traveled to Kansas City, San Diego and Oakland. As I mentioned, I ventured out to a Royals baseball game in Kansas City, had dinner at the home of relatives in San Diego and nursed a hangover in Oakland. In each case I was distracted by the reason I was in those cities in the first place to really take note of what those cities had to offer.

So here we were spending three nights in the non-NFL city of Salt Lake City. With our game not until Sunday we had time to clear our heads and soak in the ambience.

I didn't take any sightseeing trips. I was still able to enjoy what I saw from the area of our hotel on South Temple and during the rides to and from the University of Utah. That consisted primarily of the Wasatch Mountains.

But that was from a distance, albeit a short one. I did take a leisurely walk through Temple Square and had a pleasant chat with some missionaries there. At the time I didn't have an especially high opinion of the Church of Jesus Christ of Latter-day Saints although knowing Phil Hoddesson the way I did softened whatever negative opinions I may have had.

Of course. our primary purpose for being in Salt Lake City was to prepare for Sunday's game. Walker was going to make sure we didn't get too impressed with ourselves after the Oakland victory.

"You have no idea of how rough you have made things for yourselves," Walker stressed during our meeting at the conclusion of our film session on

Wednesday. "You beat the Raiders . . . on *Monday Night Football* no less. You played like champions. Everybody in the NFL has taken notice."

I believe we had the right attitude. By the time we began our workout on Wednesday we were no longer talking about what we did against the Raiders. Although the workout was for loosening up the way a Tuesday workout would be after a Sunday game, everybody seemed to be fairly serious. There was good-natured banter, of course, but not to the point of it getting out of hand.

On Thursday we worked out with emphasis on the offense. On Friday we worked out with emphasis on the defense and then took some extra time to work on our special teams. On both days we worked very well together with everybody encouraging everybody else.

Walker allowed the Salt Lake City media limited access to us. The TV stations all wanted clips and comments from an NFL team working out in the neighborhood. On Thursday Walker gave each station time to get footage of that day's workout. In doing so he made certain that we only ran plays that had been seen already, holding the new plays until after the media faction was gone. As I said, coaches have a way of being paranoid about spies.

Hoddesson and Billingsley were the darlings of the media since they were both from Utah and had both played for Brigham Young University. Joe was from Ogden, which was north of Salt Lake City while Phil was from Orem which was to the south near Provo. I happened to catch their feature on the late evening news on Thursday.

"I miss my family and friends," Billingsley replied when asked if he missed being in Utah. "What I miss most is my girlfriend although I'm glad I get to spend a little time with her this week. She's still going to BYU but Hawaii's a nice place to play football. The people are nice, and the team is pretty good."

"I don't have more than a couple of years left in the NFL but I'd like to finish my career in Hawaii," Hoddesson said when Billingsley's previous remark immediately segued to Hoddesson. "It's changed a lot since I was there on a mission but it's still a really nice place. The people are nice and the guys on the team are great."

On Friday morning we had our final meeting and workout session at the University of Utah. From there we went to Salt Lake City Airport to fly to Denver.

About halfway between Salt Lake City and Denver I finally finished *Shogun*. Jennings was sitting a couple of rows ahead of me. I got up and handed the book to him.

"Finally," he said. "So how'd you like it?"

"It was interesting," I replied, standing in the aisle. "The story in general was interesting anyway. Sometimes Clavelle was hard to follow. It doesn't flow as well as a book should at times but it's still worthwhile reading."

261

Ed nodded and said it would be interesting to see how long it would take him to read the book.

"How long did it take you?" he asked.

"Let's see. I bought it just before we went to San Diego. Then we had Dallas, Houston and the Raiders. I guess about four weeks."

"Four weeks, huh? I guess it's quite an accomplishment reading a book this size."

"I guess," I replied in a mock sigh. "I think I'll go see if I can find an *Archie* comic book or something on that level now. I need to give my brain cells a rest."

After dinner with a few teammates in Denver on Friday I ventured out on my own. I hadn't had a drink since my birthday disaster. I figured I was ready to have a beer or two but no more than that. I had learned my lesson from my experience six days earlier.

There was no prohibition on drinking in the bar of the hotel where the team was staying. Some teams have rules against that but not the Hawaiians. Walker actually preferred that we do our drinking in the hotel bar since he or one of the other coaches could monitor the activity and step in if one of the players started to get out of hand. That was better than having to deal with a player getting in trouble in another part of the city.

I simply felt like spending a little time away from the team. I went to a lounge in a hotel about a block away. Restricting myself to a two-beer limit, I sat at a small table and ordered a Coors which still wasn't available in Hawaii.

At the table next to me was a voluptuous young woman with long wavy dark blonde hair. She sat down right after I did and ordered a gin and tonic.

Although I had gone to the lounge to merely enjoy a couple of beers and think about Sunday's game, I made inadvertent eye contact with the young woman. She seemed to be looking at me as if trying to place me.

"Excuse me," she said a moment later. "Are you Jay Dockman?"

I hesitated, momentarily taken aback. This was the first time I was ever recognized by a total stranger outside of Hawaii. I responded in the affirmative.

Her name was Kim Van Buren. She was a 21-year-old senior at the University of Wyoming from Chappell, Nebraska. She had driven down earlier that day with a girlfriend to spend the weekend in Denver and attend Sunday's game. Her friend dropped Kim off before proceeding to Brewster, Kansas, to visit family and then would return to Denver on Sunday morning to attend the game. She and Kim would return to Laramie after the game.

Had I not played in my first nationally televised NFL game four nights earlier Kim would not have recognized me. Our earlier game with the Broncos had been televised in the region but that was a month earlier and I wasn't featured prominently enough to be memorable. Since I had played a really good game on Monday night I was shown a few times on the sideline with my helmet off. There was also a still photo of me shown during the Monday night telecast so Kim and the rest of the country got a glimpse of what I looked like without being disheveled and perspiring.

Being from Nebraska, Kim was a football fan. She and several other students had gathered at an off-campus tavern to watch Monday night's game. She said she was occasionally needled back home about choosing Wyoming over Nebraska although the Wyoming campus was more than 100 miles closer to her home than the Nebraska campus. There was an unwritten rule that people from Nebraska should be fervently loyal to the University of Nebraska.

"Is it true that you have a sister at Wyoming?" Kim asked.

"Yeah, Linda. She's a junior sociology major. Do you know her?"

"No," Kim replied. "Somebody just mentioned while we were watching the game on Monday that you had a sister on campus."

After a few minutes of conversing from table to table we moved to a booth. It was all intended to be very innocent. We were two people taking a little time to get to know each other and nothing more. Kim was a very intelligent, self-confident woman.

At about the time I was ordering my second beer and her second gin and tonic I spotted a few of my teammates walking in. Eric Hamer, Gary Giametti, Gavin Pratt and Stuart Arroyo grabbed a booth on the opposite side of the lounge. They didn't notice Kim and me until several minutes later when we got up to leave. I pretended not to notice them.

My experience with Kim was the subject of inquiries and needling from my teammates the next day. It went with being a part of a phalanx of men, I guess. I was regarded as a hustler although I never put myself in that category even though the media even joined the ranks of those who did. I simply got along reasonably well with women just like thousands of other single men my age.

What I did with Kim was never confirmed or denied. If there is any way in which I could give myself credit, I was always pretty strict with myself when it came to keeping that aspect of my life private. In laymen's terms, I didn't kiss and tell.

I did see Kim one more time. On Saturday night I returned to her hotel to have one drink with her. I never saw her again after that although I did hear about her once about six months later. While visiting my family in California my sister told me that Kim had sought her out on campus to tell her she had met me.

Injuries are a part of the game. Coaches and players point that out as routinely as they would say that income taxes are a part of being employed.

Unfortunately injuries can sure screw up a good game plan.

Grummon injured his shoulder during Thursday's workout in Salt Lake City. By Sunday morning it was obvious he was still too sore to play. He had worked out lightly since hurting himself and X-rays were negative but there was still too much pain. Even the injections didn't help much.

Kamanu would be starting in Rich's place. He was a capable replacement.

This is the type of thing we had been preparing for since training camp. While I had done work as the team's emergency quarterback, Jurgens had worked out as a backup tight end. Jon wasn't expected to be in more than a handful of plays, at most, unless Kamanu got hurt. In that event he would become our primary tight end.

At least we finally had Pratt back at defensive end. He was even getting the starting nod over Jurgens. That had nothing to do with Jurgens's role as the emergency tight end. Pratt had simply outplayed Jurgens during the week. Pratt was expected to be an All-Pro defensive end in the near future while Jurgens was considered to be near the end of his career.

It was a cold day in Denver. By that I mean the temperature seemed to be in the 40s or 50s. That wasn't uncomfortable, even for those of us from the tropics. The Broncos would be more used to this but it would not be an impediment for the Hawaiians. The few days we had worked out in Salt Lake City helped us to prepare. It also helped that the weather was reasonably pleasant instead of the blizzards that could hit Denver even this early in the season.

I felt loose as I ran my pregame laps. I felt even better still as I went through the pregame warmup with my teammates. Nobody seemed affected by the not very tropical temperature or the thin air.

In the locker room before kickoff I went through my normal routine. I visited the urinal, drank some Gatorade, visited the urinal, took care of a few other things and visited the urinal. My cleats were not yet getting a muddy buildup; something I needed to check throughout the course of the game. I always wore white regulation football cleats whenever we played on grass as opposed to the white all-purpose shoes I wore on artificial surfaces. I preferred the all-purpose shoes because they were lighter but the cleats gave me better traction on grass, especially if conditions were moist.

Pratt led us in *The Lord's Prayer*. Like most teams who utilized a pregame prayer, this was not a prayer for victory. All we were asking for was the strength to play to the best of our ability and that injuries be kept to a minimum.

"Thanks, Gavin," Walker said after the prayer had concluded. "We're moving into the second half of the season now. We can even our record with a victory. We built some momentum last Monday, I believe, but we're playing a team now that knows you are capable of beating them and are going to be giving it your all. Let's go out and play hard, play smart and execute. Let's put it to them."

264

We stood up almost in unison. I grabbed my helmet and headed out to the field with most of my teammates and coaches. As I stood in the end zone, I caught an arbitrary sighting of my sister who was sitting a few rows behind the Hawaiians bench. She and a friend drove down from Laramie that morning and picked up the tickets I'd left at the box office. She wasn't able to come down sooner because of a campus project which she had been committed to the night before. At the age of 20 she was developing into a nice-looking young woman.

Linda and I still weren't especially close. She was my sister and I knew I loved her but we still never really connected. She had always been "my pesky kid sister" while I was growing up.

The age gap played a role in our distance. She started high school the same year I started college. As she grew into a more sophisticated young lady I was rarely around, especially after I transferred from USC to the Hawaii.

I didn't acknowledge my sister's presence. She understood that gestures to people in the bleachers was something I didn't do. To me it simply wasn't in the makeup of football. In college I didn't even acknowledge my girlfriend's presence and she was right behind our bench with the other cheerleaders.

It was a different matter for pro baseball players. I've seen baseball players in the major and minor leagues mingle with fans during pregame activity. They'll talk to fans, sign autographs and occasionally even slip somebody a baseball.

Most football players have totally different psyches. Each game represents a week's worth of work. Some subtly wave to somebody in the crowd or even briefly speak. Most simply focus on the field.

Dating back to high school football I was totally detached from the crowd. I observed some of the people coming in or would notice something about somebody if I happened to glance in their direction. Only if my team was securing a rout did I finally loosen up. At that point I would smile and nod and occasionally wave if I saw somebody I knew. Even then it was very brief.

The pregame introductions got underway. Dietrich, Abraham and Nelson, as usual, were introduced first among the offense.

"At center, number 59, from Brigham Young University, Phil Hoddesson," reported the public address announcer as Phil jogged toward the middle of the field.

Phil actually got a smattering of cheers. He had played for Denver over the previous six seasons and had been active with several local charity groups. Obviously there are people who will remember even an offensive lineman. They will even remember a lineman like Phil who was a nice guy who simply did his job and didn't cause trouble.

We won the toss. I hoped that meant that we would draw first blood and never look back. I wanted this road trip to culminate in perfection.

"Let's do it," I said as I slapped five with Ozzie as we assumed our posts on the goal line. I resisted the urge to try to be too clever with my dialogue. I was thinking about how it would be better to have a perfect road trip and go home with a break-even record than to have a break-even road trip and go home with a losing record. It seemed clever when I thought it but I figured that something would get lost in the translation if I tried to orally convey that thought.

The kick came. It was heading toward Ozzie. Ozzie backpedaled as he got set to catch the ball.

I took a quick glance upfield and ran into the end zone.

"Down it! Down it!" I barked, gesturing downward with my left hand. The Broncos were converging and there was no way that Ozzie was going to be able to run from seven yards deep in the end zone to the 20. I doubted that he would even make it to the ten.

Ozzie followed my advice. We had first and ten at our own 20.

Feeling like champions after our stunning upset six days earlier, we went to work. Bender opened with a pass to Dietrich at the 30. Ted eluded a defensive back by running around him and reached the 35 before being brought down.

It was a good start. That seemed essential. We needed to grab the momentum and try not to surrender it. It was only one play but it sure beat getting off to a sluggish start.

We decided to stay with our air attack. Bender tried to hit Kamanu but the ball was tipped at the line of scrimmage. The ball continued moving forward but toward the center of the field instead of near the left sideline. A defensive back got his hands on the ball at the 50 but I was right behind him. I leaped up and reached around him to swat the ball away.

I stumbled when I came down, going down on one knee. It was a great relief to see the ball hit the ground without anybody intercepting the pass. I don't know what the play did for our momentum but at least it didn't give them any.

The defensive back who nearly intercepted the pass was not happy. I turned and looked at him. The expression on his face was one of surprise. It was as if he was a child who had had a favorite toy taken away.

I rose up and ran to our huddle. Bender shook my hand.

"Good play, Jay."

We went to the air again. This time the pass was to me over the middle. I caught the ball at the 50 and tried to maneuver around a defensive back. I ran about ten yards but primarily sideways before being thrown to the ground, having moved forward only one yard.

"Penalty marker on the play," I heard over the public address system.

"Oh, man," I moaned. "Don't tell me somebody was holding."

266

Fortunately the Broncos were offside. We declined the penalty. We had a first down at the Denver 49.

After Scott hit a wall for no gain through the right, Kamanu got his first reception of the year. Bender hit him at the 37. He picked up an additional three yards before being knocked out of bounds.

A two-yard gain by Scott up the middle, an incompletion and a pass to Giametti that was nearly intercepted stalled the drive. Guinn led the field goal unit on the field. He would be attempting a 49-yard field goal.

"It's okay. We've got plenty of time for touchdowns," Walker reminded us as we exited the field.

Having to settle for a field goal was not equated with a national tragedy. We would settle for three.

"No sweat," Grummon said from behind the bench, dressed in street clothes except he was wearing his white road jersey. "The air here is thin. Guinn will make this one easily."

Of course the air was thin in Denver. Guinn had no trouble getting the distance. Unfortunately he had a little trouble with direction. The ball hit the left upright and bounced back. The crowd reacted as if the Broncos had just scored a touchdown.

I shook my head in frustration and grabbed a cup of Gatorade. As I sat on the bench I resigned myself to the fact that Guinn wasn't going to make every field goal attempt. I was disappointed but I wasn't going to get down on him. Nobody felt as bad about the missed field goal as he did.

"It's all right, man," I said sympathetically as Eric walked past where I was sitting.

I turned my focus to the field. Denver began its drive by rushing four yards around left end.

The following play was unbelievable. Denver's quarterback dropped back. He hit his receiver about 40 yards downfield. The receiver went the rest of the way unmolested. The crowd roared twice as loud as it did when Guinn missed the field goal.

"What the hell were you doing out there, Rodgers?" Walker bellowed.

Rodgers stood on about the Hawaii 20 with his hands on his hips. The receiver had simply faked him out. He faked toward the sideline so effectively that he had Carl beat by about ten yards before Carl could recover. He caught the pass over the middle and almost could have walked the rest of the way.

As I headed out to receive the kickoff after the successful extra point I crossed paths with Rodgers as he was leaving the field. He was heading for the sideline at about the 30. Walker was standing near the 50 and it was obvious that Carl didn't feel like dealing with him.

"It's okay, Carl," I said discreetly. "We'll get it back."

It would be easy to get down on a defensive back who got burned on occasion. It would be easy to get down on a ball carrier who fumbled or a receiver who dropped a pass. It would be easy to get down on somebody who missed a tackle or a kicker whose field goal attempt was not true. Such acts would be counterproductive.

I was focused on a touchdown as the kickoff was made. The touchdown was not going to come on the kickoff itself. I caught the ball eight yards deep in the end zone and immediately downed it. Had I tried to run that one out Walker would have forgotten that he was angry at Rodgers. I would have been the new scapegoat and deservedly so.

"Okay, let's go to work," said Bender as we huddled for the opening play. "We'll have this baby tied up before the end of the quarter."

Bender went to me first. He hit me over the middle at the 26. I turned upfield as I was being hit and managed to get to the 28 before going down.

We managed a first down before having to run another play. A defensive tackle jumped offside, bumping Hoddesson as he remained poised to snap the ball. As soon as the whistle blew Phil rose from his position with a contented smirk on his face and headed back to the huddle.

An incompletion was followed by a pass near the right sideline. Dietrich twisted his body as he caught the pass in the air. He moved down to the Denver 45 before being knocked out of bounds. He was hit pretty hard and went down but it was a clean hit.

"Nice job, Ted," I said as I reached down to help Ted up. "That was a helluva catch."

Scott picked up three yards around right end before we went to our double double formation, an uncharacteristic move since that was a formation we normally reserved for obvious passing situations, and resumed our air attack. Bender looked down the left sideline and found Giametti. Gary caught the ball in stride at the 21 and got down to the 12.

"All right. Now we're moving," Bender remarked in the huddle. "The Broncos are now finding out who they're messing with."

"Whom," Kerner corrected lightly.

"What?"

"It's whom. Whom they're messing with."

"If you say so," Bender chuckled. I guess we felt we could loosen up a little.

It took only two more plays. Kerner went up the middle for two yards. Bender then hit Kamanu in the back of the end zone. Kamanu's second career reception resulted in his first career touchdown. He raised the ball over his head and jumped up and around before using both hands to spike the ball.

"Now that's what I call style, my man," Abraham said as he reached Kamanu and whacked him on the back. "You were perfect, man! You put egg all over the defender's face."

268

What Craig did was abruptly shift direction in the back of the end zone. That caused the defensive back guarding him to fall down.

Our extra point attempt was true. The game was tied at seven with 5:27 left in the quarter. Bender's prophecy had come true.

"I want this one," I said to nobody in particular as I grabbed my cup of Gatorade after the extra point. I noticed that Bender was standing right there. "I want this one. They beat us on our field. Let's stick it to them here."

"I understand," Steve said. "Just don't get too hung up on revenge. The game in Honolulu doesn't matter now. Last Monday's game doesn't matter. The only thing that matters is this game right here."

"I know," I replied. "The game last month is just a little extra incentive. It's the same as if they made disparaging remarks about us in the paper. It's another reason to want to stick it to them."

Steve nodded. We sat down on the bench together and watched our defense in action.

Actually we sat down just in time to see the kickoff. The kick was fielded two yards deep in the end zone. The return man decided to run it out.

The return man had gotten to about the five when he saw Hasegawa breaking through. Rich was fast and fought off a block to enable himself to get downfield in a hurry. The return man tried to run around Rich but to no avail. Rich and the return man were rolling on the ground at the eleven.

"Yeah, Hasegawa! That's the way to go, baby! That's the way to go!" a jubilant Allen cried out after jumping up as he waited to take the field with the rest of the defense. Russ ran on the field but made sure that he ran a path that enabled him to meet Rich and give him a congratulatory whack on the helmet as Rich ran off the field.

I stood and joined those who greeted Rich. It was potentially a very key play. Rich was primarily a substitute but he had a way of coming up with big plays when he got an opportunity.

The Bronco offense seemed to believe it was not a setback. They methodically moved downfield. By making a couple of big plays to augment a series of smaller plays they made two first downs and had a first down at the Denver 49. Two plays later they had a first down at the Hawaii 34.

As if they weren't doing well enough on their own, we gave them a boost. Prendergast jumped prematurely and got cited for encroachment. They had first and five at the 29.

The Broncos went up the middle for three yards. A sweep around left end put them back at the 28 when the running back was given a violent reception by Pratt. Then the quarterback had reasonably good protection but no receivers open. He threw the ball out of the end zone to prevent an interception.

269

It was fourth and four. The Bronco field goal unit took the field. The clock was ticking with less than a minute to play in the quarter.

"I guess we won't have the lead at the end of the quarter," I said to Kerner as I stood up and prepared to run on the field for the kickoff.

My prediction was a little premature. The kick was wide to the left. We were still tied at seven with 28 seconds left in the first quarter. Since the field goal was not made I would not be returning a kickoff. We had the ball at the 28.

We started our drive with an incompletion. Scott then went through the left and picked up seven yards to the 35. We had a third and three as the first quarter expired.

"What do you think?" Marv asked me as we moved to the opposite end to change directions.

"I think we'd better pull this one out," I replied evenly before looking around and making sure there were no Broncos around. I didn't want to fuel their fire.

Marv and I happened to be looking downfield. Three eggs suddenly flew out of the seats behind the end zone and landed near the ten-yard line.

"What was that for?" Marv wondered.

"It's Halloween," I reminded him.

"Oh, right. But why are they throwing eggs here?"

I shrugged. My guess was a combination of Halloween spirit and an overabundance of Coors.

Kerner got us off to a flying start in the second quarter. He went through the left and picked up 12 yards to the 47 for a first down.

We nearly faltered after that. Bender threw a pass that was off Dietrich's hands and nearly intercepted. Scott then went up the middle and lost his footing after gaining only a yard.

There is a lot to be said for having a veteran quarterback like Bender. Physically he was past his prime but he had poise and the smarts that befit his veteran status. He hit Giametti with a pass on a slant at the Denver 49. Gary went all the way to the 32 before a pair of defensive backs brought him down.

We were looking good. Not every play worked to perfection but we were able to recover. We were coming up with big plays when we needed them.

Bender hit me at the 16 next. I broke a couple of tackles but still managed to pick up three more yards to the 13. It was another first down.

Dietrich was next. Bender hit him on the numbers at the two. Ted dove into the end zone to give us our first lead of the game.

"Yeah, baby!" I cried out, raising my arms in triumph before running over to Ted who was a few yards away from me.

270

Ted rolled over on his back. He had a huge grin on his face. Scott and I helped him to his feet before he spiked the ball where he stood.

We were hot. Monday night's victory was obviously no fluke. Denver was going to have to rise to the occasion if the Broncos expected to beat us. The Broncos were capable and a lot could happen in the 43 and-a-half minutes left in the game. For the moment we had the momentum.

From the sideline I watched contentedly as Guinn split the uprights. It was 14-7 with 13:29 left in the half.

I sat on the bench. I felt that it was extremely imperative that we win this game. I believed that losing would tarnish Monday night's victory. It would also cut into our playoff hopes.

The Broncos downed the kickoff in the end zone and began their drive from the 20. They picked up two first downs and had a first down at their own 45.

"Geez," I muttered under my breath, losing my patience. I knew better than to believe that our defense would stop the Broncos cold every time. I simply was impatient to return to the field and run up the score.

A two-yard run and an incomplete pass followed. That created an obvious pass situation.

The heat was on but the quarterback got the pass off. Unfortunately for him, Prendergast tipped the ball up. McDaniel managed to catch the tipped pass before going down. We had the ball at the 50. It was an ideal opportunity to resume our quest to pull away.

"Yes! Yes! Yes!" I exclaimed as I grabbed my helmet and headed to the field. I suddenly was very embarrassed with the way I had lost my patience a few minutes earlier. I figured we had no alternative but to score a touchdown since we were beginning our drive at midfield.

Unfortunately we didn't go anywhere. Scott picked up two yards up the middle and Bender hit Kerner with a pass at the 38 but the latter was nullified because Dietrich was offside. It was second and 13 at our own 47.

This was not a scenario for panic. Unfortunately two consecutive incompletions forced us to punt. It was a virtual waste of a turnover that enabled us to start the drive in excellent field position. I heaved a sigh of frustration as I stood on the sideline.

The situation only got worse. A sick feeling washed over me as Jablonski's punt was blocked. I won't document the language I used. Denver recovered the ball at the Hawaii 29.

"Geez," I muttered as I sat on the bench next to Giametti. "We just blew a big opportunity."

Gary looked at me and nodded. He had only been in one play during the abbreviated series but he appeared equally as frustrated.

"Maybe they'll blow their opportunity," Gary suggested.

"Maybe," I agreed although I had my doubts.

The Broncos found themselves in a third and eight at the 27. I silently hoped that our defense would hold them one more time to force them to kick a field goal and keep us in the lead. That was when the quarterback found a receiver inside the 15. The receiver was brought down at the eleven for a first down.

Two plays later the Broncos had a third and seven at the eight. A pass in the left corner of the end zone and the subsequent extra point tied the game. There was 3:22 left in the half.

"All right, gang," Walker called in a tone that did not mask his exasperation. "It's a brand-new game. This is the time to show them what we're made of. Let's start with a good return."

I ran to my post at the goal line. NBC was still in commercial so I did some stretching. I figured we had just enough time to put together a touchdown drive without allowing Denver another possession before halftime.

The kick was made and it came in my direction. I caught the ball a yard deep in the end zone and headed upfield.

Ozzie laid out a good block against the first Bronco downfield. That was all I had time to notice. Before I could observe anything else I had a collision with an orange jersey at the 20.

Actually I didn't see the orange jersey until after the fact. It was one of those times where one is looking at one location and is hit from a different location. I was suddenly lying on the ground and looking at grass and the chalk on the 20-yard line.

"Wow," I gasped as I rose up and headed to our huddle, catching up with Kerner who was heading to the huddle from the sideline. "That guy came out of nowhere."

"Are you all right?" Jeff asked.

"I'll feel great if we score a touchdown," I replied.

We started in that direction. We even got some help from the opposition. Scott rushed four yards. The entire play was nullified because Denver was offside, giving us a first and five at the 25 instead.

Our drive nearly ended on the next play. Bender unleashed a pass to Kamanu. A Bronco defensive back stepped in front of Craig and headed the pass off. It was a sure six points for Denver except the defensive back appeared to make the mistake of starting to run before he had possession. He juggled the ball momentarily before the ball dropped incomplete. The crowd groaned in unison.

Bender hit me on the following play. I caught the pass just before I was hit from behind and dropped at the 31. It was still good for a first down.

Scott rushed up the middle for three yards. Bender followed by hitting me with another pass. I caught the ball on the run at our 45 and picked up three more yards for another first down.

This was when we hit the two-minute warning. The play actually ended with 1:56 showing. That was how much time we had to travel 53 yards.

When play resumed Denver wasted no time in serving notice that the Broncos intended to fight us every step of the way. Bender's pass to Slater was batted away.

We stayed on the ground on the next play to let the Broncos know we were not necessarily going to the air on every play. Scott picked up four yards although a yellow flag nullified the gain. Kohl was cited for unnecessary roughness. He got a tad overzealous in his blocking technique, moving us back to our own 33. It was second and 25 with 1:36 left in the half.

Bender hit Slater at the 47 on the next play. Joe was about five yards in from the sideline when he made the catch. He raced for the sideline and just barely made it as he was being tackled. That stopped the clock with 1:23 left. It was third and five.

That was where the drive ended. An incompletion followed and we were forced to punt.

Jablonski took advantage of the thin air and skied his punt. It was fielded at the nine and the return man just barely eluded Hasegawa a yard or two later. He got as far as the 19 before being brought down.

That was the final effort of the first half. The Bronco quarterback took two snaps and dropped to a knee to allow the clock to run out. The very audible boos were not enough to compel the Broncos to try for a long play. The clock ran down and both sides retreated to their respective locker rooms.

"You stink, number 59," I heard a young voice from the stands call out. I happened to catch a glimpse of the young fan and he actually resembled a 12-year-old Danny Bonaduce.

"Hey, 77. You stink. You also stink, 24. Hey, number eleven. How come your uniform's all clean? Aren't you good enough to play? Hey, 25. What makes you think you're so great?"

Of course we ignored the remarks. It was part of the game. He was probably just a nice kid having a little fun. The worst remarks usually come from adults who have had a few too many. Some make remarks that are not suitable for the children nearby who can't help but hear what an alcohol-induced stupor causes.

"We have a very inconsistent running game," Walker reported before we were to return to the field. "We need for the offensive line to do a better job of blocking."

Whether our offensive line was doing an inadequate job of blocking or not, Walker was right about our running game being substandard. I found out later that we had only nine rushes in the first half for a paltry 26 yards.

"We could have broken this game open," Walker pointed out in a tone that was not demeaning. "We forced a turnover at midfield. We didn't do anything with it and that stupid penalty was totally inexcusable."

Walker paused. He shook his head. I think he was trying to make his point without discouraging us. He had to utilize a semblance of self-control. He could save his screaming for Tuesday.

"Men, I know you're a better team than this. You have to give the Broncos some credit because they are rising to the occasion but you have it in you to get through all of that. The Broncos are a good team but we're better. Now let's get out there and show the world who we are."

We had made adjustments before Walker's talk. There was no doubt that the Broncos had also made adjustments. The second half promised to be very intense.

Guinn set the ball on the tee at the 35. When he got the signal from the referee he approached the ball and put his foot into it. The ball arched up end over end and then came down.

The kick was fielded at the one. The return man made a decent return, getting all the way to the 25.

"Stick it to 'em, defense!" I called as our defensive unit ran on the field.

"Sock it to 'em, you guys!" Dietrich called.

"'Sock it to 'em?'" Kerner echoed inquisitively. "What is this? *Laugh In?*"

Whatever it was, a two-yard loss on the opening play was nullified when we accepted a holding penalty. This put them in a hole with a first and 20 at the 15.

An incompletion was followed by an 18-yard reception at the 33. The quarterback did an outstanding job of getting the pass off because he was hotly pursued by Allen and McDaniel. Rodgers had the receiver covered but the pass was right on the numbers and Carl could only drop him almost where the reception was made. They now had a third and two.

The Broncos went off left tackle and reached the 36. They had a first down.

Two rushes and one pass later resulted in a pair of first downs. The Broncos were moving deeper into Hawaii territory. Their second first down was at the Hawaii 33. I was getting sick to my stomach.

A run up the middle netted them all of one yard. Before they could get the next play off their right tackle jumped and pushed them back to the 37. That was followed by an incomplete pass to give them a third and 14.

For me the drive was a roller coaster of emotions. I felt so helpless as the Broncos picked up chunks of yardage, then hopeful when it appeared that our defense might be able to stop them. I recalled high school when I was a two-way player and could play a role in stopping them. As a pro I was a mere spectator when the defense was on the field.

The Broncos tried to convert but came up short. A receiver got a violent reception from Blakely and Hasegawa after he caught the pass which we hoped would discourage him from catching any more passes that day. He had still gained 12 yards to give them a fourth down at the 25. The field goal unit ran on the field.

"Do you think they'll fake it?" I asked Stanek.

"It wouldn't be a bad strategy. They probably just want to get the lead but even if they faked a field goal and didn't make it, it wouldn't be a bad place to leave the ball."

The Broncos didn't fake. The kick was up and through the uprights to give them a 17-14 lead with 9:43 left in the third quarter.

"All right," I said somewhat flippantly as I prepared to head out for the kickoff. "They got a field goal so we'll respond with a touchdown."

Suddenly I noticed that Walker had turned around to look at me. He nodded very slightly. It was as if he was saying that he liked my positive attitude.

We started our drive on the 20 after Ozzie downed the kickoff five yards deep in the end zone. Kerner began the drive with a four-yard run up the middle. Dietrich promptly erased the gain with a yard to spare when he jumped before the next snap.

Ted redeemed himself on the ensuing play. He caught a pass at the 36 and picked up three more yards to give us a first down at the 39.

As we huddled up I happened to notice the faces of some of my teammates. Scott, Marv, Hayer and Dietrich all looked very determined. It had been a hard-hitting game that was wearing on us a little and the third quarter was only a little more than half finished. We still had it in us to pull this game out. It was at a time like this that we could see how it worked to our advantage to spend the week in Salt Lake City where the elevation and climate were similar to Denver's. We may have already been physically spent had we returned to Honolulu after Oakland.

Scott only picked up a yard on the first-down play. I went through on the next play and took advantage of the huge hole opened by Stanek, Hayer and Kamanu. It was a power play since Hayer and Kamanu double-teamed the defensive end. I picked up seven yards to give us a third and two at the Hawaii 47.

On the following play Scott went right up the gut. He picked up the yardage we needed for the first down and broke a tackle to get past midfield to the 49.

"Helluva job, Larry!" Marv exclaimed as he helped Larry to his feet. "That's what I call running!"

I have to admit that Marv's remarks would not have gained him entrance into an Ivy League school or even landed him a job as a color commentator. It did, however, epitomize the situation. Had Marv gone to an Ivy League school or even Oxford he probably would have made the same remarks. It was not necessary to speak Cosellese to speak intelligently. In fact, it was preferable that he not speak Cosellese.

For an encore Scott picked up eight yards around right end. Kerner picked up two more yards through the left. It looked like a first down for us.

The referee wasn't willing to concede the first down. Neither, I'm sure, were the Broncos. The referee blew his whistle and waved his arms over his head to signal a time out. He ordered the chain on the field.

We were slightly short. Scott immediately fixed the problem by going up the middle for ten yards. Larry was generally a mellow guy but on the field he was often capable of impersonating a bull being taunted by a matador. He simply charged ahead and refused to go down.

On first down I got the call. We did a sweep around the left. Following the path of blockers, I managed four yards to the 25.

That was as far as the drive went. On the following play none of the receivers could get open and Bender had to throw the ball away. He tried to hit me inside the ten on the third-down play but a defensive back stepped in and knocked the ball down. His effort was aided by the fact that he actually pressed down on my shoulder to give himself leverage to get to the ball. As I positioned myself for the reception, I suddenly found myself slightly paralyzed on my right side because of the pressure the defensive back was putting on me.

"Interference!" I called, pointing to the defensive back and looking at the official. "He interfered with me!"

"No, no," the official replied calmly. "He was going for the ball."

"But he can't put his hand on me the way he did!" I insisted.

"I'm sorry, Dockman. I can't call it if I don't see it. From my angle it was a clean defensive play."

I happened to look into the face of the perpetrator. To his credit, his face was blank. He didn't make a face to taunt me. He was probably grateful to have gotten away with his violation.

As football players are human and make mistakes, so are the officials. No matter how well the league tries to cover the field with officials, they are not going to see everything. No official was in the right position to see the infraction, I realized, although that didn't make me feel any better. It deprived us of an opportunity to go for a touchdown that would give us the lead.

"What happened?" Walker asked when I reached the sideline.

"He used my body to get to where he needed to go to knock the pass down," I replied dejectedly. "The official said he didn't see it."

Walker clenched his jaw and nodded. He also understood that the officials were human. That didn't make *him* feel any better.

At least we salvaged something. Guinn kicked a 42-yard field goal. The score was tied at 17 with 2:27 left in the third quarter.

276

I grabbed my Gatorade and sat on the bench. I was perspiring but not as much as one might expect. It was a chilly day in Denver and that worked to keep our bodies reasonably cool. In Honolulu, with its humidity, I perspired profusely throughout each game. At home I actually normally began perspiring during our pregame warmup.

Denver fielded the kickoff two yards deep in the end zone. I started worrying when they got as far as the 30. All I could see was Hawaiians getting blocked while the return man gained yardage. It was finally Zanakis, the rookie linebacker out of Washington State, who got him in a bearhug and brought him down.

The Broncos picked up two first downs. One was the result of good execution on their part. The other came as a result of McWilliams' facemask penalty that cost us 15 yards and gave them a first down at the Hawaii 39.

Of course Walker was not pleased. Sometimes when something aggravated him he would simply stand with his arms folded and his jaw clenched. This was one of those times when he expressed his displeasure in a somewhat different manner. He faced the bench and addressed anybody who happened to be within earshot.

"This is how you lose football games! It's stupid penalties like that! There was no reason for McWilliams to grab the facemask! If you want to lose this game, keep committing stupid infractions like that one!"

I don't think the guys on the field heard Walker although those of us on the bench sure felt guilty even though we had nothing to do with the penalty. Regardless, the defense bore down and held the Broncos to three yards on the next two plays. As the clock got to within the final 20 seconds of the third quarter the quarterback took the snap and dropped back on third and seven.

From where I sat I could literally see the quarterback's eyes widen. Allen was heading his way. The quarterback tried to elude him by dropping back further and rolling to his left.

It wasn't enough as Allen caught him. Zanakis arrived on the scene to hit the quarterback at a full clip before he and Allen drove the quarterback to the ground.

"Now that's the way to play football!" Walker exclaimed, clenching his fists and waving them around.

It was an eleven-yard sack, giving Denver a fourth and 18 at the Hawaii 47 as the third quarter expired. NBC was going to show commercials and I was going to take the field.

"Jay," Walker called as I took my first steps toward the field. I took a detour to confer with my coach.

"Yeah, Coach."

"How do you feel?"

"Fine," I replied, puzzled because I couldn't think of anything that would suggest otherwise.

"What I mean is, do you feel like you can break one? I'd like to get a good return on this. What do you think?"

I looked at the line of scrimmage. As a rule I didn't try to return anything that came down within the ten yard line. That meant anything longer than a 43-yard punt.

"I'll be lined up on the ten," I said. "If it's in front of me I'll try to get something out of it. Do you want me to try to return it if it is inside the ten?"

Walker paused. He considered the possibility.

"No, I guess not. Just try to get some kind of halfway decent return if you can. If they kick it away from you, let it go, but let's see if we can get a return out of this. A good return will fire everybody up. Let's give it a shot, okay?"

I responded in the affirmative, as if I could do otherwise, and ran out to the field. This would be the Broncos' first punt of the game. I stood on the ten-yard line and waited for action to resume.

The punt was made. I didn't have to move forward or backward to field it. I simply had to move a few steps to my right.

"You've got room, Jay!" I heard Hasegawa call from a few yards in front of me. He was the one designated to be my eyes on the opposition since my own eyes were on the descending ball.

I fielded the punt and ran forward. I got past one defender by sidestepping him but was caught at about the 17. That was where we would start our drive.

Did I say something about a drive? Eight yards does not constitute much of a drive. The offense had barely taken the field when we had to make way for the punting unit. We didn't even get a first down.

Of course it happens that way. I knew that and so did everybody else. The three-and-out is just as much a part of football as the touchdown. I just hate to see it happen to my own team. If we had at least picked up a few first downs we could have at least pinned the Broncos back.

Jablonski took some of the sting out of that abbreviated drive. He unleashed a booming punt. It was one of those punts that made the crowd gasp at the sight of the ball seeming to leave the atmosphere. The punt sailed out of bounds at the Denver 26.

"Okay, defense! Three and out!" I called.

I almost felt like a hypocrite. We didn't exactly do our job. How could I expect our defense to do its job?

Yet that's the nature of the game. If one unit falters the other is expected to carry the load. There were many times during my career when one unit had miserable experiences and the other made up for it. It is part of what playing as a team is all about. We pick each other up.

278

Unfortunately our defense wasn't having much more success than we did. I watched helplessly as the Broncos moved down the field. After a few first downs they had a first down at the Hawaii 34.

They went through the right. The ball carrier picked up a few yards and then was hit by Jennings. That knocked the ball loose.

"Fumble!"

I shot up from my seat. I anticipated our recovery.

Unfortunately the Broncos recovered their own fumble. It was second and five at the 29.

"Damn, that would've been just the break we needed," I muttered to whoever happened to be nearby.

A draw play got them to the 26. That was followed by an incompletion. The Broncos sent their field goal unit out.

"Okay," I sighed, "if they make the field goal we'll follow it up with a touchdown."

What blew me away wasn't that the field goal attempt was no good. It was that it was actually short.

Granted, there is still gravity in Denver despite the thinner air. Still, this was only a 43-yard attempt. The kicker simply didn't get enough foot into it.

"All right, offense. Let's capitalize on this!" Walker directed as the offensive unit ran on the field.

Apparently we weren't listening or didn't understand what Walker meant. We got off to a good start when Scott shot up the middle for five yards. A sweep around the right on second down went nowhere. We followed that up with an incompletion and headed back to the sideline. It was our second consecutive three and out and that did nothing for our confidence. The crowd, however, seemed rather pleased.

Jablonski got off another good punt although not as good as his previous punt. The Denver return man caught the punt at his own 23. He was brought down at the 32. The clock showed 7:28 left in the game.

The Broncos proceeded to march down the field again. A five-yard rush was followed by a 19-yard pass play to give them a first down at the Hawaii 44. Two rushes later they had third and three at the 37. If we could hold them to no gain a field goal would have to travel 54 yards; doable, especially in Denver, but not a piece of cake.

With three yards to go for a first down there was nothing certain about what the Broncos would run. They opted for a pass. Richards and Jennings both rushed the quarterback, forcing him to scramble. He finally tucked the ball away and got down to the 31 before stepping out.

I held my tongue. Every expletive known to man, and perhaps a few originals, came to mind. I didn't say a word because I didn't want to sound as if I was lambasting the defense. I understood that our defense was giving 100 percent. It was simply the resulting circumstance that I objected to.

The Broncos were doing more than trying to score. They were also winding down the clock. They were well within field goal range and were content to move closer to the goal line a short chunk at a time.

After two rushing plays they had a first down at the 19. They lost two yards on the following play when Prendergast got into the backfield and dropped the ball carrier, then attempted a pass.

This time it was Pratt applying the pressure. He had the Bronco quarterback in his grasp. As Pratt and the quarterback headed toward the ground the quarterback threw the ball that landed untouched.

"Grounding! That's intentional grounding!" Walker charged, pointing toward where the ball had landed.

Unfortunately Walker's allegation produced nothing. There was actually a receiver in the vicinity. He was about 15 yards beyond where the ball hit the ground but the ball was thrown in his direction, even if only by accident.

The following play was more successful for the Broncos. The quarterback hit his receiver over the middle at about the ten. He spun his way to the seven before going down. It was first and goal and the Broncos allowed the clock to run down to the two-minute warning. The crowd was loving it!

"Geez, what a game," I muttered, looking at the scoreboard and noting the tie score with only two minutes to play. With the Broncos pounding on the door it was going to take a big play by the defense to keep the game tied when we got the ball back.

The Broncos tried to run up the middle. The ball carrier hit little more than a wall of white jerseys. He still managed to pick up a yard.

We called time out. By the time the clock stopped it was down to 1:52.

The Broncos went back to the air on the following play. Initially I was grateful since an incompletion would stop the clock and save us a time out. My optimism was crushed when the quarterback found a receiver in the end zone. The extra point made it a 24-17 game with 1:45 left.

A sense of foreboding swept over me as I returned to the field. I knew we were capable of getting into the end zone and forcing the game into overtime. If the rest of our fourth quarter was any indication, we were going to have to wake ourselves up. On offense our entire fourth quarter was comprised of two three and out possessions.

The kick was made. It was a deliberately low kick and rolled and arbitrarily bounced up as it headed our way. It was heading toward Ozzie who fielded the ball about a yard deep in the end zone. He had stepped back so I assumed he was going to down the ball.

Ozzie surprised me. He actually tried to return the kick. Instead of downing the ball and taking the ball on the 20 without running any time off the clock, Ozzie made a rookie mistake and tried to return it. He wound up down at the eleven.

It was partially my fault, I suppose. I should have told him to down the ball. Instead I assumed that he would know to do it on his own.

At least the play was a relatively quick one. Only six seconds ticked off the clock. We had 1:39 to go 89 yards. Had Ozzie played it smart, however, we would have had 1:45 to go 80 yards. The six fewer seconds and nine extra yards could prove to be fatal.

I was furious with Ozzie, as well as myself, but couldn't get caught up in that. It was Walker's job to be angry at him and he definitely was. I was too far downfield to hear what Walker was saying but I could see Walker giving Ozzie an earful as Ozzie approached the sideline. I also knew that I was going to be asked about my role in the faux pas, on Tuesday if not that day.

"They know we're going to be passing," Bender pointed out as we began our huddle. "Receivers, do your best to get open and then be looking for the sideline. We need to preserve our time outs."

Steve called the play and the receivers jockeyed for position. Before Steve could even begin to look downfield he was sacked for a three-yard loss. A Denver linebacker successfully anticipated the snap and shot through at exactly the right moment and caught Steve just as Steve was starting to drop back.

We called time. There was 1:31 left by the time the clock stopped. We had one time out left.

Marv moved us closer to the end zone. Unfortunately it was the one behind us. He jumped prior to the snap. That moved the ball half-the-distance to the goal line. We had second and 17 at the four.

Bender's pass on second down fell incomplete. He was met by a heavy rush on the next attempt and had to scramble. He got the pass off but that also fell incomplete. We had fourth and 17 with 1:12 to play.

The Broncos had their dime defense on the field in response to the double-double formation that we were using. That would make it harder to get a receiver open but we had to give it a shot. We had a little more than a minute to travel 96 yards.

Bender had time. He unleashed a pass to Dietrich near the right sideline.

A defensive back stepped in and picked off the pass at the 26. His momentum carried him out of bounds at the 25. The Broncos had a first down with 1:04 left. The game was as good as over.

Three snaps later it was officially over. Our winning streak was halted at one. Instead of evening our record at 4-4 we had a dismal 3-5 record. It was hard to believe that we had beat the Raiders only six nights earlier.

As I shook hands with some of my opponents I looked as cheery as possible. I still tried to ponder what had gone wrong. Had we been that bad or had the Broncos been that good?

I had no way of knowing. All I knew was our flight to Honolulu was going to seem longer than it actually would be.

It was special teams coach Ken Holcomb who volunteered to give the postgame prayer. Perhaps he knew that the players weren't up for doing it themselves. I know I wasn't.

Walker addressed the team as he always did. I didn't hear a word he said. I was replaying the game over and over in my head. We made mistakes and the Broncos made mistakes. It simply boiled down to the Broncos outscoring us by a touchdown.

Two meetings with the Broncos and two losses. The losses were by a combined ten points.

The latter probably explains why the loss hurt so much. We had a good team. We believed we were better than our record indicated. We were gelling rapidly as a unit. The victory over Oakland, at least as far as we were concerned, was no fluke.

Neither was our loss to Denver. The Broncos simply outplayed us by seven points. That was the only honest way to summarize the game.

"Hey, Sis," I greeted cheerily as I approached my sister who was waiting near the team bus.

That was probably the only time I ever referred to Linda as "Sis." I would not have even done so this time had I not been conscious of several teammates in the vicinity. I figured it was best to make it clear that this was my sister to stave off any lewd remarks about her or any suggestions of carnal activity between us. Whenever they kidded me about other women who had been with me I normally bypassed their levity with a smile. Any suggestions regarding my sister would not have been dealt with so easily, I'm sure.

Linda had come down from Laramie with a cute redhead named Christine. We had a little time to talk before I had to board the bus that would take my teammates and me to Stapleton Airport.

"You played a good game," Linda remarked.

"Not good enough," I replied in a partial sigh. "We really wanted this one and came up short."

Linda, Christine and I talked for about ten minutes. I was also able to introduce them to Hamer, Prendergast, McDaniel, Stanek, Marv and Bender as they came by. With the dozen or so who had heard me refer to Linda as "Sis" and the six who were introduced to her, that meant that almost half of my teammates knew that Linda was my sister. My hope was that word would spread quickly that this was not some groupie or barroom pickup. When I thought about it later, I couldn't believe how paranoid I seemed to be.

I was actually more surprised by how concerned I was about my sister's reputation. I didn't realize I cared as much as I did. I had never been so protective of her.

282

Hoddesson, Billingsley, Joseph and I were the only players visiting with relatives and/or friends after the game. When we got word that the bus was ready to leave I hugged my sister and boarded the bus. Nobody made any lewd remarks so I figured that word had spread that Linda was not some conquest.

I sat next to Grummon. As we headed to Stapleton he asked me what my sister was doing in Denver.

"She drove down from Laramie," I replied. "She goes to the University of Wyoming."

It suddenly dawned on me that Linda may have chosen Wyoming for a reason similar to why I chose the University of Hawaii. I suspected that she was no longer comfortable in southern California. While I specifically earmarked Hawaii for my change of venue, she later confided in me that she had been willing to go anywhere that sharply contrasted the Los Angeles area. She settled on Wyoming after also considering Nevada-Las Vegas, Washington State, New Mexico and even the University of Hawaii.

CHAPTER THIRTEEN
Retaliation Against the Chiefs

We licked our wounds on Monday. The Bronco game had been tough to lose but it was behind us. It was nice to be home again after being gone for slightly more than a week.

Tuesdays were easily my longest days. Most of the day was fairly typical when it began with a full day of football and then ended with my sports highlight show. I went to the stadium and sat through the film session.

The film session was not especially pleasant. The mistakes that killed us were there for all to see. Walker didn't rant and rave as much as I thought he would. He did wonder out loud on a few occasions if our upset of Oakland made us complacent in Denver.

Walker knew, though, that we had played hard. Perhaps a few of the guys did get overconfident after we beat the Raiders but they shouldn't have. It was a great victory, to be sure, but all it really proved was that even an expansion team can square off and do well against a championship caliber team.

At least after the film session I enjoyed the light workout with my teammates. Of course it would have been more fun had we beaten the Broncos. It would have been something to have spent a week on the road and come home with a sweep instead of breaking even. If overconfidence was the reason we lost in Denver, our collective cocksurety prevented us from being at the break even mark just after the halfway point of the season. A 4-4 record would have looked far more impressive than our actual 3-5. Our loss to Denver seemed to make a substantial difference in our record even though it was only one loss.

"Our victory over the Raiders convinced us that we could beat the Broncos," I said to my roommate on Tuesday morning. "Unfortunately it also convinced the Broncos that we could beat the Broncos. They made sure they were ready just like Walker told us they would do."

There was one thing that was atypical for this particular Tuesday. For the second time in my life I would be voting in a presidential election. Four years earlier I voted for George McGovern, much to the chagrin of my Nixon-loving parents. This time I was hoping to pick a winner.

My polling place was at Fort DeRussy. I decided it would be more practical to walk down than to fight for a parking space in that part of Waikiki.

When I set out I still didn't know for whom I was going to vote, at least in the race to the White House. Incumbent Mayor Frank Fasi would get my vote, as would first time Congressional candidate Cec Heftel but not because he also happened to be the majority owner of the Hawaiians although it also didn't work against him.

I debated in my head all the way down. I liked Jimmy Carter. I also couldn't say that I didn't like Gerald Ford.

When I got to my voting booth I settled on Ford. He had done a reasonably credible job of bringing respectability to the White House in the wake of Watergate. I figured he deserved an opportunity to show how well he would do with a full term.

It might surprise at least a few people, including my parents and President Ford himself, that I would vote for Ford after being an antiwar demonstrator who voted for McGovern four years earlier. Some people would insist that I was changing my ways but that was not the case. Vietnam was no longer an issue. As always, I considered each issue and candidate individually. I believed that Ford had earned my vote after taking over the Oval Office during a very tumultuous time in history.

There were those who voted against Ford because he pardoned Nixon. Some even claimed that that was what ultimately cost Ford the election.

Whether the pardon cost Ford the election, I don't know. As much as I opposed Nixon dating back to his handling of Vietnam, I believed that Ford had acted correctly in pardoning Nixon. It was time for the country to move on and heal its wounds. I agreed with Ford during one of his debates with Carter that Nixon paid for his role in Watergate with his disgrace. It was something Nixon was going to have to live with for the rest of his life.

During my sports highlight show my only focus was on football. Most of my show had been prepared the day before so I wasn't under a lot of stress on Tuesday. I was glad that I didn't have to do the show from Salt Lake City the way I did the previous week although the Salt Lake City show was a nice change. I still preferred the confines of my own studio.

I left the studio immediately after finishing the live show. Rather than go home, I decided to treat myself to a brew at the Nest which I occasionally frequented dating back to my junior year in college. I usually ran into somebody I knew whenever I stopped in. If nothing else, I knew most of the employees.

Don Simmons was there so I joined him at a table near the back. The place was actually fairly crowded for a Tuesday night. Normally attendance didn't pick up until later in the week.

"That was a helluva couple of games you guys played on the road," Don remarked after we had ordered beers from the waitress.

"Well, we won one and lost one. It was great to beat Oakland. It was tough losing to Denver."

"Did the altitude in Denver bother you?"

I thought for a moment and shook my head. The beers we had ordered were placed in front of us by an attractive blonde waitress in white shorts.

"There's no way in hell that Walker would allow us to use that for an excuse but I don't think it did anyway," I replied. "It shouldn't affect you if you're in good shape. It also helped that we worked out all week in Salt Lake City and that it didn't get nearly as cold as it could have. The altitude and the temperature in the 50s probably would have been a problem had we simply flown over the day before from Honolulu."

The conversation drifted to the Oakland game. Don said that Howard Cosell did not mince words about being unhappy having to do a Monday night game with an expansion team.

"It was typical Howard," Don said, chuckling lightly. "During the first part of the game he kept insisting that this was something that simply slipped through the cracks. He blasted the NFL for scheduling you guys on a Monday night. By the time the second half rolled around he could see how competitive you were and, of course, you eventually won. You wouldn't believe the praise he was heaping on you."

"Did he also praise the NFL for having the brilliance to schedule us on a Monday night?"

"No, he didn't go that far," Don chuckled.

The game, I learned later, was actually originally scheduled to be in Honolulu so that the telecast could include shots of Hawaii's scenery with our rematch later in the season in Oakland. For reasons unknown to virtually everybody except for whoever made the decision, the locales were switched, but somebody decided to keep the game on Monday night anyway. The switch had to do with kickoff for a Monday night game being right in the middle of rush hour in Honolulu, creating a lot of empty seats at Aloha Stadium for the national TV audience to see, so they switched the sites when they should have simply scheduled us to play the Raiders on Sunday and given up their desire to give us a Monday night game.

I understand that most of the folks at ABC weren't happy when this game slipped through the cracks. They stopped complaining when we gave them exactly the kind of game they looked for on a Monday night. Our team may have been comprised primarily of rookies and alleged castoffs. We still knew how to play good football.

"They'll never doubt you guys again," Don remarked.

"They'd better not," I replied somewhat lightly.

At the next table sat three very lovely young ladies. The one I considered to be the prettiest was a slender brunette whose long hair was permed at the ends. She frequently exchanged eye contact with me. I decided to see if I could take it further.

I've met some very nice women in some very unique ways. I have also heard of other men and women coming together in some very bizarre ways. I suppose it is simply spontaneity that makes it possible in each situation.

This time I used peanuts as an ice breaker. She was drinking a mai tai that was served in a wide mouth glass referred to as a "bucket." I shelled

286

some peanuts that were in the bowl on my table and started using her glass for basketball practice. From a distance of about ten feet, I was surprisingly accurate.

I was testing her to see how she would react. If she appeared in any way annoyed I would have simply gone about my business. Instead she watched the peanuts fly into her drink and giggled, then looked at me with dark eyes that sparkled.

Still spontaneous, I abruptly got up from my chair. I darted over to her and kissed her square on the mouth, meeting no resistance. We still hadn't said a single word to each other.

We did eventually speak. I sat with her for a moment. Her name was Bonnie. She was visiting from Burnaby, British Columbia, Canada. She would be in Hawaii for ten more days.

And she wanted to go out with me!!!!

That was the impression I got, anyway. I didn't exactly ask her out and she didn't exactly beg me to take her out. She simply gave me the name of her hotel and room number and invited me in her sweet soft voice to call when I got a chance. She still knew nothing about me except that my name was Jay.

I called Bonnie the following evening. We had a nice chat. She was a very unpretentious young lady who worked as a sales assistant for a Vancouver TV station.

Bonnie was a year younger than me. She and her two friends had rented a car and were spending their days at various spots around the island. They would leave Honolulu for Maui on Monday morning but would return to Honolulu two days later to spend two final nights in Waikiki.

Initially I thought I would ask Bonnie out for Saturday night, then thought better of it since we had a game the next day. I didn't think Bonnie or I would have an especially good time if I took her out when my mind was certain to be on the Chiefs.

I asked her out for Friday instead and she accepted.

The workouts on Thursday and Friday were occasionally arduous. It wasn't as if they were anything out of the ordinary. I was simply looking forward to spending time with the pretty visitor from Canada.

It isn't as if I didn't date other women during the season since I very obviously did. Bonnie, for whatever the reason, struck me as being out of the ordinary. My initial impression was that I would like her a little more than the others. I had no expectations of any permanence. I was still anxious to spend whatever time I was able to with this pretty lady.

We had a great time. Not a wild time by any stretch of the imagination but great nonetheless. We started the evening by dining at Rudy's; an Italian restaurant on Kuhio Avenue that also happened to be my favorite of all restaurants.

Whenever I was with a young lady I tried not to talk too much about football. It was still a focal point of my life so it was inevitable that football was discussed. It could turn a date into a total bore if I allowed football to dominate the evening. When the subject came up I tried to talk as much as possible about the team or football in general. I wanted to avoid going into a boring speech about my own personal alleged highlights.

"Are you good?" she asked lightly.

"Well," I began equally as light. "The season's a little more than half over and they haven't cut me yet. I guess I'm doing okay so far."

At least we had television work as a common bond. I didn't even want to spend too much time talking about that. I was allegedly a star with my own show and she was simply a part of the office staff.

I was curious about Vancouver since I had never been to Canada. The closest I had ever come was my senior year in high school when I visited the University of Washington on a recruiting visit and my senior year in college when I played a football game on that same campus in Seattle.

"It's just like any other city," she said, somewhat surprised that I hadn't understood that.

After dinner I took Bonnie dancing at the Tiki in the International Marketplace. I took her back to her hotel at a respectable enough hour so that I wouldn't have any difficulty getting up in time for the morning workout at Aloha Stadium and she wouldn't have any difficulty getting up in time to do whatever it was she and her friends were planning.

"What time is your game on Sunday?" she asked as I was driving her back to her hotel.

Out of habit I almost answered ten o'clock, then replied, "Eleven o'clock" when I recalled that our games would start an hour later. The change came as a result of the rest of the country being back on standard time.

"Can I go?" she asked.

"You want to go?" I responded in surprise, having erroneously assumed that she would have no interest in going to a football game.

"Sure. Do you mind? I would love to see you play."

"Well, you're more than welcome but if you ride with me it'll be a long day for you. I'll probably leave at about 7:30."

Bonnie suggested the possibility of her friends going if I could get them tickets. If that were the case the three of them could ride to the game together at a later time in their rental car. Otherwise she was willing to ride with me at the earlier time. I would call her the next day and we would work out the details.

"How was it?" Hamer asked while I was stretching on the turf at Aloha Stadium prior to Saturday's light workout.

"How was what?" I asked back.

288

"Last night. I saw you dancing with that little dolly."

"You were at the Tiki?"

"Um-hmm. Rich and some girl he picked up and Sandy and me."

I shrugged casually. I didn't want to make a big deal out of it.

"We had a good time," I said.

That seemed to satisfy Eric for the moment. He began stretching on his own a few feet away.

I actually felt sorry for Eric. He was positively mad about Sandy Ishikawa; one of the most gorgeous women I had ever seen. Despite her pulchritude, the Japanese lady with hair cut in something similar to a page boy was not hung up on herself in any way. She liked Eric okay but only as a friend. Eric reluctantly understood that his devotion to her far outweighed her devotion to him. He hoped she would eventually fall for him.

"Nice looking lady you were with last night," Hasegawa remarked when he showed up a few minutes later.

"Of course" I replied jocularly. "You don't think I'd want to be seen in public with somebody who looks like Tiny Tim, do you? Why didn't you guys come over and say hello? I didn't even know you were there."

"Ah, well, we didn't want to interfere. Besides that, you left right after we spotted you."

I managed to get three tickets. When I spoke to Bonnie that afternoon she told me her companions were planning to go to the Polynesian Cultural Center. It was a trip that they had been planning since their arrival a week earlier and had been putting off.

They didn't know that the Polynesian Cultural Center was closed on Sundays. Neither did I so there was no way that I could set them straight. They would spend Sunday making the drive of roughly 40 miles before discovering that the attraction was closed for the day.

"Are you going with them?" I asked.

"I'd rather go with you if you don't mind."

"Pick you up about 7:30?"

"Sure," she replied happily. "Shall I just wait out in front?"

"That'd be perfect," I said. "Oh and be prepared for me not saying much. I rarely talk a lot before a game so don't worry if I'm not very talkative."

"Okay."

I also suggested that she not worry about breakfast. I told her I had a way to get her fed at the stadium.

I set the alarm for six. Naturally I was out of bed a little before five. Throughout my entire career I don't believe I heard an alarm clock more than three or four times on gamedays. I still always set the alarms just in case.

As usual I couldn't wait to get started. I may have even been a little extra anxious to go because of Bonnie. It would be the first time in my professional career that I would actually take a date to a game I was to play in. However active I may have been with the opposite sex, I usually kept that facet of my life separate from my life on the gridiron. The last romantic tie I had in connection with football was my senior year in college and only because my girlfriend happened to be a cheerleader.

I took a shower while I waited for the coffee to brew. It seemed almost ludicrous that I would take a shower when I was going to be soaked with perspiration a few hours later. The shower helped me to relax a little and kill time.

The rest of the morning was spent drinking coffee, smoking cigarettes and trying to focus on the morning paper. When I was still a smoker it was the hours prior to my departure for a game when I smoked the heaviest. Looking back, I don't understand why but that's the way it was until I finally quit smoking after the 1980 season. Once I left home I was a more moderate smoker. In the anxious hours prior to departure I turned a handsome profit for the Marlboro people and had the oncologists standing by at the local hospitals.

I pulled up to Bonnie's hotel on Ala Moana Boulevard shortly before 7:30. She was waiting out front. Although my mind was on the game, I took note of how beautiful she looked in her white shorts and pink T-shirt that she'd bought from one of the local merchants. With her petite figure and girlish face she was more likely to be described as "cute" than "beautiful." She was still definitely a beauty.

There was sporadic conversation. I was glad, though, that I had advised Bonnie ahead of time about my taciturn pregame state. Despite the pulchritude in the seat next to me as I maneuvered my Porsche along the H-1 and Moanalua freeways, my mind was on the Kansas City Chiefs no matter how hard I tried to give Bonnie a fair amount of attention.

I parked in the players' area and walked Bonnie down the ramp and through the tunnel that led to the north end zone. As we made our way across the length of the field I could see her checking out the stadium that had opened only a little more than a year earlier. I could tell that she was impressed.

"There's nobody in the stands," she said.

"Kickoff's still about three hours away. They don't open the gates until 9:30. The fans who are already here are in the parking lot having tailgate parties."

I took Bonnie to the hospitality room. She helped herself to a decent breakfast from the buffet while I got a small plate of fruit and glass of orange juice for myself.

"That's not much of a breakfast," Bonnie observed amusedly.

"It'll hold me over," I replied.

I ate my pregame meal while Bonnie and I conversed casually. Although I was still plagued by pregame jitters, I always became more gregarious once I had reached the hospitality room. I could engage in normal conversations although I also checked my watch frequently.

Several teammates were on hand for their pregame bites and conversation. Among those Bonnie met were Ed, Marv and Bender. She even met Coach Walker who was very gracious as he always was whenever he met somebody's guest. Bonnie also met a handful of wives and girlfriends.

At about 8:45 I excused myself to begin my pregame ritual. Karla Nelson graciously volunteered to guide Bonnie to the seats when it was time to move upstairs and guide her back to the hospitality room where I would pick her up after the game.

My pregame ritual was done. I had run my laps and joined my teammates for our pregame warmup. I felt loose and ready to tangle with the Chiefs.

In the closing minutes before kickoff I sat in front of my locker and drank a Pepsi. I was flanked by Rodgers and Kerner who, like me, seemed to be in a different world.

I wanted this game bad. We still had a shot at a winning record. We were even still technically in contention for a playoff berth.

The playoff berth seemed like a longshot. The wild card was still possible if we could keep winning. We could begin that quest with this game. In the process we could avenge the three-point defeat in September.

Walker came in and stood in the center of the room. I gulped down the last of my Pepsi. Everybody else stopped whatever they were doing. Ozzie had been reading a sports publication and put it away. Black did the same with his girlie magazine. Billingsley, sitting on the opposite side of Rodgers from me, put away what I later learned was *The Doctrine and Covenants*, a Latter-day Saints publication.

"All right, men," Walker began. "We are ready to go. At least I assume we're ready to go. Is there anybody here who isn't ready to play?"

It was a rhetorical question. Walker paused anyway to give anybody who wanted to an opportunity to admit to being less than ready. I don't know what Walker would have done had anybody, even jocularly, suggested that he was not quite ready.

"Okay, good. Who's going to lead us this week?"

Rodgers had chosen that moment to scratch his head. Walker only saw Carl's hand starting to go up. He was designated to lead us in *The Lord's Prayer*.

"Our Father who are art in heaven. . . ."

At this juncture we all joined in. It was obviously a set prayer which literally came about during Biblical times. It still had its spiritually cleansing power that we needed.

Or so I believed. I only knew that I wanted God on my side. Years later I came to be amazed at how little I knew about God at the time. I suppose I could not have classified my desire as being in earnest as long as I was polluting my lungs with cigarette smoke and viewing sex as something that could be regarded as recreational.

But my covenant with God would come in time. For the moment my focus was on football and the Kansas City Chiefs. I listened intently as Walker implored us to put everything we had into our rematch with them.

"Let's go," he said, waving his arm to direct us out of the locker room.

I headed out as far as the end zone. My offensive colleagues and I were to be introduced this week. I took a moment and looked into the sideline seats in the orange section. I spotted Bonnie in the top row sitting next to Karla Nelson and then put her out of my mind.

We lost the toss. I stood impatiently on the sidelines as our kickoff unit lined up and prepared to head toward the south end zone. Five Hawaiians in brown jerseys stood at the ready on each side of Guinn. Eleven Chiefs in white jerseys and red helmets stood ready to do battle with my teammates.

Guinn, as usual, got off a pretty good kick. A Kansas City return man fielded the kick at the three and headed upfield. A few seconds later he collided with Zanakis and went down at the 23.

Our defense went to work but got off to a slightly dubious start. McDaniel immediately got called for encroachment. Without having snapped the ball the Chiefs had a first and five at the 28.

The Chiefs only needed one play to get a first down. They didn't get much else beyond that. They faced a third and eight at their own 35.

It was an obvious passing situation. That was exactly what was going on. Ed blitzed and forced the Kansas City quarterback to hurry his throw. The pass was picked off by Blakely at the Kansas City 47.

"Go, Ben!" I yelled, jumping from my seat on the bench as the crowd roared.

Ben broke a tackle shortly after he picked the pass off, sidestepped another tackler wannabe and got down to the 31 before being brought down.

"Let's go! Offense!" Walker called, turning to face the bench with a huge smile on his face as the eleven members of the offense hurried to the field. We were 93 feet from our first score of the day.

There is a lot of pressure on a team that starts a drive with such outstanding field position. Not only is there virtually no excuse for not

292

scoring, there is virtually no excuse for having to settle for a field goal. Anything less than a touchdown is a major letdown.

We immediately went to the air and Bender's pass dropped untouched.

Bender hit me near the makai sideline on second down. I made the reception at the 21 and eluded a defensive back, then got down to the 14 before I was knocked out of bounds.

Scott got the next two calls. He ran through the left and managed to get to the ten. That was followed by a kama'aina right where he was hit at the line but managed to keep his feet. He got all the way to the four before a pair of Chiefs wrestled him to the ground.

"First down! That's a first down!" Kerner called.

The officials stopped the clock to measure. It turned out that Jeff knew what he was talking about.

"See? I'd never lie to them about something like that?" Jeff jocularly said to Marv and me.

We only needed one more play. Bender took the snap and dropped back. Dietrich was open in the rear of the end zone. Bender hit him in the numbers.

Ted did a little pirouette and spiked the ball behind the end zone. His fellow offensive teammates converged on him to offer congratulations. He received a few more handshakes from the members of the PAT unit as they came on the field.

The extra point was true. We had a 7-0 lead with 11:14 left in the first quarter.

"That was easy enough," Slater remarked lightly on the sidelines.

"It's only going to get harder," Bender reminded him. "We've got to keep our heads in the game. We might not start with such good field position next time."

Steve was right, of course. I still felt pretty good as I watched the kickoff unit prepare to go to work again. The whistle blew to indicate that NBC was back to show the game in Kansas City and a few other markets. Guinn approached the ball.

The kick was fielded two yards deep in the end zone. The return man headed out. He got the same distance he would have gotten had he simply downed the ball. He went down on the 20 in the loving arms of at least three different Hawaiians.

The tackle looked impressive. So did the return man's effort to try to get a few extra yards than he would have had he downed the ball. The entire effort was nullified by the yellow flag near midfield.

Hamer had been overzealous. He crossed the Hawaii 35 before Guinn kicked the ball. We were penalized five yards and had to kick again.

"Take it easy, Hamer!" Walker called. "Watch what you're doing out there!"

The return man didn't have to make a decision this time. He fielded the ball on the two and shot forward.

He didn't get far. Black busted through and met him at the 13. Running at a full clip, Black was like a truck bearing down on an old man with a walker. It was one of those hits that caused virtually everybody in the stadium to cringe. It seemed amazing that the return man bounced up immediately and appeared totally unscathed.

I shook my head and grabbed a cup of Gatorade. The penalty against us had actually worked to our advantage. The end result was that the Chiefs would start the drive at their own 13 instead of their 20. For the moment nothing seemed to be going their way.

For the second time the Chiefs needed only one play to pick up a first down. They started with a rush for seven yards. Jurgens then got called for encroachment to give the Chiefs a first down at the 25.

The Chiefs managed to put together a sustained drive this time. I sat on the bench and sipped Gatorade and tried to remain as patient as possible.

After two more first downs the Chiefs had crossed midfield. They had a first down at the Hawaii 37. They tried a sweep around left end but lost two yards when Pratt, temporarily filling in for Jurgens, fought off a block and upended the ball carrier.

The Chiefs faced third and 12 after an incompletion. They managed to convert on a pass over the middle. The receiver caught the ball at the 25 and managed to fight to the 23 for another first down.

I muttered a few things I would rather not admit to. At least I was cognizant of the close proximity of the spectators to our bench. In some stadia I could almost scream at the top of the lungs and not be heard. At Aloha Stadium the spectators in the front row could hear almost anything that was slightly louder than a normal conversation.

Two rushing plays later the Chiefs had a third and five at the 18. Nobody could be certain if they would pass or rush on the next play. All I knew was I was willing to concede the field goal.

It was a pass. The Kansas City quarterback dropped back. He spotted a receiver crossing the field at about the ten-yard line and fired in his direction.

There was one obstacle in the form of Allen. Russ leaped up and just managed to get his hands on the ball. He stumbled back a little before regaining his balance and moving forward. He was brought down at the 15.

"All right!" I cheered as I leaped up, putting my helmet on and fastened the chin strap as I ran on the field. My path crossed Russ's as I headed toward where our huddle would form up near the north end zone.

"Way to go, Russ!" I hollered as I held my hand out for him to slap with his as our paths crossed.

It felt great to have held the Chiefs to a goose egg after their long drive. Both of their possessions ended in turnovers. I looked up at the scoreboard and grinned at the sight of our seven-point lead. I could also see that there was 4:13 left in the first quarter.

We wasted no time in moving the ball. Scott went up the middle for six yards. Bender then found Dietrich at the Hawaii 42. Ted easily hauled the pass in and turned toward the south end zone. He picked up an additional four yards before being brought down.

Unfortunately this drive fizzled on us. A four-yard rush by Kerner where he fumbled but managed to recover got us as far as the midfield stripe. After an incompletion we faced a third and six.

The blitz was on. Bender tried to elude his attackers but it was a tall order for his 36-year-old legs that had toiled in the NFL for 14 seasons. He was smothered at our 40 to force the punting unit to take the field.

Walker was shaking his head as we approached the sideline. He was showing great restraint in not lashing out. He knew that there would be times when a blitz would lead to a quarterback sack. It still was hard for him to accept.

Jablonski's punt was a good one. The ball was fielded at the Kansas City 18. The return man fought his way to the 25.

As the final minutes of the first quarter wound down the Chiefs weren't able to do much. They picked up a first down but that was about it. They had a third and ten at their own 38 when their quarterback rolled to his right to pass. Jennings was in hot pursuit.

"Get him, Ed!" Marv and I called in unison as we both rose from our seats on the bench.

Ed had the quarterback in his grasp. The quarterback seemed to still be searching for a receiver. The delay enabled Allen to join Ed. The three of them went down on the Kansas City 29.

It is always great to hear the crowd cheer.

At least it is great to hear the crowd at Aloha Stadium cheer. Hearing the crowd cheer a week earlier at Mile High Stadium in Denver didn't make me happy at all.

"All right! All right! We're looking good!" I cheered as I ran on the field. I looked up at the scoreboard and saw the clock ticking with less than 40 seconds left in the first quarter.

I stood at about the 25 and awaited the punt. As the Chiefs broke out of their huddle I turned and looked at the clock again. It was ticking away with less than 15 seconds.

The Chief punter got the punt off. It was a high punt over near the makai sideline. It took a couple of bounces but I decided to take a chance. I got a high hop at the 14 and started heading upfield.

I had to straight-arm a defender shortly after I reached the 20. I broke a tackle between the 25 and 30 before continuing on. I was finally hit and dropped at the 34. It was a 20-yard return. That was the final play of the quarter.

We were changing sides so we would be heading toward the north end zone. As I made my way toward our huddle inside the 25 on the south end zone side I pondered the situation. I was grateful that we were leading by a touchdown. I was also surprised that Kansas City hadn't scored. The Chiefs had one drive where a score seemed to be a certainty. I was grateful that our defense dug in when it needed to and turned the Chiefs away.

We went right to work to begin the second quarter. We crossed midfield on the first play when Bender hit Grummon on the Kansas City sideline of the 50. Rich maneuvered his way to the 45 before being wrestled down.

I got the call next. I went through the right and picked up seven yards to the 38.

Our momentum got disrupted when Stanek jumped before the snap. That moved us back to the 43. Stanek was livid with himself. He didn't say anything but the expression on his face made it obvious.

"It's okay," Bender said as we regrouped in the huddle. "We'll get it back. Let's not sweat it."

There is no way to discern if Stanek's faux pas truly killed our drive. All I know is we got nowhere after that. Scott's sweep around left end only got as far as the line of scrimmage. Bender's pass to me was out of reach. I dove for the ball at about the 25 but couldn't get close enough. The ball sailed past and hit the ground, bouncing its way to just behind the end zone.

I laid on the ground for a few seconds. Out of frustration I took a deep breath and exhaled. I wanted this game. A 7-0 lead was never secure.

"Are you okay there, Dockman?" the field judge asked.

I rose up and nodded.

"There's nothing wrong with me that a few more touchdowns won't cure," I said.

The official grinned at my remark. He'd been around long enough to know that occasionally football players need a few seconds of meditation to deal with having things not go as planned.

At least Jablonski pinned the Chiefs back. He went for the proverbial coffin corner. His punt went out of bounds at the six.

The Chiefs had to go 94 yards for a score. It appeared as if they were going to cover the entire distance. After only seven plays they had achieved three first downs. It was first down at the Kansas City 47.

"How much more are you clowns going to give them?" Walker called. "We should already have the ball back. Let's get tough out there."

The Chiefs went up the middle to create a second and seven at the 50. They went to the air on the following play but the ball landed at least ten yards from the nearest receiver. Out defensive backs did an excellent job of covering all of the receivers.

On third down the Chiefs went to the air again. They were focused on a first down and a pass was thrown in the direction of a receiver at about the 40. Rodgers managed to jump in and knock the ball away.

"All right, Rodgers! That's the way to do it!" Walker cheered. "Good coverage! Good coverage!"

I was back on the field again. I stood on the ten-yard line in anticipation of a punt return. I was grateful that the Chiefs still had a goose egg on the scoreboard.

There wouldn't be any return. The punt went out at the nine. There was 9:37 left in the half.

"This is perfect," Bender said as we huddled in the south end zone. "We can just about kill the clock if we do this drive right. We can go into the locker room with a two-touchdown lead."

The Chiefs didn't seem to want to cooperate. Our opening play was a screen pass. I caught the ball at the seven and was actually lucky to get back to the line of scrimmage. I was hit almost immediately but fought my way forward. I managed to get as far as the ten.

Our next play left us back at the original line of scrimmage. Scott rushed through the left and lost a yard.

Since we were in an obvious pass situation we went into our double double. Dietrich was wide to the right while I formed up in the right slot. Slater was wide to the left and Giametti was in the left slot. Kerner was the lone setback.

Bender spotted Giametti open over the middle at about the 25. He got the pass off.

Unfortunately a linebacker leaped up and tipped the ball at about the 12. The ball arched up and came down at about the 20 into the waiting arms of a Kansas City defensive back. Dietrich was nearby and brought the man down at the 18.

"So much for killing the clock and being two touchdowns ahead at halftime," I muttered. I was angry but I didn't want it to show. A display of anger might have been construed as anger toward Bender. The interception was truly not his fault. It was the result of a good play by the defense.

Regardless of who was to blame, our seven-point lead was in jeopardy. The Chiefs needed to travel a mere 54 feet to tie the game. That distance was less than the distance between bases on a Little League field.

The Chiefs picked up four yards through the left on their first play. They followed that up with a pass to the six for a first and goal. They had traveled 36 feet in two plays and had only 18 feet to go.

Most of my teammates were standing in front of the bench. I stood near the 40. I had consumed my Gatorade and crumpled the cup and threw it down.

"Let's go, defense!" I called. A lot of my teammates were yelling to encourage the defense. Nobody's focus was anywhere but the field.

The next play produced nothing for the Chiefs. Their quarterback rolled to his right but had no receivers open. Had he tried to run he would have been pulverized by McDaniel who was in hot pursuit. He wisely opted to throw the ball out of the end zone.

A four-yard rush up the middle got the Chiefs to the two. That was followed by a sweep around right end that fell just short of the end zone. They called a time out to decide whether to go for a field goal and be satisfied by simply getting on the scoreboard or going for the tie.

Giametti was standing next to me. I looked at him and raised my eyebrows.

"Do you think they'll go for it?" he asked.

"That's what I would want to do," I replied. "It depends on what the coach wants."

Coaches have a tendency to be more practical than players. There probably wasn't a single Chief who wanted to settle for a field goal. Doing so almost seemed like a surrender. What they would ultimately do was contingent on whether the coach believed they could push the ball in or not.

Secretly I hoped that they would settle for the field goal. I didn't want to say anything because I didn't want to give the impression that I lacked confidence in my defensive teammates. With guys like Richards, McDaniel, Allen, Jennings and Blakely we had a defense that could stand up to just about anybody. Still, it seemed feasible that the Chiefs could gain the six inches or so that they needed for a touchdown.

The Chiefs were going for it. We put in our goal line defense. There were six down linemen, two linebackers and three defensive backs. Different teams have different goal line defenses. This was our primary one although we also had others.

I practically held my breath as I anticipated the play. Our crowd roared to do its part in making things difficult for the Chiefs. Jennings and Allen looked like they were revving their engines as they chugged their legs while they awaited the snap. Black, Blakely and Morrissey were ready in case the Chiefs decided to surprise us with a pass, but they were playing very tight.

At the snap the quarterback wheeled around and handed the ball to a running back. At the line of scrimmage there was a solid wall of humanity in brown jerseys and white jerseys. After a few seconds the officials were blowing their whistles.

"They didn't make it! They didn't make it!" Walker exclaimed.

A few Chiefs disagreed. They were holding their arms straight up to try to coerce a touchdown. The officials did not seem to agree although they didn't signal anything one way or the other right away.

Suddenly the referee pointed toward the north end zone, leading to a huge roar from our crowd. That meant that our defense had held and we had a first down. Our defensive unit ran off the field clapping their hands. Our offense did the same thing as we ran on the field.

298

I also happened to notice the dejected manner in which the Kansas City offense left the field. The way one of their linemen was jerking his head I could tell that his mouth was a free flow of expletives. I actually started to laugh as I approached our huddle at the back of the south end zone.

That goal line stand was one of the last spectacular plays of the half. We managed to move the ball and picked up a couple of first downs. Our drive was climaxed by another interception, this time in Kansas City territory. On second and three from the Kansas City 44 Bender tried to hit Dietrich near the mauka sideline. The ball was picked off at the 25. The defensive back started upfield but stepped out of bounds at the 26. At this point there was 1:34 left in the half.

The Chiefs also picked up a couple of first downs before their drive started bogging down after they got into Hawaii territory. After Jennings sacked the quarterback at the 50 to give them a third and 18 the Chiefs went to the air against our dime defense.

Hasegawa got the pick. He sandbagged a little and then stepped in front of the receiver at the 25 to intercept the pass. He headed up the field before the Kansas City quarterback brought him down at the Hawaii 47.

Kerner and I spontaneously ran on the field. We got out there so quick that Hasegawa was still on the ground when we reached him. Jeff and I reached down and pulled Rich to his feet, whacking him on the back and his helmet as we enthusiastically lauded his clutch play.

We wanted a touchdown but were willing to settle for a field goal. With only 12 seconds left we wanted to get a quick pass completion to within field goal range. We had two of our time outs left so it wasn't imperative that we get out of bounds. We simply had to be careful not to run out the clock.

One play meant it was touchdown or nothing before the end of the half. Bender was under heavy pressure to the surprise of virtually nobody. He had to quickly find an open receiver or else throw the ball away before the clock ran out. He managed to throw the ball away just as he was about to be sacked. Four seconds remained.

The Chiefs had been in a nickel defense on the preceding play. With time for only one more play they went with seven defensive backs. That meant that Bender would probably have more time to get the pass off but there would be very little room for the receivers to maneuver before and after the reception.

It was a *Hail Mary* situation. We didn't go quite to that extreme. Bender hit Dietrich at the 25. Ted got as far as the 20 before going down. That ended the first half.

"You have a seven-point lead," Walker pointed out before we were to return to the field for the second half. "Seven points on the scoreboard.

You should have more. Let's not get lost on the way to the end zone in the second half."

While I was on the field, I wasn't one to think about statistics. I felt as if I had played a long and hard first half. I was surprised to learn later that it hadn't quite been that way.

It turned out that Hawaii had only 22 plays from scrimmage in the first half. The Chiefs had exactly double that. Obviously time of possession is often a very misleading statistic. All Kansas City had to show for its effort was futility.

Of course we didn't have much more than that ourselves.

We were to receive the second half kickoff. I stood on the goal line to the left of Ozzie as I always did. My thoughts were almost exclusively on breaking this game open.

The Kansas City kicker put his foot into the ball. It was heading my way.

I didn't know exactly where I was when I got the ball. All I knew was that I had backpedaled a few yards and was closer to the rear of the end zone than the front of it. Officially it turned out that I was seven yards deep. A gut feeling told me to take a chance. I wanted to portray a catalyst who made things happen.

The Chiefs' kickoff unit probably expected me to kneel down. They may have let up a little, buying me a few steps. I still had a long way to go to get to at least the 20. That was how far I had to get to justify the return.

There were some good blocks ahead of me. That helped a lot. I still had to do a lot on my own. I spun my way out of a tackle just inside the 20 and continued forward. I sidestepped another Chief and got all the way to the 28 before a Chief got me around the ankles.

Officially it was a 35-yard return . . . and the crowd loved it!

"Okay, good job," the referee said. "Let's get up there. Everybody okay? Let's get up from there, guys."

I was getting up as the rest of our offensive unit was coming on the field. I happened to catch a glimpse of Walker before I joined everybody in the huddle. He had an incredulous look on his face. There wasn't much he could say since I had done a good return. Had I not got to the 20 Walker's expression would have been radically different. I also would have been in for a butt chewing when I returned to the sideline or during Tuesday's film session or both.

We began with a 3 Mililani right. Scott took the handoff and shot forward. He broke a couple of tackles and wound up with a 21-yard run to the Hawaii 49.

We went to the air next. Bender hit yours truly a yard beyond the first down marker. I scooted around a defender and picked up an additional seven yards to the 33.

300

Two plays for 39 yards. That was an impressive way to start the half.

But not as impressive as the next play. Larry Scott left his 21-yard rush in the dust. On a 3 Waikiki left, which was a trap, Larry picked up about ten yards before anybody even got a hand on him. They didn't stop him, though, and Larry shot all the way to the end zone to get us that second touchdown we wanted.

Three plays for 72 yards. Our time of possession was still way down but who cared? The Chiefs could have all the possession time they wanted as long as they didn't score.

As I returned to the sideline Walker congratulated Scott for his 54 rushing yards on two plays. After Guinn's PAT gave us a 14-0 lead Walker came over to me as I grabbed a cup of Gatorade.

"What made you decide to run the kickoff back so deep in the end zone?" he asked in a tone that was not critical.

"Something told me I could," I replied. "I wanted to get something going."

"I think it worked."

Whatever impact my decision to return the kick had was minimal. I think the entire offensive unit was frustrated and determined after our performance in the first half. I might have inspired something but I believe those plays would have taken place even if I had downed the ball.

Our fired-up performance carried into the kickoff. The kick was fielded at the one. Hamer hustled downfield and dropped the return man at the 17.

The crowd was into the game as much as ever by this time. Our rapid score and Hamer's hustle got the fans going. I hoped our defense was as fired up as the crowd was.

Kansas City went to work. They continued to pad their time of possession by picking up a couple of first downs. That was all right with me as long as the score didn't change. I was kind of anxious, though, to get back on the field. It could also help the Chiefs if our defense was overworked.

The Chiefs got to the 50 and no further. On fourth and six I assumed my post to receive the punt.

I stood between the hashmarks at the ten. I figured it didn't matter where I was. They were probably going to punt it away from me. I was still hoping to get to the ball and try to help fire my teammates up again. I wanted for us to have the game put away by the time the fourth quarter was about half over, if not sooner.

The punt was away from me, as expected. It wasn't kicked as high as I would normally come to expect and that enabled the ball to hit the ground before I could get to it. The ball bounced and rolled a little before it was finally downed at the five.

Obviously we were in a big hole for this drive. With a 14-point lead this could work to our advantage as long as we moved the ball. The Chiefs were still in striking distance but time would ultimately be a factor if we played it right. If we didn't turn the ball over we could eat up a large chunk of the clock and get at least a field goal if not a touchdown. The Chiefs would probably still be in striking distance but it would be a more arduous task for them.

Scott got us started. He went through the right to the nine. The four-yard gain almost seemed like a letdown compared to his 21-yard and 33-yard gains from his previous two carries but this was all right. We could use up a huge chunk of the clock if we could score by picking up four yards at a time.

I got the call next on a 4 kama'aina right. I was hit in the backfield but managed to break the tackle. With Kerner, Stanek, Nelson and even Bender leading the way I managed to pick up seven yards to the 16. We had a first down.

We went for a short pass next. Bender took the snap and immediately fired to his left to Slater at the 17. Joe got up to the 21 before he went down.

Another pass followed. Bender threw it my way over the middle. It was low but I made a sliding catch at the Hawaii 41. A Kansas City defensive back touched me before I could rise up to keep me from advancing. I gave the ball to the nearest official and headed back to our huddle.

"Jay!" I heard.

I looked and saw Giametti. He was coming on the field to relieve me. I ran off, slapping palms with Gary as our paths crossed, and stood near Walker.

"I'll let Gary relieve you for a couple of plays," Walker said. "Stay close. I'll send you back in in a minute."

I stood a couple of feet behind Walker. I watched as Bender dropped back to pass. He had to try to scramble before he could find a receiver. He was sacked for a five-yard loss.

One of Bender's many attributes was that he was resilient. He got up without a second thought and presided over the huddle.

Bender went to the air again. This time he got the pass off. He found Giametti at the Kansas City 43. Gary tried to elude a defender by running across the field. He had gone almost from the right hash mark to the left sideline before he was brought down. He was still at the 43 but we had a first down again.

Walker turned around. He looked at me.

"Ready?" he asked.

"I'm ready."

"Okay, tell Bender to run a 3 Wahiawa right."

"Gotcha," I replied, heading back to the field. "Giametti!"

We ran the play. Scott picked up seven yards to the 36. We were in position for a long field goal although we still had a reasonable expectation of a touchdown.

Bender hit Dietrich on the next play at the 25. Ted's momentum took him out of bounds to prevent a further advance. It was another first down.

Scott didn't get anywhere on a sweep around the right. A short pass from Bender to Slater netted only three yards to give us a third and seven at the 22. We were close to having to settle for a field goal.

"We don't want a field goal," Bender told us in the huddle. "They'll be looking for a pass. We'll go with the Kailua. Let's pick up about ten yards on this. Kailua right on two, on two. Ready?"

"Break!"

We followed Bender's orders very well. Scott went through the right and got us the first down. He even did Bender's suggestion of ten yards one better, finally being stopped at the eleven. The clock was ticking with a little more than two minutes left in the third quarter.

I was feeling great. I was drenched with perspiration and there were scrapes on parts of my body from sliding around on the turf but I had an incredible sense of well-being. At this juncture I was almost totally sure that we would win this game. Somehow I sensed the right level of confidence among my teammates.

A short pass to Kerner got us to the four. Perhaps remembering that I had picked up seven yards on the 4 kama'aina right during the early part of this drive, Bender called the play again.

The play had the desired effect. I followed my blockers around right end. The Chiefs had tightened up but I dove from about a yard out and came down in the end zone.

"Jay Dockman the ball carrier," came the announcement over the public address system. "Gain of four yards on the play. Touchdown Hawaii."

Naturally the crowd erupted. Our fans had actually been very vocal through the entire drive. We picked up chunks of yardage on almost every play. In the end it had taken us 13 plays to move 95 yards.

With the extra point our lead was expanded to 21-0. There were 51 seconds left in the third quarter.

"There's still a whole quarter to go," offensive line coach Jerry Meacham reminded us. "Take it easy and drink some Gatorade but be ready to go. We want to get at least one more score to put the game away."

I did as Meacham directed. It was what I normally did after every offensive drive anyway but I understood how imperative it was this time. If the Chiefs were able to put together any type of scoring drive it was imperative that we retaliate.

Guinn's kick was out of the end zone to give the Chiefs a first down at the 20. That was the beginning of a three and out. They rushed for five yards and then threw an incomplete pass. On third down they went to the air again and were nearly picked off. The pass was in and out of Rodgers' hands.

Carl dropped to his knees momentarily. He shook his head and then looked at his hands as if he was searching for a hole in them. He then got up and ran off the field.

"It's all right," I heard Allen tell Carl. "We're getting the ball back."

The clock was stopped with eight seconds left in the third quarter. I stood at about the 35 as I waited for Kansas City to punt. I figured that the punt would exhaust what was left of the quarter. A sustained drive, even if it didn't lead to a score, could just about put the Chiefs on the ropes.

Suddenly the punt was in the air. I had to run up a couple of steps. I fielded the punt at the 39 as I heard Hasegawa a few yards ahead of me letting me know I had room to run.

I shot forward. I was almost to midfield before any Chief got close to me. I cut obliquely to elude the defender and moved into Kansas City territory, turning straight to about the 40 about five yards from the makai sideline. There were a couple of good blocks to aid in my progress and the crowd of 46,106 was standing and yelling. The punter himself grabbed my shoulder pads and got me down at the 25.

As the cheers washed over me I bounced up and flipped the ball to an official. I almost regretted that we were at the break between quarters. I was so stoked that I wanted to get the next play off immediately.

A few teammates from the punt return team offered their congratulations as I headed toward where we would be huddling on the south end zone side of the field. I also received the congratulations of my colleagues from the offensive unit. What I didn't realize at the time was that I had wiped out the entire punt. I was brought down exactly where the line of scrimmage had been when the Chiefs punted. It was a 36-yard punt and a 36-yard return.

"Our people are happy," Scott observed, indicating the crowd as we killed time while NBC was showing commercials. "This'll have them out here next week."

"Do you really think they'll be out here next week?" Kerner asked, trying to sound serious.

"Of course they will," Scott replied.

"Then our fans are idiots," Kerner remarked lightly. "We play in Philadelphia next week."

We broke out laughing in the huddle. I noticed a couple of the Chiefs defensive players giving us strange looks. We were probably looser than we should have been. A three-touchdown lead following a big play to end the third quarter does that to a team, I guess.

304

The strategy was to run off as much of the clock as possible enroute to a score. We only had to travel 25 yards so we couldn't run off too much time, especially if we didn't succeed in getting even one first down, but the idea was to take off as much time as we could to turn this into a four-score game.

Scott picked up three yards on the first play. Kerner followed up the middle for no gain but the futility was nullified by an offsides penalty against the Chiefs. We had a second and two at the 17.

It was Scott again going around right end. He got as far as the 15. The officials called time to measure. The measurement proved that we had a first down by about five or six inches.

Scott went up the middle on the next play. He was hit a few times but managed to keep his feet. He was all the way down to the three before he went down. It was first and goal.

Kerner got the call on the next two plays. On a Kaneohe left he managed only a yard. He caught a swing pass at the one on the following play and fought his way into the end zone.

The crowd exploded again. The fans were having as much fun as we were. I was on my knees in the center of the end zone after throwing a block when Jeff crossed the goal line. I raised my arms in triumph and ran over to Kerner to join my teammates in congratulating him.

Guinn's kick was straight through the uprights. That gave us a 28-0 lead with 12:16 left.

Theoretically the game was over. That's what I believed, anyway. There was still technically time for the Chiefs to score four touchdowns. I suspected that our defense would not allow that.

I sat on the bench and joked with a few of my teammates. I barely paid attention as the Chiefs put together their best drive of the day. They began on their own 20 after downing the kickoff three yards into the end zone. They mixed a series of rushes and passes to give themselves a first down at the Hawaii 21.

At this point I got more serious. My greed was showing its ugly head. Although I believed that victory was secure, I wanted the shutout. It was a minor inconvenience but I still preferred that the Chiefs leave town with nothing but goose eggs on the scoreboard.

The Chiefs rushed to the 16. That was followed by a pass to the two. The receiver spun around to elude Black and stepped into the end zone for the Chiefs' first score of the game with 8:49 left to play.

"So much for the shutout," I remarked lightly to Marv.

"Yeah, well, a shutout is next to impossible in the NFL. With a lead like we've got this late in the game we can't blame the defense for not digging in the way they did earlier."

As the Chiefs prepared to kick the extra point Walker turned and said something to special teams coach Ken Holcomb. Holcomb nodded and turned to face the players on the sideline.

"We're going with the hands team," Holcomb announced, giving us protection from an onside kick.

The Chiefs surprised us by not going with the onside kick. They may have been surrendering or simply putting faith in their defense that it would stop us on a three and out. They may also have been hoping to pin us back.

It also wasn't a normal end over end kick. It was actually a low liner that hit the ground at about the 25 and continued to hop in my direction. I fielded the ball at the six and headed upfield.

I wasn't in the mood to go down too soon. With a front line comprised of people who weren't used to playing on the kick return unit there was more penetration than normal by the Chiefs. I had to bob and weave a little and add the occasional straight-arm to pick up yardage. I managed to get to the 32 before a pair of Chiefs brought me down.

Whether or not the Chiefs had surrendered, Walker ostensibly decided that they had. He sent Joseph in at quarterback, Danny Edwards in at fullback, Ozzie in at tailback and Giametti in at halfback.

"Good game, Jay," Walker said with a warm smile as he offered his hand to me when I exited the field.

It was a three and out. Jablonski punted from the 38. The ball landed untouched and bounced and rolled before coming to rest on the Kansas City eleven.

The Chiefs fared a little better than we did on our previous effort. They managed a first down at the 28. That was followed by three incompletions including one that was nearly intercepted by Blakely. The Chiefs, definitely conceding defeat, opted to punt.

As I stood on about the 30 I decided that the most I would do was call for a fair catch. I changed my mind when I fielded the punt at the 31. I decided to try to put together a return but only got as far as the 35. I suppose my earlier punt return inspired me to try to return this one all the way.

Unfortunately I came up about 65 yards short.

Billingsley went in at quarterback this time. He fared slightly better than Joseph since the offense picked up a first down. After that we were well inside the two-minute warning so Walker called on Billingsley to take a few snaps and drop to his knee. The purpose was simply to give Joseph and Billingsley a little bit of playing time, not to run up the score.

We were 4-5. It was also our first home victory since we opened against St. Louis. That was almost two months earlier.

Kerner gave the postgame prayer. When he finished Walker held up a football as he always did after a victory."

Overall it seemed to be a good team effort," Walker remarked. "I think one play may have deflated the Chiefs and kept them from being more fired up in the second half. That interception that halted their scoring drive late in the first half was a key play."

Walker then flipped the ball to Hasegawa. Rich was rewarded with a round of cheers from his teammates.

It was a good overall effort as Walker suggested. One of the highlights was Scott. He had another 100-yard game, gaining 111 yards on only 14 carries.

As I showered and dressed I thought about how happy I actually was for Bonnie that we had won. It wasn't that a loss would have screwed up her day. It was simply the fact that football is a very emotional game. I would have been okay but not as much fun to be with had we lost.

I suppose it also helped my mood that I had personally played a good game. I preferred not to dwell on that although it did help shape my mood.

In its own way this had been a milestone victory. I had read in some publication prior to the season that the best expansion teams could expect to win about three games during their maiden seasons. This fourth victory obviously meant we had surpassed somebody's allegedly expert projection. Although we were one game below breaking even, we still had some hope for a postseason berth.

Bonnie was beaming when she spotted me entering the hospitality room. The sight of her made me feel so good that I actually regretted that we were having nothing more than a temporary fling. She had a lot of qualities that I liked in a woman. She was intelligent and self-assured although she was also soft spoken. She also had a sense of humor . . . and pulchritude.

"You played a good game," Bonnie said sincerely.

"Thanks," I responded, always slightly embarrassed whenever I received a compliment although I never understood why. "Ready to go?"

As we walked the length of the field Bonnie and I talked a little about the game. She grabbed my left arm and felt the gauze covering a scrape just below my elbow. It wasn't painful but it was conspicuous.

"You're hurt," she said.

"Not really. It's just what happens when you slide around on this artificial turf. It happens on grass, too, but it's worse on turf."

Bonnie liked football but had never watched anybody she knew play the game since she was in high school. Attending the game as my guest caused her to view the game from an unprecedented perspective for her. She said that a few times when I took hits she held her breath until I got up. It is what most wives, girlfriends and mothers also experience.

"You remind me of the girlfriend I had in college," I said. "She said that every time I got hit she vicariously took it with me. She drove me nuts sometimes with the way she worried."

"It sounds like she really cared about you."

I nodded.

"She did," I admitted while hoping we wouldn't spend any more time talking about my college girlfriend. Carol had been wonderful but I was with Bonnie for the moment. It wouldn't have been fair to her if I spent the time talking, or thinking, about Carol.

"Was this a good team you played?" Bonnie asked as we reached the tunnel that connected the field and the parking lot.

"We have a better record than them right now but I don't think they're a bad team. They beat us earlier this year in Kansas City so we got our revenge today. The game in Kansas City was a lot closer."

Bonnie and I had a pleasant time the rest of the afternoon and into the evening. We shared a pizza at the Shakey's on Kamehameha Highway in Aiea before returning to Waikiki and taking in some of the attractions there. We also had a nice walk on the beach before I took her back to her hotel.

I considered her itinerary to be strange. She and her friends were going to Maui and then would return to Honolulu. The other tourists I had dated who were going to neighbor islands would return to Honolulu only to catch their flights home. I never knew of anybody who sandwiched a neighbor island trip between stays in Honolulu.

"Can I call you when I get back in town on Wednesday?" she asked.

"Of course."

CHAPTER FOURTEEN
Philly

I felt great when I woke up on Monday morning. I wasn't totally sure of why. Perhaps it was the company I had kept. Perhaps it was our rematch victory. It could even have been the fact that the lowly expansion team in Hawaii was still technically in the playoff hunt even though we needed at least a few other teams to completely collapse before we could have a realistic expectation of the postseason.

In all probability all of these factors played roles in my sense of well-being.

I spent the morning at the beach in Waikiki. It was conveniently located since it was within walking distance of my home. It was also inhabited primarily by tourists so it seemed less likely that I would be recognized. I valued my privacy but rarely had any.

What I wanted in the worst way was to go surfing. Unfortunately I was cursed with a nasty streak of integrity. I wasn't willing to break my contractual agreement that I not surf between the first day of training camp and our final game of the season. I figured that the odds were that I wouldn't get caught but I would always know that I had breached the agreement. I settled for a nice refreshing swim.

The water felt wonderful. It always did. I've known people who don't like to swim in salt water but I have always loved it. Growing up in southern California, I spent many a free day at the various beaches along the coast. I was often found at beaches in Santa Monica, Venice and Malibu. I also ventured down to the likes of Huntington, Newport and Laguna. There were even rare occasions when I ventured as far south as San Clemente, Oceanside and San Diego.

In Hawaii the water was infinitely more refreshing than that of southern California. Of course the water in Hawaii is warmer although I was not as cognizant of that as I was when I first visited Hawaii more than six years earlier. Being in the ocean was simply a wonderful way to relax.

As a teenager I was the quintessential diehard when it came to swimming. Contrary to what some people believe, it gets cold in sunny California during the winter months. Once all of the holiday excitement had passed I would start getting cravings in January and head to the beach with a friend or two. It wasn't until my senior year in high school that I finally invested in a wet suit. Prior to that I would swim or surf in the frigidly cold water in an ordinary pair of swimming trunks. I would then lie on the beach and shiver furiously for a half-hour or so without any regret that I was willing to swim without a wet suit at such an unseasonal time.

But this was Hawaii. I still owned the wet suit but rarely used it. Since this was November a wet suit at the beaches in southern California would have been extremely prudent. In Hawaii the water was refreshingly cool.

For lunch I went over to the smorgasbord on Lewers Street. This was ideal for me because I could get a well-balanced meal without having to put up with my own cooking. The smorgasbord was a relatively inexpensive venture and I could go back for seconds or even fifths if I wanted.

The smorgasbord was something I could do without any problem as long as I went early in the week. I didn't gain weight back in those days although I would have had I made the smorgasbord a daily ritual. Later in life I had to be more careful but at 25 I could pig out on occasion with no negative effects.

On Tuesday it was back to the regimented football routine. I was still feeling good about everything. I looked forward to our encounter in Philadelphia. The Eagles were not having a good season. I believed we would win as long as we didn't get overconfident or make stupid mistakes.

Naturally the day started with the film session. Walker wasn't jovial when he ran the offensive films but he also generally wasn't negative. He pointed out mistakes and a few times seemed angry but not in a volatile way. He also handed out compliments during situations that warranted them.

One of the highlights was my 35-yard kick return from seven yards deep in the end zone to start the second half. Walker ran the projector straight through without a word. Once I was down Walker paused the film.

"When I saw you running the kick back from that deep in the end zone, I wanted to shoot you on the spot," Walker said lightly. "Afterward I was glad you decided to run it back. If you go by the book you would automatically down the ball that deep. Sometimes you have to throw the book out the window and take a gamble."

Walker paused for a moment, creating an air where everybody knew there was more to come.

"Of course Mr. Dockman," he continued somewhat lightly, "it's pretty darn lucky for you that the gamble paid off."

That busted everybody up.

"Gentlemen, we're still contending for a playoff spot," Walker announced to the entire team after our film sessions. "We're even technically alive to win the division if we keep winning, Denver loses a few more and Oakland totally collapses. I wouldn't count on Oakland losing even half of its remaining games, let alone all of them, but stranger things have happened. It is still technically possible for you to win the division."

Walker paused to let it all sink in. Nobody, Walker included, expected us to win the division. Walker was right, though, that it was technically possible. The important thing was for us to keep believing in ourselves. If we could continue winning and about half-a-dozen or so teams from our conference went into slumps, we could beat the odds and win the wild card berth.

"I don't expect to win the division," Walker admitted. "Even the wild card seems remote but we're still in it. I want you to understand that although I don't want you looking too far ahead. If we're destined to reach the postseason, we're going to have to keep our focus on the present. We play one game at a time, one quarter at a time and one play at a time. Between now and Sunday I don't want anybody even thinking about the Chargers, Raiders, Bengals or Browns. The first thing we have to do is conquer Philadelphia."

Walker went over the week's schedule. This included the plan for Friday's flight to Philadelphia.

"We're scheduled to leave at four o'clock on Friday afternoon. We'll have a good practice Friday morning which should wrap up in time for you to be showered and dressed by noon. Make your arrangements to be driven to Air Service if you haven't already done so. Everybody should be at Air Service by 3:30. If you haven't been able to arrange for transportation by Thursday morning, let me know and we'll work something out."

This talk took place on the Tuesday of every week we were scheduled to travel. He would repeat most of it at the beginning of whatever day we were to travel, in this case Friday. It might have seemed redundant but Walker didn't take any chances. He wanted as few distractions as possible, and few distractions would have been more severe than somebody missing the plane. Since everybody had a specific role, it was important that everybody make the flight.

"I hate the idea of you guys having to scramble for rides to Air Service," Walker muttered for the nth time. "We'll try to find a way for you guys to park your cars somewhere next season. The way we have to do it now is too big a distraction."

I survived the routine as we looked ahead to Philadelphia. Casual workout on Tuesday, film of the Eagles' previous game on Wednesday. That was followed by a meeting and a workout with emphasis on the offense on Wednesday.

Bonnie called me early on Wednesday evening, having returned from Maui a short time earlier. I wanted to see her that night but used restraint. We agreed to have one final rendezvous the following night.

"I prefer to do something casual and quiet if you don't mind," I told her. "That will be fine."

On our final night together I took Bonnie to the Sizzler in the Koko Marina Shopping Center in Hawaii Kai. We followed that with a few hours at Sandy Beach, talking while the waves broke near the shore with a thundering crash. Sandy Beach is probably the most dangerous beach on Oahu. This is because the waves appear innocuous but are actually deadly. Many a neck was broken for those unenlightened about the perils of Sandy.

311

The hazard of Sandy didn't affect Bonnie and me. We sat in the sand and shared a six-pack, breaking a law that was rarely enforced in those days as long as people were discreet. As we talked we gradually moved closer together until we were holding each other close.

It had all been very casual to this point. We had held hands some, danced several times including a few slow dances on our first night out and exchanged a few sweet kisses. It wasn't until this moment, though, that the affection got more serious.

I suppose Bonnie and I were thinking alike. We liked each other. We cared about each other. We were strongly attracted to each other. If we were living in the same locale we could even fall in love with each other and continue from there.

In retrospect, it was the first time since I had been with my college girlfriend that I actually felt a desire to love.

The key was that Bonnie and I did not live in the same locale. We didn't even live in the same country. We were simply making the most of a wonderful experience we were having. Neither of us expected anything more than what we would have during Bonnie's visit. The next day she would fly to Vancouver and I would fly to Philadelphia. Although I suppose I would not have been averse to us reuniting in the near future, I believe we both knew that whatever we might have had together was fated to end at the end of the evening.

Bonnie did not attract me as the promiscuous type although she also wasn't a prude. I doubted that she was a virgin and I most definitely wasn't. Looking back, it surprises me that I somehow knew that having sex with Bonnie or simply trying to have sex with her would have diminished the significance of the experience. Given my attitude about sex at the time, it is downright amazing.

Yet somehow I knew that Bonnie was somebody to be enjoyed simply for the joy of being with her. That was the way it had been with Carol a few years earlier. When I was with Carol was when I truly understood the sheer joy of simply being with somebody extraordinarily special. Sex had nothing to do with it.

At the door to Bonnie's hotel room we hugged and kissed one final time.

"I'm glad I met you," she said with eyes that were even slightly glazed.

I'm glad, too," I said.

She watched while I got on the elevator. As the door closed we smiled, waved and savored our last seconds of eye contact.

In almost every man's life, I believe, there will be an occasional woman who has a lasting impact. He doesn't necessarily fall in love with her and might not even spend a substantial amount of time with her. Somehow she stands out in a very gratifying way.

312

There were several women who passed through my life. Most were almost completely forgotten soon after I last encountered them. There were still a few who warranted fond memories.

Although I never saw Bonnie again, I did hear from her once. She sent me a nice letter in care of the team at the end of my career.

Dear Jay,

You probably don't remember me but I remember you. In 1976 I visited Hawaii. Because of you I had a holiday that was even better than I ever dared dream.

I know you are happily married and I am happy for you. A couple of times when I was watching your games on TV they showed your wife. She is really pretty.

I am also happily married now with two children. I think we were both destined to be with other people. That doesn't mean we can't have fond memories of a special time in our lives.

All I really want to do is congratulate you on a great career. I am going to miss seeing you play. I always watched whenever possible whenever your games were shown in Vancouver. I always enjoyed hearing the announcers saying such nice things about you. It means a lot to me to know that people share my opinion of you.

In case you don't remember me, I was the girl you took to your game against Kansas City. I was amazed that you could play so hard and still be such a gentleman. You treated me like a lady. I will always be grateful for that.

I did see you play in person one more time. A couple of years after we met you played a game in Seattle. I drove down with a friend to see the game. Of course you played a good game.

Anyway I just wanted to thank you again for being so nice to me. The time I got to spend with you is a very wonderful memory. I am glad that you had such a great career.

Have a wonderful life,

Bonnie

That letter meant a lot. Treating a lady like a lady definitely has its rewards. An arbitrary sexual encounter generally lasts for one evening and the two parties might forget each other. The experience of being part of a twosome focusing on the sheer joy of simply being together, even if only ephemerally, can be a lasting experience.

Our flight was delayed. It was an annoyance, albeit a petty one. It wasn't an especially lengthy delay. It rarely happened throughout the course of my career but it was something that was bound to happen on occasion.

Despite the delay, it was a pleasant flight. The lasagna was good even though it was the kind with spinach in it. Although one cannot taste the spinach when it is included in lasagna, I prefer to do without.

Spinach was about the only vegetable I didn't like. My mother tried to feed it to me when I was a kid and I learned at first bite that spinach and I would have a very acrimonious association. Even Popeye couldn't cause the overall nutritional value, which would allegedly enable me to beat the daylights out of any bully who dared cross my path, to supersede the distasteful flavor my taste buds experienced with spinach. As an adult the only time I consumed spinach was when it was adulterating my lasagna.

"What can you tell me about Philadelphia?" Giametti asked Jennings during the flight.

Ed, Gary, Abraham, Scott and I had gathered at the back of the plane. We were about 90 minutes out of Philadelphia at the time, making it about midnight in Honolulu but five o'clock on Saturday morning in Philadelphia. I had been to Philadelphia since it had been a franchise city in the WFL. Ed, of course, was taken from the Eagles in the expansion draft.

"What do you want to know?" Ed asked. "Do you want to know about the city or the team or what?"

"I don't know," Gary replied. "I'm sure it's like most cities we visit. What's it like to play there?"

Ed hesitated. He had a thoughtful expression.

"It's funny but I never really thought about it," Ed said. "I don't know what it'll be like playing on the visiting team. I liked playing for the home team while I was there although the fans could get downright mean if we screwed up, which we often did. As far as the visitors go. . . . I honestly don't know. I never really paid attention."

I couldn't recall anything special about when I played in Philadelphia. There may have been a hostile reception although nothing different from the other WFL cities. The crowds we encountered in the WFL weren't nearly as large as what we were certain to experience as the NFL version of the Hawaiians.

"I've been to Philadelphia a few times," Clint said. "They're really not much different than the fans anywhere else. They're a noisy bunch but they make a lot of noise in Cleveland and New York, too."

"Somebody threw a whiskey bottle at me once," Larry added. "It happened while we were running off at halftime."

"What did you do that made somebody do that?" Ed asked.

"Nothing, really, except that I had the audacity to play on the other team. I think the fan was just throwing it at our team in general. I just happened to be the one who came closest to being hit. That doesn't reflect on Philadelphia itself. It can happen anywhere when some idiot has too much to drink and loses control of himself."

It was known as "The Vet." Veteran's Stadium was one of the cookie cutter stadiums built for both baseball and football. Aloha Stadium was also built for baseball and football but with a totally different design that wound up never being duplicated. Four sections of bleachers moved on cushions of air at Aloha Stadium so that it would have a semblance of an oval figure for football and a more symmetrical figure for baseball.

As we went through our light Saturday workout I looked around. Other cookie cutter facilities had been built in St. Louis, Cincinnati, Atlanta, Pittsburgh and Washington. The only other such facility I had been to at this point was in Washington although I would see Cincinnati a few weeks later.

"What are you thinking about?" Hoddesson asked.

"Just checking the place out. This was where baseball had the All-Star Game this year . . . and the Phillies and Reds played here for the National League championship last month."

"You're unbelievable, Jaybird," Kerner remarked. "It's about 90 below and you're thinking about baseball. What do you think about in the summer? Figure skating?"

"Hockey," I replied wryly.

"Where'd you go last night?" Marv asked Ed as he, Ed, Scott, Rodgers and I drank coffee in the lobby of the hotel. Kickoff was at one o'clock. Our pregame meal was at 8:30. We had congregated at slightly before seven.

"I had dinner with some old friends," Ed replied.

"Former teammates?" Larry asked.

"Nah, just some neighbors. This guy and his wife lived next door to Jennifer and me. He's always inventing things and marketing them. I think that someday he's either going to be a millionaire or blow himself up in his garage."

Ed talked about how strange it was to return. He spent the evening in the house next to the one he had lived in during the majority of his tenure in Philadelphia. He felt as if an invisible shield had been built to prevent him from returning to his old house.

"Would you rather have stayed in Philadelphia?" I asked.

"No, not really. I wouldn't have been disappointed to stay here but I really like Hawaii. If we don't make the playoffs I'm going to go lie on the beach the day after the season ends. That beats hell out of shoveling snow in Philadelphia.

It was interesting that Ed mentioned the playoffs and the possibility of the Hawaiians actually qualifying. Our fellow expansionists in Memphis, Seattle and Tampa Bay were as good as dead on opening day. Also dead were the likes of the Giants, Chiefs, Bills and 49ers as well as the Eagles. We were still technically contenders and it felt great.

It was the defense's turn to be introduced. That worked out well for Ed since he would be introduced to his former home fans.

315

"At left outside linebacker, number 57, from California, Ed Jennings," the PA announcer announced as Ed ran from the end zone to midfield.

I guess I should have said that it worked out well for the fans that the defense was introduced. It gave them an opportunity to boo at several more decibels than normal. The entire defensive unit was greeted with boos, of course. When Ed was announced the crowd turned it up enough to be heard in Pittsburgh.

"I see you left an indelible impression here," Kerner remarked when Ed and the rest of the defense came to the sideline.

"Oh, hell yes," Ed replied, shaking his head in amused disbelief. "I showed my disloyalty to the city when the Eagles made me available in the expansion draft and the Hawaiians took me."

"That's okay," I remarked. "The fans here can shovel snow while you're lying on the beach."

"Well right now they're shoveling something other than snow," Ed quipped. "Or I guess they're just dishing it out."

As far as the weather went, there was no snow on the ground but it was cold. The temperature was in the 40s at gametime. That was the coldest we had endured thus far but we dealt with it. Most of us were wearing thermals and those who weren't didn't seem uncomfortable. It would have had to have been a lot colder to cause thoughts about the temperature to supersede our focus on the game.

The Eagles won the toss. I shrugged my shoulders and patiently stood by. The kicking team and defense would get their licks in. My hope was that they would leave us good field position.

Guinn kicked off. The ball was taken two yards deep in the end zone. The Eagle return man didn't hesitate as he headed upfield. He quickly got to the 20 where he broke Hasegawa's tackle. He also broke tackles by Morrissey and K.T. Smith.

"What the hell are you guys doing out there?" I heard Walker bark, probably out of having nothing more intelligent to say under the circumstances. I don't know exactly what my teammates were doing but what they *weren't* doing was tackling.

The ball carrier crossed midfield and headed down the far sideline. It was Zanakis who finally caught him. He pursued the ball carrier obliquely after previously being knocked down. He finally hammered the return man at the Hawaii 21. It was obviously not an auspicious start for us although it could potentially demoralize the Eagles if our defense prevented them from scoring.

"Let's go, guys," Allen beckoned as he and the others on our starting defense ran out to the field.

I shook my head and sat down. At the same time the fans were quieting down. Legend has it that Philadelphia fans love to boo. They sure weren't booing that kick return.

"Maybe we can hold them to a field goal," Kerner said optimistically as he sat next to me.

"Or turn it over," I suggested.

"That would take the wind out of their sails," Jeff remarked.

The Eagles went off left tackle. They got three yards.

It only took one more play. The Eagles opted to go to the air. The quarterback threw a strike to a receiver being covered by Black. Mark had the man well covered but the pass was perfect. The receiver caught the ball just as he was crossing the goal line.

There was a penalty marker down. I saw it fly up at the snap. Either one of our defensive linemen was offsides or else he was drawn offsides. I couldn't think of any other possibility.

Unfortunately the penalty was against Richards. He had lined up in the neutral zone. The Eagles declined the penalty.

The extra point gave the Eagles a 7-0 lead. Counting the kick return, the opening drive covered 102 yards on three plays and ate up exactly one minute.

"Okay, okay. Let's get it back," Walker encouraged in a somewhat exasperated tone.

I ran to my post on the goal line. I focused on getting myself hyped. I felt demoralized by the kick return that led to a touchdown two plays later. I wanted to put our inauspicious start behind us and do some damage myself.

The kick came. It was heading my way. I moved back a few steps and caught the ball. With a mob of green jerseys coming after me, I noticed that I was about eight yards deep in the end zone. I suspected that I shouldn't tempt fate by doing a runback from so deep in the end zone two weeks in a row. I downed the ball.

That was probably the highlight of our entire drive. Bender's pass to Dietrich was batted down. He wanted to go to the air again and was sacked at the 16. The raucous fans who loved to boo seemed to be enjoying the opportunity to cheer. There hadn't been that many in Philadelphia over the previous few years; at least not in football.

On third and 14 Bender tried to hit Giametti on the sideline just beyond the first down marker. A defensive back stepped in and nearly intercepted the pass. He batted the ball about three feet up in the air like a child would bat a toy balloon. When the ball came down it went right through his hands to the ground.

And they were cheering in Philadelphia. If anybody was booing the defensive back for muffing the interception that would have been a sure six points, I couldn't hear them.

Actually I couldn't hear anything. All I recall noticing was the scowl on Walker's face as my teammates and I headed for the sideline. A drive that lasts for three plays and totals a loss of four yards was the type of thing that rarely made him smile.

Of course nobody on our team was too happy. The players on the offensive unit were the most unhappy of the bunch.

At least Jablonski did some good for us. He got off a booming punt despite a heavy rush. The punt traveled 47 yards to the 38. The return man got as far as the Philadelphia 45 before going down.

This drive would not prove to be a carbon copy of the Eagles' previous drive. They went to the air on the opening play and Black nearly came up with an interception. He was just getting his hands on the ball when it squirted out. Mark reacted by taking a mini hop and waving his fists through the air a couple of times before putting his hands on his knees and glaring at his feet. Thus far in the game it did not seem to be his day.

"It's all right, Mark! You'll get the next one!" defensive coordinator Max Crawford called to try to encourage him.

The Eagles went around right end and picked up four yards on the following play. That put us in our nickel defense.

On the snap the quarterback dropped back. Ed penetrated through the line and went after him. The quarterback tried to scramble away but Ed had him in his grasp. A split-second later McDaniel also had his arms around the quarterback and the three of them went down on the Philadelphia 42.

This produced the booing we were expecting. It probably would have happened anyway but we suspected it was more intense because it was a former Eagle who made the sack. Ed would only be credited with a half sack but he had been the catalyst.

It was fourth and 13. That meant that I was back on the field. I fielded the punt at the Hawaii 20 and tried to run it back. I got as far as the Hawaii 30 before I was mauled by a pair of Eagles.

This alleged drive didn't do much better than our first possession. We picked up three yards when Scott ran through the right on the opening play. The Eagles gave us an additional five yards before the next snap which produced no gain but then we gave the five yards right back after Hayer jumped prematurely. Bender threw an incompletion under a heavy rush on third down.

Neither side had managed a first down by this time although the Eagles did have a touchdown. We had now run six plays from scrimmage. Our overall offensive total was still one yard shy of breaking even.

"You guys ought to be thinking about moving the ball out there," Walker instructed us in one of his better displays of sarcasm as we exited field. "Just because you won last week doesn't mean you're not allowed to win this week. Let's see if we can win two in-a-row for a change."

318

Jablonski gave us another good punt. This time there would be no return. The ball went out of bounds at the Philadelphia 24. Thus far that was the worst field position the Eagles had that day.

They wouldn't have the ball long. After a five-yard gain on the ground they went to the air. A swing pass was picked off by Jennings at the Philadelphia 33. Ed stumbled a little, then took off. He was brought down at the 24.

That fired up the offense, if not the entire team. Amid the loud boos from the crowd were exultant cheers among the Hawaiian players.

I ran on the field with my teammates from our offensive unit. It worked that I would cross paths with Ed as he was running off. As we approached each other I pointed at him with a big smile on my face.

"Obviously you still love playing in Philadelphia," I said, stopping briefly to shake Ed's hand.

"Yeah, they love me here," Ed replied jocularly. "You can tell by the crowd."

I met my teammates in the huddle. Thanks to Ed we were only 72 feet from a touchdown. It didn't seem like it was asking too much for us to actually score.

Scott went through the left on the first play. He was hit near the line but kept his feet. He got as far as the 18.

Kerner was next. He also went through the left. He picked up six yards to the 12. With 6:12 remaining in the first quarter we had just secured the first first-down of the game by either team.

Scott played philanthropist before the next snap. He jumped after I had already gone in motion. That cost us five yards to the Philadelphia 17.

"Okay, okay. Don't worry about it," Bender told us in the huddle. "We'll make it up."

I got the call. I went around right end. Amid the grunts and the sound of pads colliding I felt myself getting hit at about the 15. Somebody hit against my thigh pad. I spun around and continued forward until I reached the 12. That was when I was brought down and was lying on my back.

The whistles blew. Directly above me I could see an official in his striped shirt. He was blowing his whistle and holding an upraised arm to signal that the play was dead.

"Okay, everybody up," the official instructed after he finished blowing his whistle.

The Eagle who tackled me raised himself up. He reached down to offer me his hand and pulled me up.

"Good run," he said as he whacked me on the derriere.

"Thanks. Good tackle," I answered as I handed the ball to the official and headed to the huddle. I suppose the man who tackled me and I were simply trying to soften each other up.

319

We tried to score through the air on the following play. Bender was under a heavy rush. He still spotted Grummon in the left corner of the end zone. He unleashed the ball but a defensive back batted it away.

Another pass was called on third down. Bender didn't meet as heavy a rush but the receivers were pretty well covered. He spotted Giametti and tried to get the ball to him. Unfortunately that pass was also batted down.

I was near the back line in the center of the end zone when the play was blown dead. I stood for a moment with my hands on my hips. I didn't blame anybody but it was frustrating. I believed we should have scored a touchdown.

It came as no surprise that the field goal unit came out. Had it been a fourth and one or fourth and two or possibly even a fourth and three Walker might have been amenable to going for the touchdown. On fourth and ten, especially with the way we had barely been able to move the ball thus far, he was willing to settle for the field goal.

At least Guinn put us on the scoreboard. His 29-yard effort was true.

"That's better than nothing," I muttered.

"Nah, it's okay," Bender responded, standing next to me. "We've got plenty of time. They seem to have the momentum at the moment but we're gradually taking it away from them. We just have to hang in there. We'll wear them down."

I was again reminded of why Bender was such a good quarterback. There was a lot to be said for confidence.

Guinn kicked as if he had his share of confidence. The kick was fielded about eight yards deep in the end zone. The return man wisely opted to down the ball.

While I looked forward to shifting the momentum to us, it didn't appear as if it was going to happen right away. A rush up the middle went to the 24. That was followed by a pass to the Philadelphia 36.

The latter was for a first down. With 2:13 left in the first quarter the Eagles finally got their first first-down.

Not that I would ever make fun of them for it. It is hard to make fun of them when they are still holding a four-point lead.

The Eagles seemed to be feeling a little better about themselves. An end sweep picked up seven yards. They went through the right on the next play to get about three yards. That was close to a first down.

It wasn't close enough. The officials called time and brought the chain out. The measurement showed them about two inches short.

We went to our 44 defense: four down linemen and four linebackers. The defense was rounded out by three defensive backs in zone coverage.

I stood and watched as the quarterback took the snap. My defensive teammates seem to build a fairly impressive wall to prevent the inches necessary for a first down. I could hear a lot of grunting and pads violently colliding at the snap. The ball carrier took the handoff and leaped up. . . .

320

"He got it," I said in exasperation.

"No, maybe he's short," Dietrich replied.

"No, he made it," I said, shaking my head. "I don't know exactly where they're going to spot the ball but I'm sure he got enough yardage."

Unfortunately I happened to be right. The ball was marked at the Philadelphia 47. That was enough for a first down. The crowd that allegedly loved to boo was cheering again.

The Eagles picked up four yards to the Hawaii 49 on first down. They tried a sweep around right end on the next play and lost a yard. Once again it was former Eagle Ed Jennings in the limelight. He was the one who made the tackle on what turned out to be the final play of the first quarter.

"We shouldn't be losing to these guys," I muttered to myself although Bender heard me. "These guys are not that good."

"Hang in there, Jay," Steve said, optimistically tapping my back. "We've got three quarters left. We'll get the job done."

The Eagles got the second quarter off to a good start, at least for them. They completed a pass over the middle at the Hawaii 40. Black was right there to prevent any further gain. It was still enough for a first down.

I found myself getting anxious. I knew there was still plenty of football left and that their four-point lead was hardly insurmountable. I suddenly found myself worrying about the Eagles gradually pulling away from us to the point where we would not be able to come back. A victory would put us at the .500 mark ten games into the season. I wanted this one very badly.

The Eagles didn't seem impressed. As I watched helplessly on the bench the Eagles achieved two more first downs. The latter first down was at the eleven.

We were an expansion team. I should have been grateful for the four wins we had already achieved. Despite that, being willing to settle for those four wins seemed tantamount to conceding the final five games. I was still thinking about the possibility of achieving the impossible by making the playoffs.

The crowd was getting raucous. Allen dampened their spirits on the next play. The Eagles tried to go up the middle and the ball carrier found a violent reception with Russ. That was two yards behind the line of scrimmage to give them a second and 12 at the 13.

"Okay, that's the way to play it!" Walker called although it was very unlikely that the defense heard his words of approbation. "Let's keep pushing them back!"

Whether the defense heard Walker or not was not important. It was as if the defense did hear him. The Eagle quarterback dropped back. Jurgens caught up with him at the 20. The quarterback tried to scramble but Jon reached out and dragged him down by the shoulder pads.

"Yeah!" I cried out, jumping from my seat on the bench. The fans were booing. I was thrilled.

"One more play," I said to Scott. "We just need to hold them for one more play. If we can push them back one more time it will make it harder for them to get even a field goal."

"It would sure deflate their spirits," the tailback from LSU added, looking at me with his crooked smile.

I would have been happy with another sack. I was happier when the Eagles turned the ball over. As I knew they would, the Eagles went to the air to try to get through our dime defense. Rodgers picked the ball off at the ten; his first interception of the season. Carl fought off a couple of Eagle receivers and made his way to the 17 before a pair of linemen brought him down.

Walker turned around to call the offense. Before he could utter a single word the entire unit ran past him. We were stoked.

One of the hottest songs on the charts at the time was *Nadia's Theme*. It was a very beautiful song titled in honor of Romanian gymnast Nadia Comaneci. As pleasant as the song was to listen to, its beauty was nothing compared to the sound of the booing at Veterans Stadium at that moment. Philly fans hadn't had much to cheer about that season. I was determined to keep it that way.

And so we began a drive. Our objective was 83 yards away. We were going to begin by utilizing our air attack.

I ran about 20 yards downfield and turned around. That was just in time to see an Eagle defensive back cut in front of Dietrich and pick off the pass intended for him at the 32. Ted tried to tackle him but was off balance and fell down while trying to reverse direction. The defensive back weaved his way to the 23 before Marv brought him down.

They weren't booing anymore. I hated every fan in attendance because of that. I wasn't there to listen to the fans cheer. I wanted them to have the most miserable day they'd had all year. Given the Eagles' record, that would have been a major achievement.

I was angry as I left the field and grabbed my cup of Gatorade. The interception came as a result of an outstanding play by the defensive back. It wasn't something I could blame on Bender.

Even if it was Bender's fault, I wasn't going to blame him. Interceptions were simply a frustrating part of the game. Interceptions, regardless of whether they were the fault of the quarterback or somebody else on offense or the result of a great defensive play, were no worse than a lineman missing a block or a ball carrier fumbling. My anger was at the circumstance.

I understood how Bender was feeling. I had spent four years being a quarterback in high school. I wasn't picked off very often but it did happen. The only thing to do was suck it up and go from there.

322

The Eagles were anxious to capitalize to extend their lead to 14-3. They went through the left on the opening play for four yards. A screen pass to the right on the following play got them a first down at the eleven.

"Let's go, defense. Come on," I mumbled to myself as if my words would reach them by telekinetic power.

My words were of no help on the next play. The Eagles went up the middle for five yards.

The Eagles attempted to pass but the quarterback was forced to throw the ball out of the end zone. That led to a sweep around left end that left them in a fourth and one at the two.

It was decision time for the Eagles. A field goal was almost a sure thing since it was the same distance as an extra point. I was actually hoping they would go for the first down if our defense could rise to the occasion.

They were going for it. As the crowd roared its approval the Eagles lined up. The quarterback held his hands up to quiet the crowd so that his teammates could hear his signals.

On our sideline Stanek, who was occasionally known to portray a clown, started waving his hands up and down as if trying to encourage the crowd to raise the volume.

"Yeah, like they're going to listen to you," Marv said lightly.

As nervous as I was, I still managed to laugh a little.

The Eagles attempted a sweep around right end. The pulling guard managed to fight off McDaniel but Ed and Black were right there. They teamed up to stop the Eagles for no gain.

"Yeah!" I exclaimed, heading to the field with my offense colleagues. We had a first down at the two. Only 98 yards to go for a touchdown.

As I headed toward where we would huddle in the end zone, I watched a commotion going on near the line of scrimmage. A couple of Eagles were conferring with an official and pointing. It appeared that they were not happy with where the ball was spotted. I could tell that they were not acting with any civility.

The latter was confirmed when a yellow flag suddenly shot up in the air. Apparently one of the disgruntled Eagles said something that was better left unsaid. The Eagles were cited for unsportsmanlike conduct. Instead of starting our drive at the two, our original line of scrimmage would be the 17. I was tempted to thank the offending Eagle.

They were booing again. My assumption was that they were not booing the Philly player's alleged misconduct but the fact that the Eagles were penalized. All I cared about was the fact that we didn't have the goal line and a potential safety lurking at our back

The Eagles continued their transgressions as we prepared to start the first play of the drive. As the booing continued, one of the Eagle linemen jumped too soon and made contact with Hayer. That cost them another five yards.

"All right, they're helping us bigtime," Bender remarked in the huddle to get us thinking positive. "We can't help but go all the way this time. Let's do it. Here we go."

Bender called a Kailua right. Scott took the handoff and picked up four yards.

I got the call next. I raced around left end. I managed to spin my way to the 30 for a first down.

Scott got the next two calls. He went up the middle for a hard fought six-yard gain. On a sweep around right end he was hit in the backfield and broke loose, then hustled his way to the Hawaii 49 for a 13-yard gain. We had another first down.

This was where it appeared that our drive would stall. Bender passed to nobody in particular on first down. He tried to hit me downfield on the next play but the pass was batted down.

The Eagles blitzed on the next play. Bender knew it was coming and dumped a quick pass off to me at the Philadelphia 49. I picked up another ten yards before being knocked out of bounds at the 39.

Surprisingly enough, that was our first completion of the day. The deep coverage had simply been too good. We finally decided to sneak one in underneath. Fortunately I managed to pick up enough yardage to keep the drive alive.

After Scott picked up only two yards through the left, Kerner got the call. He was hit at the line while going through the right, then broke the tackle and got to the 30.

It was Scott again on a 3 Wahiawa right. He bulldozed his way to the 26 for still another first down. We were almost completely guaranteed three points by this time but I was already thinking about how I wouldn't be happy with that. A touchdown would give us the lead.

Another Philadelphia penalty got us another first down. On third and seven at the 23 Bender's incompletion was nullified by a roughing the passer penalty. Three plays later Bender hit Dietrich in the middle of the end zone to give us a 9-7 lead with 44 seconds left in the half. Ted was hit as he caught the ball but held on for the score.

Guinn's extra point extended our lead to 10-7. The Eagles downed the kickoff in the end zone and then the quarterback dropped to his knee on the following two snaps to end the half.

There was plenty of booing as the two sides left the field but I wasn't certain of what the crowd was booing this time.

I ate a Hershey bar and drank some Gatorade at halftime. The offense and defense made some adjustments before Walker addressed the entire team.

"The receivers aren't getting open," Walker announced in what may have been the quintessential understatement of the day. "We can do better.

We've got to find a way to do it. We can't depend exclusively on the defense and we can't limit ourselves to grinding it out on the ground. We've got to get our passing game working."

I didn't find out how right Walker was about our passing ineptitude until I saw the statistics later. At halftime we had 66 rushing yards. We had gained only 20 yards in the air on only two completions. That was a very anemic total.

We returned to the field amid the expected boos. I actually smiled to myself as I listened to the crowd." I love it when they boo us in Philadelphia," I remarked to Allen on the sideline. "If they're booing it means we're probably winning."

"I know what you mean," Russ replied with a chuckle. "I've always loved being booed . . . at least when I was on the visiting team. Our fans in Hawaii haven't really booed us but I remember a time or two when I was with the Lions that we got booed in Detroit. Of course we might have deserved it but it still hurts the ego. All you can do is just try to ignore it and go out and play as hard as you can."

We were struggling to beat a team that had only two victories to that point. Both victories were against the New York Giants who would finally get into the win column against the Redskins in a game being played concurrent with ours. The Eagles were reportedly rebuilding under new head coach Dick Vermeil but their record with only two victories against a very week team compared to ours with victories over much tougher teams suggested that we should already be leading by at least a couple of touchdowns. Perhaps we weren't taking the Eagles seriously.

I stood in my designated spot on the goal line as I awaited the kick to start the second half. The familiar butterflies gathered in my stomach as I waited for NBC to come out of commercial. Despite our slender three-point lead, I felt cocky. I actually envisioned us having a lead of about four touchdowns by the time the third quarter ended.

But the rout would have to start with the kickoff. I decided that I was going to run it all the way back.

Unfortunately the kicker didn't cooperate with my fantasy. He squibbed it. The ball was fielded by Giametti at the 20.

I shot forward in hope of laying a good block. Unfortunately Gary fielded the ball too far ahead of me and the play was over in a few seconds. He returned the ball to the Hawaii 38 before being brought down by a pair of Eagles. I didn't get to hit anybody.

Another Eagle decided that he wanted to be in on the tackle. I was sure that the whistle was blowing when he fell on top of Gary and his two teammates. I was just reaching the scene when the extra hit took place.

"Late hit! Late hit!" I called, pointing downward at the guilty party.

I looked around. There wasn't a yellow flag anywhere.

"Didn't you see that?" I asked the nearest official. "That was a late hit."

The official shook his head.

"It was close," he said, "but not close enough. His momentum was carrying him and he was already going down when the play was blown dead."

I didn't agree with the explanation but there was no point in arguing. Having played organized football since I was 14 and organized baseball since I was eight, there were occasions when I questioned the rulings on the field. At no time did I ever succeed in getting a call reversed.

At least we had reasonably good field position. Our own 38 was not a bad place to start our first drive of the half.

Scott managed only two yards on a sweep around right end. I followed up by picking up four yards through the right.

On the following play Dietrich ran a quick button hook that had him turned in right about at the point where we needed to go for a first down. Bender hit him on the numbers and Ted did a great job of maneuvering around a linebacker who had visions of pulverizing his smaller opponent. I did my part by putting my shoulder into the midsection of a defensive back and driving him out of the play. Ted got to the Philadelphia 45 before he was finally brought down.

Slater relieved Ted for one play and made the most of it. He caught a pass on the 41 while running a cross pattern. He turned toward our goal line and managed to pick up an additional seven yards. We had our second first down in as many plays, this time at the Philadelphia 34.

I got into the act to give us our third consecutive first down. I caught a pass at the 19 near the left sideline. I was tripped up immediately by a defensive back who lunged in my direction and somehow managed to grab me by the ankle. I reached down to try to right myself but my knee hit the ground at the 16. It was still an 18-yard gain and I probably would not have gotten more than another yard or two since another defensive back was coming right at me when I was ruled down.

We had a free play after that. One of the Eagle linemen jumped before the snap. Kerner went up the middle and got as far as the 12. We took the penalty which gave us a first and five at the eleven.

The fans were booing. That seemed to fire up their defense.

"We're making it too easy for them!" I heard one of the Eagle defenders bark.

"We're better than this! We've got to stop them now!"

I was feeling as if they couldn't and the effect of the chiding was not immediate. Bender hit Grummon with a short pass at the seven. Although Rich was hit and dropped immediately, we only had a yard to go for another first down.

Scott picked that up for us. He picked up three yards through the left. It was first and goal.

That was when the Eagle determination kicked in. They guessed that we were going to pass on first down and, Unfortunately they were right. Bender dropped back and was brought down by a blitzing linebacker at the eleven.

Scott got three of those yards back on a run through the middle to give us a third and goal at the eight. The fans had stopped booing when Bender was sacked and were now hollering encouragement to the defense to hold us at bay.

Bender was cool under pressure. That would befit somebody with his experience. He found Dietrich in the end zone and fired a bullet in his direction. Unfortunately a defensive back just barely managed to reach over with one hand and knock the pass down. We now had fourth and goal and I knew exactly what Walker was going to call.

I said a few choice words that befit my vernacular of the day. I didn't blame anybody for our inability to score a touchdown. I didn't blame Walker for sending in the field goal unit. I was simply frustrated over our inability to climax the drive with the full seven points.

"Shake it off, men," Walker directed as my offensive colleagues and I reached the sideline. "That was a good drive. We'll punch it in next time."

I knew that Walker was right. It wasn't a bad drive and it also wasn't a total loss. Guinn converted on his field goal attempt to give us a 13-7 lead.

As sick as I felt over having to settle for a field goal, at least I was able to console myself for the moment. What was about to happen would ultimately make me extremely sick.

We started our defensive effort on a dubious note. We were late getting our kicking team on the field and lost five yards for delay of game.

"That's Pop Warner crap!" Walker bellowed with good reason. "That's about as inexcusable as any penalty we can create! What's so hard about getting the kicking team on the field?"

I was right behind Walker when he went into this tirade. I understood his feelings but felt very uncomfortable standing so close to him. I almost felt guilty even though I was not guilty of anything. I quickly but subtly moved as far away from Walker as I could get simply to be out of his line of fire.

It turned out that Guinn was the guilty party although he was primarily a victim of circumstance. Somehow on his field goal the lace on his right shoe snapped. One of the attendants had to dig for a replacement lace and it took longer than it should have. Somebody should have allowed us a special time out for an equipment adjustment but very few people, and none of the officials, knew what was causing the delay. Guinn was running on the field just as the yellow flag was tossed up.

And the fans weren't booing. I was hoping we would do something to change that.

Guinn ultimately kicked the ball to the four. The Eagles got a good return out of the deal. Zanakis brought the return man down after a 31-yard gain to the 35.

"That's way too far," I muttered under my breath as I grabbed a windbreaker and put it on. I wasn't especially cold but I still felt a little more comfortable with the windbreaker on. At least it wasn't raining.

The Eagles immediately went to the air. The Eagle quarterback pinpointed a pass to his receiver at the Hawaii 48. Rodgers was right there, sticking to the receiver like flypaper and hitting him immediately. It was simply a picture-perfect pass and the receiver's concentration was such that he was able to hang on to the ball and give his team a first down.

After a rush to the 44 the Eagles decided to go for a longer trek through the air. The quarterback hit a receiver near the right sideline at the 20. The receiver picked up an additional 13 yards before he was hit and dropped by Black, whom the receiver had beaten on the play, and Blakely. They had first and goal.

"Dammit, defense! Halftime is over!" Walker called, cupping his hands near his mouth to amplify his voice. "Didn't you notice the kickoff to start the half? It's time to play ball!"

It's not likely that the defensive unit heard Walker or cared to note his sarcastic remarks. The crowd had become so raucous that Walker's voice would have been muffled, assuming that it could be heard at all so far down the field.

Regardless of Walker's sarcasm, the Eagles wasted no time in giving our defense a porous appearance. A running back went right up the middle and didn't stop until he reached the end zone. The extra point gave them a 14-13 lead with 5:20 left in the third quarter.

"All right, all right," Walker remarked, turning to face us. "They adjusted and got a score. Let's stick it to them."

Walker suddenly looked right at me.

"We'll start with a good kick return," he added. He was addressing the entire kick return unit but looking directly at me since I happened to be the first member of the kick return unit his eyes fell on.

I took my place on the goal line again. In keeping with custom, I slapped five with Rich Hasegawa, my fellow ex-Rainbow who had replaced Ozzie as my partner on the goal line.

"You guys stink!" exclaimed an inebriated sounding voice in the seats directly behind the end zone. That led to more taunts from the spectators in the immediate vicinity. Rich and I wisely ignored them.

The Philly kicker put his foot into the ball as soon as NBC said it was okay. It was high this time and coming into my area. I moved slightly to my left and caught the ball on the goal line.

328

I headed upfield determined to make something happen. One Eagle managed to get close at about the 15 but I straight-armed him and kept going. It wasn't until I reached the 29 that I was finally caught from behind and brought down.

Whistles were blowing. The momentum caused my tackler and me to roll on the ground until he wound up on top of me. He was positioned so that I could barely see. I could see a small patch of the green artificial turf and a few sets of feet. I could also tell that my tackler outweighed me by about 75 pounds.

"Okay, good play all around," an official nearby was saying. "Let's get up there. Let's get the game going again."

As soon as my tackler was off, I got up without difficulty. I joined my teammates in the huddle. We were going to go to the air on the opening play.

At least that was the plan. Bender took the snap and found himself being rushed. I was about 20 yards downfield and open but Steve was scrambling and couldn't see me. I waved to get his attention just as he was about to be hit two yards behind the line of scrimmage after scrambling forward.

As Steve was about to hit the ground I saw the ball hit the ground and roll away. Suddenly there was a handful of white jerseys and green jerseys diving after the pigskin. I ran toward the fumble but was so far away that there was little that I could do except be a witness. There was a pile of men in either green or white jerseys right around where the line of scrimmage had been. A couple of men in green jerseys standing above the pile were pointing in one direction. Hoddesson and Marv in white jerseys were pointing in the other direction. A couple of officials were still trying to sort out the pile.

"Who's got it?" Dietrich asked as he stood beside me.

I turned and spread my palms out. As soon as I did that the crowd let out a sustained roar. At that moment I knew exactly who had possession. If the roar of the crowd didn't tip me off, the sight of guys in green jerseys jumping up in exultation did the trick. The Eagles had recovered at the 29.

Dejectedly I headed to the sideline. Walker was in his trademark angriest stance with his arms folded and his jaw clamped shut. He kept his mouth shut tight because he knew that anything he had to say in this mood, regardless of how much we might have deserved it, would be counterproductive.

"It's all right, man," I saw Kerner saying to Bender.

Steve had an expression on his face that could have cut through steel. He was angry at himself. It probably also didn't help his disposition that he had to ignore one fan in particular who was taunting him in the section behind our bench.

"Way to go, Bender! Thank you very much, Bender! You're the best player the Eagles have right now! No wonder the Vikings got rid of ya!"

A few of us smirked at that. Even Steve seemed to find it amusing although we were careful not to let it show. The allegedly learned fan obviously didn't know that Steve had never played for the Vikings.

At least our defense knew more about football than the pickled fan did. It rose to the occasion. Two rushes and an incomplete pass netted the Eagles eight yards. They had fourth and two at the 21.

The Eagles' field goal unit took the field. The ball was spotted at the 28. The kicker got his foot into it, but the ball appeared to be veering. It was hard to tell from my angle on the sideline but it didn't look as if it was. . . .

Suddenly the ball hit the right upright. I started to raise my arms in jubilation but the ball didn't bounce back on the field the way I expected it to. The ball caromed off the upright and went over the crossbar. The Eagles had extended their lead to 17-13.

As much as the three points disgusted me, it could be argued that we got a break. Turning the ball over to them at our 29 was roughly the equivalent of inviting them to a free touchdown. We were lucky that we only gave up a field goal.

For the third time in the third quarter I stood on the goal line to receive a kickoff. After Rich and I did our customary slap fives he looked at me and shook his head with a bewildered expression showing beyond his facemask.

"I can't believe this Mickey Mouse team is beating us this late in the game," he remarked.

"It's okay. Their lead won't last much longer," I replied although I wasn't certain of how sure I should be. The Eagles, while possibly dejected after having to settle for a field goal on their last drive, clearly had the momentum. I wondered if we could get it back.

The kick came my way again. I fielded the ball at the four. There was good blocking in front of me. Slater held one Eagle at bay well enough to prevent him from making a direct hit on me. The Eagle broke loose but had momentarily lost his balance. He stumbled into my right hip but I spun around and moved away from him, then leaped over one of his teammates who had been laid out by Edwards. For the second kick return in a row I was brought down at the 29.

Not that the return did any good. Just as I was being hit by one Eagle, Giametti was blocking another right around the 29. Unfortunately Gary caught him slightly from behind. As I was going down I noticed the yellow flag flying up. The clip took us back to just inside the 15.

This was obviously not an auspicious start. It didn't get any better when Bender threw an incompletion and Scott lost two yards to give us a third and 12 near the 12.

"We're better than this," Bender chided at the beginning of the huddle. "Let's play like we want to win. Everybody, including me, is screwing up. Let's play the way we're supposed to."

Bender called the play. A moment later I had my second reception of the second half and third of the game. Steve hit me while I was on the run at about the 22. I continued to the 29, seemingly a magnetic spot for me, before being knocked out of bounds on the left sideline.

"All right. That's what we needed," Bender remarked as we huddled inside the 20.

My reception was fairly routine but it was exactly what we needed.

Scott carried twice to get us a first down at our own 43. Kerner went up the middle to the Philadelphia 43 to get us another first down. We were recapturing the momentum.

The Eagles helped our cause. They stopped Scott for a gain of only three yards but their effort was nullified when one of their defensive tackles was called for holding. That gave us a first and five at the Philadelphia 38.

Scott took the ball around right end on the next play. He was hit at the line. Somehow he managed to pick up a couple of yards before three Eagles brought him down. It was the final play of the third quarter.

As the officials moved the ball to the other side of the field, Bender went to the sideline to converse with Walker while Joseph, Billingsley and the offensive coaching staff stood nearby. I joined Marv, Clint and the rest of my offensive colleagues just across midfield where we were to huddle prior to the first play of the final quarter.

Nobody said anything. We still somehow communicated. If we weren't watching Bender and Walker conversing on the sideline, we were looking at each other. Each expression seemed to indicate a determination to pull this game out.

On the first play of the quarter I made my best catch of the day. Bender's pass was coming in too low so I made the catch while going into a slide at the 18. It was a perfect baseball popup slide although I will never understand how I was able to pull it off. I never used my hands to pop myself back up since both hands were cradling the ball. Somehow my momentum enabled me to pop back up anyway and I got down to the 12 before finally going down.

"Helluva catch, Jay," Dietrich remarked as he helped me to my feet. "That's going to be on the highlight shows."

It was a good feeling but I couldn't afford to get too full of myself. There is that small matter of being on the right end of the scoreboard before one thinks about where he might fit in during the highlight shows. We were still trailing and would still be trailing if we ultimately had to settle for a field goal.

"Dockman!" I heard as I headed toward where we were huddling. I could see that Giametti was being sent in. I ran toward our sideline.

"Great catch, man," Gary said as we met.

I reached the sideline. Walker whacked me on the rear and signaled for me to stay close. He was going to send me back in after a play or two. I stood behind him and watched as my offensive colleagues went to the line.

As Bender was calling the signals one of their linebackers jumped forward. He tried to correct himself but ran into Stanek. The Eagles were called for encroachment to give us a first and five at the seven.

"Okay, that's five free yards!" Walker hollered although he couldn't be heard because the crowd was booing again. "Let's take it in!"

I stood and watched as Giametti ran through the left. He managed only a yard. The Eagles did a great job of plugging the hole, giving Gary a nice green brick wall to crash into.

Walker turned toward me. He looked thoughtful for a few seconds. He then probably feared that he had consumed too much time in trying to decide on a play. Our offense was already in the huddle and the referee had signaled the ball ready for play.

"One more play and I'll send you back in," Walker said before turning around in time to see our offense break the huddle and head to the line.

Bender hit Scott with a swing pass. Scott caught the ball at the five and zigzagged. He was hit and dropped but not before he was two yards deep in the end zone.

"All right!" I exclaimed, somewhat sorry that I hadn't been on the field but elated that we had recaptured the lead.

It was interesting to note the enthusiasm of our defense and substitutes when we scored. It wasn't any great shock that they were thrilled but this was about the first time I had seen it up close.

Scott was slow in getting up. When he was hit he had the wind knocked out of him. After a few long moments he finally rose and trotted to the sideline. He even got polite applause from the fans although there were also some boos tossed in.

Guinn's kick was dead on target. We had a 20-17 lead. There was 12:50 left.

"I guess the thing to do now is hold them and then score again while running out the clock," I remarked to Bender as he and I grabbed cups of Gatorade.

"That's it," he agreed. "It sounds pretty simple but they're not going to be easy. These guys are really up for us."

That was very true. The Eagles were obviously having a terrible year. At some point in their lackluster season they probably started looking ahead to their date with the expansion team from Hawaii. Although we were obviously playing much better than the average expansion franchise, they were looking at this as a game that they had to win.

I was sipping my Gatorade as I watched the referee signal that action could resume. I found out later that the only market showing this game was

Honolulu. NBC deduced that a game between the Hawaiians and Eagles would not be a ratings bonanza in too many places. The game hadn't sold out so it wasn't even being shown in Philadelphia.

Guinn approached the ball and put his foot into it. It sailed end over end as our kicking unit chased after it while a group of players in green helmets with silver wings got set to impede my teammates.

The ball was fielded on the goal line and the return man sprinted forward. He got as far as the 31 before Pratt and Zanakis teamed up to bring him down.

I looked at the scoreboard. I recalled thinking about beginning the half with the notion that we should have a four-touchdown lead by this point. Instead we were leading by a mere field goal. That seemed ominous.

"Let's go, defense!" I called out before putting on my windbreaker and taking a seat on the bench.

The Eagles seemed to have two ideas. The first was to score, which was fairly obvious since there was no reason to believe that anybody on the team had ties to the mob and would prefer to shave points. The other idea, although not as obvious, was that they would eat up as much of the clock as possible. They seemed to be taking as much time as possible between plays without being cited for delay of game. Their first two plays were rushing plays that resulted in a combined total of about ten yards. It was close enough that the officials called time out to measure.

I stood up as the chain was brought out. The ball was at the Philadelphia 41 which was about where they needed to go to pick up that first down. The measurement indicated that they were about three inches short.

"All right! Let's hold 'em!" I called.

I put on my helmet, perhaps as some form of superstition. If we held them, they would probably punt. I was counting on taking the field to field a punt after the following futile play.

The Eagles went up the middle. Richards seemed to greet the ball carrier at the line of scrimmage. Unfortunately the ball carrier managed to lunge forward and got to the Philadelphia 43 before going down.

I sighed in frustration and returned to the bench. I took off my helmet and decided to try to relax. I didn't want to burn all of my energy cheering on the defense. With guys like Allen, McDaniel, Jennings, Black and Rodgers on our defense I knew I could count on them.

Kerner sat next to me. He seemed to be reading my thoughts.

"So our guys hold them and we drive downfield for an insurance touchdown, running out the clock in the process," he said.

"Sounds good to me," I replied.

The Eagles refused to cooperate. As the clock wound down, which wasn't that critical because there was still plenty of time and would ultimately work to their disadvantage if they didn't score, they continued

333

moving toward their goal. Eventually they wound up with a first down at the Hawaii 28.

"If they get a field goal out of this it still works to our advantage," Bender remarked, sitting on the other side of Kerner. "We drive downfield and run out most of the clock before we score. All we would need is a field goal."

The Eagles finally lost track of time and got cited for delay. That gave them a first and 15 at the Hawaii 33.

Two rushing plays netted them ten yards. Thanks to the penalty they faced third and five at the Hawaii 23.

"Okay, we hold them on this play, they blow the field goal attempt and we run out the clock," I remarked hopefully. We always talked a great game on the sideline.

Perhaps I should have kept my mouth shut. The Eagle quarterback dropped back. Allen blitzed but the quarterback got the pass off just before Russ hammered him.

The receiver caught the ball at about the 15 and got as far as the 12 before Rodgers brought him down. The receiver even made it a point to avoid going out of bounds. The Eagles were definitely working the clock. There was still almost five minutes left so it wasn't as if we wouldn't have time. Still, every second ticked off would work against whichever team was on the lower end of the scoreboard when this drive finished. The Eagles would be all but completely dead if they didn't score.

Two plays got them down close to the two. It was time for another measurement.

This time they were short by about the length of a football. It was third and short.

The quarterback called his own number. He lunged forward on a quarterback sneak and picked up about a yard. The Eagles had first and goal at the one.

And the crowd was loving it!

"Dig in, guys!" I called, knowing that the defense couldn't hear me unless I had some type of telekinetic power.

The Eagles tried going around left end on the next play. Zanakis shot through the line and dropped the ball carrier for a one-yard loss.

My heart was pounding. I was no longer sitting. Nobody on the sideline was sitting. We were collectively hollering, or at least willing, our encouragement to our defensive teammates. Our guys were very capable of erecting a wall of human steel at the goal line.

The Eagles decided to go to the air on second down. The quarterback spotted a receiver in the left corner of the end zone. Unfortunately for him, Morrissey was also in the vicinity. Jim deflected the ball and knocked it up, then got both of his hands on the ball that seemed to have the feel of a bar of wet soap in the shower. Jim juggled the ball for a moment before it fell to the artificial turf.

A sick feeling engulfed me. It was nothing compared to what Jim must have felt. It was a wonderful opportunity for the rookie from Villanova. Unfortunately it was one of those fluky events that happen to human beings. Jim actually made a great play to prevent the receiver from making the reception. A combination of factors probably prevented him from making the interception. Instead, the Eagles had third and goal at the two with 2:47 left.

I couldn't stand still. I found myself walking a somewhat erratic pattern in front of our bench as the Eagles called the next play. I finally stood still when the Eagles broke their huddle and headed up to the line.

It was a rush off left tackle. The ball carrier was met by no fewer than four Hawaiian defenders. It appeared as if the ball carrier may have been stopped short but the officials suddenly raised their arms, triggering that sick feeling in my stomach again as the crowd went wild.

"Oh, sh . . . !"

Never mind what I said. I muttered a steady stream of expletives. I wasn't angry at our defense. I had simply counted heavily on preventing the Eagles from scoring, or at least limiting them to a field goal, and was frustrated.

The extra point made it 24-20 with 2:43 left to play. That meant that we couldn't settle for a field goal to tie the game. We had to go for the TD.

As I stood on the goal line I had an unobstructed view of the scoreboard. It didn't lie. We were losing by four points. I was hoping to use up the final two minutes and 43 seconds to put us in what I considered to be our rightful spot on the scoreboard as the final gun went off. That, I figured, would put another crack in the replica of the Liberty Bell that hung at the top of the stadium and make our flight home so festive that it would seem like it was only two minutes and 43 seconds long.

With the clock being a factor, I made what could be classified as a mistake on the kick return. It was a low kick that bounced toward me. What I should have done was simply step back into the end zone and field the ball there by downing it, saving precious seconds and giving us a first and ten at the 20. Instead I fielded the ball on the goal line, starting the clock, and headed upfield.

I was hit just after I crossed the 20 but fought for more yardage. That second effort, which was purely instinctive, knocked off an extra second or two. I was finally ruled down at the 23. The clock was stopped at 2:35.

"Okay, 77 yards to victory," Bender stated optimistically as soon as we were huddled. "Let's go to work."

That's exactly what we did. Cognizant of the clock and the number of yards we needed, we began our march without regard for the crowd that made as much noise as possible to drown out our signals.

Bender had to scramble a little on the first play. He was hit but not before getting a pass off to Dietrich near the right sideline. Ted stepped out of bounds to stop the clock with 2:28 left, giving us a second down at the Hawaii 29.

Slater was next. Bender hit Joe at about the 40. Joe was between the left sideline and left hashmark but ran obliquely and managed to get out of bounds at the Hawaii 44. We had a first down with the clock stopped at 2:16. It was hard for me to believe that it took us 12 seconds to move 15 yards, but Bender was under a heavy rush again and Slater took a few extra seconds off the clock to get out of bounds since he had to dodge and weave around a couple of defenders.

Bender was pressured again on the next play but held his ground. He spotted Slater over the middle near the Philadelphia 40 and got the pass off.

An Eagle safety made a good play on this. He wasn't able to pick the pass off but he was able to knock the pass away.

That stopped the clock at 2:08. The partisan fans who reportedly loved to boo could smell a rare 1976 victory and continued to raucously support their team. Our goal was obviously to get them booing again.

The Eagle defense also smelled a potential victory and were hyped to avoid letting it get away. They pulled out all the stops on the next play. As expected, they forced Bender to scramble. He cocked his arm and fired, having spotted Giametti downfield, but the pass was knocked back at the line of scrimmage. A couple of Eagles batted the ball around and one lineman appeared to have an interception before losing his grip.

The ball dropped incomplete.

We were at the two-minute warning. Officially there was 1:59 left. We were in a third and ten situation, seemingly stalled at our own 44. We had all three of our time-outs left.

"Two minutes to travel 56 yards," Marv observed, seeming to be thinking out loud. "We can do it, baby."

That was all that was said in the huddle while Bender conversed with Walker. We all nodded while looking at the goal line that was a mere 168 feet from the line of scrimmage.

A more immediate goal was moving 30 feet over the next two plays. If we couldn't achieve that much it was all over.

We took care of the immediate dilemma on the next play. Bender, under the expected rush, scrambled to his right and spotted me past the first down marker. He hit me at the Philadelphia 44. I rushed to the sideline to stop the clock with 1:49 left.

Dietrich was the receiver on the following play. Bender hit him at the 30. Instead of running out of bounds, Ted decided he had room to run and headed toward the end zone. He was finally dropped at the 22. He was near the sideline but didn't quite make it out of bounds.

It took us a few seconds to realize that the clock was still running. Hayer was the one who seemed to make the discovery first.

"Time! Time! Time!" he cried, making a "T" by placing the palm of his hand on top of the fingertips of his other hand.

An official blew his whistle and waved his hands over his head to stop the clock. We were down to 1:32. That still seemed like enough time to travel a mere 66 feet.

The Eagles were relentless. They continued to put pressure on Bender. Steve scrambled to his left and spotted Giametti in the end zone. We didn't necessarily want to score this soon since it would give the Eagles an opportunity to score again but we had to utilize the opportunity if it was there. He unleashed the pass in Gary's direction. An Eagle defender knocked the ball away to stop the clock at 1:23

Second down produced another rush. Bender toyed with the idea of running out of bounds as he scrambled since he couldn't find an open receiver. I was near the goal line but I had two defensive backs on me.

Bender spotted Dietrich at about the five near the right sideline. He had a defender nearby but Steve tried to thread the needle. It was a good pass but the defensive back managed to reach around and bat the ball away. The play ate up 14 seconds.

As I headed toward where we would huddle I could see Walker near the 30 hollering at the officials. Ted was pointing so it was obvious that he thought that pass interference should have been called. I also thought that should have been the case but the officials ruled that any contact was the result of the defensive back going for the ball. They were probably right but I didn't want to make that concession in my partisan state of mind.

The following play had the predictable start. Bender met a heavy rush and was forced to scramble. He wasn't able to find an open receiver since the Eagle defense had all receivers covered. Bender finally heaved the ball out of the end zone to stop the clock at 57 seconds.

It was fourth and ten. We had 22 yards to go for the touchdown. We needed to get to the 12 to keep the drive alive.

Bender took matters into his own hands. Four receivers in or near the end zone fought in vain to get loose. At the same time Bender met a heavy rush. He actually managed to break a tackle about eight yards behind the line of scrimmage before deciding to try to pick up the first down with his legs. He was forced to run a pretty erratic course but managed to get down to the ten before finally being brought down.

Steve was still in bounds. He knew it and wasted no time. While still down he called time out. The clock was stopped with 39 seconds left.

The ball was marked just inside the ten. That meant we had a maximum of four chances to get into the end zone. We would not be able to pick up another first down; a seemingly moot point since we only had 39 seconds and one time out remaining.

We ate up one third of what was left on the clock on the next play. Steve, naturally, was forced to scramble. Perhaps he should have conceded the sack but that is something nobody expected him to do. He finally did get sacked after trying to scramble away. He was dropped at the 18. We used our final time out to stop the clock with 26 seconds left.

"Just get open," Steve instructed after calling the play. "Try to get to the end zone. If you can't get that far, get to the sideline."

It was a good idea. We were in our double-double, as we had been throughout the drive. Scott had spent the entire drive on the sideline as Dietrich was wide to the right and Slater was wide to the left on each play. I had been in the slot on the right and Giametti was in the left slot.

Unfortunately Bender never got the pass off. He was sacked at the 22. We hurried back to the line to enable Bender to take another snap and throw the ball away. It was fourth and goal at the Philadelphia 22. There were four seconds left.

This was it. As opposed to every previous play, the last thing we wanted to do was make a reception and step out of bounds. This play had to end in the end zone or else our entire effort would have been in vain. Only a defensive penalty could give us another breath of life if we didn't score.

I lined up in my usual spot and headed for the end zone when the ball was snapped. I actually managed to slightly fake the safety and gain a step or two on him. As I prepared to cross the goal line I looked back. The ball was already heading in my direction. The films would show that I was the only receiver open and Bender noticed immediately.

It was a perfect pass. Everything seemed to be going in slow motion. My eyes were fixed on the ball as my mind happily focused on catching the winning touchdown pass. I reached out just enough for the ball and. . . .

Unbelievable! I dropped the ball! I was all by myself about five yards into the end zone and dropped the bloody ball!

I was completely out of the end zone by the time I was able to stop my momentum. I looked back and saw the ball I should have caught slowly rolling out of the end zone. I stood and stared at the ball as if it was a best friend that had just betrayed me.

The crowd was cheering wildly. I had just made their day. All I could do was stand with my hands on my hips. My impulse was to flip them the. . . .

No, that would have been the absolute wrong thing to do. It was a rare happy Sunday in Philadelphia that season. They were supportive of their team which needed all the help it could get in 1976. I never dreamed that I would play such a prominent role in the Eagles' victory.

I looked up. Giametti and Slater were a few feet away. The rookies from Long Beach State and Baylor, respectively, seemed to be looking at me with pity. At the time I believed it would have served me right had they called me every dirty name in the book.

There was nothing I could do. I decided it was best to simply head to the locker room. As I headed in that direction I accepted handshakes from a few of my opponents but otherwise didn't acknowledge anybody, especially the crowd. It was simply best to seek refuge away from the field.

I honestly wanted to cry. There were worse things I could have done but it was something I tried to consider beneath me. I fought off the urge although it was difficult.

Football is an emotional game. That's why it is not necessarily unusual to see or hear about football players who cry after a tough loss. In high school I recall a few occasions when I fought off the urge to cry after a tough loss. In my final game as a senior, where our season ended with a defeat in a CIF Playoff game, I actually did shed a quick tear or two but was generally able to control myself. I didn't look down on teammates who weren't as successful in controlling themselves.

As soon as I was out of sight from the crowd I took my jersey off. I hadn't reached the locker room yet but I couldn't wait to get out of my uniform. It was as if my uniform was tainted by my faux pas to end the game.

I didn't want to talk to anybody in the locker room. Not my teammates, not the coaches and definitely not the media. I did my best to avoid eye contact, even with the teammates who were giving me pats on the back and encouraging words.

It might seem callous that I didn't want to talk to the media, especially since my TV show technically made me a part of the media, but I had just dropped a pass I knew I should have caught to end the game. Had I not muffed the pass we would have been five and five instead of four and six.

The locker room was almost completely devoid of conversation. That's the way it always was after a loss. There were sounds of uniforms being shed and a potpourri of other noises but very little else.

Walker and his staff entered the room. Walker stood in the middle.

"Volunteer?" he asked somberly.

Believe it or not, I was tempted to volunteer to give the postgame prayer. It was as if the prayer would give me the absolution I needed. Perhaps I even thought that I could somehow use the prayer to turn the clock back and return to the field to catch the pass.

Regardless, I didn't volunteer. Coach Wilson wound up giving the prayer.

Walker didn't say much. He rarely did immediately after a tough loss. Whether he was angry or felt sorry for us or was simply downtrodden, he always waited. He didn't want to act impulsively. We had a home game against San Diego the following week. He didn't want to lambaste us so severely that we would still have a chip on our shoulders seven days later.

Members of the media were finally allowed in. Most spoke in respectably subdued voices to Walker. I couldn't hear what was being said but I could hear the voices as I hurried out of my uniform.

A beat writer from a Philadelphia newspaper turned up a few moments later. He came directly to me as I was stark naked except for a towel around my waist. I was halfway between my locker and the shower room when he caught up with me.

"Excuse me," he said. "How did it feel to drop the pass that would have won the game for you?"

I could see that this reporter was young; probably about the same age as me. He probably didn't mean to phrase himself the way he did. There were so many respectable ways he could have asked the same question. His apparent inexperience caused him to ask in probably the worst way possible. It was as if he was asking me how I felt about blowing the game for my team.

Initially I thought I might have misunderstood. Even a rival team's beat reporter wouldn't ask such a stupid, demeaning question, would he?

It took only an instant to realize I had heard correctly. In the subdued locker room everybody not already in the showers could hear the question. Giametti, Hayer, Clint, Dietrich, Arroyo, Richards and a few others were in my line of sight. They all seemed to be frozen with incredulous expressions.

"Take that tape recorder and . . . ," I responded in a tone that befit my words, literally telling him where he could shove the tape recorder. As the reporter's jaw abruptly dropped to the floor I headed to the showers.

I honestly tried not to respond that way. I tried to say nothing at all. I should have simply headed to the showers. Unfortunately it was as if he had pushed a button that forced me to say what I said.

"No wonder Cosell hates sportswriters," I mumbled to myself as the hot water rapidly shot over my body in the shower.

The reporter had left by the time I returned to the locker room. I felt a little better but was still fuming. I wasn't sure if I was more angry at myself for dropping the pass or the reporter for asking such an insensitive question.

I found out later that after I went into the shower the young reporter, who had covered the Eagles the year before when Jennings was still with the team, told Ed that I needed to adjust my attitude toward the media.

"Like hell he does," Ed reportedly replied in his authoritative voice. "You ask him a stupid question like that after he dropped a pass he normally would have caught, who can blame him? Are you really that stupid? If it had been me, I would have done the same thing. Some of these guys would have shoved that microphone down your throat."

That was Ed, to be sure. He was always on the side of right regardless of who it might have been. If even Adolf Hitler was ever right about anything he would have argued for hours in support of Hitler on that single issue.

The flight home was long. It was a long flight anyway but that was compounded by us losing a tough game and, of course, my dropping a pass that would have won it for us. Had I caught the pass it would have changed a sullen flight into something more festive. It was a critical blow to

340

whatever remote hopes we might have had for making the playoffs. We now needed to win all four of our remaining games just to finish the season with a winning record.

Our playoff hopes were not totally dead. We knew we would have to sweep our final four games and hope that New England, Denver and any other wild card contenders fell short. Standing in our way were the Chargers, Raiders, Bengals and Browns. We had to win three just to break even.

San Diego and Oakland we had already beat on their own home turfs. We knew that they would both be looking to return the favor. The Raiders especially would want our heads on a platter. Not only were we still the only team to beat them to this point in the season, we did it during a nationally televised Monday night game.

Cincinnati and Cleveland had no cause for vengeance but they were still fighting for playoff berths and might very well consider us to be a major key, I figured. They were also certain to know that we were not to be taken lightly. No team should be taken lightly anyway but our four victories, especially the one against the Raiders, and the way we were generally tough in defeat should have set off alarms around the league. The Bengals and Browns would have to be on top of their games if they wanted to beat us.

We wanted a winning record and the games against the Bengals and Browns would be major impediments regardless of what we did against the Chargers and Raiders. The games against the Bengals and Browns would be in their home stadiums in Cincinnati and Cleveland. There was no reason to believe that these games in Ohio in December would be played in a heat wave. As cold as it may have been in Philadelphia in mid-November, the weather in Ohio seemed likely to be even worse in December.

I didn't get up during the flight except for a couple of times to use the lavatory. Having lost such a tough game, everybody was pretty subdued anyway. A few guys came over along the way to ask me how I was doing, which was appreciated, while the rest opted to leave me alone. That was also appreciated.

An attractive blonde flight attendant named Charlene brought me dinner. It was roast beef with an assortment of trimmings. I ate the meal although I didn't really enjoy it. I wasn't sulking but was very deep in thought throughout the entire flight. I wanted to get past this so that it wouldn't affect me against San Diego.

"Do you mind if I sit for a minute?" I heard a familiar voice inquire about 15 minutes after we passed over the lights of San Francisco and began our crossing of the Pacific.

It was Walker. The master psychologist had a somewhat paternal grin on his face.

"Not at all," I replied, forcing an empty smile as I gestured to the empty seat next to me.

Walker sat and offered me a Winston. I picked up my lighter from my tray table and lit his cigarette, then mine.

"It's been about eight hours since the game ended," Walker pointed out. "How do you feel now?"

I hesitated and shrugged my shoulders.

"I'll get over it. Right now I don't feel too good. I know I'm not the first guy to drop a pass and it's not even the first pass I've ever dropped. It is the first time I ever dropped a pass that would have won a game."

Walker nodded thoughtfully. He drew into his cigarette. He continued to look thoughtful as he exhaled a stream of smoke.

"It's tough to deal with something like that," he said, "but I don't want you thinking that you lost the game for us. I'm sure that when we watch the films on Tuesday we'll see tackles that didn't get made, blocks that were ineffective, passes that missed their marks and an assortment of other mistakes. It's true that we would have won the game had you caught the pass but no game is won or lost as a result of a single play."

Walker was so compassionate that in some ways I felt even worse. Just the same, I was glad that Walker was the type of coach who understood. He ranted and raved about stupid mistakes. He also understood that physical errors were part of the game.

"You mean you didn't want to tear my head off when I dropped that pass?" I asked half-facetiously.

"The thought may have crossed my mind," he replied, chuckling. "Why do you think I waited so long to come back here? You're entitled to something like that on occasion. I know it's not going to do any good to make you feel worse. No doubt the media will show that play on their so-called highlight films. What you have to do is ignore all of that. Once we've gone over the game films on Tuesday you can put the whole thing behind you and look ahead to next week."

I told Walker that I would. I was worried, though, that this might happen again. That idea was what I had to get out of my mind. I didn't want to psych myself into dropping more routine passes.

We landed in Honolulu at about midnight. By about 12:30 the plane was unloaded and we collected our baggage. Marv and Karla Nelson drove me home.

"Don't sweat it, my man," Marv said after I got out of the car in front of the building I lived in.

I truly appreciated the support from my teammates and coaches. Nobody was happy that I had dropped the pass but everybody seemed to understand that it was the kind of thing that could have happened to anybody.

342

Bill was sitting in the living room when I got upstairs, having just gotten home from work. Since he worked the later shift that Sunday he was able to watch the game on TV before leaving for work.

"Don't let it get to you," was the first thing he said. Having been my teammate during my last two years in college, he understood me as well as anybody. I was always among the first to tell a teammate not to worry if he made a mistake but I tended to get down on myself when I made such a mistake. I was very much a perfectionist when it came to my own performance. The support from Bill, my teammates, Walker and the other coaches helped me to keep things in the proper perspective.

Or at least I was heading toward the proper perspective.

Suddenly my romantic rendezvous with a pretty Canadian named Bonnie seemed light years away. I could have used her warm embraces at about this time. Unfortunately she was back in Vancouver.

CHAPTER FIFTEEN
The Charger Rematch

It was a good thing that I was tired when we returned to Honolulu. I had no trouble getting to sleep. Instead of tossing and turning and replaying the final play of the game in my mind I dropped off to sleep shortly after I got into bed.

Of course I still felt some regrets when I woke up on Monday morning. Just the same, the good night's sleep helped to rejuvenate my spirits. It was a new day and I wanted it to represent a new beginning.

I spent Monday trying to enjoy life. I laid on Waikiki Beach and took a swim, reveling in the opportunity for anonymity among the tourists. Later I had a beer at the Nest, talked to a few friends and generally enjoyed myself. The subject of the game inevitably came up but in a respectable manner. I was able to reroute the conversations to other things once an acceptable amount of time had been spent discussing the game.

On Tuesday I returned to the world of pro football. I got to Aloha Stadium determined to look ahead to the Chargers. The Eagles were behind us and I didn't care to look back.

Well, there was that small matter of the game films. True to form, Walker was guardedly critical of our performance. There were mistakes that needed to be pointed out and he did but he was careful not to go too far with it.

We spent a lot of time reviewing our final drive. There was a lot of focus on the amount of pressure on Bender.

"We have to concede that the Eagle defenders did their jobs when they got into our backfield," Walker admitted. "They had a well-orchestrated plan to blitz and stunt and do whatever else it took. We all knew that they were going to penetrate but they shouldn't have been able to get through as much as they did. We need to block better than we did. We've got to protect our quarterback and give him time to find his receivers. We did an outstanding job of moving downfield on this drive but Steve spent too much time having to scramble. Those scrambles took a lot of time off the clock. Had we had a little more time we wouldn't have felt so much pressure after we got that final first down. We might have had time to throw in one or two rushing plays to force them to stop keying on the pass."

Walker did me a big favor. He actually shut off the projector as the grand finale was coming up.

"I think we've seen all that we needed to see," he remarked.

I was grateful and I suppose my teammates might have been as well. We didn't have to relive the horror of certain victory literally dropped to defeat.

"The season will end for us December 11," Walker announced to begin the meeting after the offense and defense had both concluded their films and had come together. "The best we can wind up is eight and six. I honestly don't believe that will be good enough to earn the wild card berth. In all probability we lost whatever hope we had when we lost in Denver."

The latter remark made me feel not quite so bad. Regardless of how close we would ultimately come to the wild card spot, I knew that one miscue to turn a victory in Philadelphia into a defeat would not figure prominently in our failure to make the playoffs. One play is literally not the difference between success and failure but my miscue loomed larger from the Philadelphia game because of the timeliness of the miscue. It was, as Walker projected, shown during several highlight segments across the country. It was even shown during the halftime highlight segment of *Monday Night Football*.

"We've still got a shot at a winning record," Walker continued. "That would far surpass what everybody expected for a first-year team. If we win three out of our final four we can break even. If we win all four we wind up with a winning record. Shall we give it everything we've got left to give for the season?"

"Yeah!" we all cried in unison.

"What was that?"

"YEAH!" we repeated louder than ever.

"All right then. First thing's first. We've got five days to prepare for the Chargers. They're mad at us because of what we did to them in front of their fans. Let's do the same thing in front of our fans."

And so we began preparing for San Diego. The Tuesday workout was light, as usual, but everybody seemed hyped to kick okole. It was as if our next opponent was somebody we were meeting in the first round of the playoffs, not somebody simply trying to finish ahead of us in the division. Our focus was solely on the Chargers. Whatever happened in Philadelphia was now officially history.

Well, there was the matter of the bruised ego of a certain Philadelphia sportswriter who asked a very stupid question. Ferd Borsch from *The Honolulu Advertiser* told me that I had fueled his fire. A very unflattering article was written about me in Monday's edition of a Philadelphia newspaper.

I didn't actually see the article but Ferd filled me in. The Philadelphia sportswriter dedicated an entire column to accusing me of being a vulgar, arrogant snob when he insisted that all he was trying to do was his job.

"Who cares if they hate me in The City of Brotherly Love?" I told Ferd.

That quote appeared in Wednesday's edition of the *Advertiser* and was picked up by the national wire services. Philadelphia was one of the locales where my quote was printed. My next visit to Philadelphia promised to be very interesting. I was certain to be the recipient of a generous assortment of boos.

But I loved getting boos in places like Philadelphia. I wasn't one to incite the crowd but I never felt insulted or discouraged if I or my teammates were booed in an opposing stadium. The boos often meant that we were doing well. If the fans in Philadelphia wanted to put my ego to the test they should give me a long standing ovation.

"Keep your cool, Jay," Walker whispered to me as I exited the locker room tunnel to the field prior to Wednesday's workout. "Don't try to overcompensate. You're a Pro Bowl caliber player having a Pro Bowl year. Just play your game and everything will work out okay."

I understood what Walker was doing. He was trying to take the pressure off of me. He truly understood the psychological difference between dropping a pass during an insignificant moment and dropping a pass that would have been the winning touchdown. He knew it was better for me, as well as the team, if he showed that he still had confidence in me.

Walker's encouragement meant a lot. I have to admit that. I was still stinging from my infamous drop, especially since I felt that I had no choice but to include it on my own TV show the night before, but Walker's words were soothing and even healing.

And I had a good workout. Through the course of our first padded workout of the week I caught about half-a-dozen passes and didn't drop a single one. That also helped to rebuild my shattered ego.

As far as the entire team went, Wednesday's workout was great. So were the workouts on Thursday and Friday. Walker rode us a bit but not too much. Nobody was dogging it.

I suppose there was still some aspect of Philadelphia on my mind as I went through the week even though I tried not to think about it. Every pass I caught was another step to segregate myself from the pass I dropped on Sunday.

It was a confidence booster. Each pass I caught, regardless of how routine or difficult, was a major stroke to my bruised ego. I needed to eradicate the idea that even I was capable of dropping a routine pass in the end zone. It wasn't that I was putting myself above anybody else. I simply felt that the natural order of things was that it was understandable that others dropped routine passes but for me it was a cardinal sin.

I suppose it was akin to the guy who believes it's okay for others to strike out with the bases loaded and the game on the line but not him.

There was a change made. Sterling Burgess had a broken ankle and was placed on injured reserve, ending his season. He was a backup tackle in his sixth year in the NFL, having played five years in Green Bay before being taken by Hawaii in the 31st round of the expansion draft. The red-haired alumnus of San Diego State was good, having even made the Pro Bowl one year in Green Bay, but was simply beaten out for the starting spots by Abraham and Hayer.

Replacing Burgess was Vince Daniels from Cal Poly-San Luis Obispo. Daniels had actually started the season with us, having been taken from Cleveland in the 19th round of the expansion draft. He spent the first three games on the taxi squad, then was activated in time to play in San Diego. After playing against Dallas the following week he was waived.

I was glad to see Vince come back. He was a congenial individual with a sense of humor whom I had gotten to know fairly well. He was what one might refer to as a "gutsy" player since he was actually fairly small for a tackle but played hard and well.

"It's great to be back," Vince told me as we prepared for Wednesday's workout. "I could have stayed had I agreed to return to the taxi squad but I didn't feel I could handle it after getting to play in those two games."

Vince said that he wanted to try to hook on with somebody else so Walker agreed to release him instead of returning him to the taxi squad.

"After the first couple of weeks I figured my career was about over," Vince said. "When Walker called me Monday night I was so eager to come back that I wanted to fly back that night. There were no more flights to Honolulu left but I would have almost been willing to hijack a plane."

Rather than hijack a plane, Vince happily flew back on Tuesday. He arrived early on Tuesday afternoon.

"The Chargers must be my good luck charm," Vince observed just as our Wednesday workout was about to start. "I was activated from the taxi squad just before we played them in San Diego. Now I'm back in time to play them here."

"Yeah, I guess they are your good luck charm," Grummon remarked. "We'll have to celebrate by kicking the Chargers' cans."

Our entire roster featured 43 different names. That meant there were 43 different personalities. Some personalities had very subtle differences but no two were exactly alike.

Black and Joseph enjoyed staying out all night although they generally curtailed that activity as gameday approached. Hoddesson's idea of a wild night was taking his wife and kids out to dinner. Allen and Bender were also good family men although they were not LDS members and did not earmark Monday for Family Home Evening the way Hoddesson did. Marv and Kerner were good-natured individuals who would walk ten miles to help somebody in need. Hamer was a free spirit who was somewhat careless with his money, especially when it came to betting on frivolous things since he usually lost those bets. McWilliams was a savvy business type who not only invested on Wall Street but Jennings insisted that he would someday own Wall Street. Scott was a congenial individual while his backup, Ozzie Roberts, was more aloof. Billingsley was a surly rookie.

Despite the diverse makeup of the team, we had a fairly strong bond. Teammates with practically nothing else in common were working together in unprecedented harmony. We had an opportunity to make history even though we were out of the playoff picture. Every game we won would separate us further from the prototype expansion team. Everybody was encouraging everybody else with unbridled enthusiasm.

Jim Martinez dropped by my place on Thursday night. It wasn't unusual for the Marine from my old neighborhood in Azusa to drop by on occasion. He was scheduled to leave the islands the day before our season finale in Cleveland to be separated from the Marine Corps.

"You mean you're not going to become a . . . a . . . ? What's that they call somebody who reenlists?" I asked jocularly.

"A lifer?"

"Yeah, a lifer. You mean you're not going to become a lifer?"

"Nope. Once was enough for me," Jim replied good naturedly.

I got up and got Jim and me beers, then returned to the living room. My roommate was working so Jim and I had the place to ourselves.

"How does the team look for Sunday?" Jim asked.

"I think we're ready . . . or at least we will be. Of course the Chargers will come here with a score to settle after what we did to them in San Diego. Then the Raiders will be coming to town with the same attitude. I think we'll be ready for that one, too."

Jim nodded and took a swig of his beer. I noticed that he seemed to be pondering something.

"What are you going to do when you get back to Azusa?" I asked.

"Well first thing I'll do is go back to my job at Sav-On. Do you remember the Sav-On on Foothill?"

I nodded and smirked at that. The Sav-On was a memory from my youthful days in Azusa. I wasn't one who normally shoplifted but the rare occasions I did were at the Sav-On. I stole about half-a-dozen candy bars from there, meaning I still owed the facility about 30 cents since candy bars were a nickel back then.

"What did you do at Sav-On?" I asked.

Jim said he was a stock clerk. He was guaranteed to have his job back since it was required by federal law to allow anybody spending up to four years in the military to have their old jobs back. Jim was planning to work through the summer and then go to college on the GI Bill.

"At Citrus, right?"

"Yeah."

"Are you still planning to play football and then transfer to Hawaii?"

"I hope so," he said. "Do you really think I would have a shot?"

I pondered that question for a moment. It seemed like a lofty goal when considering that he would be a college freshman at the age of 21 and 22 or

23 before he would transfer to Hawaii but no more lofty than an NFL expansion team trying to have a winning record in its first season.

"Keep yourself in shape," I suggested. "If you report in good shape you'll have a real shot at playing college football. There are guys older than you who have played football as freshmen. It'll also help that you played while you were stationed in the Philippines."

Jim was among those getting passes from me for our game against the Chargers. My roommate, Bill, was also getting a pass. Also attending the game would be Bill's girlfriend, Cherie, who still sadly believed that she and Bill were forever while everybody else had a better concept of the truth. Don Simmons would also be getting a pass and would be attending the game stag since his girlfriend, who was a nurse, would be working.

"You're looking good," Walker told us as we gathered around him on the turf at Aloha Stadium after our light Saturday workout. "Just remember that you have a team coming tomorrow that wants to beat you as badly as any team you've faced this season. Know that you're good but not so good that you can't be beat. You have to be at your best for 60 minutes and then we'll savor the fruits of victory."

Walker dismissed us and we headed to the locker room. I did feel confident about our rendezvous with the Chargers. As long as the praise didn't go to our heads the Chargers were going to have a tough time getting revenge.

"What are you going to do today?" Giametti asked in the locker room.

"Just be a lazy bum," I replied lightly. "I'm going to go home, open a beer, turn on the TV and spend some time kicking back on the couch. After I've done that for a while, I don't know."

That nonplan was my actual plan. I felt quietly content and confident. I wanted to savor a little enjoyment with a reasonably quiet afternoon. Unfortunately after I got home, I found myself in the presence of some company I preferred not to keep.

I honestly prefer not to judge people harshly. I have to admit, though, that there are people I have known that I wish I hadn't. One such individual is a character named Ron Whitcomb.

Whitcomb is somebody I met while I was in college. As I was entering my junior year three teammates and I rented a house on University Avenue just down the road from the university.

"I know what it's like to be young," Mr. Kobayashi, our fiftyish landlord, told us when we signed the lease. "Have a good time. I won't bother you as long as you pay your rent on time, maintain the yard and make restitution for any damage."

Initially it was a junior tight end named Chris Alexander, a junior wide receiver named Phil Hewitt and a sophomore center named Keith Maldaur renting the place with me in August 1972. It was actually Chris who invited me to join the threesome after he transferred to the University of Hawaii. Chris was from Glendora, California, which was the very place I was born. He had even played against me once in high school during a CIF Playoff game; a game I remembered although I didn't remember him even though he had known who I was. He had played his first two years of college ball at Citrus Junior College.

Although our residence was officially inhabited by four student-athletes, it became a landmark for the party crowd. It wasn't unusual to have as many as 20 athletes, non-athletes and even a few non-students crashing in various parts of the three-bedroom house on any given night. It became a veritable commune.

"Can you imagine what the walls would've thought if they could've seen what went on here the last few months?" Chris jocularly asked during a rare quiet moment at the end of the semester.

"It's quite a zoo we've got here," I agreed. "The Manoa Zoo."

The name stuck. Until the day that I finally vacated the place after my first pro season, the place was widely known as the Manoa Zoo. There were various combinations of roommates including Bill Trimble but, due primarily to graduations and dropouts, I was the only tenant in the house when I began my pro career.

Among those appearing frequently at the Manoa Zoo was Whitcomb. How he found the place was unknown to me although it wasn't unusual for somebody to appear out of nowhere with a reasonable expectation of blending in. Whitcomb wasn't a student and it wouldn't surprise me to find out that he never even graduated from high school. He was a short, tough-talking individual. He changed jobs a lot and at this point in 1976 was working as a security guard somewhere in Waikiki.

I didn't care for Whitcomb much dating back to the day I met him although I generally tolerated him. He had a stronger bond with Bill even though Bill didn't especially care for him either. Somehow he found out where Bill and I were living and never hesitated to drop by unannounced and make himself welcome. From what I understood, he also never hesitated to tell the gritty crowd he usually ran with that he and I were close friends.

Why Bill and I let Whitcomb hang out at our place is beyond me. Bill and I often needled each other about him.

"Your brother called while you were at practice," Bill would say.

"Craig?" I replied, believing he was referring to the brother I actually did have.

"No. Ron. Ron Whitcomb."

Whitcomb somehow sensed that I didn't care for him. He was obviously more perceptive than I realized because I was never actually rude to him. He usually showed up only when he was reasonably certain that Bill would be there.

Perhaps he recalled the incident when he aroused my ire during my final semester as an undergraduate. I was at the Blue Goose with Don Simmons one night. Don and I were having a beer and discussing my future since I had just been drafted by the WFL Hawaiians, the Dallas Cowboys and the Boston Red Sox.

Whitcomb suddenly appeared and invited himself to join us. Bill also arrived just as Whitcomb was beginning to explain to me why it was in my best interests to sign with the Cowboys.

Initially it was amusing and baffling. Whitcomb insisted that I should sign with the Cowboys because he believed the best women were in Texas. Despite the fact that he had never been anywhere near Texas, he insisted that he knew that the best women were there. He was even undeterred when I pointed out that I had a girlfriend to whom I was very devoted.

"Hey, slick, she's cool," Whitcomb said pompously. "But you're a man. Ya gotta try new stuff. She's gonna wait for ya. That's what she's for, man.

I responded only by looking at Dave and Bill who were sitting across the booth from me. I remember thinking that his logic was obtained simultaneously with his grammar. I suppose the low-esteemed women Whitcomb knew might agree with him but my girlfriend wasn't one to put up with the kind of man who wanted to play around and I was too much in love to want to anyway.

"See what I'm sayin', man?" Whitcomb continued. "The bitch'll wait."

At that point I was no longer amused. I never called my girlfriend a bitch and I wasn't going to allow anybody else to. Although nobody would have blamed me had I chosen to clean Whitcomb's clock, it wouldn't have been right. To resist the urge to give him what he deserved but would also have put me on the front page of both Honolulu newspapers, I took a swig of beer and lit a cigarette. I looked at Don and Bill and exhaled a stream of smoke.

"If I ever treat Carol the way he says I should," I said slowly to try to buy some time to regain my composure. "If I ever call her a bitch . . . you guys hire a hitman to knock me off. If I ever treat a lady like Carol like that then I don't deserve to live."

That was the only truly negative incident I'd had with Whitcomb prior to 1976 although I trusted him even less than I did prior to that. He still seemed to believe it was all right to hang around and drop by unannounced. I suppose I could have gotten rid of him quickly had I insisted on playing music from my John Denver collection. Whitcomb hated John Denver.

On that Saturday in 1976 I didn't play my John Denver music because I was watching USC play football on television. Like most of what was seen in Hawaii in 1976, the game was a week old. All pro football games were shown on the same day they were played, if not live, as were most other sporting events. Prime time programs, game shows, soap operas and most other network shows were shown a week later in Hawaii than on the

351

mainland and so were USC football games unless they were nationally televised games such as the Trojans' annual matchup with UCLA.

USC happened to be playing Washington. I already knew the outcome of the game since I kept tabs on USC. Although I transferred to the University of Hawaii after one year at USC, I still maintained a loyalty to USC. I loved USC and had looked forward to playing in the Los Angeles Coliseum with the Trojans. My reason for leaving USC after only one year was because I simply realized that I would be happier in Hawaii.

It just so happened that Whitcomb was from Washington. In fact, he had never ventured outside of Washington until he moved to Hawaii. He began to insist that Washington was going to win.

"The game was played last week," I pointed out. "USC won."

Whitcomb, who knew everything there was to know in the world, insisted that the game was being shown live. I was trying to be fair and honest but he wouldn't buy my explanations. I knocked myself out trying to explain the process to him in minute detail. He wasn't willing to shut up until I agreed to bet on the game.

The easiest 20 bucks I ever made.

To Whitcomb's credit, which was a phrase rarely expressed, he paid up without complaint. It funded my dinner that night which I shared with a friend. A comely blonde named Nicole East and I ate Korean food at a restaurant near the university. I was very big on kal bi ribs and kimchee.

Despite an allegation or two to the contrary, Nicole and I were nothing more than friends. That was all she needed in the wake of her husband abruptly leaving her for another woman a couple of months earlier. Although Nicole was the type of woman who appealed to me physically and mentally, she was never anything more than a friend whose husband had also been a friend of mine.

I heard later that the husband, in the presence of his new lover, became insanely jealous when he heard that Nicole and I had dinner together. He was convinced that there was something more than friendship between Nicole and me. Obviously some very interesting people passed through my life in the mid-70s.

Vince Daniels, perhaps feeling rejuvenated for his second tenure with the Hawaiians, led us in *The Lord's Prayer*. When the prayer was finished Walker stood in the middle of the room and prepared to address us before we would take the field.

"We have four games left. We will take them one at a time. We start with this one. Think of nothing but the San Diego Chargers."

Walker slowly started walking around the room. His latter sentence probably seemed vital to him since we had Oakland coming to town the following week. We couldn't very well beat the Chargers if we were already worrying about the Raiders.

352

"You beat the crap out of these guys in San Diego," Walker pointed out for the nth time that week. "That was simply part one. It won't mean a thing if you don't take them now. You have it in you to do it again. I know what you are capable of doing. You've shown the capability of being one of the most formidable teams in the NFL. Let's be that team. Let's go."

We won the toss and I was psyched to go. I was so psyched that I might have tried to return the kickoff even if the San Diego kicker knocked the ball out of the end zone. As I stood on the goal line of the south end zone I silently willed the kicker to kick it to me. I suppose I was determined to start redeeming myself for Philadelphia right from the very beginning.

The kick was suddenly up. My alleged psychic powers seemed to be working. I backed up a few steps and fielded the kick.

Officially I was four yards deep in the end zone. If anybody was instructing me to down the ball, I wasn't about to heed the call. This was one return I was absolutely determined to make. My overzealous desire to redeem myself may have been superseding common sense.

I charged out. Some good blocks were made but a couple of Chargers fought off the blocks. I broke a tackle at the 15 and another one at about the 22. A few yards later I hurdled a downed Charger before a pair of Chargers brought me down at the 35.

It was an awesome feeling! I quickly bounced up and clapped my hands.

"All right! Let's go!" I exclaimed as I exchanged pats with a few of my teammates and headed to our huddle at the 25. At that moment I believed I could bend steel with my bare hands and leap tall buildings in a single bound. All that was missing was a phone booth where I could change into my cape and tights.

Two plays later I was returned to mortal status. That was when I carried through the right and was stopped for no gain. As soon as I hit the hole I was greeted by a wall of white jerseys with blue and gold trim. Something told me Superman probably would have gone further.

"You ain't goin' nowhere, Dockman," one of the Chargers muttered as I lay on the ground amid half-a-dozen or so other bodies from both sides. "You lost the game for your team last week and you ain't gonna do any better this week."

Remarks like that were not necessarily atypical. The trick was to not take them personally. I had left myself wide open to such remarks when I dropped the pass in Philadelphia in such a high-profile scenario. I had to simply disregard the remarks, which wasn't easy, and carry on.

My rush for no gain was indicative of our first series. The only highlight was just before my rush when the Chargers got called for encroachment to give us a second and four instead of second and nine after Kerner's whopping one-yard gain.

Our drive became a three and out after Bender was sacked for a seven-yard loss at the 34.

"See? They're not going to make it easy for you guys," Walker remarked calmly as the offense ran to the sideline. He was simply making a point but I was still annoyed. I found it hard to accept the fact that the Chargers held us to only three plays on our opening drive. I was hoping my kick return would fire up the Hawaiians but apparently it only fired up the Chargers.

Jablonski got off an excellent punt that went out of bounds at the San Diego 20. At least he prevented the Chargers from starting with what the NBC commentators would have referred to as "excellent field position."

The Chargers opened with a pass to the San Diego 37 to give them a first down. Fortunately their drive was not much more successful than ours after that. They wound up with a fourth and one at their own 46. I ran on the field to field the punt.

Actually the Chargers were not in a bad place to fake a punt. As I stood near the Hawaii 25 I silently prayed that if they did fake the punt that my teammates would stop them. An ugly feeling swept over me as I visualize the Chargers doing the fake and either running or passing for a first down.

Just the thought of it made me angry. The Chargers were still in their huddle and I was already angry at them over a fake punt that they hadn't even attempted and might not have even considered. I silently resolved that if I was in a position to make a tackle that I would make their ball carrier pay for the arrogance of faking the punt, succeeding in picking up the first down and getting far enough downfield to force me to make the stop. I was developing a pretty good hatred for my opponents.

My alleged psychic powers ostensibly soured them on the idea of trying a fake. Perhaps out of fear that I would make a dynamic return, or so I chose to believe, the punter aimed for the left sideline. That kept me from fielding the punt. All I could do was watch as the ball was downed on the Hawaii six.

"Okay, we're all warmed up now," Bender said to begin the huddle. "We're going to blow these guys away with this drive."

I had no objections to a 94-yard drive. The Chargers seemed pretty impressed with themselves for pinning us back on the six. It would be very humbling for them if we could score.

We got off to a good start. Bender dropped back and hit Scott over the middle at the eight. Larry picked up five more yards to the 13.

The next play wasn't quite as successful but at least it did pick up a couple of yards. Bender rolled to his right and saw that his primary receivers, Dietrich and me, were covered. He dumped a pass off to Grummon who had initially been blocking on the play and then became a safety valve just beyond the line of scrimmage. Rich caught the ball at the 15 just as he was being hit and dropped.

Kerner went up the middle and picked up the necessary yard. For good measure he picked up a second yard to give us a first and ten at our own 17.

Unfortunately two yards seemed to suddenly be the trend. Scott carried on the next two plays and managed all of two yards both times. Our "drive" was climaxed by Bender getting sacked at the 15.

I was downfield and watched helplessly as Steve tried to scramble. I was open but he had a pair of Chargers moving in on him. One grabbed him by the back of his shirt to slow him up and the other plowed into him.

Slater was nearby. We both stopped as soon as Bender went down. Joe and I simultaneously looked at each other and shook our heads before heading to the sideline.

"What's going on here?" Walker asked rhetorically as the offense returned too soon to the sidelines. "They're killing you guys. You're supposed to be better than this."

Nobody had any explanation. We had started to move and then we stopped. It was a numbing experience.

As I grabbed my cup of Gatorade I happened to glance into the first few rows behind our bench. The spectators seemed to have dumbfounded expressions on their faces. One 30ish shirtless man had such an intense ponderous expression on his face that he looked like he was in a classroom trying to study the board for the answer to a complex math problem. I assumed he was trying to find the answer to our problem.

The problem certainly wasn't Jablonski. He got his foot into the ball so well that it almost looked as if it was going to leave the atmosphere. The hang time enabled our coverage to move downfield and force the Charger return man to call a fair catch at the San Diego 45.

If the first quarter was any indication, this game was a boon for the concessionaires. Both sides seemed reluctant to move. It reminded me of a comedian's routine where he referred to two teams "tearing up the middle of the field." The Chargers managed a first down before the drive stalled to give them a third and seven at the Hawaii 37. If we could hold them to an incomplete pass the best they could do was a 54-yard field goal.

Allen had a better idea. He charged in and hammered the quarterback at the Hawaii 45. For the first time since the opening kickoff the crowd had reason to cheer. The Chargers had fourth and 15. A field goal, if they were to attempt one, would have to be attempted about a yard short of the NFL record.

A field goal attempt would have been feasible had this game been played three years earlier. At that time the goal posts were positioned at the goal lines, making this a 52-yard attempt. Also, under the old rules a missed field goal was essentially a touchback, meaning the defensive team at the time of the field goal attempt would start its next drive at the 20. The new rule called for the ball to be spotted at the failed field goal attempt's line of scrimmage.

The Chargers punted in a manner that prevented me from making a return. It was off to the right this time and bounced inside the ten. I tried to block a Charger who was shooting downfield but stalled him only minimally. He downed the ball at the two.

There were 46,112 fans in attendance at Aloha Stadium. The sound of the crowd was such that it almost seemed as if we were playing for that many empty seats. Although the game was still scoreless, it felt as if the Chargers were beating the crap out of us. They definitely had the advantage to this point.

Fortunately we started chipping away at that advantage. We ran a Kailua left and Scott picked up eight yards. The same play to the right picked up seven yards to give us a first down at the 17 and get the crowd to stop yawning.

I got the call next. I headed around right end and got good protection from our pulling guards, Marv and Stanek, as well as Kerner who ran directly ahead of me. The Charger defenders closed in on me but not before I had picked up four yards to the 21.

We had picked up 19 yards on this drive. With the way the rest of the quarter had gone, the 19 yards felt pretty good. At this juncture it still appeared that our punter was the front-runner to be awarded the game ball.

Kerner picked up four more yards up the middle to give us a third and two. He carried again through the left and was hit a yard later, then squirmed loose and continued. I took out a defensive back just as he was about to bear down on Jeff, giving me an ephemeral sense of euphoria. Jeff finally went down at the 38.

I looked at the scoreboard clock as I rose to my feet to take my place in our huddle between the 25 and 30. The clock showed 44 seconds and was still running. I figured we had one play left in the quarter.

That play wound up being a swing pass. Bender hit me on the right about a yard beyond the line of scrimmage. I was hit at the 40 but spun around. I wasn't able to shake my tackler. I still managed to get to the 42.

The clock continued to tick. There were less than ten seconds left in the quarter. I began moving to the opposite side of the field with my teammates while Bender went to the sideline to converse with Walker.

Our drive to close out the quarter had covered 40 yards in only six plays. We were finally playing like we were capable of playing although we still had a long way to go. The fact that the Chargers were hyped for the game played a major role in our somewhat futile beginning. Also factored in was that we simply hadn't played especially well prior to this drive. Our passing game had been especially inept. We had three completions for 13 yards.

We got the second quarter off to a great start. Scott went up the middle. He went from the Hawaii 42 to the San Diego 42 for a gain of 16 yards.

356

Unfortunately that was the last hurrah of the drive. Bender passed on the next play and the ball seemed to slip out of his hand. The ball was so far off the mark that nobody was sure of who the intended receiver was. The only one who had a decent shot at the ball was a defensive back who nearly intercepted it.

Steve was sacked again on the following play, giving us a third and 17 at the Charger 49. He was pressured again on the following play although he managed to get the pass off that fell incomplete about seven or eight yards in front of Giametti. It was time again for *The Ray Jablonski Show*.

Walker had no remarks for us as we ran off the field. He simply stood with his arms folded and glared at us. There was no doubt that he was really ticked off.

I hoped that Jablonski lifted his spirits a little. Ray got off another great punt. Our ineptitude was making him a very viable candidate for the Pro Bowl.

The ball bounced inside the ten. Hasegawa hustled down and stayed with the ball that took a couple of bounces and then started to roll. He touched the ball down at the one, drawing a roar from the crowd.

"This is sad," I said to Marv as we stood at the Gatorade table. "So far the biggest cheer of the day was on one of our punts."

"I hear ya, brah. We've got to do a better job of moving that ball. I hope that last drive gave us a little momentum."

I watched as the Chargers broke their huddle in the back of the south end zone and headed for the line of scrimmage. I considered the possibility of our defense throwing them for a loss to create a safety for an ultimate 2-0 victory. With our inability to move the ball, I was willing to settle for that. A win is a win regardless of how ugly and boring.

The Chargers didn't feel like yielding the safety. They picked up a total of six yards on two rushing plays before a short pass gave them a first down at their 19. After a five-yard rush that was countered by an illegal procedure penalty prior to the next play, the Chargers went for a longer pass. The ball was caught at the 35 before the receiver turned upfield with Black and Blakely in pursuit. The two defensive backs weren't able to bring the receiver down until he had reached the Charger 42.

"Let's go, defense! Stick it to them!" I barked as I rose from the bench. It was another example of me feeling guilty about hollering for the defense when our offense wasn't exactly stealing the show.

A pass over the middle was called. The receiver caught the ball at the 50 and was hammered immediately by Rodgers. He didn't gain any extra yardage after the reception but it was still an eight-yard gain.

Our defensive line rose to the occasion on the next two plays. A rush up the middle was met by a solid wall that produced no gain. The Chargers tried to rush off right tackle on the next play but Richards was there to drop him a yard behind the line of scrimmage. It was fourth and three in a game where the Charger punter was just as viable a candidate for the Pro Bowl as our punter.

"Punt return team!" I heard Walker bark although not until I was crossing the sideline to the field. I was all too aware that the time had come to return to the field. Silently I hoped that we would finally succeed in putting some points on the board.

The Charger punter went for the sideline again. This time he wasn't as successful. I was able to field the punt at the Hawaii 14.

"Fair catch" was not in my vernacular this time. I could have heard a herd of buffalo charging in my direction and I still would have attempted to return the punt. It was another case of my determination superseding common sense but I wanted to get something going.

At least I was able to get away. I sidestepped a defender about two yards after I fielded the punt. I tried to run past another but he caught me from the side and brought me down at the 21. It was a respectable seven-yard return.

The whistles blew and I got up. This time I guarded my enthusiasm. A seven-yard return, while better than nothing, was below average. I simply accepted it and joined the rest of the offense in the huddle.

Once again our drive got off to a promising start. Bender hit Dietrich near the makai sideline at the 34. He fought for three more yards before being knocked out of bounds.

Another pass was called. This one was intended for Grummon.

Unfortunately a Charger defensive back played the pass perfectly. He stepped in front of Grummon and picked the pass off at the Hawaii 48. I was further downfield; too far away to do anything more than watch helplessly. I still gave chase although I knew it was futile. It appeared to be an easy touchdown.

Kerner quashed the Chargers' touchdown hopes. He had stayed back to block for Bender and was able to pursue the defensive back. He was actually closer to the opposite sideline as the defensive back when the interception was made but was fast enough and able to move at the right angle to bring the defensive back down on the Hawaii 13.

The whistles blew and I slowed up. I reached down and helped Kerner up just as a Charger behind me loudly questioned Bender's masculinity.

"Hey, cool it, man!" his Charger teammate loudly responded to possibly prevent an all-out brawl. There was still some repercussion. I turned around just in time to see Stanek shove the Charger who had the offending mouth.

About a dozen of us from both sides got between Stanek and the loudmouth. I think all of the officials were blowing their whistles and a few of them stepped in to help the players separate the combatants. There was also a roar from the crowd; something that hadn't happened much to this point.

358

At least the alleged rhubarb got our minds off of a more immediate concern . . . such as the fact that the Chargers were going to start a drive 39 feet from the end zone. The most we could hope for was a turnover. If we couldn't do that, I was hoping we would limit them to a field goal. Even if they succeeded I was hoping that having to settle for three points on a drive that began 13 yards from paydirt would deflate their egos.

Two plays later the Chargers picked up a first down at the two. On the next play the Charger quarterback rolled to his right and passed. McDaniel got his hand on the ball but only managed to tip it up. The intended receiver dove from his position in the right corner of the end zone and managed to get his hands on the ball just before the ball hit the ground.

A sick feeling washed over me as the officials' arms shot up. It was only one touchdown but with the way we had been playing that might have been all that the Chargers needed.

"What are you going to do about that?" Walker bellowed, turning and looking at his players on the sidelines. "Are you going to start playing now or was this week just a wasted effort?"

I was fortunate enough to be able to take my place on the kick return unit. I wasn't in the mood to listen to Walker who was still ranting as I ran on the field. I stood on the goal line of the north end zone and thought about the situation at hand. That 7-0 score might as well have been 70-0. We had to quickly make something happen.

The kick was up. It was coming in my direction. I could also tell that it was going to be a short kick so I started to move forward.

My hope was that my running start would produce extra yardage. I was on the run as I caught the ball at the nine and shot forward. There was a nice little hole for me to move through. I was feeling almost invulnerable until a pair of Chargers hit me simultaneously. The three of us remained upright for about two or three yards before we all went down on the 30.

Officially it was only a 21-yard return but it wasn't bad. The 30 wasn't a bad place to start. All we had to do was remember how to move the ball from scrimmage. We had done a pretty fair job of it during our first ten games but suddenly we seemed to be suffering from amnesia. It seemed like a lost art.

That includes this drive. In three plays we managed to move a total of three feet. After Scott's one-yard gain Bender threw two incomplete passes; one of which was nearly intercepted.

As much as I hate to admit it, we were looking like an expansion team. We were no longer defying the expectations of an expansion team by being competitive. Tampa Bay, Seattle and Memphis all could have beaten us with the way we were playing.

Our saving grace was the way the defense was keeping the Chargers in check. The Chargers' lone score came on a short drive in the wake of a turnover. Otherwise our defense was flawless, but if we couldn't put together sustained drives the defense was going to wear down.

The fans weren't going to let us get away with the expansion team excuse. For the first time during the season they were booing us. Most of our fans, I believe, were not booing but there was enough for us to notice. That really struck a blow.

"Listen to that!" Walker barked as we reached the sideline. "You're getting what you deserve! With the way you're playing you should be grateful that they're not throwing things at you!"

"Don't give them any ideas, Coach," I muttered under my breath, careful to express myself softly enough to avoid being heard although I was slightly miffed at Walker and would have loved to have gotten into his face. It wasn't enough that we averaged only one foot per play during our previous series. Walker was doing the equivalent of giving a drowning man a glass of water. I was fired up to turn things around but not because of Walker's verbal abuse.

But I also have to admit that he was right. We flat out sucked!

Jablonski got off a decent punt. It was fielded at the Charger 30.

Unfortunately the return man managed to dodge and weave enough to cause Hasegawa to lose his balance and fall on his face. The return man dodged a couple of other tacklers. It almost seemed as if he shaved 30 seconds off the clock while making a 14-yard return. It wasn't that long, of course, but it seemed to be an eternity before Daniels finally brought him down on the San Diego 44. They were in good field position.

I attribute that 14-yard return to excellent work by the return man. As a punt returner myself I could not help but, at least grudgingly, be impressed with the effort. Our fans, however, did not concur. They were booing so loud that I almost thought that we were back in Philadelphia.

On the sidelines I felt totally helpless. My job while the defense was on the field was to drink my Gatorade, listen to whatever words of wisdom members of the coaching staff had and do whatever it took to will the defense on. In high school I was a two-way player but in college and the pros the two-way player was virtually obsolete. That left me helpless in the defensive effort.

Then again, our offensive unit wasn't racking up chunks of yardage. I guess I felt pretty helpless there, too.

After two plays the Chargers had picked up close to ten yards to mark the ball on the Hawaii 46. The officials called time out to measure. Our luck being what it was, on top of our inept play, mandated that the Chargers had the first down.

"Come on, Hawaiians! Dig in! Let's go!" I heard a male voice call from somewhere in the bleachers. I was reminded of how we had silenced the crowd in San Diego before almost everybody gave up during the fourth quarter and left. Our crowd, when it wasn't showering us with the occasional round of boos, was in a relatively taciturn state. Anybody watching us for the first time would find it hard to believe that we already had four victories . . . or even one victory.

The Chargers' strategy was obvious. They were going for another score, of course. What they also wanted to do was run out the clock. They had a third and three at the Hawaii 39 when they ran the clock down to the two-minute warning. We had two time-outs to burn.

We used our first time out after the next play. The play still ate up eleven seconds before we finally got the clock stopped. The Chargers tried to run through the right, but Richards and Jennings set up a fairly impressive roadblock. The running back backpedaled and then shifted toward the middle. He was brought down by Allen and Blakely after picking up two yards.

It was fourth and one at the Hawaii 37 with 1:49 left in the half. The question remained whether they would go for a 54-yard field goal, punt toward the coffin corner or try to pick up the first down. I stood at the ready in case their punting unit ran on the field. I watched the other side of the field as the Charger quarterback conversed with the head coach.

The quarterback ran back on the field to huddle with his offensive colleagues. The Charger field goal unit and punting unit stayed in place.

"Let's go, defense!" I called, standing behind the sideline with my helmet on in anticipation of returning to the field. "Get us the ball back!"

The Chargers tried a draw play. The running back headed up the middle and was met by a solid wall of brown jerseys. His own linemen also unwittingly comprised a part of the wall since they were trying in vain to block our defensive linemen and linebackers and they were in the path of the ball carrier. It took a couple of seconds but the ball carrier was brought down.

It took a moment to determine the outcome but we had a first down at our 37.

The crowd let out a huge roar. The fans were obviously cheering the defense's effort. I also wanted to believe they were cheering because they were optimistic that the offense would do something this time even though there was very little evidence to suggest that we were capable of such a thing.

There was 1:42 left in the half. We had one time out left. Our strategy was the same as the Chargers'. We obviously wanted to score while leaving no time on the clock.

Of course we hadn't moved the ball very well through the rest of the first half. What made us think this drive would be different?

It wasn't. Two rushes by Scott netted us a total of one yard. The crowd was back in its Philadelphia mode.

Bender dropped back to pass on third down. He met a heavy rush. He hit Kerner just before Kerner was hit by a Charger lineman at the Hawaii 40. Jeff got to the 43 before he was dragged down. It was fourth and four.

Do I need to mention the boos?

"Why don't they go to the concourse and buy hot dogs or something?" I muttered as I ran off the field.

Dietrich was a few feet in front of me. He heard what I said and turned to face me.

"The fact is, we suck," he said.

"I know that," I grumbled. "I don't need the crowd to remind me. Believe me, I'm no happier about it than they are."

Walker didn't say anything. He didn't have to. His stance with his arms folded and clenched jaw said everything. As we reached the sideline the story in his eyes suggested that we had just murdered a member of his family.

Jablonski continued to be the lone bright spot for the Hawaiians. It's pretty pathetic when your star player is the punter.

Well, okay, the defense was having a good enough day. We still win as a team and lose as a team but if the score was still 7-0 after four quarters nobody was going to blame the defensive players if they beat the daylights out of the offensive players in the locker room.

But Jablonski did what he was hired to do. He sent the ball toward the stratosphere. The Charger return man called a fair catch on the 16. It was a 41-yard punt. With only seven seconds left in the half the Charger quarterback took the snap and dropped to his knee. We headed to the locker room amid a moderate combination of booing and cheering. It could have been worse.

I made my obligatory trip to the urinal and grabbed a cup of Gatorade. What we normally did was meet in offensive and defensive groups to review the first half and plan the second half. Afterward Walker would offer us a few words of encouragement.

We broke from the norm. The defensive unit went over its game plan, but the entire halftime show for the offense was comprised of a screaming martinet. The offense had played so poorly that Walker ostensibly felt that planning new strategies would not do any good.

"How bad do you want to be?" he barked rhetorically. "The season isn't over yet! Did you know that?"

Walker stormed around the room as he made his motivational speech. I actually felt bad for the defense since it obviously wasn't their fault that we weren't moving the ball. They were trying to plan their strategies but they were having a hard time hearing their coaches while Walker was yelling. Since we were on the wrong side of a 7-0 score the defensive players weren't feeling any satisfaction. I'll bet even Jablonski was feeling like crap right about now.

"I'll tell you what we're going to do!" Walker continued. "We're going to score touchdowns, that's what we're going to do! That's the way you win football games!"

An official poked his head in and caught Walker's eye. He let Walker know that we were expected to return to the field.

"Jablonski!" Walker bellowed to wrap up his address. He turned and faced Jablonski but continued loud enough for everybody to hear. "You're having a helluva game! That's the one positive observation I can make but you might as well go take your shower right now! We are going to score touchdowns in the second half! Your services will not be needed in the second half!"

I didn't realize that Walker was so prophetic. After the defense held the Chargers at bay during the opening series we took over. I caught a pass on our third play from scrimmage at the Charger 45 and got down to the 39 before I coughed up the ball. A Charger recovered at the 37 so it was obvious that Jablonski wasn't needed on this drive.

On the third play of our next drive Bender's pass to Giametti was intercepted at the Hawaii 29 and returned to the 27 before Giametti took him down. Once again Walker was right. We didn't need Jablonski.

It's funny to reflect back on now. It wasn't so funny then. I was fuming as I returned to the sideline. I also made it a point to avoid Walker even though the interception obviously wasn't my fault. If I could have gotten away with taking refuge on the Chargers' side of the field, I would have.

What saved us was that Black interrupted the Chargers' drive after my fumble with an interception. After Bender threw the interception to climax our ephemeral second possession Blakely intercepted a pass on about the goal line and returned the ball to the Hawaii 22. Thanks to the defense we still trailed by only a touchdown. That was still a monumental margin with our offensive effort.

Our possession after Blakely's interception started out as inept as the previous possessions. All we had to show for our first two snaps were two incomplete passes. Although the booing was not universal, there was enough of it going on for us to know that our fans were not pleased.

We actually did something right on third down. Bender hit me over the middle at about the 32. I picked up four more yards to the 36.

"First down, Hawaiians," the public address announcer reported after giving the other information pertaining to the previous play. It was a phrase that almost seemed obsolete that day.

That one play seemed to give us momentum. Bender hit me again at midfield. I was hit immediately but hung on to the ball. We had another first down.

It was nice to hear the crowd cheering again. I suspect, though, that many of our fans were taking a "wait and see" attitude about how they felt about our chances of putting together something worthwhile.

We tried to do our part. Scott picked up our third first down in as many plays. He went up the middle and fought his way to the 37 before being brought down. The boos were continuing to turn into raucous cheers. I was no longer hearing any booing.

"All right. The Hawaiians are finally starting to arrive," Bender remarked to fire us up as we formed our huddle. "I formation, split left, wing left, four kama'aina pitch right. On two, on two. Ready?"

"Break!"

This was the kama'aina play similar to the Green Bay sweep but Bender would pitch the ball to me instead of handing it off. We executed it perfectly as I followed a few of my teammates around right end. Marv threw the most hellacious block of the play as he knocked a Charger right on his derriere. It wasn't until I reached the 30 that I was finally tripped up.

"Okay, good job. Good job," Bender said as we began our next huddle. "We've come too far to fall short now."

Scott went up the middle and picked up two of the three yards we needed for a first down. Kerner finished the job by going up the middle and grinding his way to the 22. He did a remarkable tank impersonation whenever he carried the ball through the line. Scott and I were both quicker and faster but Kerner was like a piece of heavy equipment.

The Chargers gave us a little assistance on the next play. Scott only managed one yard up the middle. One of the Charger linemen went for the fake and thought that Kerner was carrying the ball. He grabbed Jeff and threw him down pretty hard, ostensibly conscious of just how difficult Jeff was to bring down but unconscious of the fact that Jeff didn't have the ball. The unnecessary roughness penalty against his team gave us a first down at the eleven.

We must have really been in love with plays up the middle. For the fourth consecutive play we went up the gut. Scott picked up two yards.

The next play ended the third quarter. It also prevented us from having goose eggs on the scoreboard for three consecutive quarters. Scott ran around right end and fought his way through the last three yards. He was brought down but not until he had crossed the goal line just inside the pylon.

Of course I did my part to help out the officials, as did a few of my teammates. I had been blocking a defensive back when I saw Larry go down a few yards away. I naturally had to raise my arms as if it was my job to make the touchdown official.

"Now we're cookin'!" Marv exclaimed as he and Grummon helped Larry to his feet.

"We're playing like a team now," Larry observed truthfully and happily. For good measure he gave Marv the ball and told him to spike it.

364

We, as well as our fans, were in much better spirits than we were through the majority of the game. Walker was even smiling as we ran off the field.

"Okay, that's more like it," he remarked as he slapped a few of us on the back. "Let's keep it up."

After Guinn kicked the extra point we had only tied the game but the momentum had shifted and the defense was well-rested. I was reasonably confident that we would pull the game out. I was also reasonably certain that the Chargers weren't going to lay down for us.

A few of us congregated at the Gatorade table. We were a little giddy. It was a relief to finally get on the scoreboard and shift the momentum.

"Okay, don't get too far ahead of yourselves," Coach Tipton told us in a diplomatic way. "We still have a whole quarter to play, and we need to score at least once more. Twice would be better."

There was no argument. There was also no doubt that the 37-year-old former guard from SMU knew that we were taking the game seriously.

If the Chargers wanted to grab the momentum from us they didn't succeed on the kickoff. The kick was fielded four yards deep in the end zone. The return man, perhaps zealous to make something happen, did not even hesitate.

"Get him! Get him!" I heard a fan loudly direct above the roar of the rest of the crowd.

Black hammered him at the 14. As the ball carrier was going down I saw the ball come loose.

"Fumble! Fumble!"

"Loose ball!"

It was a mad scramble among players in white jerseys and brown jerseys. From where I stood I couldn't see the ball. All I could see was an assortment of players diving inside the 20.

Ultimately the action stopped. The referee pointed toward the south end zone. The Chargers had recovered. Although the ball had bounced and rolled around, it was recovered at about the point of the fumble.

"Damn!" I said out loud while some of my teammates employed a more colorful vernacular. If our earlier play suggested a lack of desire to win, we definitely wanted the game now.

The Chargers managed to make some noise at the start of the drive. They picked up four yards to the 18 by opening with a run around left end. A perfectly placed pass over the middle, despite Blakely providing tight coverage, then gave them a first down at the San Diego 34.

"Okay, okay! Don't worry about it!" Walker called. "They made a helluva play on that one! Just dig in and don't let them get any further!"

The Chargers fought for three yards by going off right tackle. They went to the air again on the next play. Rodgers batted the ball down to give them a third down.

"Okay, 33 nickel!" Walker commanded, turning and pointing at Hasegawa. That sent Rich in and brought Prendergast out. This formation meant three down linemen, three linebackers and five defensive backs.

"Hukilau! Hukilau!" our defenders barked. Of course it wasn't uncommon for our defense to call out the Hawaiian word for a large net-fishing party which we used as our term for a blitz. It was designed to get the offense thinking about a blitz even though it didn't necessarily mean a blitz. We could use the term on every play but it only meant blitz if it was called in the huddle. In this case I suspected that a blitz was on the menu.

Allen wasted no time. He charged in on the snap. The Charger quarterback tried to scramble away and moved toward the right sideline. It was there that he was met by Richards. Norm and Russ worked together to throw the quarterback for a sack at the 28; a nine-yard loss.

The people in the crowd were jumping out of their seats as they cheered at this point. Of course the defense had played well all day. It simply took a surge by the offense to get the crowd to fully appreciate the defense.

I appreciated the defense. For the moment, though, the pressure was on me. I was back on the field, standing near the Hawaii 30 to field the punt. With the momentum going our way I knew that a good return would enable us to keep the momentum.

This was the time when I needed to remind myself to not try to do anything stupid. I had to be prudent enough not to try to return the punt if a fair catch was the only solution. I also didn't want to call for a fair catch if I had room to run.

The punt was off and heading my way. It was a good punt although it wouldn't get the hang time the Chargers probably wanted.

"Run it, Jay!" I heard Hasegawa direct as I positioned myself to make the catch.

I fielded the punt right on the 30. As soon as I looked toward the north end zone I could see that I had plenty of room. Immediately I figured I would get close to ten yards. There was some outstanding blocking and I also managed to straight-arm a Charger near the 40. I was hit at the 44 but still managed to get to the 46 before I went down.

It was a 16-yard return which is excellent on a punt. Most importantly, we had very good field position.

"Okay, okay!" Walker called with his hands cupped around his mouth as soon as the play was blown dead. "That was a great effort all around! Now let's put some more points on the board!"

There was no argument from any of my teammates and most definitely not from me. The more I thought about the possibility of two losses in a row after how tough our loss was in Philadelphia, the more determined I was to pull this game out.

Unfortunately we didn't get off to an auspicious start. We were a little overzealous with our opinions on how to go about winning the game. With

366

eleven men in the huddle there were at least seven or eight different ideas of what play we should run first.

Bender finally restored order and called a play. We headed toward the line.

Suddenly there was a whistle accompanied by a yellow flag in the air. All of the commotion forced us to use up too much time.

"Brilliant! Brilliant!" Walker barked from the sideline. "I guess that good field position was a little too much for you. Do you guys want to win this game or not?"

We finally did get the play off. I managed to catch a pass that was slightly behind me near the right hashmark of the San Diego 47. There was a defender right there to hit me immediately. I still managed to fight for another two yards to give us a second and one at the Charger 45.

The second and one quickly turned into a third and three. Scott went through the left and got nowhere. A Charger linebacker penetrated and brought Larry down at the 47.

Walker said nothing. I happen to catch a glimpse of him. He stood stoically with his hands on his hips. I guess he decided that his sarcastic remarks weren't going to help.

Besides, he couldn't possibly have felt more angry than my colleagues on offense and I did. These setbacks were killing us.

There was another slight setback. Grummon hurt his ankle trying to block the linebacker who brought Scott down. He hobbled off the field to polite applause after the trainer attended to him. Fortunately it was only a temporary problem. He would be able to return after a few minutes.

Scott made up for the yardage he lost. He was so angry about the previous play that a rhinoceros would not have been able to stop him. He went up the middle and broke two tackles before finally going down at the 39. It was first down and the crowd was cheering again.

Kerner went up the middle next. He didn't do quite as well as Scott but it was good enough. He powered his way for a four-yard gain to the 35. At the very least, we were moving more and more into field goal range.

We went back to the air on the next play. It wound up being another completion in my hands. I caught the pass near the left sideline at the 12. I eluded a tackle for another five yards before being knocked out of bounds.

"Good job, Jay," Grummon said over the roar of the crowd as he reached down to help me up, having returned just before the start of the previous play.

I was feeling effervescent. Once again my confidence was up.

"Dockman!" I heard as I headed toward our huddle. I saw that Giametti was coming in to spell me for a play or two. As much as I wanted to score the touchdown to try to compensate for the touchdown that I should have scored the week before, I left the field without argument. Gary and I slapped fives as we normally did as our paths crossed.

"Good play," Walker told me when I returned to the sideline. "Stay close."

From my vantage point directly behind Walker I watched as Bender took the snap and dropped back. The Charger defense broke through and put pressure on Steve. He had no choice but to throw the ball out of the end zone.

"Damn, why can't the line hold those guys up?" I heard Walker mutter as he put his hands on his knees and looked down at the artificial turf. I was hoping to go back in, but Walker appeared set to rest me for at least one more play. He sent Ozzie in instead to give Scott a rest.

"How do you feel?" Walker asked Scott when Scott reached the sideline.

"I feel great, Coach."

"Okay, good," Walker said. "Stand by. You and Jay are going back in on the next play if we don't score on this one."

Larry and I stood side by side as we watched the next play. Ozzie went through the left. The determined Charger defense was all over him. He still managed to pick up two yards.

"What did we get? Two yards? Three yards?" Walker wondered out loud as he tried to decipher what was taking place near the north end zone before turning to face Larry and me. "They're probably going to be looking for a pass. Jay, you and Larry go back in. Tell Bender to run the 3 kama'aina left."

"Right, Coach," I said as Larry and I headed to where our huddle was getting ready to form. "Gary!"

"Ozzie!" Larry called.

I gave Bender the play and we formed up after Bender called the play in the huddle. The formation had me in the right slot before going in motion toward the left. This way I would be part of the contingent running interference for Scott as he carried the ball around left end.

As the play developed there was a mass of humanity on the left side. I put my shoulder in the midsection of the first white jersey I saw to try to keep him out of the play. In the same general vicinity were other bodies. The brown jerseys were trying to keep the white jerseys from stopping the brown jersey carrying the ball. There were numerous grunts and groans along with the sounds of equipment colliding. Scott finally went down near the left pylon just short of the goal line. It was fourth and inches.

The whistles were blowing. I could see one official holding his foot where he believed the play ended. Although a field goal could ultimately prove to be the winning margin for us, I wanted to go for a touchdown. We were too close, at least as far as I was concerned, to go for a field goal.

"Time!" I heard Bender request, causing more whistles as the referee waved his hands over his head, then gesture with his hands to let everybody in the stadium know that we had used our first time out of the half.

368

The rest of the offense huddled near the ten as Bender went to converse with Walker. Most of our heads were turned as we watched the conference. We obviously couldn't hear what was being said but that wasn't what we were concerned about anyway. Although we all knew that a field goal could only help us, none of us wanted to see the field goal unit run on the field.

Walker wasn't afraid to gamble, I knew. Had we only gained a couple of yards on the previous play there is no doubt that Walker would not have hesitated to send the field goal unit out. Since we only had a few inches to go he was willing to consider going for the entire wad. That would force the Chargers to go for the touchdown if they got far enough downfield toward the end of the game. A field goal would be of no use to them if enough time passed before they got into scoring position.

Bender returned to the huddle. The field goal unit stayed put. The crowd roared its approval. The only addition was Craig Kamanu since we were going with two tight ends. Dietrich returned to the sideline.

It was a 1 Wahiawa right; another name for a quarterback sneak. I was to line up on the right wing and head into the end zone. That way Bender would have a receiver if he saw that he wouldn't be able to get through before he reached the line of scrimmage. I was still more of a decoy since if Bender couldn't penetrate he probably wouldn't have time to look for a receiver.

We didn't need my services as a receiver. Steve took the snap and shot forward behind Hoddesson. The first thing I saw when I turned to see how the play was unfolding was an official raising his arms. That produced the sweetest roar of the crowd I had heard all day.

"Steve Bender the ball carrier," I heard over the public address system as I joined my teammates in congratulating Steve. "Touchdown, Hawaii."

It was our first lead of the day. Guinn made it a seven-point lead with the extra point. The clock showed 7:39. That was plenty of time for the Chargers to tie and then retake the lead.

"You guys have to hold 'em," I said to Richards on the sideline to try to encourage him and his defensive colleagues.

"They're not going anywhere against us," he said assuredly. "This is our game to win."

Norm seemed totally determined. We all did and none of the defensive players appeared to be wearing down. I was reasonably confident.

But I wasn't cocky. I knew that a lot could happen over the next seven minutes and 39 seconds and a lot of it was not good. I had to hope that the defense was up to the challenge and that the offense was up to the challenge when we had the ball again.

Guinn's kickoff was fielded at the five. The Charger return man got all the way to the 32. That wasn't a bad place for them to start. I still refused to panic over one halfway decent kick return.

After two plays the Chargers had gained exactly three feet. A rush for one yard and an incomplete pass gave them a third and nine at the 33. I stood up as if I believed that would somehow help the defense to stop them.

The Chargers weren't waving any white flags. Their quarterback rolled out and fired a pass that was caught near the sideline right in front of where I stood at the San Diego 45. Black muffed a tackle and the receiver got as far as the Hawaii 48 before Blakely drove him down. The Chargers had new life.

"Geez," I muttered under my breath. I grabbed another cup of Gatorade and sat back down on the bench. The Gatorade wasn't because I was thirsty. I was simply using it as a diversion.

At least we continued to hold San Diego's ground attack in check. A rush up the middle netted them two yards. A rush through the left got them only to the line of scrimmage.

Everybody knew that a pass was coming. We were back in our 33 nickel. It was important to stop them here because they weren't even in field goal range. If they kicked a field goal and got the ball back they could win the game with a touchdown. We did not want to concede even a field goal if we could avoid it.

I was standing again. Everybody on the sideline was standing. We rooted our defense on as the Charger quarterback took the snap and dropped back. Jennings and Richards were doing an impeccable job of putting pressure on him as the crowd roared its encouragement.

The quarterback did get the pass off. Unfortunately for him, he didn't have an open receiver. He threw the ball over the middle in the vicinity of where he had a receiver running a cross pattern with Hasegawa on his tail. The receiver attempted to make a diving catch but the ball still hit the ground about seven or eight feet away.

"All right! Way to go, guys!" I cheered as I put my helmet on and took the field for the punt.

Suddenly I noticed the yellow flag in the vicinity of the line of scrimmage. My heart sank.

I worried for nothing. The Chargers were offside. We declined the penalty.

There were only two things I feared at this juncture. One was that they would try a fake punt. The other was that they would pick up the eight yards they needed.

Actually there was a third fear. I was afraid that I would try to field the punt and wind up muffing it. Although I had been very sure handed as a receiver on this particular day, I was still suffering slightly from the aftereffects of the previous Sunday's muffed reception. The only way I was going to get over it was by getting through the entire game without screwing up in a key situation. I could just as easily drop a punt as a pass. Walker wouldn't be so understanding about it this time around, I was sure.

The punter ostensibly didn't sense how paranoid I had become. He kicked it to my left. The ball bounced near where I had positioned myself on the ten-yard line but well to my left. Knowing that there was no way that I could field the ball cleanly, I stayed away and focused on blocking a Charger chugging downfield who was trying to down the ball deep in our territory. We wound up with a pretty intense collision that knocked us both down. It was all in vain since the ball went out of bounds at the five.

"Are you all right?" I asked the Charger as I rose to my knees.

"Yeah, I'm okay, man. What happened?"

"You mean with the punt?"

"Yeah."

"It went out of bounds, I think. Yeah, they're spotting it at the five."

We both stood up and looked at each other with raised eyebrows. I think we were both thinking about the wasted effort when the punt went out of bounds. I was also relieved that I was given an excuse not to try to field the punt. Had I muffed it I probably would have broken down and cried right in front of everybody. In eleven seasons of football dating back to my freshman year of high school I had never cried during a football game but I am certain to this day that a muffed punt would have opened up the water fountains in my eyes.

"This is just what we need," Bender remarked in the huddle. "As long as we keep moving and picking up first downs we can run out the clock."

The clock was frozen at 4:27. It started to run as soon as the ball was snapped. We had to avoid running out of bounds and incomplete passes that would automatically stop the clock. A score would pretty much ice the game away but it wasn't imperative that we score. Not scoring was all right as long as we ran down the clock. With 95 yards in front of us we could keep the ball out of the Chargers' hands as long as we kept picking up first downs.

Scott got us off to a good start. He picked up four yards up the middle.

The following play didn't work quite as well. Larry went through the right but picked up only one yard. It was a suddenly precarious situation. The clock was running but there was still more than three minutes left. If we didn't convert on third down we would have to punt which probably would leave the Chargers in good field position with plenty of time to get to the end zone. Another critical point was that the Chargers still had all three of their time-outs.

Bender took the snap and quickly stepped back. The blitz was on but he looked to his left and found Grummon who had slanted outward. The former New York Giant caught the pass at the 13 as Bender was getting hit and avoided a Charger who made a desperation lunge at him. Rich got as far as the 19 before a pair of Chargers took him down. We had the first down that we desperately needed.

Equally as important, the clock continued to run. It was at about 3:10 when the referee signaled that the ball was ready for play.

The clock was stopped briefly when the Chargers got called for encroachment. An overzealous linebacker shot through the line and tried to stop but brushed against Marv. He gave us five of the ten yards we needed for another first down.

Scott picked up four of the remaining five yards through the right. Precious seconds continued to tick away as we approached the two-and-a-half-minute mark.

I was given the honor of trying to pick up the first down on the following play. I rushed through the left and was grabbed near the line of scrimmage but stayed up. I kept my feet moving and managed to get to the 30 before being brought down by a trio of visitors from San Diego. We had the first down and allowed the final few seconds to tick down to the two-minute warning.

Hayer whacked me on the rear as I casually made my way back toward where we were huddling near the 20 while Bender headed to the sideline. Although I was hit near the line, it wasn't Carl's fault. I was initially hit by a defensive back who had read the play and charged in. Carl and Stanek both did outstanding jobs of handling their blocking assignments. It was obvious that the Charger defensive unit was getting tired. That would definitely work to our advantage if we didn't screw things up on our own.

What was great about the first two plays after the two-minute warning was that they both took a little longer than they were designed to. Scott went up the middle on the first play and picked up five yards to the Hawaii 35. Because of his tenacious refusal to go down immediately after he was hit the clock had wound down to 1:51 before the Chargers were able to use their first time out.

The next play didn't work quite as well for us. Scott lost a yard going through the left. He still fought hard against going down. The Chargers didn't get to use their second time out until the clock was down to 1:43.

As Bender conversed with Walker I wondered if Walker was willing to gamble with a pass. It would look like a stroke of genius if it worked. If it fell incomplete it would not only stop the clock, it would allow the Chargers to save their final time out and open the gates for the second-guessers.

"Do you think Walker's going to send in a pass play?" Dietrich asked me as if he had been reading my thoughts.

"I don't know," I replied thoughtfully. "The only thing I can say about Walker at a time like this is he doesn't go by the book. The book would say keep the ball on the ground and chew up as much of the clock as you can. Walker doesn't mind taking a gamble."

I knew that if we kept the ball on the ground and didn't make the first down the Chargers would probably go ahead and use their final time out. A good Jablonski punt would mean that the Chargers would have very little time to cover about 70 yards.

Kerner got the call. He went through the right on a Kaneohe right. It was sheer determination, coupled with the exhaustion of the San Diego defense, that enabled Jeff to keep going as the crowd roared its encouragement. A couple of Chargers got their hands on him but he continued until he was finally brought down at the 41. That was one more yard than we needed for another first down.

The clock ran down to 1:26 before the Chargers used their final time out. It was a formality since we had achieved that final hurdle to certain victory. Bender took three snaps and dropped down to run out the clock.

I joined my colleagues in heaving sighs of relief. This had to have been the longest game of the season. It only went 60 minutes of actual playing time, of course, but in such a tight game that you feel is imperative that you win the time seems to drag on. It looked like we were going to let this one get away. Fortunately we wore the Chargers down.

We actually owed it to our defense. Our defensive unit did a phenomenal job of keeping the score down. It would have been an injustice to the defense had the offense not put those two touchdowns on the board and then had that final sustained drive.

The Chargers almost seemed dazed but were gracious in defeat. I shook hands with the victims of the Hawaiians' first ever NFL season sweep and headed toward the locker room. Black and Jablonski were walking just ahead of me when I reached the south end zone.

"Did you ever punt in the second half?" Black asked.

Jablonski hesitated, then shook his head. He looked at Black and raised his eyebrows.

"I guess Walker knew what he was talking about," Black remarked. "He said you weren't going to be used and you weren't."

Apparently Walker didn't forget his halftime prophecy. All smiles in the locker room after our victory. He even awarded the game ball to Jablonski.

It wasn't a pretty victory. We still weren't turning it down.

Scott came up short in his quest for another 100-yard game although I don't think he was worried about it. He had a solid game with 23 carries for 87 yards.

I narrowly missed a 100-yard game as a receiver. I didn't even think about it until I read in the paper the next day that I had six receptions for 98 yards. It would have been nice to have picked up those extra two yards but a 100-yard game means very little if the team doesn't win. What we accomplished as a team, regardless of how ugly or improbable, was much more important than individual statistics.

For whatever it was worth, Larry and I both seemed certain to eclipse the 1,000-yard marks in rushing and receiving, respectively. With three games to go Larry had 202 carries for 875 yards. I had 51 receptions for 946 yards.

Dietrich was technically within striking distance but he probably needed to have 100-yard games in each of our final three contests. He had 39 receptions for 689 yards.

But these were individual achievements. Walker would breathe fire if he knew of anybody thinking about those even though it would almost be inhuman not to. Our focus was to have a winning season. If we could sweep the remaining three games against one team assured of a playoff spot and two teams still in contention. . . .

First thing's first. The Raiders were next. Not only were we the only team to beat the Raiders to this point, we wanted to be the only two teams to beat the Raiders.

CHAPTER SIXTEEN
The Oakland Raid

Monday was a day to rest. The victory over the Chargers enabled me to simply enjoy myself. That meant nothing connected to football, no commercials to shoot and no fighting traffic.

That also meant doing nothing connected to my TV show. In order to be free on Monday I spent a few hours at the studio immediately after the game putting together the bulk of the videotaped segment, leaving a two-minute window open for highlights of the Monday night game. I had also done the narration over the videotaped segment and had written the bulk of the script for my live portions. All that was left aside from the Monday night highlights, assuming there would be any, was some footage of the University of Hawaii's basketball team going through its paces. The Rainbow hoopsters would be opening their season on Friday night. A camera man and I would capture the footage Tuesday afternoon at Klum Gym on the University of Hawaii campus.

But 24 hours would pass before I had to report for my Tuesday film session, meeting and workout with the team and then put the final touches on my TV show. On Monday I was free to simply bask in the sun on the beach. Since I didn't feel like battling traffic I settled on Fort DeRussy since it was within walking distance of where I lived. Armed with a beach mat, a towel and a paperback book, I spent the better part of the day alternating between swimming and lying on the beach.

I suppose there were people who recognized me. The spot I chose, though, was relatively safe. Most of the locals who would normally frequent this spot were working. Many of the tourists in the area may have known my name but I still hadn't had the exposure that would have enabled most of them to recognize me.

"Hey, are you Jay Dockman?" I heard a young male voice inquire.

I looked up from *A Tale of Two Cities*, the book I had bought a few days earlier but didn't open until that day. I saw that I was being addressed by two boys and a girl of about 15 or 16. One boy was fairly large with features that suggested Polynesian ancestry. The other boy was of medium height and stocky and appeared to be 100 percent haole (Caucasian) with dark blonde hair and blue eyes. The attractive girl with shoulder-length raven hair was probably Japanese or possibly Korean.

"What are you kids up to?" I asked congenially.

"We were just wondering. Are you Jay Dockman?" the Polynesian boy repeated.

Feeling self-conscious about whatever attention was suddenly dropped on my shoulders, I nodded subtly with a polite smile.

"Do you go to school?" I asked.

"Roosevelt," the haole boy responded, referring to the school at the base of the Punchbowl crater a few miles away. To honor the high school's namesake, the school's nickname was the Rough Riders.

"Why aren't you there?" I asked in a nonjudgmental way.

"Eh, school's out, brah. We got out a little while ago," the Polynesian boy answered while the haole boy nodded and the girl looked out toward the ocean.

I didn't necessarily believe the boy until I looked at my watch. It was almost four o'clock.

"Can we get an autograph?" the Polynesian boy asked.

"Yeah, sure," I said politely. "I don't have a pen or paper, though."

"Oh. Eh, Denise. You get pen and paper?" the Polynesian asked in a local vernacular.

The girl opened her purse and thumbed through. She had paper in a small spiral notebook. Amid the chewing gum, lipstick and Milk Duds she eventually found a pen.

I signed autographs for each of the three teenagers, personalizing them for Ken, Kaipo and Denise. The boys were almost effervescent while Denise politely thanked me.

As the three teenagers headed down the beach toward the Cinerama Reef Hotel I suddenly felt conspicuous. The autograph session got people's attention. Nobody approached me but it seemed as if a lot of the people in the area were sizing me up. I jocularly wondered if they were trying to ascertain what movie I was in or what soap opera I was on or if I was John Denver wearing a dark wig and phony moustache. With a least a couple dozen people trying to be subtle while they looked me over, it was fortunate that it was about the time I had planned to leave anyway. I went home and took a shower, walked down to the Red Lion on Kuhio Avenue to pick up a pizza to take home, then returned just in time to catch the start of *Monday Night Football*.

"Your brother came by after you left this morning," my roommate remarked after he returned home from work in time to catch the second half kickoff.

"My brother?" I answered quizzically, still not used to Bill's jocular attempt to label somebody other than the 14-year-old brother I actually had in California as my brother.

"You know. Ron."

I shook my head in amusement. I had forgotten about Whitcomb. How I could have forgotten him was hard to comprehend although he really wasn't worth remembering.

"He told me that you and I should start moving up in the world," Bill continued lightly.

"What? Are you kidding?"

376

"No, that's really what he was saying when he came over today. He said that it was about time that you and I started trying to move up in the world."

Whitcomb's opinion was very interesting. Bill had a business degree and was doing very well as an assistant manager at a Waikiki restaurant. I had a bachelor's degree, would begin work toward a master's degree in January, was having a good season as a pro football player and had a weekly sports highlight TV show.

"I didn't realize that Whitcomb thought that we were just too complacent with our lives," I remarked facetiously.

"I guess we must be."

"And this from a high school dropout making minimum wage."

It was a good thing for Ozzie Roberts that we beat San Diego. It was good for all of us but most definitely Ozzie. Walker might not have been such a good sport about Ozzie's faux pas had we lost on Sunday.

We were having our scheduled game film session on Tuesday. It was definitely not a pleasant experience for the offense during the first half when we didn't move the ball especially well. Everything that could possibly have gone wrong seemed to go wrong. There were incomplete passes, missed blocks and shabby running. The temperature in the room seemed to be on the rise as Walker breathed fire.

Of course we finally got it together and won the game despite a lackluster start to the second half. Walker was in a better mood when we reached the fourth quarter segment.

One drive contained nothing unexpected. The more the game progressed, the more focused we were and the more the momentum favored us.

At one point Walker paused the project while the screen showed us in the "I" formation. I was set in a three-point stance on the right wing obliquely behind Abraham, Kerner was in a three-point stance at fullback and Ozzie was directly behind Kerner, giving Scott a breather.

"Now before I run this," Walker announced, "I want everybody to count the number of men we have on the field."

We all took a moment and silently counted. Everything looked normal to me. We had two tackles, two guards, a center, a tight end, a wide receiver, a quarterback, a fullback, a tailback and a halfback. In my estimation that added up to eleven. The only other players on the field were on the other team.

"Abraham!" Walker called in a way that made Clint wonder what he had done wrong. "How many do you see?"

"Eleven?" Clint replied tentatively.

"How many, Scott?"

"I count eleven."

"Grummon, how about you?"

"Eleven, Coach."

"Everybody says eleven," Walker reported. "Well, everybody's wrong. We only had ten on this play."

This naturally led to some murmurs throughout the room. Walker started the film in slow motion.

The play was a 2 Mililani right. In a mode that ran one frame at a time we watched as Bender took the snap, turned and moved back, and handed the ball to Kerner who headed toward the line.

What Walker wanted us to see was Roberts. He didn't move a muscle throughout the entire sequence. Prior to the snap the fourth-round draft choice from Austin Peay was positioned directly behind Kerner crouched slightly with his hands on his thigh pads. He stayed in that position as the ball was snapped and never moved until the play was finally over. It was as if somebody had erected a statue on the playing field.

As the play progressed we started a ripple of muffled laughter. The laughter got louder and louder until everybody was nearly hysterical. The super slow motion made Ozzie's enigmatic bout with rigor mortis that much more comical.

Even Walker was laughing. That was probably lucky for Ozzie.

"Okay, okay," Walker finally called to restore order although he was still laughing slightly. "Now Ozzie . . . when you're out on the field we expect you to do something when the play starts. Run through the line, block somebody or do a handspring. Next time you just stand there I'll send the team doctor out to do an autopsy on you."

That set the tone for the rest of the session. There wasn't that much left anyway, and this session had a happy ending since we did actually win the game. There was still some muffled laughter taking place when the session ended.

Walker stood and pondered as the defense joined us and the room started to return to a more serious mode. Once the projector was off the Chargers were history. We couldn't revel in the victory anymore. Our immediate concern was the imminent arrival of the Oakland Raiders.

I sat quietly while flanked by Scott and Abraham. Marv, who was sitting directly behind me, remarked in a somewhat loud whisper that Larry, Clint and I looked like an Oreo.

That was heard by virtually everybody including Walker. The players and assistant coaches tried to stifle their giggles but Walker didn't seem to mind. The good-natured remark and subsequent laughter defined the cohesiveness of the team. If anybody had any major prejudices, they kept them to themselves. What little racial humor there was would not have offended most people. We were very careful in how we dealt with such humor.

I suppose that cohesiveness was partially the reason we had played so well. Granted, a five-and-six record kept us far from the NFL elite. It was still phenomenal for a team added to the league less than a year earlier.

The cohesiveness is not to imply that we were all chummy with each other. We were not. I do believe, though, that as a unit we were more cohesive than most of the players on other teams were with their teammates, at least when it came to playing together.

A local sportswriter theorized that one of the reasons we started so much better than other expansion franchises was the smallness of the community we represented. Although my teammates had their own interests and went their own ways most of the time, we saw a lot of each other off the field, even if only by accident. It wasn't unusual to go to a grocery store or shopping center in or around Honolulu and run into a teammate or two. The arbitrary encounters, regardless of how ephemeral, allegedly enabled us to get to know each other better and, therefore, play together better.

At least that was the opinion of a local sportswriter. I am not especially quick to disagree with him even though it is not quite as simple as he made it sound. We had that advantage over players from virtually everywhere with the probable exception of Green Bay. Players from places such as Los Angeles would see their teammates during practices and games before getting swallowed up in the neighboring communities. Arbitrary encounters for most were probably once in a blue moon.

Of course there had to be other factors in our success. We had to have the ability in the first place, we had to be willing to work hard and we had to be coached well, among other things. Whatever cohesiveness we had was simply a small piece to the puzzle.

Thursday was Thanksgiving. We still had practice, to the surprise of nobody. Walker trimmed as much fat as he felt he could. We still needed a good workout to help us get ready for Sunday's matchup with Oakland.

Aside from wanting to win the game under any fair circumstance, this game was extra special because it was our last home game of the season. We were also constantly being reminded by everybody from TV sports anchors to total strangers that we were still the only team to have beaten Oakland.

There was also no doubt that the Raiders were aware of who had beaten them. Although teams are not supposed to use revenge as a primary motive, the idea of revenge was stamped on their minds. They wouldn't have been human otherwise.

We were motivated for a variety of reasons. Among everything else, a victory would get us back to the .500 level for the first time since our fourth game of the season.

It was a pretty good workout. We arrived earlier than normal so that we were all dressed and ready to work precisely at eight o'clock. Normally our Thursday workouts went at least two hours. Walker terminated the workout at about 9:30 and there were no meetings.

"I want you to have a nice Thanksgiving," Walker told us as we knelt on the turf that was damp from the overnight rain. "Anybody who doesn't have anywhere to go, drop by my place. You're welcome to come by to fix a plate of turkey and trimmings and have a drink or two. The turkey will be ready at about one."

That was vintage Walker. Sometimes he pushed us the way a Marine Corps drill instructor pushes his recruits. He still had a truly big heart.

I didn't go to Walker's. I spent part of the day watching football and eating dinner with friends.

My big event of the day was that night. That was when I had a date with a young lady named Christie Carlisle. She was an attractive brunette who looked a lot like actress Lesley Ann Warren. She was a nurse at Straub Hospital who lived in the Punchbowl area of Honolulu.

I had actually met Christie several months earlier at a bar and grill on Kapiolani Boulevard called the Columbia Inn. Since that time we had several arbitrary encounters around town. I ran into her a week earlier at the Safeway on Beretania Street and asked her out. This would be our first, and only, time out together.

This is not to say there was anything wrong with her. She was a little nutty at times but not an airhead. The chemistry between us simply wasn't there.

We were going to the Neal Blaisdell Arena to see Olivia Newton-John. It worked out that I was contemplating whom to invite to the concert when I happened to run into Christie at the Safeway.

It was a fantastic concert. Olivia was vibrant and sang flawlessly with a band behind her that performed equally as well. She closed with her signature piece, *I Honestly Love You*.

When she finished her finale she was rewarded with polite applause. . . .

And then everybody quietly left! I was dumbfounded as those in attendance simply made an orderly exit.

By this time I had been to several concerts. I had seen everybody from Gordon Lightfoot to the Rolling Stones to Joni Mitchell to the Moody Blues. In each case the audience stood and cheered for more when the performers left the stage. I couldn't understand why that didn't happen with Olivia. Didn't everybody think she did a show worthy of more than polite applause at the end? I thought she was wonderful.

After I got over the shock of the apparent lack of appreciation I took Christie down the street to the Columbia Inn for a nightcap. That was when I discovered how well Christie and I actually knew each other.

"What kind of work do you do?" she asked during the course of our conversation.

It took me a moment to recover from that. It wasn't that I expected everybody I came into contact with to know who I was. However, I had known Christie for about seven or eight months.

"I, uh, play for the Hawaiians."

"The football team? You play football?"

I guess the subject had never come up. I would have loved to have seen her face had she surfed through the channels on a Tuesday night and stumbled across my TV show.

As we went through our light Saturday workout I knew that we were ready. We had worked hard during the week. The opportunity to finish the Hawaiians' inaugural season with a winning record and the opportunity to close out our home schedule with a victory gave us the incentive we needed. There was also one other factor.

"You men already beat these guys in Oakland," Walker pointed out; not for the first time as he employed every tactic possible to pump us up. "Nobody else has beaten them this season. You are the only blemish on their record. After tomorrow you can be the only two blemishes on their record."

Walker wanted this one bad. I suppose that he was partially thinking about how good he would look if he guided an expansion team to a winning record in its maiden season and rightfully so. There was also the matter of momentum going into our two final games.

Besides that, Walker wanted his players to be happy. As long as we played hard and fair there was happiness in victory.

I sure wanted to win. The Raiders, to me, were the preeminent NFL team. They were the NFL team I most loved to watch during my WFL days. I revered the opportunity to beat a second time the team I considered to be the most preeminent in 1976.

Just the same, I needed to focus on other things. Beginning on Friday I seemed to see nothing but silver and black. Even the most ostentatiously outrageous aloha shirts and matching muumuus seemed to be silver and black in my mind's eye. Every man, woman and child I saw seemed to also be wearing eye patches.

Put another way, I had Oakland Raiders on the brain.

This had also been true on Friday night when I was back at the Blaisdell Arena. This time I was there to watch the University of Hawaii basketball team open its season against Oregon State. Don Simmons was with me but I barely noticed that he was there.

Not that I didn't enjoy watching the game which the Rainbows lost, 91-76. There were even a few instances when I didn't think at all about the Raiders.

Very few.

On Saturday night I declined an offer to attend the University of Hawaii's football game against Oregon State's gridiron contingent. I wanted to be loyal to my alma mater. I simply felt that I needed to avoid football for one night. The Rainbow Warriors were having an off year and I was afraid that being in attendance during what was potentially a lopsided loss would leave me in the wrong frame of mind for the Raiders. I had to focus on winning and I was afraid that a poor game by the Rainbow Warriors, if that was the way it was going to be, would send me to bed in a losing frame of mind.

I didn't even listen to the game on the radio. Instead I spent the evening at Maunalua Bay in relative solitude. I sat on the rocks that lined the banks of the bay and essentially meditated as I looked out to sea.

It was still daylight when I arrived. There were people water skiing, fishing and having picnics nearby. They all seemed to be wearing silver and black and black eye patches.

At least that's the way they looked to me. Had my imagination run away further I might have seen Jolly Roger flags on the sailboats.

I was still at Maunalua Bay after the sun went down. To my left I could see the lights in the homes along the Portlock peninsula. Off in the distance to my right were the lights of Kahala. I could also see the lights of various aircraft that had just taken off or were about to land at Honolulu International Airport.

Growing tired of just sitting, I went to my car and pulled out. Instead of heading west toward my home in Waikiki, I headed east. I drove through some of the side streets in Hawaii Kai. This was one of the nicer suburbs in Honolulu; one that I always enjoyed cruising through. I especially enjoyed driving up Poipu Drive which rose up along the side of the Koko Head crater and was one of the more affluent sections of Hawaii Kai. I even enjoyed this drive at night although it was better in the daylight hours since it afforded one a beautiful view of Maunalua Bay. Often I used this drive as a way of pondering all that was going on in my life.

Ultimately I returned to Kalanianaole Highway and continued east. I drove past Hanauma Bay, headed around the curve by the rocky cliffs and then past the Halona Blow Hole and Sandy Beach. Around Makapuu Point I continued, through Waimanalo and then Kailua before returning to Honolulu via Pali Highway. Somewhere along the way I turned on the radio just in time to hear one of my favorite Christmas classics, Stan Freberg's *Green Christmas*. It was a piece that managed to capture the true meaning of Christmas while also displaying the exploitation of the sacred holiday.

Sleep was hard to come by.

382

Okay, that wasn't unusual the night before a game. This time it seemed extreme. I even considered staying up all night.

At about one o'clock I was still wide awake even though I had been in bed for about 90 minutes. I decided to get up and get dressed. I figured a walk would calm me down.

I actually got as far as the front door before I had second thoughts. No matter what, I was better off staying home. I went back to my bedroom and got undressed.

It didn't take long after that for me to fall asleep. I even slept straight through for a change. I still didn't hear the alarm clocks which were set for about six o'clock. It was shortly before five that I awoke and jumped out of bed.

"Okay, let's play some football," I enthusiastically told myself in a low voice. As soon as my eyes had opened, I was wide awake.

During the pregame warmup I watched as the spectators gradually filed in. Many were still enjoying tailgate parties in the parking lot but plenty opted to sit in their seats and watch us warm up. Like our opening game against the Cardinals, this game had sold out although not in time to lift the local television blackout.

Exactly two weeks later our season would be over. While the thought of the season coming to an end for us saddened me some, the date seemed a long way away.

What was most sad for the moment was the fact that this was our final 1976 home game. Through three years of football at the University of Hawaii, two WFL seasons and one NFL season there was always something extra special about playing for the home crowd.

But this would be it for 1976. It was our seventh and final home game. In my opinion it would also be the toughest of the entire bunch.

That says a lot. Going into the season I considered Dallas and Oakland to be about equal on our home level of difficulty. The Cowboys had gone to the Super Bowl in January and the Raiders would have been the Cowboys' opponent had they not been bumped by the Steelers in the AFC Conference Championship. We had also faced tough competition at home from the Cardinals who had the misfortune of squaring off against a team determined to make a positive first impression in the NFL, the Broncos, the Oilers who were making a rise from obscurity and the Chargers who came at us hard and heavy a week earlier before we finally wore them down.

But at this juncture I realized that this would be our toughest home opponent of the season. The Raiders had a lot of incentive since they were vying for the home field advantage in the playoffs. They also wanted to continue building momentum as the playoffs neared.

And, of course, there was that one unsightly blemish on their record. They were going to square off against a team they already knew was very capable of beating them. There was no doubt that they had fine-tuned their game plan to make sure it wouldn't happen again.

For all of the factors involved, I believed I was accurate in labeling this as our toughest home game of the season. It would make for a very strong statement about the Hawaiians if we could win this one.

"You know you can beat this team," Walker pointed out just before we were to leave the locker room for the final time before kickoff. "You proved that in October. You beat them on their turf and now you can beat them here."

When Walker spoke he was fired up. He still paused to weigh his words carefully. Often he seemed to be looking at the area above the lockers as if he had a script written there, then would look down at arbitrarily selected players.

"This is our final home game," he continued as he slowly paced in front of us as we sat in front of our lockers. "The stadium is sold out. Fifty-thousand people are here to show their support. At home and on the road, you've given them a fairly good season; something far better than what they projected at the start of the season. We won't be going to the Super Bowl this year and our opponent for today just might but. . . ."

Another pause. I am not sure if Walker needed to collect himself or if he simply wasn't sure of what to say next. He might even have paused deliberately for effect. I know I was pumped up.

"Those fans out there are very proud of you," Walker said, lowering his voice and displaying a faraway look as if he could literally see every paying customer in their seats. "You have an opportunity to go out there and give them a lot to look forward to in 1977. Let's give them a preview of coming attractions by being the best damn football players you can be. I know you can rise to the challenge so let's go."

With that we simultaneously rose and headed out of the locker room. A phalanx of active players, players on injured reserve, players on the taxi squad and coaches all had one very common goal. We were determined to beat the Raiders.

The fans displayed their approbation as we appeared on the field from the tunnel. Most of them seemed to be standing as they cheered. I was only a few feet behind Joseph and Grummon as they became the first players to step on the field and the relative quiet erupted into an explosive roar. If the fans had any say in the outcome of this game, there was a group of athletes in store for a very long flight to Oakland that day.

"How do you feel?" I asked Hamer on the sideline just prior to the coin toss. "Are you ready to go?"

"I'm ready," he replied.

It was a big opportunity for him. He was starting at left cornerback. Black had been listed as questionable after injuring his knee in the San Diego game. By Saturday it was obvious that Mark wouldn't be ready, giving Eric the starting nod.

I happened to spot Mark behind the bench. He had a strange expression on his face. Standing in street clothes except for his game jersey, which was standard attire for all members of the team not suited up including taxi squad members, he looked slightly angry and somewhat bored. For all of his debauchery, he was a very intense football player.

"How's the knee feeling?" Rodgers asked as he happened to pass Mark.

Black shrugged. In all probability he wanted to play. I believe his inactivity was not his idea. He was benched, I believed, by the team physician.

I was so immersed in trying to read Black's mind that I didn't even notice the coin toss. It was one of those rare times in 1976 that Hawaii actually won the toss. I wondered if I should ignore the toss more often.

The kick came. Ozzie was deep with me again. It headed Ozzie's way.

"It's all yours!" I cried out and ran forward to head off the first person in a white jersey I saw.

Ozzie fielded the kick on the five. I managed to help him since I put a good block on somebody in a white jersey. I managed to knock the defender back a little and then turn him around. Somewhere along the way Ozzie ran past us.

I looked up and saw Ozzie getting hit. I also saw the ball pop loose as he started going down, causing the crowd noise to go from a loud roar to a collective groan. I was about six or seven yards behind him and bolted forward to try to recover the ball. Fortunately Ozzie managed to recover his own fumble since his tacklers actually brought him down on top of it. We had a first down at our own 29.

"Good return, Ozzie," I heard Giametti say as he helped Ozzie to his feet.

"I can't believe I fumbled that damn ball," Ozzie muttered.

"It's all right," Hasegawa said as he whacked Ozzie on the derriere. "We've still got the ball. Don't worry about it."

As the members of the kick return unit who were not in the starting lineup headed to our sideline, I went to where our huddle was forming up. It may have been my imagination but everybody looked more determined than normal.

"Okay, let's make history," Bender commented before calling the play.

We got off to a reasonably good start when Kerner went through the left and picked up three yards. We then lost all of those yards and two others when Dietrich started running his pass pattern before the snap. An incomplete pass made it third and 12.

Unfortunately for the Raiders, they weren't playing against a team that made concessions on third and long. With four receivers on the field in an obvious pass situation, Bender hit Giametti near the left sideline at the Hawaii 43. That was more than enough for a first down but Gary could pick up more. He spun around to elude a tackler and was finally knocked out of bounds at the Oakland 48.

That ignited the crowd. We still had almost half the distance of the field to go from where we started but our conversion on third and long probably assured them that we were playing to win. No doubt the Raiders were also cognizant of that.

I got the call next. Bender hit me over the middle at the 39. That was a yard short of the yardage needed for a first down and I was hit as soon as I had the ball but I managed to do a spin of my own. The defensive back didn't lose his grip on me, but I still managed to get to the 37 before he and another defensive back got me down. It was our second first down in as many plays.

The crowd was happy and the scoreboard encouraged the crowd further while we were in our huddle. As Steve was calling the play I happened to glance up and see the animated cheerleader appear and wave her pom poms over her head.

"Go! Go! Go! Go! Go!" the crowd yelled on cue from the animated cheerleader.

Perhaps that fired up the Raiders. They dug in and made it difficult for us to pick up any substantial amount of yardage. We managed only five yards on the next two plays to give us a third and five at the Oakland 32. It became fourth and five when Bender's pass to Dietrich was batted down near the 15.

I was near the right sideline at the 20 and well-covered when I saw the pass knocked away. The crowd seemed to let out another collective groan and whistles were blowing all over to signify that the play was over. I stood for a moment with my hands on my hips, then headed to our sideline in resignation. It had been a moderately successful drive since we were at least in field goal range.

"Three points are better than no points," I heard Stanek say to Clint in front of the bench. It was still frustrating for all of us. We wanted to knock the Raiders off balance by picking up the full seven during the opening drive.

As we were all forcing ourselves to be grateful that we at least managed to get three points something totally unexpected happened.

Guinn missed the field goal!

Eric got his foot into it and got the height and distance. From where I stood it looked like it would split the uprights until it suddenly seemed to hook. My heart sank as I realized that the kick was wide to the left.

"All right, all right. It happens, it happens," Walker remarked to try to build us back up. "Even the best kickers miss on occasion."

Guinn came to the sideline and stood by himself behind the bench. Like most kickers, Eric's helmet contained a single facebar. It was easy to see how angry he was with himself since he couldn't hide his face behind a larger mask. He even seemed to have tears stinging his eyes.

"It's all right, man," I said as I casually walked in front of where Eric was standing. "We've got plenty of time to put points on the board."

About half-a-dozen teammates gave encouraging words to him. He was down on himself and that was understandable. He wanted to win this game as badly as the rest of us did. His missed field goal was still no worse than any mistake any of his teammates had made on the field. It was important that he know that his teammates were behind him.

I grabbed a cup of Gatorade and sat down in time to see a Raider running back pick up four yards. I also saw Richards move slightly over to the Oakland side of the ball and try in vain to get back before the snap. It was a free play for the Raiders and they wisely took the penalty since it gave them a first and five at their own 37 instead of second and six at the 36.

It took only one play for the Raiders to pick up the five yards they needed for a first down. They went around left end and got up to the Oakland 42. A measurement was called for and the Raiders had picked up the first down with about three inches to spare.

The Raiders managed only a yard on the next play but that was nullified. One of their linemen was called for holding. We accepted the penalty to force them back to the 32.

"All right! We can hold them!" I called out, rising from my seat and moving into position behind the bench where I could watch the action on the field and do a few stretching exercises to simply occupy the time before I would return to the field.

Jennings held the Raiders at bay on the next play. Moving into the flat, he knocked down a pass near the Oakland 40.

"All right, Ed! That's the way to play it, baby!" I called before running in place for a few seconds. I would have given almost anything for a turnover. I couldn't wait to return to the field.

The Raiders were more successful on the ensuing play. A pass was caught on the run, over the middle just inside the Oakland 45. The receiver broke Blakely's tackle and managed to get to the Hawaii 49 before Rodgers drove him down.

"Damn!" I heard Marv remark from directly in front of me where he sat on the bench.

At least they still hadn't picked up the first down. It was third and one. I hoped we could hold them to no gain if we couldn't push them back or turn the ball over. That would force them into a situation where they would be expected to punt.

Our defensive line was determined to stop the Raiders. Unfortunately their running back was even more determined not to be stopped. He was hit near the line but refused to concede anything. By the time he was finally brought down he had fought his way to the 47. It was another first down.

I decided that there was no point in getting myself too psyched up to return to the field. Since our aluminum benches at Aloha Stadium had no backrests I casually stepped over the bench from behind and sat next to Marv.

"I can't stand this," I said. "I just want to get out there and put some points on the board."

"I hear ya," Marv replied. "We knew that they would move the ball. I just wish they wouldn't."

Move the ball they did as Marv and I helplessly observed from the bench. A half-dozen plays later the Raiders had a first down at the Hawaii 23. That was when we came to fully appreciate the athletic ability of Pratt, our injury prone rookie defensive end from Arkansas.

Gavin had been an all-around athlete in high school. He had been a two-way player on his high school football team as a defensive end and fullback, a guard on his high school basketball team and a third baseman on his high school baseball team. He was good enough to receive scholarship offers in each one and had also been a middle round draft choice of the newly transplanted Texas Rangers in 1972. He was big but solidly built with great leaping ability. That leaping ability is what enabled him to go up the ladder and bat away a pass near the line of scrimmage.

The ball went slightly to Gavin's right. He stumbled forward and wasn't able to intercept the pass but Prendergast did manage to grab it just before it hit the ground at the 22. The big black defensive tackle lumbered forward until he was wrestled down at the Hawaii 28.

"All right!" I cried out as I leaped up from my seat, thrusting my arms in the air with my left hand holding my helmet by the facemask. As soon as the play was blown dead I charged on the field, leading my offensive colleagues toward where we would form up our huddle. I managed to slap fives with both Pratt and Prendergast as our paths crossed while also noticing the roar of the crowd. That was like hearing symphony music during home games but it may have sounded like a dirge to the Raiders.

"Okay, the defense forced a break for us," Bender remarked as we formed up in the huddle. "Let's not waste it."

Scott went up the middle but managed only two yards on the opening play. We made up for the short yardage on the next play when Bender hit Dietrich at the 41. Ted eluded a tackler by side-stepping him and got as far as the Hawaii 48 before being tackled.

"All right. We're moving. We're moving," I said to nobody in particular as I headed back to the huddle.

388

Bender met a heavy rush on the following play. He managed to scramble away and got the pass off in my direction. It was a pretty good pass but a defender made a good play and batted the ball away near the Oakland 35.

"(Expletive deleted)!" I snapped before the defender caught my eye. "Good play," I told him sincerely although I really wanted to cut his hands off. He smiled in a way that was either expressing gratitude for the compliment or flippantly mocking me.

We went for a sweep around right end on the following play. Scott only managed a yard. The Raider defense had been quick and managed to head Larry off despite the number of blockers trying to run interference for him.

It was third and nine. We had good field position but that came as a result of our only first down of this drive. I dreaded the thought of having to punt after our defense had turned the ball over for us.

The Raiders knew that a pass was in the works. Bender dropped back and met another heavy rush. He managed to get the pass off while on the run, putting more juice on the ball than intended.

I was the intended receiver. I leaped up in the air as I ran toward the right sideline near the 30 and tipped the errant pass slightly upward. It came back down in my hands and I set my feet before my momentum carried me out of bounds.

Whistles were blowing and the crowd was cheering. I could still hear an Oakland defender over the noise.

"He caught it out of bounds! He caught it out of bounds!"

As I turned to return to the field and huddle with my teammates, I could see the Oakland defensive back pointing at the sideline as if that was where I had stepped before securing the ball. If it was any comfort to me, and it was, it was the same defensive back who had knocked the pass away from me two plays earlier.

The official seemed oblivious to the defender's contention as he simply stood to mark where I had gone out at the 28. The Raider defender, recognizing the futility of his argument, threw up his arms in frustration and headed toward his team's defensive huddle.

I know for a certainty that I had made a legitimate catch. I recall looking down at my toes as they hit the ground. I could still see a small portion of green artificial turf between my toes and the white paint on the sideline. I wasn't in by more than an inch or two but that was enough.

Our drive stalled after that. Scott managed two yards through the right. I went through the left and managed only three yards to the 23. Bender then threw a pass out of reach of everybody when none of his receivers could get open. We had no choice but to once again try to get on the scoreboard with a field goal. The clock was stopped with 1:24 left in the first quarter.

"You can do it, Eric," I said to try to encourage Guinn as our paths crossed while I ran off the field.

It would be a 40-yard attempt. It was a respectable distance but very doable for Eric. He had done an outstanding job for us all season.

What nobody counted on was Billingsley muffing the snap. He bobbled it briefly before he set it down. Guinn had to hesitate, forcing him to be slightly off balance as he kicked. This time the ball headed in the right direction but came down near the rear of the end zone underneath the cross bar and bounced out.

"Geez, that still would have been good a few years ago," Daniels remarked as he stood next to where I was.

Initially I didn't understand what Vince was saying. After a moment I realized he was referring to the placement of the goal posts. The ball would have cleared the uprights prior to the 1974 season when the goal posts were in the front of the end zone.

"Not that it does us any good now," Vince continued, looking at me and shrugging in resignation.

Guinn had the angry expression on his face again as he returned to the sideline and stood behind the bench. Billingsley also looked angry and sought refuge behind the bench but not where Guinn was hanging out.

"Shake it off," Bender told Billingsley.

"I can't believe I muffed the snap like that," Billingsley grumbled.

"You're not the first person to muff a snap," Bender continued. "You've got to put it behind you."

What was interesting was hearing Guinn telling reserve fullback Danny Edwards that it wasn't Billingsley's fault that he missed the field goal.

"He did a good job in getting the ball down after he muffed the snap. I was the one who didn't recover. I've made field goals after muffed snaps before. I just missed this one."

Regardless of who was at fault, we didn't get the score we wanted. Two drives were climaxed by missed field goals. The game was scoreless as we prepared to close out the first quarter and the Raiders had the ball.

Two pass plays produced two first downs. The Raiders then went through the left for six yards to give them a second and four at the Hawaii 41. That was when time expired in the quarter.

I wasn't sure of what to do during the break. Being somewhat superstitious, I thought about remaining seated or getting up and walking around. I finally settled for getting up and grabbing another cup of Gatorade, then sitting back down.

Whatever I did, it didn't seem to work. Hamer batted down a pass on the opening play of the second quarter but the Raiders got a pass completion to the 33 on the next play. Since taking over they had picked up 44 yards and three first downs in five plays.

The Raiders continued to move. They mixed rushes with passes and a few minutes later had a first and goal at the four. That was when I decided

390

to stand and watch our defense try to keep the Raiders out of the north end zone.

It would take more than one play. The Raiders tried going up the middle again. They got to the one before their running back was brought down by Allen and Blakely.

The Raiders set up on the line on second down. As the signals were being called an overzealous Pratt jumped and came into contact with the Raiders' tight end. The encroachment penalty, which would normally cost us five yards but couldn't be more than half-the-distance to the end zone, moved the Raiders about 18 inches forward.

On the ensuing play a Raider running back headed into the line. There was a lot of compression of bodies wearing white jerseys and brown jerseys. For one split second I thought we might have held them until I saw officials' arms going up. The Raiders had drawn first blood three minutes and 42 seconds into the second quarter.

"Okay, okay," I muttered under my breath as I put my helmet on. "So we don't shut them out."

The Raiders had no trouble with the extra point. I headed to the north end zone for the kickoff. I reminded myself that there was still plenty of time. It was obvious but I felt compelled to remind myself anyway.

As I was moving into my position I happened to arbitrarily glance into the seats behind the end zone. I happened to look directly into the eyes of an attractive blonde of about 21. I had never seen her before to the best of my knowledge but that didn't stop her from blowing kisses at me. It still wasn't enough to make me forget about how badly I wanted to win this game. My immediate priority was the Raiders. I had no intention of trying to find out who the young woman was. She could have been a hooker who happened to enjoy football for all I knew.

The kick came and once again it was to Ozzie. He prepared to field the ball about two yards deep in the end zone.

"Run it out, Ozzie!" I called before running forward to block.

I was just about to zero in on a white jersey when I thought I detected a joint groan from the crowd and then a series of whistles telling me the play was dead. I turned to look to see how far Ozzie had gotten and was surprised to see him so far behind me.

As I would see on the film a few days later, Ozzie hesitated when he fielded the ball. On top of that, Giametti missed his block. The Raider in question seemed to find a way around Gary and had a clear shot at Ozzie. He buried Ozzie at the ten.

"Now that sucks," I muttered once I had assessed the situation. I didn't know the particulars of why at the time. All I knew was that we had lousy field position.

What followed was a drive that Kerner probably hated for the rest of his life. It wasn't that he did anything that never happened to anybody else. It was simply a situation where he couldn't seem to do right.

Jeff went up the middle and managed only a yard. It was a disappointment to all of us that he didn't pick up more but the Raiders didn't have a 10-1 record to this point by having a defense that was incapable of stopping people like Jeff. Nobody thought less of Jeff for picking up a mere three feet.

Bender and I teamed up, with the aid of nine other Hawaiians on the field, to get us some breathing room. Steve rolled to his right and hit me near the right sideline at the 26. I managed to brake instead of going out of bounds and turned upfield. One Oakland defender got his hand on my shoulder pad but I was already moving forward and slipped away. Jack Tatum hammered me at the 31.

"Ol' Dockman ought to be hearing whistles and seein' stars after that hit," I overheard one of the Oakland defenders remark as Tatum and I rose to our feet.

It was tempting to respond to that. The fact is the shot I took looked far more brutal when I saw it later than it actually felt. It was primarily a matter of being up one second and then suddenly lying on the ground. I had virtually no recollection of the shot itself or of the trip to the turf.

Prudently I didn't respond but casually joined my teammates in the huddle. Whatever temptation I might have had to swear, smile, thumb my nose or taunt in some other manner, I ignored.

Scott ran through the right and picked up seven yards to the 38. Unfortunately it was Kerner's time to prove that even the best players are human. He got cited for an illegal block below the waist at about the line of scrimmage. That cost us 15 yards, not to mention the seven yards that were nullified by the penalty, to give us a first and 25 at our own 16.

"Okay, okay. We'll make up for it," Bender stated in the huddle. "Shake it off, Jeff."

It would have been easy for any of us to have been momentarily angry at Jeff. All of us put together could not have been more angry at him than he was at himself. Sensing this, Scott whacked him on the back to encourage him as we were breaking out of the huddle.

"It's okay, man," Larry whispered.

We got six of the yards back on the following play when Scott went around right end on a 3 kama'aina right. Bender then hit Dietrich at the 41 in front of the Raider bench on the right sideline. The pass was actually high and Ted had to make a leaping catch. He was rewarded with a brutal hit at about the time his feet touched the ground.

"Hoo, baby, that was one bad hit," I heard a Raider happily remark as I ran toward Ted who was about ten yards from me when he went down.

"Great catch," I said as I grabbed Ted's hand to help him to his feet. "Are you okay?"

"Damn right I am," he replied casually.

Suddenly more whistles. I turned and saw the referee waving his arms over his head and then pointing to himself. He was indicating an official time out for a measurement.

In all of the excitement from Ted's great catch and his ensuing hit, I had forgotten to gauge how close we were to the first down. The measurement showed that we were about six inches from that milestone.

"Third and inches," I could visualize the NBC commentator in the booth reporting.

We lined up in our dotted "I" and ran a 2 Mililani right. This was a draw play with Kerner taking the ball. Unfortunately one of the Raiders shot through the line with impeccable timing. Not only did he wait just long enough to avoid being called for offsides or encroachment, he got into our backfield quick enough to drop Jeff for a three-yard loss.

I felt helpless. I didn't even see it coming. Scott and I were positioned right behind Jeff at the snap. I saw Jeff take the handoff and then there was suddenly a large man in a white jersey stuck to Jeff like Velcro and knocking him down. Somebody somewhere must have done something that tipped the defender off. Either that or he had simply made a lucky guess that Jeff would be carrying the ball.

Needless to say, Kerner wasn't very happy. He had carried twice on the drive for a net loss of two yards and was responsible for a penalty that cost us an additional 22 yards. It obviously wasn't his fault that he lost the three yards on the previous play but who could convince him of that at the moment? Football players with any sense of dedication tend to believe that if they need to pick up six inches that they should be able to do so even if they have to run through a wall of solid steel.

At least I was of that frame of mind. I believe Jeff was no different.

Fortunately we had Jablonski to provide us with our silver lining. Ray got off a pretty good punt that was downed at the Oakland 14.

"Well at least they also get to start with lousy field position," Hoddesson remarked.

I grabbed a cup of Gatorade and sat on the bench. Tipton called the entire offensive unit together.

Tipton knelt directly in front of me so I didn't have to move from my seat on the bench. The rest of the offensive unit huddled around him either by sitting on the bench or kneeling around him.

"What's going on here?" Tipton asked rhetorically. "We've got no running game. We've got to get the running game going or else they'll also shut down our passing attack. We can beat these guys but we have to execute. Linemen, do a better job of opening the holes. Backs, be quicker.

These guys are no better than you but they're shutting you down and have a one-touchdown advantage."

Of course the Raiders wanted to extend that advantage to two touchdowns. By the time our meeting ended I noticed that the Raiders had a second and four at midfield. Two plays later they had a first down at the Hawaii 45.

"Oh, geez. Come on, defense," I muttered, feeling somewhat guilty since my own unit hadn't exactly been doing its job.

The defense did its job on the very next play. The Raiders opted to pass. Richards penetrated into the backfield and grabbed Stabler at the Oakland 45. Stabler went down easily.

"Fumble!" I heard myself calling as I jumped to my feet. The ball was bouncing around erratically near where Norm had sacked Stabler.

Norm was up in an instant. He fielded the ball at about the Oakland 42 and started to run with it. He managed to pick up an additional four yards before being dragged down from behind.

To this point that was the play of the game for us. Suddenly we had come to life. Our crowd was cheering loud enough to leave no doubt that our fans were still on our side. It was up to us to capitalize on this break.

I happened to look toward the sideline as I reached our huddle. Walker was absolutely radiant with an end zone-to-end zone smile. He gave Norm a hard whack to his shoulder pads before Norm continued toward the area behind Walker where he was greeted by more enthusiastic coaches and teammates.

Walker's radiance told me we had better score a touchdown or else. If we didn't make the most of this opportunity. . . .

We were inside the two-minute warning by this time. That could work to our advantage. We were close enough to the goal line to prevent the clock from being a major factor. We could also shave enough time off to prevent the Raiders from putting together a sustained drive.

I was the recipient of the first pass. I ran to just a little beyond the first down marker near the makai sideline. Bender had rolled out to his right, fought off a modest rush and hit me with a perfect pass. I stepped out of bounds at the 26 to give us a first down with the clock stopped at 1:22.

We were close enough and had two time-outs left so the Raiders could not assume that we would not attempt to rush. That was what we were counting on and we tried a play-action pass on the following play. Bender faked a handoff up the middle to Scott, dropped back and then hit Scott over the middle at the 23.

The play didn't work as well as we had hoped. Scott was hit immediately to prevent the gain from being more than three yards. The clock even moved down to 1:09 before somebody thought to call time out. There was still plenty of time for us and that much less time for the Raiders to put something together.

394

I am sorry to say our drive didn't go any further than that. Bender was forced to throw a pass away under a heavy rush when he couldn't find an open receiver. On the next play he found Giametti open inside the ten and fired a bullet in his direction.

Unfortunately a defensive back was close enough to adjust and knock the ball down. It was a miracle that the defensive back didn't hang on to the ball. It was very close to an interception and the defensive back might even have had a long return for a touchdown.

While heaving a sigh of relief that that play didn't result in seven points for the enemy, we knew what was coming next. The field goal unit did not hesitate to head to the field. The offensive unit did not hesitate to leave the field.

At least we were getting three points. That wasn't as many as we wanted but it was better than nothing. We were very much in the game.

Guinn's field goal attempt kept us down by a touchdown. His kick was wide to the right. The Raiders had the ball on their own 23 with 47 seconds left in the half.

For what seemed like an eternity but was actually only a few seconds, Guinn stood doubled over as if he suddenly had stomach cramps. For the third time that day he had missed a field goal. Adding salt to his wound, he had to face his teammates on the sideline.

Guinn stood by himself as far away from everybody as he could. Nobody tried to approach him; probably because nobody knew exactly what to say to him. No doubt he was inconsolable. The best thing to do seemed to be to leave him alone.

The Raiders opted to take a couple of snaps and let the clock run out. They went into their locker room on the makai side of the south end zone content with their one-touchdown lead.

"We can't seem to get our running game going," Walker pointed out near the end of the break. "How come? Don't tell me these guys are that good. We should be able to pick up some yardage on the ground but we're not. We're not doing that and we're not converting on our field goal attempts. It's killing us."

Walker wasn't speaking in an angry tone. He was simply pointing out the obvious. He probably regretted that he included the field goal remark. He definitely did not bolster Guinn's confidence.

The statistics backed up the obvious fact that we did not have a running game of any significance. During the first half we had rushed nine times for 16 yards. Our passing game had been sound with nine completions in 15 attempts for 135 yards. We still needed to balance it out with a quality ground attack. No amount of yardage was of any use if we didn't put points on the board.

As we were leaving the locker room I saw Walker ostensibly confirm my belief that he regretted what he said about our field goal game. He pulled Guinn off to the side to have a word with him. Several of us overheard what he said in a very paternal, understanding tone.

"Just shake the first half off. You've done really well for us all year long. Just put the first half out of your mind. Everything will be okay."

I had a pretty good idea of how Eric felt. After all, I was the guy who dropped what would have been the winning touchdown pass in Philadelphia two weeks earlier. I had moved on but hadn't forgotten. I even made it a point to remind myself of Philadelphia when I had the urge to be angry at Eric. He was a good guy and was normally a pretty dependable kicker.

The second half opened as either a study of two very good defenses or else two very inept offenses. We got off to a good start when Guinn's kickoff was fielded seven yards deep in the south end zone. The Raider return man prudently opted not to try to run it out despite the fact that everybody on our side of the field was hoping he would.

A holding penalty and not much else gave the Raiders a third and 13 at their own 17. It was obvious that they were going to pass and Rodgers managed to reach around the receiver and deflect the ball away near the 30. The Raiders were going to have to punt.

"Their punter is at about the same level of excellence as Jablonski," special teams coach Ken Holcomb said to me as I prepared to take my position on the field. "Don't do anything stupid but I still want you to do whatever you can to put together a return. The better your return, the better field position we'll have when we start our first drive of the half."

This was a very critical point. Since our defense had held the Raiders' opening drive of the second half to a loss of three yards, we had an opportunity to start our first drive of the half with some excellent field position. I had to try to do whatever I could to prevent the punt from getting behind me. It was a formidable task when considering that the Raiders had just about the best punter in the NFL.

It was a good punt and off to my right. I still managed to glide over and field the ball at the Hawaii 43 although I felt awkward catching it. I had good protection and also managed to maneuver around a defender. I got to the Oakland 48 before I was finally brought down. It was a respectable nine-yard return.

Such great field position . . . followed by a futile drive. Bender started the drive by dropping back and having the ball slip out of his hands as he threw. The intended receiver was Grummon but nobody could have known that. Because the ball slipped out of his hand the only one reasonably close was a defender. The pass was nearly intercepted.

396

Bender didn't get a chance to throw a near interception on the next play. He was sacked at the Hawaii 45. We had third and 17.

It was frustrating. We were not incapable of converting on third and long but the opening two plays of this drive seemed to be indicative of how our day was going. The defense had held what was arguably the best team in the NFL to a mere seven points. The offense was stuck at the starting gate.

Bender called a pass to the surprise of nobody. He met a heavy rush which was also to the surprise of nobody. He still managed to scramble and get the pass off before being hit.

It wasn't a bad pass. It was heading my way and catchable with a reasonable effort. What I didn't count on, primarily because a receiver rarely does, was a defensive back coming from nowhere and cutting in front of me. He picked off the pass at the 28 and headed upfield. Bender and Hayer teamed up to bring him down in front of the Oakland sideline but not until he had picked up 32 yards to the Hawaii 40.

I felt sick. I am normally able to be optimistic about our chances of winning, but my thoughts were getting increasingly more negative. We were only down by a touchdown but that could stand up easily with the way we were playing. Nothing seemed to be going our way.

At least on the offensive end.

The defense rose to the occasion which kept us in the game. A rush and an incomplete pass gave them a third and seven at the Hawaii 37. If our defense could hold them to no gain a field goal attempt would be about 54 yards; very doable but difficult.

Whatever thoughts the Raiders had of attempting a field goal were forgotten on the ensuing play. The Raiders were a team which wasn't averse to rushing in what is normally an obvious passing situation. Just the same, our defense guessed correctly that they would attempt a pass. Childhood friends Norm Richards and Russ Allen teamed up to sack Stabler at the Hawaii 46. A field goal at this range would have been about 63 yards, tying the NFL record.

The Oakland punting unit took the field as we knew it would. With 16 yards to go for a first down it was too risky to try pick it up even though our offense hadn't been showing too many signs of life. It was better that they should try to pin us back before shutting down our inept offense. If they held us they would almost be certain of excellent field position when they got the ball back.

I took my place with my back to the north end zone. I considered standing at the five to give myself a running start, then took my regular post at the ten. I wanted to do something to get us back in the game but I didn't want to take any unnecessary risks. I was determined to not try to field anything that I couldn't field cleanly. I did not want to run the risk of fumbling because I was overzealous to do something heroic. By standing at the ten I knew that anything over my head was something I should simply allow to bounce into the end zone.

The punt wasn't over my head but it was far to my left. I ran over to try to cut down a Raider wideout who was charging downfield. I actually threw a pretty good block on him even momentarily knocking him in the air before he came down on his back. Unfortunately he wasn't the only Raider trying to get to the ball and the punt was downed at our one-yard line.

I suppose it could be argued that I blew an opportunity to make up for not being able to return the punt. Bender called my number and handed off to me. I charged up the middle and got as far as the two.

Scott fared a little better. He ran through the right as far as the six. That gave us a semblance of breathing room but we still needed to pick up at least five yards for the first down. We had one chance to get it.

An incomplete pass ended that quest. Feeling sick to my stomach over our futility, I ran off the field and hoped that Jablonski would put one of his booming punts together. We definitely needed it now. The Raiders stood to have pretty good field position anyway but a better than average punt would help our cause.

Jablonski didn't let us down. He put together one of those punts that gets the crowd putting together a simultaneous "ooooooh." It was one of those punts that makes one wonder how close to the ceiling of the Superdome it would have come.

The Raiders were able to put together a return. The return man fielded the punt on the Oakland 47. He weaved his way to the Hawaii 46 before being brought down by Hamer.

Despite the booming punt and return of only seven yards, the Raiders still had excellent field position. After forgetting how in awe I had been of Jablonski's punt, I took note of the precariousness of our situation as the Raiders began their drive.

Two plays and a facemask penalty later the Raiders had a first down on the Hawaii 14. Ed was guilty of the facemask infraction. Walker's face turned the hue of a sunburned tourist.

Things didn't work for us even when they seemed to go our way. On the second play after the facemask the Raiders rushed to the five and Blakely hammered the ball carrier, knocking the ball loose. There was the predicted mad scramble for the ball that went out of bounds at the five. Since the Raiders were the last team to possess the ball, they retained possession. It was third and one.

The Raiders didn't get the first down. They didn't have to. On the very next play they carried the ball in. The extra point extended their lead to 14-0.

I didn't show it but I was livid inside. I knew we were better than this. All things considered, the defense was doing well but the offense had the appeal of a sewage spill. Since I was a prime part of the offensive unit I considered myself to be among the effluent. I wanted to single-handedly make something happen.

Ozzie may have been thinking the same thing. He took the kick about six yards deep in the end zone and didn't hesitate to run it out. It wasn't a wise move but he seemed to get away with it. He got as far as the 19, only a yard short of what one should be able to pick up when returning the ball from the end zone, before being brought down. All things considered, it was an impressive effort.

At long last we came to life. After Scott's four-yard rush, Bender hit me with a pass at the Hawaii 38. I was hit at the 40 but still managed to fight for two more yards before going down. The cheers of the crowd washed over me as I bounced up and ran to where our huddle was to form up.

There was more to come. Scott went up the middle and got all the way to the 50. Bender then hit Grummon at the Oakland 34. Rich was brought down immediately but that was all right. We had a first down and were moving the ball.

The Raiders obviously weren't happy about that. They came hard at Bender on the next play. Steve scrambled and rushed forward and managed to get up to the 30 before being knocked out of bounds.

Suddenly there was no doubt in my mind. I knew we were going to score. We had been held scoreless at this point for the first time in our brief history but that didn't matter. I was certain that we were finally going to get on the scoreboard.

I also knew we were going to win. I even believed that the Raiders were going to sue the NFL for awarding Hawaii a franchise. We were going to be their Achilles heel for 1976.

Perhaps Bender sensed my cocksure attitude. He called on me to throw a pass. Although he had me running to my right when I am a left-handed passer, I managed to get the pass off to Dietrich. Ted caught the ball at the nine and got as far as the two before going down.

And oh, the roar of the crowd! It was one of those moments a professional athlete lives for. The offense came to life and so did the crowd.

Bender and I teamed up to end the drive on the very next play. He hit me over the middle about three yards deep in the end zone. I was hit but managed to remain on my feet and hold on to the ball. The officials shot their arms up to produce another roar from the crowd.

I sprinted to the sideline after spiking the ball. The clock showed 1:58 left in the third quarter. With the extra point we trailed by only a touchdown.

"Now that's the way to do it, men," Walker encouraged from his post on the sideline as our kicking team prepared to kick off to the Raiders. "Let's keep it up. You can beat this team."

I believed it. I also saw that it was going to become a more formidable challenge. A probable combination of their offense being fired up and well-rested and our defense wearing down enabled the Raiders to move the ball. As time expired in the third quarter the Raiders had a first down at their own 45.

The tension was too heavy as we changed sides of the field. I paced a little, grabbed some more Gatorade and probably tried to will our defense into turning the ball over.

"We can't lose to these guys," I muttered to Dietrich when I stood next to him in front of our bench. "We have to win this game."

Of course Ted wasn't arguing. Nobody on our side wanted to lose.

Naturally our opponents were also pretty determined to win. They had clinched the division a week earlier but they were still playing for the home field advantage throughout the playoffs as well as for pride. One loss to us destroyed their hopes for a perfect season while a second loss to us could be the reason why they would have to play a postseason game on the road.

On the first play of the fourth quarter McDaniel managed to throw the Raiders for a one-yard loss. That was followed by an incompletion so my level of optimism was on the rise again.

I did a few seconds of stretching and running in place. If we could hold the Raiders for one more play they would be forced to punt. I was looking forward to putting together a return that would break their backs.

Unfortunately the Raiders converted on third down. They passed to the Hawaii 44 to give them a first down.

It was a roller coaster of emotion. I was down and then I was up and then I was down again.

The Raiders seemed to know what to do. They gradually tore up chunks of real estate in their quest to reach the end zone again. Twice they converted on third down to give them first downs at the 27 and 16. A field goal would force us to score twice and a touchdown was something I didn't care to consider.

They only managed two yards on first down. After two incompletions they sent their field goal unit out.

"Now if we can just get them to miss it," I said to nobody in particular as I stood among a cluster of teammates on the sideline. I suddenly spotted Guinn standing a few feet away. No doubt he was wishing that his bad luck would rub off on the Raider kicker.

The ball was spotted at the 21. They got the kick off. It went through the uprights. The Raiders had extended their lead to 17-7 with 9:53 left in the game.

"All right, we've still got plenty of time," I heard Walker point out as I ran to the field for the kickoff.

Walker was right, of course. It was simply a matter of whether we could score twice and hold the Raiders in the process. The Hawaiians, as much as any other team in the NFL, knew how to move down the field while keeping their opponents at bay. If we could pull this game out it would be the comeback of the year.

Perhaps the Raiders were starting to worry about what my teammates and I were thinking. They actually did the unthinkable by not getting to the field on time. They got cited for delay of game and were forced to kick from their 30. It was something I couldn't recall seeing happen on a kickoff since. . . .

Oh, right. We got nailed for the same thing a week earlier. Prior to that I couldn't recall seeing it since high school.

I was determined to break the kick into a long gain.

Perhaps they read my mind. The kick went directly to Ozzie who fielded it at the 14.

"Move it, Ozzie!" I barked as I charged forward in search of the first white jersey that had the nerve to try to penetrate through our wedge. It didn't take long and I pulverized him, striking him in his midsection and knocking us both to the ground.

My effort wasn't enough. Ozzie simply wasn't an especially elusive return man. He had power and speed but he wasn't especially quick with his moves. He only managed to pick up 13 yards to the 27.

The drive itself was a disappointment. It was another three and out. Kerner picked up three yards but that was followed by a pair of incompletions. Before I knew it I was back on the sidelines watching Jablonski punt.

At least the punt was halfway decent although not up to Ray's usual standard. The punt traveled a respectable 38 yards to the Oakland 32. The Oakland return man bobbed and weaved his way to the 39.

I grabbed some Gatorade and analyzed the situation. We were down by ten, obviously needing two scores. We had reached the point where the clock could work against us although that would be less critical if the defense could put the Raiders away quickly.

It took the defense a little longer than I had hoped. The defense still limited the Raiders to one first down so it wasn't bad. K.T. Smith did a brilliant play in dropping a running back for a two-yard loss at the Hawaii 44 to give them a third and nine. That was followed by a determined rush by Richards that nearly resulted in a sack. Stabler managed to get the pass off before Norm nailed him but the ball fell untouched.

"Grounding! Grounding!" Walker barked to the officials.

I believe Walker may have had a case. I didn't see any eligible receivers near where the ball landed. There was a receiver in the same general direction but the ball fell well short and to the right of that receiver.

Regardless of what I thought or Walker thought or any of my teammates thought or even what the jeering crowd thought, we were all overruled by the officials. There wasn't a yellow flag in sight.

At least the Raiders had to punt. Before I ran on the field I was confronted by Walker and Holcomb.

"If you can put together a return, do it," Walker directed. "If the ball is inside the ten don't automatically decide not to put together a return. If you think you've got room to run, go for it."

That was just what I wanted to hear. If I could put together a good return, especially one that took me all the way in, the clock would be less of a factor.

I stood on the five in front of the south end zone instead of the ten the way I normally did on a punt. The five was going to be my demarcation line. If the ball was coming down inside the five I would let it go. If it was outside the five I would be open to a return.

The punt was up and heading slightly to my right. I had to move forward and, unfortunately moved a little too quickly. I had hoped to catch the punt while moving forward to give me a good head start. Instead I had to pause and wait for the ball to come down.

I still got off and was determined to get at least to the 20. Unfortunately I saw some white jerseys heading my way. Some were headed off but others I had to elude.

As I reached the 15, I tried to arch my way around a white jersey. He still managed to grab my arm and drag me down at the 17.

It was a disappointment. I had tried to make something happen that would shift the momentum our way and didn't succeed. I still couldn't dwell on it.

Dietrich nearly killed our drive on the first play. He turned to receive what was about as close to perfect a pass as one can imagine but apparently didn't turn quickly enough. The ball hit him square on the chest at about the 35 and bounced off. A Raider defensive back actually slid and got his hands on the ball but couldn't hang on. The game would have been as good as over had he held the ball.

On the following play Ted got new life. It was practically the same play and Ted caught the ball at the Hawaii 36. He managed to scramble for four more yards, giving us a first down at the Hawaii 40.

I was next but didn't get to produce the desired result. Bender's pass to me over the middle at about the 50 was slightly off the mark. I still could have caught the ball had I been able to lunge for it but a Raider defensive back managed to swat the ball away from me just before I was able to get my hands on it.

We had better luck on the next play. Bender hit me on the right sideline at the Oakland 46. Seeing that I had nowhere to go from there, I stepped out of bounds.

At least we were showing our vocal fans what we were made of. We had had trouble moving the ball through much of the day but we weren't giving up. All we had to do was make up the ten points.

Bender's next pass netted only three yards. Under a heavy rush he hit Giametti as a safety valve near the line of scrimmage. Gary only managed to get to the 43.

Slater got the call on the next play. He was just inside the 30 when Bender's pass headed his way.

A Raider defensive back stepped in front of Slater. He appeared to have the interception but juggled the ball. He still didn't have possession until after he stepped out of bounds. We got another much-needed break on that one.

Things weren't looking good. I sized up the situation and realized we had two chances to get seven yards. There was no way that we were going to punt if we didn't convert on third down. We might go for a field goal if we could get a little closer but a punt was out of the question with the clock stopped at 2:18.

Bender met a heavy rush. The Raiders didn't have to be geniuses to know we were going to pass on third and long. Steve had to scramble a little before he managed to get the ball away but it was out of bounds. I was the closest Hawaiian to the ball but there was no way that I could field the ball and come down in bounds.

This was do or die time. If we didn't convert we still might wind up with the ball one more time but there wouldn't be enough time to get the two scores we needed.

Bender did what an outstanding veteran quarterback will do in the clutch. He eluded the rush and found Slater at about the 31. Joe picked up four more yards to get us a first down. The clock was stopped for the two-minute warning with 1:57 showing.

The fans were pleased with our effort. They were standing and cheering as Bender headed over to the sideline. We were giving them a game. In the end I hoped to reward their loyalty with a victory. It was within reach.

I happened to notice Guinn. He was working feverishly on the sideline. He was kicking the ball into the net he had standing up behind the bench. No doubt his missed field goals were heavy on his mind and he was looking to redeem himself. I sensed that he would be under almost unbearable pressure if he was called on to try another field goal.

When play resumed the Raider defense sent out a very strong statement that they weren't giving anything away. Bender took the snap and met a very heavy blitz. He managed to elude the blitz by scrambling away, having no option but to chew up precious seconds. He even got the pass off and tried to hit me near the goal line just before he was finally hammered.

I was also hammered simultaneously with the arrival of the ball. I am sorry to say I wasn't able to hang on. The clock was stopped at 1:45.

Bender was rushed again and had to eat up a few more extra precious seconds to scramble. Once again he got the pass off and even avoided being hit this time.

Grummon caught the ball at the six and headed toward the goal line. He was hit but kept his feet chugging. I managed to block another Raider who was moving in for the kill a few feet away. Rich didn't go down until just after he crossed the goal line.

I was lying on the ground at about the three when Rich got into the end zone. I jumped up and ran over to him. He got up as quickly as possible and slammed the ball into the turf before accepting the congratulations of his teammates.

As my teammates and I ran off the field I was aware of the crowd once again. They were definitely with us. All were standing and cheering as loud as they could. I could hear several who were capable of whistling. Many were jumping up and down as they clapped their hands.

What was critical was the extra point. This obviously hadn't been Guinn's day and I had a feeling that he had butterflies over a simple extra point attempt. If he missed we would not be able to tie the score with a field goal.

Fortunately Eric's kick was true. That had to have been a heavy load off his mind. He had made an extra point earlier but this one was the more critical. We trailed 17-14 with 1:34 left. That meant that our home season had only a little more than a minute and-a-half remaining unless we forced the game into overtime.

For the first time since I played in the 1974 Hula Bowl I was on a kicking team. That is because we were going to do an onside kick and would be using only our kicker and ten players who normally handled the ball. There could be occasions when an onside kick was an option and we would use our regular kicking unit. In this case we wouldn't be fooling anybody if we used our regular kicking unit. Everybody knew we were going for the onside kick so it was prudent that we utilize our ball handlers.

Eric kicked the ball to his left. He kicked it a little too hard but a Raider on their front line had difficulty with it. The ball actually hit him on the shin and went behind him. Suddenly there was a mix of white jerseys and brown jerseys scrambling for the ball.

I wasn't able to be a part of the pile. I stood above it as a group of players lay on the ground. The officials waved their arms over their heads to stop the clock which started as soon as the ball hit the Raider players' shin, and started sorting through the pile.

Suddenly I spotted the ball. So did at least one or two of my teammates. I leaped in the air and pointed toward the north end zone.

That produced a reaction from the crowd but it still wasn't official. Suddenly the referee pointed toward the north end zone and the place exploded. It was Gary Giametti who managed to gain possession of the ball. A couple of Raiders were still trying to get the ball away from him but he had it well-protected while lying in the fetal position.

We had a first down at the Oakland 48. The clock showed 1:28.

We wasted no time. I was smelling another upset and was almost giddy in anticipation. No doubt the Raiders were feeling twinges of paranoia. It may have stopped a few of their hearts when Bender hit me at the 36. I managed to fight for four more yards before stepping out of bounds. The clock was stopped with 1:21 left.

Suddenly I spotted a yellow flag near the line of scrimmage. I hoped that the Raiders had jumped offside. It seemed more likely, though, that somebody was going to get cited for holding.

That was exactly what it was. Kerner was the guilty party. His hold may have prevented Bender from getting sacked so it wasn't necessarily a negative development. It was still disheartening to have a first and 20 at our own 42 instead of a first and ten at the Oakland 32. The difference of 26 yards could prove to be especially critical with so little time left.

We regained most of the yardage almost immediately. Bender hit Dietrich at the Oakland 36. He managed another yard but wasn't able to make it out of bounds. We had a first down but were forced to use one of our three time-outs. By the time the clock stopped it was down to 1:09.

At least we were back in field goal range. It was simply a matter of whether Guinn was psychologically ready. I personally preferred to score a touchdown and prevent sending the game into overtime although if Guinn converted on a field goal, especially if he added one more in overtime, the three field goals that he missed would be forgotten.

Bender was rushed on the next play. He couldn't find an open receiver and was forced to scramble. He managed to step out of bounds but got no further than the line of scrimmage. That stopped the clock at 1:01.

On the next play Bender had more time to get set. He spotted Giametti over the middle at about the 20. He threw a frozen rope to Gary . . . that he immediately dropped.

Suddenly I was in Philadelphia again except I was seeing it happen to somebody else. Remembering helped to enable me to sympathize with Gary as he jumped up in the air in frustration about ten yards away from me and held his hands over his helmet at the temples. In retrospect, I could recall the sudden groan from the crowd. I hoped that they knew that this was the type of thing that could happen to anybody. It was good to note that I couldn't hear any booing.

"Let's go. We'll get it back," I said to Gary as I patted him on the back and tried to nudge him toward our huddle. I looked back at the clock and saw that 54 seconds remained. It was third down.

"Shake it off, Gary," Bender said when Gary reached the huddle. I sensed that Bender didn't feel like being so compassionate but it was better for the team that he not get down on Gary. He knew that Gary was a good receiver and simply had one get away from him.

Unfortunately our situation deteriorated on the next play. The blitz was on. I ran a pattern that took me to about the 15 and saw Bender trying to scramble for his life. I started running back toward the line of scrimmage to give Steve a better target but my effort was in vain. Steve was swallowed up by a trio of Oakland defenders and dropped at the Oakland 49.

It took us a few seconds but we finally called time. There were 39 seconds left. It wasn't much time but a more critical dilemma was our yardage situation. The sack clearly took us out of field goal range. Not only would a field goal attempt have been about 66 yards but the attempt would have been toward the north end zone which was against the wind. We had one play to travel 24 yards or else the game was as good as over.

My heart pounded as Bender talked the situation over with Walker on the sideline. The obvious choice was to have the receivers run out to inside the 25. That way we could get the first down and try to get out of bounds without having to spend our final time-out. If we did have to use our final time-out we could still run a couple of plays as long as we managed to get out of bounds each time.

Our plan was exactly as it should have been. The Raiders put a mild rush on Bender but they were primarily in a prevent defense. Bender got the pass off, trying to hit Slater near the left sideline inside the 25. The pass was batted away to turn the ball over to the Raiders. The clock was stopped with 32 seconds left.

I almost cried as I ran to the sideline. I don't like to admit that but I honestly almost cried just like I almost did in Philadelphia. That is indicative of how badly I wanted to win this game.

Stabler, as expected, took a snap and simply dropped to one knee. We didn't bother calling our final time-out so they didn't have to take another snap.

Game over, game lost. The outcome can't be changed. It went into the record books as a loss for us. It didn't matter if we lost by three points or 30 points. A loss is a loss in the standings. Only those who bet on us to beat the spread came out victors. Despite the fact that we had beaten the Raiders in Oakland, the Raiders were 13 and-a-half point favorites.

Probably the worst thing about this loss was it was our last home game of the season. We had good crowds for all of our home games and their enthusiasm was overwhelming. We usually gave them good games but when the final gun went off we had a 3-4 home record for 1976.

Of course Oakland was more than ready for us. We had beaten them a month earlier and, believe me, there was no lapse in memory. The Raiders did not come to Hawaii for a vacation but they wanted to enjoy their stay.

And they seemed to enjoy their visit. At least they were on the side of the scoreboard that they wanted to be.

"I've gotta hand it to you, Dockman," John Matuszak remarked as we headed toward our respective locker rooms. "You guys are pretty (expletive deleted) good."

"Good game, Jay," said the ever-congenial Ken Stabler who had also greeted me with the same demeanor after we beat the Raiders in Oakland. "You have one of the toughest teams we've had to play this year. It's hard to believe that this is your team's first year in the NFL."

That seemed to be the general consensus of everybody from the Oakland coaching staff on down. The Oakland players and coaches told my teammates and me that they were overwhelmed by how good we were.

"I've got to tell you, Jay," one of the coaches said to me behind the south end zone. "I am damn glad you guys won't be in our division or even in our conference next year. You guys got too good too fast. You're probably going to be even better next year."

"Thanks," I replied graciously as I shook the coach's hand. "We've got some good players and some great coaches."

"You sure do. Good luck the rest of the way."

I admit that the praise felt good. It still wasn't quite enough. Nobody was sure at the start of the season if we would gel soon enough to win more than a few games. It wasn't that long before that we had a legitimate, albeit remote, shot for the wild card berth although that was now long gone.

We were 5-7. The best we could do was break even. We needed to win two games on the road in conditions that were not expected to be tropical in order to achieve that objective.

Breaking even is still a mediocre record. Maybe we were officially an expansion team, but a mediocre record suggests a mediocre team regardless of how long the team has been in existence. Perhaps we weren't really worthy of the high praise.

Then again, maybe I needed to stop beating myself up over it.

The locker room was about as solemn as it had been all season. Never had we made such a determined effort, at least in defeat, over the course of the season. We played our hearts out but it obviously wasn't quite enough.

Hayer had tears in his eyes. So did Kerner and Grummon and probably a few others. We wanted this game badly and played accordingly. They shut down our running game and held us scoreless in the first half but we didn't quit. We were proud of our determination and effort but that is never enough when you wind up on the wrong end of the scoreboard.

Suddenly I looked over at Eric Guinn. He was sitting and looking down. Had he made even one of the field goals that he attempted we would have gone to overtime. Perhaps if Billingsley hadn't muffed the snap on the second field goal attempt Eric would have converted and been in a better frame of mind on his third attempt, meaning that we would have won by three points instead of losing by three points. It still wasn't Eric's fault that we lost, nor was it Billingsley's. Unfortunately some of the so-called experts among the general public were going to blame Eric while a few others might even blame Billingsley just as there were those who blamed me when we lost in Philadelphia two weeks earlier. It wouldn't matter as long as Eric and Joe didn't blame themselves.

Guinn suddenly looked up. He and I then made eye contact. I subtly gave him a thumb's up gesture and mouthed the words "It's okay."

Walker suddenly appeared. He stood silently in the middle of the room for a couple minutes.

"Men," he finally began. "That was obviously one tough game to lose. I'll have to look at the films and find the mistakes but our loss wasn't because of a lack of effort. We'll go over the mistakes on Tuesday but nobody is going to accuse you of not putting your hearts into this one."

Walker paused for a moment. He looked around the room in an effort to briefly make eye contact with everybody.

"Go out and relax and unwind," he continued. "We'll see you on Tuesday."

My roommate had to go directly to work after the game so I had the place to myself when I got home. Five minutes after I arrived Don Simmons called from the intercom phone in the lobby. I buzzed him up.

"It was a good game," he said as he cracked open the beer I had waiting for him when he arrived.

"Thanks," I replied. "Not good enough, though."

"Hey, it was Oakland. You are the only team to have beat them so far this year."

"Yeah," I said wryly. "Too bad we had to play them twice."

Don nodded and took a sip of his beer. He raised his eyebrows.

"You've won five games with two to go. That's a heck of a lot better than anybody had a right to expect."

"I know," I agreed. "But if you were in my shoes, would you be satisfied with a losing record?"

Don shrugged and took another swig of his beer. He pursed his lips as he pondered.

"I guess not," he admitted. "At least you're not in Tampa Bay's shoes."

"Oh, I forgot. Did they finally win?"

Don shook his head.

"Memphis put 'em away, 24-13."

"Geez."

I honestly wasn't feeling sorry for myself regardless of Tampa Bay's 12th consecutive misfortune. It is simply that football is a game where one must be dedicated and work extremely hard. Since the Hawaiians fit into that mold it was hard for my teammates and me to accept losses, especially in tight games that could have gone either way, and a mediocre record. We worked as hard as champions. Our record suggested mediocrity at best.

We were still five victories better than Tampa Bay. I honestly felt sorry for the Bucs and had actually rooted for them throughout the season, especially since John McKay was their head coach. I had enjoyed knowing him when he recruited me to play football for USC and during the one year I attended USC. My decision to leave USC for the University of Hawaii had nothing to do with McKay or the school he represented.

"I can't imagine being winless after 12 games," I said. "Eventually, though, everything will fall into place for them. McKay's too good a coach for the team to continue losing."

It turned out to be a total loss for all of Hawaii's sports fans that day and throughout the entire weekend. Don and I went to the Neal Blaisdell Arena that night and watched the University of Hawaii's basketball team take on Oregon State. Despite a hot hand from UCLA transfer Gavin Smith and his 37 points, Hawaii fell on the short end of a 96-78 score.

Of course I never mentioned that the night before the University of Hawaii football team fell on the short end of a 59-0 rout with Oregon State. As loyal as I have always been to my alma mater, I made the right decision by staying away from that game.

CHAPTER SEVENTEEN
Cage That Tiger

I woke up on Monday morning still smarting from the tough loss. Losses were hard to accept sometimes, even in games we were expected to lose.

As I read the account of the game in the afternoon newspaper I discovered that Dietrich and I had both had 100-yard receiving games. That didn't take the sting out of the loss.

Ted had five receptions for 111 yards. That was his third 100-yard game of the season. His totals for the season were 44 receptions for an even 800 yards.

I had seven receptions for 101 yards. That was my fourth 100-yard game. I also went over the 1,000-yard mark with 58 receptions for 1,047 yards.

So what did it mean?

It meant that we still lost 17-14.

And it wasn't Guinn's fault. Walker drove that point home with the media.

"Those missed field goals were not the difference in the game," Walker pointed out. "You reporters like to dwell on a good player having a bad day but that wasn't what lost the game for us. The difference was our inability to get a touchdown on at least one of those drives where we attempted the field goals."

That was the beauty of Walker. He would dress us down in practices, meetings and film sessions but he never hesitated to stick up for us with the media.

There was also something more ominous in the newspaper. The game in Cincinnati the day before was played in a virtual blizzard. Not only were we playing in Cincinnati the following Sunday but the Steelers had beaten the Bengals in the aforementioned blizzard. The Bengals were certain to be a hungry team since they had to beat us or else be virtually eliminated in the playoff hunt.

The game was still six days away.

I wanted to play now!

The advantage of playing in Hawaii is we play in a tropical climate. The disadvantage of playing in Hawaii is we play in a tropical climate.

Both statements apply. Playing in a tropical climate means we play under generally favorable conditions at home. It may rain but the rain does not create bitter cold the way it will elsewhere. A passing shower on a warm Hawaii day is very refreshing.

The warm climate, especially on artificial turf, meant for some excessively warm conditions on the field. That worked more to the disadvantage of our opponents, especially if the opponents were from

410

locales such as Green Bay, Buffalo and Minnesota (in the days prior to the Metrodome) than for us. They could bask in the warmth early in the game before the comparably higher temperatures and humidity wore them down if they were not mentally and physically prepared.

Of course the advantage went to the opponents on their home turf as the approach of winter meant colder temperatures. Entering frigid conditions from a tropical environment was brutal. The best we could do was try not to focus on the cold while on the field. It wasn't easy.

We ended the 1976 campaign with back-to-back games in Ohio. After Cincinnati we would head to Cleveland.

There was a lot at stake even though we were well out of the playoff picture. If we could play through the cold and win both games we would break even. That, as I have said, suggests mediocrity but it is phenomenal for an expansion team full of older castoffs and young upstarts. The fact that we had won five games seemed phenomenal enough since expansion teams were not expected to win more than two or three. Four meant better than expected and five was considered almost scandalous. Since we were leaving town with a chance to return home with seven wins we definitely had everybody's attention.

It would actually be an even more formidable task than I previously described. We hadn't won back-to-back games all season. We had never lost more than two in-a-row but we had never won more than one in-a-row.

We also knew that Cincinnati and Cleveland would not be laying down for us, especially since both teams were still hoping for playoff berths. It didn't take long for word to spread that the Hawaiians could match up with anybody. Our opening day victory against St. Louis opened some eyes. Our nationally televised Monday night upset in Oakland was definitely a selling point. We proved to any remaining doubters up to and including Howard Cosell that the Hawaiians were a formidable force.

The weather we were certain to encounter made Walker decide even before training camp started that we would fly to Cincinnati on Wednesday, December 1. Normally we would have left on Friday afternoon. Walker decided to take an extra couple of days to get us adjusted to the cold. We had a solid workout at Aloha Stadium preceding our flight after we watched films of the Bengals' loss to the Steelers.

"Work hard," Walker instructed as we went through our paces, knowing that working anything less than hard was a capital crime with him. "If you work hard and believe in yourselves you will have a golden opportunity to make a name for yourselves."

Throughout the week it was obvious that there would be some changes for the Cincinnati game. Mark Black was still nursing a sore knee and would not be 100 percent. He would play but only as a reserve. Hamer would be starting at left cornerback.

There would also be a change on the kick return unit. Rich Hasegawa would be joining me as a deep back again. The coaching staff simply wasn't satisfied with Ozzie Roberts as a return man so the staff moved him forward and stationed my former University of Hawaii teammate on the goal line with me. It was done earlier in the season on a temporary basis but this appeared to be the likely scenario for both of our remaining games.

Speaking of the University of Hawaii, the Rainbow Warriors would be closing out their season on Saturday night with an encounter that some were comparing to a mouse in a rattlesnake cage. The Rainbow Warriors, at 3-7, were not having much of a season and would climax their year of futility against the Nebraska Cornhuskers who were having an outstanding season. Although I tried to maintain a positive attitude the way I would if I were actually playing the game myself, I was actually glad that I would be in Cincinnati during the Rainbow Warriors' grand finale. I was ashamed to admit that I knew in my heart that the only way Hawaii would beat Nebraska was if the Huskers' plane crashed.

The streets of Waikiki and vicinity reminded me of Nebraska's previous game in Hawaii during my sophomore season at the university five years earlier. Probably the most loyal college football fans in the country were those from Nebraska and it almost appeared as if the entire population of Nebraska was in Hawaii. Everywhere one looked there would be people decked out in their red shirts. Hawaii had become a sea of red.

But they were very nice people. Nebraska fans were among the nicest people I ever encountered.

Of course they could afford to be nice with the way their team played.

Shortly after our Wednesday workout I went to a gym in Pearl City. I lifted weights and then decided to run from the gym to the Arizona Memorial landing and back; a total distance of about six miles. The run actually was very relaxing.

On the way back I happened to encounter Russ Allen who had taken his wife Ellen to lunch at a local eatery on Kamehameha Highway in Aiea. Ellen was an attractive, sophisticated woman with platinum blonde hair she always kept cut to slightly above the shoulders. She was a witty woman, making her a good match for Russ since he was not short on humor. She had worked as a flight attendant while Russ was playing in Detroit but switched to being a reservations agent at Honolulu International Airport for the same airline after moving to Hawaii.

Russ had just let Ellen in on the passenger side as I approached on the sidewalk in front of where he was parked. He was getting in on his side and did a double-take when he spotted me running at a fairly brisk pace.

"Didn't you get enough of that at our workout?" he called out lightly.

"I'm too wound up," I replied honestly before accelerating. It wasn't that I wanted to run faster, but I needed to get home. I had actually lost track of

412

time and needed to rush home, grab my already packed suitcase and head downstairs where Ed Jennings and his girlfriend would be picking me up.

I enigmatically felt pangs of sadness as we took off from Honolulu. As I looked down at the beaches, office buildings, residential areas and Koolau Mountains I thought about how the season would be over when I saw these sights again. Although we still had a losing record with no chance of doing anything better than breaking even, I was having the time of my life. We had a good team. I didn't want to stop playing.

Of course other thoughts entered my mind as we headed toward frigid Ohio. As I read the afternoon newspaper my mind digressed to the close games we had lost. Guinn's sudden slump was obviously the difference in the game a few days earlier against the Raiders although, again, he didn't lose the game for us. My sudden slump on the final play of our game in Philadelphia was the difference in that contest.

Looking back further as I looked down at the ocean far below, I recalled how difficult we had made it for the Cowboys and Oilers before they finally outscored us. We had also lost games against the Chiefs and Broncos by three points apiece.

Had we pulled about three of those contests out we would still be in the playoff hunt. If one of those victories had been against the Raiders on Sunday we could still technically be in contention for the division title.

Suddenly I felt that it was absurd to be rehashing the season to focus on what might have been. My focus had to be on Cincinnati. I subconsciously shook my head.

"What are you shaking your head for?" Ed Jennings asked from the seat next to me.

"Huh?"

"What are you shaking your head for?"

"Oh, I don't know," I replied haltingly, slightly flustered. "I guess I was just thinking about something."

We reached Cincinnati at about 6:30 on Thursday morning, Cincinnati time. It was about eight o'clock when I finally got to my hotel room; three o'clock in the morning, body time. I had less than four hours to sleep since we had to be on the bus at noon to have a full-padded workout at Riverfront Stadium.

Walker had meticulously planned the entire thing. The purpose of the long overnight flight, the few hours of sleep and the workout was another way of getting us adjusted to where we would be playing. Although some of us, including me, grumbled a time or two about how we could have stayed in Honolulu for another day or two, it was probably Walker's attention to minute detail that made him the great coach that he was.

413

"That damned Lombardi was a bad influence on Walker," Ted Dietrich, who had played for the legendary Vince Lombardi in Washington, muttered facetiously at one point during the bus ride to our first workout in Cincinnati when he was reasonably certain that Walker couldn't hear him. "Lombardi's the reason Walker's so nitpicky."

If anybody was half-asleep at the workout, the cold woke them up. It wasn't as cold as we had expected but it was still cold by our standards with temperatures consistently near the freezing level. It was a stark contrast to our workout the day before in our tropical environment.

Nobody seemed adverse to having the workout on so little sleep in the cold. Everybody was psyched to continue our ascent to levels nobody had expected when we were added to the league. Never in the history of the NFL was a team so determined to rise to mediocrity.

Or, as Kerner so eloquently put it, "I didn't come all this way to freeze my butt off and lose."

Of course that was the way Walker was thinking although he didn't express himself that way. He definitely wasn't taking any chances. During our workouts he actually had some of his assistants positioned in different parts of the stadium to monitor for spies.

It was a full practice on Thursday but the one on Friday was much more intense.

On Saturday we had our typical walk-through. Most of us were decked out in sweatshirts and sweatpants as we went through a workout that was primarily a formality. I continued my tradition of wearing my Dodger cap and t-shirt but I wore sweatpants in lieu of gym shorts and I had a thermal top under my t-shirt.

On Saturday night I went out to dinner with Ed, Marv and Kerner. We were joined by Bender and Dietrich. Bender told us that he definitely planned to play again in 1977. That was welcome news to all of us.

There was nothing unusual about the pregame warmup. We went through our usual paces. I watched some as the fans gradually came in and took their seats. At one point I unconsciously had a big smile on my face.

"What are you so happy about?" Giametti asked; himself bearing a big smile after noting mine.

"I don't know," I said, momentarily stunned that I had had the smile on my face and then realized what had made me smile. "I was just watching some of these people coming in. I started thinking about how I hope we ruin their entire day."

Gary shook his head and looked around at the handful of fans who had arrived early at this cookie cutter facility. After pondering for a moment, he looked back at me with the same smile.

"I guess it would be nice to ruin everybody's day," he concurred lightly. "The weather will seem a lot warmer if we win."

414

As I usually did in a stadium that also housed a baseball team, I allowed myself to digress a little as I studied the stadium. In its short seven-season history it had already played host to five World Series and one All-Star Game. I visualized the stars of the day such as Johnny Bench, Pete Rose, Don Gullett and Joe Morgan playing on this turf. Although I was earning my living as a football player, I still tended to idolize baseball players. Baseball was still my favorite sport although I didn't publicly admit that until much later in my career. The reason I opted to play football instead of baseball was because I figured that I would know much sooner in my career whether I would be successful or not.

Suddenly I wondered how I might have fared as a player in the Reds' organization. I had almost forgotten that the Reds had drafted me out of high school. At the time I was set on going to college with my athletic scholarship; a decision I never regretted. Just the same, I wondered how far I would have gone in the Reds' organization had I opted to sign to play with them instead.

Of course it is a question I will never be able to answer. There were teams who wanted me and I continued getting drafted during and after college. That might suggest to some an automatic ticket to superstardom in the major leagues but I'm not so sure. I knew a lot of outstanding baseball players who seemed earmarked for long careers in the majors who never got beyond the low minors. I had also observed several outstanding players with the Hawaii Islanders and their opponents who spent very little or no time in the majors.

Gameday was chilly but not like the snowy day from a week earlier. The temperature was in the 30s with a slight breeze. However, there was absolutely no precipitation. There were lingering traces of the snow from a week earlier around the city but not a single snowflake had fallen since our arrival.

We won the toss. That alone got Walker hyped up.

"All right!" Walker exclaimed as he visualized first blood. "Let's stick it to them right away!"

It sounded like a good plan. Unfortunately the maximum we could do was jump off to a seven-point lead. No matter how impressive our opening drive might have seemed, the most we could get was seven points. That probably would not have been enough to persuade the Bengals to recognize the futility of taking us on.

I was hyped for a big return. I watched the airborne ball and realized it was heading Hasegawa's way. He caught the ball about five yards deep in the end zone and sized up the situation. The number of enemy jerseys heading his way convinced him a runback was out of the question and I relayed that type of information to him in case he didn't notice it on his own. He prudently downed the ball. Had Rich tried to run the kick back he would have been lucky to reach the ten-yard line.

We decided to come out the gate hard. We were going straight to the air.

Unfortunately the Bengals also decided to come out the gate hard. A couple of linebackers charged in and forced Bender to rush his pass. Fortunately he got the pass off which fell incomplete in the general vicinity of Dietrich.

Of course the Bengals were hollering for a grounding penalty and I am not sure that it wasn't justified. The ball may have been in the general vicinity of Dietrich but that is tantamount to saying that San Diego is in the general vicinity of Los Angeles. I believe we dodged a bullet on that one.

The Bengal defense charged in again on the following play. It was obvious that they had a lot at stake. They knew that they had to win to have a reasonable shot at a playoff berth, even controlling their own destiny since they would still be a game up on the Steelers if they won, but they did not have the tiebreaker advantage over the Steelers and couldn't afford to lose. They also knew that we were determined to hammer another nail into their 1976 coffin and were very capable of doing so.

Bender tried to scramble but he was about five or six years past his prime as a scrambler. I was running a post and couldn't help but notice the crescendo in the roar of the crowd. When I looked back I saw three defenders taking Steve down. He had scrambled forward but it was still a three-yard loss.

Walker didn't have to say a single word. As I headed to our huddle I caught a glimpse of him and could tell that he was a very unhappy camper. His arms were folded and his jaw was clenched tight. That pose said it all.

The next play didn't help Walker's disposition. Bender was under a heavy rush again. This time he got the pass off that was intended for Dietrich. Unfortunately the pass was picked off at the Hawaii 29. The cornerback who made the interception spun around and got as far as the 24 before Slater brought him down. The Bengals were 72 feet from drawing first blood and smelling playoffs.

That definitely got the crowd to remind us that we were not playing at home. Everybody seemed to be shouting at the top of their lungs. In that cookie-cutter facility the crowd noise seemed to bounce off the walls, making the roar seem even louder.

Emotionally I was a cross between anger and depression as I ran off the field. I was angry that we had turned the ball over and that the partisan crowd seemed overjoyed. It also depressed me that we weren't able to simply charge out of the gate and put the game away on the first series. I focused on the fact that a loss guaranteed a losing record and I wasn't willing to settle for that without a fight. I was still determined to send the Bengals and their fans home unhappy.

416

The drama continued. I sat helplessly with a cup of Gatorade in my hand as the Bengals picked up eleven yards on the very first play from scrimmage. They ran a quick pass over the middle that was completed before Rodgers brought the receiver down at the 13.

Two rushing plays later had the Bengals down to the Hawaii three. The officials stopped the clock to measure. They had picked up just barely enough for a first down. They were nine feet from a TD.

"Maybe the defense will hold 'em," Scott muttered as he took the seat next to me.

"Maybe," I remarked dryly, sounding about as convinced as Larry did. We were both resigned to the notion of being down by a touchdown before getting an opportunity to shift the momentum our way.

On the next play I realized our defense was going to make the Bengals earn all 108 inches to the goal line. The Bengals tried going to the air and all receivers were well-covered. At the same time the quarterback met a very determined rush from McDaniel, Jennings and Allen. The quarterback managed to avoid going down but he was forced to throw the ball over the end zone.

I am ashamed to say that I apparently had a deplorable lack of confidence in our defense. Feeling as if the sky was going to fall after the interception, I sat glumly as if the incomplete pass had merely delayed the inevitable. I hadn't lost confidence in our ability to win but I couldn't concede that the Bengals might end this ephemeral drive with fewer than seven points.

The Bengals picked up two yards through the right to give them a third and one. They went through the left on the next play and appeared to have scored. About half-a-dozen Bengals were standing with their arms raised as if they had. I also noted that none of the officials had their arms raised.

In the end it was fourth and inches. By this time we were all standing and crowding the sideline as far as we could without being penalized. We still couldn't get to within 30 yards of the line of scrimmage so we didn't have the kind of view we wanted.

The Bengals never seemed to even consider a field goal. They broke out of their huddle and headed up to the line as if the only option was to go for the full seven. They had two tight ends while we were stacked at the line in our 62 wall: six down linemen and two linebackers. Jennings and Zanakis were the only two linebackers while Allen stayed in but was down. I actually started to believe that the Bengals would come away empty.

Zanakis timed the snap perfectly. He actually penetrated into the Cincinnati line and was waiting for the ball carrier who just happened to be running through the left and into Kevin's path. The ball carrier tried to leap over but Kevin caught him and toppled over with the ball carrier in his grasp. The ball carrier had lost almost a full yard, leaving the Bengals with a goose egg still on the scoreboard.

It goes without saying that there was jubilation on our sideline. We were celebrating in such a manner that one would believe we had just won the game. I leaped up a couple of times with my arms raised before taking my parka off and grabbing my helmet.

"Let's capitalize on this, offense!" Walker instructed.

Zanakis was obviously the hero of the moment. As he ran off the field he was flanked by Allen, Rodgers, Richards and Prendergast. The rookie from Bellingham, Washington, had risen to the occasion in grand fashion. As I ran past him I could see a radiant smile beneath his facemask. There is very little in football that can compare with what one feels after making such a huge play.

With the ball on the one our huddle was in the back of the end zone. As Bender prepared to call a play he seemed to take a second to check out the crowd. There was no rush since NBC was in commercial.

"Let's piss these people off," Bender said once he turned his attention back to the huddle. It is another example of why he was such a good veteran quarterback. Forgotten was his interception. Bender's demeanor suggested that the interception he'd thrown was the furthest thing from his mind.

"Two Mililani left," he ordered. We were opening with a draw play that would send Kerner up the middle between the center and left guard.

Kerner and everybody else rose to the occasion. Jeff went up the middle and blasted his way to the seven.

"They'll be looking for Scott this time," Bender remarked as we huddled prior to the next play. He called a Kaneohe right, meaning that Kerner was going to carry again, this time off right tackle.

The play worked great. Kerner got all the way to the 12. It was first down.

After that the Cincinnati defense tightened up. Bender tried to get a pass off but was met by a heavy rush. He managed to avoid a couple of tackles and shot forward but was still brought down for a loss of a yard at the eleven. That preceded Scott's first carry of the day that netted nothing. It was third and eleven.

Despite another heavy rush, Bender got his first completion of the day.

I was happy to be the recipient. He hit me at the right sideline at about the first down marker. I managed to elude a tackle and raced forward for another eleven yards, giving us a first down at our 33.

It felt great. I bounced up and practically sprinted to where we would huddle. We had the momentum and I wanted it to continue at least for the next 67 yards.

I didn't even mind the cold. My nose was running but I was undaunted. The temperature was slightly above freezing so there was virtually no chance of having to play the game on the blanket of snow that covered the field a week earlier.

418

Scott only managed to pick up a yard on a sweep so we went to the air again. This time Bender hit Dietrich at the Hawaii 45. He arched around a defender before being hit by another defender and dropped at midfield. It was another first down.

"All right, all right. Let's keep moving forward," Bender suggested in the huddle before calling the next play.

Two rushes by Scott netted us four yards to the Cincinnati 46. That was when we went to the air again.

I wound up being the designated receiver again. Bender hit me at the 27. I was well covered but Steve deliberately threw the ball low. I caught the ball in a slide and was touched at the 27 to halt my forward progress. It was another first down on a drive that had consumed 72 yards thus far.

Dietrich held his hand out so that he could help me up. As we headed toward the huddle I heard my name called. It was Giametti coming in to spell me. We slapped fives as our paths crossed.

"Great catch," he commented.

Walker whacked me on the shoulder pads as I reached the sideline. He no longer had his scowl on his face although we still hadn't scored. He told me to stay close.

Giametti suddenly found himself in the spotlight. He ran a sweep around left end that picked up four yards. Since Gary rarely carried the ball Bender decided that the last thing the Bengals would be looking for was another Giametti rush.

This didn't produce quite the desired result. Gary managed only one yard through the left. That gave us a third and five at the Cincinnati 22.

I went back in. In this case it was Scott who came out since Walker wanted to go to our double-double formation.

Bender dropped back. I was well-covered on the right, as was Dietrich. It was Giametti he spotted near the end zone.

Gary made the grab on the one. He bobbled the ball slightly but managed to regain control just as he was crossing the goal line near the left sideline. We were on the board with 4:02 left in the first quarter.

The negatives were forgotten. The interception that climaxed what little we had on our first drive happened in another lifetime. However inept we may have appeared the first time we had the ball, it was superseded by a 99-yard drive that put us on the scoreboard.

Guinn's PAT was true. We had a 7-0 lead.

"Okay, that was a good drive," Bennici remarked. "Let's keep in mind that we have to keep putting points on the board. This is a hungry team we're playing today."

My mood had done a metamorphosis from the previous time I sat on this same bench. After once being resigned to the idea of us surrendering a touchdown, I was suddenly cocksure. I had a smirk on my face as I thought about the Bengals virtually kissing their playoff hopes goodbye. There were still 49 minutes left and we led by a mere touchdown but I was so full of myself that I was already writing the Bengals off even though they would still be technically alive even if they did lose to us.

At least all was going our way for the moment. I knew that they were capable of wiping us out. I simply felt extremely good about our situation at the moment.

The kickoff was totally unspectacular. The ball was fielded about two yards deep in the end zone. The return man seemed almost determined not to run the ball back. He caught the ball, paused and then dropped to a knee.

"Aw, come on. Let our guys have a shot at you," Dietrich remarked jocularly although not loud enough to be heard away from the confines of our bench. It was indicative of our mood, I suppose. We were savoring the moment. If the momentum shifted we would not be quite so loose.

The Bengals weren't waving any white flags. We probably didn't want them to. We wanted to beat them by outplaying them, not because they surrendered in the first quarter.

Although our defense was pretty determined, the Bengals managed to pick up a couple of first downs. The latter was at their own 46.

"That's far enough!" Walker called from his sideline post. "Let's stop them right now!"

I guess Walker's directive needed time to sink in. The Bengals immediately moved into Hawaii territory, going up the middle to the Hawaii 49. It was second and five.

The fans were enjoying the drive. We had silenced them with our scoring drive. Now they were getting back into the game.

An errant pass that fell untouched about ten yards beyond a well-covered receiver did not silence the crowd. It gave us optimism, though, since the Bengals were not in field goal range. If we could hold them one more time they would be forced to punt.

Morrissey rose to the occasion. He blitzed from the right corner on the next play and forced the quarterback to scramble. He shot through the line, sidestepped a block and caught up with the laterally moving quarterback at the Cincinnati 46. The quarterback had no choice but to tuck the ball away and go down in Morrissey's grasp.

"All right, rookie!" Kerner hollered as some of my other teammates and I expressed similar laconic approbation.

I was smiling again. I took off my parka and put my helmet on. I was met by Walker as I headed out to the field.

"If you have any chance at all, do a return," Walker instructed. "They're obviously going to try to pin us back but let's try to prevent that. Don't do anything foolish but go for it if a return is at all possible."

I took my place at the 15; 39 yards from the line of scrimmage. The punt got off and was slightly to my left. It was also destined to come down in front of me. I ran up to make the grab.

Officially I caught the punt at the 21. I had timed it so that I would catch it on the run. This obviously enables one to get off to a fast start although it also increases the possibility of a fumble.

Fortunately I didn't fumble. I shot forward although I didn't stay up for very long. Almost immediately I found myself in a game of chicken with somebody in an orange helmet and dark jersey. I tried to run right through him but he was relentless. He got me down at the 31 to climax a ten-yard return.

It all happened so fast that I thought I had only picked up a yard or two. It took me by surprise to learn that I had gone as far as I did. The first clue that I had done better than originally thought was when I caught a glimpse of Walker as I rose from the artificial turf. He was nodding his head and displaying a grin of approval.

"Good job, Jay," Bender commented as he slapped me on the back. I joined my offensive colleagues in the huddle at about the 20.

The punt return was the second to last play of the first quarter. There were eleven seconds left. Scott ran out the clock by going up the middle for seven yards.

NBC went to commercial and we changed sides. Scott's gain to end the quarter was a good momentum builder.

"Keep it up. Keep it up," Walker called in encouragement to us as he prepared to greet Bender for their between-quarter conference.

It was only 7-0 with three full quarters to go. It still had to be demoralizing for the Bengals. They missed a golden opportunity to score. We countered by marching 99 yards for the only score of the game thus far. It was a pretty good comeback after our less than auspicious opening drive.

Abraham must have had the jitters going into the second quarter. After Kerner opened the quarter by rushing to the Hawaii 44 to give us a first down, Clint jumped before the snap on the following play to give us a first and 15 at our own 39. It was the first penalty of the game for either team, coming with 14:33 left in the second quarter.

Obviously we had a little further to go for our next first down. Scott went around left end and managed only two yards. Bender then hit me over the middle at the Cincinnati 45. I was hit almost immediately but managed to struggle to the 43 before going down. Despite the extra five yards we had to cover because of the penalty, we had the first down.

Ozzie got the call on the next play since Scott was on the sideline adjusting his shoulder pads. He went up the middle for a yard.

To complete an earlier thought, Abraham continued his overzealousness. He jumped before the snap again, giving us a second and 14 at the Cincinnati 47.

I didn't even have to look at Walker on the sideline to know that he was bearing his trademark scowl. I was probably even subconsciously afraid that

421

if I looked in his direction that he would blame me for the faux pas. Walker had a way of bringing out the paranoia in a man.

"Man, I can't believe I did it again," Clint bellowed as we moved back to the huddle.

"Take it easy," Bender calmly assured him. "It's all right. We'll get it back."

Bender wasted no time in proving that he knew what he was talking about. He proceeded to fire a perfect pass to Dietrich. Ted caught the ball at the 25 and picked up three more yards to give us a first down. It was Bender's sixth consecutive completion.

The completion streak ended at six but we did avert disaster in the process. Bender tried to hit Grummon at the left sideline inside the ten. A defensive back jumped in front of Rich and appeared to have an interception. Fortunately he dropped the ball.

I was standing at the front of the goal line as this was going down. An expletive was right on the tip of my tongue as the defensive back seemed to make a spectacular play to pick off the pass. Before I could utter the aforementioned expletive I was heaving a sigh of relief. There were probably several sighs of such relief among the Hawaii contingent.

As I reached the huddle I noticed two contrasting expressions on Bender's face. There were traces of pain for having almost thrown an interception to kill an impressive drive. There was also a look of relief.

The interception would not have been Steve's fault. The defensive back simply made an outstanding play. It still would have reflected in Steve's statistics. It also would have brought the Bengals to life, especially if the interception was returned for a touchdown which is what might have happened had the defensive back hung on to the ball.

Apparently undaunted by what almost happened, Steve went to the air again. He dropped back and had good protection. He spotted me in the end zone as I was trying to shake my defender.

I was about six yards deep when the ball arrived. I was on the run and reached out to pull in a nearly perfectly placed pass. I was hit from behind and dropped immediately but I hung on. It was a fantastic feeling to look up and see an official towering over me with his arms raised.

Grummon was first on the scene. He pulled me up and gave me a bear hug.

"That's the way! That's the way!" he cried out as my other teammates arrived.

I'm sure I was smiling as I ran toward the sideline. I slapped fives with some members of the extra point unit as our paths crossed. I received a few more congratulations from teammates and coaches on the sideline.

"Now I don't feel so bad," Abraham remarked in slight embarrassment as he shook my hand.

422

"Good," Kerner remarked lightly. "We knew we had to hurry and score before you jumped offside again."

The PAT was good. That gave us a 14-0 lead. The clock showed 11:48 remaining in the first half.

I put on my parka and took my helmet off. I grabbed a cup of Gatorade and sat on the bench. Dietrich occupied the seat on my right, Marv was on my left . . . and the crowd was not especially noisy.

"Ah, nothing beats a quiet Sunday afternoon in beautiful downtown Cincinnati," Hayer quipped.

"Yeah, it sure beats a quiet Sunday in Honolulu," Slater added.

"Ain't it the truth?" Scott chimed in.

Guinn got his foot solidly into the ball on the kickoff. The ball once again came down about two yards deep in the end zone. Like before, the return man didn't attempt a return. That produced some boos from the taciturn crowd.

"Yeah, they're right," I deadpanned. "I would've run the kick back."

Of course those words were the result of the ego of one who had just scored a touchdown. Our kicking team actually did a good job of hustling downfield. The ball carrier probably would not have made it to the 20 had he attempted a return. I just happened to feel invincible at the moment.

The Bengals made a semblance of noise on the first play from scrimmage. A slant pattern produced a seven-yard reception. The receiver was immediately hammered by Ed who read the play and dropped back to make the tackle.

It was a wasted effort. A sweep around right end produced a one-yard loss when McDaniel dropped the ball carrier behind the line. That led to a pass that was broken up by Blakely.

"Yeah!" I cheered, leaping to my feet and thrusting my fists in the air. "Way to go, defense!"

I was pumped like never before. I shed my parka, grabbed my helmet and ran on the field. I was extremely grateful to the defense for holding the Bengals without yielding even one first down. A long punt return, I believed, would have the Bengals almost ready for the white flags.

Unfortunately I didn't get my punt return although, the reason had its demoralizing effect on the Bengals. The punt went off the side of the punter's foot. The ball went out of bounds at the Hawaii 41. My ego found the fact that I couldn't return the punt somewhat disturbing but I was grateful for the field position.

In the huddle I could see it in my teammates' faces. Every one of them was determined to add another touchdown to our tally.

And we became human battering rams. Thanks to great blocking and powerful running, Scott headed up the middle to the 45. I followed by going through the left across midfield to the Hawaii 49. Kerner then carried and was hit behind the line before powering his way to the Cincinnati 48 for a first down.

Each successful play shot up our level of confidence. We were strutting like peacocks as we headed to the huddle.

Scott picked up nine yards over the next two plays. He managed only two yards through the right on the first play but picked up seven on a 3 kama'aina right to give us a third and one. Kerner ensured the first down by picking up five yards off left tackle.

We were hot!

But then our drive stalled. A pass to Grummon fell incomplete. I managed all of four yards on a sweep around right end to give us a third and six. Bender then was sacked at the 36 to create a fourth and 12.

This may have been the moment that Guinn dreaded. He had had such a disappointing performance against Oakland the previous week that he must have very badly wanted to redeem himself while simultaneously dreading the prospect of having to kick a field goal. His teammates and the coaching staff spent much of the week trying to help him keep his confidence up. He was probably hoping his first field goal attempt of the game would be something less formidable than 53 yards.

Of course if he converted on a field goal attempt of only ten yards less than the NFL record his confidence would soar to new heights.

We were all standing on the sideline and rooting Eric on as much for his sake as the team's. He was a nice guy and a good teammate. Everybody wanted to see him come through.

It was a good snap from Stuart Arroyo. Billingsley fielded it cleanly and put it down. Eric approached the ball and put his foot into it solidly.

The ball arched up. It looked like it had the distance. From our vantage point on the sideline it appeared to be fairly accurate.

Unfortunately it missed the mark. The kick was slightly to the left. Guinn had now missed on four consecutive attempts. This was after he converted on 13 out of 16 over the first eleven games. He was definitely in a slump.

Guinn ran off the field. He sat down at the far end of the bench and bowed his head. From a distance a few of us watched mournfully as he occasionally shook his head in bewilderment. A couple of teammates tapped him on the shoulder as they went by to try to lift his spirits. Holcomb sat with him; perhaps giving him some pointers.

Walker kept glancing in Guinn's direction. It probably helped that we were still up by two touchdowns. Walker's expressions appeared to be those of sympathy and not anger. He knew that nobody wanted Guinn to get back on track more than Guinn himself did.

Meanwhile the Bengals were experiencing their own brand of futility, much to our delight. They managed a first down at our 48 but then a short gain followed by sacks by Zanakis and Allen gave them a fourth-and-16 at their own 46.

I assumed my post at the 15. This time the punter got a pretty good punt off with good hang time. Sensing a fast pursuit and heeding Hasegawa's instruction, I raised my hand and made a fair catch at the 16. There was 1:18 left in the half.

"We're going for it," Bender announced in the huddle. "Let's get to at least field goal range."

On the very first play the Bengals served notice that it wouldn't be so bloody simple. Bender dropped back and saw a hard charge of Bengal defenders. He scrambled and finally got the pass off to Grummon at the 20. Rich went up to the 25 before stepping out of bounds. The clock stopped at 1:06.

Our nine-yard gain came with a price. Marv had dropped back to protect Bender. He did a good job but managed to sprain his ankle. He limped off the field and Hubert ran on in his place. Marv would be sidelined for the rest of the game but was expected to be back the following week.

When play resumed Bender hit Dietrich over the middle at our 36. Ted picked up nine more yards before being brought down about two yards inbounds.

"Time out!" I barked, making a "T" with my hands. At least three of my teammates were doing the same thing. We got the clock stopped with 55 seconds left in the half.

An incompletion, thanks partially to a heavy rush, preceded a pass that I caught near the right sideline at the Cincinnati 44. I was hit immediately and knocked out of bounds, apparently in an effort to save me the bother of stepping out on my own. That stopped the clock with 38 seconds showing.

With the Bengal's determined rush and Guinn's bad luck we decided to play it safe. Rather than risk an interception that could take the momentum away or a sack that would force Guinn to attempt a longer field goal than he might have been comfortable with at the time, we decided to keep the ball on the ground. We lined up in the dotted "I" and ran a 4 Mililani right. I charged up the middle all the way to the 18 before being brought down.

What I will never understand is why we didn't try to run at least one more play. Instead we let the clock tick down to three seconds before we used our final time out. Whatever the reason may have been was not known by me. All I know is the field goal unit was dispatched to the field.

"You can do it," I said as my path crossed with Guinn's on my way to the sideline.

Although I wasn't about to say so at the time, I was glad we were going for a field goal instead of a touchdown. With our two-touchdown lead I didn't feel it was especially imperative that we score a touchdown. I believed a successful field goal would rekindle Guinn's confidence. That was probably more critical at that juncture than the extra four points we would have had we successfully gone for a touchdown.

Everybody seemed to want Guinn to succeed. Every player, every coach and everybody else on the sideline was standing. During Guinn's sudden slump I didn't hear a single disparaging word about him by anybody connected to the team.

It was a good snap. Billingsley had no trouble getting the ball down. Guinn approached the ball and there was the sound of the "thump" when his foot connected with the ball.

I watched as the ball headed toward the uprights. It looked good but I was watching from an angle several yards away. It wasn't until the officials raised their arms that the apparent jinx had been taken off of Guinn.

It was only the final play of the first half of a game where the outcome was still in doubt. Judging by the reaction of the players and coaches, one would think we were the Baltimore Colts after the field goal on the final play of Super Bowl V. Normally a field goal to expand our lead by three points would have generated a guardedly positive reaction before we casually headed to the locker room for halftime. In this case a lot of us rushed out to greet Guinn like a conquering hero.

"Thanks, I needed that," he said with an expression that didn't defy his relief.

This is an example, I guess, of how football truly is a team game. Guinn got along with his teammates but wasn't especially close to anybody. With his medium height and thin frame he had never been anything other than a kicker dating back to high school near Searchlight, Nevada. That may have been why he sometimes felt somewhat detached from his brawnier teammates.

Yet he was a vital part of our team. His job was to kick and he did it well, just as he had done during his four previous seasons in Buffalo and Washington. Not only did he have a high field goal percentage on the season, his kickoffs were high enough and deep enough to enable our kicking team to converge on the ball carriers. He also wasn't one to shy away from contact.

Guinn didn't profess to be anything other than what he was. Unlike Jablonski who had been a split end and safety at his high school in Asheville, North Carolina, and a substitute defensive back at Clemson besides being his teams' punter, Guinn's football skills were limited. He still wasn't totally devoid of athletic skills since he ran the mile for his high school track team and was a pretty adept bowler.

Despite the celebration on the field, we knew we still had another half to play. Things had settled down by the time we got to the locker room. I was among those visiting the urinal before getting a cup of Gatorade and making my perpetual mistake of keeping profits up for the Marlboro people. I joined my offensive colleagues in going over a couple of plays to be

426

adjusted with Tipton while the defense did the same thing with Crawford. There wasn't time to do much but we wanted to do all we could to expand our 17-point lead.

"You know that the Bengals are regrouping and adjusting," Walker reminded us just before our return to the field. "You have to be ready. A 17-point lead is nothing, especially against a team like this. You have to put together 30 minutes of solid football."

Please pardon the pun when I say that the Bengals came at us like a caged tiger breaking loose. Their very determined game plan seemed obvious from the kickoff, which was fielded three yards deep in the end zone and returned to the 24.

Immediately they passed over the middle to about the 35. The receiver broke Morrissey's tackle and headed upfield. He was brought down at the 45 in a joint effort by Rodgers and Blakely.

It was only one good play but it was enough to get the crowd back into it. I was starting to worry. I sat on the bench to try to calm myself down a little.

Our fortune seemed to change slightly when their three-yard rush was nullified by a holding penalty. That was followed by a pass that was slightly off target near midfield to give them a second and 20.

The Bengals weren't still in the playoff hunt for nothing. One of their receivers made a diving catch of a pass near midfield. He managed to get back to his feet before anybody could touch him down. He got all the way to the Hawaii 43 before Hamer caught him from behind and threw him down.

Eric's not especially tender tackle did not go over well with some of the Bengals. There was a little bit of shoving going on before the officials restored order. It was a pretty brutal tackle but I don't believe it was malicious. It was simply Eric's momentum.

"Man, this is really getting intense," Abraham remarked from where he sat about five feet to my right. "We've really got to turn up the heat."

"I hear ya," Grummon replied. "If they score we had better score."

"We had better score even if they don't score," offered Hubert.

"Right on," said Marv who was now in street clothes. "We're too good to blow a 17-point lead."

Those of us in the vicinity all seemed to agree. It was best that we look at it that way. That beat thinking about the fact that the Bengals were a team capable of overcoming a 17-point deficit, especially against an expansion team hoping to simply break even on the season.

Two plays later the Bengals had another first down at the Hawaii 24. Two plays after that they had a third and one at the 15. The crowd continued to be very vocal.

427

"Let's go Bengals!" we could hear from behind our bench amid the crowd noise generated throughout all of Riverfront Stadium.

"You stink, Hawaii!"

"What makes you think you can hold on to a 17-point lead?"

"The Bengals are going to grind you into the turf!"

"Get it in the end zone, Cincinnati!"

The Bengals did a sweep around left end. They only needed to get to the 14 for a first down. The ball carrier was brought down by Morrissey at the 13.

"Fumble!"

I didn't see the fumble. All I could see after I knew that the ball was loose was several black jerseys and white jerseys scrambling around in what had been the Bengal's backfield during the previous play. This meant that if the Bengals recovered they would probably wind up having to settle for a field goal.

Things settled down a little near the 15. There was a small pile of humanity over what I assumed was the football. The officials were sorting through the pile to ascertain possession.

Suddenly the referee stood erect. He pointed to indicate that Hawaii had recovered the fumble.

"All right!" I hollered, grabbing my helmet and shedding my parka before heading toward the field. At the same time Walker turned and was waving us on. He was wearing a huge smile.

It was Allen who recovered the fumble. He stood up and briefly held the ball aloft, then flipped it to an official and ran triumphantly off the field.

In retrospect, that was vintage Allen. Not only was he the anchor of our defense, he was the one most likely to make the crucial big play when we needed it the most.

What we needed now were big plays from the offense. Our defense had continued to hold the Bengals to a goose egg on the scoreboard. The offense needed to put more points on the board so that if the Bengals did score it would be more for the sake of their pride and not something likely to put them back in the game.

We got off to a reasonably good start. A short pass to Dietrich and a rush by Scott gave us a first down at our own 28.

Unfortunately we started to sputter amid Cincinnati's determined defense. Scott managed only one yard on a sweep around right end. On the following play Bender was nearly intercepted at the Hawaii 40. The defensive back had tipped the ball up on a pass to Slater, then made a diving lunge for the ball but fell inches short of making the interception. We had third and nine.

The task of picking up the first down fell on my shoulders. I ran to the first down marker and was hit by one of Bender's bullets. I was hit

428

immediately from behind, going down at the 32 although I had actually caught the ball just beyond the first down marker at the 33.

As soon as I went down the whistles blew. I rose quickly and tossed the ball to a nearby official. I casually headed back to where we would be huddling up near our own 20.

"What are you spotting it there for?" I heard Walker suddenly bellow from the sideline adjacent to where I had gone down. "You're marking it where he went down. His forward motion was just beyond the first down marker."

Walker continued to plead his case. I stood by helplessly as I awaited the final outcome. Walker continued yelling and pointing while I sensed an inferno building inside of me. I knew that Walker's argument was going to be in vain even though the replays showed that my forward motion was definitely beyond the first down marker. We had no choice but to send the punting unit on the field.

"They sure screwed us out of that one," Walker muttered while looking at me as I exited the field. I somehow managed to keep my mouth shut although I definitely had an editorial of my own that I wanted to express to the officials. As I grabbed a cup of Gatorade I noticed that virtually everybody on the sideline appeared extremely angry.

As I sat on the bench and tried to cool my volatile insides Tipton came over to me. He handed me the headset.

"Wilson wants to talk to you," he said.

I put the headset on. I expected Wilson to tell me that the officials blew the mark; something I already knew.

"Yeah, Coach," I said.

"What happened?" Wilson asked from his post in the press box. "Didn't you get to first down territory?"

"Yeah I did. They just spotted the ball wrong."

"Well next time get a little further downfield. You just cost us a first down."

I stood up and, in my livid state, expressed a few expletives at Wilson. I told him that I had done my job and wasn't about to take the blame for the officials' mistake.

Tipton was standing nearby. He held his hand out.

"I'll take the headset," he said.

I gratefully handed the headset to Tipton.

"It wasn't Jay's fault so don't blame him," I heard Tipton bark as he moved away from me. "He was where he was supposed to be. The officials didn't mark the ball right."

After that Tipton was far enough away to where I couldn't hear him. I tried to put the bad spot behind me and focus on what was going on at the time. The Bengals had a first down at their own five. Guinn may have cooled off but Jablonski was hot. He had just punted 58 yards to pin the Bengals back. They had to travel 95 yards to put points on the board.

We gave them a little bit of a boost. Their three-yard run was nullified by Jennings jumping offside. In his zeal he jumped into the backfield, somehow doing so without touching any of the Bengal players but wasn't able to get back before the ball was snapped.

A rush to the 19 gave them a first down and brought the crowd back to life. This was the beginning of a steady march from one end of the field to the other. The Bengals still appeared to be undaunted by their 17-point deficit.

If the Bengals didn't do it on their own, we helped them. After picking up three more first downs they had a second and five at the Hawaii 28. An incomplete pass was nullified because Jurgens jumped offside. That moved the ball to the 23.

The referee blew his whistle and waved his hands over his head. Time was called to measure. The Bengals would ultimately have a first down by about two inches.

"That's far enough! Don't let them get any more!" Walker called from his post. "Stop them right there! Force the turnover!"

It appeared that the defense was heeding Walker's demand that the Bengals be stopped cold. An incompletion and a rush for no gain followed Walker's demand.

Unfortunately the Bengals succeeded on a play that we had attempted at the end of our previous drive. The receiver went to just beyond the first down marker and caught a pass. He was hit and dropped immediately by Black. The officials this time spotted the ball at the right spot.

There was a penalty marker on the play. Zanakis had jumped offside. The Bengals declined the penalty. It was first and ten.

Walker's jaw was clenched. He stood with his hands on his hips. Despite the fact that our defense had gone through almost three full quarters without yielding a single point to a playoff contender, Walker looked like he wanted to tear the entire unit to shreds.

The defense didn't falter. Richards shot through the line and dropped a running back for a two-yard loss at the 14. After an incompletion the Bengals faced a third and 12.

It was obviously a passing situation. Our defensive backs provided tight coverage. It didn't matter anyway since McDaniel charged the quarterback. The quarterback appeared poised to run to his left away from Jim but that route was blocked by our other defensive end, Jurgens. He was sandwiched by McDaniel and Jurgens at the 19 to give the Bengals a fourth and 19.

"Now that's the way to play it!" Walker called as he raised his fists in the air.

The Bengals sent their field goal unit to the field. There were some boos among the crowd but it was actually a smart move. The Bengals needed a minimum of three scores to catch up to us. Had they gone for the touchdown, which would have been a stupid move although the Bengal coaches would have looked like geniuses had they succeeded, and failed to deliver they still would have needed three scores.

It became a two-score game when the placekicker put the ball through the uprights. It was 17-3 with eight seconds left in the third quarter. Time was running out but there was still more than enough time for the Bengals to catch us and even move ahead of us. We needed to score again and run as much time off the clock as we could.

I was feeling good but not overconfident as I took my spot for the kickoff. Both of our offensive and defensive units seemed fairly sound. We might even have expanded our lead had the officials placed the ball correctly after my reception although there was nothing I could do to rectify that. The defense did well to hold the Bengals to three points despite the penalties against us. I was feeling strong and believed our offense could move the ball again.

The kickoff was out of the end zone so we began our drive at the 20 with those same eight seconds still showing on the clock. Scott began the drive by picking up 15 yards to run out the third quarter, clarifying my belief that we could move the ball. I was hoping the pattern would carry through the fourth quarter.

And it did. It was pretty much all Hawaii the rest of the way. We marched toward the end zone with the same success as General Sherman's march to the sea during the Civil War. I had one reception during the drive for 18 yards and two carries for six total yards. Scott climaxed the drive by banging it in from the one to give us a 24-3 lead.

Equally as important, we used up virtually half of the final quarter. By the time Scott slammed into the end zone the clock showed 7:36. It was still possible for the Bengals to catch us but the extra score would make it a much more formidable task.

The Bengals gave it their best shot. They began with a good kick return. The ball was fielded at the two. The return man got all the way to the 33 before Pratt brought him down.

They weren't going down easy. A few plays later they had a first down at the Hawaii 48 with 6:41 showing.

While the Bengals were determined to force us to earn the victory if we were to get it, our defense served notice that they would have to earn any scores they made. The quarterback was rushed on the very next play and forced to scramble. He did manage to pick up two yards before stepping out of bounds. That stopped the clock with 6:32 left.

"That's good, defense!" Walker called. "They can have all the short yardage they want!"

Allen blitzed on the next play. The quarterback tried to drop back to get a pass off. He spotted a receiver and unleashed the ball but Allen tipped the ball, knocking it well off course.

The ball arched up and was traveling end over end. It was caught by Zanakis at the Hawaii 45. Kevin returned the ball to the 50. The interception represented another nail in the Bengals' coffin.

"All right, offense. Let's eat up that clock," Walker directed. The clock showed 6:22. The issue was not whether we could score but how much time we could burn. They were still three scores away and all of their scores had to be touchdowns.

We ran a few plays and found ourselves in a third and 12. With the clock ticking away we didn't feel there was any urgency in getting a first down. The Bengals could still catch us but only if our defense totally collapsed.

Bender had me run a slant. I caught the ball at the Cincinnati 47. I still needed seven yards to get to the first down. If not, Jablonski was likely to pin the Bengals back with one of his punts.

I managed to spin away from a defender and outran another. I could see a couple of others a little further upfield who had been covering Dietrich and Grummon. They were heading in my direction but I still managed to get to the 39 before they brought me down. That was good enough for a first down with a yard to spare.

With less than five minutes to play Walker apparently decided the outcome was no longer in doubt. In came Kamanu, Ozzie, Edwards, Slater and Giametti to replace Grummon, Scott, Kerner, Dietrich and me. There were also some changes made on the interior line.

Joseph went in at quarterback. It was hoped that he and the other fresh bodies could keep the drive going to run out the clock.

The replacements did exactly as they were expected to do. Joseph ultimately climaxed the drive on a fourth down with only about six inches to the goal line. He did a quarterback sneak to ultimately extend our lead to 31-3 with 49 seconds left.

By this time the stadium was emptying out. The Bengals had lost the game and diminished their hopes for the playoffs. They were still technically alive in the playoff hunt but they needed a collapse by the Steelers who were in the process of routing the Tampa Bay Buccaneers to move them into a tie with the Bengals for the division lead while also holding the tiebreaker advantage. The loss also moved the Bengals a game behind the New England Patriots for the wild card spot since the Patriots were wrapping up their victory over the New Orleans Saints. The Bengals' best hope for a playoff spot was by winning their regular season finale over the Jets while hoping that the Steelers would fall to the Houston Oilers. The Patriots had virtually secured the wild card berth since they would be closing out their regular season schedule against the hapless Buccaneers.

432

The Bengals ran a few plays to try to narrow the score but Rodgers ultimately came up with an interception on the final play at the Hawaii 15. Rather than run up the score for no particular reason, he took a few steps before dropping to one knee at the 17. At that point we were officially 6-7.

It was Tipton who gave the postgame prayer. He was not someone I considered to be devoutly religious even though he was from SMU. He still managed to give a good prayer. He was probably also thinking about how the postgame beer was going to taste.

"Thanks, Mike," Walker said at the conclusion of the prayer. "This week I want to give out two game balls."

Walker held a ball up while a second one sat on a table. He tossed it to Guinn who received a round of cheers even though probably nobody expected him to get the ball.

"I honestly believe your field goal to end the first half gave us a little extra adrenalin," Walker stated. "It gave us that little extra strength that we needed to carry us through the second half, and I think it also got you back on track."

It made sense, I believed. Had Guinn missed that field goal he might have been on a negative mindset that was irreversible.

Walker picked up the second ball and held it up. That caused the cheers to die down again.

"This ball goes to another unsung hero," Walker announced. "Sometimes you don't realize how important a player is to a club until you look back and see what he's accomplished. He's done an outstanding job for us all season. When he made that punt that put the Bengals back on the five I decided that he had earned his game ball."

Walker tossed the ball to Jablonski. He was also given a round of cheers.

Unlike earlier in the season when we went to a neutral site between two road games, we stayed in Cincinnati. The whole point of our earlier trip to Salt Lake City was to help us adjust to the altitude and climate we would experience in Denver while being far enough away to make it difficult for the opposition to spy on us. In this case we were already in a similar altitude and climate while still relatively distant from Cleveland. Why move?

A group of us staged a semblance of a bachelor party on Sunday night. Jablonski was getting married exactly one week after our final game in his hometown in North Carolina. Since we weren't going home and would not be practicing the next day, we staged an impromptu bachelor party in Jablonski's hotel room.

The party was the brainchild of Allen and Rodgers and, I'm sure, would not have happened had we lost that day. Supposedly at about ten o'clock that night a small group of players had congregated in the hotel lobby when Allen suddenly said, "Let's have a bachelor party for Jablonski."

At that point they went to a nearby store where they purchased a large supply of beer, soda and snacks and then pounded on Jablonski's door for his surprise bachelor party. It would have been a bigger surprise had they discovered that Jablonski had gone out for the night although I guess they would have *forced themselves* to consume the refreshments in Jablonski's honor.

I had been out with Ed, Marv and Prendergast. We had dinner together and then went to a nearby lounge to quietly converse over a couple of beers.

A bluegrass trio was performing at the lounge. We were treated pretty well even after the patrons realized that we were part of the contingent that beat the hometown team earlier that day.

We arrived back at the hotel at about eleven. We bought a couple of six-packs and were going to lounge around in one of our rooms when Black appeared in the lobby. He told us about the bachelor party in Jablonski's room.

As I recall, the celebrants besides the guest of honor were Black, Allen, Richards, Dietrich, Rodgers, Stanek, Jurgens, Marv, Ed, Pratt and me. Bender also appeared and drank two beers before departing. Giametti, Kerner and Slater also showed up eventually.

The coaching staff was also represented. Tipton, Jerry Meacham, Bennici and Max Crawford took part in the festivities. There wasn't much empty space in that hotel room.

It wasn't really as big a deal as it sounded. We simply crowded into a single hotel room and drank beer and talked and laughed until about four in the morning. Nobody got especially drunk or rowdy.

At one point I looked around the room and felt a momentary wave of sadness. Five months had passed since training camp. That was when this group began to form. We had come a long way since then and nobody could deny that we rose well above expectations. Contrasting personalities notwithstanding, we gelled into an unbelievably good unit. After one more week that unit would no longer be intact.

Throughout the party it was primarily a phalanx of males bonding. At one point Black suggested getting Jablonski a hooker but Jablonski vetoed the idea.

I was glad that he did. Although I was an allegedly swinging bachelor, I didn't want to be a party to somebody cheating on his fiancée. I actually believed in men and women being faithful to each other even before they were officially bound in wedlock.

CHAPTER EIGHTEEN
The Climax

I slept until almost noon on Monday. I got up, took a shower, got dressed and went out for something to eat. After that I returned to my hotel room, turned on the TV and promptly fell asleep. I woke up about two hours later.

We resumed our routine on Tuesday. Five months after the beginning of training camp it was our final week of workouts. It was a bittersweet experience.

The routine remained the same except we had to adapt to the road version. That meant we had to have our film sessions and meetings in the hotel before boarding a bus for our workouts. Walker arranged for us to use a high school field in Covington, Kentucky.

We could have practiced at Riverfront Stadium. We might have had our next game been at a stadium with artificial turf. Since Cleveland's Municipal Stadium had grass Walker arranged to use a facility with grass.

I am not saying Walker was wrong. I am simply saying I disagreed with him. I don't believe it would have made any discernable difference if we had practiced on artificial turf. I personally preferred to play on grass and always regretted that Aloha Stadium used artificial turf. I do believe our practices before the Cleveland game would have been just as effective had we worked out at Riverfront Stadium. That seemed preferable to a high school that could not provide us with a dressing facility. After our films and other meetings we got dressed in our hotel rooms, conspicuously walked through the lobby to the bus, crossed the Ohio River into Kentucky and had our workout before backtracking to our hotel.

Once again there was the matter of my TV show. As had been the case in Salt Lake City several weeks earlier, arrangements were made with a local TV station to hire a small crew to shoot and edit my show. I went to the studio to voice over the highlight clips. My intros and segues into commercials were shot at Riverfront Stadium.

"Hi, I'm Jay Dockman addressing you from Riverfront Stadium in Cincinnati; the scene of the Hawaiians' latest triumph," I greeted while looking into a camera from my initial post on the turf at midfield. "We squared off against a very determined team on Sunday but the Hawaiians rose to the occasion."

Highlights of the Hawaiians' victory led off the show. That was followed by a few highlights from other NFL games. In the interest of time, we only showed highlights of games involving teams in contention for playoff spots. The Hawaiian-Bengal highlights segued into highlights of these other games with my prerecorded voice doing the narration. I didn't appear on camera again until it was time to go to commercial.

"When we come back we'll show some of the week's NBA highlights," I announced, this time sitting in a bleacher seat that was in the front row behind what had been the Hawaiians' bench on Sunday.

The show concluded with highlights from the University of Hawaii's 1976 football season. With a 3-8 record that climaxed three nights earlier with the team obliterated 68-3 by the Nebraska Cornhuskers, meaning that my alma mater's football team lost the final two games of the season by a combined score of 127-3, there weren't that many highlights.

"Obviously it wasn't a banner year for the University of Hawaii Rainbow Warriors," my prerecorded voice reported as the highlight clip began. I essentially gave an editorial as a potpourri of shots from throughout the season was shown. There was a liberal assortment of plays that led to triumph and plays that fell way short of triumph.

"What can I say?" I asked rhetorically when the highlight tape ended and the scene returned to Riverfront Stadium; this time with me standing against a goal post with the blank scoreboard in the background. "Even the best of teams have their difficult times. This is only the Rainbow Warriors' third season as a Division I school. As a fan as well as a loyal alumnus of the University of Hawaii, I have to believe that better days are just around the corner."

On that note I closed the show. The entire package was sent by satellite to Honolulu where the crew there put everythng in the proper sequence.

On Friday morning we checked out of the hotel. We crossed into Kentucky again and headed to the Cincinnati-Northern Kentucky International Airport. We boarded our plane, flew to Cleveland, checked into our hotel and then went to Municipal Stadium for our workout.

It was our final workout of the season. Workouts were often rigorous or boring and there were times when I wondered if Walker was in reality a sadist disguised as a human being. I still regretted that there wouldn't be any workouts after this.

Earlier on that same field the Cleveland Browns had what they hoped would not be their final workout of the season. They had to beat us or else it was all over for them. If they did beat us they had to hope that the Steelers and Bengals both would lose on Sunday. If the Browns beat us and the Steelers and Bengals both lost, the Browns' season would be extended for at least one more week as division champions.

We were very aware of the scenario. We had a chance to play the spoiler. That was why I didn't get too wrapped up in the thought of this being our final workout of the season. It wasn't as if we were playing a team that was also eliminated from playoff contention and simply playing out its schedule. This was a game that meant something. It was a good way to end the season if we weren't going to the playoffs ourselves.

436

The pregame breakfast was set for eight o'clock. I requested a seven o'clock wakeup call from the desk. That didn't prevent me from getting out of bed at about 5:30.

I showered and dressed and went down to the lobby. The lobby was relatively uninhabited except for hotel personnel who quietly went about their business.

And then I spotted Jennings.

Ed was sitting by himself on a soft chair near the lobby entrance. He seemed to be staring at the wall directly opposite. He moved only to draw off of his cigarette.

"How long have you been here?" I asked.

"Oh, hey, Jay. About five minutes is all. I was just thinking about getting a cup of coffee. Want to join me?"

"Sure."

We sat in a booth in the hotel coffee shop. At this hour there were only three other customers. Two of them appeared to be a middle-aged couple comprised of a stocky black man and a slightly plump but still attractive white woman with red hair. The other patron may have been a travelling businessman who was staying at the hotel.

A pretty waitress with extremely black skin came over. Her name tag identified her as Diane.

"Hey, I recognize you," Diane immediately said to Ed. "You play for the Philadelphia Eagles, right?"

"I used to," Ed replied good naturedly. "I play for Hawaii now."

"Hawaii? Hawaii's got a team?"

"We sure do. We play the Browns this afternoon."

Once Diane got over the apparent shock of even a remote locale like Hawaii having an NFL franchise, she took our orders. We both ordered coffee while Ed also ordered a sweet roll.

"You know what I think?" Ed asked after our orders were placed.

"What?"

"I think we'd better play so well today that nobody in Cleveland ever forgets that Hawaii has a pro football team."

"I'm up for that," I said.

One final pregame meal of steak and eggs in a hotel dining room. All players were present, as were all coaches and other team personnel. This was traditionally an event where members of the media who accompanied the team were not welcome. This final pregame meal of the season was not the exception.

This appeared to be like the other pregame breakfasts we enjoyed on the road. The room was filled with relatively subdued conversation. In order to keep the focus, most of the team talked about things pertaining to the game or else said nothing at all. Nobody seemed to be asking anybody what they were doing for Christmas or what their plans may have been for the offseason. Those issues could be taken up later.

One final bus ride to the stadium. I sat by a window on the right side of the bus and watched the scenery without really noticing it. My focus was on football.

I was completing my third year in a Hawaiians uniform. It was the completion of my first year in the NFL version of the Hawaiians.

How unreal it seemed. My first season in the NFL; a league I had essentially rejected a few years earlier in favor of an opportunity to remain in the place I had begun to call home to play for a brand-new team in a brand-new league.

During my tenure in the WFL there were no trips to Cleveland. NFL cites such as Chicago, Detroit, Houston and Philadelphia had WFL franchises but not Cleveland. The entire state of Ohio was never the site of a WFL matchup.

So my presence in Cleveland meant that I was definitely in the NFL. After almost a full season it still sometimes seemed unreal. We wore identical uniforms as those from the WFL but each week on the opposite side of the field we saw nothing but uniforms from established NFL franchises. Of the four expansion franchises, we were the only one who didn't match up with a fellow expansion team during the regular season. The other three expansion teams actually squared off against the remaining two expansion teams. There was no explanation for why the Hawaiians faced only established NFL teams although it was probably simply a fluke.

Of course I could have played in the NFL for somebody other than Hawaii. Had Hawaii not been added to the NFL I would have been the property of the Cowboys. I would like to believe that I would have been good enough to make the team had I opted to play for, the Cowboys instead of turning to baseball.

Suddenly it dawned on me that this was a very significant anniversary. Our final game of our maiden NFL season was being played on the first anniversary of the first signing of a player to the NFL version of the Hawaiians.

Of course that player was yours truly. Within days of the announcement that Hawaii would be included in the NFL there was a modest upheaval regarding where I would play since I had played for Hawaii of the WFL but it was Dallas that owned the NFL rights to me. While the Cowboys were focusing their primary attention on the playoffs that would ultimately lead them to the Super Bowl, the management agreed to a deal that would keep me in Hawaii. I was officially signed by the NFL Hawaiians on December 11, 1975.

438

Before I knew it I was doing my pregame ritual of running laps. It was a reasonably sunny day, but it was still December. The temperature that day was reported to have reached a high of 34 and it wasn't quite that warm yet. Unlike my ritual in Honolulu where I ran with gym shorts and an LA Dodger T-shirt and cap, I was wearing my game pants although I did hold out for my Dodger shirt. Underneath the T-shirt I was once again wearing thermals that I would also wear under my game jersey.

The bleachers were empty. Later they would be filled with ravenous Brown fans who resented the notion that a team from the tropics came determined to knock the hometown team out of the playoff picture. I wanted every one of those fans to go home disappointed. That would be Hawaii's Christmas present to Cleveland.

In the locker room I prepared for the pregame warmup. I took off my game pants and put on the shoulder pads and game jersey for the final time in the Bicentennial year. I put a pair of stirrup socks over the white socks I was wearing, then put a second pair of white socks over the stirrup socks. After that I slipped into my girdle pads and pulled my game pants on.

Of course I continued another pregame tradition by visiting the urinal every five minutes or so. Hoddesson, as usual, read from *The Book of Mormon*. Jurgens sat with his eyes closed, ostensibly in silent prayer since he crossed himself periodically. Others went through their own religious and secular rituals.

I lit a cigarette. Years later with nicotine eradicated for several years, I shake my head in disbelief that I ever found enjoyment in such a deadly habit. Smoking cigarettes seemed innocuous and natural at the time. Now I pity those who feel as I once did.

But, of course, this is the way it was in 1976. Several teammates and coaches were smokers. I sat on the stool in front of my locker and puffed away. Those who didn't smoke had to live with it since there were very few laws that protected the nonsmoker from second-hand smoke. Since smoking was still fairly commonplace they were probably used to being around smokers.

The absolute last game of the season. No matter what, we wouldn't be watching game films on Tuesday. The entire team could screw up so badly that we could create new definitions for ineptitude and Walker would not be able to chastise anybody two days later.

Of course I still wanted to play well and I wanted to win. I was hoping that everybody on the team felt that way. We could ensure that the Browns also wouldn't be watching game films two or three days later.

As the time approached to take the field for the official pregame warmup, I put on my cleats and grabbed my helmet. I felt great. There were a few butterflies but that wasn't unusual. Dating back to high school, I never began a game devoid of pregame jitters. If I ever began a game without pregame butterflies I would probably believe I hadn't properly prepared.

Back in the locker room we took care of last-minute details. Hoddesson led us in *The Lord's Prayer*. Walker then addressed the team.

"All right, men. It has been a pretty good season for us when considering the fact that this is an expansion team. You've played hard and well all season, even in most of the games that you didn't win."

Walker paused and slowly turned a 360. He attempted to look each player and coach directly in the eye as we stood or sat around the perimeter of the room.

"Sizing ourselves up against the other expansion teams, Memphis has won two games, Seattle has won two and Tampa Bay. . . . Well, I hope for their sake that they can end the season with their first victory although they will have their hands full with the Patriots. I would definitely hate to go through what John McKay's going through. I know that the Bucs are a better team than that."

Walker paused again. For a moment he looked directly at me as if he was going to address me specifically. I was sitting on a stool in front of my locker and waited before he looked at a few other teammates and continued.

"There is no tomorrow for us as far as 1976 goes. We play one final game and go home. With the exception of Marv Nelson who will be going to the Pro Bowl, any further involvement you'll have with pro football this season will mean that you'll either watch it on television or buy a ticket to a game. You've had a pretty good season but this is as far as you go."

Walker hesitated. He seemed to be looking up. He took a deep breath and continued.

"Six victories is outstanding for an expansion team. I am personally not satisfied with it since I would much rather have done well enough to make the playoffs but it still isn't bad. Those six victories you've racked up are two or three times more than what anybody expected. What I want to know is, shall we go out for the next few hours and go through the motions while watching the clock tick down and being content with those six victories? Or shall we go out there and play hard, smart football the way I know you can and see if you can run your victory total up to seven? What's it going to be?"

There was a momentary silence but one could literally feel the spirit in the locker room gradually build. Marv finally stood up.

"I want seven!" he shouted.

"I want seven!" Allen concurred.

"I want seven!" chimed in Jablonski.

The next thing I knew, every player and coach was clapping and chanting in unison.

440

"Seven! Seven! Seven! Seven! Seven! Seven! Seven! Seven! Seven! Seven! Seven! Seven! Seven . . . !"

It was unlike anything we'd experienced all season long. We played well throughout the majority of the season because we gelled so well as a unit. Never were we as cohesive as we were going into our final game of 1976. If our spirit was indicative of the kind of day we were going to have, the Browns were in, as we say in Hawaii, "deep kim chee."

"All right!" Walker intervened brightly, obviously very pleased with the collective attitude of the team. "Let's not stand here and talk about it! Let's go out and do it!"

Out of the locker room we went with a collective roar, through the tunnel and up the steps of the baseball dugout to the field. As I ran to the sideline with my teammates, excluding the starting defensive unit, which hung by the dugout for individual introductions, I was so pumped that I swore my feet never touched the ground. Our record may have been mediocre but I believed that Lombardi's Green Bay Packers in their prime would have no chance of beating us on this day.

Our defensive players were introduced amid a loud chorus of boos and then Cleveland's offensive lineup was introduced amid raucous cheers. All the while we ignored the crowd by milling about the sideline. We pumped each other up by smacking shoulder pads, slapping helmets, shaking hands and simply giving verbal encouragement.

Marv grabbed my helmet by the facemask. He shook it hard enough to get my attention but not so hard that he snapped my neck out of place.

"Let's do it, Jaybird! Let's do it, my man!"

"I'm up for that!" I replied enthusiastically as I slapped the side of his helmet.

The *National Anthem* was played and then our four captains joined Cleveland's captains at midfield. The coin was tossed and Cleveland won, choosing to receive.

Like our season opener at home, I was disappointed that I wouldn't be on the field for the opening kickoff. Unlike the season opener, I didn't allow it to affect my patience. I reminded myself that I would get my licks in soon enough.

As I stood on the sideline and waited for NBC to give its blessing to start the game, I looked around the stadium. There was a very enthusiastic crowd on hand bundled up in winter clothing. Heavy jackets and wool caps were virtually everywhere. As I took note of the long sleeves of my thermals protruding beyond the limits of my white game jersey, I reminded myself for the nth time that this was not Aloha Stadium.

It was Municipal Stadium, the home of the Cleveland Indians and Cleveland Browns. At one time it had also been the home of the Cleveland Rams until these same Browns, then of the AAFC, stole their thunder and forced the Rams to expatriate themselves to Los Angeles.

The facility had been home to some outstanding football teams in its history. It had also been home to some outstanding baseball teams although it hadn't hosted a postseason baseball game since 1954.

That was the World Series which is best remembered for a sparkling catch Willie Mays made during a game at the Polo Grounds in New York but two of the games were played in Cleveland on the very field where I stood. The New York Giants swept the Indians in that series despite the presence of Indian greats such as Bob Feller and Bob Lemon. I was hoping to do for the Browns that day what the Giants did for the Indians in 1954.

The Browns started fast, raising their fans' excitement level a couple of notches. They took the opening kickoff from the one to their own 26 for a reasonably good return. That was followed by a rush up the middle to the 33 and then a pass which gave them a first down at the Hawaii 48.

"They're up for this one," Dietrich remarked as he sat next to me on the bench.

"They sure are," I replied, showing my flare for the obvious that would not qualify me to be a Rhodes Scholar.

The Browns stayed on the ground for a few plays. They went off left tackle to the 43 to give them a second and five. That was followed by a sweep around left end which picked up four more yards. On the next play they went up the middle but managed only a single yard.

Whistles blew and the officials signaled for a time out. The chain was brought out to measure.

I happened to notice Walker who stood adjacent to where the ball was being measured. He stood bent over with his hands on his knees as the measurement was made.

"That's short! That's short!" he bellowed before the chain was even stretched out.

It turned out that Walker was right. The Browns were short by a few inches. Their options included trying a field goal which would have been about 55 yards. They could also try a short punt to force us to start our first drive with our backs to the end zone. They could also try to pick up the first down.

The crowd didn't hesitate to let the Browns know what they wanted.

"Go! Go! Go! Go! Go! Go! Go! Go!"

The crowd chant probably had nothing to do with the ultimate decision but the Browns did go for it.

"Let's go, defense! Let's hold 'em!" I called as I rose from my seat. I was determined to take the field after only one more play.

It was another rush up the middle. The ball carrier seemed to be stopped at the line. Allen seemed to get a good grip on him although he was also being blocked.

The ball carrier suddenly slipped away enough to lunge forward for a gain of one yard. The Browns had their first down.

I felt let down. I also knew that this was part of the game. The Browns didn't become playoff contenders by routinely choking on these short yardage situations. They had it in them to get the first down and they obviously did.

Our defense dug in. Following an incompletion and a rush of only two yards, the Browns approached the line on third and eight at the 35. It was most likely going to be a pass although we will never know. The right tackle jumped and yellow flags flew up. The Browns suddenly had third and 13 at the 40.

We were in a nickel defense with Hasegawa inserted as the extra defensive back. Originally we were in our 33 nickel formation but after the penalty Walker decided to switch to the 24 nickel, meaning two down linemen and four linebackers.

"Hukilau! Hukilau!" I could hear among the Hawaiian defenders. That suggested that a blitz was possible and I was pretty sure that it was. Allen did his thing by chugging in place while he awaited the snap of the ball. Ed was in his customary stance whenever it was possible that he would be blitzing, leaning forward with his right leg planted behind him almost as if he had his own starting block.

"Man, this is gonna be good," I said to Hoddesson. I was standing again and anticipating the Browns' quarterback lying under a barrage of white jerseys.

The blitz was on. It wasn't Allen or Jennings. It was Hasegawa. Rich was quick but the quarterback was good at scrambling. He got away and managed to get to the 36 before being hit hard and dropped near our sideline by Black who had returned to the starting lineup after an injury had limited his playing time against Cincinnati.

Walker looked slightly exasperated although I think he realized that the four-yard gain was the result of good play on their part, not poor play on our part. Rich had gotten through quickly but the quarterback was also quick. Their receivers were covered so the quarterback had no choice but to scramble.

They still hadn't come even close to a first down. On fourth and nine it appeared that the Browns were forced to try a field goal. Had Hasegawa been able to drop the quarterback for a sack they probably would have been forced to punt.

The Browns' field goal unit lined up. The snap was down and the kick was up. The ball seemed to barely have the distance but it was on target. We were down by a field goal with 10:03 left in the first quarter.

"All right! All right! No harm done!" Walker called. "Let's have a good return and then take it in for seven!"

I ran to my post on the goal line. I looked at Hasegawa and smiled as we slapped fives. He did not look happy.

"I should have had that (expletive deleted) quarterback," he muttered.

"He was too quick," I said. "Don't worry about it. We'll get it all back right now."

We were teammates. Good teammates work together and try to keep each other from getting down. Had I not come through with a play I know that Rich would have tried to boost my spirits. Our bond was even stronger since we had also played college football together and been teammates with the WFL Hawaiians.

The kick was up and headed in Rich's direction. He backpedaled a few steps and caught the ball about six yards deep in the end zone. I looked upfield and saw enough of a charge to tell me it wouldn't be wise for Rich to try a return.

"Down it! Down it!" I called out.

Rich didn't hear me above the roar of the crowd. He still knew exactly what to do. He dropped to one knee to give us a first down at the 20.

We began the drive in very determined fashion. Bender hit Dietrich with a bullet at the 31. Ted was hit and dropped immediately but he had still picked up a first down.

Grummon then ran a short slant. Bender hit him at the 34. The tight end from Syracuse managed to fight for four more yards to give us a second down at the Hawaii 38.

"All right! We're moving! We're moving!" I remarked enthusiastically as the huddle formed.

"Yeah, we're moving all right," Marv concurred. "Let's keep it up, guys."

Scott got his first carry of the day and didn't waste it. A sweep around right end got outstanding blocking. Larry got all the way to the 44 before a pair of Browns knocked him down. It was our second first down of the drive.

Unfortunately it was our last first down of the drive as well. The Brown defense was suddenly relentless. Before I knew it I was running off the field. It was fourth and eleven at our own 43.

I guess I looked angry as I stood on the sideline and watched as I awaited Jablonski's punt. Clint seemed to notice it as he headed in my direction.

"It's all right, man," he said assuredly. "We're gonna be all right."

I had no retort for that. All I could do was shake my head. I probably wanted this game worse than any game we'd played all season. A victory could speak volumes about my teammates and me. In some ways it would even mean more than our victory in Oakland.

Jablonski did his job. He got off a booming punt that was fielded at the Cleveland 14. The Cleveland punt returner seemed unimpressed with the 43-yard distance and decided to return it.

444

It was a fairly good return, much to my chagrin. The return man avoided Hamer's determined charge. He got as far as the 28 before a pair of University of Hawaii alums, Kupau and Hasegawa, teamed up to bring him down.

The Browns picked up one first down but had little success aside from that. They wound up with a fourth and four at the Hawaii 45. A field goal attempt seemed unlikely since it would have been about 62 yards. They sent their punting unit to the field.

"Obviously they want to pin us back," Walker told me as I prepared to head to my post. "Don't be a fool but don't make it easy on them. If you have a shot at making a good return, go for it."

I stood on the ten-yard line. I thought about my options. It appeared likely that they would try to get the punt past me and down it near the goal line. That's what I had to try to prevent.

The punter went for the sideline to my left. It had a good hang time which enabled their coverage men to get downfield. That also enabled me to see where the ball was likely to touch down. It would still be a few yards inside the playing field but then it would probably bounce toward the sideline. In all probability it would bounce out of bounds inside the five.

I raised my hand to signal a fair catch. I caught the ball cleanly with two Brown defenders nearby. It was a moral victory for us, I guess, since I probably prevented the ball from bouncing out of bounds closer to the end zone. We still had a long way to go since I caught the ball on the eight.

"We've got a long way to go," Bender observed in an obvious understatement as we huddled up in the end zone, "but we've got plenty of time to get there."

Initially it didn't seem to matter how long we had since we didn't seem to be going anywhere in particular. Scott and Kerner both carried for gains of one yard to give us a third and eight.

After that we started to move. Bender hit me with a slightly errant pass. I had to leap up and pull it down near the right sideline. As I came down I was hit and dropped at the Hawaii 28 to give us a first down.

Our ground game continued to struggle. Scott went off left tackle and was dropped a yard behind the line. I had a little more success through the same hole since I managed to pick up three yards to the 30. Once again we were facing a third and eight.

The Browns knew that a pass was coming. I am reasonably sure that everybody in the stadium knew that a pass was coming as well as everybody following the game on TV and radio.

Bender was rushed and had to scramble. He found Slater open at the Cleveland 48 and managed to get the pass off to him just as he was being hit by a linebacker. Slater picked up seven more yards to the 41 to give us our best field position of the day to this point.

That was the final play of the first quarter. I hadn't even been paying attention to the clock. As I was congratulating Slater on making such a good play I noticed that the officials were changing directions.

"Wow, that was a fast quarter," I remarked to Slater.

I was in good spirits. I sensed that we were rising to the occasion. Since this was a Saturday game it was even one shown to the entire country instead of to only a select few regional markets. Football fans all over America were once again getting a glimpse of how well this mere expansion team from Hawaii could play football. If the Oakland upset didn't convince them, this one should.

Of course we still had a goose egg on the scoreboard and trailed by a field goal. The upset hadn't happened yet.

But we were on the move.

And we continued to move from the beginning of the second quarter. Bender hit Dietrich at the 29 near the right sideline. Ted spun for two more yards to give us another first down at the 27.

"All right! That's the way to play it!" I exclaimed as I headed to where we would huddle. This time I didn't bother trying to keep my voice down. I figured that the Browns would know that we would be cheering each other on when things were going well. That's exactly what they were doing when things were going their way.

Bender tried to hit Grummon near the ten but the pass was offline. Scott then ran a sweep around left end and managed to pick up three yards. We had third and seven at the 24.

It was another probable pass situation. Dietrich was wide to the right. I was wide to the left although a yard behind the line of scrimmage. This left Grummon as an eligible receiver since he was tight on the left.

I was covered but still managed to gain a step on my defender. Bender spotted me near the left hash mark and unleashed a pass before sidestepping a rusher. I caught the ball at the six and was hit but managed to squirm away. I was hit again at about the two but lunged forward and crossed the goal line on the fly. It was a great way to climax a 92-yard drive.

"Yeah, Jay! Way to go! Way to go!"

Those words came from Dietrich. He came over and helped me up and ran with me to the sideline.

"Great job, Jay! Fantastic!" Walker complimented, showing one of his broad smiles.

Of course it felt good. I accepted the congratulatory pats and handshakes from my teammates and took note of how quiet the crowd was.

Just the same, there was a long way to go. The extra point gave us a 7-3 lead but there was still 13:36 left in the first half.

The Browns put together a drive that produced a couple of first downs. When they got near midfield our defense dug in. On third and seven at the

Hawaii 42 Richards and Prendergast reached the quarterback. They sacked him at the Cleveland 47, giving them a fourth and 18.

Obviously the Browns set up to punt. I fielded the punt at the 15 without even considering the possibility of a fair catch. My mind was made up that I was going to make something happen and I did have a decent return. I was hit at about the 18 but still managed to keep my feet. I zigzagged around defenders in brown jerseys to the 26 before I was finally dragged down.

Of course I wanted to take it all the way in and was somewhat disappointed. Just the same, an eleven-yard punt return is fairly good. Eleven yards on a kick return is considered atrocious but it is above average on a punt return.

Unfortunately my punt return was pretty much the highlight of our subsequent drive. A six-yard sack and a delay of game penalty gave us a second and 21 at our own 15. We managed to get as far as the 31 over the next couple of plays but that was still five yards short of what we needed for the first down. Jablonski came on and did his thing, punting to the 28 with no return.

"You guys have to get back on track," Tipton told the offense as we sat in a group on the bench. "That sack on the opening play killed your momentum. You guys on the line have got to do a better job of protecting the quarterback. You receivers have to find a way to get open sooner. That one touchdown we've got is not going to win this game for us. I guarantee it."

Tipton tried not to show it but he was very upset with the line. Although Bender was only sacked once on the previous series, he was under heavy pressure on the subsequent two plays prior to getting the passes off. In both cases he couldn't find his primary receivers so he had to go underneath to Kerner and Scott.

By the time Tipton finished talking we noticed that the Browns were on the move again. They had a second and five at the Hawaii 39 when I was able to resume focusing on what was happening on the field. A sweep around left end picked up ten yards to give them a first down at the 29.

"Geez, we've got to stop these guys," Hoddesson muttered from where he stood next to me.

"We've also got to move the football," Marv pointed out. "Even if we don't always score, we've got to move the ball. Otherwise the defense won't get any time to rest."

A pass near the sideline was caught at the eight. Morrissey hit the receiver immediately but he held on to the ball. It was first and goal.

The Browns were in the so-called *red zone*. The Hawaii defense rose to the occasion. A rush up the middle got the Browns only one yard. Richards then foiled what appeared to be a sweep when he tackled the ball carrier in the backfield, giving the Browns a third and goal at the nine. That was

447

followed by an incomplete pass that was highlighted by a heavy rush from Zanakis.

"All right! All right!" I exclaimed, certain that we had prevented a touchdown. I hadn't felt this giddy since our opening game.

The Browns' field goal unit ran on the field. Although I preferred that the Browns not pick up any points, I was willing to concede the field goal that wasn't expected to be especially difficult. We would still have the lead.

As expected, the Browns converted on the field goal. We held a 7-6 lead. We had a little extra time to prepare for our offensive series since we were at the two-minute warning.

"We've got plenty of time to put together another score before the half," Tipton reminded us. "They know what's coming but we can do it if we execute. We're just going to focus on those short sideline passes to try to get to at least field goal range. We've also got two time-outs that we can use. Just play it smart and we'll be okay."

I took my place on the goal line with Hasegawa. Neither of us said anything but we looked at each other with expressions that told me we were thinking identical thoughts. We were both determined to have a solid return that would start our drive in good, if not excellent, field position.

Perhaps the Cleveland kicker read our thoughts. He kicked a low line drive. The ball hit the ground near the 20 and continued moving in our direction.

I charged forward and fielded the ball at the nine. Since I fielded the ball on the run I had to be careful to not fumble. Fortunately the ball took a hop that came up to my belt buckle and I was able to get a firm grip on the ball.

It wasn't until I got to the 31 that I was hit. Fielding the ball on the run gave me a flying start. I was determined not to go down and ran a slightly erratic pattern before I was hit while still keeping my feet. A second Brown charged into me before I finally went down.

I wasn't sure of how far I'd gotten. As I bounced up I noticed where they were spotting the ball. I was satisfied that I had put together a reasonably good return. We had 1:52 to travel 69 yards.

As Tipton told us a few minutes earlier, the Browns were going to know what was coming. It was up to us to execute.

I was the intended receiver on the first play. I ran a flare toward the right sideline. The ball was heading my way but a Brown defensive back jumped in and picked the ball off at the 36. I hit him immediately and got him down at the 34. All of a sudden our hopes to pad our lead were dashed by an excellent opportunity for the Browns to take the lead.

Of course the crowd was jacked up over that. There was a thunderous roar washing over the field. The Browns were still trailing but they had 1:45 to travel a mere 102 feet. Even a field goal could send them to the locker room with a halftime lead.

"What happened?" Tipton asked me on the sideline.

"What happened? What happened was that he cut in front of me," I replied, angry over the circumstance but not that Tipton asked me the question even though it should have been very obvious to him what had happened.

"You've got to get that ball," Tipton said, apparently chastising me for the interception.

"Come on, man," I answered, starting to get excited and a little angry at Tipton. "There was no way that I could have prevented that. The best I could do was tackle him to prevent a long runback. I was looking at the ball. I didn't see him coming ov. . . ."

"It was my fault," I heard from my right. I turned to look and saw that Bender was joining in the conversation. "Jay ran the right pattern. I just didn't throw it hard enough. That enabled the defensive back to have time to step in and pick it off."

Tipton looked at me and then at Bender. He appeared to be at a loss for words. He shook his head and moved away.

"You didn't have to do that," I said to Bender.

"Why not? It was the truth. I didn't have a very tight grip on the ball. That slowed the ball down and enabled the defensive back to pick it off."

"Well, maybe," I said. "Whatever the reason, we lost the ball and an opportunity to score."

Steve nodded as we both moved over to the Gatorade table. Few people had more integrity than Steve. I never knew of him to make lame excuses or shift the blame to where it didn't belong. Whenever he was at fault, he took his medicine.

The Browns had run one play by this time. They had rushed off right tackle and picked up seven yards to the 27. They called time out with 1:37 left in the half.

"That might not have been a smart move on their part," Bender remarked. "If they use up their time-outs and don't score they'll enable us to take over with time left on the clock."

Of course we were hoping for that. We also hoped that they wouldn't gain any more ground. The more ground they gained, the easier a field goal would be for them.

The Browns picked up two yards on each of the next two plays. That gave them a first down at the 20. We called time out with 58 seconds left in the half.

Between plays the crowd continued to be raucous. They toned down as the Browns broke out of their huddles but roared otherwise. The fact that this was the first of two steps toward getting the Browns into the playoffs was not lost on them.

Allen briefly dashed the Browns' playoff hopes on the next play. He clobbered the ball carrier up the middle at the 17.

"Fumble!" several of us hollered in unison. The ball popped out of the ball carrier's hands when Russ hit him and shot up in the air. There was suddenly a mad scramble for the ball although only a few members from each team seemed to know that there was a live ball rolling on the ground.

It wasn't as dramatic as it seemed. The massive cardiac arrest among the Cleveland faithful seemed to be a false alarm. After a few seconds the officials indicated that the Browns still had the ball. They hurried to line up on the ball as the clock started back up with 47 seconds left in the half.

An incomplete pass stopped the clock with 38 seconds. It was third and seven. If we could hold them for one more play the Browns would probably run the clock down to the final few seconds before using another time out and calling on their field goal unit.

Of course the Browns preferred a touchdown. The quarterback took the snap and rolled to his left. He was under a slight rush but nothing menacing. He fired the ball toward the end zone where a slightly open receiver was positioned in the center a couple of yards forward of the back line.

Touchdown!

"Oh, geez," I muttered, looking down at the ground. A sick feeling washed over me.

We no longer had the lead. The touchdown gave the Browns a 12-7 lead. The extra point extended the lead to 13-7.

"Yeah, you bums may have gotten lucky in Cincinnati the other day but here in Cleveland you have to play against a *real* football team!" I heard one raucous fan remark among the general cheering that was taking place.

Hasegawa and I took our usual places on the goal line. Neither of us seemed to be in high spirits. I looked at the scoreboard and noticed the clock. There were only 29 seconds left.

"We've got to try to run it all the way back," I told Rich. "We should at least try to get past midfield. If we can do that we can at least try to kick a field goal. If we stay on this side of the field Bender's just going to drop to one knee and that'll be it."

"Yeah, I know man," Rich agreed wearily. "We've got to run it back no matter what."

The kick was high and headed Rich's way. He fielded the ball four yards deep in the end zone.

I ran up to head off the first brown jersey I saw. Rich bobbled the ball slightly and then ran forward, getting only as far as the nine.

There were 23 seconds left. Bender and the rest of the offense ran on the field. Bender took a snap, dropped to one knee and that wound up being the final play of the first half. I looked at the scoreboard as the final seconds ticked away. We were still losing 13-7.

"This doesn't look like the same bunch that was psyched up before the game," Walker angrily remarked at halftime. "You men are blowing it. You've had opportunities but you're not making the most of them."

"This is a big opportunity for you. It's one final chance to make a really impressive name for yourselves. There's 30 minutes left of the season for us and I don't want to waste a single second of it."

Walker drew into his cigarette and looked around the room before continuing.

"You're got six victories. That's not good enough. If we finish with only six victories it means we finish with a losing record. Seven gets us to the break-even mark and will force people to notice us. I personally am not willing to settle for six victories."

Walker continued his spiel until it was time to return to the field. Instead of the offensive and defensive units meeting in their respective groups to plan the second half, we were told to empty our bladders and sit in front of our lockers so that Walker could give us one final dressing down for 1976.

"You're on the wrong end of the scoreboard," Walker continued, exhaling a plume of smoke as he spoke. "You can't let it end this way. You're too good of a team for that with too much self-respect."

An official poked his head in and held up two fingers. Walker nodded and gave a thumb's up.

"All right. Let's go," he said, leading us to take the last drags off of our cigarettes, gulp the last of our Gatorade and file out. A few of the guys ran to the urinals for one final opportunity for relief.

I was extremely anxious to resume play and do whatever it was that we had to do to win. We may have been trailing but we were far from out of this game.

For whatever it was worth, we found out later that Scott was approaching a significant milestone at halftime. He was a mere one-yard shy of 1,000 rushing yards on the season. Nobody was aware of it at the time and at the time nobody really cared. He was virtually guaranteed to achieve the milestone. It would be tainted if the milestone didn't come with a victory.

Hasegawa started the second half by fielding the kick a yard deep in the end zone. When it was clearly going to be his return I shot forward in search of an enemy brown jersey. I found one at about the 15 and threw myself into him. Somehow I managed to keep my feet and stay with him, forcing him toward the sideline while Rich ran past.

By the time the enemy defender broke free it was too late. Having finally gone down when the defender broke away, I rose to my knees and looked upfield. Rich was in the grasps of a pair of Browns and going down but he had already reached the 28.

It was a good runback. The field position wasn't great but it wasn't bad. Feeling extremely good about the block I had thrown, I was confident that we would have little trouble covering the 72 yards we needed for the score.

Scott went up the middle for two of those yards. That obviously gave us a second and eight. It also gave him 1,001 rushing yards on the season. They announced it over the PA system although none of us on the field noticed it. We were too busy trying to win a football game.

Dietrich slanted in and caught a quick pass at the 34. He managed to sidestep a defender and get all the way to the Hawaii 40. That gave us a first down.

Scott went up the middle again and had a much better result than his previous carry. He gutted his way to the 47. We were on the move and that was great. We were playing like the quality team we knew we were.

A 4 kama'aina left was called. That meant that I would be running a sweep around left end. A couple of Browns got into the backfield but I managed to run away from them. Following my convoy of blockers, I passed midfield and got to the Cleveland 45 before a defensive back managed to charge in from my right. It was a pretty hard tackle but I felt no ill effects.

"Good job, Jay," Scott complimented as he reached down to help me up.

"Thanks but I owe most of it to those three Sherman tanks running interference for me," I replied as we headed toward our huddle. I was referring to Marv, Stanek and Kerner who led the way around left end. One by one they knocked defenders out of the play. It wasn't until I was completely alone that I was finally brought down.

"Okay, we're looking good," Bender remarked before calling the next play. We were going back to the air. Thus far in the early moments of the second half we were having success with both our air and ground attacks. That gave us more freedom to mix things up.

Slater was the recipient of Bender's pass. He caught the ball at the 31 on a post. It was a pretty good pass although Joe had to slow up a little to keep from overrunning the ball. That enabled the defensive back covering him to hit him as soon as he made the reception. Slater went down immediately but held on to the ball. It was another first down for us, this time at the Cleveland 31.

Bender's next pass wasn't quite on the mark. I made the reception but had to dive for it. I caught the ball at about the 12 while parallel to the ground. Since I had been running at an angle I still managed to slide forward to the ten before a Brown defensive back wound up on top of me. He did so cleanly, simply falling on top of me to make sure that I didn't attempt to get up and run.

I felt pretty impressed with myself. Unfortunately it was all in vain. We were penalized for illegal motion, nullifying my brilliant effort. We found ourselves having a first and 15 at the 36.

452

The next play killed the drive. Going to the air again, Bender aimed for Grummon. It wasn't a bad pass but it was indicative of what can happen if a defensive back makes a good play. The defensive back reached in as Grummon was in the process of catching the ball. He swatted the ball up in the air and made the interception at the 24, running up four yards before being hit and dropped by Kerner.

I was cognizant of the crowd as I ran off the field in frustration. Needless to say, the fans were cheering pretty loud. It had been a fairly quiet second half as far as crowd noise went until this point. One play changed the ambience and switched the momentum.

At least Walker was quiet. He looked very confused. I think he wanted to say something but wasn't sure of what to say. We had had a fairly impressive drive and he may have wanted to touch on that point. He probably also wanted to be critical but didn't want to discourage us.

I was extremely downtrodden. I realized that the Browns' playoff hopes hinged on this game. Although we were not going to the playoffs, I felt that there was more at stake for us for some reason. It somehow seemed more imperative that we end the season with a victory than for the Browns to go to sleep knowing they were still in the playoff hunt. This game was, at least in a sense, our Super Bowl.

There was 11:03 left in the third quarter. That meant 26:03 left in the 1976 season for us. We were hoping that would also be all that the Browns had left. We knew that it might work out that way for them even if they beat us but we wanted to dash their hopes for the postseason ourselves.

The interception gave the Browns new life. The roar of the crowd told us they were fired up and we were in big trouble. They were moving the ball and had momentum. I tried to accept the notion of a losing season where we actually won twice as many games as an expansion team has the right to expect but I wasn't going to concede that unless it became official.

As I sat on the bench and sipped my Gatorade I looked at my pants. The field was in pretty good shape and wasn't wet, so my uniform still looked fairly white to those who didn't see me up close. I could see subtle grass stains and some areas of dirt on my pants and the part of my jersey that I could see. It would be the last time that I would see this on myself for a little while. I wanted it to be memorable for all the right reasons.

Before I knew it the Browns had a first down at the Hawaii 28. A score would obviously be difficult on us. There was still plenty of time but even a field goal would force us to have to score twice if we wanted to win this game. We had it in us to do it. They had it in them to stop us.

A rush up the middle got the Browns to the 23. They went to the air on the next play.

This turned into one of Rodgers' finer moments. He had a receiver fairly well covered inside the ten. When the pass reached the receiver at about the five Carl batted the ball away. His momentum enabled him to follow the general path of the ball which was still in the air. He stumbled forward and went down, then managed to get his hand on the ball just before it hit the ground.

Unfortunately he wasn't able to get his other hand on the ball. The ball bounced off of one hand and hit the ground before Carl could grab it. The play was listed simply as an incomplete pass.

I was sick for Carl. From my position on the sideline near midfield I wasn't able to see the play clearly but I had a pretty good idea of what had transpired. As a two-way player in high school I had had my share of interceptions but there were also a few interceptions I thought I should have had but didn't. Carl's effort was enormous. I thought he deserved a better fate.

At least the crowd was happy. Too bad it was somebody else's crowd.

The Browns went back to the ground on third down. Going off left tackle, they got as far as the 19. That gave them a fourth and one. It was decision time.

It would have been prudent of the Browns to go for the field goal. Succeeding in that, their lead would expand to 16-7. It wasn't an insurmountable lead, especially since we were only about halfway through the third quarter. It still would force us up a steeper hill since we would need two scores if they succeeded.

Those in the crowd did not seem to be thinking prudently. Either that or they knew we were capable of putting together a touchdown and field goal that would give us the lead if the Browns didn't score the rest of the way.

"Go! Go! Go! Go! Go! Go! Go! Go! Go! Go!"

And so they went for it. I couldn't believe it. Neither did some of my teammates and our coaches on the sideline.

"They're out of their minds," remarked Randy Hubert.

There were a few other remarks. It is interesting to note how rationally we were thinking on the sideline. If our offense was on the field in a similar situation, we would have been very upset if our field goal unit ran out. The Browns were doing exactly what we would have wanted to do in that situation. From our vantage point on the sideline the Browns were certifiably insane.

Of course our disparaging thoughts and remarks would have been utterly meaningless if the Browns managed to get the yard they needed for the first down. We fervently hoped our defense would justify our remarks.

Those of us on the sideline were all standing as the Browns got set. We all stood near the 30 which was the demarcation line for us. We might never have recovered had the Browns got the first down because we were penalized for having players too far down the sideline so we were careful about that. That would have been one of the most inexcusable penalties in the history of the NFL.

454

We were all yelling from the sideline as the Browns got ready to snap the ball. We tried to give our defense whatever encouragement we could during this very critical play.

The snap was made. Then came the handoff. The Browns were trying to go around left end, running a sweep with pulling guards.

Jurgens was waiting. He fought off a block and shot into the backfield. He brought the ball carrier down at the 20, forcing him to lose a yard.

"All right!" I exclaimed, jumping up in the process. We were all cheering on the sideline for a few seconds before those of us with the offensive unit headed to the field.

There was a multitude of enthusiastic exchanges as the offense crossed paths with the defense. What nobody seemed to notice right away was that we had an injured player on the field near the line of scrimmage. Zanakis was having trouble getting up.

Time was already out but the injury caused a little more of a delay. As selfish as it seems, I was almost annoyed with our rookie linebacker out of Washington State for being injured at this point. The mindset of a football player can often be very enigmatic. We were fired up to move the ball and I was afraid that the delay for the injury would douse some of our fire.

Zanakis was able to leave the field under his own power. He did so with polite applause ringing the stadium. It was time to get down to business.

It wasn't Kevin's fault that we didn't do anything with the ball once we had it. Two incompletions were sandwiched around a three-yard rush. In no time at all I found myself running off the field in frustration as Jablonski and the rest of the punting unit ran on.

"Men, you've got to move the ball if you want to win this game," Tipton said as we reached the sideline.

I glared at Tipton and walked past him to don my parka and head to the Gatorade table. I was already upset about our inability to move the ball, if not blatantly angry, and that can sometimes bring out the worst in me. I still recall the temptation to sarcastically ask him if that was the kind of logic they taught at SMU or if he managed to pick up such a profound observation elsewhere. Fortunately I held my tongue.

At least the Browns seemed to subscribe to Tipton's game plan. They were moving the ball. Although they started the drive off inauspiciously with a delay of game penalty, they moved the ball at a steady clip. Before long they were measuring for a first down at the Hawaii 39.

The measurement proved the Browns short but they picked up two yards on the next play to give them a first down. That was followed by a five-yard rush which was followed by an illegal procedure penalty against them. That moved the Browns back to the 37 to give them a second and ten.

They went to the air. A Cleveland receiver made the reception inside the 25. He tried to race around Rodgers but was brought down by Rodgers with assistance from Black.

The Browns still had a first down at the Hawaii 21. I suspected that if they wound up in a fourth down situation again they would go for the field goal this time.

Blakely rose to the occasion before the Browns could even consider a field goal. On first down he made an off-balance interception at the eight near the right sideline. His momentum carried him out of bounds to prevent him from advancing. It didn't matter since we had a first down at our own eight with four seconds left in the third quarter.

"Let's move that ball, offense," Walker directed as the offensive unit started heading for the field. "Let's put seven big ones on that scoreboard. We've gone long enough without scoring."

"No kidding," I muttered under my breath only loud enough for me to hear. We hadn't put up a single point in the second half. That just didn't seem right.

As I joined my teammates in the huddle I figured we at least owed it to the defense to put something on the board. Although the defense had surrendered two sustained drives, it came through when we needed it to the most. We rewarded their initial effort with a three and out. I was hoping for something much better this time.

It only took one play to outdo our previous series. Scott went off right tackle and picked up seven yards.

That play also ended the third quarter. Dutifully we strolled to the other end of the field. Bender went to the sideline to converse with Walker, the Cleveland defensive captain went to his sideline to converse with his coach and NBC made money by showing commercials.

"This is it," I mentioned to Marv as we headed toward the opposite end of the field. "We have 15 minutes left in the season."

"Yeah," he replied reflectively. "Unless we take it into overtime."

Overtime was a reasonable possibility. If all we managed were two field goals and the Browns didn't score at all we would wind up in overtime. That would extend our season to a maximum of 15 extra minutes.

"Let's win it in regulation," I suggested, keeping my voice down to prevent any of our opponents from hearing me and having extra fuel in their fire.

"Good idea," Kerner agreed lightly. "It's (expletive deleted) cold out here."

Kerner was unofficially the designated comedian of the offense. Although his remark wasn't especially clever, and probably not even original, it loosened us up a bit. Some of us laughed lightly at the remark, leading the Cleveland defense to look our way with quizzical looks on their faces.

This was going to be it. Counting the six preseason games, we had played for 19 hours, 45 minutes. Barring overtime, we were down to the final 15 minutes. For all I knew it could have been the last 15 minutes of my career. Although I was coming to the end of a very productive season, there were no guarantees that I would be on the roster for 1977's opening kickoff. A lot could happen between now and then.

At the time I was not thinking about my chances for 1977. There was still a formidable hurdle to climb to close out the final 15 minutes of 1976. It was very important that we find a way to pull the game out. Although the difference would have been only one victory, a mediocre break-even mark would make a substantially stronger statement than if we settled for a losing record.

The Brown defense seemed rejuvenated after the break. They came out charging on the opening play. Bender dropped back to pass and found himself having to scramble. He somehow managed to pick up a yard to the 16 before being hammered. Bender bounced right up.

Perhaps Kerner was thinking revenge over the way Bender was hit even though the shot Bender took was totally clean. Whatever the case, he went off right tackle and seemed determined not to be brought down. He fought off a tackle at the line, then picked up a few more yards and broke another tackle. He got all the way to the 28 before he finally went down.

"That ought to start shutting those (expletive deleted) fans up," Grummon remarked as we started forming a huddle.

I sensed that we were regaining the momentum. A pair of carries by Scott strengthened that belief. The two plays combined for a dozen yards to give us another first down at the 40.

"All right," said Bender as he got set to call another play. "We're not going to screw it up this time."

Of course the Browns weren't laying down for us. They may even have been somehow tipped off that Bender was going to pass. They put another heavy rush on him. Bender somehow managed to throw the ball away to where it was dropped untouched down the field before they could sack him. The ball dropped about ten yards short of where I was but I was also well covered.

Bender was rushed again on the following play but he must have anticipated that. He got rid of the ball just as he was going to be hit, throwing a swing pass to me on his right side. I caught the ball just behind the line and scampered to the Hawaii 46 to give us a third and four.

"Okay, we've got 'em on the ropes," Bender remarked. It was a pretty bold statement since anything less than four yards on the next play would force us to punt. I still don't know if he actually believed that or if he simply wanted for us to believe it.

Whatever the case, he hit me again. This time it was a slant pattern over the middle. I made the reception at the Cleveland 49 so that alone was enough for a first down. I managed five more yards before I was tackled.

"All right! Another first down for us!" Marv exclaimed as we headed toward the huddle. He didn't seem the least bit concerned about what impact such exuberance might have on our opposition. I probably didn't care, either, although they still had the lead and we needed to travel another 44 yards if we wanted to take the lead. A field goal meant we would still be trailing although there was still plenty of time.

The Browns rose to the occasion on the next play and seemed to do the same on the play after that. On first down they stuffed Scott after a gain of only one yard. They did the same with Kerner to put us in a third and eight.

But wait! The whistle blew when Kerner's forward momentum was stopped. That didn't stop a Cleveland lineman from wrestling Kerner to the ground. I spotted at least two airborne yellow flags.

This could easily have started a brawl. There was some pushing and shoving but very little and it ended quickly. It was probably a matter of the Browns having so much at stake while having to deal with a team that was determined to knock them out of contention.

The unnecessary roughness penalty moved the ball to the 28. It was a stupid penalty for the Browns to commit. Their playoff hopes were on the line and they would have had us in a difficult scenario with a third and eight outside a reasonable field goal range. Instead we had a first down at the 28; a good field goal range although we were determined to keep Guinn off the field except to kick a PAT.

That's the way Scott made it look on the next play. Following his convoy of determined blockers including yours truly on a 3 kama'aina right, Scott scooted effortlessly around right end. He sped his way to the 17 where he was tackled. On one single play we had another first down.

Scott wasn't through yet. He went off tackle on the next play. It took more strength and determination than on the previous play but he still managed to pick up five yards.

Kerner gave Scott a breather on the next play. Jeff took the handoff on a 2 Wahiawa right and headed up the middle between Hoddesson and Marv. It was another determined effort to remain upright. He had secured another first down at the six before the play ended.

We were 18 feet from the end zone. I was at the highest level of optimism I had experienced that entire day. I was certain that this drive would end with us taking the lead. Sometimes you just know.

Or at least you *think* you know.

And I was right. It only took one play to prove me right. Bender found Dietrich about seven yards deep in the end zone. The ball hit him in the numbers to tie the game with 7:42 left in the season.

458

Now we had to win. That's the way I saw it. I could not stand the thought of flying home from Cleveland without a victory. Football is a very emotional game and to lose in a game we wanted to win as badly as this one would be devastating, especially since it was now our game to win.

Guinn did his part to aid in the effort. A chip shot through the uprights gave us the lead for the first time since we essentially gift-wrapped it and gave it away near the end of the first half.

"Okay, good work, men," Tipton remarked as the offensive unit gathered after the PAT. "Just keep in mind that it's not over yet. If the defense can hold them during this drive we will have to focus on putting together another score while running down the clock."

Slightly more than half of the final quarter remained. That was plenty of time for things to happen. Some of those things were very good. Some of them I preferred not to even consider.

Guinn continued to do his part. The subsequent kickoff didn't return to Earth until it was fielded three yards deep in the end zone. The Cleveland return man opted to simply down the ball.

How I wished the two-way player in the NFL wasn't obsolete. In high school I would have been on the field with the defense. In the NFL I could only sit on the bench while wearing my parka and sipping my Gatorade as my heart pounded. I desperately wanted to contribute to the effort of shutting down the Browns' offense.

Our defensive unit actually didn't seem to need me. The line built a wall on the first play from scrimmage. The running back tried to run off right tackle. He managed one token yard.

"Yeah, that's the way to do it!" I hollered, grateful to my defensive colleagues for doing their part to protect our lead.

I was slightly less enthused after the next play. The Browns decided to go to the air. The quarterback found a receiver near the 40. He scampered to the Cleveland 44 before Rodgers wrestled him down.

"What's wrong with you guys?" defensive backs coach William Pickett barked. "You gave them all of that space. Let's have some tight coverage. We need for you to get the ball back for us."

I was starting to worry again. The only advantage I saw to the Browns making such huge gains was that if they were destined to continue in that pattern and would ultimately score there would still be time for us to put together a drive. A check of the clock showed that it was running just inside the seven-minute mark.

The Browns decided to try a pass underneath. Zanakis, fully recovered from his injury, reached out and picked it off at the Cleveland 47.

"Go, Kevin!" I hollered, jumping from my seat as Zanakis started heading toward our end zone. He was fairly fast for a man his size and was fearless when it came to confrontations with the opposition. Although he had never been a ball carrier, even in high school, he managed to break a couple of tackles before he was finally knocked out of bounds at the Cleveland 30.

"All right, offense! There's the opportunity you've been looking for!" Walker enthusiastically pointed out. "You can just about put the game away here."

We were a mere 90 feet from making things virtually impossible for the Browns. That was nothing more than the distance between bases on a baseball field. If we could go all the way, we could run off a fairly large chunk of the clock. There would still be time for them, but a Hawaii touchdown would force them to have to score twice. A field goal would render a Cleveland field goal virtually useless in their quest.

The Cleveland defense came through in the clutch. Scott went up the middle and managed only a single yard. That was followed by a pair of incompletions.

Critics would say that we should not have called those pass plays since the incompletions stopped the clock. Our way of thinking was that we had the guts to pass even in a situation such as that. We also didn't want the Browns thinking they could simply anticipate the run on every play.

Regardless, our strategy didn't quite work. Before I knew it I was running off the field while our field goal unit ran on. All I could do was hope that Guinn was still over his slump. We definitely needed this field goal to prevent the Browns from winning the game with a field goal.

Arroyo got the snap back to Billingsley without a hitch. Billingsley put the ball down and Guinn put his foot into it.

"Looks good! Looks good!" I remarked from the sideline as I watched the ball head toward the end zone. It had the height and appeared as if it would have the distance. The only question was whether it had the accuracy.

Suddenly the arms were raised by the two officials under the goal posts. The kick was right on target. We now had a 17-13 lead with 5:59 left in the game and season.

"We've got about six minutes left," I remarked to Clint after I grabbed a cup of Gatorade and sat on the bench next to him. "This is going to be the longest six minutes of my life."

"Yeah, what we need is for the defense to get us another turnover," Clint replied.

"That would help," I concurred. "But I don't mind telling you, I'm having a blast out here. I almost hate to see the season end."

I watched as Guinn teed up the ball on the Hawaii 35 and stepped back. As soon as NBC was back he approached the ball and put his foot into it. It was fielded about a yard deep in the end zone.

This time there was a runback. The return man darted out past the 20. He was stopped by Pratt at the 25.

The Browns made a tactical mistake that could potentially harm them down the road. They had trouble getting organized in their huddle. The

460

smart thing probably would have been to accept the delay of game penalty since the clock was going to be more of a factor fairly soon. Instead they used a time out; their second of the half since they had also used one during the third quarter. They only had one left.

Yet it might not have been a critical issue. What remained to be seen was how much time the Browns needed to drive down the field. It could even be that they wouldn't need a time-out.

The Browns started on a determined note. A pass was completed just beyond the first down marker. The receiver turned and tried to go further but was hit immediately by Black. He still had gone all the way to the 36 to give the Browns a first down after the opening play of the drive.

Of course they wanted to mix it up to prevent us from keying on the pass. There was enough time left that it didn't hurt to burn some time with a few rushing plays. The Browns picked up four yards and then one yard on consecutive rushes, giving them a third and five at their own 41.

By this time, I was standing again. I simply could not stay seated. The excitement had me too hyper. With the opportunity to finish at the break-even mark, the opportunity to knock the Browns out of the playoff picture and the opportunity to simply end the season as a winner, there was simply too much at stake. I was hoping to smile all the way from Cleveland to Honolulu.

The Browns wanted to wipe the smile right off of my face. We knew that a pass was coming, and Allen staged a pretty impressive blitz. He was cut down in the backfield but Jennings and Richards managed to put some heat on the quarterback. The quarterback still managed to get the pass off which was completed at the Hawaii 41 where the receiver stepped out of bounds. The Browns had another first down.

"Damn!" I muttered under my breath.

Of course these plays brought the fans back into it. The stadium was completely full and as loud as possible after each play that netted the Browns a positive result. I tried to ignore the fans but there was no way to avoid noticing how enthusiastic they were. By this time six days earlier we had the fans in Cincinnati heading for the exits but things were different in Cleveland.

The Browns went back to their ground attack and managed three yards. That was followed by an attempt through the air that put their quarterback under pressure. Before he could get the pass off Jurgens had him sacked at the Hawaii 45, creating a collective groan from the crowd and a boisterous cheer on our sideline. That meant third and 14.

My heart felt as if it was going to bust out of my chest. The clock had moved to inside three minutes. That meant that we had to hold the Browns on two more plays since failure on the next play obviously would not mean a punt. I knew that I had fielded my last punt for 1976.

There was no blitz on the next play despite the cries of "hukilau." There was a rush but the quarterback had fairly good protection while he set up to throw.

Unfortunately for him, his receivers were pretty well recovered by our nickel defense. He had nowhere to run and no receivers so he did the smart thing by throwing the ball away but close enough to a receiver to where the receiver might make a spectacular catch. At the very least, he wouldn't get cited for intentional grounding.

There was no spectacular catch. The ball dropped untouched. The Browns had to do it now or else it was all but completely over.

We stayed in our nickel defense instead of going to the dime. I thought it was strange but it was actually the right thing to do. The Browns were likely to try to go for a mere 14 yards. A dime defense could defend against something like that effectively but the nickel was better in a shorter pass situation since it enabled us to put more pressure on the quarterback.

There was pressure on the quarterback although once again there was no blitz despite more cries of "hukilau." Our defensive backs covered the receivers and our three linebackers also dropped back. The Browns were welcome to the first 13 yards. It was that 14th yard that we didn't want them to get.

The quarterback spotted a receiver near the left sideline. He appeared to be far enough downfield to pick up the first down. Morrissey was covering him but seemed to have lost his balance when the receiver shifted direction and moved in to just beyond the yardage necessary for the first down. The quarterback fired the ball in his direction.

Once again it was Zanakis shining for the Hawaiians. He had dropped back with Allen and Jennings and was covering the right side of the field. As soon as he saw where the ball was going he hustled over. He just barely managed to reach out and get his hand on the ball, knocking it away and out of bounds before leaping up in triumph with his fists thrust in the air.

"All right, Z-man!" Marv exclaimed.

Of course we were all understandably ecstatic about this development. On the sideline there was a lot of yelling and backslapping and other forms of celebration. In the bleachers there was a lot of downtrodden emotion.

I ran on the field for what I figured would be the last time in 1976. With a four-point lead and 2:06 to play it seemed very unlikely that the game would go into overtime. We would have to kick a field goal and then the Browns would have to retort with a touchdown for that to happen.

The first play went to me. I took a handoff and went off left tackle. I managed to pick up only three yards to the Hawaii 48. That play ended right at the two-minute warning.

I was feeling good but was also apprehensive. I knew that there was still time for us to screw things up. I tried not to think that way but couldn't help myself.

462

At the same time I was a little sad. As Bender conversed with Walker on the sideline I thought about the fact that these two minutes were the last two minutes of the season. For all of the torture of training camp, the lambasting during film sessions and other inconveniences, I had enjoyed the season. I knew that there were other things I would enjoy once we were finished and I could go surfing again but was still sorry to end the season.

But there was still the matter of the final two minutes. We had to use the time wisely if we wanted to win. We needed to pick up a first down in order to prevent the Browns from having one more shot.

Scott carried around right end when play resumed. He picked up three yards to the Cleveland 49 where he was hit pretty hard.

"Fumble!"

I joined several players in white jerseys and brown jerseys in the scramble for the loose ball. As it was, the ball didn't travel very far. Scott managed to recover his own fumble at about the same spot where he was hit.

What a relief that was. The last thing anybody wanted to do was give the Browns the ball back on a play like that. Nobody felt that way more than Scott did.

The Browns used their final time out. By that time the clock had run down to 1:46. The scramble for the ball shaved a few extra seconds off the clock. The Browns also waited a few extra seconds before they thought to burn the time out.

"It's okay, man," I said as I patted Scott on the arm while we waited in the huddle for Bender who was talking to Walker on the sideline. "You're having a helluva great game."

If we could move the ball another 12 feet it would be virtually over. Otherwise we could run as much time as possible off the clock, call a time out before being hit with a delay of game penalty and Jablonski could pin them back with another impeccable punt.

Nobody expected a pass and we didn't pass. Instead we ran a Kailua right. Scott took the handoff and shot through the line. Protecting the ball with both hands, he battled his way to the 42. That was three more yards than we needed for the first down.

As soon as the play was blown dead I looked up at the clock. It was running with less than 1:40 left. I also noticed that the some of the 56,025 Cleveland faithful were heading for the exits. They wouldn't be standing in line for playoff tickets even if the Steelers lost to the Oilers and the Bengals lost to the Jets the following day. Unless we fouled up in the worst conceivable way, the season was over in Cleveland.

Three snaps and it was officially all over. The game was over and the 1976 season, at least for the Hawaiians and Browns, was over.

I shook hands and spoke briefly with a few of the Cleveland players before leaving the field. The Brown players who were willing to meet with us, and nobody could really blame those who weren't although there were only a few, were very gracious in defeat.

"We knew we had to be at the top of our game to beat you guys," a Black defensive lineman said as he shook my hand. "We saw it when you beat the Raiders and the way you handled the Bengals last week got our attention. You guys can play with anybody."

Before I left the field Browns Head Coach Forrest Gregg crossed my path. The former offensive tackle for Vince Lombardi's Green Bay Packers who was there when Walker was one of Lombardi's assistants wasn't smiling but he also wasn't scowling. He stopped and looked me over for a second, then stuck out his hand.

"You played a good game, Jay," he said sincerely. "Your team is definitely on its way."

"Thanks, Coach. Good luck next season," I replied before heading off the field.

We were all smiles as the players and coaches gradually trickled into the locker room. We had shown that this expansion team could compete with the best of them.

Walker stood in the middle of the room once everybody was inside. As we knelt, stood, or sat and bowed our heads, Walker announced that he would like to do the prayer this final time.

"Oh God. We are very grateful for all that you have given us. We are grateful for the good fortune to be a part of the National Football League. We are grateful for the determination we have to give it our best, win or lose. We are grateful that injuries were kept to a relatively low number and that most of them were not serious. We are grateful for this season just completed."

"We ask that you bless us and guide us as we move into the offseason. We ask that you heal the injured. We ask that you bless our families."

"We also ask that you bless the less fortunate. We are grateful that we are physically able to perform as a football team, but we know that there are many with deformities which prevent them from being in our position. We ask that you please bless them as well as those who are sick. Please bless the impoverished and those who are otherwise unfortunate. Please keep the world peaceful and please keep us strong so that we may enjoy another productive season. Amen."

"Amen," we repeated in unison.

Walker looked around the room. He was smiling broadly and his eyes were slightly welled with happy tears. He looked as happy as he did in later years when we won Super Bowls.

"First thing," Walker said, holding up a football. "There were some great plays today. I wish I could give out a dozen or so game balls. This time I'd like to single out one rookie who really came of age today. He has made

464

some good plays all season long but today he made a couple of big plays that were keys to our victory."

On that note Walker tossed the ball to Zanakis who received cheers from his teammates. The cocky rookie looked surprised and even moved by the display of approbation. Although I was modestly disappointed that I was never singled out for a game ball during the season, I was happy for Zanakis who clearly deserved the recognition this time around.

"Now that it's over," Walker continued hoarsely after the applause had died down, "I have to say that you men did everything I could possibly have asked of you. I'm including all of you coaches as well as the players."

Walker took a deep breath. Although visibly moved by the experience, his voice was back to normal when he resumed.

"There are some good teams going to the playoffs. One from each conference will go to the Super Bowl. My hat's off to them but . . . I'll take this team any day."

Walker's talk was briefly interrupted by a roar from the players and assistant coaches.

"I want to thank you for all you did this season. You earned the right to be on this team and you maintained that right by the way you performed. You did the fans proud, you did the league proud, you did your families proud, you did yourselves proud and you even did all of Hawaii proud."

Again there was a raucous roar. This was one of those moments in a person's life that one would like to see never end.

"We know we're not going to the playoffs but you know we will real soon if you guys continue to play as hard as you played this year. What you did this season, especially at the end, built momentum that should carry into next season. Have a great time in the offseason but stay in shape and come back to camp ready to play ball."

With that we let out another celebratory roar and shed our uniforms for the final time in 1976. As I shed each article of clothing and equipment I experienced a mixture of melancholy and fulfillment. I was sad to see it end but glad that it had gone so well. I also recall hoping that the 1977 season would prove to be even better.

Only a few players didn't fly back to Hawaii. It was never mandatory anyway since some players had friends or family in the cities we visited and opted to stay an extra day. As long as they were back in Honolulu in time for our first gathering after each game there was never a problem with a player staying over as long as Walker knew who would be staying behind for a day.

Although most of my teammates would be leaving Honolulu for their offseason homes within the next few days, they returned to Hawaii with the rest of the team. Perhaps they wanted that final flight as a unit. Some may have simply wanted to experience Hawaii for a short time without having to deal with the pressure associated with pro football. Some probably didn't feel like dealing with the hassle of packing up until after the season. Some, like myself, were officially residents of Hawaii.

It was a happy flight. It was also somewhat sad. We were returning home in triumph after winning two games on the road to climax an outstanding, by expansion team standards, season. It was sad, though, because this was our final time as a unit. Not everybody would be with the team when we kicked off in 1977. Most probably would be around, I reasoned, but a few members of a special 1976 team would be gone in 1977.

I sat next to Ed Jennings on the flight home. I drank my allotted three beers and then added a fourth when Walker decided that an extra-long flight at the end of a good season mandated that it wouldn't hurt to allow one more for the road.

It was a fun flight. Although not everybody was friendly toward some people, there were no enemies. Everybody was visibly relaxed as we had achieved the impossible by rising to the ranks of mediocrity in our maiden season. Everybody was smiling and engaging in conversation with everybody else. Adding to the casually relaxed ambience of the flight was that nobody was worried about how he would look during our game film session. We knew we probably would never see films of this contest until the Browns appeared on our schedule again.

What a way to end the season! We were not close to making the playoffs but we definitely played the spoiler. We officially ended the Browns' playoff hopes and put a damper on the Bengals' playoff hopes although they were still technically alive going into the final weekend. If the Bengals beat the Jets and the Steelers lost to the Oilers the next day then the Bengals would clinch the division. Had the Bengals beat us they could clinch their division with a victory over the Jets who had won three games all season. The odds were in favor of the Steelers since they had the tiebreaker as well as momentum. After getting off to a 1-4 start, the Steelers had won eight in-a-row.

It could even be argued that we knocked the Cardinals out of the playoff picture even though our match with them was in the season opener. At 9-4, they were one game behind the Cowboys and Redskins who would be squaring off against each other the following day for the division championship. Had they beat us they would be in the thick of the playoff hunt with their only obstacle being the New York Giants who were 3-10 at this point. If they beat the Giants they could win the division if the Cowboys and Redskins played to a tie. Otherwise, they could have secured the wild card with a victory, having no tiebreaker advantage with either the Cowboys or the Redskins.

All of these things were discussed during the flight home. Probably no 7-7 team was ever more full of itself.

But I guess we had a right to be. Of our seven victories, three were against teams who were fighting for playoff spots. One of the others was against a team who was not only going into the postseason but would also have had an unblemished record were it not for us. We could also finish tied for second place in our division if the Broncos lost to the Bears the next day. If the Broncos won we would have sole possession of third place unless the Chargers added a second blemish to the Raiders' schedule the next day.

Seemingly too soon our DC-8 touched down in Honolulu shortly before midnight. As we claimed our luggage on the tarmac outside of Air Service the players and coaches shook hands in farewell.

"Jay, I hope to get an All-Pro performance out of you next year," Walker said as he shook my hand.

"I hope to give it to you," I replied sincerely.

Marv and Karla Nelson gave me a ride home. We waved to our remaining teammates as we left the airport parking lot and pulled out on Lagoon Drive.

The season wasn't entirely over for Marv. He would be travelling to Seattle the following month to participate in the Pro Bowl. He would be Hawaii's only representative. I would watch the game with Ed Jennings and find myself somewhat proud and envious of Marv.

I also set a new goal to meet while watching the game. I wanted to play in a Pro Bowl myself.

I took a little time off from football.

At least as a player. I got up early on Sunday morning, put on a pot of coffee and watched football on TV. In the space of a single day I was transformed from football player to football fan but with an insider's perspective.

Throughout the remainder of December I socialized and had a good time. I still did my TV show, of course, but also watched the struggling University of Hawaii basketball team, attended a few holiday parties and resumed surfing. With the season over I no longer had the $5,000 fine hanging over my head if I got caught surfing.

It only took two days before part of the 1976 Hawaiians team started to come undone. Phil Hoddesson announced his retirement. He said pro football had been wonderful to him but it was time to return to his home in Orem, Utah, to get on with his life. Years later he told me he had contemplated retirement a year earlier but opted to give it one more season when he was taken by Hawaii in the expansion draft. He wanted to take advantage of the opportunity to play football in the same locale where he had served his church mission.

Phil was a guy I hated to lose. He was friendly with virtually everybody but not necessarily chummy. He was the type of guy who had the wisdom to count his blessings. He had enjoyed playing football and was grateful for the privilege but was infinitely more grateful for his beautiful wife and his children. His church and his family were his top priorities.

I wasn't disappointed with my 1976 performance. In 14 games I caught 69 passes for 1,218 yards and seven touchdowns and rushed 46 times for 212 yards and one touchdown. I also completed two of three passes for 55 yards. As a special-teams performer I returned 21 kickoffs for 614 yards and 18 punts for 188 yards.

The stats weren't bad although I wanted to improve on them. It wasn't necessarily the numbers I wanted to improve on although I wasn't averse to that since personal improvement could only help the team. What I wanted to do in 1977 was do whatever it took to help my team go to the playoffs if not the Super Bowl itself.

Wasn't that a lofty goal for a second-year expansion team?

October 15, 2000.

We were gathered behind the south end zone just as we did whenever we were introduced while still active. The former coaches wore brown polo shirts with the Hawaiians logo while the former players wore brown game jerseys. The jerseys had our names on the backs and numbers to match our attire from America's Bicentennial except these jerseys did not include the Bicentennial patch that all NFL teams wore in 1976.

A total of 34 former players and six former coaches were on hand for the special ceremony. The former coaches were introduced first, making their way to midfield at whatever paces pleased them. The former players were then introduced in numerical order to make the same sojourn to midfield.

The reunion officially began the night before. All players and coaches were required to furnish their own transportation to Hawaii but the team managed to arrange up to three nights in a Waikiki hotel, wheeling and dealing in exchange for advertising. This didn't affect me since I was among a handful still residing in Hawaii. The night before we all, along with our wives, reunited for a dinner arranged by the team in another advertising exchange.

Among those at the reunion was Marv Nelson. He was the only man to have an unbroken tenure with the Hawaiians. He retired as a player after our first Super Bowl victory and became the offensive line coach. He moved up quickly, becoming offensive coordinator a few years later and then became Walker's top assistant. That wasn't bad for somebody who once told me his being Black would impede his chances of coaching in any capacity in the NFL.

Walker suffered a fatal heart attack after the 1990 season. Marv was named to replace him.

468

"It's not the way I wanted to get the job," Marv recollected. "I know that Walker would have wanted me to take it."

Although Marv normally handled the pregame rituals in the locker room as head coach, he agreed to break away long enough to take part in the pregame ceremony. His mind was on that day's game but he dutifully stood behind the end zone awaiting the festivities while chatting and shaking hands with players he hadn't seen in several years.

Marv was one of my two business partners in a local sporting goods chain. The other partner was Ed Jennings who retired one season after Marv. Ed stayed in football although not in Hawaii since there were no openings on Walker's staff when Ed retired as a player. He coached in San Francisco and Kansas City before becoming the head coach in Memphis in 1988. Although he was still a business partner and very good friend, Ed spent very little time in Hawaii over the dozen years since becoming top man in Memphis.

Ed was in Hawaii on this day since the Hawaiians' opponent was Ed's team. Ed figured it didn't hurt to ask the team's brass if they minded if he took a few minutes to take part in the pregame introduction of the charter Hawaiian players. The Memphis brass surprised him by giving their consent as long as it didn't create a distraction for his team.

So there we were, older versions of the 1976 team in replicas of the jerseys we wore a quarter-century earlier. There was a lot of gray hair in this group and some had lost their hair. Gary Giametti, my backup wearing his number 25, was bald after telling us in 1976 that his baldness was inevitable. Mark Black, a defensive back who probably led the 1976 team in beer drinking and missed curfews, was also bald as he wore his familiar number 40.

Backup quarterback Frank Joseph in his number 11 was also present with a full head of hair that was about 75 percent salt and 25 percent pepper. Unlike Black, who had done about half-a-dozen short terms behind bars and was cut from the team in 1978 after an incident in Atlanta, Joseph had done some hard time. After his career ended he got himself involved in the drug trade and spent eight years in prison in New York.

Free for almost a full decade at the time of the reunion, Joseph was humbled by his incarceration.

"Those eight years gave me a lot of time to think," he admitted remorsefully during a newspaper interview. "I figured drugs were easy money without giving any thought to the lives they were ruining, including my own. I probably would be dead now if I hadn't gotten busted because I was pretty heavy into the coke. Those eight years were long but I got what I deserved . . . and I got to know God while I was there. Prison was probably the best thing to ever happen to me."

Joseph had been such a cocksure, often flippant, individual. I liked him all right in 1976 but the change in him in 2000 warmed me in some enigmatic way. It was good to see him striving to follow a straight path. He spent a lot of his spare time talking to young people about why they should stay away from drugs. His repentance was inspiring.

Black appeared to be the same as he had always been. He was likable but was still a 50ish juvenile delinquent. He was still the biggest beer drinker among his old teammates. He had been married and divorced twice, reportedly having wives who didn't appreciate his infidelity. He had gotten along with his teammates during his tenure with the team but had always been primarily concerned with doing what was according to his desires regardless of the effect on anybody else.

Joe Billingsley was present. Although we can't be totally certain, the time on the sideline during the first part of his career affected the former BYU quarterback's personality. He was often hostile toward his teammates, creating a barrier between his teammates and himself.

Billingsley, like Joseph, was a totally different person at the reunion. He still had an aloofness about him but had gravitated to a more humble and congenial demeanor. He and I spent about 20 minutes in conversation. Previously our longest conversations were a maximum of about 20 words.

Among those also in attendance were Russ Allen and Norm Richards, wearing 62 and 77 respectively. Allen was assistant coach for the Hawaiians in 2000, returning to the team shortly before Walker's death after coaching on the high school level in Van Nuys, California. Richards owned a few motorcycle dealerships in the Los Angeles area.

Allen and Richards seemed fated to spend a lot of time together, having grown up a block apart in Glendale, California. They played Pop Warner and high school football together before heading down the road to USC. It took the NFL draft to pry them apart with Richards heading to Houston and Allen to Detroit. They were reunited as teammates when they were taken by Hawaii one round apart in the expansion draft. Everybody involved with the draft process swore that they knew nothing about this duo's history together aside from the fact that they had been teammates at USC.

Conspicuously absent was Jeff Kerner. He readily accepted the invitation to attend the reunion, then suffered a fatal heart attack while quietly watching television at his home two months earlier. He had been a popular teammate and the emptiness from his passing, especially since it happened so close to the reunion, was felt by everybody.

Jeff was represented. His wife Susan decided to attend to reconnect with some of the players and wives she had known. Some of us persuaded her to wear her husband's jersey number 24 and represent him on the field instead of sitting in the bleachers with the other wives. She reluctantly agreed and later said she was glad she did. I think it even helped her to cope with her new status as a widow.

470

Jeff wasn't the only former Hawaiian player to have passed away at this point. He simply had been the only player from the 1976 team to have passed away. A handful of others from later teams, as well as the earlier WFL teams, had also died from various causes.

A sad postscript to this is that Pam Bender was not at the 1976 team's reunion in 2000. Three years earlier she passed away after a brief illness. Since she and Steve had taken up permanent residence in Hawaii, I got to know her very well. I was deeply saddened by her sudden death. While Steve had always displayed a businesslike demeanor while occasionally showing a sense of humor, Pam displayed a terrific sense of humor. She was a fun person to know.

The most conspicuously absent was Walker. I honestly had a great deal of respect for the man.

Of course he pushed us hard. There were times when he ranted and raved and made us feel as valuable as something the neighbor's dog deposits on your lawn. He was also an outstanding football coach and a wonderful human being. Behind the facade of cantankerous outbursts was a man who was a true friend to every man who ever played for him.

If I was a good football player, I owe that success primarily to Marcus Farnwell, my high school coach, and Walker. There were other coaches and teammates who were vital to my success at South Valley High School, USC, the University of Hawaii and both the WFL and NFL Hawaiians. Farnwell and Walker still get most of the credit.

Walker had an uncanny knack for bringing out the best in people as long as those in question allowed him to. He worked us hard but with a righteous purpose. He wanted us to be absolutely the best we could be. He wanted to win, naturally, but knew that the winning stemmed from putting our best effort into what we did.

Some coaches on all levels work players hard solely for the sake of working them hard. Often it is punishment for being on the short end of the scoreboard without regard for how well the team actually played. Those arc the teams that wind up, at best, mediocre with little or no sense of achievement. They are not motivated to win as much as they are afraid to lose since winning is merely a temporary exile from retribution and not a reward that comes from playing to the best of one's ability.

Walker simply got us to be the best we could be. Win or lose, there was no satisfaction unless we played our best. He carried that further by also encouraging us to be the best we could be off the field. I would like to believe that among the dozens of rookie prospects he had to cut before they had the opportunity of playing even a single down in the NFL, there are at least a few who are better men for having briefly associated with Walker.

I remained friends with Walker even after my retirement and found his sudden death to be a crushing blow. The two greatest influences in my life,

Walker and Farnwell, have passed on but there probably aren't any days when I don't think of them. I hope they understand just how much I appreciate what they did for me.

As far as the reunion went, it was a rousing success. It was a wonderful opportunity for most of the players and coaches from that charter NFL team to briefly bond once again. We were the franchise that materialized almost from nowhere but made its mark in a hurry. The 1976 team laid the foundation for our success in ensuing years. It was a very special group of football players that I will never forget.

About The Author

Jim Gardner grew up in West Covina, California, then moved to Hawaii after high school where he lived for 50 years. Like the main character in the trilogy, Gardner is an alumnus of the University of Hawaii, earning his degree in journalism before embarking on a career as a broadcast journalist and freelance writer. In 2021 he retired to Union, Missouri, to be closer to his son, Reggie, but his heart will always be in Hawaii.

Made in the USA
Columbia, SC
31 January 2023

11357027R00263